CRIME NOVELS

AMERICAN NOIR
OF THE 1930S AND 40S

CRIME NOVELS

AMERICAN NOIR

OF THE 1930S AND 40S

The Postman Always Rings Twice
James M. Cain

They Shoot Horses, Don't They?
Horace McCoy

Thieves Like Us
Edward Anderson

The Big Clock
Kenneth Fearing

Nightmare Alley
William Lindsay Gresham

I Married a Dead Man
Cornell Woolrich

THE LIBRARY OF AMERICA

The Postman Always Rings Twice copyright 1934 James M. Cain;
copyright renewed 1962 by James M. Cain. Published by
arrangement with Alfred A. Knopf, Inc. *They Shoot Horses, Don't
They?* copyright 1935 by Horace McCoy. Published by arrangement
with the Estate of Horace McCoy. *Thieves Like Us* copyright 1937 by
Edward Anderson. *The Big Clock* copyright 1946 by Kenneth
Fearing, copyright renewed in 1973 by Bruce Fearing. Reprinted by
the permission of Russell & Volkening as agents for the author.
Nightmare Alley copyright 1946 by William Lindsay Gresham.
Reprinted by permission of Renee Gresham, David Gresham, and
Douglas H. Gresham. *I Married a Dead Man* copyright 1948 by
William Irish. Copyright assigned to Sheldon Abend D/B/A
Author's Research Company, 1982. Published by arrangement with
Viking Penguin, a division of Penguin Books USA, Inc.

The paper used in this publication meets the
minimum requirements of the American National Standard for
Information Sciences—Permanence of Paper for Printed
Library Materials, ANSI Z39.48—1984.

Distributed to the trade in the United States
by Penguin Books USA Inc
and in Canada by Penguin Books Canada Ltd.

Library of Congress Catalog Number: 97–2485
For cataloging information, see end of Notes.
ISBN 1–883011–46–9

First Printing
The Library of America—94

Manufactured in the United States of America

ROBERT POLITO

SELECTED THE CONTENTS AND WROTE
THE NOTES FOR THIS VOLUME

Contents

The Postman Always Rings Twice
James M. Cain 1

They Shoot Horses, Don't They?
Horace McCoy 97

Thieves Like Us
Edward Anderson 215

The Big Clock
Kenneth Fearing 379

Nightmare Alley
William Lindsay Gresham 517

I Married a Dead Man
Cornell Woolrich 797

Biographical Notes 977

Note on the Texts 983

Notes 987

THE POSTMAN
ALWAYS RINGS TWICE

by James M. Cain

To
Vincent Lawrence

I

THEY threw me off the hay truck about noon. I had swung on the night before, down at the border, and as soon as I got up there under the canvas, I went to sleep. I needed plenty of that, after three weeks in Tia Juana, and I was still getting it when they pulled off to one side to let the engine cool. Then they saw a foot sticking out and threw me off. I tried some comical stuff, but all I got was a dead pan, so that gag was out. They gave me a cigarette, though, and I hiked down the road to find something to eat.

That was when I hit this Twin Oaks Tavern. It was nothing but a roadside sandwich joint, like a million others in California. There was a lunchroom part, and over that the house part, where they lived, and off to one side a filling station, and out back a half dozen shacks that they called an auto court. I blew in there in a hurry and began looking down the road. When the Greek showed, I asked if a guy had been by in a Cadillac. He was to pick me up here, I said, and we were to have lunch. Not today, said the Greek. He layed a place at one of the tables and asked me what I was going to have. I said orange juice, corn flakes, fried eggs and bacon, enchilada, flapjacks, and coffee. Pretty soon he came out with the orange juice and the corn flakes.

"Hold on, now. One thing I got to tell you. If this guy don't show up, you'll have to trust me for it. This was to be on him, and I'm kind of short, myself."

"Hokay, fill'm up."

I saw he was on, and quit talking about the guy in the Cadillac. Pretty soon I saw he wanted something.

"What you do, what kind of work, hey?"

"Oh, one thing and another, one thing and another. Why?"

"How old you?"

"Twenty four."

"Young fellow, hey. I could use young fellow right now. In my business."

"Nice place you got here."

"Air. Is a nice. No fog, like in a Los Angeles. No fog at all. Nice, a clear, all a time nice a clear."

3

"Must be swell at night. I can smell it now."

"Sleep fine. You understand automobile? Fix'm up?"

"Sure. I'm a born mechanic."

He gave me some more about the air, and how healthy he's been since he bought this place, and how he can't figure it out, why his help won't stay with him. I can figure it out, but I stay with the grub.

"Hey? You think you like it here?"

By that time I had put down the rest of the coffee, and lit the cigar he gave me. "I tell you how it is. I got a couple of other propositions, that's my trouble. But I'll think about it. I sure will do that all right."

Then I saw her. She had been out back, in the kitchen, but she came in to gather up my dishes. Except for the shape, she really wasn't any raving beauty, but she had a sulky look to her, and her lips stuck out in a way that made me want to mash them in for her.

"Meet my wife."

She didn't look at me. I nodded at the Greek, gave my cigar a kind of wave, and that was all. She went out with the dishes, and so far as he and I were concerned, she hadn't even been there. I left, then, but in five minutes I was back, to leave a message for the guy in the Cadillac. It took me a half hour to get sold on the job, but at the end of it I was in the filling station, fixing flats.

"What's your name, hey?"

"Frank Chambers."

"Nick Papadakis, mine."

We shook hands, and he went. In a minute I heard him singing. He had a swell voice. From the filling station I could just get a good view of the kitchen.

2

About three o'clock a guy came along that was all burned up because somebody had pasted a sticker on his wind wing. I had to go in the kitchen to steam it off for him.

"Enchiladas? Well, you people sure know how to make them."

"What do you mean, you people?"

"Why, you and Mr. Papadakis. You and Nick. That one I had for lunch, it was a peach."

"Oh."

"You got a cloth? That I can hold on to this thing with?"

"That's not what you meant."

"Sure it is."

"You think I'm Mex."

"Nothing like it."

"Yes you do. You're not the first one. Well, get this. I'm just as white as you are, see? I may have dark hair and look a little that way, but I'm just as white as you are. You want to get along good around here, you won't forget that."

"Why, you don't look Mex."

"I'm telling you. I'm just as white as you are."

"No, you don't look even a little bit Mex. Those Mexican women, they all got big hips and bum legs and breasts up under their chin and yellow skin and hair that looks like it had bacon fat on it. You don't look like that. You're small, and got nice white skin, and your hair is soft and curly, even if it is black. Only thing you've got that's Mex is your teeth. They all got white teeth, you've got to hand that to them."

"My name was Smith before I was married. That don't sound much like a Mex, does it?"

"Not much."

"What's more, I don't even come from around here. I come from Iowa."

"Smith, hey. What's your first name?"

"Cora. You can call me that, if you want to."

I knew for certain, then, what I had just taken a chance on when I went in there. It wasn't those enchiladas that she had to cook, and it wasn't having black hair. It was being married to that Greek that made her feel she wasn't white, and she was even afraid I would begin calling her Mrs. Papadakis.

"Cora. Sure. And how about calling me Frank?"

She came over and began helping me with the wind wing. She was so close I could smell her. I shot it right close to her ear, almost in a whisper. "How come you married this Greek, anyway?"

She jumped like I had cut her with a whip. "Is that any of your business?"

"Yeah. Plenty."

"Here's your wind wing."

"Thanks."

I went out. I had what I wanted. I had socked one in under her guard, and socked it in deep, so it hurt. From now on, it would be business between her and me. She might not say yes, but she wouldn't stall me. She knew what I meant, and she knew I had her number.

That night at supper, the Greek got sore at her for not giving me more fried potatoes. He wanted me to like it there, and not walk out on him like the others had.

"Give a man something to eat."

"They're right on the stove. Can't he help himself?"

"It's all right. I'm not ready yet."

He kept at it. If he had had any brains, he would have known there was something back of it, because she wasn't one to let a guy help himself, I'll say that for her. But he was dumb, and kept crabbing. It was just the kitchen table, he at one end, she at the other, and me in the middle. I didn't look at her. But I could see her dress. It was one of these white nurse uniforms, like they all wear, whether they work in a dentist's office or a bakeshop. It had been clean in the morning, but it was a little bit rumpled now, and mussy. I could smell her.

"Well for heaven's sake."

She got up to get the potatoes. Her dress fell open for a second, so I could see her leg. When she gave me the potatoes, I couldn't eat. "Well there now. After all that, and now he doesn't want them."

"Hokay. But he have'm, *if* he want'm."

"I'm not hungry. I ate a big lunch."

He acted like he had won a great victory, and now he would forgive her, like the big guy he was. "She is a all right. She is my little white bird. She is my little white dove."

He winked and went upstairs. She and I sat there, and didn't say a word. When he came down he had a big bottle and a guitar. He poured some out of the bottle, but it was sweet Greek wine, and made me sick to my stomach. He started to sing. He had a tenor voice, not one of these little tenors like you hear on the radio, but a big tenor, and on the high notes he would put in a sob like on a Caruso record. But I couldn't listen to him now. I was feeling worse by the minute.

He saw my face and took me outside. "Out in a air, you feel better."

" 'S all right. I'll be all right."

"Sit down. Keep quiet."

"Go ahead in. I just ate too much lunch. I'll be all right."

He went in, and I let everything come up. It was like hell the lunch, or the potatoes, or the wine. I wanted that woman so bad I couldn't even keep anything on my stomach.

Next morning the sign was blown down. About the middle of the night it had started to blow, and by morning it was a windstorm that took the sign with it.

"It's awful. Look at that."

"Was a very big wind. I could no sleep. No sleep all night."

"Big wind all right. But look at the sign."

"Is busted."

I kept tinkering with the sign, and he would come out and watch me. "How did you get this sign anyway?"

"Was here when I buy the place. Why?"

"It's lousy all right. I wonder you do any business at all."

I went to gas up a car, and left him to think that over. When I got back he was still blinking at it, where it was leaning against the front of the lunchroom. Three of the lights were busted. I plugged in the wire, and half the others didn't light.

"Put in new lights, hang'm up, will be all right."

"You're the boss."

"What's a matter with it?"

"Well, it's out of date. Nobody has bulb signs any more. They got Neon signs. They show up better, and they don't burn as much juice. Then, what does it say? Twin Oaks, that's all. The Tavern part, it's not in lights. Well, Twin Oaks don't make me hungry. It don't make me want to stop and get something to eat. It's costing you money, that sign is, only you don't know it."

"Fix'm up, will be hokay."

"Why don't you get a new sign?"

"I'm busy."

But pretty soon he was back, with a piece of paper. He had drew a new sign for himself, and colored it up with red, white, and blue crayon. It said Twin Oaks Tavern, and Eat, and Bar-B-Q, and Sanitary Rest Rooms, and N. Papadakis, Prop.

"Swell. That'll knock them for a loop."

I fixed up the words, so they were spelled right, and he put some more curley cues on the letters.

"Nick, why do we hang up the old sign at all? Why don't you go to the city today and get this new sign made? It's a beauty, believe me it is. And it's important. A place is no better than its sign, is it?"

"I do it. By golly, I go."

Los Angeles wasn't but twenty miles away, but he shined himself up like he was going to Paris, and right after lunch, he went. Soon as he was gone, I locked the front door. I picked up a plate that a guy had left, and went on back in the kitchen with it. She was there.

"Here's a plate that was out there."

"Oh, thanks."

I set it down. The fork was rattling like a tambourine.

"I was going to go, but I started some things cooking and I thought I better not."

"I got plenty to do, myself."

"You feeling better?"

"I'm all right."

"Sometimes just some little thing will do it. Like a change of water, something like that."

"Probably too much lunch."

"What's that?"

Somebody was out front, rattling the door. "Sounds like somebody trying to get in."

"Is the door locked, Frank?"

"I must have locked it."

She looked at me, and got pale. She went to the swinging

door, and peeped through. Then she went into the lunch-room, but in a minute she was back.

"They went away."

"I don't know why I locked it."

"I forgot to unlock it."

She started for the lunchroom again, but I stopped her. "Let's—leave it locked."

"Nobody can get in if it's locked. I got some cooking to do. I'll wash up this plate."

I took her in my arms and mashed my mouth up against hers. . . . "Bite me! Bite me!"

I bit her. I sunk my teeth into her lips so deep I could feel the blood spurt into my mouth. It was running down her neck when I carried her upstairs.

3

For two days after that I was dead, but the Greek was sore at me, so I got by all right. He was sore at me because I hadn't fixed the swing door that led from the lunchroom into the kitchen. She told him it swung back and hit her in the mouth. She had to tell him something. Her mouth was all swelled up where I had bit it. So he said it was my fault, that I hadn't fixed it. I stretched the spring, so it was weaker, and that fixed it.

But the real reason he was sore at me was over the sign. He had fallen for it so hard he was afraid I would say it was my idea, stead of his. It was such a hell of a sign they couldn't get it done for him that afternoon. It took them three days, and when it was ready I went in and got it and hung it up. It had on it all that he had drew on the paper, and a couple of other things besides. It had a Greek flag and an American flag, and hands shaking hands, and Satisfaction Guaranteed. It was all in red, white, and blue Neon letters, and I waited until dark to turn on the juice. When I snapped the switch, it lit up like a Christmas tree.

"Well, I've seen many a sign in my time, but never one like that. I got to hand it to you, Nick."

"By golly. By golly."
We shook hands. We were friends again.

Next day I was alone with her for a minute, and swung my fist up against her leg so hard it nearly knocked her over.
"How do you get that way?" She was snarling like a cougar. I liked her like that.
"How are you, Cora?"
"Lousy."
From then on, I began to smell her again.

One day the Greek heard there was a guy up the road undercutting him on gas. He jumped in the car to go see about it. I was in my room when he drove off, and I turned around to dive down in the kitchen. But she was already there, standing in the door.
I went over and looked at her mouth. It was the first chance I had had to see how it was. The swelling was all gone, but you could still see the tooth marks, little blue creases on both lips. I touched them with my fingers. They were soft and damp. I kissed them, but not hard. They were little soft kisses. I had never thought about them before. She stayed until the Greek came back, about an hour. We didn't do anything. We just lay on the bed. She kept rumpling my hair, and looking up at the ceiling, like she was thinking.
"You like blueberry pie?"
"I don't know. Yeah. I guess so."
"I'll make you some."

"Look out, Frank. You'll break a spring leaf."
"To hell with the spring leaf."
We were crashing into a little eucalyptus grove beside the road. The Greek had sent us down to the market to take back some T-bone steaks he said were lousy, and on the way back it had got dark. I slammed the car in there, and it bucked and bounced, but when I was in among the trees I stopped. Her arms were around me before I even cut the lights. We did plenty. After a while we just sat there. "I can't go on like this, Frank."
"Me neither."

"I can't stand it. And I've got to get drunk with you, Frank. You know what I mean? Drunk."

"I know."

"And I hate that Greek."

"Why did you marry him? You never did tell me that."

"I haven't told you anything."

"We haven't wasted any time on talk."

"I was working in a hash house. You spend two years in a Los Angeles hash house and you'll take the first guy that's got a gold watch."

"When did you leave Iowa?"

"Three years ago. I won a beauty contest. I won a high school beauty contest, in Des Moines. That's where I lived. The prize was a trip to Hollywood. I got off the Chief with fifteen guys taking my picture, and two weeks later I was in the hash house."

"Didn't you go back?"

"I wouldn't give them the satisfaction."

"Did you get in movies?"

"They gave me a test. It was all right in the face. But they talk, now. The pictures, I mean. And when I began to talk, up there on the screen, they knew me for what I was, and so did I. A cheap Des Moines trollop, that had as much chance in pictures as a monkey has. Not as much. A monkey, anyway, can make you laugh. All I did was make you sick."

"And then?"

"Then two years of guys pinching your leg and leaving nickel tips and asking how about a little party tonight. I went on some of them parties, Frank."

"And then?"

"You know what I mean about them parties?"

"I know."

"Then he came along. I took him, and so help me, I meant to stick by him. But I can't stand it any more. God, do I look like a little white bird?"

"To me, you look more like a hell cat."

"You know, don't you. That's one thing about you. I don't have to fool you all the time. And you're clean. You're not greasy. Frank, do you have any idea what that means? You're not greasy."

"I can kind of imagine."

"I don't think so. No man can know what that means to a woman. To have to be around somebody that's greasy and makes you sick at the stomach when he touches you. I'm not really such a hell cat, Frank. I just can't stand it any more."

"What you trying to do? Kid me?"

"Oh, all right. I'm a hell cat, then. But I don't think I would be so bad. With somebody that wasn't greasy."

"Cora, how about you and me going away?"

"I've thought about it. I've thought about it a lot."

"We'll ditch this Greek and blow. Just blow."

"Where to?"

"Anywhere. What do we care?"

"Anywhere. Anywhere. You know where that is?"

"All over. Anywhere we choose."

"No it's not. It's the hash house."

"I'm not talking about the hash house. I'm talking about the road. It's fun, Cora. And nobody knows it better than I do. I know every twist and turn it's got. And I know how to work it, too. Isn't that what we want? Just to be a pair of tramps, like we really are?"

"You were a fine tramp. You didn't even have socks."

"You liked me."

"I loved you. I would love you without even a shirt. I would love you specially without a shirt, so I could feel how nice and hard your shoulders are."

"Socking railroad detectives developed the muscles."

"And you're hard all over. Big and tall and hard. And your hair is light. You're not a little soft greasy guy with black kinky hair that he puts bay rum on every night."

"That must be a nice smell."

"But it won't do, Frank. That road, it don't lead anywhere but to the hash house. The hash house for me, and some job like it for you. A lousy parking lot job, where you wear a smock. I'd cry if I saw you in a smock, Frank."

"Well?"

She sat there a long time, twisting my hand in both of hers. "Frank, do you love me?"

"Yes."

"Do you love me so much that not anything matters?"

"Yes."

"There's one way."

"Did you say you weren't really a hell cat?"

"I said it, and I mean it. I'm not what you think I am, Frank. I want to work and be something, that's all. But you can't do it without love. Do you know that, Frank? Anyway, a woman can't. Well, I've made one mistake. And I've got to be a hell cat, just once, to fix it. But I'm not really a hell cat, Frank."

"They hang you for that."

"Not if you do it right. You're smart, Frank. I never fooled you for a minute. You'll think of a way. Plenty of them have. Don't worry. I'm not the first woman that had to turn hell cat to get out of a mess."

"He never did anything to me. He's all right."

"The hell he's all right. He stinks, I tell you. He's greasy and he stinks. And do you think I'm going to let you wear a smock, with Service Auto Parks printed on the back, Thank-U Call Again, while he has four suits and a dozen silk shirts? Isn't that business half mine? Don't I cook? Don't I cook good? Don't you do your part?"

"You talk like it was all right."

"Who's going to know if it's all right or not, but you and me?"

"You and me."

"That's it, Frank. That's all that matters, isn't it? Not you and me and the road, or anything else but you and me."

"You must be a hell cat, though. You couldn't make me feel like this if you weren't."

"That's what we're going to do. Kiss me, Frank. On the mouth."

I kissed her. Her eyes were shining up at me like two blue stars. It was like being in church.

4

"Got any hot water?"

"What's the matter with the bathroom?"

"Nick's in there."

"Oh. I'll give you some out of the kettle. He likes the whole heater full for his bath."

We played it just like we would tell it. It was about ten o'clock at night, and we had closed up, and the Greek was in the bathroom, putting on his Saturday night wash. I was to take the water up to my room, get ready to shave, and then remember I had left the car out. I was to go outside, and stand by to give her one on the horn if somebody came. She was to wait till she heard him in the tub, go in for a towel, and clip him from behind with a blackjack I had made for her out of a sugar bag with ball bearings wadded down in the end. At first, I was to do it, but we figured he wouldn't pay any attention to her if she went in there, where if I said I was after my razor, he might get out of the tub or something and help me look. Then she was to hold him under until he drowned. Then she was to leave the water running a little bit, and step out the window to the porch roof, and come down the stepladder I had put there, to the ground. She was to hand me the blackjack, and go back to the kitchen. I was to put the ball bearings back in the box, throw the bag away, put the car in, and go up to my room and start to shave. She would wait till the water began dripping down in the kitchen, and call me. We would break the door down, find him, and call the doctor. In the end, we figured it would look like he had slipped in the tub, knocked himself out, and then drowned. I got the idea from a piece in the paper where a guy had said that most accidents happen right in people's own bathtubs.

"Be careful of it. It's hot."

"Thanks."

It was in a saucepan, and I took it up in my room and set it on the bureau, and laid my shaving stuff out. I went down and out to the car, and took a seat in it so I could see the road and the bathroom window, both. The Greek was singing. It came to me I better take note what the song was. It was Mother Machree. He sang it once, and then sang it over again. I looked in the kitchen. She was still there.

A truck and a trailer swung around the bend. I fingered the horn. Sometimes those truckmen stopped for something to eat, and they were the kind that would beat on the door till you opened up. But they went on. A couple more cars went by. They didn't stop. I looked in the kitchen again, and she wasn't there. A light went on in the bedroom.

Then, all of a sudden, I saw something move, back by the porch. I almost hit the horn, but then I saw it was a cat. It was just a gray cat, but it shook me up. A cat was the last thing I wanted to see then. I couldn't see it for a minute, and then there it was again, smelling around the stepladder. I didn't want to blow the horn, because it wasn't anything but a cat, but I didn't want it around that stepladder. I got out of the car, went back there, and shooed it away.

I got halfway back to the car, when it came back, and started up the ladder. I shooed it away again, and ran it clear back to the shacks. I started back to the car, and then stood there for a little bit, looking to see if it was coming back. A state cop came around the bend. He saw me standing there, cut his motor, and came wheeling in, before I could move. When he stopped he was between me and the car. I couldn't blow the horn.

"Taking it easy?"

"Just came out to put the car away."

"That your car?"

"Belongs to this guy I work for."

"O.K. Just checking up."

He looked around, and then he saw something. "I'll be damned. Look at that."

"Look at what?"

"Goddam cat, going up that stepladder."

"Ha."

"I love a cat. They're always up to something."

He pulled on his gloves, took a look at the night, kicked his pedal a couple of times, and went. Soon as he was out of sight I dove for the horn. I was too late. There was a flash of fire from the porch, and every light in the place went out. Inside, Cora was screaming with an awful sound in her voice. "Frank! Frank! Something has happened!"

I ran in the kitchen, but it was black dark in there and I

didn't have any matches in my pocket, and I had to feel my way. We met on the stairs, she going down, me going up. She screamed again.

"Keep quiet, for God's sake keep quiet! Did you do it?"

"Yes, but the lights went out, and I haven't held him under yet!"

"We got to bring him to! There was a state cop out there, and he saw that stepladder!"

"Phone for the doctor!"

"You phone, and I'll get him out of there!"

She went down, and I kept on up. I went in the bathroom, and over to the tub. He was laying there in the water, but his head wasn't under. I tried to lift him. I had a hell of a time. He was slippery with soap, and I had to stand in the water before I could raise him at all. All the time I could hear her down there, talking to the operator. They didn't give her a doctor. They gave her the police.

I got him up, and laid him over the edge of the tub, and then got out myself, and dragged him in the bedroom and laid him on the bed. She came up, then, and we found matches, and got a candle lit. Then we went to work on him. I packed his head in wet towels, while she rubbed his wrists and feet.

"They're sending an ambulance."

"All right. Did he see you do it?"

"I don't know."

"Were you behind him?"

"I think so. But then the lights went out, and I don't know what happened. What did you do to the lights?"

"Nothing. The fuse popped."

"Frank. He'd better not come to."

"He's got to come to. If he dies, we're sunk. I tell you, that cop saw the stepladder. If he dies, then they'll know. If he dies, they've got us."

"But suppose he saw me? What's he going to say when he comes to?"

"Maybe he didn't. We just got to sell him a story, that's all. You were in here, and the lights popped, and you heard him slip and fall, and he didn't answer when you spoke to him. Then you called me, that's all. No matter what he says, you got to stick to it. If he saw anything, it was just his imagination, that's all."

"Why don't they hurry with that ambulance?"

"It'll be here."

Soon as the ambulance came, they put him on a stretcher and shoved him in. She rode with him. I followed along in the car. Halfway to Glendale, a state cop picked us up and rode on ahead. They went seventy miles an hour, and I couldn't keep up. They were lifting him out when I got to the hospital, and the state cop was bossing the job. When he saw me he gave a start and stared at me. It was the same cop.

They took him in, put him on a table, and wheeled him in an operating room. Cora and myself sat out in the hall. Pretty soon a nurse came and sat down with us. Then the cop came, and he had a sergeant with him. They kept looking at me. Cora was telling the nurse how it happened. "I was in there, in the bathroom I mean, getting a towel, and then the lights went out just like somebody had shot a gun off. Oh my, they made a terrible noise. I heard him fall. He had been standing up, getting ready to turn on the shower. I spoke to him, and he didn't say anything, and it was all dark, and I couldn't see anything, and I didn't know what had happened. I mean I thought he had been electrocuted or something. So then Frank heard me screaming, and he came, and got him out, and then I called up for the ambulance, and I don't know what I would have done if they hadn't come quick like they did."

"They always hurry on a late call."

"I'm so afraid he's hurt bad."

"I don't think so. They're taking X-Rays in there now. They can always tell from X-Rays. But I don't think he's hurt bad."

"Oh my, I hope not."

The cops never said a word. They just sat there and looked at us.

They wheeled him out, and his head was covered with bandages. They put him on an elevator, and Cora, and me, and the nurse, and the cops all got on, and they took him up and put him in a room. We all went in there. There weren't enough chairs, and while they were putting him to bed the nurse went and got some extra ones. We all sat down. Somebody said something, and the nurse made them keep quiet. A doctor came in and took a look, and went out. We sat there a hell of a while. Then the nurse went over and looked at him.

"I think he's coming to now."

Cora looked at me, and I looked away quick. The cops leaned forward, to hear what he said. He opened his eyes.

"You feel better now?"

He didn't say anything, and neither did anybody else. It was so still I could hear my heart pounding in my ears. "Don't you know your wife? Here she is. Aren't you ashamed of yourself, falling in the bathtub like a little boy, just because the lights went out. Your wife is mad at you. Aren't you going to speak to her?"

He strained to say something, but couldn't say it. The nurse went over and fanned him. Cora took hold of his hand and patted it. He lay back for a few minutes, with his eyes closed, and then his mouth began to move again and he looked at the nurse.

"Was a all go dark."

When the nurse said he had to be quiet, I took Cora down, and put her in the car. We no sooner started out than the cop was back there, following us on his motorcycle.

"He suspicions us, Frank."

"It's the same one. He knew there was something wrong, soon as he saw me standing there, keeping watch. He still thinks so."

"What are we going to do?"

"I don't know. It all depends on that stepladder, whether he tumbles what it's there for. What did you do with that slungshot?"

"I still got it here, in the pocket of my dress."

"God Almighty, if they had arrested you back there, and searched you, we'd have been sunk."

I gave her my knife, made her cut the string off the bag, and take the bearings out. Then I made her climb back, raise the back seat, and put the bag under it. It would look like a rag, like anybody keeps with the tools.

"You stay back there, now, and keep an eye on that cop. I'm going to snap these bearings into the bushes one at a time, and you've got to watch if he notices anything."

She watched, and I drove with my left hand, and leaned my right hand on the wheel. I let one go. I shot it like a marble, out the window and across the road.

"Did he turn his head?"

"No."

I let the rest go, one every couple of minutes. He never noticed it.

We got out to the place, and it was still dark. I hadn't had time to find the fuses, let alone put a new one in. When I pulled in, the cop went past, and was there ahead of me. "I'm taking a look at that fuse box, buddy."

"Sure. I'm taking a look myself."

We all three went back there, and he snapped on a flashlight. Right away, he gave a funny grunt and stooped down. There was the cat, laying on its back with all four feet in the air.

"Ain't that a shame? Killed her deader than hell."

He shot the flashlight up under the porch roof, and along the stepladder. "That's it, all right. Remember? We were looking at her. She stepped off the ladder on to your fuse box, and it killed her deader than hell."

"That's it all right. You were hardly gone when it happened. Went off like a pistol shot. I hadn't even had time to move the car."

"They caught me down the road."

"You were hardly out of sight."

"Stepped right off the ladder on to the fuse box. Well, that's the way it goes. Them poor dumb things, they can't get it through their head about electricity, can they? No sir, it's too much for them."

"Tough, all right."

"That's what it is, it's tough. Killed her deader than hell. Pretty cat, too. Remember, how she looked when she was creeping up that ladder? I never seen a cuter cat than she was."

"And pretty color."

"And killed her deader than hell. Well, I'll be going along. I guess that straightens us out. Had to check up, you know."

"That's right."

"So long. So long, Miss."

"So long."

5

We didn't do anything about the cat, the fuse box, or anything else. We crept into bed, and she cracked up. She cried, and then got a chill so she was trembling all over, and it was a couple of hours before I could get her quiet. She lay in my arms a while, then, and we began to talk.

"Never again, Frank."

"That's right. Never again."

"We must have been crazy. Just plain crazy."

"Just our dumb luck that pulled us through."

"It was my fault."

"Mine too."

"No, it was my fault. I was the one that thought it up. You didn't want to. Next time I'll listen to you, Frank. You're smart. You're not dumb like I am."

"Except there won't be any next time."

"That's right. Never again."

"Even if we had gone through with it they would have guessed it. They *always* guess it. They guess it anyway, just from habit. Because look how quick that cop knew something was wrong. That's what makes my blood run cold. Soon as he saw me standing there he knew it. If he could tumble to it all that easy, how much chance would we have had if the Greek had died?"

"I guess I'm not really a hell cat, Frank."

"I'm telling you."

"If I was, I wouldn't have got scared so easy. I was *so* scared, Frank."

"I was scared plenty, myself."

"You know what I wanted when the lights went out? Just

you, Frank. I wasn't any hell cat at all, then. I was just a little girl, afraid of the dark."

"I was there, wasn't I?"

"I loved you for it. If it hadn't been for you, I don't know what would have happened to us."

"Pretty good, wasn't it? About how he slipped?"

"And he believed it."

"Give me half a chance, I got it on the cops, every time. You got to have something to tell, that's it. You got to fill in all those places, and yet have it as near the truth as you can get it. I know them. I've tangled with them, plenty."

"You fixed it. You're always going to fix it for me, aren't you, Frank?"

"You're the only one ever meant anything to me."

"I guess I really don't want to be a hell cat."

"You're my baby."

"That's it, just your dumb baby. All right, Frank. I'll listen to you, from now on. You be the brains, and I'll work. I can work, Frank. And I work good. We'll get along."

"Sure we will."

"Now shall we go to sleep?"

"You think you can sleep all right?"

"It's the first time we ever slept together, Frank."

"You like it?"

"It's grand, just grand."

"Kiss me goodnight."

"It's so sweet to be able to kiss you goodnight."

Next morning, the telephone waked us up. She answered it, and when she came up her eyes were shining. "Frank, guess what?"

"What?"

"His skull is fractured."

"Bad?"

"No, but they're keeping him there. They want him there for a week, maybe. We can sleep together again, tonight."

"Come here."

"Not now. We've got to get up. We've got to open the place up."

"Come here, before I sock you."
"You nut."

It was a happy week, all right. In the afternoon, she would drive in to the hospital, but the rest of the time we were together. We gave him a break, too. We kept the place open all the time, and went after the business, and got it. Of course it helped, that day when a hundred Sunday school kids showed up in three busses, and wanted a bunch of stuff to take out in the woods with them, but even without that we would have made plenty. The cash register didn't know anything to tell on us, believe me it didn't.

Then one day, stead of her going in alone, we both went in, and after she came out of the hospital, we cut for the beach. They gave her a yellow suit and a red cap, and when she came out I didn't know her at first. She looked like a little girl. It was the first time I ever really saw how young she was. We played in the sand, and then we went way out and let the swells rock us. I like my head to the waves, she liked her feet. We lay there, face to face, and held hands under water. I looked up at the sky. It was all you could see. I thought about God.

"Frank."
"Yes?"
"He's coming home tomorrow. You know what that means?"
"I know."
"I got to sleep with him, stead of you."
"You would, except that when he gets here we're going to be gone."
"I was hoping you'd say that."
"Just you and me and the road, Cora."
"Just you and me and the road."
"Just a couple of tramps."
"Just a couple of gypsies, but we'll be together."
"That's it. We'll be together."

Next morning, we packed up. Anyway, she packed. I had bought a suit, and I put that on, and it seemed to be about

all. She put her things in a hatbox. When she got done with
it, she handed it to me. "Put that in the car, will you?"

"The car?"

"Aren't we taking the car?"

"Not unless you want to spend the first night in jail, we're
not. Stealing a man's wife, that's nothing, but stealing his car,
that's larceny."

"Oh."

We started out. It was two miles to the bus stop, and we
had to hike it. Every time a car went by, we would stand
there with our hand stuck out, like a cigar store Indian, but
none of them stopped. A man alone can get a ride, and a
woman alone, if she's fool enough to take it, but a man and
a woman together don't have much luck. After about twenty
had gone by, she stopped. We had gone about a quarter of a
mile.

"Frank, I can't."

"What's the matter?"

"This is it."

"This is what?"

"The road."

"You're crazy. You're tired, that's all. Look. You wait here,
and I'll get somebody down the road to drive us in to the
city. That's what we ought to done anyhow. Then we'll be all
right."

"No, it's not that. I'm not tired. I can't, that's all. At all."

"Don't you want to be with me, Cora?"

"You know I do."

"We can't go back, you know. We can't start up again, like
it was before. You know that. You've got to come."

"I told you I wasn't really a bum, Frank. I don't feel like
no gypsy. I don't feel like nothing, only ashamed, that I'm
out here asking for a ride."

"I told you. We're getting a car in to the city."

"And then what?"

"Then we're there. Then we get going."

"No we don't. We spend one night in a hotel, and then we
start looking for a job. And living in a dump."

"Isn't that a dump? What you just left?"

"It's different."

"Cora, you going to let it get your goat?"

"It's got it, Frank. I can't go on. Goodbye."

"Will you listen to me a minute?"

"Goodbye, Frank. I'm going back."

She kept tugging at the hatbox. I tried to hold on to it, anyway to carry it back for her, but she got it. She started back with it. She had looked nice when she started out, with a little blue suit and blue hat, but now she looked all battered, and her shoes were dusty, and she couldn't even walk right, from crying. All of a sudden, I found out I was crying too.

6

I caught a ride to San Bernardino. It's a railroad town, and I was going to hop a freight east. But I didn't do it. I ran into a guy in a poolroom, and began playing him one ball in the side. He was the greatest job in the way of a sucker that God ever turned out, because he had a friend that could really play. The only trouble with him was, he couldn't play good enough. I hung around with the pair of them a couple of weeks, and took $250 off them, all they had, and then I had to beat it out of town quick.

I caught a truck for Mexicali, and then I got to thinking about my $250, and how with that much money we could go to the beach and sell hot dogs or something until we got a stake to take a crack at something bigger. So I dropped off, and caught a ride back to Glendale. I began hanging around the market where they bought their stuff, hoping I would bump into her. I even called her up a couple of times, but the Greek answered and I had to make out it was a wrong number.

In between walking around the market, I hung around a poolroom, about a block down the street. One day a guy was practicing shots alone on one of the tables. You could tell he was new at it from the way he held his cue. I began practicing shots on the next table. I figured if $250 was enough for a hot dog stand, $350 would leave us sitting pretty.

"How you say to a little one ball in the side?"

"I never played that game much."

"Nothing to it. Just the one ball in the side pocket."

"Anyhow, you look too good for me."

"Me? I'm just a punk."

"Oh well. If it's just a friendly game."

We started to play, and I let him take three or four, just to feel good. I kept shaking my head, like I couldn't understand it.

"Too good for you hey. Well, that's a joke. But I swear, I'm really better than this. I can't seem to get going. How you say we put $1 on it, just to make it lively?"

"Oh well. I can't lose much at a dollar."

We made it $1 a game, and I let him take four or five, maybe more. I shot like I was pretty nervous, and in between shots I would wipe off the palm of my hand with a handkerchief, like I must be sweating.

"Well, it looks like I'm not doing so good. How about making it $5, so I can get my money back, and then we'll go have a drink?"

"Oh well. It's just a friendly game, and I don't want your money. Sure. We'll make it $5, and then we'll quit."

I let him take four or five more, and from the way I was acting, you would have thought I had heart failure and a couple more things besides. I was plenty blue around the gills.

"Look. I got sense enough to know when I'm out of my class all right, but let's make it $25, so I can break even, and then we'll go have that drink."

"That's pretty high for me."

"What the hell? You're playing on my money, aren't you?"

"Oh well. All right. Make it $25."

Then was when I really started to shoot. I made shots that Hoppe couldn't make. I banked them in from three cushions, I made billiard shots, I had my english working so the ball just floated around the table, I even called a jump shot and made it. He never made a shot that Blind Tom the Sightless Piano Player couldn't have made. He miscued, he got himself all tangled up on position, he scratched, he put the one ball in the wrong pocket, he never even called a bank shot. And when I walked out of there, he had my $250 and a $3 watch that I had bought to keep track of when Cora might be driving in to the market. Oh, I was good all right. The only trouble was I wasn't quite good enough.

"Hey, Frank!"

It was the Greek, running across the street at me before I had really got out the door.

"Well Frank, you old son a gun, where you been, put her there, why you run away from me just a time I hurt my head I need you most?"

We shook hands. He still had a bandage around his head and a funny look in his eyes, but he was all dressed up in a new suit, and had a black hat cocked over on the side of his head, and a purple necktie, and brown shoes, and his gold watch chain looped across his vest, and a big cigar in his hand.

"Well Nick! How you feeling, boy?"

"Me, I feel fine, couldn't feel better if was right out a the can, but why you run out on me? I sore as hell at you, you old son a gun."

"Well, you know me, Nick. I stay put a while, and then I got to ramble."

"You pick one hell of a time to ramble. What you do, hey? Come on, you don't do nothing, you old son a gun, I know you, come on over while I buy'm steaks I tell you all about it."

"You alone?"

"Don't talk so dumb, who the hell you think keep a place open now you run out on me, hey? Sure I'm alone. Me a Cora never get to go out together now, one go, other have to stay."

"Well then, let's walk over."

It took him an hour to buy the steaks, he was so busy telling me how his skull was fractured, how the docs never saw a fracture like it, what a hell of a time he's had with his help, how he's had two guys since I left and he fired one the day after he hired him, and the other one skipped after three days and took the inside of the cash register with him, and how he'd give anything to have me back.

"Frank, I tell you what. We go to Santa Barbara tomorrow, me a Cora. Hell boy, we got to step out a little, hey? We go

see a fiesta there, and you come with us. You like that, Frank?
You come with us, we talk about you come back a work for
me. You like a fiesta a Santa Barbara?"

"Well, I hear it's good."

"Is a girls, is a music, is a dance in streets, is swell. Come
on, Frank, what you say?"

"Well, I don't know."

"Cora be sore as hell at me if I see you and no bring you
out. Maybe she treat you snotty, but she think you fine fellow,
Frank. Come on, we all three go. We have a hell of a time."

"O.K. If she's willing, it's a go."

There were eight or ten people in the lunchroom when we
got there, and she was back in the kitchen, washing dishes as
fast as she could, to get enough plates to serve them.

"Hey. Hey Cora, look. Look who I bring."

"Well for heaven's sake. Where did he come from?"

"I see'm today a Glendale. He go to Santa Barbara with
us."

"Hello, Cora. How you been?"

"You're quite a stranger around here."

She wiped her hands quick, and shook hands, but her hand
was soapy. She went out front with an order, and me and the
Greek sat down. He generally helped her with the orders, but
he was all hot to show me something, and he let her do it all
alone. It was a big scrapbook, and in the front of it he had
pasted his naturalization certificate, and then his wedding certificate, and then his license to do business in Los Angeles
County, and then a picture of himself in the Greek Army, and
then a picture of him and Cora the day they got married, and
then all the clippings about his accident. Those clippings in
the regular papers, if you ask me, were more about the cat
than they were about him, but anyway they had his name in
them, and how he had been brought to the Glendale Hospital, and was expected to recover. The one in the Los Angeles
Greek paper, though, was more about him than about the cat,
and had a picture of him in it, in the dress suit he had when
he was a waiter, and the story of his life. Then came the X-
Rays. There were about a half dozen of them, because they
took a new picture every day to see how he was getting along.
How he had them fixed up was to paste two pages together,

along the edges, and then cut out a square place in the middle, where the X-Ray was slipped in so you could hold it up to the light and look through it. After the X-Rays came the receipted hospital bills, the receipted doctors' bills, and the receipted nurses' bills. That rap on the conk cost him $322, believe it or not.

"Is a nice, hey?"

"Swell. It's all there, right on the line."

"Of course, is a not done yet. I fix'm up red, a white, a blue, fix'm up fine. Look."

He showed me where he had put the fancy stuff on a couple of the pages. He had inked in the curley cues, and then colored it with red, white, and blue. Over the naturalization certificate, he had a couple of American flags, and a eagle, and over the Greek Army picture he had crossed Greek flags, and another eagle, and over his wedding certificate he had a couple of turtle doves on a twig. He hadn't figured out yet what to put over the other stuff, but I said over the clippings he could put a cat with red, white, and blue fire coming out of its tail, and he thought that was pretty good. He didn't get it, though, when I said he could have a buzzard over the Los Angeles County license, holding a couple of auctioneer's flags that said Sale Today, and it didn't look like it would really be worth while to try to explain it to him. But I got it, at last, why he was all dressed up, and not carrying out the chow like he used to, and acted so important. This Greek had had a fracture of the skull, and a thing like that don't happen to a dumb cluck like him every day. He was like a wop that opens a drug store. Soon as he gets that thing that says Pharmacist, with a red seal on it, a wop puts on a gray suit, with black edges on the vest, and is so important he can't even take time to mix the pills, and wouldn't even touch a chocolate icecream soda. This Greek was all dressed up for the same reason. A big thing had happened in his life.

It was pretty near supper time when I got her alone. He went up to wash, and the two of us were left in the kitchen.

"You been thinking about me, Cora?"

"Sure. I wouldn't forget you all that quick."

"I thought about you a lot. How are you?"

"Me? I'm all right."

"I called you up a couple of times, but he answered and I was afraid to talk to him. I made some money."

"Well, gee, I'm glad you're getting along good."

"I made it, but then I lost it. I thought we could use it to get started with, but then I lost it."

"I declare, I don't know where the money goes."

"You sure you think about me, Cora?"

"Sure I do."

"You don't act like it."

"Seems to me I'm acting all right."

"Have you got a kiss for me?"

"We'll be having supper pretty soon. You better get ready, if you've got any washing to do."

That's the way it went. That's the way it went all evening. The Greek got out some of his sweet wine, and sang a bunch of songs, and we sat around, and so far as she was concerned, I might just as well have been just a guy that used to work there, only she couldn't quite remember his name. It was the worst flop of a home-coming you ever saw in your life.

When it came time to go to bed, I let them go up, and then I went outside to try and figure out whether to stay there and see if I couldn't get going with her again, or blow and try to forget her. I walked quite a way off, and I don't know how long it was, or how far away I was, but after a while I could hear a row going on in the place. I went back, and when I got close I could hear some of what they were saying. She was yelling like hell and saying I had to leave. He was mumbling something, probably that he wanted me to stay and go back to work. He was trying to shut her up, but I could tell she was yelling so I would hear it. If I had been in my room, where she thought I was, I could have heard it plain enough, and even where I was I could hear plenty.

Then all of a sudden it stopped. I slipped in the kitchen, and stood there listening. But I couldn't hear anything, because I was all shook up, and all I could get was the sound of my own heart, going bump-bump, bump-bump, bump-bump, like that. I thought that was a funny way for my heart to sound, and then all of a sudden I knew there was two hearts in that kitchen, and that was why it sounded so funny.

I snapped on the light.

She was standing there, in a red kimono, as pale as milk, staring at me, with a long thin knife in her hand. I reached out and took it away from her. When she spoke, it was in a whisper that sounded like a snake licking its tongue in and out.

"Why did you have to come back?"

"I had to, that's all."

"No you didn't. I could have gone through with it. I was getting so I could forget you. And now you have to come back. God damn you, you have to come back!"

"Go through with what?"

"What he's making that scrapbook for. *It's to show to his children!* And now he wants one. He wants one right away."

"Well, why didn't you come with me?"

"Come with you for what? To sleep in box cars? Why would I come with you? Tell me that."

I couldn't say anything. I thought about my $250, but what good was it telling her that I had some money yesterday, but today I lost it playing one ball in the side?

"You're no good. I know that. You're just no good. Then why don't you go away and let me alone instead of coming back here again? Why don't you leave me be?"

"Listen. Stall him on this kid stuff just a little while. Stall him, and we'll see if we can't figure something out. I'm not much good, but I love you, Cora. I swear it."

"You swear it, and what do you do? He's taking me to Santa Barbara, so I'll say I'll have the child, and you—you're going right along with us. You're going to stay at the same hotel with us! You're going right along in the car. You're—"

She stopped, and we stood there looking at each other. The three of us in the car, we knew what that meant. Little by little we were nearer, until we were touching.

"Oh, my God, Frank, isn't there any other way out for us than that?"

"Well. You were going to stick a knife in him just now."

"No. That was for me, Frank. Not him."

"Cora, it's in the cards. We've tried every other way out."

"I can't have no greasy Greek child, Frank. I can't, that's all. The only one I can have a child by is you. I wish you were some good. You're smart, but you're no good."

"I'm no good, but I love you."

"Yes, and I love you."

"Stall him. Just this one night."

"All right, Frank. Just this one night."

7

"There's a long, long trail a-winding
    Into the land of my dreams,
    Where the nightingale is singing
    And the white moon beams.

"There's a long, long night of waiting
    Until my dreams all come true,
    Till the day when I'll be going down
    That long, long trail with you."

"Feeling good, ain't they?"

"Too good to suit me."

"So you don't let them get hold of that wheel, Miss. They'll be all right."

"I hope so. I've got no business out with a pair of drunks, I know that. But what could I do? I told them I wouldn't go with them, but then they started to go off by themselves."

"They'd break their necks."

"That's it. So I drove myself. It was all *I* knew to do."

"It keeps you guessing, sometimes, to know what to do. One sixty for the gas. Is the oil O.K.?"

"I think so."

"Thanks, Miss. Goodnight."

She got in, and took the wheel again, and me and the Greek kept on singing, and we went on. It was all part of the play.

I had to be drunk, because that other time had cured me of this idea we could pull a perfect murder. This was going to be such a lousy murder it wouldn't even be a murder. It was going to be just a regular road accident, with guys drunk, and booze in the car, and all the rest of it. Of course, when I started to put it down, the Greek had to have some too, so he was just like I wanted him. We stopped for gas so there would be a witness that she was sober, and didn't want to be with us anyhow, because she was driving, and it wouldn't do for her to be drunk. Before that, we had had a piece of luck. Just before we closed up, about nine o'clock, a guy stopped by for something to eat, and stood there in the road and watched us when we shoved off. He saw the whole show. He saw me try to start, and stall a couple of times. He heard the argument between me and Cora, about how I was too drunk to drive. He saw her get out, and heard her say she wasn't going. He saw me try to drive off, just me and the Greek. He saw her when she made us get out, and switched the seats, so I was behind, and the Greek up front, and then he saw her take the wheel and do the driving herself. His name was Jeff Parker and he raised rabbits at Encino. Cora got his card when she said she might try rabbits in the lunchroom, to see how they'd go. We knew right where to find him, whenever we'd need him.

Me and the Greek sang Mother Machree, and Smile, Smile, Smile, and Down by the Old Mill Stream, and pretty soon we came to this sign that said To Malibu Beach. She turned off there. By rights, she ought to have kept on like she was going. There's two main roads that lead up the coast. One, about ten miles inland, was the one we were on. The other, right alongside the ocean, was off to our left. At Ventura they meet, and follow the sea right on up to Santa Barbara, San Francisco, and wherever you're going. But the idea was, she had never seen Malibu Beach, where the movie stars live, and she wanted to cut over on this road to the ocean, so she could drop down a couple of miles and look at it, and then turn around and keep right on up to Santa Barbara. The real idea was that this connection is about the worst piece of road in Los Angeles County, and an accident there wouldn't surprise anybody, not even a cop. It's dark, and has no traffic on it hardly, and no houses or anything, and suited us for what we had to do.

The Greek never noticed anything for a while. We passed a little summer colony that they call Malibu Lake up in the hills, and there was a dance going on at the clubhouse, with couples out on the lake in canoes. I yelled at them. So did the Greek. "Give a one f' me." It didn't make much difference, but it was one more mark on our trail, if somebody took the trouble to find it.

We started up the first long up-grade, into the mountains. There were three miles of it. I had told her how to run it. Most of the time she was in second. That was partly because there were sharp curves every fifty feet, and the car would lose speed so quick going around them that she would have to shift up to second to keep going. But it was partly because the motor had to heat. Everything had to check up. We had to have plenty to tell.

And then, when he looked out and saw how dark it was, and what a hell of a looking country those mountains were, with no light, or house, or filling station, or anything else in sight, the Greek came to life and started an argument.

"Hold on, hold on. Turn around. By golly, we off the road."

"No we're not. I know where I am. It takes us to Malibu Beach. Don't you remember? I told you I wanted to see it."

"You go slow."

"I'm going slow."

"You go plenty slow. Maybe all get killed."

We got to the top and started into the down-grade. She cut the motor. They heat fast for a few minutes, when the fan stops. Down at the bottom she started the motor again. I looked at the temp gauge. It was 200. She started into the next up-grade and the temp gauge kept climbing.

"Yes sir, yes sir."

It was our signal. It was one of those dumb things a guy can say any time, and nobody will pay any attention to it. She pulled off to one side. Under us was a drop so deep you couldn't see the bottom of it. It must have been 500 feet.

"I think I'll let it cool off a bit."

"By golly, you bet. Frank, look a that. Look what it says."

"Whassit say?"

"Two hundred a five. Would be boiling in minute."

"Letta boil."

I picked up the wrench. I had it between my feet. But just then, away up the grade, I saw the lights of a car. I had to stall. I had to stall for a minute, until that car went by.

"C'me on, Nick. Sing's a song."

He looked out on those bad lands, but he didn't seem to feel like singing. Then he opened the door and got out. We could hear him back there, sick. That was where he was when the car went by. I looked at the number to burn it in my brain. Then I burst out laughing. She looked back at me.

" 'S all right. Give them something to remember. Both guys alive when they went by."

"Did you get the number?"

"2R-58-01."

"2R-58-01. 2R-58-01. All right. I've got it too."

"O.K."

He came around from behind, and looked like he felt better. "You hear that?"

"Hear what?"

"When you laugh. Is a echo. Is a fine echo."

He tossed off a high note. It wasn't any song, just a high note, like on a Caruso record. He cut it off quick and listened. Sure enough, here it came back, clear as anything, and stopped, just like he had.

"Is a sound like me?"

"Jus' like you, kid. Jussa same ol' toot."

"By golly. Is swell."

He stood there for five minutes, tossing off high notes and listening to them come back. It was the first time he ever heard what his voice sounded like. He was as pleased as a gorilla that seen his face in the mirror. She kept looking at me. We had to get busy. I began to act sore. "Wot th' hell? You think we got noth'n t' do but lis'n at you yod'l at y'self all night? C'me on, get in. Le's get going."

"It's getting late, Nick."

"Hokay, hokay."

He got in, but shoved his face out to the window and let go one. I braced my feet, and while he still had his chin on the window sill I brought down the wrench. His head cracked, and I felt it crush. He crumpled up and curled on the seat like a cat on a sofa. It seemed a year before he was still. Then Cora, she gave a funny kind of gulp that ended in a moan. Because here came the echo of his voice. It took the high note, like he did, and swelled, and stopped, and waited.

8

We didn't say anything. She knew what to do. She climbed back, and I climbed front. I looked at the wrench under the dash light. It had a few drops of blood on it. I uncorked a bottle of wine, and poured it on there till the blood was gone. I poured so the wine went over him. Then I wiped the wrench on a dry part of his clothes, and passed it back to her. She put it under the seat. I poured more wine over where I had wiped the wrench, cracked the bottle against the door, and laid it on top of him. Then I started the car. The wine bottle gave a gurgle, where a little of it was running out the crack.

I went a little way, and then shifted up to second. I couldn't tip it down that 500-foot drop, where we were. We had to get down to it afterward, and besides, if it plunged that far, how would we be alive? I drove slow, in second, up to a place where the ravine came to a point, and it was only a 50-foot drop. When I got there, I drove over to the edge, put my foot on the brake, and fed with the hand throttle. As soon as the right front wheel went off, I stepped hard on the brake. It stalled. That was how I wanted it. The car had to be in gear, with the ignition on, but that dead motor would hold it for the rest of what we had to do.

We got out. We stepped on the road, not the shoulder, so there wouldn't be footprints. She handed me a rock, and a piece of 2 × 4 I had back there. I put the rock under the rear axle. It fitted, because I had picked one that would fit. I slipped the 2 × 4 over the rock and under the axle. I heaved down on it. The car tipped, but it hung there. I heaved again.

It tipped a little more. I began to sweat. Here we were, with a dead man in the car, and suppose we couldn't tip it over?

I heaved again, but this time she was beside me. We both heaved. We heaved again. And then all of a sudden, there we were, sprawled down on the road, and the car was rolling over and over, down the gully, and banging so loud you could hear it a mile.

It stopped. The lights were still on, but it wasn't on fire. That was the big danger. With that ignition on, if the car burned up, why weren't we burned too? I snatched up the rock, and gave it a heave down the ravine. I picked up the 2 × 4, ran up the road with it a way, and slung it down, right in the roadway. It didn't bother me any. All over the road, wherever you go, are pieces of wood that have dropped off trucks, and they get all splintered up from cars running over them, and this was one of them. I had left it out all day, and it had tire marks on it, and the edges were all chewed up.

I ran back, picked her up, and slid down the ravine with her. Why I did that was on account of the tracks. My tracks, they didn't worry me any. I figured there would be plenty of men piling down there pretty soon, but those sharp heels of hers, they had to be pointed in the right direction, if anybody took the trouble to look.

I set her down. The car was hanging there, on two wheels, about halfway down the ravine. He was still in there, but now he was down on the floor. The wine bottle was wedged between him and the seat, and while we were looking it gave a gurgle. The top was all broken in, and both fenders were bent. I tried the doors. That was important, because I had to get in there, and be cut up with glass, while she went up on the road to get help. They opened all right.

I began to fool with her blouse, to bust the buttons, so she would look banged up. She was looking at me, and her eyes didn't look blue, they looked black. I could feel her breath coming fast. Then it stopped, and she leaned real close to me.

"Rip me! Rip me!"

I ripped her. I shoved my hand in her blouse and jerked. She was wide open, from her throat to her belly.

"You got that climbing out. You caught it in the door handle."

My voice sounded queer, like it was coming out of a tin phonograph.

"And this you don't know how you got."

I hauled off and hit her in the eye as hard as I could. She went down. She was right down there at my feet, her eyes shining, her breasts trembling, drawn up in tight points, and pointing right up at me. She was down there, and the breath was roaring in the back of my throat like I was some kind of a animal, and my tongue was all swelled up in my mouth, and blood pounding in it.

"Yes! Yes, Frank, yes!"

Next thing I knew, I was down there with her, and we were staring in each other's eyes, and locked in each other's arms, and straining to get closer. Hell could have opened for me then, and it wouldn't have made any difference. I had to have her, if I hung for it.

I had her.

9

We lay there a few minutes, then, like we were doped. It was so still that all you could hear was this gurgle from the inside of the car.

"What now, Frank?"

"Tough road ahead, Cora. You've got to be good, from now on. You sure you can go through it?"

"After that, I can go through anything."

"They'll come at you, those cops. They'll try to break you down. You ready for them?"

"I think so."

"Maybe they'll pin something on you. I don't think they can, with those witnesses we got. But maybe they do it. Maybe they pin it on you for manslaughter, and you spend a year in jail. Maybe it's as bad as that. You think you can take it on the chin?"

"So you're waiting for me when I come out."

"I'll be there."

"Then I can do it."

"Don't pay any attention to me. I'm a drunk. They got tests that'll show that. I'll say stuff that's cock-eyed. That's to cross them up, so when I'm sober and tell it my way, they'll believe it."

"I'll remember."

"And you're pretty sore at me. For being drunk. For being the cause of it all."

"Yes. I know."

"Then we're set."

"Frank."

"Yes?"

"There's just one thing. We've got to be in love. If we love each other, then nothing matters."

"Well, do we?"

"I'll be the first one to say it. I love you, Frank."

"I love you, Cora."

"Kiss me."

I kissed her, and held her close, and then I saw a flicker of light on the hill across the ravine.

"Up on the road, now. You're going through with it."

"I'm going through with it."

"Just ask for help. You don't know he's dead yet."

"I know."

"You fell down, after you climbed out. That's how you got the sand on your clothes."

"Yes. Goodbye."

"Goodbye."

She started up to the road, and I dived for the car. But all of a sudden, I found I didn't have my hat. I had to be in the car, and my hat had to be with me. I began clawing around for it. The car was coming closer and closer. It was only two or three bends away, and I didn't have my hat yet, and I didn't have a mark on me. I gave up, and started for the car. Then I fell down. I had hooked my foot in it. I grabbed it, and jumped in. My weight no sooner went on the floor than it sank and I felt the car turning over on me. That was the last I knew for a while.

Next, I was on the ground, and there was a lot of yelling

and talking going on around me. My left arm was shooting pain so bad I would yell every time I felt it, and so was my back. Inside my head was a bellow that would get big and go away again. When it did that the ground would fall away, and this stuff I had drunk would come up. I was there and I wasn't there, but I had sense enough to roll around and kick. There was sand on my clothes too, and there had to be a reason.

Next there was a screech in my ears, and I was in an ambulance. A state cop was at my feet, and a doctor was working on my arm. I went out again as soon as I saw it. It was running blood, and between the wrist and the elbow it was bent like a snapped twig. It was broke. When I came out of it again the doctor was still working on it, and I thought about my back. I wiggled my foot and looked at it to see if I was paralyzed. It moved.

The screech kept bringing me out of it, and I looked around, and saw the Greek. He was on the other bunk.

"Yay Nick."

Nobody said anything. I looked around some more, but I couldn't see anything of Cora.

After a while they stopped, and lifted out the Greek. I waited for them to lift me out, but they didn't. I knew he was really dead, then, and there wouldn't be any cock-eyed stuff this time, selling him a story about a cat. If they had taken us both out, it would be a hospital. But when they just took him out, it was a mortuary.

We went on, then, and when they stopped they lifted me out. They carried me in, and set the stretcher on a wheel table, and rolled me in a white room. Then they got ready to set my arm. They wheeled up a machine to give me gas for that, but then they had an argument. There was another doctor there by that time that said he was the jail physician, and the hospital doctors got pretty sore. I knew what it was about. It was those tests for being drunk. If they gave me the gas first, that would ball up the breath test, the most important one. The jail doctor won out, and made me blow through a glass

pipe into some stuff that looked like water but turned yellow
when I blew in it. Then he took some blood, and some other
samples that he poured in bottles through a funnel. Then they
gave me the gas.

When I began to come out of it I was in a room, in bed,
and my head was all covered with bandages, and so was my
arm, with a sling besides, and my back was all strapped up
with adhesive tape so I could hardly move. A state cop was
there, reading the morning paper. My head ached like hell,
and so did my back, and my arm had shooting pains in it.
After a while a nurse came in and gave me a pill, and I went
to sleep.

When I woke up it was about noon, and they gave me
something to eat. Then two more cops came in, and they put
me on a stretcher again, and took me down and put me in
another ambulance.

"Where we going?"

"Inquest."

"Inquest. That's what they have when somebody's dead,
ain't it."

"That's right."

"I was afraid they'd got it."

"Only one."

"Which?"

"The man."

"Oh. Was the woman bad hurt?"

"Not bad."

"Looks pretty bad for me, don't it?"

"Watch out there, buddy. It's O.K. with us if you want to
talk, but anything you say may fall back in your lap when you
get to court."

"That's right. Thanks."

When we stopped it was in front of a undertaker shop in
Hollywood, and they carried me in. Cora was there, pretty
battered up. She had on a blouse that the police matron had
lent her, and it puffed out around her belly like it was stuffed
with hay. Her suit and her shoes were dusty, and her eye was
all swelled up where I had hit it. She had the police matron

with her. The coroner was back of a table, with some kind of a secretary guy beside him. Off to one side were a half dozen guys that acted pretty sore, with cops standing guard over them. They were the jury. There was a bunch of other people, with cops pushing them around to the place where they ought to stand. The undertaker was tip-toeing around, and every now and then he would shove a chair under somebody. He brought a couple for Cora and the matron. Off to one side, on a table, was something under a sheet.

Soon as they had me parked the way they wanted me, on a table, the coroner rapped with his pencil and they started. First thing, was a legal identification. She began to cry when they lifted the sheet off, and I didn't like it much myself. After she looked, and I looked, and the jury looked, they dropped the sheet again.

"Do you know this man?"

"He was my husband."

"His name?"

"Nick Papadakis."

Next came the witnesses. The sergeant told how he got the call and went up there with two officers after he phoned for an ambulance, and how he sent Cora in by a car he took charge of, and me and the Greek in by ambulance, and how the Greek died on the way in, and was dropped off at the mortuary. Next, a hick by the name of Wright told how he was coming around the bend, and heard a woman scream, and heard a crash, and saw the car going over and over, the lights still on, down the gully. He saw Cora in the road, waving at him for help, and went down to the car with her and tried to get me and the Greek out. He couldn't do it, because the car was on top of us, so he sent his brother, that was in the car with him, for help. After a while more people came, and the cops, and when the cops took charge they got the car off us and put us in the ambulance. Then Wright's brother told about the same thing, only he went back for the cops.

Then the jail doctor told how I was drunk, and how examination of the stomach showed the Greek was drunk, but Cora wasn't drunk. Then he told which cracked bone it was that the Greek died of. Then the coroner turned to me and asked me if I wanted to testify.

"Yes sir, I guess so."

"I warn you that any statement you make may be used against you, and that you are under no compulsion to testify unless you so wish."

"I got nothing to hold back."

"All right, then. What do you know about this?"

"All I know is that first I was going along. Then I felt the car sink under me, and something hit me, and that's all I can remember until I come to in the hospital."

"*You* were going along?"

"Yes sir."

"You mean you were driving the car?"

"Yes sir, I was driving it."

That was just a cock-eyed story I was going to take back later on, when we got in a place where it really meant something, which this inquest didn't. I figured if I told a bum story first, and then turned around and told another story, it would sound like the second story was really true, where if I had a pat story right from the beginning, it would sound like what it was, pat. I was doing this one different from the first time. I meant to look bad, right from the start. But if I wasn't driving the car, it didn't make any difference how bad I looked, they couldn't do anything to me. What I was afraid of was that perfect murder stuff that we cracked up on last time. Just one little thing, and we were sunk. But here, if I looked bad, there could be quite a few things and still I wouldn't look much worse. The worse I looked on account of being drunk, the less the whole thing would look like a murder.

The cops looked at each other, and the coroner studied me like he thought I was crazy. They had already heard it all, how I was pulled out from under the back seat.

"You're sure of that? That you were driving?"

"Absolutely sure."

"You had been drinking?"

"No sir."

"You heard the results of the tests that were given you?"

"I don't know nothing about the tests. All I know is I didn't have no drink."

He turned to Cora. She said she would tell what she could.

"Who was driving this car?"

"I was."

"Where was this man?"

"On the back seat."

"Had he been drinking?"

She kind of looked away, and swallowed, and cried a little bit. "Do I have to answer that?"

"You don't have to answer any question unless you so wish."

"I don't want to answer."

"Very well, then. Tell in your own words what happened."

"I was driving along. There was a long up-grade, and the car got hot. My husband said I had better stop to let it cool off."

"How hot?"

"Over 200."

"Go on."

"So after we started the down-grade, I cut the motor, and when we got to the bottom it was still hot, and before we started up again we stopped. We were there maybe ten minutes. Then I started up again. And I don't know what happened. I went into high, and didn't get enough power, and I went into second, right quick, and the men were talking, or maybe it was on account of making the quick shift, but anyhow, I felt one side of the car go down. I yelled to them to jump, but it was too late. I felt the car going over and over, and next thing I knew I was trying to get out, and then I was out, and then I was up on the road."

The coroner turned to me again. "What are you trying to do, shield this woman?"

"I don't notice her shielding me any."

The jury went out, and then came in and gave a verdict that the said Nick Papadakis came to his death as the result of an automobile accident on the Malibu Lake Road, caused in whole or in part by criminal conduct on the part of me and Cora, and recommended that we be held for the action of the grand jury.

There was another cop with me that night, in the hospital, and next morning he told me that Mr. Sackett was coming over to see me, and I better get ready. I could hardly move yet, but I had the hospital barber shave me up and make me look as good as he could. I knew who Sackett was. He was the District Attorney. About half past ten he showed up, and the cop went out, and there was nobody there but him and me. He was a big guy with a bald head and a breezy manner.

"Well, well, well. How do you feel?"

"I feel O.K., judge. Kind of shook me up a little, but I'll be all right."

"As the fellow said when he fell out of the airplane, it was a swell ride but we lit kind of hard."

"That's it."

"Now Chambers, you don't have to talk to me if you don't want to, but I've come over here, partly to see what you look like, and partly because it's been my experience that a frank talk saves a lot of breath afterwards, and sometimes paves the way to the disposition of a whole case with a proper plea, and anyway, as the fellow says, after it's over we understand each other."

"Why sure, judge. What was it you wanted to know?"

I made it sound pretty shifty, and he sat there looking me over. "Suppose we start at the beginning."

"About this trip?"

"That's it. I want to hear all about it."

He got up and began to walk around. The door was right by my bed, and I jerked it open. The cop was halfway down the hall, chinning a nurse. Sackett burst out laughing. "No, no dictaphones in this. They don't use them anyway, except in movies."

I let a sheepish grin come over my face. I had him like I wanted him. I had pulled a dumb trick on him, and he had got the better of me. "O.K., judge. I guess it was pretty silly, at that. All right, I'll begin at the beginning and tell it all. I'm in dutch all right, but I guess lying about it won't do any good."

"That's the right attitude, Chambers."

I told him how I walked out on the Greek, and how I bumped into him on the street one day, and he wanted me back, and then asked me to go on this Santa Barbara trip with them to talk it over. I told about how we put down the wine, and how we started out, with me at the wheel. He stopped me then.

"So you *were* driving the car?"

"Judge, suppose *you* tell *me* that."

"What do you mean, Chambers?"

"I mean I heard what she said, at the inquest. I heard what those cops said. I know where they found me. So I know who was driving, all right. She was. But if I tell it like I remember it, I got to say I was driving it. I didn't tell that coroner any lie, judge. *It still seems to me I was driving it.*"

"You lied about being drunk."

"That's right. I was all full of booze, and ether, and dope that they give you, and I lied all right. But I'm all right now, and I got sense enough to know the truth is all that can get me out of this, if anything can. Sure, I was drunk. I was stinko. And all I could think of was, I mustn't let them know I was drunk, because I was driving the car, and if they find out I was drunk, I'm sunk."

"Is that what you'd tell a jury?"

"I'd have to, judge. But what I can't understand is how she came to be driving it. I started out with it. I know that. I can even remember a guy standing there laughing at me. Then how come she was driving when it went over?"

"You drove it about two feet."

"You mean two miles."

"I mean two feet. Then she took the wheel away from you."

"Gee, I *must* have been stewed."

"Well, it's one of those things that a jury might believe. It's just got that cock-eyed look to it that generally goes with the truth. Yes, they might believe it."

He sat there looking at his nails, and I had a hard time to keep the grin from creeping over my face. I was glad when he started asking me more questions, so I could get my mind on something else, besides how easy I had fooled him.

"When did you go to work for Papadakis, Chambers?"

"Last winter."

"How long did you stay with him?"

"Till a month ago. Maybe six weeks."

"You worked for him six months, then?"

"About that."

"What did you do before that?"

"Oh, knocked around."

"Hitch-hiked? Rode freights? Bummed your meals wherever you could?"

"Yes sir."

He unstrapped a briefcase, put a pile of papers on the table, and began looking through them. "Ever been in Frisco?"

"Born there."

"Kansas City? New York? New Orleans? Chicago?"

"I've seen them all."

"Ever been in jail?"

"I have, judge. You knock around, you get in trouble with the cops now and then. Yes sir, I've been in jail."

"Ever been in jail in Tucson?"

"Yes sir. I think it was ten days I got there. It was for trespassing on railroad property."

"Salt Lake City? San Diego? Wichita?"

"Yes sir. All those places."

"Oakland?"

"I got three months there, judge. I got in a fight with a railroad detective."

"You beat him up pretty bad, didn't you?"

"Well, as the fellow says, he was beat up pretty bad, but you ought to seen the other one. I was beat up pretty bad, myself."

"Los Angeles?"

"Once. But that was only three days."

"Chambers, how did you come to go to work for Papadakis, anyhow?"

"Just a kind of an accident. I was broke, and he needed somebody. I blew in there to get something to eat, and he offered me a job, and I took it."

"Chambers, does that strike you as funny?"

"I don't know how you mean, judge."

"That after knocking around all these years, and never doing any work, or even trying to do any, so far as I can see, you suddenly settled down, and went to work, and held a job steady?"

"I didn't like it much, I'll own up to that."

"But you stuck."

"Nick, he was one of the nicest guys I ever knew. After I got a stake, I tried to tell him I was through, but I just didn't have the heart, much trouble as he had had with his help. Then when he had the accident, and wasn't there, I blew. I just blew, that's all. I guess I ought to treated him better, but I got rambling feet, judge. When they say go, I got to go with them. I just took a quiet way out."

"And then, the day after you came back, he got killed."

"You kind of make me feel bad now, judge. Because maybe I tell the jury different, but I'm telling you now I feel that was a hell of a lot my fault. If I hadn't been there, and begun promoting him for something to drink that afternoon, maybe he'd be here now. Understand, maybe that didn't have anything to do with it at all. I don't know. I was stinko, and I don't know what happened. Just the same, if she hadn't had two drunks in the car, maybe she could have drove better, couldn't she? Anyway, that's how I feel about it."

I looked at him, to see how he was taking it. He wasn't even looking at me. All of a sudden he jumped up and came over to the bed and took me by the shoulder. "Out with it, Chambers. Why did you stick with Papadakis for six months?"

"Judge, I don't get you."

"Yes you do. I've seen her, Chambers, and I can guess why you did it. She was in my office yesterday, and she had a black eye, and was pretty well banged up, but even with that she looked pretty good. For something like that, plenty of guys have said goodbye to the road, rambling feet or not."

"Anyhow they rambled. No, judge, you're wrong."

"They didn't ramble long. It's too good, Chambers. Here's an automobile accident that yesterday was a dead open-and-shut case of manslaughter, and today it's just evaporated into nothing at all. Every place I touch it, up pops a witness to tell me something, and when I fit all they have to say together, I haven't got any case. Come on, Chambers. You and that woman murdered this Greek, and the sooner you own up to it the better it'll be for you."

There wasn't any grin creeping over my face then, I'm here to tell you. I could feel my lips getting numb, and I tried to speak, but nothing would come out of my mouth.

"Well, why don't you say something?"

"You're coming at me. You're coming at me for something pretty bad. I don't know anything to say, judge."

"You were gabby enough a few minutes ago, when you were handing me that stuff about the truth being all that would get you out of this. Why can't you talk now?"

"You got me all mixed up."

"All right, we'll take it one thing at a time, so you won't be mixed up. In the first place, you've been sleeping with that woman, haven't you?"

"Nothing like it."

"How about the week Papadakis was in the hospital? Where did you sleep then?"

"In my own room."

"And she slept in hers? Come on, I've seen her, I tell you. I'd have been in there if I had to kick the door down and hang for rape. So would you. So *were* you."

"I never even thought of it."

"How about all those trips you took with her to Hasselman's Market in Glendale? What did you do with her on the way back?"

"Nick told me to go on those trips himself."

"I didn't ask you who told you to go. I asked you what you did."

I was so groggy I had to do something about it quick. All I could think of was to get sore. "All right, suppose we did. We didn't, but you say we did, and we'll let it go at that. Well, if it was all that easy, what would we be knocking him off for? Holy smoke, judge, I hear tell of guys that would commit murder for what you say I was getting, when they weren't getting it, but I never hear tell of a guy that would commit murder for it when he already had it."

"No? Well I'll tell you what you were knocking him off for. A piece of property out there, for one thing, that Papadakis paid $14,000 for, cash on the nail. And for that other little Christmas present you and she thought you would get on the boat with, and see what the wild waves looked like. *That little $10,000 accident policy that Papadakis carried on his life.*"

I could still see his face, but all around it was getting black and I was trying to keep myself from keeling over in bed. Next thing, he was holding a glass of water to my mouth. "Have a drink. You'll feel better."

I drank some of it. I had to.

"Chambers, I think this is the last murder you'll have a hand in for some time, but if you ever try another, for God's sake leave insurance companies out of it. They'll spend five times as much as Los Angeles County will let me put into a case. They've got detectives five times as good as any I'll be able to hire. They know their stuff from A to izzard, and they're right on your tail now. It means money to them. That's where you and she made your big mistake."

"Judge, I hope Christ may kill me, I never heard of an insurance policy until just this minute."

"You turned white as a sheet."

"Wouldn't you?"

"Well, how about getting me on your side, right from the start? How about a full confession, a quick plea of guilty, and I'll do what I can for you with the court? Ask for clemency for you both."

"Nothing doing."

"How about all that stuff you were telling me just now? About the truth, and how you'd have to come clean with the jury, and all that? You think you can get away with lies now? You think I'm going to stand for that?"

"I don't know what you're going to stand for. To hell with that. You stand for your side of it and I'll stand for mine. I didn't do it, and that's all I stand for. You got that?"

"The hell you say. Getting tough with me, hey? All right, now you get it. You're going to find out what that jury's really going to hear. First, you were sleeping with her, weren't you? Then Papadakis had a little accident, and you and she had a swell time. In bed together at night, down to the beach by day, holding hands and looking at each other in between. Then you both had a swell idea. Now that he's had an accident, make him take out an accident policy, and then knock him off. So you blew, to give her a chance to put it over. She worked at it, and pretty soon she had him. He took out a policy, a real good policy, that covered accidents, and health, and all the rest of it, and cost $46.72. Then you were ready. Two days after that, Frank Chambers accidentally on purpose

ran into Nick Papadakis on the street, and Nick tries to get
him to go back to work for him. And what do you know
about that, he and his wife had it already fixed up they were
going to Santa Barbara, had the hotel reservations and everything, so of course there was nothing to it but Frank Chambers had to come with them, just for old times' sake. And you
went. You got the Greek a little bit drunk, and did the same
for yourself. You stuck a couple of wine bottles in the car, just
to get the cops good and sore. Then you had to take that
Malibu Lake Road, so she could see Malibu Beach. Wasn't
that an idea, now. Eleven o'clock at night, and she was going
to drive down there to look at a bunch of houses with waves
in front of them. But you didn't get there. You stopped. And
while you were stopped, you crowned the Greek with one of
the wine bottles. A beautiful thing to crown a man with,
Chambers, and nobody knew it better than you, because that
was what you crowned that railroad dick with, over in Oakland. You crowned him, and then she started the car. And
while she was climbing out on the running board, you leaned
over from behind, and held the wheel, and fed with the hand
throttle. It didn't need much gas, because it was in second
gear. And after she got on the running board, she took the
wheel and fed with the hand throttle, and it was your turn to
climb out. But you were just a little drunk, weren't you? You
were too slow, and she was a little too quick to shoot the car
over the edge. So she jumped and you were caught. You think
a jury won't believe that, do you? It'll believe it, because I'll
prove every word of it, from the beach trip to the hand throttle, and when I do, there won't be any clemency for you, boy.
It'll be the rope, with you hanging on the end of it, and when
they cut you down they'll bury you out there with all the
others that were too goddam dumb to make a deal when they
had the chance to keep their neck from being broke."

"Nothing like that happened. Not that I know of."

"What are you trying to tell me? That *she* did it?"

"I'm not trying to tell you that anybody did it. Leave me
alone! Nothing like that happened."

"How do you know? I thought you were stinko."

"It didn't happen that I know of."

"Then you mean she did it?"

"I don't mean no such a goddam thing. I mean what I say and that's all I mean."

"Listen, Chambers. There were three people in the car, you, and she, and the Greek. Well, it's a cinch the Greek didn't do it. If you didn't do it, that leaves her, doesn't it?"

"Who the hell says anybody did it?"

"I do. Now we're getting somewhere, Chambers. Because maybe you didn't do it. You say you're telling the truth, and maybe you are. But if you are telling the truth, and didn't have any interest in this woman except as the wife of a friend, then you've got to do something about it, haven't you? You've got to sign a complaint against her."

"What do you mean complaint?"

"If she killed the Greek, she tried to kill you too, didn't she? You can't let her get away with that. Somebody might think it was pretty funny if you did. Sure, you'd be a sucker to let her get away with it. She knocks off her husband for the insurance, and she tries to knock off you too. You've got to do something about that, haven't you?"

"I might, if she did it. But I don't know she did it."

"If I prove it to you, you'll have to sign the complaint, won't you?"

"Sure. *If* you can prove it."

"All right, I'll prove it. When you stopped, you got out of the car, didn't you?"

"No."

"What? I thought you were so stinko you didn't remember anything. That's the second time you've remembered something now. I'm surprised at you."

"Not that I know of."

"But you did. Listen to this man's statement: 'I didn't notice much about the car, except that a woman was at the wheel and one man was inside laughing when we went by, and another man was out back, sick.' So you were out back a few minutes, sick. That was when she crowned Papadakis with the bottle. And when you got back you never noticed anything, because you were stinko, and Papadakis had passed out anyhow, and there was hardly anything to notice. You sat back and passed out, and that was when she slid up into second, kept her hand on the hand throttle, fed with that, and as soon as she had slid out on the running board, shot the car over."

"That don't prove it."

"Yes it does. The witness Wright says that the car was rolling over and over, down the gully, when he came around the bend, *but the woman was up on the road, waving to him for help!*"

"Maybe she jumped."

"If she jumped, it's funny she took her handbag with her, isn't it? Chambers, can a woman drive with a handbag in her hand? When she jumps, has she got time to pick it up? Chambers, it can't be done. It's impossible to jump from a sedan car that's turning over into a gully. She wasn't in the car when it went over! That proves it, doesn't it?"

"I don't know."

"What do you mean you don't know? Are you going to sign that complaint or not?"

"No."

"Listen, Chambers, it was no accident that car went over a second too soon. It was you or her, and she didn't mean it would be you."

"Let me alone. I don't know what you're talking about."

"Boy, it's still you or her. If you didn't have anything to do with this, you better sign this thing. Because if you don't, then I'll know. And so will the jury. And so will the judge. And so will the guy that springs the trap."

He looked at me a minute, then went out, and came back with another guy. The guy sat down and made out a form with a fountain pen. Sackett brought it over to me. "Right here, Chambers."

I signed. There was so much sweat on my hand the guy had to blot it off the paper.

10

After he went, the cop came back and mumbled something about blackjack. We played a few rounds, but I couldn't get my mind on it. I made out it got on my nerves to deal with one hand, and quit.

"He kind of got to you, hey?"

"Little bit."

"He's tough, he is. He gets to them all. He looks like a preacher, all full of love for the human race, but he's got a heart like a stone."

"Stone is right."

"Only one guy in this town has got it on him."

"Yeah?"

"Guy named Katz. You've heard of him."

"Sure, I heard of him."

"Friend of mine."

"It's the kind of a friend to have."

"Say. You ain't supposed to have no lawyer yet. You ain't been arraigned, and you can't send for nobody. They can hold you forty eight hours incommunicado, they call it. But if he shows up here, I got to let him see you, you get it? He might show up here, if I happened to be talking to him."

"You mean you get a cut."

"I mean he's a friend of mine. Well, if he didn't give me no cut, he wouldn't be no friend, would he? He's a great guy. He's the only one in this town can throw the headlock on Sackett."

"You're on, kid. And the sooner the better."

"I'll be back."

He went out for a little while, and when he came back he gave me a wink. And pretty soon, sure enough, there came a knock on the door, and in came Katz. He was a little guy, about forty years old, with a leathery face and a black moustache, and the first thing he did when he came in was take out a bag of Bull Durham smoking tobacco and a pack of brown papers and roll himself a cigarette. When he lit it, it burned halfway up one side, and that was the last he did about it. It just hung there, out the side of his mouth, and if it was lit or out, or whether he was asleep or awake, I never found out. He just sat there, with his eyes half shut and one leg hung over the arm of the chair, and his hat on the back of his head, and that was all. You might think that was a poor sight to see, for a guy in my spot, but it wasn't. He might be asleep, but even asleep he looked like he knew more than most guys awake, and a kind of a lump came up in my throat. It was like the sweet chariot had swung low and was going to pick me up.

The cop watched him roll the cigarette like it was Cadona doing the triple somersault, and he hated to go, but he had to. After he was out, Katz motioned to me to get going. I told him about how we had an accident, and how Sackett was trying to say we murdered the Greek for the insurance, and how he made me sign that complaint paper that said she had tried to murder me too. He listened, and after I had run down he sat there a while without saying anything. Then he got up.

"He's got you in a spot all right."

"I ought not to signed it. I don't believe she did any such a goddam thing. But he had me going. And now I don't know where the hell I'm at."

"Well, anyhow, you ought not to have signed it."

"Mr. Katz, will you do one thing for me? Will you see her, and tell her—"

"I'll see her. And I'll tell her what's good for her to know. For the rest of it, I'm handling this, and that means I'm handling it. You got that?"

"Yes sir, I've got it."

"I'll be with you at the arraignment. Or anyhow, somebody that I pick will be with you. As Sackett has made a complainant out of you, I may not be able to appear for you both, but I'll be handling it. And once more, that means that whatever I do, I'm handling it."

"Whatever you do, Mr. Katz."

"I'll be seeing you."

That night they put me on a stretcher again, and took me over to court for the arraignment. It was a magistrate's court, not a regular court. There wasn't any jury box, or witness stand, or any of that stuff. The magistrate sat on a platform, with some cops beside him, and in front of him was a long desk that ran clear across the room, and whoever had something to say hooked his chin over the desk and said it. There was a big crowd there, and photographers were snapping flashlights at me when they carried me in, and you could tell from the buzz that something big was going on. I couldn't see much, from down there on the stretcher, but I got a flash at Cora, sitting on the front bench with Katz, and Sackett, off to one side talking to some guys with briefcases, and some of the cops and witnesses that had been at the inquest. They set me down in front of the desk, on a couple of tables they had shoved together, and they hadn't much more than got the blankets spread over me right than they wound up a case about a Chinese woman, and a cop began rapping for quiet. While he was doing that, a young guy leaned down over me, and said his name was White, and Katz had asked him to represent me. I nodded my head, but he kept whispering that Mr. Katz had sent him, and the cop got sore and began banging hard.

"Cora Papadakis."

She stood up, and Katz took her up to the desk. She almost touched me as she went by, and it seemed funny to smell her, the same smell that had always set me wild, in the middle of all this stuff. She looked a little better than she had yesterday. She had on another blouse, that fitted her right, and her suit had been cleaned and pressed, and her shoes had been polished, and her eye was black, but not swelled. All the other people went up with her, and after they had spread out in a line, the cop told them to raise their right hand, and began to mumble about the truth, the whole truth, and nothing but the truth. He stopped in the middle of it to look down and see if I had my right hand raised. I didn't. I shoved it up, and he mumbled all over again. We all mumbled back.

The magistrate took off his glasses, and told Cora she was charged with the murder of Nick Papadakis, and with assault against Frank Chambers, with intent to kill, that she could make a statement if she wanted to, but any statement she made could be used against her, that she had the right to be represented by counsel, that she had eight days to plead, and the court would hear her plea at any time during that period. It was a long spiel, and you could hear them coughing before he got done.

Then Sackett started up, and told what he was going to prove. It was about the same as he had told me that morning, only he made it sound solemn as hell. When he got through,

he began putting on his witnesses. First there was the ambulance doctor, that told when the Greek had died, and
where. Then came the jail doctor, that had made the autopsy,
and then came the coroner's secretary, that identified the
minutes of the inquest, and left them with the magistrate, and
then came a couple of more guys, but I forget what they said.
When they got done, all that the whole bunch had proved
was that the Greek was dead, and as I knew that anyway, I
didn't pay much attention. Katz never asked any of them anything. Every time the magistrate would look at him, he would
wave his hand and the guy would step aside.

After they had the Greek dead enough to suit them, Sackett
really straightened out, and put some stuff in that meant
something. He called a guy that said he represented the Pacific
States Accident Assurance Corporation of America, and he
told how the Greek had taken out a policy just five days before. He told what it covered, how the Greek would get $25
a week for 52 weeks if he got sick, and the same if he got hurt
in an accident so he couldn't work, and how he would get
$5,000 if he lost one limb, and $10,000 if he lost two limbs,
and how his widow would get $10,000 if he was killed in an
accident, and $20,000 if the accident was on a railroad train.
When he got that far it began to sound like a sales talk, and
the magistrate held up his hand.

"I've got all the insurance I need."

Everybody laughed at the magistrate's gag. Even I laughed.
You'd be surprised how funny it sounded.

Sackett asked a few more questions, and then the magistrate
turned to Katz. Katz thought a minute, and when he talked
to the guy, he did it slow, like he wanted to make sure he had
every word straight.

"You are an interested party to this proceeding?"

"In a sense I am, Mr. Katz."

"You wish to escape payment of this indemnity, on the
ground that a crime has been committed, is that correct?"

"That is correct."

"You really believe that a crime has been committed, that
this woman killed her husband to obtain this indemnity, and
either tried to kill this man, or else deliberately placed him in

jeopardy that might cause his death, all as part of a plan to obtain this indemnity?"

The guy kind of smiled, and thought a minute, like he would return the compliment and get every word straight too. "Answering that question, Mr. Katz, I would say I've handled thousands of such cases, cases of fraud that go over my desk every day, and I think I have an unusual experience in that kind of investigation. I may say that I have never seen a clearer case in all my years' work for this and other companies. I don't only believe a crime has been committed, Mr. Katz. I practically know it."

"That is all. Your honor, I plead her guilty on both charges."

If he had dropped a bomb in that courtroom, he couldn't have stirred it up quicker. Reporters rushed out, and photographers rushed up to the desk to get pictures. They kept bumping into each other, and the magistrate got sore and began banging for order. Sackett looked like he had been shot, and all over the place there was a roar like somebody had all of a sudden shoved a seashell up against your ear. I kept trying to see Cora's face. But all I could get of it was the corner of her mouth. It kept twitching, like somebody was jabbing a needle into it about once every second.

Next thing I knew, the guys on the stretcher picked me up, and followed the young guy, White, out of the courtroom. Then they went with me on the double across a couple of halls into a room with three or four cops in it. White said something about Katz, and the cops cleared out. They set me down on the desk, and then the guys on the stretcher went out. White walked around a little, and then the door opened and a matron came in with Cora. Then White and the matron went out, and the door closed, and we were alone. I tried to think of something to say, and couldn't. She walked around, and didn't look at me. Her mouth was still twitching. I kept swallowing, and after a while I thought of something.

"We've been flim-flammed, Cora."

She didn't say anything. She just kept walking around.

"That guy Katz, he's nothing but a cop's stool. A cop sent

him to me. I thought he was on the up-and-up. But we've been flim-flammed."

"Oh no, we ain't been flim-flammed."

"We been flim-flammed. I ought to have known, when the cop tried to sell him to me. But I didn't. I thought he was on the level."

"I've been flim-flammed, but you haven't."

"Yes I have. He fooled me too."

"I see it all now. I see why I had to drive the car. I see it, that other time, why it was me that had to do it, not you. Oh yes. I fell for you because you were smart. And now I find out you're smart. Ain't that funny? You fall for a guy because he's smart and then you find out he's smart."

"What are you trying to tell me, Cora?"

"Flim-flammed! I'll say I was. You and that lawyer. You fixed it up all right. You fixed it up so I tried to kill you too. That was so it would look like you couldn't have had anything to do with it. Then you have me plead guilty in court. So you're not in it at all. All right. I guess I'm pretty dumb. But I'm not that dumb. Listen, Mr. Frank Chambers. When I get through, just see how smart you are. There's just such a thing as being too smart."

I tried to talk to her, but it wasn't any use. When she had got so that even her lips were white, under the lipstick, the door opened and Katz came in. I tried to jump for him, off the stretcher. I couldn't move. They had me strapped so I couldn't move.

"Get out of here, you goddam stool. *You* were handling it. I'll say you were. But now I know you for what you are. Do you hear that? Get out of here!"

"Why, what's the matter, Chambers?"

You would have thought he was a Sunday school teacher, talking to some kid that was crying for his chewing gum that had been taken away. "Why, what's the matter? I *am* handling it. I told you that."

"That's right. Only God help you if I ever get you so I got my hands on you."

He looked at her, like it was something he just couldn't understand, and maybe she could help him out. She came over to him.

"This man here, this man and you, you ganged up on me so I would get it and he would go free. Well, he was in this as much as I was, and he's not going to get away with it. I'm going to tell it. I'm going to tell it all, and I'm going to tell it right now."

He looked at her, and shook his head, and it was the phoniest look I ever saw on a man's face. "Now my dear. I wouldn't do that. If you'll just let me handle this—"

"You handled it. Now I'll handle it."

He got up, shrugged his shoulders, and went out. He was hardly gone before a guy with big feet and a red neck came in with a little portable typewriter, set it on a chair with a couple of books under it, hitched up to it, and looked at her.

"Mr. Katz said you wanted to make a statement?"

He had a little squeaky voice, and a kind of a grin when he talked.

"That's right. A statement."

She began to speak jerky, two or three words at a time, and as fast as she said it, he rattled it off on the typewriter. She told it all. She went back to the beginning, and told how she met me, how we first began going together, how we tried to knock off the Greek once, but missed. A couple of times, a cop put his head in at the door, but the guy at the typewriter held up his hand.

"Just a few minutes, sarge."

"O.K."

When she got to the end, she said she didn't know anything about the insurance, we hadn't done it for that at all, but just to get rid of him.

"That's all."

He gathered his sheets together, and she signed them. "Will you just initial these pages?" She initialed them. He got out a notary stamp, and made her hold up her right hand, and put the stamp on, and signed it. Then he put the papers in his pocket, closed his typewriter, and went out.

She went to the door and called the matron. "I'm ready now." The matron came in and took her out. The guys on the stretcher came in and carried me out. They went on the double, but on the way they got jammed in with the crowd that was watching her, where she was standing in front of the elevators with the matron, waiting to go up to the jail. It's on the top floor of the Hall of Justice. They pushed on through, and my blanket got pulled so it was trailing on the floor. She picked it up and tucked it around me, then turned away quick.

II

They took me back to the hospital, but instead of the state cop watching me, it was this guy that had taken the confession. He lay down on the other bed. I tried to sleep, and after a while I did. I dreamed she was looking at me, and I was trying to say something to her, but couldn't. Then she would go down, and I would wake up, and that crack would be in my ears, that awful crack that the Greek's head made when I hit it. Then I would sleep again, and dream I was falling. And I would wake up again, holding on to my neck, and that same crack would be in my ears. One time when I woke up I was yelling. He leaned up on his elbow.

"Yay."

"Yay."

"What's the matter?"

"Nothing's the matter. Just had a dream."

"O.K."

He never left me for a minute. In the morning, he made them bring him a basin of water, and took out a razor from his pocket, and shaved. Then he washed himself. They brought in breakfast, and he ate his at the table. We didn't say anything.

They brought me a paper, then, and there it was, with a big picture of Cora on the front page, and a smaller picture of me on the stretcher underneath it. It called her the bottle killer. It told how she had pleaded guilty at the arraignment, and would come up for sentence today. On one of the inside pages, it had a story that it was believed the case would set a record for speed in its disposition, and another story about a preacher that said if all cases were railroaded through that quick, it would do more to prevent crime than passing a hun-

dred laws. I looked all through the paper for something about the confession. It wasn't in there.

About twelve o'clock a young doctor came in and went to work on my back with alcohol, sopping off some of the adhesive tape. He was supposed to sop it off, but most of the time he just peeled it, and it hurt like hell. After he got part of it off, I found I could move. He left the rest on, and a nurse brought me my clothes. I put them on. The guys on the stretcher came in and helped me to the elevator and out of the hospital. There was a car waiting there, with a chauffeur. The guy that had spent the night with me put me in, and we drove about two blocks. Then he took me out, and we went in an office building, and up to an office. And there was Katz with his hand stuck out and a grin all over his face.

"It's all over."

"Swell. When do they hang her?"

"They don't hang her. She's out, free. Free as a bird. She'll be over in a little while, soon as they fix up some things in court. Come in. I'll tell you about it."

He took me in a private office and closed the door. Soon as he rolled a cigarette, and half burned it up, and got it pasted on his mouth, he started to talk. I hardly knew him. It didn't seem that a man that had looked so sleepy the day before could be as excited as he was.

"Chambers, this is the greatest case I ever had in my life. I'm in it, and out of it, in less than twenty four hours, and yet I tell you I never had anything like it. Well, the Dempsey-Firpo fight lasted less than two rounds, didn't it? It's not how long it lasts. It's what you do while you're in there.

"This wasn't really a fight, though. It was a four-handed card game, where every player has been dealt a perfect hand. Beat that, if you can. You think it takes a card player to play a bum hand, don't you. To hell with that. I get those bum hands every day. Give me one like this, where they've all got cards, *where they've all got cards that'll win if they play them right*, and then watch me. Oh, Chambers, you did me a favor all right when you called me in on this. I'll never get another one like it."

"You haven't said anything yet."

"I'll say it, don't worry about that. But you won't get it, you won't know how the hand was played, until I get the cards straightened out for you. Now first. There were you and the woman. You each held a perfect hand. Because that was a perfect murder, Chambers. Maybe you don't even know how good it was. All that stuff Sackett tried to scare you with, about her not being in the car when it went over, and having her handbag with her, and all that, that didn't amount to a goddam thing. A car can teeter before it goes over, can't it? And a woman can grab her handbag before she jumps, can't she? That don't prove any crime. That just proves she's a woman."

"How'd you find out about that stuff?"

"I got it from Sackett. I had dinner with him last night, and he was crowing over me. He was pitying me, the sap. Sackett and I are enemies. We're the friendliest enemies that ever were. He'd sell his soul to the devil to put something over on me, and I'd do the same for him. We even put up a bet on it. We bet $100. He was giving me the razz, because he had a perfect case, where he could just play the cards and let the hangman do his stuff."

That was swell, two guys betting $100 on what the hangman would do to me and Cora, but I wanted to get it straight, just the same.

"If we had a perfect hand, where did his hand come in?"

"I'm getting to that. You had a perfect hand, but Sackett knows that no man and no woman that ever lived could play that hand, not if the prosecutor plays his hand right. He knows that all he's got to do is get one of you working against the other, and it's in the bag. That's the first thing. Next thing, he doesn't even have to work the case up. He's got an insurance company to do that for him, so he doesn't have to lift a finger. That's what Sackett loved about it. All he had to do was play the cards, and the pot would fall right in his lap. So what does he do? He takes this stuff the insurance company dug up for him, and scares the hell out of you with it, and gets you to sign a complaint against her. He takes the best card you've got, which is how bad you were hurt yourself, and makes you trump your own ace with it. If you were hurt

that bad, it had to be an accident, and yet Sackett uses that to make you sign a complaint against her. And you sign it, because you're afraid if you don't sign it he'll know goddam well you did it."

"I turned yellow, that's all."

"Yellow is a color you figure on in murder, and nobody figures on it better than Sackett. All right. He's got you where he wants you. He's going to make you testify against her, and he knows that once you do that, no power on earth can keep her from ratting on you. So that's where he's sitting when he has dinner with me. He razzes me. He pities me. He bets me $100. And all the time I'm sitting there with a hand that I know I can beat him with, if I only play the cards right. All right, Chambers. You're looking in my hand. What do you see in it?"

"Not much."

"Well, what?"

"Nothing, to tell you the truth."

"Neither did Sackett. But now watch. After I left you yesterday, I went to see her, and got an authorization from her to open Papadakis's safe deposit box. And I found what I expected. There were some other policies in that box, and I went to see the agent that wrote them, and this is what I found out:

"'That accident policy didn't have anything to do with that accident that Papadakis had a few weeks ago. The agent had turned up on his calendar that Papadakis's automobile insurance had pretty near run out, and he went out there to see him. She wasn't there. They fixed it up pretty quick for the automobile insurance, fire, theft, collision, public liability, the regular line. Then the agent showed Papadakis where he was covered on everything but injury to himself, and asked him how about a personal accident policy. Papadakis got interested right away. Maybe that other accident was the reason for that, but if it was the agent didn't know anything about it. He signed up for the whole works, and gave the agent his check, and next day the policies were mailed out to him. You understand, an agent works for a lot of companies, and not all these policies were written by the same company. That's No. 1 point that Sackett forgot. But the main thing to remember

is that Papadakis didn't only have the new insurance. He had
the old policies too, *and they still had a week to run.*

"All right, now, get this set-up. The Pacific States Accident
is on a $10,000 personal accident policy. The Guaranty of
California is on a $10,000 new public liability bond, and the
Rocky Mountain Fidelity is on an old $10,000 public liability
bond. So that's my first card. He had an insurance company
working for him up to $10,000. I had two insurance com-
panies working for me up to $20,000, whenever I wanted to
call them in. Do you get it?"

"No, I don't."

"Look. Sackett stole your big card off you, didn't he? Well,
I stole the same card off him. You were hurt, weren't you?
You were hurt bad. Well, if Sackett convicts her of murder,
and you bring suit against her for injuries sustained as a result
of that murder, then a jury will give you whatever you ask for.
And those two bonding companies are liable for every cent of
their policies to satisfy that judgment."

"Now I get it."

"Pretty, Chambers, pretty. I found that card in my mitt,
but you didn't find it, and Sackett didn't find it, and the Pacific States Accident didn't find it, because they were so busy
playing Sackett's game for him, and so sure his game would
win, that they didn't even think of it."

He walked around the room a few times, falling for himself
every time he passed a little mirror that was in the corner, and
then he went on.

"All right, there it was, but the next thing was how to play
it. I had to play it quick, because Sackett had already played
his, and that confession was due any minute. It might even
come at the arraignment, as soon as she heard you testify
against her. I had to move fast. So what did I do? I waited
till the Pacific States Accident man had testified, and then got
him on record that he really believed a crime had been committed. That was just in case I had a false arrest action against
him later on. And then, wham, I pleaded her guilty. That
ended the arraignment, and for that night, blocked off Sackett. Then I rushed her in a counsel room, claimed a half hour
before she was locked up for the night, and sent you in
there with her. Five minutes with you was all she needed.

When I got in there she was ready to spill it. Then I sent Kennedy in."

"The dick that was with me last night?"

"He used to be a dick, but he's not a dick any more. He's my gum-shoe man now. She thought she was talking to a dick, but she was really talking to a dummy. But it did the work. After she got it off her chest, she kept quiet till today, and that was long enough. The next thing was you. What you would do was blow. There was no charge against you, so you weren't under arrest any more, even if you thought you were. Soon as you tumbled to that, I knew no tape, or sore back, or hospital orderly, or anything else would hold you, so after he got done with her I sent Kennedy over to keep an eye on you. The next thing was a little midnight conference between the Pacific States Accident, the Guaranty of California, and the Rocky Mountain Fidelity. And when I laid it in front of them, they did business awful quick."

"What do you mean, they did business?"

"First, I read them the law. I read them the guest clause, Section 141¾, California Vehicle Act. That says if a guest in an automobile gets hurt, he has no right of recovery, *provided*, that if his injury resulted from intoxication or willful misconduct on the part of the driver, then he can recover. You see, you were a guest, and I had pleaded her guilty to murder and assault. Plenty of willful misconduct there, wasn't there? And they couldn't be sure, you know. Maybe she did do it alone. So those two companies on the liability policies, the ones that had their chin hanging out for a wallop from you, they chipped in $5,000 apiece to pay the Pacific States Accident policy, and the Pacific States Accident agreed to pay up and shut up, and the whole thing didn't take over a half hour."

He stopped and grinned at himself some more.

"What then?"

"I'm still thinking about it. I can still see Sackett's face just now when that Pacific States Accident fellow went on the stand today and said his investigation had convinced him that no crime had been committed, and his company was paying the accident claim in full. Chambers, do you know what that feels like? To feint a guy open and then let him have it, right on the chin? There's no feeling like it in the world."

"I still don't get it. What was this guy testifying again for?"

"She was up for sentence. And after a plea of guilty, a court usually wants to hear some testimony to find out what the case is really about. To determine the sentence. And Sackett had started in howling for blood. He wanted the death penalty. Oh, he's a blood-thirsty lad, Sackett is. That's why it stimulates me to work against him. He really believes hanging them does some good. You're playing for stakes when you're playing against Sackett. So he put his insurance man on the stand again. But instead of it being *his* son of a bitch, after that little midnight session it was *my* son of a bitch, only Sackett didn't know it. He roared plenty when he found it out. But it was too late. If an insurance company didn't believe she was guilty, a jury would never believe it, would it? There wasn't a chance in the world of convicting her after that. And that was when I burned Sackett. I got up and made a speech to the court. I took my time about it. I told how my client had protested her innocence from the beginning. I told how I didn't believe it. I told how I knew there existed what I regarded as overwhelming evidence against her, enough to convict her in any court, and that I believed I was acting in her best interest when I decided to plead her guilty and throw her on the mercy of the court. But, Chambers, do you know how I rolled that *but* under my tongue? But, in the light of the testimony just given, there was no course open to me but to withdraw the pleas of guilty and allow the cases to proceed. Sackett couldn't do a thing, because I was still within the limit of eight days for a plea. He knew he was sunk. He consented to a plea for manslaughter, the court examined the other witnesses itself, gave her six months, suspended sentence, and practically apologized even for that. We quashed the assault charge. That was the key to the whole thing, and we almost forgot it."

There came a rap on the door. Kennedy brought Cora in, put some papers down in front of Katz, and left. "There you are, Chambers. Just sign that, will you? It's a waiver of damages for any injuries sustained by you. It's what they get out of it for being so nice."

I signed.

"You want me to take you home, Cora?"

"I guess so."

"One minute, one minute, you two. Not so fast. There's one other little thing. That ten thousand dollars you get for knocking off the Greek."

She looked at me and I looked at her. He sat there looking at the check. "You see, it wouldn't be a perfect hand if there hadn't been some money in it for Katz. I forgot to tell you about that. Well. Oh, well. I won't be a hog. I generally take it all, but on this, I'll just make it half. Mrs. Papadakis, you make out your check for $5,000, and I'll make this over to you and go over to the bank and fix up the deposits. Here. Here's a blank check."

She sat down, and picked up the pen, and started to write, and then stopped, like she couldn't quite figure out what it was all about. All of a sudden, he went over and picked up the blank check and tore it up.

"What the hell. Once in a lifetime, isn't it? Here. You keep it all. I don't care about the ten grand. I've got ten grand. This is what I want!"

He opened his pocketbook, took out a slip, and showed it to us. It was Sackett's check for $100. "You think I'm going to cash that? I am like hell. I'm going to frame it. It goes up there, right over my desk."

12

We went out of there, and got a cab, because I was so crippled up, and first we went to the bank, and put the check in, and then we went to a flower shop, and got two big bunches of flowers, and then we went to the funeral of the Greek. It seemed funny he was only dead two days, and they were just burying him. The funeral was at a little Greek church, and a big crowd of people was there, some of them Greeks I had seen out to the place now and then. They gave her a dead pan when we came in, and put her in a seat about three rows from the front. I could see them looking at us, and I wondered what I would do if they tried to pull some

rough stuff later. They were his friends, not ours. But pretty
soon I saw an afternoon paper being passed around, that had
big headlines in it that she was innocent, and an usher took
a look at it, and came running over and moved us up on the
front bench. The guy that did the preaching started out with
some dirty cracks about how the Greek died, but a guy went
up and whispered to him, and pointed at the paper that had
got up near the front by that time, and he turned around and
said it all over again, without any dirty cracks, and put in
about the sorrowing widow and friends, and they all nodded
their head it was O.K. When we went out in the churchyard,
where the grave was, a couple of them took her by the arm,
and helped her out, and a couple more helped me. I got to
blubbering while they were letting him down. Singing those
hymns will do it to you every time, and specially when it's
about a guy you like as well as I liked the Greek. At the end
they sang some song I had heard him sing a hundred times,
and that finished me. It was all I could do to lay our flowers
out the way they were supposed to go.

The taxi driver found a guy that would rent us a Ford for
$15 a week, and we took it, and started out. She drove. When
we got out of the city we passed a house that was being built,
and all the way out we talked about how not many of them
have gone up lately, but the whole section is going to be built
up as soon as things get better. When we got out to the place
she let me out, put the car away, and then we went inside. It
was all just like we left it, even to the glasses in the sink that
we had drunk the wine out of, and the Greek's guitar, that
hadn't been put away yet because he was so drunk. She put
the guitar in the case, and washed the glasses, and then went
upstairs. After a minute I went up after her.

She was in their bedroom, sitting by the window, looking
out at the road.
"Well?"
She didn't say anything. I started to leave.
"I didn't ask you to leave."
I sat down again. It was a long while before she snapped
out of it.

"You turned on me, Frank."

"No I didn't. He had me, Cora. I had to sign his paper. If I didn't, then he would tumble to everything. I didn't turn on you. I just went along with him, till I could find out where I was at."

"You turned on me. I could see it in your eye."

"All right, Cora, I did. I just turned yellow, that's all. I didn't want to do it. I tried not to do it. But he beat me down. I cracked up, that's all."

"I know."

"I went through hell about it."

"And I turned on you, Frank."

"They made you do it. You didn't want to. They set a trap for you."

"I wanted to do it. I hated you then."

"That's all right. It was for something I didn't really do. You know how it was, now."

"No. I hated you for something you really did."

"I never hated you, Cora. I hated myself."

"I don't hate you now. I hate that Sackett. And Katz. Why couldn't they leave us alone? Why couldn't they let us fight it out together? I wouldn't have minded that. I wouldn't have minded it even if it meant—you know. We would have had our love. And that's all we ever had. But the very first time they started their meanness, you turned on me."

"And you turned on me, don't forget that."

"That's the awful part. I turned on you. We both turned on each other."

"Well, that makes it even, don't it?"

"It makes it even, but look at us now. We were up on a mountain. We were up so high, Frank. We had it all, out there, that night. I didn't know I could feel anything like that. And we kissed and sealed it so it would be there forever, no matter what happened. We had more than any two people in the world. And then we fell down. First you, and then me. Yes, it makes it even. We're down here together. But we're not up high any more. Our beautiful mountain is gone."

"Well what the hell? We're together, ain't we?"

"I guess so. But I thought an awful lot, Frank. Last night. About you and me, and the movies, and why I flopped, and the hashhouse, and the road, and why you like it. We're just two punks, Frank. God kissed us on the brow that night. He gave us all that two people can ever have. And we just weren't the kind that could have it. We had all that love, and we just cracked up under it. It's a big airplane engine, that takes you through the sky, right up to the top of the mountain. But when you put it in a Ford, it just shakes it to pieces. That's what we are, Frank, a couple of Fords. God is up there laughing at us."

"The hell he is. Well we're laughing at him too, aren't we? He put up a red stop sign for us, and we went past it. And then what? Did we get shoved off the deep end? We did like hell. We got away clean, and got $10,000 for doing the job. So God kissed us on the brow, did he? Then the devil went to bed with us, and believe you me, kid, he sleeps pretty good."

"Don't talk that way, Frank."

"Did we get that ten grand, or didn't we?"

"I don't want to think about the ten grand. It's a lot, but it couldn't buy our mountain."

"Mountain, hell, we got the mountain and ten thousand smackers to pile on top of that yet. If you want to go up high, take a look around from that pile."

"You nut. I wish you could see yourself, yelling with that bandage on your head."

"You forgot something. We got something to celebrate. We ain't never had that drunk yet."

"I wasn't talking about that kind of a drunk."

"A drunk's a drunk. Where's that liquor I had before I left?"

I went to my room and got the liquor. It was a quart of Bourbon, three quarters full. I went down, got some Coca Cola glasses, and ice cubes, and White Rock, and came back upstairs. She had taken her hat off and let her hair down. I fixed two drinks. They had some White Rock in them, and a couple of pieces of ice, but the rest was out of the bottle.

"Have a drink. You'll feel better. That's what Sackett said when he put the spot on me, the louse."

"My, but that's strong."

"You bet it is. Here, you got too many clothes on."

I pushed her over to the bed. She held on to her glass, and some of it spilled. "The hell with it. Plenty more where that came from."

I began slipping off her blouse. "Rip me, Frank. Rip me like you did that night."

I ripped all her clothes off. She twisted and turned, slow, so they would slip out from under her. Then she closed her eyes and lay back on the pillow. Her hair was falling over her shoulders in snaky curls. Her eye was all black, and her breasts weren't drawn up and pointing up at me, but soft, and spread out in two big pink splotches. She looked like the great grand-mother of every whore in the world. The devil got his money's worth that night.

13

We kept that up for six months. We kept it up, and it was always the same way. We'd have a fight, and I'd reach for the bottle. What we had the fights about was going away. We couldn't leave the state until the suspended sentence was up, but after that I meant we should blow. I didn't tell her, but I wanted her a long way from Sackett. I was afraid if she got sore at me for something, she'd go off her nut and spill it like she had that other time, after the arraignment. I didn't trust her for a minute. At first, she was all hot for going too, spe-cially when I got talking about Hawaii and the South Seas, but then the money began to roll in. When we opened up, about a week after the funeral, people flocked out there to see what she looked like, and then they came back because they had a good time. And she got all excited about here was our chance to make some more money.

"Frank, all these roadside joints around here are lousy. They're run by people that used to have a farm back in Kansas or somewhere, and got as much idea how to entertain people as a pig has. I believe if somebody came along that knew the business like I do, and tried to make it nice for them, they'd come and bring all their friends."

"To hell with them. We're selling out anyhow."

"We could sell easier if we were making money."

"We're making money."

"I mean good money. Listen, Frank. I've got an idea people would be glad of the chance to sit out under the trees. Think of that. All this nice weather in California, and what do they do with it? Bring people inside of a joint that's set up ready-made by the Acme Lunch Room Fixture Company, and stinks so it makes you sick to your stomach, and feed them awful stuff that's the same from Fresno down to the border, and never give them any chance to feel good at all."

"Look. We're selling out, aren't we? Then the less we got to sell the quicker we get rid of it. Sure, they'd like to sit under the trees. Anybody but a California Bar-B-Q slinger would know that. But if we put them under the trees we've got to get tables, and wire up a lot of lights out there, and all that stuff, and maybe the next guy don't want it that way at all."

"We've got to stay six months. Whether we like it or not."

"Then we use that six months finding a buyer."

"I want to try it."

"All right, then try it. But I'm telling you."

"I could use some of our inside tables."

"I said try it, didn't I? Come on. We'll have a drink."

What we had the big blow-off over was the beer license, and then I tumbled to what she was really up to. She put the tables out under the trees, on a little platform she had built, with a striped awning over them and lanterns at night, and it went pretty good. She was right about it. Those people really enjoyed a chance to sit out under the trees for a half hour, and listen to a little radio music, before they got in their cars and went on. And then beer came back. She saw a chance to leave it just like it was, put beer in, and call it a beer garden.

"I don't want any beer garden, I tell you. All I want is a guy that'll buy the whole works and pay cash."

"But it seems a shame."

"Not to me it don't."

"But look, Frank. The license is only twelve dollars for six months. My goodness, we can afford twelve dollars, can't we?"

"We get the license and then we're in the beer business. We're in the gasoline business already, and the hot dog business, and now we got to go in the beer business. The hell with it. I want to get out of it, not get in deeper."

"Everybody's got one."

"And welcome, so far as I'm concerned."

"People wanting to come, and the place all fixed up under the trees, and now I have to tell them we don't have beer because we haven't any license."

"Why do you have to tell them anything?"

"All we've got to do is put in coils and then we can have draught beer. It's better than bottled beer, and there's more money in it. I saw some lovely glasses in Los Angeles the other day. Nice tall ones. The kind people like to drink beer out of."

"So we got to get coils and glasses now, have we? I tell you I don't *want* any beer garden."

"Frank, don't you ever want to *be* something?"

"Listen, get this. I want to get away from this place. I want to go somewhere else, where every time I look around I don't see the ghost of a goddam Greek jumping out at me, and hear his echo in my dreams, and jump every time the radio comes out with a guitar. I've got to go away, do you hear me? I've got to get out of here, or I go nuts."

"You're lying to me."

"Oh no, I'm not lying. I never meant anything more in my life."

"You don't see the ghost of any Greek, that's not it. Somebody else might see it, but not Mr. Frank Chambers. No, you want to go away just because you're a bum, that's all. That's what you were when you came here, and that's what you are now. When we go away, and our money's all gone, then what?"

"What do I care? We go away, don't we?"

"That's it, you don't care. We could stay here—"

"I knew it. That's what you really mean. That's what you've meant all along. That we stay here."

"And why not? We've got it good. Why wouldn't we stay here? Listen, Frank. You've been trying to make a bum out of me ever since you've known me, but you're not going to do it. I told you, I'm not a bum. I want to *be* something. We stay here. We're not going away. We take out the beer license. We amount to something."

It was late at night, and we were upstairs, half undressed. She was walking around like she had that time after the arraignment, and talking in the same funny jerks.

"Sure we stay. We do whatever you say, Cora. Here, have a drink."

"I don't want a drink."

"Sure you want a drink. We got to laugh some more about getting the money, haven't we?"

"We already laughed about it."

"But we're going to make more money, aren't we? On the beer garden? We got to put down a couple on that, just for luck."

"You nut. All right. Just for luck."

That's the way it went, two or three times a week. And the tip-off was that every time I would come out of a hangover, I would be having those dreams. I would be falling, and that crack would be in my ears.

Right after the sentence ran out, she got the telegram her mother was sick. She got some clothes in a hurry, and I put her on the train, and going back to the parking lot I felt funny, like I was made of gas and would float off somewhere. I felt free. For a week, anyway, I wouldn't have to wrangle, or fight off dreams, or nurse a woman back to a good humor with a bottle of liquor.

On the parking lot a girl was trying to start her car. It wouldn't do anything. She stepped on everything and it was just plain dead.

"What's the matter? Won't it go?"

"They left the ignition on when they parked it, and now the battery's run out."

"Then it's up to them. They've got to charge it for you."

"Yes, but I've got to get home."

"I'll take you home."

"You're awfully friendly."

"I'm the friendliest guy in the world."

"You don't even know where I live."

"I don't care."

"It's pretty far. It's in the country."

"The further the better. Wherever it is, it's right on my way."

"You make it hard for a nice girl to say no."

"Well then, if it's so hard, don't say it."

She was a light-haired girl, maybe a little older than I was, and not bad on looks. But what got me was how friendly she was, and how she wasn't any more afraid of what I might do to her than if I was a kid or something. She knew her way around all right, you could see that. And what finished it was when I found out she didn't know who I was. We told our names on the way out, and to her mine didn't mean a thing. Boy oh boy what a relief that was. One person in the world that wasn't asking me to sit down to the table a minute, and then telling me to give them the low-down on that case where they said the Greek was murdered. I looked at her, and I felt the same way I had walking away from the train, like I was made of gas, and would float out from behind the wheel.

"So your name is Madge Allen, hey?"

"Well, it's really Kramer, but I took my own name again after my husband died."

"Well listen Madge Allen, or Kramer, or whatever you want to call it, I've got a little proposition to make you."

"Yes?"

"What do you say we turn this thing around, point her south, and you and me take a little trip for about a week?"

"Oh, I couldn't do that."

"Why not?"

"Oh, I just couldn't, that's all."

"You like me?"

"Sure I like you."

"Well, I like you. What's stopping us?"

She started to say something, didn't say it, and then laughed. "I own up. I'd like to, all right. And if it's something

I'm supposed not to do, why that don't mean a thing to me. But I can't. It's on account of the cats."

"Cats?"

"We've got a lot of cats. And I'm the one that takes care of them. That's why I had to get home."

"Well, they got pet farms, haven't they? We'll call one up, and tell them to come over and get them."

That struck her funny. "I'd like to see a pet farm's face when it saw them. They're not that kind."

"Cats are cats, ain't they?"

"Not exactly. Some are big and some are little. Mine are big. I don't think a pet farm would do very well with that lion we've got. Or the tigers. Or the puma. Or the three jaguars. They're the worst. A jaguar is an awful cat."

"Holy smoke. What do you do with those things?"

"Oh, work them in movies. Sell the cubs. People have private zoos. Keep them around. They draw trade."

"They wouldn't draw my trade."

"We've got a restaurant. People look at them."

"Restaurant, hey. That's what I've got. Whole goddam country lives selling hot dogs to each other."

"Well, anyway, I couldn't walk out on my cats. They've got to eat."

"The hell we can't. We'll call up Goebel and tell him to come get them. He'll board the whole bunch while we're gone for a hundred bucks."

"Is it worth a hundred bucks to you to take a trip with me?"

"It's worth exactly a hundred bucks."

"Oh my. I can't say no to that. I guess you better call up Goebel."

I dropped her off at her place, found a pay station, called up Goebel, went back home, and closed up. Then I went back after her. It was about dark. Goebel had sent a truck over, and I met it coming back, full of stripes and spots. I parked about a hundred yards down the road, and in a minute she showed up with a little grip, and I helped her in, and we started off.

"You like it?"

"I love it."

We went down to Caliente, and next day we kept on down the line to Ensenada, a little Mexican town about seventy miles down the coast. We went to a little hotel there, and spent three or four days. It was pretty nice. Ensenada is all Mex, and you feel like you left the U.S.A. a million miles away. Our room had a little balcony in front of it, and in the afternoon we would just lay out there, look at the sea, and let the time go by.

"Cats, hey. What do you do, train them?"

"Not the stuff we've got. They're no good. All but the tigers are outlaws. But I do train them."

"You like it?"

"Not much, the real big ones. But I like pumas. I'm going to get an act together with them some time. But I'll need a lot of them. Jungle pumas. Not these outlaws you see in the zoos."

"What's an outlaw?"

"He'd kill you."

"Wouldn't they all?"

"They might, but an outlaw does anyhow. If it was people, he would be a crazy person. It comes from being bred in captivity. These cats you see, they look like cats, but they're really cat lunatics."

"How can you tell it's a jungle cat?"

"I catch him in a jungle."

"You mean you catch them *alive*?"

"Sure. They're no good to me dead."

"Holy smoke. How do you do that?"

"Well, first I get on a boat and go down to Nicaragua. All the really fine pumas come from Nicaragua. These California and Mexican things are just scrubs compared to them. Then I hire me some Indian boys and go up in the mountains. Then I catch my pumas. Then I bring them back. But this time, I stay down there with them a while, to train them. Goat meat is cheaper there than horse meat is here."

"You sound like you're all ready to start."

"I am."

She squirted a little wine in her mouth, and gave me a long look. They give it to you in a bottle with a long thin spout

on it, and you squirt it in your mouth with the spout. That's
to cool it. She did that two or three times, and every time she
did it she would look at me.

"I am if you are."

"What the hell? You think I'm going with you to catch
them goddam things?"

"Frank, I brought quite a lot of money with me. Let's let
Goebel keep those bughouse cats for their board, sell your car
for whatever we can get, and hunt cats."

"You're on."

"You mean you will?"

"When do we start?"

"There's a freight boat out of here tomorrow and it puts
in at Balboa. We'll wire Goebel from there. And we can leave
your car with the hotel here. They'll sell it and send us whatever they get. That's one thing about a Mexican. He's slow,
but he's honest."

"O.K."

"Gee I'm glad."

"Me too. I'm so sick of hot dogs and beer and apple pie
with cheese on the side I could heave it all in the river."

"You'll love it, Frank. We'll get a place up in the mountains,
where it's cool, and then, after I get my act ready, we can go
all over the world with it. Go as we please, do as we please,
and have plenty of money to spend. Have you got a little bit
of gypsy in you?"

"Gypsy? I had rings in my ears when I was born."

I didn't sleep so good that night. When it was beginning
to get light, I opened my eyes, wide awake. It came to me,
then, that Nicaragua wouldn't be quite far enough.

14

When she got off the train she had on a black dress, that
made her look tall, and a black hat, and black shoes and stockings, and didn't act like herself while the guy was loading the
trunk in the car. We started out, and neither one of us had
much to say for a few miles.

"Why didn't you let me know she died?"

"I didn't want to bother you with it. Anyhow, I had a lot to do."

"I feel plenty bad now, Cora."

"Why?"

"I took a trip while you were away. I went up to Frisco."

"Why do you feel bad about that?"

"I don't know. You back there in Iowa, your mother dying and all, and me up in Frisco having a good time."

"I don't know why you should feel bad. I'm glad you went. If I'd have thought about it, I'd have told you to before I left."

"We lost some business. I closed down."

"It's all right. We'll get it back."

"I felt kind of restless, after you left."

"Well my goodness, I don't mind."

"I guess you had a bad time of it, hey?"

"It wasn't very pleasant. But anyhow, it's over."

"I'll shoot a drink in you when we get home. I got some nice stuff out there I brought back to you."

"I don't want any."

"It'll pick you up."

"I'm not drinking any more."

"No?"

"I'll tell you about it. It's a long story."

"You sound like plenty happened out there."

"No, nothing happened. Only the funeral. But I've got a lot to tell you. I think we're going to have a better time of it from now on."

"Well for God's sake. What is it?"

"Not now. Did you see your family?"

"What for?"

"Well anyway, did you have a good time?"

"Fair. Good as I could have alone."

"I bet it was a swell time. But I'm glad you said it."

When we got out there, a car was parked in front, and a guy was sitting in it. He got a silly kind of grin on his face and climbed out. It was Kennedy, the guy in Katz's office.

"You remember me?"

"Sure I remember you. Come on in."

We took him inside, and she gave me a pull into the kitchen.

"This is bad, Frank."

"What do you mean, bad?"

"I don't know, but I can feel it."

"Better let me talk to him."

I went back with him, and she brought us some beer, and left us, and pretty soon I got down to cases.

"You still with Katz?"

"No, I left him. We had a little argument and I walked out."

"What are you doing now?"

"Not a thing. Fact of the matter, that's what I came out to see you about. I was out a couple of times before, but there was nobody home. This time, though, I heard you were back, so I stuck around."

"Anything I can do, just say the word."

"I was wondering if you could let me have a little money."

"Anything you want. Of course, I don't keep much around, but if fifty or sixty dollars will help, I'll be glad to let you have it."

"I was hoping you could make it more."

He still had this grin on his face, and I figured it was time to quit the feinting and jabbing, and find out what he meant.

"Come on, Kennedy. What is it?"

"I tell you how it is. I left Katz. And that paper, the one I wrote up for Mrs. Papadakis, was still in the files, see? And on account of being a friend of yours and all that, I knew you wouldn't want nothing like that laying around. So I took it. I thought maybe you would like to get it back."

"You mean that hop dream she called a confession?"

"That's it. Of course, I know there wasn't anything to it, but I thought you might like to get it back."

"How much do you want for it?"

"Well, how much would you pay?"

"Oh, I don't know. As you say, there's nothing to it, but I might give a hundred for it. Sure. I'd pay that."

"I was thinking it was worth more."

"Yeah?"

"I figured on twenty five grand."

"Are you crazy?"

"No, I ain't crazy. You got ten grand from Katz. The place has been making money, I figure about five grand. Then on the property, you could get ten grand from the bank. Papadakis gave fourteen for it, so it looks like you could get ten. Well, that makes twenty five."

"You would strip me clean, just for that?"

"It's worth it."

I didn't move, but I must have had a flicker in my eye, because he jerked an automatic out of his pocket and leveled it at me. "Don't start anything, Chambers. In the first place, I haven't got it with me. In the second place, if you start anything I let you have it."

"I'm not starting anything."

"Well, see you don't."

He kept the gun pointed at me, and I kept looking at him. "I guess you got me."

"I don't guess it. I know it."

"But you're figuring too high."

"Keep talking, Chambers."

"We got ten from Katz, that's right. And we've still got it. We made five off the place, but we spent a grand in the last couple weeks. She took a trip to bury her mother, and I took one. That's why we been closed up."

"Go on, keep talking."

"And we can't get ten on the property. With things like they are now, we couldn't even get five. Maybe we could get four."

"Keep talking."

"All right, ten, four, and four. That makes eighteen."

He grinned down the gun barrel a while, and then he got up. "All right. Eighteen. I'll phone you tomorrow, to see if you've got it. If you've got it, I'll tell you what to do. If you haven't got it, that thing goes to Sackett."

"It's tough, but you got me."

"Tomorrow at twelve, then, I phone you. That'll give you time to go to the bank and get back."

"O.K."

He backed to the door and still held the gun on me. It was late afternoon, just beginning to get dark. While he was backing away, I leaned up against the wall, like I was pretty down in the mouth. When he was half out the door I cut the juice in the sign, and it blazed down in his eyes. He wheeled, and I let him have it. He went down and I was on him. I twisted the gun out of his hand, threw it in the lunchroom, and socked him again. Then I dragged him inside and kicked the door shut. She was standing there. She had been at the door, listening, all the time.

"Get the gun."

She picked it up and stood there. I pulled him to his feet, threw him over one of the tables, and bent him back. Then I beat him up. When he passed out, I got a glass of water and poured it on him. Soon as he came to, I beat him up again. When his face looked like raw beef, and he was blubbering like a kid in the last quarter of a football game, I quit.

"Snap out of it, Kennedy. You're talking to your friends over the telephone."

"I got no friends, Chambers. I swear, I'm the only one that knows about—"

I let him have it, and we did it all over again. He kept saying he didn't have any friends, so I threw an arm lock on him and shoved up on it. "All right, Kennedy. If you've got no friends, then I break it."

He stood it longer than I thought he could. He stood it till I was straining on his arm with all I had, wondering if I really could break it. My left arm was still weak where it had been broke. If you ever tried to break the second joint of a tough turkey, maybe you know how hard it is to break a guy's arm with a hammerlock. But all of a sudden he said he would call. I let him loose and told him what he was to say. Then I put him at the kitchen phone, and pulled the lunchroom extension through the swing door, so I could watch him and hear what he said and they said. She came back there with us, with the gun.

"If I give you the sign, he gets it."

She leaned back and an awful smile flickered around the corner of her mouth. I think that smile scared Kennedy worse than anything I had done.

"He gets it."

He called, and a guy answered. "Is that you, Willie?"

"Pat?"

"This is me. Listen. It's all fixed. How soon can you get out here with it?"

"Tomorrow, like we said."

"Can't you make it tonight?"

"How can I get in a safe deposit box when the bank is closed?"

"All right, then do like I tell you. Get it, first thing in the morning, and come out here with it. I'm out to his place."

"His *place*?"

"Listen, get this, Willie. He knows we got him, see? But he's afraid if she finds out he's got to pay all that dough, she won't let him, you get it? If he leaves, she knows something is up, and maybe she takes a notion to go with him. So we do it all here. I'm just a guy that's spending the night in their auto camp, and she don't know nothing. Tomorrow, you're just a friend of mine, and we fix it all up."

"How does he get the money if he don't leave?"

"That's all fixed up."

"And what in the hell are you spending the night there for?"

"I got a reason for that, Willie. Because maybe it's a stall, what he says about her, and maybe it's not, see? But if I'm here, neither one of them can skip, you get it?"

"Can he hear you, what you're saying?"

He looked at me, and I nodded my head yes. "He's right here with me, in the phone booth. I want him to hear me, you get it, Willie? I want him to know we mean business."

"It's a funny way to do, Pat."

"Listen, Willie. You don't know, and I don't know, and none of us don't know if he's on the level with it or not. But maybe he is, and I'm giving him a chance. What the hell, if a guy's willing to pay, we got to go along with him, haven't we? That's it. You do like I tell you. You get it out here soon as you can in the morning. Soon as you can, you get it? Because I don't want her to get to wondering what the hell I'm doing hanging around here all day."

"O.K."

He hung up. I walked over and gave him a sock. "That's just so you talk right when he calls back. You got it, Kennedy?"

"I got it."

I waited a few minutes, and pretty soon here came the call back. I answered, and when Kennedy picked up the phone he gave Willie some more of the same. He said he was alone that time. Willie didn't like it much, but he had to take it. Then I took him back to the No. 1 shack. She came with us, and I took the gun. Soon as I had Kennedy inside, I stepped out the door with her and gave her a kiss.

"That's for being able to step on it when the pinch comes. Now get this. I'm not leaving him for a minute. I'm staying out here the whole night. There'll be other calls, and we'll bring him in to talk. I think you better open the place up. The beer garden. Don't bring anybody inside. That's so if his friends do some spying, you're right on deck and it's business as usual."

"All right. And Frank."

"Yes?"

"Next time I try to act smart, will you hang one on my jaw?"

"What do you mean?"

"We ought to have gone away. Now I know it."

"Like hell we ought. Not till we get this."

She gave me a kiss, then. "I guess I like you pretty well, Frank."

"We'll get it. Don't worry."

"I'm not."

I stayed out there with him all night. I didn't give him any food, and I didn't give him any sleep. Three or four times he had to talk to Willie, and once Willie wanted to talk to me. Near as I could tell, we got away with it. In between, I would beat him up. It was hard work, but I meant he should want that paper to get there, bad. While he was wiping the blood off his face, on a towel, you could hear the radio going, out in the beer garden, and the people laughing and talking.

About ten o'clock the next morning she came out there. "They're here, I think. There are three of them."

"Bring them back."

She picked up the gun, stuck it in her belt so you couldn't see it from in front, and went. In a minute, I heard something fall. It was one of his gorillas. She was marching them in front of her, making them walk backwards with their hands up, and one of them fell when his heel hit the concrete walk. I opened the door. "This way, gents."

They came in, still holding their hands up, and she came in after them and handed me the gun. "They all had guns, but I took them off them in the lunchroom."

"Better get them. Maybe they got friends."

She went, and in a minute came back with the guns. She took out the clips, and laid them on the bed, beside me. Then she went through their pockets. Pretty soon she had it. And the funny part was that in another envelope were photostats of it, six positives and one negative. They had meant to keep on blackmailing us, and then hadn't had any more sense than to have the photostats on them when they showed up. I took them all, with the original, outside, crumpled them up on the ground, and touched a match to them. When they were burned I stamped the ashes into the dirt and went back.

"All right, boys. I'll show you out. We'll keep the artillery here."

After I had marched them out to their cars, and they left, and I went back inside, she wasn't there. I went out back, and she wasn't there. I went upstairs. She was in our room. "Well, we did it, didn't we? That's the last of it, photostats and all. It's been worrying me, too."

She didn't say anything, and her eyes looked funny. "What's the matter, Cora?"

"So that's the last of it, is it? Photostats and all. It isn't the last of me, though. I've got a million photostats of it, just as good as they were. Jimmy Durante. I've got a million of them. Am I mortified?"

She burst out laughing, and flopped down on the bed.

"All right. If you're sucker enough to put your neck in the

noose, just to get me, you've got a million of them. You sure have. A million of them."

"Oh no, that's the beautiful part. I don't have to put my neck in the noose at all. Didn't Mr. Katz tell you? Once they just made it manslaughter, they can't do any more to me. It's in the Constitution or something. Oh no, Mr. Frank Chambers. It don't cost me a thing to make you dance on air. And that's what you're going to do. Dance, dance, dance."

"What ails you, anyhow?"

"Don't you know? Your friend was out last night. She didn't know about me, and she spent the night here."

"What friend?"

"The one you went to Mexico with. She told me all about it. We're good friends now. She thought we better be good friends. After she found out who I was she thought I might kill her."

"I haven't been to Mexico for a year."

"Oh yes you have."

She went out, and I heard her go in my room. When she came back she had a kitten with her, but a kitten that was bigger than a cat. It was gray, with spots on it. She put it on the table in front of me and it began to meow. "The puma had little ones while you were gone, and she brought you one to remember her by."

She leaned back against the wall and began to laugh again, a wild, crazy laugh. "And the cat came back! It stepped on the fuse box and got killed, but here it is back! Ha, ha, ha, ha, ha, ha! Ain't that funny, how unlucky cats are for you?"

15

She cracked up, then, and cried, and after she got quiet she went downstairs. I was down there, right after her. She was tearing the top flaps off a big carton.

"Just making a nest for our little pet, dearie."

"Nice of you."

"What did you think I was doing?"

"I didn't."

"Don't worry. When the time comes to call up Mr. Sackett, I'll let you know. Just take it easy. You'll need all your strength."

She lined it with excelsior, and on top of that put some woolen cloths. She took it upstairs and put the puma in it. It meowed a while and then went to sleep. I went downstairs to fix myself a coke. I hadn't any more than squirted the ammonia in it than she was at the door.

"Just taking something to keep my strength up, dearie."

"Nice of you."

"What did you think I was doing?"

"I didn't."

"Don't worry. When I get ready to skip I'll let you know. Just take it easy. You may need all your strength."

She gave me a funny look and went upstairs. It kept up all day, me following her around for fear she'd call up Sackett, her following me around for fear I'd skip. We never opened the place up at all. In between the tip-toeing around, we would sit upstairs in the room. We didn't look at each other. We looked at the puma. It would meow and she would go down to get it some milk. I would go with her. After it lapped up the milk it would go to sleep. It was too young to play much. Most of the time it meowed or slept.

That night we lay side by side, not saying a word. I must have slept, because I had those dreams. Then, all of a sudden, I woke up, and before I was even really awake I was running downstairs. What had waked me was the sound of that telephone dial. She was at the extension in the lunchroom, all dressed, with her hat on, and a packed hat box on the floor beside her. I grabbed the receiver and slammed it on the hook. I took her by the shoulders, jerked her through the swing door, and shoved her upstairs. "Get up there! Get up there, or I'll—"

"Or you'll what?"

The telephone rang, and I answered it.

"Here's your party, go ahead."

"Yellow Cab."

"Oh. Oh. I called you, Yellow Cab, but I've changed my mind. I won't need you."

"O.K."

When I got upstairs she was taking off her clothes. When we got back in bed we lay there a long time again without saying a word. Then she started up.

"Or you'll what?"

"What's it to you? Sock you in the jaw, maybe. Maybe something else."

"Something else, wasn't it?"

"What are you getting at now?"

"Frank, I know what you've been doing. You've been lying there, trying to think of a way to kill me."

"I've been asleep."

"Don't lie to me, Frank. Because I'm not going to lie to you, and I've got something to say to you."

I thought that over a long time. Because that was just what I had been doing. Lying there beside her, just straining to think of a way I could kill her.

"All right, then. I was."

"I knew it."

"Were you any better? Weren't you going to hand me over to Sackett? Wasn't that the same thing?"

"Yes."

"Then we're even. Even again. Right back where we started."

"Not quite."

"Oh yes we are." I cracked up a little, then, myself, and put my head on her shoulder. "That's just where we are. We can kid ourself all we want to, and laugh about the money, and whoop about what a swell guy the devil is to be in bed with, but that's just where we are. I was going off with that woman, Cora. We were going to Nicaragua to catch cats. And why I didn't go away, I knew I had to come back. We're chained to each other, Cora. We thought we were on top of a mountain. That wasn't it. It's on top of us, and that's where it's been ever since that night."

"Is that the only reason you came back?"

"No. It's you and me. There's nobody else. I love you, Cora. But love, when you get fear in it, it's not love any more. It's hate."

"So you hate me?"

"I don't know. But we're telling the truth, for once in our life. That's part of it. You got to know it. And what I was lying here thinking, that's the reason. Now you know it."

"I told you I had something to tell you, Frank."

"Oh."

"I'm going to have a baby."

"*What?*"

"I suspicioned it before I went away, and right after my mother died I was sure."

"The hell you say. The hell you say. Come here. Give me a kiss."

"No. Please. I've got to tell you about it."

"Haven't you told it?"

"Not what I mean. Now listen to me, Frank. All that time I was out there, waiting for the funeral to be over, I thought about it. What it would mean to us. Because we took a life, didn't we? And now we're going to give one back."

"That's right."

"It was all mixed up, what I thought. But now, after what happened with that woman, it's not mixed up any more. I couldn't call up Sackett, Frank. I couldn't call him up, because I couldn't have this baby, and then have it find out I let its father hang for murder."

"You were going to see Sackett."

"No I wasn't. I was going away."

"Was that the only reason you weren't going to see Sackett?"

She took a long time before she answered that. "No. I love you, Frank. I think you know that. But maybe, if it hadn't been for this, I would have gone to see him. Just *because* I love you."

"She didn't mean anything to me, Cora. I told you why I did it. I was running away."

"I know that. I knew it all along. I knew why you wanted to take me away, and what I said about you being a bum, I didn't believe that. I believed it, but it wasn't why you wanted to go. You being a bum, I love you for it. And I hated her for the way she turned on you just for not telling her about something that wasn't any of her business. And yet, I wanted to ruin you for it."

"Well?"

"I'm trying to say it, Frank. This is what I'm trying to say. I wanted to ruin you, and yet I couldn't go to see Sackett. It wasn't because you kept watching me. I could have run out of the house and got to him. It was because, like I told you. Well then, I'm rid of the devil, Frank. I know I'll never call up Sackett, because I had my chance, and I had my reason, and I didn't do it. So the devil has left me. But has he left you?"

"If he's left you, then what more have I got to do with him?"

"We wouldn't be sure. We couldn't ever be sure unless you had your chance. The same chance I had."

"I tell you, he's gone."

"While you were thinking about a way to kill me, Frank, I was thinking the same thing. Of a way you could kill me. You can kill me swimming. We'll go way out, the way we did last time, and if you don't want me to come back, you don't have to let me. Nobody'll ever know. It'll be just one of those things that happen at the beach. Tomorrow morning we'll go."

"Tomorrow morning, what we do is get married."

"We can get married if you want, but before we come back we go swimming."

"To hell with swimming. Come on with that kiss."

"Tomorrow night, if I come back, there'll be kisses. Lovely ones, Frank. Not drunken kisses. Kisses with dreams in them. Kisses that come from life, not death."

"It's a date."

We got married at the City Hall, and then we went to the beach. She looked so pretty I just wanted to play in the sand with her, but she had this little smile on her face, and after a while she got up and went down to the surf.

"I'm going out."

She went ahead, and I swam after her. She kept on going, and went a lot further out than she had before. Then she stopped, and I caught up with her. She swung up beside me, and took hold of my hand, and we looked at each other. She knew, then, that the devil was gone, that I loved her.

"Did I ever tell you why I like my feet to the swells?"

"No."

"It's so they'll lift them."

A big one raised us up, and she put her hand to her breasts, to show how it lifted them. "I love it. Are they big, Frank?"

"I'll tell you tonight."

"They feel big. I didn't tell you about that. It's not only knowing you're going to make another life. It's what it does to you. My breasts feel so big, and I want you to kiss them. Pretty soon my belly is going to get big, and I'll love that, and want everybody to see it. It's life. I can feel it in me. It's a new life for us both, Frank."

We started back, and on the way in I swam down. I went down nine feet. I could tell it was nine feet, by the pressure. Most of these pools are nine feet, and it was that deep. I whipped my legs together and shot down further. It drove in on my ears so I thought they would pop. But I didn't have to come up. The pressure on your lungs drives the oxygen in your blood, so for a few seconds you don't think about breath. I looked at the green water. And with my ears ringing and that weight on my back and chest, it seemed to me that all the devilment, and meanness, and shiftlessness, and no-account stuff in my life had been pressed out and washed off, and I was all ready to start out with her again clean, and do like she said, have a new life.

When I came up she was coughing. "Just one of those sick spells, like you have."

"Are you all right?"

"I think so. It comes over you, and then it goes."

"Did you swallow any water?"

"No."

We went a little way, and then she stopped. "Frank, I feel funny inside."

"Here, hold on to me."

"Oh, Frank. Maybe I strained myself, just then. Trying to keep my head up. So I wouldn't gulp down the salt water."

"Take it easy."

"Wouldn't that be awful? I've heard of women that had a miscarriage. From straining theirself."

"Take it easy. Lie right out in the water. Don't try to swim. I'll tow you in."

"Hadn't you better call a guard?"

"Christ no. That egg will want to pump your legs up and down. Just lay there now. I'll get you in quicker than he can."

She lay there, and I towed her by the shoulder strap of her bathing suit. I began to give out. I could have towed her a mile, but I kept thinking I had to get her to a hospital, and I hurried. When you hurry in the water you're sunk. I got bottom, though, after a while, and then I took her in my arms and rushed her through the surf. "Don't move. Let me do it."

"I won't."

I ran with her up to the place where our sweaters were, and set her down. I got the car key out of mine, then wrapped both of them around her and carried her up to the car. It was up beside the road, and I had to climb the high bank the road was on, above the beach. My legs were so tired I could hardly lift one after the other, but I didn't drop her. I put her in the car, started up, and began burning the road.

We had gone in swimming a couple of miles above Santa Monica, and there was a hospital down there. I overtook a big truck. It had a sign on the back, Sound Your Horn, the Road Is Yours. I banged on the horn, and it kept right down the middle. I couldn't pass on the left, because a whole line of cars was coming toward me. I pulled out to the right and stepped on it. She screamed. I never saw the culvert wall. There was a crash, and everything went black.

When I came out of it I was wedged down beside the wheel, with my back to the front of the car, but I began to moan from the awfulness of what I heard. It was like rain on a tin roof, but that wasn't it. It was her blood, pouring down on the hood, where she went through the windshield. Horns were blowing, and people were jumping out of cars and running to her. I got her up, and tried to stop the blood, and in between I was talking to her, and crying, and kissing her. Those kisses never reached her. She was dead.

16

They got me for it. Katz took it all this time, the $10,000 he had got for us, and the money we had made, and a deed for the place. He did his best for me, but he was licked from the start. Sackett said I was a mad dog, that had to be put out of the way before life would be safe. He had it all figured out. We murdered the Greek to get the money, and then I married her, and murdered her so I could have it all myself. When she found out about the Mexican trip, that hurried it up a little, that was all. He had the autopsy report, that showed she was going to have a baby, and he said that was part of it. He put Madge on the stand, and she told about the Mexican trip. She didn't want to, but she had to. He even had the puma in court. It had grown, but it hadn't been taken care of right, so it was mangy and sick looking, and yowled, and tried to bite him. It was an awful looking thing, and it didn't do me any good, believe me. But what really sunk me was the note she wrote before she called up the cab, and put in the cash register so I would get it in the morning, and then forgot about. I never saw it, because we didn't open the place before we went swimming, and I never even looked in the cash register. It was the sweetest note in the world, but it had in it about us killing the Greek, and that did the work. They argued about it three days, and Katz fought them with every law book in Los Angeles County, but the judge let it in, and that let in all about us murdering the Greek. Sackett said that fixed me up with a motive. That and just being a mad dog. Katz never even let me take the stand. What could I say? That I didn't do it, because we had just fixed it up, all the trouble we had had over killing the Greek? That would have been swell. The jury was out five minutes. The judge said he would give me exactly the same consideration he would show any other mad dog.

So I'm in the death house, now, writing the last of this, so Father McConnell can look it over and show me the places where maybe it ought to be fixed up a little, for punctuation and all that. If I get a stay, he's to hold on to it and wait for what happens. If I get a commutation, then, he's to burn it, and they'll never know whether there really was any murder or not, from anything I tell them. But if they get me, he's to take it and see if he can find somebody to print it. There won't be any stay, and there won't be any commutation, I know that. I never kidded myself. But in this place, you hope anyhow, just because you can't help it. I never confessed anything, that's one thing. I heard a guy say they never hang you without you confess. I don't know. Unless Father McConnell crosses me, they'll never know anything from me. Maybe I'll get a stay.

I'm getting up tight now, and I've been thinking about Cora. Do you think she knows I didn't do it? After what we said in the water, you would think she would know it. But that's the awful part, when you monkey with murder. Maybe it went through her head, when the car hit, that I did it anyhow. That's why I hope I've got another life after this one. Father McConnell says I have, and I want to see her. I want her to know that it was all so, what we said to each other, and that I didn't do it. What did she have that makes me feel that way about her? I don't know. She wanted something, and she tried to get it. She tried all the wrong ways, but she tried. I don't know what made her feel that way about me, because she knew me. She called it on me plenty of times, that I wasn't any good. I never really wanted anything, but her. But that's a lot. I guess it's not often that a woman even has that.

There's a guy in No. 7 that murdered his brother, and says he didn't really do it, his subconscious did it. I asked him what that meant, and he says you got two selves, one that you know about and the other that you don't know about, because it's subconscious. It shook me up. Did I really do it, and not know it? God Almighty, I can't believe that! I didn't do it! I loved her so, then, I tell you, that I would have died for her! To hell with the sub-conscious. I don't believe it. It's just a lot of hooey, that this guy thought up so he could fool the judge. You know what you're doing, and you do it. I didn't do it, I know that. That's what I'm going to tell her, if I ever see her again.

*

I'm up awful tight, now. I think they give you dope in the grub, so you don't think about it. I try not to think. Whenever I can make it, I'm out there with Cora, with the sky above us, and the water around us, talking about how happy we're going to be, and how it's going to last forever. I guess I'm over the big river, when I'm there with her. That's when it seems real, about another life, not with all this stuff how Father McConnell has got it figured out. When I'm with her I believe it. When I start to figure, it all goes blooey.

No stay.

Here they come. Father McConnell says prayers help. If you've got this far, send up one for me, and Cora, and make it that we're together, wherever it is.

THEY SHOOT HORSES, DON'T THEY?

DON'T THEY?

by Horace McCoy

To
Michael Fessier
and
Harry Clay Withers

THE
PRISONER
WILL
STAND.

I

I STOOD UP. *For a moment I saw Gloria again, sitting on that bench on the pier. The bullet had just struck her in the side of the head; the blood had not even started to flow. The flash from the pistol still lighted her face. Everything was plain as day. She was completely relaxed, was completely comfortable. The impact of the bullet had turned her head a little away from me; I did not have a perfect profile view but I could see enough of her face and her lips to know she was smiling. The Prosecuting Attorney was wrong when he told the jury she died in agony, friendless, alone except for her brutal murderer, out there in that black night on the edge of the Pacific. He was as wrong as a man can be. She did not die in agony. She was relaxed and comfortable and she was smiling. It was the first time I had ever seen her smile. How could she have been in agony then? And she wasn't friendless.*

I was her very best friend. I was her only friend. So how could she have been friendless?

IS THERE

ANY LEGAL CAUSE

WHY

SENTENCE

SHOULD NOT NOW

BE PRONOUNCED?

2

WHAT could I say? . . . All those people knew I had killed her; the only other person who could have helped me at all was dead too. So I just stood there, looking at the judge and shaking my head. I didn't have a leg to stand on.

"Ask the mercy of the court," said Epstein, the lawyer they had assigned to defend me.

"What was that?" the judge said.

"Your Honor," Epstein said, "—we throw ourselves on the mercy of the court. This boy admits killing the girl, but he was only doing her a personal favor——"

The judge banged on the desk, looking at me.

THERE BEING

NO LEGAL CAUSE

WHY SENTENCE

SHOULD NOT NOW

BE PRONOUNCED . . .

3

IT WAS funny the way I met Gloria. She was trying to get into pictures too, but I didn't know that until later. I was walking down Melrose one day from the Paramount studios when I heard somebody hollering, "Hey! Hey!" and I turned around and there she was running towards me and waving. I stopped, waving back. When she got up to me she was all out of breath and excited and I saw I didn't know her.

"Damn that bus," she said.

I looked around and there was the bus half a block down the street going towards Western.

"Oh," I said, "I thought you were waving at me. . . ."

"What would I be waving at you for?" she asked.

I laughed. "I don't know," I said. "You going my way?"

"I may as well walk on down to Western," she said; and we began to walk on down towards Western.

That was how it all started and it seems very strange to me now. I don't understand it at all. I've thought and thought and still I don't understand it. This wasn't murder. I try to do somebody a favor and I wind up getting killed myself. *They are going to kill me. I know exactly what the judge is going to say. I can tell by the look of him that he is going to be glad to say it and I can tell by the feel of the people behind me that they are going to be glad to hear him say it.*

Take that morning I met Gloria. I wasn't feeling very good; I was still a little sick, but I went over to Paramount because von Sternberg was making a Russian picture and I thought maybe I could get a job. I used to ask myself what could be nicer than working for von Sternberg, or Mamoulian or Boleslawsky either, getting paid to watch him direct, learning about composition and tempo and angles . . . so I went over to Paramount.

I couldn't get inside, so I hung around the front until noon when one of his assistants came out for lunch. I caught up with him and asked what was the chance to get some atmosphere.

"None," he said, telling me that von Sternberg was very careful about his atmospheric people.

I thought that was a lousy thing to say but I knew what he was thinking, that my clothes didn't look any too good. "Isn't this a costume picture?" I asked.

"All our extras come through Central," he said, leaving me. . . .

I wasn't going anywhere in particular; I was just riding along in my Rolls-Royce, having people point me out as the greatest director in the world, when I heard Gloria hollering. You see how those things happen? . . .

So we walked on down Melrose to Western, getting acquainted all the time; and when we got to Western I knew she was Gloria Beatty, an extra who wasn't doing well either, and she knew a little about me. I liked her very much.

She had a small room with some people over near Beverly and I lived only a few blocks from there, so I saw her again that night. That first night was really what did it but even now I can't honestly say I regret going to see her. I had about seven dollars I had made squirting soda in a drug store (subbing for a friend of mine. He had got a girl in a jam and had to take her to Santa Barbara for the operation.) and I asked her if she'd rather go to a movie or sit in the park.

"What park?" she asked.

"It's right over here a little way," I said.

"All right," she said. "I got a bellyful of moving pictures anyway. If I'm not a better actress than most of those dames I'll eat your hat— Let's go sit and hate a bunch of people. . . ."

I was glad she wanted to go to the park. It was always nice there. It was a fine place to sit. It was very small, only one block square, but it was very dark and very quiet and filled with dense shrubbery. All around it palm trees grew up, fifty, sixty feet tall, suddenly tufted at the top. Once you entered the park you had the illusion of security. I often imagined they were sentries wearing grotesque helmets: my own private sentries, standing guard over my own private island. . . .

The park was a fine place to sit. Through the palms you could see many buildings, the thick, square silhouettes of apartment houses, with their red signs on the roofs, reddening the sky above and everything and everybody below. But if you wanted to get rid of these things you had only to sit and stare at them with a fixed gaze . . . and they would begin receding. That way you could drive them as far into the distance as you wanted to. . . .

"I never paid much attention to this place before," Gloria said.

. . . "I like it," I said, taking off my coat and spreading it on the grass for her. "I come here three or four times a week."

"You do like it," she said, sitting down.

"How long you been in Hollywood?" I asked.

"About a year. I been in four pictures already. I'd have been in more," she said, "but I can't get registered by Central."

"Neither can I," I said.

Unless you were registered by Central Casting Bureau you didn't have much chance. The big studios call up Central and say they want four Swedes or six Greeks or two Bohemian peasant types or six Grand Duchesses and Central takes care of it. I could see why Gloria didn't get registered by Central. She was too blonde and too small and looked too old. With a nice wardrobe she might have looked attractive, but even then I wouldn't have called her pretty.

"Have you met anybody who can help you?" I asked.

"In this business how can you tell who'll help you?" she said. "One day you're an electrician and the next day you're a producer. The only way I could ever get to a big shot would be to jump on the running board of his car as it passed by. Anyway, I don't know whether the men stars can help me as much as the women stars. From what I've seen lately I've about made up my mind that I've been letting the wrong sex try to make me. . . ."

"How'd you happen to come to Hollywood?" I asked.

"Oh, I don't know," she said in a moment—"but anything is an improvement over the life I led back home." I asked her where that was. "Texas," she said. "West Texas. Ever been there?"

"No," I said, "I come from Arkansas."

"Well, West Texas is a hell of a place," she said. "I lived with my aunt and uncle. He was a brakeman on a railroad. I only saw him once or twice a week, thank God. . . ."

She stopped, not saying anything, looking at the red, va-porish glow above the apartment buildings.

"At least," I said, "you had a home——"

"That's what you call it," she said. "Me, I got another name for it. When my uncle was home he was always making passes at me and when he was on the road my aunt and I were always fighting. She was afraid I'd tattle on her——"

"Nice people," I said to myself.

"So I finally ran away," she said, "to Dallas. Ever been there?"

"I've never been in Texas at all," I said.

"You haven't missed anything," she said. "I couldn't get a job, so I decided to steal something in a store and make the cops take care of me."

"That was a good idea," I said.

"It was a swell idea," she said, "only it didn't work. I got arrested all right but the detectives felt sorry for me and turned me loose. To keep from starving to death I moved in with a Syrian who had a hot-dog place around the corner from the City Hall. He chewed tobacco. He chewed tobacco all the time . . . Have you ever been in bed with a man who chewed tobacco?"

"I don't believe I have," I said.

"I guess I might even have stood that," she said, "but when he wanted to make me between customers, on the kitchen table, I gave up. A couple of nights later I took poison."

"Jesus," I said to myself.

"I didn't take enough," she said. "I only got sick. Ugh, I can still taste the stuff. I stayed in the hospital a week. That was where I got the idea of coming to Hollywood."

"It was?" I said.

"From the movie magazines," she said. "After I got dis-charged I started hitch-hiking. Is that a laugh or not? . . ."

"That's a good laugh," I said, trying to laugh. . . . "Haven't you got any parents?"

"Not any more," she said. "My old man got killed in the war in France. I wish I could get killed in a war."

"Why don't you quit the movies?" I asked.

"Why should I?" she said. "I may get to be a star overnight. Look at Hepburn and Margaret Sullavan and Josephine

Hutchinson . . . but I'll tell you what I would do if I had the guts: I'd walk out of a window or throw myself in front of a street car or something."

"I know how you feel," I said; "I know exactly how you feel."

"It's peculiar to me," she said, "that everybody pays so much attention to living and so little to dying. Why are these high-powered scientists always screwing around trying to prolong life instead of finding pleasant ways to end it? There must be a hell of a lot of people in the world like me—who want to die but haven't got the guts——"

"I know what you mean," I said; "I know exactly what you mean."

Neither of us said anything for a couple of seconds.

"A girl friend of mine has been trying to get me to enter a marathon dance down at the beach," she said. "Free food and free bed as long as you last and a thousand dollars if you win."

"The free food part of it sounds good," I said.

"That's not the big thing," she said. "A lot of producers and directors go to those marathon dances. There's always the chance they might pick you out and give you a part in a picture. . . . What do you say?"

"Me?" I said . . . "Oh, I don't dance very well. . . ."

"You don't have to. All you have to do is keep moving."

"I don't think I better try it," I said. "I been pretty sick. I just got over the intestinal flu. I almost died. I was so weak I used to have to crawl to the john on my hands and knees. I don't think I better try it," I said, shaking my head.

"When was all this?"

"A week ago," I said.

"You're all right now," she said.

"I don't think so—I better not try it. I'm liable to have a relapse."

"I'll take care of that," she said.

". . . Maybe in a week—" I said.

"It'll be too late then. You're strong enough now," she said. . . .

. . . IT IS
THE JUDGMENT
AND SENTENCE
OF THIS COURT . . .

4

THE marathon dance was held on the amusement pier at the beach in an enormous old building that once had been a public dance hall. It was built out over the ocean on pilings, and beneath our feet, beneath the floor, the ocean pounded night and day. I could feel it surging through the balls of my feet, as if they had been stethoscopes.

Inside there was a dance space for the contestants, thirty feet wide and two hundred feet long, and around this on three sides were loge seats, behind these were the circus seats, the general admission. At the end of the dance space was a raised platform for the orchestra. It played only at night and was not a very good orchestra. During the day we had what music we could pick up with the radio, made loud by the amplifiers. Most of the time it was too loud, filling the hall with noise. We had a master of ceremonies, whose duty it was to make the customers feel at home; two floor judges who moved around on the floor all the time with the contestants to see that everything went all right, two male and female nurses, and a house doctor for emergencies. The doctor didn't look like a doctor at all. He was much too young.

One hundred and forty-four couples entered the marathon dance but sixty-one dropped out the first week. The rules were you danced for an hour and fifty minutes, then you had a ten-minute rest period in which you could sleep if you wanted to. But in those ten minutes you also had to shave or bathe or get your feet fixed or whatever was necessary.

The first week was the hardest. Everybody's feet and legs swelled—and down beneath the ocean kept pounding, pounding against the pilings all the time. Before I went into this marathon dance I used to love the Pacific Ocean: its name, its size, its color, its smell—I used to sit for hours looking at it, wondering about the ships that had sailed it and never returned, about China and the South Seas, wondering all sorts of things . . . But not any more. I've had enough of the Pacific. I don't care whether I ever see it again or not. *I probably won't. The judge is going to take care of that.*

Gloria and I had been tipped off by some old-timers that the way to beat a marathon dance was to perfect a system for those ten-minute rest periods: learning to eat your sandwich while you shaved, learning to eat when you went to the john, when you had your feet fixed, learning to read newspapers while you danced, learning to sleep on your partner's shoulder while you were dancing; but these were all tricks of the trade you had to practice. They were very difficult for Gloria and me at first.

I found out that about half of the people in this contest were professionals. They made a business of going in marathon dances all over the country, some of them even hitch-hiking from town to town. The others were just girls and boys who came in like Gloria and me.

Couple No. 13 were our best friends in the dance. This was James and Ruby Bates, from some little town in northern Pennsylvania. It was their eighth marathon dance; they had won a $1500 prize in Oklahoma, going 1253 hours in continuous motion. There were several other teams in this dance who claimed championships of some kind, but I knew James and Ruby would be right in there for the finish. That is, if Ruby's baby didn't come first. She expected a baby in four months.

"What's the matter with Gloria?" James asked me one day as we came back to the floor from the sleeping quarters.

"Nothing. What do you mean?" I asked. But I knew what he meant. Gloria had been singing the blues again.

"She keeps telling Ruby what a chump she would be to have the baby," he said. "Gloria wants her to have an abortion."

"I can't understand Gloria talking like that," I said, trying to smooth things over.

"You tell her to lay off Ruby," he said.

When the whistle started us off on the 216th hour I told Gloria what James had said.

"Nuts to him," she said. "What does he know about it?"

"I don't see why they can't have a baby if they want to. It's their business," I said. "I don't want to make James sore. He's been through a lot of these dances and he's already given us some good tips. Where would we be if he got sore?"

"It's a shame for that girl to have a baby," Gloria said. "What's the sense of having a baby unless you got dough enough to take care of it?"

"How do you know they haven't?" I asked.

"If they have what're they doing here? . . . That's the trouble now," she said. "Everybody is having babies——"

"Oh, not everybody," I said.

"A hell of a lot you know about it. You'd been better off if you'd never been born——"

"Maybe not," I said. "How do you feel?" I asked, trying to get her mind off her troubles.

"I always feel lousy," she said. "God, the hand on that clock moves slow." There was a big strip of canvas on the master of ceremonies' platform, painted in the shape of a clock, up to 2500 hours. The hand now pointed to 216. Above it was a sign: ELAPSED HOURS—216. COUPLES REMAINING —83.

"How are your legs?"

"Still pretty weak," I said. "That flu is awful stuff. . . ."

"Some of the girls think it'll take 2000 hours to win," Gloria said.

"I hope not," I said. "I don't believe I can hold out that long."

"My shoes are wearing out," Gloria said. "If we don't hurry up and get a sponsor I'll be bare-footed." A sponsor was a company or a firm that gave you sweaters and advertised their names or products on the backs. Then they took care of your necessities.

James and Ruby danced over beside us. "Did you tell her?" he asked, looking at me. I nodded.

"Wait a minute," Gloria said, as they started to dance away. "What's the big idea of talking behind my back?"

"Tell that twist to lay off me," James said, still speaking directly to me.

Gloria started to say something else but before she could get it out I danced her away from there. I didn't want any scenes.

"The son of a bitch," she said.

"He's sore," I said. "Now where are we?"

"Come on," she said, "I'll tell him where he gets off——"

"Gloria," I said, "will you please mind your own business?"

"Soft pedal that loud cussing," a voice said. I looked around. It was Rollo Peters, the floor judge.

"Nuts to you," Gloria said. Through my fingers I could feel the muscles twitching in her back, just like I could feel the ocean surging through the balls of my feet.

"Pipe down," Rollo said. "The people in the box can hear you. What do you think this is—a joint?"

"Joint is right," Gloria said.

"All right, all right," I said.

"I told you once already about that cussing," Rollo said. "I better not have to tell you again. It sounds bad to the customers."

"Customers? Where are they?" Gloria said.

"You let us worry about that," Rollo said, glaring at me.

"All right, all right," I said.

He blew his whistle, stopping everybody from moving. Some of them were barely moving, just enough to keep from being disqualified. "All right, kids," he said, "a little sprint."

"A little sprint, kids," the master of ceremonies, Rocky Gravo, said into the microphone. The noise of his voice in the amplifiers filled the hall, shutting out the pounding of the ocean. "A little sprint—around the track you go— Give," he said to the orchestra, and the orchestra began playing. The contestants started dancing with a little more animation.

The sprint lasted about two minutes and when it was finished Rocky led the applause, and then said into the microphone:

"Look at these kids, ladies and gentlemen—after 216 hours they are as fresh as a daisy in the world's championship marathon dance—a contest of endurance and skill. These kids are fed seven times a day—three big meals and four light lunches. Some of them have even gained weight while in the contest— and we have doctors and nurses constantly in attendance to see that they are in the best of physical condition. Now I'm going to call on Couple No. 4, Mario Petrone and Jackie Miller, for a specialty. Come on, Couple No. 4—there they are, ladies and gentlemen. Isn't that a cute pair? . . ."

Mario Petrone, a husky Italian, and Jackie Miller, a little blonde, went up to the platform to some applause. They spoke to Rocky and then began a tap dance that was very bad. Neither Mario nor Jackie seemed conscious that it was bad. When it was over a few people pitched money onto the floor.

"Give, people," Rocky said. "A silver shower. Give."

A few more coins hit the floor. Mario and Jackie picked them up, moving over near us.

"How much?" Gloria asked them.

"Feels like about six-bits," Jackie said.

"Where you from, kid?" Gloria asked.

"Alabama."

"I thought so," Gloria said.

"You and I ought to learn a specialty," I said to Gloria. "We could make some extra money."

"You're better off without knowing any," Mario said. "It only means extra work and it don't do your legs any good."

"Did you all hear about the derbies?" Jackie asked.

"What are they?" I asked.

"Some kind of a race," she said. "I think they're going to explain them at the next rest period."

"The cheese is beginning to bind," Gloria said.

. . . THAT

FOR THE CRIME

OF MURDER

IN

THE FIRST DEGREE . . .

In the dressing room Rocky Gravo introduced Vincent (Socks) Donald, one of the promoters.

"Lissen, kids," Socks said, "don't none of you be discouraged because people ain't coming to the marathon dance. It takes time to get these things going, so we have decided to start a little novelty guaranteed to pack 'em in. Now here's what we're gonna do. We're gonna have a derby race every night. We're going to paint an oval on the floor and every night everybody will race around the track for fifteen minutes and the last couple every night is disqualified. I guarantee that'll bring in the crowds."

"It'll bring in the undertaker too," somebody said.

"We'll move some cots out in the middle of the track," the promoter said, "and have the doctor and nurses on hand during the derby. When a contestant falls out and has to go to the pit, the partner will have to make two laps to make up for it. You kids will get more kick out of it because the crowds will be bigger. Say, when that Hollywood bunch starts coming here, we'll be standing 'em up. . . . Now, how's the food? Anybody got any kicks about anything? All right, kids, that's fine. You play ball with us and we'll play ball with you."

We went out to the floor. None of the contestants had anything to say about the derbies. They seemed to think that anything was a good idea if it would only start the crowds to coming. Rollo came up to me as I sat down on the railing. I had about two minutes more of rest before the next two-hour grind.

"Don't get me wrong about what I said a few minutes ago," he said. "It's not you, it's Gloria."

"I know," I said. "She's all right. She's just sore on the world, that's all."

"Try to keep her piped down," he said.

"That's a hard job, but I'll do the best I can," I said.

In a moment I looked up to the runway from the girls' dressing room and I was surprised to see Gloria and Ruby coming to the floor together. I went over to meet her.

"What do you think about the derbies?" I asked her.

"It's one good way to kill us off," she said.

The whistle started us away again.

"There's not more than a hundred people here tonight," I said. Gloria and I weren't dancing. I had my arm around her shoulder and she had hers around my waist, walking. That was all right. For the first week we had to dance, but after that you didn't. All you had to do was keep moving. I saw James and Ruby coming over to us and I could tell by the expression on his face that something was wrong. I wanted to get away, but there was no place to go.

"I told you to lay off my wife, didn't I?" he said to Gloria.

"You go to hell, you big ape," Gloria said.

"Wait a minute," I said. "What's the matter?"

"She's been after Ruby again," James said. "Every time I turn my back she's after her again."

"Forget it, Jim," Ruby said, trying to steer him away.

"Naw, I won't forget it. I told you to keep your mouth shut, didn't I?" he said to Gloria.

"You take a flying——"

Before Gloria could get the words finished he slapped her hard on the side of the face, knocking her head against my shoulder. It was a hard wallop. I couldn't stand for that. I reached up and hit him in the mouth. He hit me in the jaw with his left hand, knocking me back against some of the dancers. That kept me from falling to the floor. He rushed at me and I grabbed him, wrestling with him, trying to jerk my knee up between his legs to foul him. It was the only chance I had.

A whistle blew in my ear and somebody grabbed us. It was Rollo Peters. He shoved us apart.

"Cut it out," he said. "What's coming off here?"

"Nothing," I said.

"Nothing," Ruby said.

Rollo raised his hand, waving to Rocky on the platform.

"Give," said Rocky, and the orchestra started to play.

"Scatter out," Rollo said to the contestants, who started to move away. "Come on," he said, leading them around the floor.

"Next time I'm going to cut your throat," James said to Gloria.

"F— you," Gloria said.

"Shut up," I said.

I walked away with her, down into a corner, where we slowed up, barely moving along.

"Are you crazy?" I said. "Why don't you let Ruby alone?"

"Don't worry, I'm through wasting my breath on her. If she wants to have a deformed baby, that's okay by me."

"Hello, Gloria," a voice said.

We looked around. It was an old woman in a front row box seat by the railing. I didn't know her name but she was quite a character. She had been there every night, bringing her blanket and her lunch. One night she wrapped up in her blanket and stayed all night. She was about sixty-five years old.

"Hello," Gloria said.

"What was the matter down there?" the old woman asked.

"Nothing," Gloria said. "Just a little argument."

"How do you feel?" the old woman asked.

"All right, I guess," Gloria replied.

"I'm Mrs. Layden," the old woman said. "You're my favorite couple."

"Well, thanks," I said.

"I tried to enter this," Mrs. Layden said, "but they wouldn't let me. They said I was too old. But I'm only sixty."

"Well, that's fine," I said.

Gloria and I had stopped, our arms around each other, swaying our bodies. You had to keep moving all the time. A couple of men moved into the loge behind the old woman. Both of them were chewing unlighted cigars.

"They're dicks," Gloria said under her breath.

". . . How do you like the contest?" I asked Mrs. Layden.

"I enjoy it very much," she said. "Very much. Such nice boys and girls . . ."

"Move along, kids," Rollo said, walking by.

I nodded to Mrs. Layden, moving along. "Can you feature that?" Gloria asked. "She ought to be home putting a diaper on the baby. Christ, I hope I never live to be that old."

"How do you know those fellows are detectives?" I asked.

"I'm psychic," Gloria replied. "My God, can you feature that old lady? She's a nut about these things. They ought to charge her room rent." She shook her head. "I hope I never live to be that old," she said again.

The meeting with the old lady depressed Gloria very much. She said it reminded her of the women in the little town in West Texas where she had lived.

"Alice Faye's just come in," one of the girls said. "See her? Sitting right over there."

It was Alice Faye all right, with a couple of men I didn't recognize.

"See her?" I asked Gloria.

"I don't want to see her," Gloria said.

"Ladies and gentlemen," Rocky said into the microphone, "we are honored tonight to have with us that beautiful moving picture star, Miss Alice Faye. Give Miss Faye a big hand, ladies and gentlemen."

Everybody applauded and Miss Faye nodded her head, smiling. Socks Donald, sitting in a box seat by the orchestra platform, was smiling too. The Hollywood crowd had started coming.

"Come on," I said to Gloria, "clap your hands."

"Why should I applaud for her?" Gloria said. "What's she got I haven't? . . ."

"You're jealous," I said.

"You're goddam right I'm jealous. As long as I am a failure I'm jealous of anybody who's a success. Aren't you?"

"Certainly not," I said.

"You're a fool," she said.

"Hey, look," I said.

The two detectives had left the box with Mrs. Layden and were sitting with Socks Donald. They had their heads together, looking at a sheet of paper one of them was holding.

"All right, kids," Rocky said into the microphone. "A little sprint before the rest period. . . . Give," he said to the orchestra, clapping his hands together and stamping on the platform, keeping time to the music. In a moment the customers were clapping their hands together and stamping too.

We were all milling around in the middle of the floor, all of us watching the minute hand of the clock, when suddenly

Kid Kamm of couple No. 18 began slapping his partner on the cheek. He was holding her up with his left hand, slapping her backwards and forwards with his right hand. But she did not respond. She was dead to the world. She gurgled a couple of times and then slid to the floor, unconscious.

The floor judge blew his whistle and all the customers jumped to their feet, excited. Customers at a marathon dance do not have to be prepared for their excitement. When anything happens they get excited all at once. In that respect a marathon dance is like a bull fight.

The floor judge and a couple of nurses picked up the girl and carried her off, her toes dragging, to the dressing room.

"Mattie Barnes, of Couple No. 18, has fainted," Rocky announced to the crowd. "She has been taken to the dressing room, ladies and gentlemen, where she will have the best of medical attention. Nothing serious, ladies and gentlemen— nothing serious. It just proves that there's always something happening at the world's championship marathon dance."

"She was complaining last rest period," Gloria said.

"What's the matter with her?" I asked.

"It's that time of the month," Gloria said. "And she'll never be able to come back either. She's the type that has to go to bed for three or four days when she gets it."

"Can I pick 'em?" said Kid Kamm. He shook his head, disgusted. "Boy, am I hoodooed! I been in nine of these things and I ain't finished one yet. My partner always caves in on me."

"She'll probably be all right," I said, trying to cheer him up.

"Nope," he said, "she's finished. She can go back to the farm now."

The siren blew, meaning it was the end of another grind. Everybody ran for the dressing rooms. I kicked off my shoes, piling on my cot. I felt the ocean surge once—just once. Then I was asleep.

I woke up, my nose full of ammonia. One of the trainers was moving a bottle across my chin letting me inhale it. (This was the best way to arouse one of us from a deep sleep, the doctor said. If they had tried to wake you up by shaking you, they never would have done it.)

"All right," I said to the trainer. "I'm all right."

I sat up, reaching for my shoes. Then I saw those two detectives and Socks Donald standing near me, by Mario's cot. They were waiting for the other trainer to wake him up. Finally Mario rolled over, looking up at them.

"Hello, buddy," said one of the detectives. "Know who this is?" He handed him a sheet of paper. Now I was close enough to see what it was. It was a page torn out of a detective magazine, containing several pictures.

Mario looked at it, then handed it back. "Yeah, I know who it is," he said, sitting up.

"You ain't changed much," said the other detective.

"You wop son of a bitch," Socks said, doubling his fist. "What're you trying to pull on me?"

"Nix, Socks," the first detective said. Then he spoke to Mario. "Well, Giuseppe, get your things together."

Mario started tying his shoes. "I ain't got nothing but a coat and a toothbrush," he said. "But I would like to say good-bye to my partner."

"You dirty wop son of a bitch," Socks said. "This'll look good in the newspapers, won't it?"

"Never mind your partner, Giuseppe," the second detective said. "Hey son," he said to me, "you tell Giuseppe's partner good-bye for him. Come on, Giuseppe," he said to Mario.

"Take that wop son of a bitch out the back way, boys," said Socks Donald.

"Everybody on the floor," yelled the floor judge. "Everybody on the floor."

"So long, Mario," I said.

Mario did not say anything. It had all been very quiet, very matter-of-fact. These detectives acted as if this kind of thing happened every day.

. . . OF WHICH
YOU HAVE BEEN
CONVICTED
BY VERDICT
OF THE JURY . . .

6

So Mario went to jail and Mattie went back to the farm. *I remember how surprised I was when they arrested Mario for murder. I couldn't believe it. He was one of the nicest boys I'd ever met. But that was then that I couldn't believe it. Now I know you can be nice and be a murderer too. Nobody was ever any nicer to a girl than I was to Gloria, but there came the time when I shot and killed her. So you see being nice doesn't mean a thing. . . .*

Mattie was automatically disqualified when the doctor refused to let her continue in the contest. He said if she did go on with the dance she would injure some of her organs and never be able to have a baby. She raised hell about it, Gloria said, calling the doctor a lot of names and absolutely refusing to quit. But she did quit. She had to. They had the axe over her.

That teamed her partner, Kid Kamm, with Jackie. Under the rules you could do that. You could solo for twenty-four hours but if you didn't get a partner by then you were disqualified. Both the Kid and Jackie seemed well satisfied with the new arrangement. Jackie had nothing to say about losing Mario. Her attitude was that a partner was a partner. But the Kid was all smiles. He seemed to think that at last he had broken his hoodoo.

"They're liable to win," Gloria said. "They're strong as mules. That Alabama is corn-fed. Look at that beam. I bet she can go six months."

"I'll string along with James and Ruby," I said.

"After the way they've treated us?"

"What's that got to do with it? Besides, what's the matter with us? We've got a chance to win, haven't we?"

"Have we?"

"Well, you don't seem to think so," I said.

She shook her head, not saying anything to that. "More and more and more I wish I was dead," she said.

There it was again. No matter what I talked about she al-

ways got back to that. "Isn't there something I can talk about
that won't remind you that you wish you were dead?" I asked.

"No," she said.

"I give up," I said.

Somebody on the platform turned the radio down. The
music sounded like music now. (We used the radio all the time
the orchestra wasn't there. This was in the afternoon. The
orchestra came only at night.) "Ladies and gentlemen,"
Rocky said into the microphone, "I have the honor to announce that two sponsors have come forward to sponsor two
couples. The Pompadour Beauty Shop, of 415 Avenue B, will
sponsor Couple No. 13—James and Ruby Bates. Let's give the
Pompadour Beauty Shop, of 415 Avenue B, a big hand for
this, ladies and gentlemen—you too, kids. . . ."

Everybody applauded.

"The second couple to be sponsored," Rocky said, "is No.
34, Pedro Ortega and Lillian Bacon. They are sponsored by
the Oceanic Garage. All right, now, a big hand for the Oceanic
Garage, located at 11,341 Ocean Walkway in Santa Monica."

Everybody applauded again.

"Ladies and gentlemen," Rocky said, "there ought to be
more sponsors for these marvelous kids. Tell your friends,
ladies and gentlemen, and let's get sponsors for all the kids.
Look at them, ladies and gentlemen, after 242 hours of continuous motion they are as fresh as daisies . . . a big hand for
these marvelous kids, ladies and gentlemen."

There was some more applause.

"And don't forget, ladies and gentlemen," Rocky said,
"there's the Palm Garden right down there at the end of the
hall where you can get delicious beverages—all kinds of beer
and sandwiches. Visit the Palm Garden, ladies and gentlemen. . . . Give," he said to the radio, turning the knob and
filling the hall with noise again.

Gloria and I walked over to Pedro and Lillian. Pedro limped
from a game leg. The story was that he had been gored in a
bull ring in Mexico City. Lillian was a brunette. She too had
been trying to get in the movies when she heard about the
marathon dance.

"Congratulations," I said.

"It proves somebody is for us," Pedro said.

"As long as it couldn't be Metro-Goldwyn-Mayer it might as well be a garage," Lillian said. "Only it seems a little queer for a garage to be buying me underclothes."

"Where do you get that underclothes stuff?" Gloria said. "You don't get underclothes. You get a sweatshirt with the garage's name across the back of it."

"I get underclothes, too," Lillian said.

"Hey, Lillian," said Rollo, the floor judge, "the woman from the Oceanic Garage wants to talk to you."

"The what? . . ." asked Lillian.

"Your sponsor, Mrs. Yeargan——"

"For crying out loud," said Lillian. "Pedro, it looks like you get the underclothes."

Gloria and I walked down by the master of ceremonies' platform. It was nice down there about this time of the afternoon. There was a big triangle of sunshine that came through the double window above the bar in the Palm Garden. It only lasted about ten minutes but during those ten minutes I moved slowly about in it (I had to move to keep from being disqualified) letting it cover me completely. It was the first time I had ever appreciated the sun. "When this marathon is over," I told myself, "I'm going to spend the rest of my life in the sun. I can't wait to go to the Sahara desert to make a picture." *Of course, that won't ever happen now.*

I watched the triangle on the floor get smaller and smaller. Finally it closed altogether and started up my legs. It crawled up my body like a living thing. When it got to my chin I stood on my toes, to keep my head in it as long as possible. I did not close my eyes. I kept them wide open, looking straight into the sun. It did not blind me at all. In a moment it was gone.

I looked around for Gloria. She was standing at the platform, swaying from side to side, talking to Rocky, who was sitting on his haunches. Rocky was swaying too. (All the employes—the doctor, the nurses, the floor judges, the master of ceremonies, even the boys who sold soda pop—had been given orders to keep moving when they talked to one of the contestants. The management was very strict about this.)

"You looked very funny standing out there on your toes," Gloria said. "You looked like a ballet dancer."

"You practice up on that and I'll let you do a solo," Rocky said, laughing.

"Yes," Gloria said. "How was the sun today?"

"Don't let 'em kid you," Mack Aston, of Couple No. 5, said as he passed by.

"Rocky!" a voice called. It was Socks Donald. Rocky got down from the platform and went to him.

"I don't think it's very nice of you to razz me," I said to Gloria. "I don't ever razz you."

"You don't have to," she said. "I get razzed by an expert. God razzes me. . . . You know what Socks Donald wants with Rocky? You want some inside information?"

"What?" I asked.

"You know No. 6—Freddy and that Manski girl. Her mother is going to prefer charges against him and Socks. She ran away from home."

"I don't see what that's got to do with it," I said.

"She's jail bait," Gloria said. "She's only about fifteen. God, with all of it running around loose it does look like a guy would have better sense."

"Why blame Freddy? It may not be his fault."

"According to the law it's his fault," Gloria said. "That's what counts."

I steered Gloria back to where Socks and Rocky were standing, trying to overhear what was being said; but they were talking too low. Rather, Socks was doing all the talking. Rocky was listening, nodding his head.

"Right now," I heard Socks say, and Rocky nodded that he understood and came back on the floor, winking wisely to Gloria as he passed. He went to Rollo Peters and called him aside, whispering earnestly for a few seconds. Then Rollo left, looking around as if he were trying to find somebody, and Rocky went back to the platform.

"The kids only have a few more minutes left before they retire for their well-earned rest period," Rocky announced into the microphone. "And while they are off the floor, ladies and gentlemen, the painters will paint the big oval on the floor for the derby tonight. The derby tonight, ladies and gentlemen: don't forget the derby. Positively the most thrilling thing you ever saw—all right, kids, two minutes to go before you retire—a little sprint, kids—show the ladies and gentlemen how fresh you are— You, too, ladies and gentlemen, show these marvelous kids you're behind them with a rally——"

He turned up the radio a little and began clapping his hands and stamping his foot. The audience joined in the rally. All of us stepped a little more lively, but it was not because of the rally. It was because within a minute or two we got a rest period and directly after that we were to be fed.

Gloria nudged me and I looked up to see Rollo Peters walking between Freddy and the Manski girl. I thought the Manski girl was crying, but before Gloria and I could catch up with them the siren blew and everybody made a dash for the dressing rooms.

Freddy was standing over his cot, stuffing an extra pair of shoes into a small zipper bag.

"I heard about it," I said. "I'm very sorry."

"It's all right," he said. "Only she's the one who did the raping. . . . I'll be all right if I can get out of town before the cops pick me up. It's a lucky thing for me that Socks was tipped off."

"Where are you going?" I asked.

"South, I guess. I've always had a yen to see Mexico. So long. . . ."

"So long," I said.

He was gone before anybody knew it. As he went through the back door I had a glimpse of the sun glinting on the ocean. For a moment I was so astounded I could not move. I do not know whether I was the more surprised at really seeing the sun for the first time in almost three weeks or discovering the door. I went over to it, hoping the sun would not be gone when I got there. *The only other time I ever was this eager was one Christmas when I was a kid, the first year I was big enough to really know what Christmas was, and I went into the front room and saw the tree all lighted up.*

I opened the door. At the end of the world the sun was sinking into the ocean. It was so red and bright and hot I wondered why there was no steam. *I once saw steam come out of the ocean. It was on the highway at the beach and some men were working with gunpowder. Suddenly, it exploded, setting*

*them on fire. They ran and dived into the ocean. That was when
I saw the steam.*

The color of the sun had shot up into some thin clouds,
reddening them. Out there where the sun was sinking the
ocean was very calm, not looking like an ocean at all. It was
lovely, lovely, lovely, lovely, lovely, lovely. Several people were
fishing off the pier, not paying any attention to the sunset.
They were fools. "You need that sunset worse than you do
fish," I told them in my mind.

The door flew out of my hands, slamming shut with a bang
like that of a cannon going off.

"Are you deaf?" a voice yelled in my ear. It was one of the
trainers. "Keep that door closed! You wanna be disqualified?"

"I was only watching the sun set," I said.

"Are you nuts? You ought to be asleep. You need your
sleep," he said.

"I don't need any sleep," I said. "I feel fine. I feel better
than I ever felt in my life."

"You need your rest anyway," he said. "You only got a few
minutes left. Get off your feet."

He followed me across the floor to my cot. Now I could
notice the dressing room didn't smell so good. I am very
susceptible to unpleasant odors and I wondered why I hadn't
noticed this smell before, the smell of too many men in a
room. I kicked off my shoes and stretched out on my back.

"You want your legs rubbed?" he asked.

"I'm all right," I said. "My legs feel fine."

He said something to himself and went away. I lay there,
thinking about the sunset, trying to remember what color it
was. I don't mean the red, I mean the other shades. Once or
twice I almost remembered; it was like a name you once had
known but now had forgotten, whose size and letters and
cadence you remembered but could not quite assemble.

Through the legs of my cot I could feel the ocean quivering
against the pilings below. It rose and fell, rose and fell, went
out and came back, went out and came back. . . .

I was glad when the siren blew, waking us up, calling us
back to the floor.

. . . CARRYING
WITH IT
THE EXTREME PENALTY
OF THE LAW . . .

7

THE PAINTERS had finished. They had painted a thick white line around the floor in the shape of an oval. This was the track for the derby.

"Freddy's gone," I said to Gloria, as we walked to the table where the sandwiches and coffee had been set up. (This was called a light lunch. We had our big meal at ten o'clock at night.)

"So is the Manski girl," Gloria said. "Two welfare workers came and got her. I bet her old lady burns her cute little bottom."

"I hate to say it," I said, "but Freddy's leaving was the brightest spot of my life."

"What had he ever done to you?" she asked.

"Oh, I don't mean that," I said. "But if he hadn't left I wouldn't have got to see the sunset."

"My God," Gloria said, looking at her sandwich. "Ain't there nothing in the world but ham?"

"To you that's turkey," said Mack Aston, who was in line behind me. He was kidding.

"Here's a beef," said the nurse. "Would you rather have a beef?"

Gloria took the beef sandwich, but kept the ham too. "Put four lumps in mine," she said to Rollo, who was pouring the coffee. "And lots of cream."

"She's got a little horse in her," said Mack Aston.

"Black," I said to Rollo.

Gloria took her food over to the master of ceremonies' platform where the musicians were tuning up their instruments. When Rocky Gravo saw her he jumped down on the floor and began talking to her. There wasn't room there for me, so I went around to the opposite side.

"Hello," said a girl. The shield on her back said: 7. She had black hair and black eyes and was rather pretty. I didn't know her name.

"Hello," I said, looking around, trying to see whose partner she was. He was talking to a couple of women in a front row box.

"How are you making out?" No. 7 asked. Her voice sounded as if she had been well educated.

"What is she doing in this thing?" I asked myself. "I guess I'm doing all right," I replied. "Only I wish it was all over and I was the winner."

"What would you do with the money if you won?" she asked, laughing.

"I'd make a picture," I said.

"You couldn't make much of a picture for a thousand dollars, could you?" she asked, taking a bite of her sandwich.

"Oh, I don't mean a big picture," I explained. "I mean a short. I could make a two-reeler for that, maybe three."

"You interest me," she said. "I've been watching you for two weeks."

"You have?" I said, surprised.

"Yes, I've seen you stand over there in the sun every afternoon and I've seen you with a thousand different expressions on your face. Sometimes I got the idea you were badly frightened."

"You must be wrong," I said. "What's there to be frightened about?"

"I overheard what you said to your partner about seeing the sunset this afternoon," she said, smiling.

"That doesn't prove anything," I said.

"Suppose . . ." she said, glancing around. She looked at the clock, frowning. "We've still got four minutes. Would you like to do something for me?"

"Well . . . sure," I said.

She motioned with her head and I followed her behind the master of ceremonies' platform. This platform was about four feet high, draped with heavy, decorated canvas that fell to the floor. We were standing alone in a sort of cave that was formed by the back of the platform and a lot of signs. Except for the noise she and I might have been the only people left in the world. We were both a little excited.

"Come on," she said. She dropped to the floor and lifted the canvas, crawling under the platform. My heart was beating rapidly and I felt the blood leave my face. Through the balls of my feet I could feel the ocean surging against the pilings below.

"Come on," she whispered, pulling at my ankle. Suddenly I knew what she meant. *There is no new experience in life. Something may happen to you that you think has never happened before, that you think is brand new, but you are mistaken. You have only to see or smell or hear or feel a certain something and you will discover that this experience you thought was new has happened before. When she pulled at my ankle, trying to get me beneath the platform, I remembered the time when another girl had done exactly the same thing. Only it was a front porch instead of a platform. I was thirteen or fourteen years old then and the girl was about the same age. Her name was Mabel and she lived next door. After school we used to play under the front porch, imagining it was a cove and we were robbers and prisoners. Later on we used it to play papa and mama, imagining it was a house. But on this day I am speaking of I stood by the front porch, not thinking of Mabel or games at all, and I felt something pulling at my ankle. I looked down and there was Mabel. "Come on," she said.*

It was very dark under the platform and while I crouched there on my hands and knees trying to see through the gloom No. 7 suddenly grabbed me around the neck.

"Hurry . . ." she whispered.

"What's coming off here?" growled a man's voice. He was so close I could feel his breath against my hair. "Who is that?"

I recognized the voice now. It was Rocky Gravo's. My stomach turned over. No. 7 let go my neck and slid out from under the platform. I was afraid if I tried to apologize or say anything Rocky would recognize my voice, so I quickly rolled under the curtain. No. 7 was already on her feet moving away, looking back over her shoulder at me. Her face was white as chalk. Neither of us spoke. We strolled onto the dance floor, trying to look very innocent. The nurse was collecting our dirty coffee cups in a basket. Then I discovered my hands and clothes were filthy with dust. I had a couple of minutes before the whistle blew, so I hurried into the dressing room to clean up. When that was done I felt better.

"What a close shave that was," I told myself. "I'll never do anything like that again."

I got back on the floor as the whistle blew and the orchestra began to play. This was not a very good orchestra; but it was better than the radio because you didn't have to listen to a lot of announcers begging and pleading with you to buy something. Since I've been in this marathon I've had enough radio to last me the rest of my life. *There is a radio going now, in a building across the street from the court room. It is very distinct. "Do you need money? . . . Are you in trouble? . . ."*

"Where've you been?" Gloria asked, taking my arm.

"I haven't been anywhere," I said. "Feel like dancing?"

"All right," she said. We danced once around the floor and then she stopped. "That's too much like work," she said.

As I took my hand from around her waist I noticed my fingers were dirty again. "That's funny," I thought. "I just washed them a minute ago."

"Turn around," I said to Gloria.

"What's the matter?" she asked.

"Turn around," I said.

She hesitated, biting her lip, so I stepped behind her. She was wearing a white woolen skirt and a thin white woolen sweater. Her back was covered with thick dust and I knew where it had come from.

"What's the matter?" she said.

"Stand still," I said. I brushed her off with my hand, knocking most of the dust and lint loose from her sweater and skirt. She did not speak for a moment or two. "I must have got that when I was wrestling in the dressing room with Lillian," she said finally.

"I'm not as big a sap as she thinks I am," I told myself. "I guess you did," I said.

Rollo Peters fell in with us as we walked around the floor.

"Who is that girl?" I asked, pointing to No. 7.

"That's Guy Duke's partner. Her name is Rosemary Loftus."

"All your taste is in your mouth," Gloria said.

"I merely asked who she was," I said. "I haven't got a crush on her."

"You don't need one," Gloria said. "You tell him, Rollo."

"Leave me out of this," Rollo said, shaking his head. "I don't know a thing about her."

"What about her?" I asked Gloria, as Rollo walked away, joining James and Ruby Bates.

"Are you that innocent?" she said. "On the level—are you?" She laughed, shaking her head. "You certainly are a card."

"All right, forget it," I said.

"Why, that dame is the biggest bitch west of the Mississippi River," she said. "She's a bitch with an exclusive education and when you get that kind of bitch you've got the worst bitch of all. Why not even the girls can go to the can when she's around——"

"Hello, there, Gloria," called out Mrs. Layden. She was sitting in her usual seat in the front row box the far end of the hall, away from the master of ceremonies' platform. Gloria and I walked over to the railing. . . .

"How's my favorite couple?" she asked.

"Fine," I said. "How are you, Mrs. Layden?"

"I'm fine too," she said. "I'm going to stay a long time tonight. See?" She pointed to her blanket and her lunch basket on the chair beside her. "I'll be here to cheer you on."

"We'll need it," Gloria said.

"Why don't you take one of those boxes down there away from the Palm Garden?" I asked. "It gets pretty rowdy at the bar later on when everybody starts drinking——"

"This is fine for me," she said, smiling. "I like to be here for the derby. I want to watch them make the turns. Would you like to see the afternoon paper?" she asked, pulling the paper out from under the blanket.

"Thank you," I said. "I would like to know what's going on in the world. How is the weather outside? Has the world changed much?"

"You're poking fun at me," she said.

"No, I'm not . . . it just seems like I've been in this hall a million years . . . Thanks for the paper, Mrs. Layden. . . ."

As we moved away I unfolded the paper. Big, black headlines hit me in the face.

NAB YOUTHFUL MURDERER
IN MARATHON DANCE

———

Escaped Criminal Was Taking
Part in Beach Contest

———

Detectives yesterday picked a murderer from the marathon dance now in progress on the amusement pier at Santa Monica. He was Giuseppe Lodi, 26-year-old Italian, who escaped eight months ago from the Illinois state prison at Joliet after serving four years of a fifty-year sentence for the conviction of the hold-up slaying of an aged druggist in Chicago.

Lodi, entered in the marathon dance under the alias of Mario Petrone, offered no resistance when he was arrested by Detectives Bliss and Voight, of the Robbery Detail. The officers had dropped into the marathon dance seeking diversion from their duties, they said, and recognized Lodi through a picture they had seen in "The Line-Up," a department of a popular detective monthly which contains pictures and measurements of badly wanted criminals . . .

"Can you beat that?" I said. "I was right beside him when all that happened. I certainly feel sorry for Mario now."

"Why," said Gloria, "what's the difference between us?"

Pedro Ortega, Mack Aston and a few others gathered around us, talking excitedly. I handed the paper to Gloria and walked on alone.

"That's a hell of a thing," I thought. "Fifty years! Poor Mario . . ." *And when Mario hears the news about me, if he ever does, he will think: 'Poor guy! wasting his sympathy on me and him getting the rope. . . .'*

At the next rest period Socks Donald had a surprise for us. He issued the uniforms we were to wear in the derby races; tennis shoes, white shorts, white sweatshirts. All the boys were given thick leather belts to wear around their waists, and on either side of the belt were little handles, like those on luggage. These were for our partners to hold on when we went around the curves. It seemed very silly to me then, but later on I discovered Socks Donald knew what he was doing.

"Lissen, kids," Socks said. "Tonight we start on our first million. There'll be a lot of movie stars here for the derby and wherever they go the crowds will follow. Some team will lose tonight—some team will lose every night. I don't want no squawks about this because it's on the level. Everybody has the same chance. You'll get some extra time to get on your uniforms and some extra time to take them off. And by the way, I talked to Mario Petrone this afternoon. He told me to say good-bye to all his pals. Now, don't forget to give the customers a run for their money in the derby, kids——"

I was surprised to hear him mention Mario's name because the night before, when Mario was arrested, Socks had wanted to beat him up.

"I thought he was sore at Mario," I said to Rollo.

"Not any more," Rollo said. "That was the best break we ever had. If it hadn't been for that nobody ever would have known there was a marathon dance. That newspaper publicity was just what the doctor ordered. Reservations have been coming in all afternoon."

. . . YOU,
ROBERT SYVERTEN,
BE DELIVERED . . .

8

THAT NIGHT, for the first time since the contest started, the hall was crowded and practically every seat was taken. The Palm Garden was crowded too and there was a lot of boisterous laughing and talking at the bar. "Rollo was right," I said to myself. "Mario's arrest was the best break Socks ever had." (But not all those people had been attracted by the newspaper publicity. I found out later that Socks was having us advertised over several radio stations.)

We walked around in our track suits while the trainers and nurses set up the floor for the derby.

"I feel naked," I said to Gloria.

"You look naked," she said. "You ought to have on a jock-strap."

"They didn't give me one," I said. "Does it show that much?"

"It's not only that," she said. "You're liable to get ruptured. Get Rollo to buy you one tomorrow. They come in three sizes: small, medium and large. You take a small."

"I'm not by myself," I said, looking around at some of the other boys.

"They're bragging," Gloria said.

Most of the contestants looked very funny in their track suits. I never saw such an odd assortment of arms and legs in my life.

"Look," Gloria said, nodding to James and Ruby Bates. "Ain't that something?"

You could see Ruby was going to have a baby. It looked as if she had stuffed a pillow under her sweatshirt.

"It certainly is noticeable," I said. "But remember it's none of your business."

"Ladies and gentlemen," Rocky said into the microphone, "before this sensational derby starts I want to call your attention to the rules and regulations. Because of the number of contestants the derby will be run in two sections—forty couples in the first and forty in the second. The second derby will be run a few minutes after the first one and the entries in each one will be decided by drawing the numbers out of a hat.

"We'll run these derbies in two sections for a week, the couple in each one making the least number of laps to be eliminated. After the first week there will be only one derby. The kids will race around the track for fifteen minutes, the boys heeling and toeing, the girls trotting or running as they see fit. There is no prize for the winner, but if some of you ladies and gentlemen want to send up some prize money to encourage the kids, I know they will appreciate it.

"You will notice the cots in the middle of the floor, the nurses and trainers standing by with sliced oranges, wet towels, smelling salts—and the doctor in charge to see that none of these kids carry on unless they're in good physical condition."

The young doctor was standing in the middle of the floor, his stethoscope hanging from his neck, looking very important.

"Just a minute, ladies and gentlemen—just a minute," Rocky said. "I have in my hand a ten-dollar bill for the winner of tonight's derby, contributed by that marvelous little screen star, none other than Miss Ruby Keeler. A hand for Miss Keeler, ladies and gentlemen——"

Ruby Keeler stood up, bowing to the applause.

"That's the spirit, ladies and gentlemen," Rocky said. "And now we need some judges, ladies and gentlemen, to check the laps each couple makes." He stopped to wipe the perspiration off his face. "All right now, ladies and gentlemen, I want these judges out of the audience—forty of them. Step right up here—don't be afraid——"

Nobody in the audience moved for a moment, and then Mrs. Layden crawled under the railing and started across the floor. As she passed Gloria and me she smiled and winked.

"Maybe she'll turn out to be useful after all," Gloria said.

Soon others followed Mrs. Layden until all the judges had been selected. Rollo gave each of them a card and a pencil and seated them on the floor around the platform.

"All right, ladies and gentlemen," Rocky said. "We've got enough judges. Now we'll have the drawing for the first derby. There are eighty numbers in this hat and we'll draw forty of

them. The other couples will be in the second derby. Now we
need somebody to draw the numbers. How about you, lady?"
he asked Mrs. Layden, holding out the hat. Mrs. Layden
smiled and nodded her head.

"This is a big moment in her life," Gloria said sarcastically.

"I think she is a very sweet old lady," I said.

"Nuts," Gloria said.

Mrs. Layden began drawing out the numbers, passing them
to Rocky who announced them into the microphone.

"The first one," he said, "is couple No. 105. Right over
here, kids—all you couples who are drawn stand over here on
this side of the platform."

As fast as Mrs. Layden would draw the numbers Rocky
would announce them, then pass them to one of the judges.
That was the couple he checked, counting the number of laps
they made.

". . . Couple No. 22," Rocky said, handing the number to
a young man who wore spectacles.

"Come on," I said to Gloria. That was our number.

"I'd like that one," I heard Mrs. Layden say to Rocky.
"That's my favorite couple."

"Sorry, lady," Rocky said. "You have to take them in
order."

When the drawing was finished and we were all together
near the starting line, Rocky said, "All right, ladies and gentlemen, we're almost ready. Now, kids, all you boys remember
heel and toe. If one of you has to go to the pit for any reason
whatsoever, your partner has to make two laps of the track to
count for one. Will you start 'em off, Miss Keeler?"

She nodded and Rocky handed Rollo the pistol. He took
it to Miss Keeler, who was sitting in a front-row box with
another girl I didn't recognize. Jolson was not there.

"All right, ladies and gentlemen, hold your hats," Rocky
said. "All right, Miss Keeler. . . ." He signaled to her with
his hand.

Gloria and I had edged along the side of the platform towards the starting line and when Miss Keeler pulled the trigger we jumped away, pushing and shoving to get in front.
Gloria had me by the arm.

"Hold on to the belt," I yelled, struggling to get through

the crowd. Everybody was stumbling over everybody else, trying to get in front . . . but in a minute we spread out and
began pounding around the track. I was taking such long
steps Gloria had to trot to keep up with me.

"Heel and toe there," Rollo said. "You're running."

"I'm doing the best I can," I said.

"Heel and toe," he said. "Like this——"

He stepped in front of me, illustrating what he meant. I
had no trouble at all in learning. The trick was to keep your
shoulders and arms properly timed. I had no trouble at all in
figuring that. It seemed to come to me naturally. It was so
simple I thought for a moment I must have done some heel-
and-toe walking before. I couldn't remember it, so evidently
I hadn't. I've got a marvelous memory.

We had been going about five minutes and were well up
towards the front when I felt Gloria stop propelling herself;
that is, she stopped traveling under her own power. I was
dragging her. I felt as if she were trying to pull the belt
through my stomach.

"Too fast?" I asked, slowing down.

"Yes," she replied, almost out of breath.

One of the nurses slammed a wet bath towel around my
neck, almost knocking me off balance. "Rub your face with
it," I said to Gloria. . . . Just then couple No. 35 cut in front
of us, trying to get into the turn first. The spurt was too much
for the girl. She began to stagger, loosening her hold on his
belt.

"Stand by No. 35," yelled Rocky Gravo, but before a nurse
or trainer could reach her she had fallen on her face, sliding
a couple of feet across the floor. If I had been alone I could
have side-stepped the body, but with Gloria hanging on me I
was afraid if I dodged I would sling her off. (Making these
turns with a girl hanging on you was like playing pop-the-
whip.)

"Look out!" I yelled, but the warning was too late to do
any good. Gloria stumbled over the body pulling me down
with her, and the next thing I knew four or five couples were
piled together on the floor, struggling to get up. Rocky said
something into the microphone and the crowd gasped.

I picked myself up. I wasn't hurt, only I knew from the way

my knees were burning that all the skin was rubbed off. The nurses and trainers rushed over and began tugging at the girls, carrying Gloria and Ruby to the cots in the pit.

"Nothing serious, ladies and gentlemen," Rocky said. "Just a little spill . . . something happens every minute in the derbies . . . while the girls are in the pit the boys have to make two laps to count as one full lap for the team. All right, kids, give those solos the inside track."

I began walking very fast so as not to lose our position in the race. Now that Gloria wasn't hanging on to the strap any more I felt light as a feather. A nurse and a trainer began working over her while the doctor listened to her heart with his stethoscope. The nurse was holding smelling salts at her nose and the trainer was massaging her legs. Another trainer and nurse were doing the same thing to Ruby. I made four laps before Gloria came back to the floor. She was very pale.

"Can you hold out?" I asked, slowing down. She said yes with her head. The people were applauding and stamping their feet and Rocky was speaking words into the microphone. Ruby came back into the race, looking all in too.

"Take it easy," Rollo said, moving beside me. "You're in no danger——"

Then I felt a sharp pain in my left leg that shot up through my body and almost blew off the top of my head. "My God," I told myself; "I'm paralyzed!"

"Kick it out, kick it out," Rollo said.

I couldn't bend my leg. It simply wouldn't work. It was stiff as a board. Every time I took a step the pain went through the top of my head.

"There's a charley horse on Couple 22," Rocky said into the microphone. "Stand by there, trainers——"

"Kick it out, kick it out," Rollo said.

I kicked my leg against the floor but that was more painful than ever.

"Kick it out, kick it out——"

"You son of a bitch," I said; "my leg hurts——"

Two of the trainers grabbed me by the arms and helped me to the pit.

"There goes the brave little girl of No. 22," Rocky announced, "little Gloria Beatty. What a brave kid she is!

She's soloing while her partner is in the pit with a charley horse——look at her burn up that track! Give her the inside, kids——"

One of the trainers held my shoulders down while the other one worked my leg up and down, beating the muscles with the heels of his fists.

"That hurts," I said.

"Take it easy," said the trainer who was holding my shoulders. "Didn't you ever have one of those things before?"

Then I felt something snap in my leg and the pain was suddenly gone.

"Okay," the trainer said.

I got up, feeling fine, and went back on the track, standing there waiting for Gloria. She was on the opposite side from me, trotting, her head bobbing up and down every time she took a step. I had to wait for her to come around. (The rules were you had to come out of the pit at the point where you went in.) As Gloria neared me I started walking and in a moment she had coupled on to the belt.

"Two minutes to go," Rocky announced. "A little rally, ladies and gentlemen—" They began clapping their hands and stamping their feet, much louder than before.

Other couples began to sprint past us and I put on a little more steam. I was pretty sure Gloria and I weren't in last place, but we had both been in the pit and I didn't want to take a chance on being eliminated. When the pistol sounded for the finish half the teams collapsed on the floor. I turned around to Gloria and saw her eyes were glassy. I knew she was going to faint.

"Hey . . ." I yelled to one of the nurses, but just then Gloria sagged and I had to catch her myself. It was all I could do to carry her to the pit. "Hey!" I yelled to one of the trainers. "Doctor."

Nobody paid any attention to me. They were too busy picking up the bodies. The customers were standing on their seats, screaming in excitement.

I began rubbing Gloria's face with a wet towel. Mrs. Layden suddenly appeared beside me and took a bottle of smelling salts off the table by the cot.

"You go on to your dressing room," she said. "Gloria'll be all right in a minute. She's not used to the strain."

I was on a boat going to Port Said. I was on my way to the Sahara Desert to make that picture. I was famous and I had plenty of money. I was the most important motion picture director in the world. I was more important than Sergei Eisenstein. The critics of *Vanity Fair* and *Esquire* had agreed that I was a genius. I was walking around the deck, thinking of that marathon dance I once had been in, wondering what had become of all those girls and boys, when something hit me a terrific blow in the back of the head, knocking me unconscious. I had a feeling I was falling.

When I struck the water I began lashing out with my arms and legs because I was afraid of sharks. Something brushed my body and I screamed in fright.

I woke up swimming in water that was freezing cold. Instantly I knew where I was. "I've had a nightmare," I told myself. The thing that had brushed my body was a hundred-pound block of ice. I was in a small tank of water in the dressing room. I was still wearing my track suit. I climbed out, shivering, and one of the trainers handed me a towel.

Two other trainers came in, carrying one of the contestants who was unconscious. It was Pedro Ortega. They carried him to the tank and dumped him in.

"Is that what happened to me?" I asked.

"That's right," the trainer said. "You passed out just as you left the dance floor—" Pedro whimpered something in Spanish and splashed the water, fighting to get out. The trainer laughed. "I'll say Socks knew what he was doing when he brought that tank in here," he said. "That ice water fixes 'em right up. Get off those wet pants and shoes."

. . . BY THE
SHERIFF OF
LOS ANGELES
COUNTY
TO THE
WARDEN OF
STATE PRISON . . .

9

THE DERBY races were killing them off. Fifty-odd couples had been eliminated in two weeks. Gloria and I had come close to the finish once or twice, but by the skin of our teeth we managed to hang on. After we changed our technique we had no more trouble: we had stopped trying to win, not caring where we finished so long as it wasn't last.

We had got a sponsor too: Jonathan Beer, Non-Fattening. This came just in time. Our shoes were worn out and our clothes were ragged. Mrs. Layden sold Jonathan Beer on the idea of sponsoring us. *Sell St. Peter on the idea of letting me in, Mrs. Layden. I think I'm on my way.* They gave Gloria and me three pairs of shoes, three pairs of gray flannel trousers and three sweaters each with their product advertised on the backs of them.

I had gained five pounds since the contest started and was beginning to think that maybe we had some chance to win that thousand dollar first prize after all. But Gloria was very pessimistic.

"What are you going to do after this thing is over?" she asked.

"Why worry about that?" I said. "It's not over yet. I don't see what you're kicking about," I told her. "We're better off than we've ever been—at least we know where our next meal is coming from."

"I wish I was dead," she said. "I wish God would strike me dead."

She kept saying that over and over again. It was beginning to get on my nerves.

"Some day God is going to do that little thing," I said.

"I wish He would . . . I wish I had the guts to do it for Him."

"If we win this thing you can take your five-hundred dollars and go away somewhere," I said. "You can get married. There are always plenty of guys willing to get married. Haven't you ever thought about that?"

"I've thought about it plenty," she said. "But I couldn't ever marry the kind of man I want. The only kind that would marry me would be the kind I wouldn't have. A thief or a pimp or something."

"I know why you're so morbid," I said. "You'll be all right in a couple of days. You'll feel better about it then."

"That hasn't got anything to do with it," she said. "I don't even get a backache from that. That's not it. This whole business is a merry-go-round. When we get out of here we're right back where we started."

"We've been eating and sleeping," I said.

"Well, what's the good of that when you're just postponing something that's bound to happen?"

"Hey, Jonathan Beer," Rocky Gravo called out. "Come over here——"

He was standing by the platform with Socks Donald. Gloria and I went over.

"How'd you kids like to pick up a hundred bucks?" Rocky asked.

"Doing what?" Gloria asked.

"Well, kids," Socks Donald said, "I've got a swell idea only I need a bit of some help——"

"That's the Ben Bernie influence," Gloria said to me.

"What?" Socks said.

"Nothing," Gloria said. "Go on—you need a bit of some help——"

"Yeah," Socks said. "I want you two kids to get married here. A public wedding."

"Married?" I said.

"Now, wait a minute," Socks said. "It's not that bad. I'll give you fifty dollars apiece and after the marathon is over you can get divorced if you want to. It don't have to be permanent. It's just a showmanship angle. What do you say?"

"I say you're nuts," Gloria said.

"She doesn't mean that, Mr. Donald—" I said.

"The hell I don't," she said. "I've got no objections to

getting married," she said to Socks, "but why don't you pick out Gary Cooper or some big-shot producer or director? I don't want to marry this guy. I got enough trouble looking out for myself——"

"It don't have to be permanent," Rocky said. "It's just showmanship."

"That's right," Socks said. "Of course, the ceremony'll have to be on the square—we'll have to do that to get the crowd. But——"

"You don't need a wedding to get a crowd," Gloria said. "You're hanging 'em off the rafters now. Ain't it enough of a show to see these poor bastards falling all over the floor every night?"

"You don't get the angle," Socks said, frowning.

"The hell I don't," Gloria said. "I'm way ahead of you."

"You want to get in pictures and here's your chance," Socks said. "I already got some stores lined up to give you your wedding dress and your shoes and a beauty shop that'll fix you up—there'll be a lot of directors and supervisors here and they'll all be looking at nobody but you. It's the chance of a lifetime. What do you say, kid?" he asked me.

"I don't know——" I said, not wanting to make him sore. After all, he was the promoter. I knew if he got sore at us we were as good as disqualified.

"He says no," Gloria said.

"She does his thinking for him," Rocky said sarcastically.

"Okay," Socks said, shrugging his shoulders. "If you can't use a hundred dollars maybe some of these other kids can. At least," he said to me, "you know who wears the drawers in your family." He and Rocky both laughed.

"You just can't be polite to anybody, can you?" I said to Gloria when we had walked away. "We'll be out in the street any minute now."

"Might as well be now as tomorrow," she said.

"You're the gloomiest person I ever met," I said. "Sometimes I think you would be better off dead."

"I know it," she said.

When we came around by the platform again I saw Socks and Rocky talking earnestly to Vee Lovell and Mary Hawley, Couple No. 71.

"Looks like Socks is selling her a bill of goods," Gloria said. "That Hawley horse couldn't get in out of the rain."

James and Ruby Bates joined up and we walked four abreast. We were on friendly terms again since Gloria had stopped trying to talk Ruby into having an abortion performed. "Did Socks proposition you to get married?" Ruby asked.

"Yes," I said. "How did you know?"

"He's propositioned everybody," she said.

"We turned him down cold," Gloria said.

"A public wedding isn't so bad," Ruby said. "We had one——"

"You did?" I said, surprised. James and Ruby were so dignified and quiet and so much in love with each other I couldn't imagine them being married in a public ceremony.

"We were married in a marathon dance in Oklahoma," she said. "We got about three hundred dollars worth of stuff too. . . ."

"Her old man gave us the shotgun for a wedding present—" James said, laughing.

Suddenly a girl screamed behind us. We turned around. It was Lillian Bacon, Pedro Ortega's partner. She was walking backwards, trying to get away from him. Pedro caught up with her, slamming her in the face with his fist. She sat down on the floor, screaming again. Pedro grabbed her by the throat with both hands, choking her and trying to lift her up. His face was the face of a maniac. There was no doubt he was trying to kill her.

Everybody started running for him at the same time. There was a lot of confusion.

James and I reached him first, grabbing him and breaking his hold on Lillian's neck. She was sitting on the floor, her body rigid, her arms behind her, her head thrown back, her mouth open—like a patient in a dentist's chair.

Pedro was muttering to himself and did not seem to recognize any of us. James shoved him and he staggered backward. I put my hands under Lillian's armpits, helping her to her feet. She was shaking like a muscle dancer.

Socks and Rocky rushed up and took Pedro by either arm.

"What's the big idea?" Socks roared.

Pedro looked at Socks, moving his lips but not saying anything. Then he saw Rocky and the expression on his face changed, becoming one of ferocious resentment. He suddenly twisted his arms free, stepping backward and reaching into his pocket.

"Look out—" somebody cried.

Pedro lunged forward, a knife in his hand. Rocky tried to dodge, but it all happened so quickly he never had a chance. The knife caught him across the left arm two inches below the shoulder. He yelled and started running. Pedro turned around to follow but before he could take a step Socks hit him in the back of the head with a leather blackjack. You could hear the plunk above the music of the radio. It sounded exactly like somebody thumping their finger against a watermelon. Pedro stood there, an idiotic grin on his face and Socks hit him again with the blackjack.

Pedro's arms fell and the knife dropped to the floor. He wobbled on his legs and then he went down.

"Get him out of here," Socks said, picking up the knife.

James Bates, Mack Aston and Vee Lovell lifted Pedro, carrying him off to the dressing room.

"Keep your seats, ladies and gentlemen—" Socks said to the audience. "Please——"

I was bracing Lillian from behind. She was still shaking.

"What happened?" Socks asked her.

"He accused me of cheating—" she said. "Then he hit me and started choking me——"

"Go on, kids," Socks said. "Act like nothing has happened. Hey, nurse—help this girl to the dressing room—" Socks signaled to Rollo on the platform and the siren blew for a rest period. It was a few minutes early. The nurse took Lillian out of my arms and all the girls gathered around them, going into the dressing room.

As I went off I could hear Rollo making some kind of casual announcement over the loud speakers.

Rocky was standing at the wash basin, his coat and shirt off, dabbing at his shoulder with a handful of paper towels. The blood was streaming down his arm, running off his fingers.

"You better get the doctor on that," Socks said. "Where the hell is that doctor?" he bellowed.

"Here—" the doctor said, coming out of the lavatory.

"The only time we need you you're sitting on your ass," Socks said. "See what's the matter with Rocky."

Pedro was lying on the floor with Mack Aston straddling him, working on his stomach like a life guard with a man who has been drowning.

"Watch it—" Vee Lovell said, coming up with a bucket of water. Mack stepped back and Vee dumped the water in Pedro's face. It had no effect on him. He lay there like a log.

James Bates brought another bucket of water and doused him with that. Now Pedro began to show signs of life. He stirred, opening his eyes.

"He's coming to," Vee Lovell said.

"I better get Rocky to the hospital in my car," the doctor said, taking off his linen coat. "He's got a deep cut—almost to the bone. It'll have to be sutured. Who did it?"

"That bastard—" Socks said, pointing to Pedro with his leg.

"He must have used a razor," the doctor said.

"Here—" Socks said, handing him the knife. Socks had the leather blackjack in his other hand, the thong still around his wrist.

"Same thing," the doctor said, handing back the knife.

Pedro sat up, rubbing his jaw, a dazed look on his face.

"It wasn't your jaw," I said to him in my mind, "it was the back of your head."

"For Christ's sake, let's get going," Rocky said to the doctor. "I'm bleeding like a stuck pig. And you, you son of a bitch," he said to Pedro; "I'm going to prefer charges against you——"

Pedro looked at him fiercely, saying nothing.

"There won't be any charges filed," Socks said. "I'm having enough trouble keeping open now. Next time be careful who you cheat with."

"I wasn't cheating with anybody," Rocky said.

"Balls—" Socks said. "Take him out the back way, Doc."

"All right, Rocky," the doctor said. Rocky started out. The temporary gauze bandage on his arm was soaked already. The doctor draped a coat around Rocky's shoulders and they went out.

"Are you trying to bust up this contest?" Socks asked, turning his full attention to Pedro. "Whyn't you wait till this was over to get him?"

"I tried to cut his throat," Pedro stated calmly, in precise English. "He seduced my fiancée——"

"If he seduced your fiancée around here he's a magician," Socks said. "There's no place to seduce anybody."

"I know a place," I said in my mind.

Rollo Peters came in to the dressing room. "You guys ought to be getting your sleep," he said. "Where's Rocky?" he asked, looking around.

"The doc took him to the hospital," Socks told him. "How are they out there?"

"They're calmed down," Rollo said. "I told 'em we were rehearsing a novelty act. What was the matter with Rocky?"

"Nothing much," Socks said. "He just damn near had his arm cut off by this greaseball, that's all." He handed him Pedro's knife. "Here, take this thing and get rid of it. You do the announcing till we find out about Rocky."

Pedro got up off the floor. "I am very sorry this happened before the audience," he said. "I am very sorry I have a very quick temper——"

"I guess it could have been worse," Socks said. "It could have happened at night when we had a full house. How's your head?"

"It is sore," Pedro said. "I am very sorry this happened. I wanted to win the thousand dollars——"

"You still got a chance," Socks said.

"You mean I am not disqualified? You mean you forgive me?"

"I forgive you——" Socks said, dropping the blackjack into his pocket.

. . . TO BE
BY SAID
WARDEN . . .

```
HOURS ELAPSED . . . . . .  783
Couples Remaining  . . . . . .  26
```

LADIES and gentlemen," Rocky announced, "before the derby starts the management has asked me to tell you that there will be a public wedding here one week from to-night—a real, bona-fide wedding right here on the floor be-tween Couple No. 71, Vee Lovell and Mary Hawley. Step out there, Vee and Mary, and let the ladies and gentlemen see what a cute couple you are——"

Vee and Mary, in track suits, went to the center of the floor, bowing to the applause. The hall was packed again.

"—That is," Rocky said, "if they are not eliminated in the derby by then. We hope not, anyway. This public wedding is in line with the management's policy to give you nothing but high-class amusement——"

Mrs. Layden tugged at the back of my sweatshirt.

"What's the matter with Rocky's arm?" she asked in a whis-per. You could see Rocky had had some kind of an accident. His right arm was through his coat sleeve in the usual way, but his left arm was in a sling and on that side he wore his coat like a cape.

"He sprained it," I said.

"They only took nine stitches in it," Gloria said, under her breath.

"That's why he wasn't here last night," Mrs. Layden said. "He had an accident——"

"Yes'm——"

"Did he fall?"

"Yes'm, I think so——"

"—introducing that beautiful screen star Miss Mary Brian. Will you take a bow, Miss Brian?"

Miss Brian took a bow. The audience applauded.

"—and that master comedian, Mr. Charley Chase——"

There was more applause as Charley Chase stood up in a box seat and took a bow.

"I hate these introductions," Gloria said.

"It would be all right if you were being introduced though, wouldn't it?" I said.

"Good luck——" Mrs. Layden said as we moved towards the platform.

"I'm sick of this," Gloria said. "I'm sick of looking at celebrities and I'm sick of doing the same thing over and over again——"

"Sometimes I'm sorry I ever met you," I said. "I don't like to say a thing like that, but it's the truth. Before I met you I didn't know what it was to be around gloomy people. . . ."

We crowded behind the starting line with the other couples.

"I'm tired of living and I'm afraid of dying," Gloria said.

"Say, that's a swell idea for a song," said James Bates, who had overheard her. "You could write a song about an old nigger down on the levee who was tired of living and afraid of dying. He could be heaving cotton and singing a song to the Mississippi River. Say, that's a good title—you could call it Old Man River——"

Gloria looked daggers at him, thumbing her nose.

"Hello, there——" Rocky called out to Mrs. Layden, who had arrived at the platform. "Ladies and gentlemen——" he said into the microphone, "I want to introduce to you the champion marathon dance fan of the world—a woman who hasn't missed a single night since this contest started. This is Mrs. Layden, and the management has issued a season pass to her—good any time, good all the time. A big hand for Mrs. Layden, ladies and gentlemen.—Will you take a bow, Mrs. Layden——"

Mrs. Layden hesitated a moment, badly rattled, not knowing exactly what she should do or say. But as the audience applauded she took a couple of steps forward, bowing awkwardly. You could see this was one of the biggest surprises of her life.

"You people who are dance fans have seen her here before," Rocky said. "She is a judge in the derby every night—we couldn't have a derby unless she was here. How do you like the marathon dance, Mrs. Layden?" he asked, stooping down on his haunches and moving the microphone so she could talk into it.

"She hates it," Gloria said under her breath. "She wouldn't come to one on a bet, you dumb bastard——"

"I like it," Mrs. Layden said. She was so nervous she could hardly speak.

"Who's your favorite couple, Mrs. Layden?"

"My favorite couple is No. 22—Robert Syverten and Gloria Beatty."

"Her favorite couple is No. 22, ladies and gentlemen, sponsored by Jonathan Non-Fattening Beer— You're pulling for them to win, are you Mrs. Layden?"

"Yes, I am and if I were younger, I'd be in this contest myself."

"That's fine. Thank you very much, Mrs. Layden. All right—and now it gives me pleasure to present you with a season pass, Mrs. Layden—the gift of the management. You can come in any time without paying——"

Mrs. Layden took the pass. She was so overwhelmed with gratitude and emotion that she was smiling and crying and nodding her head at the same time.

"That's another big moment," Gloria said.

"Shut up!" I said.

"All right—are the judges ready?" Rocky asked straightening up.

"All ready," said Rollo, helping Mrs. Layden to a chair in the judges' row.

"Ladies and gentlemen," Rocky announced, "most of you are familiar with the rules and regulations of the derby—but for the benefit of those who are seeing their first contest of this kind, I will explain so they will know what is going on. The kids race around the track for fifteen minutes, the boys heeling-and-toeing, the girls running or trotting as they so desire. If for any reason whatsoever one of them goes in the pit—the pit is in the center of the floor where the iron cots are—if for any reason one of them goes in the pit, the partner has to make two laps of the track to count for one. Is that clear?"

"Get going," somebody in the audience yelled.

"Are the nurses and trainers ready? Is the doctor standing by? All right—" He handed the starter's pistol down to Rollo. "Will you start the kids off, Miss Delmar?" Rocky asked into the microphone. "Ladies and gentlemen, Miss Delmar is a famous Hollywood author and novelist——"

Rollo took the pistol to Miss Delmar.

"Hold your hats, ladies and gentlemen," Rocky sang out. "Orchestra, get ready to give. All right, Miss Delmar——"

She shot the pistol and we were off.

Gloria and I let the racehorses set the pace. We made no effort to get up in front. Our system was to set a steady clip and hold it. There was no special prize money tonight. Even if there had been it would have made no difference to us.

The audience applauded and stamped their feet, begging for thrills, but this was one night they didn't get them. Only one girl, Ruby Bates, went into the pit and that was only for two laps. And for the first time in weeks nobody collapsed on the floor when the race was over.

But something had happened that frightened me. Gloria had pulled on my belt harder and longer than she ever had before. For the last five minutes of the derby it seemed she had no power of her own. I had practically dragged her around the track. I had a feeling we had just missed being eliminated ourselves. *We had just missed. Later that night Mrs. Layden told me she had spoken to the man who had checked us. We had made only two more laps than the losers. That chilled me. I made up my mind then that from now on I had better forget my system and open up.*

The losers were Basil Gerard and Geneva Tomblin, Couple No. 16. They were automatically disqualified. I knew Geneva was glad it was over. Now she could get married to the Captain of that live bait boat she had met during the first week of the contest.

Geneva came back on the floor while we were eating. She was dressed for the street and carried a small grip.

"Ladies and gentlemen—" Rocky said into the microphone "—there's that marvelous kid who was eliminated tonight. Doesn't she look pretty? A big hand, ladies and gentlemen——"

The audience applauded and Geneva bowed from side to side as she walked towards the platform.

"That's sportsmanship, ladies and gentlemen—she and her partner lost a hard-fought derby, but she is smiling— I'll let you in on a little secret, ladies and gentlemen—" he moved his face closer to the microphone and whispered loudly: "She's in love—she's going to get married. Yes, sir, ladies and gentlemen, the old marathon dance is the original home of romance, because Geneva is marrying a man she met right here in this hall. Is he in the house, Geneva? Is he here?"

Geneva nodded, smiling.

"Where is the lucky man?" Rocky asked. "Where is he? Stand up, skipper, and take a bow——"

Everybody in the audience craned their necks, looking around.

"There he is—" Rocky shouted, pointing to the opposite end of the hall. A man had stepped over the railing from the box and was walking down the floor towards Geneva. He had the peculiar walk of a sailor.

"Say a word, skipper—" Rocky said, tilting the microphone stand over.

"I fell in love with Geneva the first time I saw her," the skipper said to the audience, "and a couple of days later I asked her to quit the marathon dance and marry me. But she said no, she didn't want to let her partner down; and there wasn't nothing for me to do but stick around. Now I'm glad she's disqualified and I can hardly wait for the honey-moon——"

The audience rocked with laughter. Rocky pulled the microphone stand upright again. "A silver shower for the new bride, ladies and gentlemen——"

The skipper grabbed the stand, yanked the microphone down to his mouth. "Never mind any contributions, folks," he said. "I guess I'm plenty able to take care of her——"

"The original Popeye," Gloria said.

There was no silver shower. Not a single coin hit the floor.

"You see how modest he is," Rocky said. "But I guess it's all right for me to tell you he is the captain of the Pacific Queen, an old four-master that's now a live-bait barge an-chored three miles off the pier. There are water taxis every hour during the day—and if any of you folks want some good deep-sea fishing go out with the skipper——"

"Kiss her, you chump," somebody in the audience yelled.

The skipper kissed Geneva, then steered her off the floor while the audience howled and applauded.

"That's the second wedding the marathon dance has arranged, ladies and gentlemen," Rocky announced. "Don't forget our big public ceremony here next week when Couple No. 71, Vee Lovell and Mary Hawley, will get married right before your very eyes. Give——" he said to the orchestra.

Basil Gerard came out of the dressing room in his street clothes and went to the table to get his last meal on the house.

Rocky sat down on the platform, swinging his legs off.

"Look out for my coffee——" Gloria said.

"Okay, okay," Rocky said, moving the cup a little. "How's the food?"

"All right," I said.

Two middle-aged women came up to us. I had seen them several times before, sitting in box seats. "Are you the manager?" one of them asked Rocky.

"Not exactly," Rocky said. "I'm the assistant manager. What was it you wanted?"

"I'm Mrs. Higby," the woman said. "This is Mrs. Witcher. Could we talk to you in private?"

"This is private as any place I got," Rocky said. "What was it you wanted?"

"We are the president and the vice-president——"

"What's the matter?" asked Socks Donald, coming around behind me.

"This is the manager," Rocky said, looking relieved.

The two women looked at Socks. "We are Mrs. Higby and Mrs. Witcher," Mrs. Higby said. "We are the president and the vice-president of the Mothers' League for Good Morals——"

"Aw-aw," Gloria said, under her breath.

"Yes?"

"We have a resolution for you," Mrs. Higby said, thrusting a folded paper into his hand.

"What's this all about?" Socks asked.

"Simply this," Mrs. Higby said. "Our Good Morals League has condemned your contest——"

"Wait a minute," Socks said. "Let's go to my office and talk this thing over——"

Mrs. Higby looked at Mrs. Witcher, who nodded. "Very well," she said.

"You kids come along—you too, Rocky. Hey nurse—take these cups and plates away——" He smiled at the two women. "You see," he said, "we don't let the kids do anything that would waste their energy. This way, ladies——"

He led the way off the floor behind the platform to his office, in a corner of the building. As we walked along Gloria pretended to stumble, falling heavily against Mrs. Higby, grabbing her around the head with her arms.

"Oh, I beg your pardon—I'm sorry——" Gloria said, looking on the floor to see what she had stumbled over.

Mrs. Higby said nothing, looking fiercely at Gloria, straightening her hat. Gloria nudged me, winking behind Mrs. Higby's back.

"Remember, you kids are witnesses——" Socks whispered as we went into his office. This office had formerly been a lounge and was very small. I noticed there had been very little change in it since the day Gloria and I had come here to make entries for the marathon. The only change was two more pictures of nude women Socks had tacked on the wall. Mrs. Higby and Mrs. Witcher spotted these instantly, exchanging significant looks.

"Sit down, ladies," Socks said. "What is it, now?"

"The Mothers' League for Good Morals has condemned your contest," Mrs. Higby said. "We have decided it is low and degrading and a pernicious influence in the community. We have decided you must close it——"

"Close it?"

"At once. If you refuse we shall go to the City Council. This contest is low and degrading——"

"You got me all wrong, ladies," Socks said. "There's nothing degrading about this contest. Why, these kids love it. Every one of them has gained weight since it started——"

"You have a girl in this contest who is about to become a

mother," Mrs. Higby said, "one Ruby Bates. It is criminal to have that girl running and walking all day when her baby is about to be born. Moreover, it is shocking to see her exhibiting herself to the world in that half-dressed condition. I should think she at least would have the decency to wear a coat——"

"Well, ladies," Socks said, "I never looked at that angle before. Ruby always seemed to know what she was doing—and I never paid no attention to her stomach. But I can see your point. You want me to put her out of the contest?"

"Most certainly," Mrs. Higby said. Mrs. Witcher nodded her head.

"All right, ladies," Socks said, "anything you say. I'm not hard to do business with. I'll even pay her hospital bills. . . . Thanks for telling me about it. I'll take care of that right away——"

"That isn't all," Mrs. Higby said. "Do you plan to have a public wedding next week or was that merely an announcement to draw a crowd of morons?"

"I never pulled nothing phony in my life," Socks said. "That wedding is on the level. I wouldn't double-cross my customers like that. You can ask anybody I do business with what kind of a guy I am——"

"We are familiar with your reputation," Mrs. Higby said. "But even at that I can hardly believe you intend to sponsor a sacrilege like that——"

"The kids who are going to get married are very much in love with each other," Rocky said.

"We won't permit such mockery," Mrs. Higby said. "We demand that you close this contest immediately!"

"What'll happen to these kids if he does?" Gloria asked. "They'll go right back on the streets——"

"Don't try to justify this thing, young woman," Mrs. Higby said. "This contest is vicious. It attracts the bad element. One of your participants was an escaped murderer—that Chicago Italian——"

"Well, ladies, you surely don't blame me for that," Socks said.

"We certainly do. We are here because it is our duty to keep our city clean and free from all such influences——"

"Do you mind if me and my assistant go outside to talk this over?" Socks asked. "Maybe we can figure this out——"

". . . Very well," Mrs. Higby said.

Socks motioned to Rocky and they went outside.

"Do you ladies have children of your own?" Gloria asked, when the door had closed.

"We both have grown daughters," Mrs. Higby said.

"Do you know where they are tonight and what they're doing?"

Neither woman said anything.

"Maybe I can give you a rough idea," Gloria said. "While you two noble characters are here doing your duty by some people you don't know, your daughters are probably in some guy's apartment, their clothes off, getting drunk."

Mrs. Higby and Mrs. Witcher gasped in unison.

"That's generally what happens to the daughters of reformers," Gloria said. "Sooner or later they all get laid and most of 'em don't know enough to keep from getting knocked up. You drive 'em away from home with your goddam lectures on purity and decency, and you're too busy meddling around to teach 'em the facts of life——"

"Why—" said Mrs. Higby, getting red in the face.

"I—" Mrs. Witcher said.

"Gloria—" I said.

"It's time somebody got women like you told," Gloria said, moving over and standing with her back to the door, as if to keep them in, "and I'm just the baby to do it. You're the kind of bitches who sneak in the toilet to read dirty books and tell filthy stories and then go out and try to spoil somebody else's fun——"

"You move away from that door, young woman, and let us out of here!" Mrs. Higby shrieked. "I refuse to listen to you. I'm a respectable woman. I'm a Sunday School teacher——"

"I don't move a f — — inch until I finish," Gloria said.

"Gloria——"

"Your Morals League and your goddam women's clubs," she said, ignoring me completely, "—filled with meddlesome old bitches who haven't had a lay in twenty years. Why don't you old dames go out and buy a lay once in a while? That's all that's wrong with you. . . ."

Mrs. Higby advanced on Gloria, her arm raised as if to strike her.

"Go on—hit me," Gloria said, not moving. "Hit me!—You even touch me and I'll kick your f — — head off!"

"You—goddam—whore!" Mrs. Higby said, furious with passion.

The door opened, bumping Gloria away from it. Socks and Rocky came in.

"This—this—" Mrs. Higby said, shaking her finger at Gloria.

"Don't stutter," Gloria said, "—say it. You know how to say the word. Whore. W-h-o——"

"Pipe down!" Socks said. "Ladies, me and my assistant have decided to take any suggestions you have to offer——"

"Our suggestion is you close this place at once!" Mrs. Higby said. "Else we shall go to the City Council in the morning——"

She started out, followed by Mrs. Witcher.

"Young woman," Mrs. Higby said to Gloria, "you ought to be in a reform school!"

"I was in one once," Gloria said. "There was a dame just like you in charge. She was a lesbian. . . ."

Mrs. Higby gasped again and went out, followed by Mrs. Witcher.

Gloria slammed the door behind them, then sat down in a chair and began sobbing. She covered her face with her hands and tried to fight it off, but it was no use. She slowly leaned forward in the chair, bending double, shaking and twitching with emotion, as if she had completely lost control of the upper half of her body. For a full moment the only sounds in the room were her sobs and the rise and fall of the ocean which came through the half-raised window.

Then Socks went over and laid his hand tenderly on Gloria's head. "Nix, kid, nix—" he said.

"Keep all this under your hat," Rocky said to me. "Don't say anything to the others——"

"I won't," I said. "Does this mean we'll have to close up?"

"I don't think so," Socks said. "It just means we'll have to try to grease somebody. I'll talk to my lawyer in the morning. In the meantime, Rocky—break the news to Ruby. She's got

to quit. A lot of women have been squawking about her—"
He looked at the door. "I should have stuck to my own
racket," he said. "Goddam bastard women . . ."

... EXECUTED AND PUT TO DEATH ...

```
HOURS ELAPSED . . . . . . 855
Couples Remaining . . . . . . 21
```

MARATHON DANCE WAR STILL RAGES

———

Mothers' League Threatens
Mass Meeting Unless City
Council Will Close Contest

———

IS THIRD DAY OF CONTROVERSY

———

The Mothers' League for Good Morals continued their war on the marathon dance today, threatening to take the issue directly to the citizens themselves unless the City Council closes the contest. The marathon dance has been in progress at a beach resort for the past 36 days.

Mrs. J. Franklin Higby and Mrs. William Wallace Witcher, president and first vice-president of the Morals League, appeared before the City Council again this afternoon, protesting the continuance of the dance. They were told by the Council that the City Attorney was making a thorough study of the law to determine what legal steps could be taken.

"We can't take any action until we know how the law reads," Tom Hinsdell, Council chief, said. "So far we have failed to find any specific statute that covers this case, but the City Attorney is examining all the codes."

"Would the City Council hesitate if a plague threatened our city?" Mrs. Higby said. "Certainly it wouldn't. If there are no specific laws to fit this situation let them pass emergency laws. The marathon dance is a plague—it is low and degrading and in the same hall there is a public bar that is a rendezvous for gangsters, racketeers and notorious criminals. Surely this is not the proper atmosphere for children . . ."

I handed the newspaper back to Mrs. Layden. "Mr. Donald told us his lawyer said the city couldn't do anything," I said.

"That doesn't make much difference," Mrs. Layden said. "Those women are out to close it and law or no law, they'll do it."

"I don't see any harm in the marathon," I said, "but they're right about the bar. I've seen a lot of tough characters in the Palm Garden. . . . How long do you think it'll take them to close us up?"

"I don't know," she said. "But they'll close it. What are you going to do then?"

"The first thing I'm going to do is get a lot of sun," I said. "I used to love the rain and hate the sun, but now it's the other way around. You don't get much sun in here——"

"After that what are you going to do?"

"I haven't made any plans," I said.

"I see. Where's Gloria?"

"She's putting on her track suit. She'll be out in a minute."

"She's beginning to weaken, isn't she? The doctor said he had to look at her heart several times a day."

"That doesn't mean anything," I said. "He looks at all of them. Gloria's all right."

Gloria wasn't all right and I knew it. We were having a lot of trouble with the derbies. I never will know how we got by the last two nights. Gloria was in and out of the pit a dozen times in the two races. But I didn't jump at conclusions simply because the doctor examined her heart six or seven times a day. I knew he could never locate her trouble with a stethoscope.

"Lean over here, Robert," Mrs. Layden said. It was the first time she had ever used my given name and I was a little embarrassed. I leaned over the railing, swaying my body so nobody could say I was violating the rules of the contest by not being in motion. The hall was packed and jammed. "You know I'm your friend, don't you?" Mrs. Layden said.

"Yes'm, I know that."

"You know I got you your sponsor, don't you?"

"Yes'm, I know that."

"You trust me, don't you?"

"Yes'm, I trust you."

"Robert—Gloria's not the right kind of girl for you."

I didn't say anything, wondering what was coming next. I had never been able to understand why Mrs. Layden had taken such an interest in me unless . . . But it couldn't be that. She was old enough to be my grandmother.

"She'll never be any good," Mrs. Layden said. "She's an evil person and she'll wreck your life. You don't want your life wrecked, do you?"

"She's not going to wreck my life," I said.

"Promise me when you get out of this you'll never see her again."

"Oh, I'm not going to marry her or anything like that," I said. "I'm not in love with her. She's all right. She just gets a little depressed sometimes."

"She's not depressed," Mrs. Layden said. "She's bitter. She hates everything and everybody. She's cruel and she's dangerous."

"I didn't know you felt that way about her, Mrs. Layden."

"I'm an old woman," she said. "I'm a very, very—old, old woman. I know what I'm talking about. When this thing is over— Robert," she said suddenly, "I'm not as poor as you think I am. I look poor but I'm not poor at all. I'm rich. I'm very rich. I'm very eccentric. When you get out of here——"

"Hello—" Gloria said, coming from nowhere.

"——Hello," Mrs. Layden said.

"What's the matter?" Gloria asked quickly. "Am I interrupting something?"

"You're not interrupting anything," I told her.

Mrs. Layden opened the newspaper and started reading it. Gloria and I walked towards the platform.

"What was she saying about me?" Gloria asked.

"Nothing," I said. "We were just talking about the marathon closing——"

"You were talking about something else too. Why did she shut up like a clam when I got there?"

"You're imagining things—" I said.

"Ladies and gentlemen—" Rocky said into the microphone, "—or maybe after reading the newspapers," he went on when the crowd had quieted down, "I should say—Fellow Morons." There was a big laugh at this; the crowd knew what he meant. "You can see we're still going in the world's champion marathon dance," he said, "and we'll keep on going until only one contestant is left—the final winner. I want to thank you very much for coming out tonight and I'd like to remind you that tomorrow night is the night you can't afford to miss—our big public wedding, when Couple No. 71—Vee Lovell and Mary Hawley—will be married right here before your very eyes by a well-known minister of the city. If you haven't made your reservations you better do so at once——

"And now, before the derby starts, I'd like to introduce a few of our celebrities—" He looked at a piece of paper. "Ladies and gentlemen, one of our honor guests is none other than that handsome screen star, Bill Boyd. Will you take a bow, Mr. Boyd?——"

Bill (Screen) Boyd stood up, taking a bow, while the audience applauded.

"Next, another screen and stage star—Ken Murray. Mr. Murray has a party of distinguished guests with him. I wonder if he'd come up to the platform and introduce them himself?——"

The audience applauded loudly. Murray hesitated, but finally stepped over the railing and went to the platform.

"All right, folks—" he said, taking the microphone. "First a young featured player, Miss Anita Louise——"

Miss Louise stood.

"——and now Miss June Clyde——"

Miss Clyde stood.

"——Miss Sue Carol——"

Miss Carol stood.

"——Tom Brown——"

Tom Brown stood.

"——Thornton Freeland——"

Thornton Freeland stood.

"——and that's all, folks——"

Murray shook hands with Rocky and went back to his party.

"Ladies and gentlemen—" Rocky said.

"There's a big director over there he didn't introduce," I said to Gloria. "There's Frank Borzage. Let's go speak to him——"

"For what?" Gloria said.

"He's a director, isn't he? He might help you get in pictures——"

"The hell with pictures," Gloria said. "I wish I was dead——"

"I'm going," I said.

I strolled down the floor in front of the boxes, feeling very self-conscious. Two or three times I almost lost my nerve and turned back.

"It's worth it," I told myself. "He's one of the finest directors in the world. Some day I'll be as famous as he is and then I'll remind him of this——"

"Hello, Mr. Borzage," I said.

"Hello, son," he said. "Are you going to win tonight?"

"I hope so . . . I saw 'No Greater Glory.' I thought it was swell," I said.

"I'm glad you liked it——"

"That's what I want to be some day," I said. "A director like you——"

"I hope you are," he said.

"Well——" I said, "good-bye——"

I went back to the platform.

"That was Frank Borzage," I said to Kid Kamm.

"Yeah?——"

"He's a big director," I explained.

"Oh—," the Kid said.

"All right—" Rocky said. "Are the judges ready? Have they got their score sheets, Rollo? —All right, kids——"

We moved out to the starting line.

"Let's not take any chances tonight," I whispered to Gloria. "We can't fool around——"

"On your marks, there, kids," Rocky said. "Stand by nurses and trainers— Hold your hats, ladies and gentlemen— Orchestra, get ready to give——"

He shot the pistol himself.

Gloria and I jumped away, pushing through into second place, directly behind Kid Kamm and Jackie Miller. They were in front, the position usually held by James and Ruby Bates. As I went into the first turn I thought about James and Ruby, wondering where they were. It didn't seem like a derby without them.

At the finish of the first lap Mack Aston and Bess Cartwright sprinted in front of us and went into second place. I began to heel-and-toe faster than I ever had before. I knew I had to. All the weaklings had been eliminated. All these couples were fast.

I stayed in third place for six or seven laps and the audience began howling and yelling for us to move up. I was afraid to try that. You can pass a fast team only on the turn and that takes a lot of energy. So far Gloria was holding up fine and I didn't want to put too much pressure on her. I wasn't worried as long as she could keep propelling herself.

After eight minutes I commenced to get hot. I yanked off my sweatshirt and tossed it to a trainer. Gloria did likewise. Most of the girls were out of their sweatshirts now and the audience was howling. When the girls removed their sweat-shirts they wore only small brassieres, and as they trotted around the track their breasts bounced up and down.

"Everything is fine now unless somebody challenges us," I told myself.

Just then we were challenged. Pedro Ortega and Lillian Bacon sped up alongside, trying to get inside at the turn. This was about the only way to pass a couple but it was not as easy as it sounds. You had to get at least two paces ahead on the straightaway and then swing sharply over at the turn. This was what Pedro had in the back of his mind. They collided with us at the turn, but Gloria managed to keep her feet and I dragged her through, holding our place.

I heard the audience gasp and I knew that meant somebody was staggering. In a moment more I heard a body hit the floor. I didn't look around; I kept pounding. This was old stuff to me now. When I got on the straightaway and could look without breaking my stride, I saw it was Mary Hawley, Vee Lovell's partner, who was in the pit. The nurses and train-ers were working on her and the doctor was using his steth-oscope——

"Give the solo the inside, kids—" Rocky yelled.

I moved over and Vee passed me. Now he had to make two laps to our one. He glanced in the pit as he passed, a look of agony on his face. I knew he was not in pain; he was only wondering when his partner would be out. . . . On his fourth solo lap she got up, coupling on again.

I signaled to the nurse for a wet towel and on the next lap she slammed it around my neck. I stuck the end of it between my teeth.

"Four minutes to go—" Rocky yelled.

This was one of the closest derbies we'd ever had. The Kid and Jackie were setting a terrific pace. I knew Gloria and I were in no danger as long as we held our own, but you never could tell when your partner would collapse. Past a certain point you kept moving automatically, without actually being conscious of moving. One moment you would be traveling at top speed and the next moment you started falling. This was what I was afraid of with Gloria—collapsing. She was beginning to drag on my belt a little.

"Keep going!" I shouted to her in my mind, slowing down a fraction, hoping to relieve the strain on her. Pedro and Lillian evidently had been waiting for this. They shot by us on the turn, taking third place. Directly behind me I could hear the pounding of the others and I realized the entire field was bunched at Gloria's heels. I had absolutely no margin now.

I hitched my hip up high. That was a signal for Gloria to shift her hold on the belt. She did, changing to the right hand.

"Thank God," I said to myself. That was a good sign. That proved she was thinking all right.

"One minute to go—" Rocky announced.

I put on the steam now. Kid Kamm and Jackie had slowed the pace somewhat, thus slowing Mack and Bess and Pedro and Lillian. Gloria and I were between them and the others. It was a bad position. I prayed that nobody behind us had the energy for a spurt because I realized that the slightest bump would break Gloria's stride and put her on the floor. And if anybody hit the floor now . . .

I used every ounce of my strength to move up, to get just one step ahead, to remove that threat from behind. . . . When the gun sounded for the finish I turned around to catch Gloria. But she didn't faint. She staggered into my arms, shiny with perspiration, fighting to get air.

"Want a nurse?" Rocky yelled from the platform.

"She's all right," I said. "Let her rest a minute——"

Most of the girls were being helped into the dressing room, but the boys crowded around the platform to see who had been disqualified. The judges had handed their tally sheets to Rollo and Rocky, who were checking them.

"Ladies and gentlemen——" Rocky announced in a minute or two. "Here are the results of the most sensational derby you have ever seen. First place—Couple No. 18, Kid Kamm and Jackie Miller. Second place—Mack Aston and Bess Cartwright. Third place—Pedro Ortega and Lillian Bacon. Fourth place—Robert Syverten and Gloria Beatty. Those were the winners—and now, the losers—the last team to finish—the couple that, under the rules and regulations, is disqualified and out of the marathon dance. That is Couple No. 11—Jere Flint and Vera Rosenfield——"

"You're crazy!" Jere Flint shouted, loud enough for everybody in the hall to hear. "That's wrong—" he said, moving closer to the platform.

"Look at 'em yourself," Rocky said, handing him the tally sheets.

"I wish it had been us," Gloria said, lifting her head. "I wish I had thrown the race——"

"Sh-h-h—" I said.

"I don't give a damn what these score cards say; they're wrong," Jere Flint said, handing them back to Rocky. "I know they're wrong. How the hell could we get eliminated when we weren't last?"

"Are you able to keep track of the laps while you're racing?" Rocky asked. He was trying to show Jere up. He knew it wasn't possible for anybody to do that.

"I can't do that," Jere said. "But I know we didn't go into the pit and Mary did. We started ahead of Vee and Mary and we finished ahead of 'em——"

"How about that, mister?" Rocky said to a man standing near-by. "You checked Couple No. 11——"

"You're mistaken, fellow," the man said to Jere. "I checked you carefully——"

"It's too bad, son," Socks Donald said, coming through the crowd of judges. "You had tough luck——"

"It wasn't tough luck; it was a goddam frame-up," Jere

said. "You ain't kidding anybody. If Vee and Mary had been eliminated you wouldn't have a wedding tomorrow——"

"Now—now—" Socks said. "You run on to the dressing room——"

"Okay," Jere said. He walked over to the man who had kept check on him and Vera. "How much is Socks giving you for this?" he asked.

"I don't know what you're talking about——"

Jere turned sidewise, slamming the man in the mouth with his fist, knocking him down.

Socks ran over to Jere, squaring off, glaring at him his hand in his hip pocket.

"If you pull that blackjack on me I'll make you eat it," Jere told him. Then he walked away, going across the floor towards the dressing room.

The audience was standing, jabbering, trying to see what was going on.

"Let's get dressed," I said to Gloria.

. . . UPON
THE 19TH DAY
OF THE MONTH
OF SEPTEMBER,
IN THE YEAR
OF OUR LORD,
1935 . . .

12

```
HOURS ELAPSED . . . . . . 879
Couples Remaining . . . . . . 20
```

ALL DAY Gloria had been very morbid. I asked her a hundred times what she was thinking about. "Nothing," she would reply. *I realize now how stupid I was. I should have known what she was thinking. Now that I look back on that last night I don't see how I possibly could have been so stupid. But in those days I was dumb about a lot of things . . . The judge is sitting up there, making his speech, looking through his glasses at me, but his words are doing the same thing to my body that his eyesight is doing to his glasses—going right through without stopping, rushing out of the way of each succeeding look and each succeeding word. I am not hearing the judge with my ears and my brain any more than the lenses of his glasses are catching and imprisoning each look that comes through them. I hear him with my feet and my legs and torso and arms, with everything but my ears and brain. With my ears and brain I hear a newsboy in the street shouting something about King Alexander, I hear the rolling of the street cars, I hear automobiles, I hear the warning bells of the traffic semaphores; in the courtroom I hear people breathing and moving their feet, I hear the wood squeaking in a bench, I hear the light splash as someone spits in the cuspidor. All these things I hear with my ears and my brain, but I hear the judge with my body only. If you ever hear a judge say to you what this one is saying to me, you will know what I mean.*

This was one day Gloria had no reason to be morbid. The crowds had been coming and going all day, since noon the place had been packed, and now, just before the wedding, there were very few vacant seats left and most of them had been reserved. The entire hall had been decorated with so many flags and so much red, white and blue bunting that you expected any moment to hear firecrackers go off and the band play the national anthem. The whole day had been full of excitement: the workmen decorating the interior, the big crowds, the rehearsals for the wedding, the rumors that the Morals League women were coming down to set fire to the hall—and the two complete new outfits the Jonathan Beer people had sent Gloria and me.

This was one day Gloria had no reason to be morbid, but she was more morbid than ever.

"Son—" a man called from a box. I had never seen him before. He was motioning for me to come over.

"You won't be in that seat long," I told him in my mind. "That's Mrs. Layden's regular seat. When she comes you'll have to move."

"Aren't you the boy of Couple 22?" he asked.

"Yessir," I said.

"Where's your partner?"

"She's down there—" I replied, pointing towards the platform where Gloria stood with the other girls.

"Get her," the man said. "I want to meet her."

"All right," I said, going to get Gloria. "Now who can that be?" I asked myself.

"There's a man down here who wants to meet you," I said to Gloria.

"I don't want to meet anybody."

"This man's no bum," I said. "He's well-dressed. He looks like somebody."

"I don't care what he looks like," she said.

"He may be a producer," I said. "Maybe you've made a hit with him. Maybe this is your break."

"The hell with my break," she said.

"Come on," I said. "The man's waiting."

She finally came with me.

"This motion picture business is a lousy business," she said. "You have to meet people you don't want to meet and you have to be nice to people whose guts you hate. I'm glad I'm through with it."

"You're just starting with it," I said, trying to cheer her up. *I never paid any attention to her remark then, but now I realize it was the most significant thing she had ever said.*

"Here she is—" I said to the man.

"You don't know who I am, do you?" the man asked.

"No, sir——"

"My name is Maxwell," he said. "I'm the advertising manager for Jonathan Beer."

"How do you do, Mr. Maxwell," I said, reaching over to shake hands with him. "This is my partner, Gloria Beatty. I want to thank you for sponsoring us."

"Don't thank me," he said. "Thank Mrs. Layden. She brought you to my attention. Did you get your packages today?"

"Yessir," I said, "and they came just in time. We certainly needed clothes. These marathon dances are pretty hard on your clothes— Have you ever been here before?"

"No, and I wouldn't be here now if Mrs. Layden hadn't insisted. She's been telling me about the derbies. Are you having one tonight?"

"A little thing like a wedding couldn't stop the derby," I said. "It goes on right after the ceremony——"

"So long—" Gloria said, walking off.

"Did I say something wrong?" Mr. Maxwell asked.

"No, sir—she's got to go down there and get her final instructions. The wedding starts pretty soon."

He frowned and I could tell he knew I was merely lying to cover Gloria's bad manners. He watched Gloria walking down the floor a minute and then looked back at me. "What chance do you have to win the derby tonight?" he asked.

"We've got a good chance," I said. "Of course, the big thing is not so much to win as it is to keep from losing. If you finish last you're disqualified."

"Suppose Jonathan Beer offered twenty-five dollars to the winner," he said. "You think you'd have a chance to get it?"

"We'll certainly try like the devil," I told him.

"In that case—all right," he said, looking me up and down. "Mrs. Layden tells me you're ambitious to get in the movies?"

"I am," I said. "Not as an actor though. I want to be a director."

"You wouldn't like a job in the brewery business, eh?"

"I don't believe I would——"

"Have you ever directed a picture?"

"No, sir, but I'm not afraid to try it. I know I could make

good," I said. "Oh, I don't mean a big feature like Boleslawsky or Mamoulian or King Vidor would make—I mean
something else at first——"

"For instance——"

"Well, like a two- or three-reel short. What a junkman does
all day, or the life of an ordinary man—you know, who makes
thirty dollars a week and has to raise kids and buy a home and
a car and a radio—the kind of a guy bill collectors are always
after. Something different, with camera angles to help tell the
story——"

"I see—" he said.

"I didn't mean to bore you," I said, "but it's so seldom I
can find anybody who'll listen to me that when I do I never
know when to stop talking."

"I'm not bored. As a matter of fact, I'm very much interested," he said. "But maybe I've said too much myself——"

"Good evening—" Mrs. Layden said, entering the box. Mr.
Maxwell stood up. "That's my seat, John," Mrs. Layden said.
"You sit over here." Mr. Maxwell laughed and took another
chair. "My, my, don't you look handsome," Mrs. Layden said
to me.

"This is the first time in my life I ever had on a tuxedo,"
I said blushing. "Mr. Donald rented tuxedoes for all the boys
and dresses for the girls. We're all in the wedding march."

"What do you think of him, John?" Mrs. Layden asked Mr.
Maxwell.

"He's all right," Mr. Maxwell said.

"I trust John's judgment implicitly," Mrs. Layden said to
me. I began to understand now why Mr. Maxwell had asked
me all those questions.

"——Down this way, you kids—" Rocky said into the microphone. "Down this way— Ladies and gentlemen. We are
about to have the public wedding between Couple No. 71—
Vee Lovell and Mary Hawley—and please remember, the entertainment for the night is not over when the marriage is
finished. That's only the beginnin'—" he said; "—only the
beginnin'. After the wedding we have the derby——"

He leaned over while Socks Donald whispered something
to him.

"Ladies and gentlemen," Rocky announced, "I take great

pleasure in introducing the minister who will perform the service—a minister you all know, Rev. Oscar Gilder. Will you come up, Mr. Gilder?"

The minister came out on the floor and walked towards the platform while the audience applauded.

"Get your places," Socks said to us. We went to our assigned positions, the girls on one side of the platform and the boys on the other.

"Before the grand march starts," Rocky said, "I want to thank those who have made this feature possible." He looked at a sheet of paper. "The bride's wedding gown," he said, "was donated by Mr. Samuels of the Bon-Ton Shop. Will you stand, Mr. Samuels?"

Mr. Samuels stood, bowing to the applause.

"Her shoes were donated by the Main Street Slipper Shop— Is Mr. Davis here? Stand up, Mr. Davis."

Mr. Davis stood.

"– —Her stockings and silken—er—you-know-whats were donated by the Polly-Darling Girls' Bazaar. Mr. Lightfoot, where are you?——"

Mr. Lightfoot stood as the audience howled.

"——and her hair was marcelled by the Pompadour Beauty Shop. Is Miss Smith here?"

Miss Smith stood.

"——And the groom's outfit, from head to foot, was donated by the Tower Outfitting Company. Mr. Tower——"

Mr. Tower stood.

"——All the flowers in the hall and that the girls are wearing are the gift of the Sycamore Ridge Nursery. Mr. Dupré——"

Mr. Dupré stood.

"——And now, ladies and gentlemen, I turn the microphone over to the Rev. Oscar Gilder, who will perform the ceremony for these marvelous kids——"

He handed the microphone stand to Rollo, who stood it on the floor in front of the platform. Rev. Gilder moved behind it, nodding to the orchestra, and the wedding march began.

The procession started, the boys on one side and the girls on the other, going down to the end of the hall and then back to the minister. It was the first time I had seen some of the girls when they weren't in slacks or track suits.

We had rehearsed the march twice that afternoon, being taught to come to a full stop after each step before taking another. When the bride and groom came into view from behind the platform, the audience cheered and applauded.

Mrs. Layden nodded to me as I passed.

At the platform we took our places while Vee and Mary, and Kid Kamm and Jackie Miller, the best man and the maid-of-honor continued to where the minister was standing. He motioned for the orchestra to stop and began the ceremony. All during the ceremony I kept looking at Gloria. I hadn't had a chance to tell her how rude she had been to Mr. Maxwell, so I tried to catch her eye to let her know I had plenty to tell her when we got together.

"——And I now pronounce you man and wife——" Dr. Gilder said. He bowed his head and began to pray:

The Lord is my shepherd; I shall not want. He maketh me to lie down in green pastures: he leadeth me beside the still waters. He restoreth my soul: he leadeth me in the paths of righteousness for his name's sake. Yea, though I walk through the valley of the shadow of death, I will fear no evil: for thou art with me; thy rod and thy staff they comfort me. Thou preparest a table before me in the presence of mine enemies: thou anointest my head with oil; my cup runneth over. Surely goodness and mercy shall follow me all the days of my life; and I will dwell in the house of the Lord for ever.

. . . When the minister had finished Vee kissed Mary timidly on the cheek and we swarmed around. The hall rocked with applause and shouts.

"Just a minute—just a minute——" Rocky yelled into the microphone. "Just a minute, ladies and gentlemen——"

The confusion died down and at that moment, at the opposite end of the hall, in the Palm Garden, there was the clear, distinct sound of glass shattering.

"Don't——" a man screamed. Five shots followed this, so close together they sounded like one solid strip of noise.

Instantly the audience roared.

"Keep your seats—keep your seats——" Rocky yelled. . . .

The other boys and girls were running towards the Palm

Garden to see what had happened, and I joined them. Socks Donald passed me, reaching into his hip pocket.

I jumped over the railing into an empty box and followed Socks into the Palm Garden. A crowd of people were standing in a circle, looking down and jabbering to each other. Socks pushed through and I followed him.

A man was dead on the floor.

"Who did it?" Socks asked.

"A guy over there—" somebody said.

Socks pushed out with me behind him. I was a little surprised to discover Gloria was directly behind me.

The man who had done the shooting was standing at the bar, leaning on his elbow. Blood was streaming down his face. Socks went up to him.

"He started it, Socks," the man said. "—He was trying to kill me with a beer bottle——"

"Monk, you son of a bitch—" Socks said, hitting him in the face with the blackjack. Monk sagged against the bar but did not fall. Socks continued to hit him in the face with the blackjack, again and again and again, splattering blood all over everything and everybody nearby. He literally beat the man to the floor.

"Hey, Socks—" somebody called.

Thirty feet away there was another group of people standing in a circle, looking down and jabbering to each other. We pushed our way through—and there she lay.

"Goddam—" Socks Donald said.

It was Mrs. Layden, a single hole in the front of her forehead. John Maxwell was kneeling beside her, holding her head . . . then he placed the head gently on the floor, and stood up. Mrs. Layden's head slowly turned sidewise and a little pool of blood that had collected in the crater of her eye spilled out on the floor.

John Maxwell saw Gloria and me.

"She was coming around to be a judge in the derby," he said. "She was hit by a stray bullet——"

"I wish it was me—" Gloria said under her breath.

"Goddam—" Socks Donald said.

We were all assembled in the girls' dressing room. There

were very few people outside in the hall, only the police and several reporters.

"I guess you kids know why I got you in here," Socks said slowly, "and I guess you know what I'm going to say. There ain't no use for anybody to feel bad about what's happened— it's just one of those things. It's tough on you kids and it's tough on me. We had just got the marathon started good——

"Rocky and I have been talking it over and we've decided to take the thousand-dollar prize and split it up between all of you—and I'm going to throw in another grand myself. That'll give everybody fifty bucks a piece. Is that fair?"

"Yes—" we said.

"Don't you think there's any chance to keep going?" Kid Kamm asked.

"Not a chance," Socks said, shaking his head. "Not with that Purity League after us——"

"Kids," Rocky said, "we've had a lot of fun and I've enjoyed working with you. Maybe some time we can have another marathon dance——"

"When do we get this dough?" Vee Lovell asked.

"In the morning," Socks said. "Any of you kids that want to can stay here tonight, just like you been doing. But if you want to leave, there's nothing to stop you. I'll have the dough for you in the morning any time after ten. Now, I'll say so-long— I got to go to police headquarters."

...IN
THE MANNER
PROVIDED BY
THE LAWS
OF
THE STATE
OF
CALIFORNIA.
AND...

13

GLORIA and I walked across the dance floor, my heels making so much noise I couldn't be sure they belonged to me. Rocky was standing at the front door with a policeman.

"Where you kids going?" Rocky asked.

"To get some air," Gloria said.

"Coming back?"

"We'll be back," I told him. "We're just going to get a little air. It's been a long time since we been outside——"

"Don't be long," Rocky said, looking at Gloria and wetting his lips significantly.

"F—— you," Gloria said, going outside.

It was after two o'clock in the morning. The air was damp and thick and clean. It was so thick and so clean I could feel my lungs biting it off in huge chunks.

"I bet you are glad to get that kind of air," I said to my lungs.

I turned around and looked at the building.

"So that's where we've been all the time," I said. "Now I know how Jonah felt when he looked at the whale."

"Come on," Gloria said.

We walked around the side of the building onto the pier. It stretched out over the ocean as far as I could see, rising and falling and groaning and creaking with the movements of the water.

"It's a wonder the waves don't wash this pier away," I said.

"You're hipped on the subject of waves," Gloria said.

"No, I'm not," I said.

"That's all you've been talking about for a month——"

"All right, stand still a minute and you'll see what I mean. You can feel it rising and falling——"

"I can feel it without standing still," she said, "but that's no reason to get yourself in a sweat. It's been going on for a million years."

"Don't think I'm crazy about this ocean," I said. "It'll be all right with me if I never see it again. I've had enough ocean to last me the rest of my life."

We sat down on a bench that was wet with spray. Up towards the end of the pier several men were fishing over the
railing. The night was black; there was no moon, no stars. An
irregular line of white foam marked the shore.

"This air is fine," I said.

Gloria said nothing, staring into the distance. Far down the
shore on a point there were lights.

"That's Malibu," I said. "Where all the movie stars live."

"What are you going to do now?" she finally said.

"I don't know exactly. I thought I'd go see Mr. Maxwell
tomorrow. Maybe I could get him to do something. He certainly seemed interested."

"Always tomorrow," she said. "The big break is always
coming tomorrow."

Two men passed by, carrying deep-sea fishing poles. One
of them was dragging a four-foot hammerhead shark behind
him.

"This baby'll never do any more damage," he said to the
other man. . . .

"What are you going to do?" I asked Gloria.

"I'm going to get off this merry-go-round," she said. "I'm
through with the whole stinking thing."

"What thing?"

"Life," she said.

"Why don't you try to help yourself?" I said. "You got the
wrong attitude about everything."

"Don't lecture to me," she said.

"I'm not lecturing," I said, "but you ought to change your
attitude. On the level. It affects everybody you come in contact with. Take me, for example. Before I met you I didn't
see how I could miss succeeding. I never even thought of
failing. And now——"

"Who taught you that speech?" she asked. "You never
thought that up by yourself."

"Yes, I did," I said.

She looked down the ocean towards Malibu. "Oh, what's
the use in me kidding myself—" she said in a moment. "I
know where I stand . . ."

I did not say anything, looking at the ocean and thinking
about Hollywood, wondering if I'd ever been there or

was I going to wake up in a minute back in Arkansas and have to hurry down and get my newspapers before it got daylight.

"—Sonofabitch," Gloria was saying to herself. "You needn't look at me that way," she said. "I know I'm no good——"

"She's right," I said to myself; "she's exactly right. She's no good——"

"I wish I'd died that time in Dallas," she said. "I always will think that doctor saved my life for just one reason——"

I did not say anything to that, still looking at the ocean and thinking how exactly right she was about being no good and that it was too bad she didn't die that time in Dallas. She certainly would have been better off dead.

"I'm just a misfit. I haven't got anything to give anybody," she was saying. "Stop looking at me that way," she said.

"I'm not looking at you any way," I said. "You can't see my face——"

"Yes, I can," she said.

She was lying. She couldn't see my face. It was too dark.

"Don't you think we ought to go inside?" I said. "Rocky wanted to see you——"

"That p——k," she said. "I know what he wants, but he'll never get it again. Nobody else will, either."

"What?" I said.

"Don't you know?"

"Don't I know what," I said.

"What Rocky wants."

"Oh——" I said. "Sure. It just dawned on me."

"That's all any man wants," she said, "but that's all right. Oh, I didn't mind giving it to Rocky; he was doing me as much of a favor as I did him—but suppose I get caught?"

"You're not just thinking of that, are you?" I asked.

"Yes, I am. Always before this time I was able to take care of myself. Suppose I do have a kid?" she said. "You know what it'll grow up to be, don't you. Just like us."

"She's right," I said to myself; "she's exactly right. It'll grow up to be just like us——"

"I don't want that," she said. "Anyway, I'm finished. I think it's a lousy world and I'm finished. I'd be better off

dead and so would everybody else. I ruin everything I get
around. You said so yourself."

"When did I say anything like that?"

"A few minutes ago. You said before you met me you never
even thought of failing. . . . Well, it isn't my fault. I can't
help it. I tried to kill myself once, but I didn't and I've never
had the nerve to try again. . . . You want to do the world a
favor? . . ." she asked.

I did not say anything, listening to the ocean sloshle against
the pilings, feeling the pier rise and fall, and thinking that she
was right about everything she had said.

Gloria was fumbling in her purse. When her hand came out
it was holding a small pistol. I had never seen the pistol before,
but I was not surprised. I was not in the least surprised.

"Here—" she said, offering it to me.

"I don't want it. Put it away," I said. "Come on, let's go
back inside. I'm cold——"

"Take it and pinch-hit for God," she said, pressing it into
my hand. "Shoot me. It's the only way to get me out of my
misery."

"She's right," I said to myself. "It's the only way to get
her out of her misery." *When I was a little kid I used to spend
the summers on my grandfather's farm in Arkansas. One day
I was standing by the smoke-house watching my grandmother
making lye soap in a big iron kettle when my grandfather came
across the yard, very excited. "Nellie broke her leg," my grandfather said. My grandmother and I went over the stile into the
garden where my grandfather had been plowing. Old Nellie was
on the ground whimpering, still hitched to the plow. We stood
there looking at her, just looking at her. My grandfather came
back with the gun he had carried at Chickamauga Ridge. "She
stepped in a hole," he said, patting Nellie's head. My grandmother turned me around, facing the other way. I started crying. I heard a shot. I still hear that shot. I ran over and fell
down on the ground, hugging her neck. I loved that horse. I
hated my grandfather. I got up and went to him, beating his
legs with my fists. . . . Later that day he explained that he loved
Nellie too, but that he had to shoot her. "It was the kindest thing
to do," he said. "She was no more good. It was the only way to
get her out of her misery. . . ."*

I had the pistol in my hand.

"All right," I said to Gloria. "Say when."

"I'm ready."

"Where?——"

"Right here. In the side of my head."

The pier jumped as a big wave broke.

"Now?——"

"Now."

I shot her.

The pier moved again, and the water made a sucking noise as it slipped back into the ocean.

I threw the pistol over the railing.

One policeman sat in the rear with me while the other one drove. We were traveling very fast and the siren was blowing. It was the same kind of a siren they had used at the marathon dance when they wanted to wake us up.

"Why did you kill her?" the policeman in the rear seat asked.

"She asked me to," I said.

"You hear that, Ben?"

"Ain't he an obliging bastard?" Ben said, over his shoulder.

"Is that the only reason you got?" the policeman in the rear seat asked.

"They shoot horses, don't they?" I said.

. . .MAY
GOD
HAVE
MERCY
ON YOUR
SOUL. . .

THIEVES LIKE US

by Edward Anderson

To
MY COUSIN AND MY WIFE
BECAUSE THERE I WAS WITH AN EMPTY GUN
AND YOU, ROY, SUPPLIED THE AMMUNITION
AND YOU, ANNE, DIRECTED MY AIM

"Men do not despise a thief, if he steal to satisfy his soul when he is hungry; but if he be found, he shall restore sevenfold; he shall give all the substance of his house."

—Proverbs of Solomon.

Chapter I

THERE was no doubt about it this time: over yonder behind the rise of scrub-oak, the automobile had left the highway and was laboring in low gear over the rutted road to where they waited. Like a saliva-wettened finger scorching across a hot iron, Bowie's insides spitted. He looked at Chicamaw.

Chicamaw's eyes were fixed up the weed-grown road, his thick-soled, convict shoes quiet on the rain-sprinkled earth that he had scarred with pacing. "That's him," he said.

Bowie looked behind him, across the creek's ridge of trees and over the field where the blades of the young corn glimmered like knives in the late-afternoon sun. Above the whitewashed walls of Alcatona Penitentiary reared the red-painted water-tank, the big cottonwood tree of the Upper Yard and the guards' towers.

The car was coming on. The jew's-harp twanging of the grasshoppers in the broomweeds seemed to heighten. I can rib myself up to do anything, Bowie thought. Anything. Every day in that place over there is wasted.

The car's springs creaked nearer. Bowie looked at Chicamaw again. "You're not planning on going some place, are you?"

Chicamaw did not move his head. "I'm just waitin' to see a horse about a feller," he said.

The taxicab bumped around the hill and wallowed toward them. Bowie squinted to see better. The figure in the back seat had on a straw hat. It was old T-Dub though. Come on, you cotton-headed old soldier!

The driver was that Kid that had been peddling marihuana to some of the boys. Jasbo they called him.

The cab stopped a few feet away and Bowie and Chicamaw moved toward it.

"Hello, Bowie," Jasbo said.

Bowie did not look at him. "Hi," he said.

T-Dub sat there with a big, paper-wrapped bundle across his knees. The yellow brightness of the new hat made his blond hair look like dry corn-silk.

"Well, what we waitin' on?" Chicamaw said. He opened the door.

T-Dub handed Chicamaw the bundle and then reached inside his blouse and pulled the gun. He scraped the barrel against the driver's cheek. "This is a stick-up, Jasbo," he said.

"Godamighty, Man," Jasbo said. His head quivered on a rigid neck.

Chicamaw ripped at the bundle strings and slapped at the paper. It contained blue denim overalls and white cotton shirts. He began stripping himself of his cotton-sacking prison clothing. Bowie and T-Dub began changing too.

Jasbo said: "Bowie, you know me. You tell these boys I'm all right."

"You just do what you're told," Bowie said.

"All you gotta do is tell me," Jasbo said.

Their clothing changed, Chicamaw pushed Jasbo over and got under the wheel and Bowie and T-Dub got in the back. They turned and went back up the road. On the highway, the wind began beating the speeding car like a hundred fly-swatters.

There was a car under the shed of the filling station on the right. A man in coveralls stood beside the red pump twisting the handle.

"Don't you let me see you throwing no winks, Jasbo," T-Dub said, "or I'll beat your ears down."

"I'll put my head 'tween my legs if you say so," Jasbo said.

They passed the filling station and Bowie looked back. The man was still twisting the pump handle. The empty highway behind looked like a stretching rubber band.

Bowie looked at the revolver in T-Dub's thick grasp. It was a silver-plated gun with a pearl handle. This old soldier knows what he is doing, Bowie thought. "Any rumbles in town?" he said.

T-Dub shook his head.

The highway still stretched emptily. They're finding out things back there now in the Warden's Office, Bowie thought. The Colonel's bowels are gettin' in an uproar now. Get out the stripes for that bunch of no-goods, he is saying. That's what you get for treatin' them like white men. No more baseball and passes to go fishing for that Bowie Bowers and Elmo Mobley. That T. W. Masefeld is not going to work in this prison commissary any more. Get out the dogs and the shotguns and the .30-30's and run them sons of bitches down. . . .

A car shot up over the rise ahead, hurtled toward them. It passed with a swooshing sound. Cars coming this way don't mean nothing, Bowie thought. No more than them crows flying over yonder. T-Dub shifted the revolver to his left hand, wiped his palm on his thigh and regrasped the gun. Old T-Dub knows what he is doing.

The tendons of Chicamaw's lean neck played into two bony knots behind each ear. That Chicamaw knows what he is doing too. A man won't get in with two boys like this just every day. No more Time for any of them. They had shook on it.

The explosion was like the highway had snapped. The escaping air of the right back tire wailed. The car began to bump. On the left was a sign post: *Alcatona . . . 14 miles.* It was right in the middle of thirteen, Bowie thought. Old unlucky *thirteen.*

They bumped across the wooden bridge and moved up the dirt side road. When they were out of sight of the highway, Chicamaw stopped. The casing looked like it had been chopped with an ax. The spare was no good either.

Dusk was smoking out the ebbing glow on the horizon. Crickets in the roadside grass sounded like wind in loose telephone wires. Old unlucky *thirteen* is getting us up tight, Bowie thought. Hundred and twenty-two miles to Keota and Chicamaw's cousin, Dee Mobley and our Hole and *thirteen* riding our sore backs.

Chicamaw yanked at the barbed wire of the fence with the pliers and then came back with a strand. He lashed Jasbo to the steering wheel.

They moved now across the field of growing cotton toward the farmhouse light. "This gentleman up here might have a car with some tires on it," T-Dub said.

The earth of the field was soft and the tough stalks whipped their legs. In the distance, back toward the Prison, there was the sound of baying dogs and Bowie stopped. "Man, listen to them dogs," he said. Chicamaw and T-Dub halted. It was a vibrant, sonorous sound like the musical notes of a deep reed instrument.

"Hell, them's possum hounds," Chicamaw said.

They walked faster. The cottonwood stumps squatted in the field like headless toads. The farmhouse light glowed nearer, a fierce orange. T-Dub broke into a lope and Chicamaw and Bowie followed.

The woman with the baby in her arms led T-Dub and Bowie back to the lamp-lighted kitchen and the little man at the table half turned in his chair, a raw, bitten onion in his left hand, and looked up at them, at the gun in T-Dub's hand.

"We need that car out there of yours, Mister," T-Dub said. "Come on up."

Little Man turned and put the onion on the table. There were fried eggs and yellow corn bread on the plate. He got up and pushed the chair against the table. "Where's them keys, Mama?" he said.

The skin about Mama's mouth was twitching and her lower lip looked like it was going to melt on her chin. "I don't know," she said. The baby in her arms began to whimper.

Little Man found the keys in his pocket.

T-Dub looked at Mama. "Lady, if you like this gentleman here and want to see him again and I think you do, you just don't open your mouth after we leave."

"Yessir," Mama said. She began jogging the baby up and down. It began to cry.

Dust was as thick as silk on the car's body and there were chicken droppings on the hood and fenders. Little Man got in front with Chicamaw. "I haven't had this car out in more than a month," he said.

The highway paralleled the high embankment of the Katy railroad now. Bowie watched the rising speedometer needle: *forty-five . . . fifty.* Stomp it, Chicamaw. Two pairs of nines riding our backs now. That kid Jasbo is squawking back yonder now all over the country. Ninety-nine years for highway robbery. Another pair for kidnaping.

The lights of the little highway town ahead spread with their approach and then scattered like flushed prey as they entered its limits. Under the filling-station sheds, swirling insects clouded the naked bulbs. The stores were closed; the depot dark. No Laws jumping us here, Bowie thought. No

Square-Johns with shotguns. He turned toward T-Dub. "How many miles you think we done?"

"Twenty," T-Dub said.

"My woman has been pretty sick," Little Man said. "Been awful torn up lately."

Chicamaw's head went up and down.

Awful sick or scared, Bowie thought. District 'Cuter shouting that all over the Court House won't sound so good, boys. Stomp it, Chicamaw. Fog right up this line. Hour and forty minutes like this and we'll be cooling off with Real People. That Dee Mobley was Real People. Him and Chicamaw had thieved together when they were kids. Chicamaw had been saving this Hole for eight years.

"Hasn't been well since the baby," Little Man said.

The motor coughed, spluttered. Chicamaw yanked out the choke button. The motor fired again, missed; the cylinders pumped with furious emptiness. Loose lugs rasped on the slowing wheels.

"Get her off the highway," T-Dub said. "Goose her. Gentlemen, this wins the fur-lined bathtub."

Bowie, T-Dub and Little Man pushed, their feet clopping on the pavement like horses. At last they reached the crossroads and they pushed the car up over the hump and out of sight of the highway.

Chicamaw started tying Little Man. T-Dub breathed like he had asthma. "I've had plenty of tough teaty in my day, but this is the toughest. I might as well turn this .38 on me and do it up right."

A car was coming; its headlights glowed above the hump. It sped on, its sound diminishing like the roll of a muffled drum.

"Let's get moving," Chicamaw said.

They crossed the highway, crawled through the fence and waded the hip-deep grass of the railroad right-of-way. They climbed the embankment and got down on the railroad bed.

"We could flag a car and throw down on them?" Chicamaw said.

"To hell with them hot cars," T-Dub said. "I'll walk it."

"We can do it by just keeping right down these ties," Chicamaw said.

"Like goddamned hoboes," T-Dub said.

The moon hung in the heavens like a shred of fingernail. There was only the sound of their feet crunching in the gravel. Chicamaw led.

The rails began to murmur. It was a train behind them. After a while, the locomotive's light showed, tiny as a lightning bug. It began to swell.

They climbed up the cut's side, clutching at the grass, and on top lay down. The earth began trembling as if the cut's sides were going to cave in and carry them under the wheels. The pounding wheels of the freight-train thundered and crashed and, after a long time, the twin red lights of the caboose passed.

"I wouldn't of minded holding that down for a while," T-Dub said.

"Why didn't you holler for them to stop, Bowie?" Chicamaw said.

"I didn't want to make them mad at us," Bowie said.

The nail in the heel of Bowie's right shoe was digging now into the flesh. To hell with it, he thought. Bad start is a good ending, boys. You can't throw snake-eyes all day. Box-cars won't jump up in your face every throw. There's a natural for us up this road.

Bowie came out of his sleep with T-Dub's voice, deep as a cistern's echo and Chicamaw's muffled rattle still stroking his ears. His feet felt like the toe-nails had been drawn out and the bits ground in his heels. The sun was piercing the plum thicket like ice picks and when Bowie turned on his back he placed his forearm over his eyes.

"I cased that bank in Zelton four times," T-Dub said. "It was a bird's nest on the ground, but every time something came up. Maybe this time will be different."

"I'm ready for a piece of it myself," Chicamaw said.

"I tell you one thing," T-Dub said. "When I rob my next bank it will be my twenty-eighth."

"I hope it's twenty-nine in a couple of weeks."

Bowie's insides quivered. I can rib myself up to do anything, he thought.

"These kids trying to rob these banks are just ding-bats,"

T-Dub said. "They'll charge a bank with a filling station across the street and a telephone office above and a hardware store next door."

"You got to watch them upstairs offices across the street from a bank too," Chicamaw said. "There's lawyers and doctors and people with shotguns just waiting for a bank to be robbed."

"I'm not going to fool with any of these clodhopper town banks," Chicamaw said. "You got to work just as hard for a thousand out of one of them as you do in a good one for fifty."

"Pick you a bank that's a depository for the county and city and you're going to find a set-up," T-Dub said. "That's why I say it don't hurt to case a bank for a week before you charge it."

Five thousand dollars and I'm backing off, Bowie thought. Five thousand salted away and I'm going back to Alky. I've done so much Time that I can do a couple of more on my ear. Go back there and grin at them from ear to ear. I can twist that Warden around my little finger. He's all right though. He'll close them books on me and my record will be clean in a couple of years. Then I'll buy me a mouthpiece for a couple of thousand that's got friends in the Capital and you'll see me coming out of that Alky squared up and with a stake.

The best way to case the Inside of a bank, T-Dub said, was by going in and cashing twenty-dollar bills. In Florida he had opened up an account in a bank just to big-eye it good.

Bowie sat up.

"The Country Boy is up," Chicamaw said. His teeth were as white as the pearl of a gun butt.

There were tiny lights in T-Dub's eyes, gray as .30-30 bullets. "What do you want for supper, Bowie? Plums or fried chicken?"

Bowie looked at a ripened plum on the stem above his head. "I'll take plums," he said.

Chicamaw had his trousers rolled to his knees and now he was pinching into his hair-matted legs.

"What the hell are you doing?" Bowie said.

"Red bugs," Chicamaw said.

Bowie looked at his blood-crusted feet; at the curled toes and grass-filled wrinkles of his shoes. Just one more night of walking though. Just a half a night. He lay back down.

Chicamaw was talking now about a bank he robbed in Kansas. "I knew I hadn't sacked up no more than two thousand out of that nigger-head and I just happened to pick up that cash slip. You know that one they put in every night to show how much cash they got on hand? . . . Well, it didn't jibe with what I had so I went back up to that Dutchman and I says to him: 'Friend, have I got everything around here?' He says: 'You got every bit of it.' I says: 'Is your cash receipt slip usually right?' He says: 'Why, yes.' I says: 'Well, I haven't got but two thousand here and this slip shows four thousand eight hundred and sixty-two dollars. Now cough it up.' That guy began swearing up and down so I just put the twitch to him. His eyes turned as red as any red you ever did see."

Bowie sat back up. "What's a twitch?" he said.

"Don't worry, you'll see one pretty soon. When I work I always carry myself one. Get you a piece of window cord and make a little stick with a hole in it and fix a loop and just put that around a man's head and give it a twist and he's gonna think his brains are coming out his ears. Anyway, this Dutchman hollers calf rope and he shows me the bottom drawer of a desk there. Sure enough, right there in it, was four little packs of the prettiest *five hundred-* and *one hundred-*dollar bills you ever saw."

A gust of wind combed the thicket and bent the stretch of high Johnston grass that separated them from the railroad. Bowie lay back.

"You know what that banker would have done if you hadn't of got onto that slip," T-Dub said. "He'd of squawked that he had been robbed of it all just the same. There's more of these bankers than you can shake a stick at that's got it stacked around over their banks and just praying every day to be robbed."

"Sure," Chicamaw said.

"They're thieves just like us," T-Dub said.

Bowie flecked an ant off the back of his hand. I'm not going to get in this too deep, gentlemen. You going to see this white child backing off when he's got five thousand.

The feet of T-Dub and Chicamaw scraped in sudden violence and Bowie jerked up like a jackknife. He looked toward
the two. They were looking into the Johnston grass. T-Dub
had the gun in his hand.

Bowie watched. Something was moving in that grass yonder
all right. It wasn't wind either. He picked up his shoes. The
grass parted again!

Chicamaw led the way, plunging through the thicket like a
football half-back; T-Dub behind and Bowie following bare-
footed and carrying his shoes. They did not stop running until
they reached the woods. Then they stopped and looked back
toward the thicket.

"What did you-all see?" Bowie said. "Jesus Christ."

"Something was in that grass," Chicamaw said.

"If there wasn't I left a damned good three-dollar hat over
there," T-Dub said. "I can see your socks hanging from here,
Bowie."

"I thought all the Laws in the county were in that grass the
way you-all tore out," Bowie said.

"I'll bet it was a hog or something," T-Dub said. "Turkey
or something. I'll bet any amount you guys want to name."

"If you think it's just a hog why don't you just trot back
over there and get that hat?" Chicamaw said.

"Ah, I want to go bare-headed anyway. Like these jelly
beans."

Bowie sat down and began putting on his shoes. His feet
were bleeding again.

"Think you going to make it, Bowie?" T-Dub said.

"The way I come across over here looks like I could run
it," Bowie said.

Chapter II

THAT rain-blurred sprinkle of lights yonder was Keota. Before
the rain commenced, Bowie had heard sounds of the town,
but now there was only the smacking of the wind-driven rain
against the shocks of old wheat around him and its clatter on

the stubbled earth. He had been alone now more than two hours and it must be getting along toward three or four o'clock. In the black depths underneath those lights yonder, T-Dub and Chicamaw were looking for Dee Mobley's place. When they found Chicamaw's cousin, they were coming back after him. Three flashes of the headlamps, if they got Dee's car, would be the signal.

Bowie reached down now and pressed his numb feet. They felt like stumps. A man on stumps couldn't do much good if he was jumped and that is why he had stayed here to wait.

The thunder in the east rumbled nearer and then cracked above him in a jagged prong of lightning. The flash bared the sodden stretch to the sagging fence and road.

I won't be hearing any more from my people, Bowie thought. Mama. Aunt Pearl. Cousin Tom. Goodbye to you people. The first thing the Law does is look up the people a man has been writing to and watch them places.

Goodbye, Mama. There's one thing about you. Whatever I ever did was all right with you. This is the only way. Maybe you'll be getting an envelope with three or four hundred dollars in it pretty soon and then you can go off and get that pellagra cured up. Get away from that husband you got for a while.

So long, Cousin Tom. Thanks for them letters and cigarettes. But all the cheering in the world don't help you none, Pal, when you're in a place like that back yonder. You know every day what is going to happen the next.

Aunt Pearl, you're a fine woman, but all the Christian Scientist stuff in the world don't help you none if you haven't got the money to buy a lawyer. And to get a good one you got to have good money.

Approaching car lights bobbed on the road and Bowie got up. The laboring machine plowed the mud of the road right on past. Bowie lowered himself back to the ground.

Them boys will be back here. Takes time to locate a man when you don't know where he lives. Let him stay out here? Them boys weren't made that way. It was getting doggone late though. There wasn't a dozen lights in the town now.

Lightning slashed the swirling heavens. Maybe a man saw something like that when they kicked the switch off on you in the Chair, Bowie thought. It didn't seem like no nine years since that morning when his lawyer came and told him they weren't going to burn him. Maybe though he had died back there in the Chair? This was just his Spirit out here in this rain? In this old world, anything happened. Maybe I'm like a cat with nine lives. I done lost one of them back there in that Alky Chair. Eight more to go. . . . Look here, Bowie, old boy, snap out of it. You're going to go ding-batty out here.

Another car was coming. It sounded like a Model-T; had one twitching feeble light.

Bowie moved toward the fence in a half crouch. The car was a Ford pick-up, its body boards thumping and rattling. That light on it was either just going off and on or signaling. What was it doing? He checked the shout in his throat. The car went on, the sound of its straining motor dying in the night.

He sat now at the side of the road. It couldn't be very long until daybreak. Well, I can't sit out here up into the day. Them boys must have got a rumble over there. They might be in trouble this very minute. They wouldn't leave me out here though. Not them boys. We've had our heads together too long on this business. Take old T-Dub. Him knocking down in that Commissary every day so they would have a stake. A man didn't start out with money that come that hard with two fellows and not intend to go through with it. Not any four hundred and twenty-five dollars. And planning as far ahead as they had? Cooling off at Dee's and then going on down into Texas and getting hold of T-Dub's sister-in-law and getting her to get them a furnished house. Nosir, that boy just wasn't made that way. And Chicamaw? Them white teeth.

The rain slapped his face and crawled on his numb feet. But I can't stay out here forever. If they ain't here by daybreak, I've just got to go on in. I can't help it. I'm going in.

The harnessed mules plowed the road's muck toward Bowie, pulling a wagon with a tarpaulin as gray and soggy as the morning. The driver, his drooping straw sombrero bowed against the drizzle, slopped along at the wagon's side. His overalls were rolled to his calves and hunks of mud leaped from his moving shoes. Now the sombrero raised.

"Good morning, Friend," Bowie said.

Sombrero shifted the wad of tobacco in his jaws. "Mornin'," he said.

Bowie pointed at his shoes. "Mind if I hang on the back of your wagon into town? My feet have plumb played out on me."

Sombrero nodded toward the wagon's rear. "Climb up in it if you want to."

Bowie went around and climbed through the canvas flap and into the wagon. The smell of alfalfa was dry and clean. He saw now the woman and the little boy. They sat on quilt-covered straw against the seat.

"Your man said I could pile in here, Lady?"

The woman nodded.

Bowie leaned back against the sides, stretched his feet in guarded relaxation. The wagon's movement was soothing and its clean dryness began to sponge him like a dry chamois skin. He closed his eyes.

"Who's that man, Ma?"

Bowie opened his eyes, looked at the child and grinned. "You don't mind me riding with you, do you, Son?"

The boy burrowed his face against his mother's bosom and she patted him. "He's a friend of your pappy's, honey."

The hoofs of the mules began clopping and Bowie asked the woman: "We in town?"

The woman nodded. "On the Square."

Bowie edged feet forward to the wagon's end, parted the flap and slid out. The pavement was like a cushion of pins.

In the center of the Square was the Court House, a two-story sandstone building with big basement signs: *Whites* . . . *Colored*. One- and two-story buildings fenced the Square: *Greenberg's Dry Goods Store* . . . *Keota State Bank* . . . *Rexall Drug Store* . . . *Hamburger's 5 & 10¢*.

The rain had stopped and the sun looked like a circle of wet, yellow paper. Bowie walked across the Court House lawn toward the dry goods store on the corner.

The clerk leaned against the doorway with his arms folded across his chest and when Bowie neared he pushed with his shoulder blades and stood erect. "Yessir?" he said.

"I got ten bucks, Pardner," Bowie said, "and I got to have

a pair of pants and a shirt and socks and shoes and some short-handled drawers."

"We'll see," Pardner said.

Bowie followed him back into the gloom and deeper into the smell of damp wool and bolted goods and floor sweep. Pardner turned on a fly-specked bulb above a table of khaki work pants.

In dry clothing now, Bowie sat on a bench while Pardner laced the new shoes on his feet. "You don't know a feller around here by the name of Tobey or Hobby or something like that, do you?" he asked.

Pardner cocked his head. "Don't believe I do."

"I used to know a feller up in Tulsy who settled down here. Been in this town a pretty good while I understand. Mobby or something like that."

"What does he look like?"

Bowie described Chicamaw. "Oh, he's sort of an Indian looking feller. Come up to about my shoulders. Black eyes and pretty skinny."

Pardner shook his head.

"He was working in a filling station up in Tulsy."

"There's a fellow named Mobley out on the Dallas highway that's got a little store and station out there."

"It wasn't Mobley, I'm sure of that."

"Did he have a girl named Keechie, little Indian-looking girl?"

"No. It don't matter. I didn't know him so well."

The new shoes made his feet feel like they were not even sore. It was good to walk. The sun was blotting the puddles and making the dry stretches of the highway glare. He passed the lumber yard with its fence of shredded show posters, the closed cotton gin, the tourist camp: *Kozy Komfort Kamp.*

That was the place yonder all right. That station right yonder with the orange-colored pump. A man sat under the shed in a tilted chair. Back of the station was a smokehouse-looking structure and then woods. Farther up the highway, on the left side, was another station.

Bowie went up under the shed toward the man in the tilted chair. "How you do, Friend?" Bowie said.

"Howdy," the man said. He had a heavy face, rough as oak

bark and long, black sideburns touched with wiry gray. The black cotton shirt had white buttons.

"Got a cold soda?" Bowie said.

The man got up and lifted the lid of the ice-box and Bowie reached in and picked up a bottle.

Bowie saw now the girl standing behind the screened doorway of the store. She was dark and small and her high pointed breasts stretched the blue cotton of the polo shirt.

Bowie looked at the man. "I wonder if I could see you private a minute?"

The man looked toward the girl and she went away.

"You're Dee Mobley, aren't you?"

"That's me."

"You haven't had a couple of visitors lately?"

Mobley looked at Bowie's shoes. "You got on some new shoes there, haven't you? Feet been hurting?"

"You doggone whistling. I just got these up town."

"New pants too?"

Bowie grinned.

"Where in the hell," Mobley said, "have *you* been?"

"Waiting for that Chicamaw and that T-Dub Masefeld."

"I went after you last night myself," Mobley said. "Raining cats and nigger babies."

"In a Model-T truck?"

"That was me."

"Well, I'll be— Can you beat that. And I just sat out there and let you go by."

Mobley made a thumbing motion toward the filling station up the highway. Two figures in uniform coveralls sat on a bench under its shed. "Them Square-Johns up yonder are always big-eyeing this way so you just go on past like you were hitch-hiking and then cut back through the woods. The boys are in that bunk of mine right back of this place."

Bowie dog-trotted through the woods toward the filling station. He could see the place that Dee called his bunk. It had a corrugated iron roof and the limbs of a big pecan tree shaded it. He crawled through the fence and went to the bunk's door and knocked. The springs of a bed inside creaked a little. He knocked again. There was no answer. "Chicamaw," he called.

Feet thumped on the floor inside, stomped toward the door. T-Dub's face was framed in the parted door. "For Christ's sake, come in," he said.

Chicamaw lay on the iron bed in his underwear. "We thought maybe you had gone back to Alky."

"I just been swimming that's all," Bowie said. "And thinking I was a lone wolf."

"I was going to go back out there tonight myself," Chicamaw said.

T-Dub pointed at the bare wooden table. On it was a bowl of pork and beans, a hunk of yellow cheese and a broken loaf of bread. "You want to glom?"

"Man, I'll say."

"We didn't get holed up here until five o'clock this morning," Chicamaw said. "I was going to go back after you tonight. I don't see how Dee missed you."

"It was my fault," Bowie said. He poured beans on a hunk of the bread and pressed it into a sandwich. He took a bite and chewed and grinned.

Chapter III

Up until a year ago, Dee Mobley had been bootlegging corn whisky, but the new Sheriff in Keota had it in for him, he said. He squatted now against the wall of the Bunk, his breath as strong as rubbing-alcohol fumes, a finger-rolled cigarette wagging on his lower lip. "The Sheriff likes these druggist boys here," Dee said. "They're doing all the booze business here now."

"Them Laws and druggists are thieves just like us," T-Dub said. He drew his hand across his sweat-beaded forehead and his fingers made a clicking sound as he slung it on the floor. "It's getting so a man has to have a gun to make a piece of money."

The afternoon sun was packing heat into the low-ceilinged, crowded room. Chicamaw sat on an up-turned bucket filing on the barrels of the 12-gauge shotgun with a hack saw. Bowie lay on the bed, a wet towel across his face.

The druggists were fixing up the cheap trade with jake and orange peel and hair tonics, Dee said, and the Indians were buying their canned heat at the five & ten. Doctors were getting the good business with prescriptions.

Dee said he had been running the grocery and filling station since fall. His daughter Keechie helped him. She stayed up in town with his sister Mara, and he stayed in the Bunk here at nights.

"That girl of yours sure mean-eyed me this morning when she brought that grub out here," T-Dub said. "I don't think she likes us around here worth a doggone."

"She don't have much to do with nobody," Dee said.

Bowie took the towel off his face so he could see Dee.

"She'll take care of you while I'm up in Tulsy," Dee said. "Just you boys don't go around in front of the station and be careful about lights at night."

T-Dub counted out three hundred and twenty-five dollars and gave it to Dee. This was to buy a second-hand car in Tulsa, cover ten dollars for the shotgun and twenty-five for Dee's trouble.

"I might be able to make it back by tomorrow night," Dee said. "But if I see I'm going to get in here after daylight I'll just wait until the next night."

"We'd like to shell out of here about eight o'clock at night," T-Dub said.

"We don't forget our friends, Dee," Chicamaw said. "You do the best you can for us and when we get in some real money, you're liable to see a piece of it."

After Dee left, T-Dub said they had ninety-five dollars left. It had to take them to Texas and pay a month's rent on a furnished house.

Chicamaw put the shotgun down and went over and picked up a road map on the bed.

T-Dub said the best way to leave a Hole was early in the evening when the traffic was heaviest. Stay off the main highways as much as you could and follow timbered country. Keep a couple of five-gallon cans filled with gasoline and circle cities like Dallas and Fort Worth where the Laws had them scout cars and radios.

The wheels of a truck ground in the gravel of the station's

driveway and they listened. Bottles rattled. "Soda-pop truck," Bowie said.

"I can run these roads all day and night through," T-Dub said. "Just keep your car clean and not let it look like it was being run hard and everybody stay shaved up and looking like you were just a fellow about town. I can count it on my hand the times I been jumped on the road."

"Just give me one man driving and me sitting in the back with a .30-30 and I can hold off any carload of Laws that ever took out after anybody," Chicamaw said.

"You can do it with a nigger-shooter," T-Dub said. "I don't see where these fellows they call G-men, them Big Shots, get that stuff about thieves not having no guts. I don't see how they get that."

"Me neither," Bowie said. "They don't do anything unless they got ten carloads and when they jump anybody they use about fourteen hundred rounds of ammunition."

"Laws never did worry me," T-Dub said. "It's the fellers you thought were your friends that beats you. And a woman mad at you. They are what beat you."

"Liquor too," Bowie said. "Some guys have to be stewed to the gills before they can work. Me, I want my head clear when I start out."

"Whiss will do it all right," T-Dub said. "But a woman mad at you can get you in a rank quicker than anything. Yessir, the Laws would be up tight if it wasn't for sore women and snitches."

"They're full of rabbit all right, them Laws," Chicamaw said.

"I wouldn't trust Jesus Christ," Bowie said.

"Listen to old Country Boy," Chicamaw said.

"Even if I saw Jesus Christ walking right in this place I wouldn't trust him," Bowie said.

The heat was getting more intense. It stuffed Bowie's nostrils and seared high up in his nose. He took the towel and soaked it again in the bucket of water.

Chicamaw started taking off his overalls.

"You ought not to do that," Bowie said. "No tellin' when that girl might come out here."

Chicamaw resnapped the overall straps.

"I'd sure like to let that sister-in-law of mine know I'm coming," T-Dub said. "But that's a good way to get a rumble. Writing letters. We'll just go on to MacMasters and I'll get her on the phone."

Chicamaw looked up from the road map. "It's three hundred and twenty-five miles from here. That country is sure bald out in there. Nothing but oil-wells and mesquite trees."

"Plenty of roads though," T-Dub said. "Man, I was raised in that West Texas country."

"I guess you know that sister-in-law of yours pretty good?" Chicamaw said.

"She's Real People," T-Dub said. "A woman that has stuck by that bud of mine like she has isn't going to turn down a chance to make some money. That bud of mine can be sprung out of Texas with a couple of thousand. He's just doing five years. On a two-for-one job now. And that woman of his is going to do all she can."

"Zelton is forty miles from MacMasters," Chicamaw said. "That's where we going to get the house, uh?"

"There's mighty nice banks in both of those towns, but Zelton, I think, takes my eye first."

Chicamaw folded the map. "I know a mouthpiece in MacMasters," he said. "Name Hawkins. Archibald J. Hawkins. Old Windy we called him. Him and me were holed up together in Mexico for a year. There's one old boy that sure beat the Law."

"What did he do?" Bowie said.

"He was a county treasurer right there in MacMasters and he sacked himself up twenty or twenty-five thousand just knocking down every month and then things started gettin' hot and he rabbited to Mexico."

"Unlatched a vault?" Bowie asked.

"Oh, no. Just knocking down. He bought all the County's stuff, see. Gravel and machinery and things like that. He would make out a voucher for five loads of gravel when he had bought only one and then go down to the bank and cash it and pocket the other four. He was in Mexico for fourteen years. All the witnesses died or forgot and then he went back just as big as you please. And on top of that took the bar examination and is practising law right there now."

"Them politicians are thieves just like us," T-Dub said. "Only they got more sense and use their damned tongues instead of a gun."

"If you ever need a mouthpiece," Chicamaw said, "Old Windy wouldn't be bad."

"I'm not needing any more lawyers myself," T-Dub said. "The way I figure is that when they get me again I won't be in any shape for a lawyer or anything else in this world to do me any good."

"That's me," Bowie said. "I mean to get me out of any new trouble."

"Well, the way I figure it," Chicamaw said, "is that two and two make five and if at first you don't suck seed, keep on sucking 'til you do suck seed."

"Aw, you damned Indian," Bowie said.

The voice of the girl, Keechie, made Bowie's veins distend and there was a velvety, fluttering sensation in his spine. She was squatting over there now by the Bunk's kerosene heater, the brown flannel of her skirt stretched tight across her bottom, showing T-Dub how to keep the wick from smoking. T-Dub had tried to boil coffee on it this morning and had only succeeded in filling everybody's noses full of soot and blacking the underwear Bowie had washed.

"Just wipe it off with a match like this," Keechie said.

"That's one thing old T-Dub don't know nothing about," Chicamaw said.

Keechie got up, holding her blackened hands out. Bowie snatched the towel off the bed post and held it toward her. "It's pretty dirty," he said.

Keechie took the towel. "Thank you."

"That big Country Boy is some gallant, ain't he, Keechie?" Chicamaw said.

Bowie's ears felt like the velvet was being pressed against them now. "Don't pay no attention to that ignoramus," he said.

"Were you raised in the country?" Keechie said.

Bowie shook his head. "Don't pay no attention to them two."

"He's just hard-headed, Miss Keechie," T-Dub said. "That's all."

"Soft-headed," Chicamaw said.

"His head looks all right to me," Keechie said.

Bowie tried hard not to swallow. "All right, you guys, that's enough."

Keechie pointed at the bed. On it was a filled paper sack and two folded newspapers. "There's some canned soup in that sack and you can heat it on that stove now." She turned toward the door.

"Thanks for the grub and papers, Miss Keechie," T-Dub said.

Bowie looked at her, the black hair, cut like a boy's; the short, strong neck and compact shoulders. "Sure thank you," he said.

"Forget it," Keechie said. She went out the door.

"That little girl don't think any too much of us, I'm here to tell you," T-Dub said. He went over to the bed and picked up a newspaper.

"She's all right," Chicamaw said. "Just stuck up."

"She acts like a little soldier to me," Bowie said.

"Old Dee just lets her do him anyway," Chicamaw said. "He won't never go on a real toot around here any more. If he wants to get boiled, he'll go clear up to Muskogee. That man's got a right to drink though. Wife leaving him like she did."

"Keechie's mother?" Bowie said.

"She run off with some damned guy. Running a medicine show."

"That little girl hasn't got no business around a bunch of criminals like us," Bowie said.

"Man, lookee here," T-Dub said. He had the Oklahoma City newspaper spread out on the bed and was tapping the left top column. "Just lookee here."

Bowie went over and he and Chicamaw looked:

ALCATONA, Okla., Sept. 15—The escape of three life-term prisoners who kidnaped a taxicab driver and a farmer in their desperate flight was announced here tonight by Warden Everett Gaylord of the State Penitentiary. Combined forces of prison, County and City officers were looking for the trio. The fugitives are:

Elmo (Three-Toed) Mobley, 35, bank robbery; T. W. (Tommy Gun) Masefeld, 44, bank robbery and Bowie A. Bowers, 27, murder.

"Pulling that toe stuff again on me," Chicamaw said. "All right, you sons of bitches."

Mobley and Bowers, Warden Gaylord disclosed, took advantage of permits allowing them to go fishing on prison property and Masefeld of a pass to town. All three were privileged trusties.

Jed Miracle, 21, Alcatona taxi driver, was bound in his own taxi which the fugitives abandoned after a tire blew out. E. T. Waters, farmer living at the edge of Akota, twelve miles south of here, gave descriptions of three men who commandeered his car at the point of a gun. After traveling with the trio for more than an hour, the fuel of the car was exhausted and Waters was tied and abandoned in his own car like Miracle.

The desperate trio are believed to be headed for the hills of Eastern Oklahoma where so many criminals have found refuge in the past few years.

Bowers, youngest of the escaped men, was serving a life sentence that had been commuted from the death penalty. He was convicted in the murder of a storekeeper in Selpa County when he was 18 years old. The killing took place during an attempted robbery. He was a member of the prison baseball team.

All of the men had good prison records, Warden Gaylord said. Masefeld had charge of the prison commissary, selling cigarettes and candies to the inmates. He had been in the prison six years. Mobley, also a member of the prison ball team, had served five years of a 99 year sentence from Larval County.

Miracle, the cab driver, described tonight how he was lured to the creek a mile from the prison by Masefeld and forced at the point of a gun to surrender his cab and accompany them.

"Masefeld told me in town he wanted to take some sandwiches and soda pop out to some friends of his who were fishing," Miracle declared. "I had done that plenty of times for some of the trusty boys and I did not think anything about it. When we reached the place, Masefeld jabbed the gun in my back and said he would kill me if I did not obey him," Miracle asserted.

"A tire blew out," Miracle went on, "and the extra was down too, so they tied me up and went on across a cotton field toward the highway. I managed to work myself loose and drove the car back to town."

The shouts of Waters, the farmer kidnaped by the men, attracted coon hunters who freed him. He declared the men treated him courteously.

"That toe stuff," Chicamaw said.

"It tickles me," T-Dub said, "about this Tommy Gun they're putting on me. I never did have but one machine gun in my life and I never did even try it out. I'll take an automatic pump gun any old day."

"It's not a very long piece about us though, is it?" Chicamaw said.

"Brother, I wish it was just two lines," Bowie said.

"Nothing at all you mean," T-Dub said. "Papers can raise more heat than anything. These Laws work like hell to get their names in the papers."

They lolled on the ground in front of the Bunk, unrecognizable bundles in the darkness, only their slapping and blowing at mosquitoes interrupting the quiet. This was the second night they had waited on Dee Mobley. The lights of the station had not been turned on this evening. Everything was set to take off. Chicamaw had the shotgun sawed off so he could carry it underneath the old lumberjacket Dee had given him. Keechie had two five-gallon cans of gasoline filled up in front of the station, two sacks of groceries and three cotton-picking sacks.

"I just hope it's not the car that's holding him up," T-Dub said. "I'll be damned if I start out in a wreck."

"He's probably drinking a little," Chicamaw said.

Bowie got up and stretched. "I wish he had picked some other time to drink if that's it." He walked over to the edge of the tree's inky shadow and stood there, looking at the back of the station. Then he came back and stood above Chicamaw and T-Dub. They were quiet again.

Bowie moved up the side of the station and peered around under the shed. He saw the figure sitting in the chair by the ice-box and his shoes rasped in the gravel with his start.

"My goodness," he said. "I didn't know that was you."

"That's all right," Keechie said.

He cleared his throat. "I didn't know anybody was around here."

"That's all right."

He looked at the Model-T pick-up parked just off the driveway. "I was thinking though that I hadn't heard it leave."

"No," Keechie said.

Bowie moved toward her.

"Sit down if you want to," Keechie said.

He lowered himself to the bottom of the doorway. There was a car under the shed of the brightly lighted filling station up the highway. Two men were standing beside it and watching the attendant fill the tank. "I don't know what could be holding that Daddy of yours," he said.

"I have an idea. If it had to be done I should have done it."

Bowie shook his head. "We don't have any business around here anyway."

The lights of a car popped around the curve from town, sprayed the highway with luminous foam. Bowie strained back against the door screen. The car passed.

"I read it in the paper about you," Keechie said.

Bowie's head went up and down.

"I guess you thought you had to leave?"

"I didn't see any use of doing any more Time. It wasn't getting me anywhere. All that was keeping me in there was money."

Keechie shook her head. "You won't get anywhere like this. Not with company like that back yonder."

"I don't know," Bowie said. "What will be, will be."

"That Chicamaw wouldn't be anything else if he could."

"I think you got them boys down wrong now. You take old T-Dub. He's got him a little farm picked out already up in Kentucky. He wants to settle down."

"That Chicamaw Mobley has never liked anything but trouble all his life."

Bowie grinned. "He's a little wild all right."

The car under the shed of the other filling station drove away. The attendant went back and sat on the bench.

"If I wasn't so hot I'd like to have me a filling station," Bowie said. "Now what I would like to have is a tourist camp."

"That would be too slow for you," Keechie said. "You want to live your life fast."

"You got me down wrong, Keechie. You'd see me following a one-eyed mule and a Georgia walking stock if I had to and what's more, like it. If I could."

Keechie took a pack of cigarettes from her polo shirt pocket, pushed up one and offered it to Bowie. When he touched her hand, the velvety glow stiffened his blood. The lighted cigarette trembled between his fingers.

"How come you to ever get in trouble?" Keechie said.

"I never was in but one."

"That one."

"You mean the Chair?"

"Yes."

"Just some fellows on the carnival I was traveling with said they knew how to make some money and I just sort of went along to see how it was done. I wanted to get some money so I could go up to Colorado and join another show. Them boys had a safe picked out and I just went along."

"You were on a carnival?"

"I went on it when I was fourteen. Just roustaboutin'."

"Did you run away from home?"

"I just left. Year after Dad died."

"Your Dad is dead?"

"Killed. Man killed him."

Shoes crunched at the side of the station and Bowie's head jerked. It was Chicamaw. "I wondered what had become of you?"

"Just talking," Bowie said.

"Don't let me bother you." Chicamaw went on back.

Keechie flipped the cigarette toward the pick-up and Bowie watched its glow on the dark ground.

"Did you shoot that man in Selpa?" Keechie said.

"It was me or him," Bowie said. "He was coming around the car after me with a gun."

The chair under Keechie creaked a little as she moved.

"If I had run like the others I wouldn't be this way now. The guy that knew all about robbing safes was the first one to run. The Big Shot."

Keechie took another cigarette.

"You smoke a lot," he said.

"I don't want it." She broke it in her hand.

"I know a man can't last Out Here long. But I'm not going to try and last. I'm going to back off and it isn't going to be long. I can still square myself up."

"No," Keechie said. "You can't beat it this way."

"Deep down in me I know I can't, but I myself says I can."

Another car was coming around the curve. Suddenly, its lights were flooding the shed under which they sat. Neither moved.

It was a coupe and Dee. He got out of the car awkwardly. He was drunk all right. "Hadtufftime," he said.

Bowie went back and told Chicamaw and T-Dub. "You think it's too late to start tonight?" he said.

"Hell, no," Chicamaw said. He and T-Dub went in the Bunk.

The motor of the Model-T around in front fired and Bowie started moving fast toward the shed. When he got around there, the pick-up was already on the highway. He watched it go, listening to the sound of the motor perishing in the darkness.

T-Dub and Chicamaw were piling things in the car. "Where's them cotton-picking sacks?" T-Dub said.

"I got them," Bowie said. He went over to the chair where she had been sitting and picked up the sacks.

"Hadtufftime," Dee said. "Tufftime."

They drove off. Shortly the wind was whipping the sacks on the fenders and insects swirled in the lamp beams and splattered on the windshield.

Chapter IV

THE two five-gallon cans rattled emptily in the coupe's rear and the red level of the gasoline gauge was below the half mark, but Fort Worth and Dallas were behind now, given the run-around without a rumble. One hundred and forty miles out this straight stretch and they would be in MacMasters. Bowie was driving.

On this side of MacMasters, at an old, abandoned wildcat well that T-Dub had described, Bowie and Chicamaw were getting out and T-Dub was going on in to contact his sister-in-law. Just as soon as he got a house, he would come back and get them.

They talked about houses now. When they had about five places, T-Dub said, and all had good hotel-lobby fronts, he would say they had a real set-up. He wanted a house in Zelton and another one in Gusherton. Then one in that resort town, Clear Waters, and one in Lothian and Twin Montes. These towns were within a radius of two hundred miles and not more than an hour's driving apart. A house in each of them would give you a Hole that you could be cooling off in within an hour after a bank was sacked.

Always get places with double garages, T-Dub said, and keep the cars out of sight. And never let the neighbors see more than one man at a time. And don't let anybody ever do any questioning. If there was any questioning, you do it yourself. Now up here in Zelton and Gusherton, they could be lease buyers or promoters as soon as they got good fronts.

"We're cotton pickers tonight and look it," Chicamaw said. "How much cotton can you pick a day, Country Boy?"

"Oh, a pound if I worked real hard," Bowie said. He looked at the fuel mark. It was getting damned low.

"And another thing," T-Dub said. "Always give the land-lady the best of the deal. Keep her satisfied."

"I had me a landlady down in Florida," Chicamaw said, "and I want you to know that there was one woman that could drink me under the table. There wasn't anything that woman wouldn't do. And just when everything was going smooth with us, they got me."

T-Dub started telling about a house he had in Colorado. The damnedest, smallest thing got him in a rank there, this right arm almost shot off and a big Law with a double-barreled shotgun jamming it in his eyes and him standing there and not even able to lift his arms. The thing he had done though was going off and staying a couple of weeks and not telling the milkman. That bastard got scared over a couple of dollars and he went to the woman that owned the house. She went over to the house and saw it all locked up and she just went in. She got an eyeful. He had that damned machine gun in that house and a bunch of shells. She goes to the Law and they show her a bunch of pictures and sure enough she picks him out. The Laws sit around that house and here he comes back. They would have killed him if it hadn't been for a woman on the porch of a house across the street. She got to shouting and screaming and telling the Laws to stop or they would have killed him. He had them black eyes where that big yellow bastard poked him with that shotgun for a month and a half.

"We sure got to stop and gas up pretty soon," Bowie said.

"That state of Colorado though," T-Dub said. "You ain't never going to get me back in it. They were going to try and put the Chair on me up there. I was praying for Oklahoma to come and get me. They had me positively identified in that state anyway. This Colorado 'cuter was after me right now and I just figured that I had been unlucky enough to draw him and I wasn't going to be lucky enough to beat that Chair. There was a little old auditor that used to come around to us boys in them death cells and talk. Kind of wanted to write pieces for the magazines or something. I got to feeling him out and finally I just showed him a *five-hundred* dollar bill. I had carried that in the sole of my shoe for six months. He tumbles and brings me a .25 automatic and some tape too just like I asked. I taped that right between my legs and Man, I was set. I had made up my mind that if they went ahead and started putting that Chair on me I was going to kill everybody around me that was man enough to die."

"They didn't even try you up there though, did they?" Chicamaw said.

"Naw. That's how come me to be back in Alky. Oklahoma finally come and got me. A little old jailer up here in the Panhandle took that gun off of me. I'd been trying to get rid of it for two weeks."

The highway turned in a banking curve and then down the highway they could see the scattered lights of a small, sleeping town. "We got to gas up here," Bowie said.

Everything was closed in the town. Small globes burned in

the rears of the stores, over the sacks of grain, the cans of oil and tire tubes in the filling stations and the show-cases in the hardware store.

"Looks like we going to have to wake somebody up," T-Dub said.

"We can just unlatch one ourselves," Chicamaw said.

Bowie drove under the shed of the filling station across the street from the Hardware Store. It was dark under the shed, but in the office a light burned. He got out and went up to the door. On the desk lay a man, suspenders down and his head on a rolled coat. There was an empty scabbard on his left hip.

"Hell, wake him up," Chicamaw said.

Bowie rattled the door and the man stirred, raised up and began to work his mouth like his jaws were sore. That old boy is a Law all right, Bowie thought.

Old Boy came out. He had a pistol in the scabbard now. "What do you boys want?" he said.

"Little gasoline, Pardner," T-Dub said.

Old Boy scratched his head. The hair looked like rope frazzle. "How much?"

"Fill it up," T-Dub said.

Old Boy moved toward the coupe; looked inside of it. T-Dub stepped toward him, brought the barrel of the revolver up into Old Boy's back like he was driving an uppercut. "Unlatch that pump, you nosy old belch before I beat your ears down good and proper."

Old Boy looked like he was trying to spit acid off the end of his tongue. Chicamaw snatched the six-shooter out of his scabbard. "And do it right now," T-Dub said.

"For God's sakes, boys," Old Boy said. "Take it easy now. I got a wife and four kids, boys. For God's sakes now. I'm an old man."

"You going to unlatch that pump?"

"For God's sakes, boys." Old Boy brought out the rattling ring of keys.

The car was serviced now and T-Dub told Old Boy to get in the car.

"We might just as well unlatch that hardware store over there while we're here and got him," Chicamaw said.

T-Dub drove with Old Boy sitting beside him; Chicamaw and Bowie stood on the running boards. They stopped in front of the Hardware Store.

Chicamaw pried at the door with the tire tool and when the lock burst, it sounded like all four tires on the coupe had blown out.

Bowie pushed back the glass door of the gun-case and began piling the weapons in his arms like sticks of wood. Chicamaw was filling the cotton sack with shells and cartridges.

The town was still undisturbed as they left it.

Behind the high signboard, twenty miles from the town, Chicamaw bound Old Boy, pulling his arms behind a post and twisting wire around the thumbs.

"You can holler somebody down in the morning," Bowie said.

"That's all right, boys. Perfectly all right. You boys are all right."

The white center line of the black asphalt was running under them again like a spout of gray water.

"I'll swear," Chicamaw said. He was looking at the six-shooter he had taken off Old Boy. It was an old frontier model, a .38 on a .45 frame. "I wish you could see this."

"What is it?" T-Dub said. "Hell, I'm driving."

There were six notches on the cedar butt of the revolver.

"I didn't know we were doing business with a bad man," T-Dub said.

"Nigger killer," Chicamaw said. "That's how he got these on here. That town was full of niggers back there."

"I ought to have stuffed it down his throat," T-Dub said. "I got fed up on him right now. Started big-eyeing this car."

"He was trying to pull a smartie all right," Bowie said.

"That back there might heat us up a little," T-Dub said. "This car here now, but I believe these cotton sacks cover it pretty well. He never saw no license on this car you can tell the world. We got to get some duplicate plates though pretty soon. You can buy all them you want for a dollar apiece. We ought to get a dozen sets."

"Naw, that old boy back there couldn't tell you whether this was a truck or a Packard," Bowie said. "Squawking the way he was."

Day began to break with a haze like cigarette smoke in a closed room and the barbed wire and cedar posts of the fences and the low, twisted mesquite trees began to take form. Bowie rubbed the bristle on his chin. "You know I haven't washed my teeth since we left Alky," he said.

The wildcat-well spot was a good place to hole up for a day or so all right. It was three miles from the Zelton Highway, a gully-scarred mesquite-clumped distance. The weed-grown road beside it was as rough as a cog wheel. It went on North, T-Dub said, beyond those cedar-timbered hills yonder and connected with a lateral road that tied up with the Gusherton Highway.

The mesquites were thick and made a fence for the clearing on which the old derrick rose. Its timbers were as gray as an old mop; away from it a little piece lay a huge wooden bull-wheel with rusty bolts.

Not even possum hunters ever came to this spot, T-Dub had said. He had holed up here three days once after he sacked a bank.

This afternoon, the second that T-Dub had been away from them, Bowie sat on a spread cotton-picking sack, trying the action again of his 12-gauge pump gun. He and Chicamaw had drawn straws for this Baby. It had a pistol grip and a ventilated rib. But the rib was coming off and about four inches of the barrel just as soon as Bowie got hold of a hack saw.

Near the edge of the sack lay more of the guns they had gotten in the Hardware Store, the polished stocks and barrels glittering in the afternoon sun. There were two 12-gauge shotguns, a .30-30 rifle and a .30-06. There was a .22 pump rifle.

Chicamaw patted the scarred stock of the shotgun he had sawed off at Dee's. "I'll still take old Betsy," he said. "All you have to do with her is point her in a general direction." He was drinking. He had found a half-gallon of whisky in the back of the coupe that Dee Mobley must have left.

"This baby here has got a trigger pull and action like a watch," Bowie said. He brought the gun to his shoulder and drew bead on the pulley at the top of the derrick. "Boy, oh boy," he said. "What I could do to a covey of quail."

Chicamaw picked up the fruit jar and started unscrewing the cap. He extended it toward Bowie.

"I'll pass this time."

Chicamaw drank and then shuddered and clenched his teeth.

"Now when I get a pistol on me I'll be willing to call it a deal," Bowie said. "There's an army store in Gusherton, T-Dub said, and I might be able to pick me up one there."

"We got us enough guns now to start us a little war all right," Chicamaw said.

Bowie squinted down the sights of the gun.

"I'll take a .30-30 myself," Chicamaw said. "I can cut capers with them little gentlemen. I know one thing though you can shoot a man through the pratt with one and it won't bring him down. I saw it happen. I did it. Me and a couple of boys were running out of Wichita and a carload of Laws jumped us. That old wreck we were in wouldn't do forty. So I just told these boys to let me out at that bridge and I'd stop them gentlemen.

"I got out and here they come. I cracked down and them Laws started flushing out of that car like it was going to explode. One of them weighed around two hundred pounds easy and I popped him while he was running across a field. He just kept going. He didn't drop until he got in the timber."

"He finally dropped though, uh?"

"He told me about it himself later. He come up to Alky. He knew who did it. Laughed about it. Thanked me for not killing him. I could have killed him all right."

"I don't care about being jumped myself," Bowie said. "I'd just as soon they stay away from me."

"The Laws never got me in a rank but twice in my life. The first time was in this State and I was just a snotty-nose punk. I'd been unlatching so many safes that I'll swear I begin to think it was on the level."

Bowie laughed.

"They got me all right in this State once. Four years I done down here on one of these prison farms, boy."

"Man, I hear they're tough. These prison farms?"

"You heard right." Chicamaw started taking the cap off the jar again. "It's not everybody that beats them farms."

Bowie placed the shotgun on the ground and picked up the .22 rifle. "I always wanted one of these little guns when I was a kid," he said.

"That time they got me in Florida," Chicamaw said, "and sent me back to Oklahoma was just my fault. That landlady I was going with and me just got a little reckless. I wish I knew where that woman was. She wasn't no spring chicken, but I'll take her to anything you could ever show me."

"How come them to ever get you down there?"

"I had a run-in with a Jew down there in a gambling place. I was drunk. I don't mind telling you. This Jew didn't want to play stud poker. He had to play draw or nothing. I called him a Christ-killer and a few other things and he said he wasn't going to take it. I told him he'd take it or else. He started out of that place and I decided I'd better frisk him. I caught him and throwed down on him. He didn't have a gun on though. I was smart enough to get out myself because you know they're hard on you in that State for showing a gun, but I got too smart and went back there the next Sunday and there was more Laws on me than I thought there was in Miami."

"A man sure ought to stay sober Out Here," Bowie said.

"What are you trying to do, preach to me?"

" 'Course not, Chicamaw."

Chicamaw took another drink.

"There I was down there in Florida with twelve thousand dollars and a woman that was the stuff. That woman just wouldn't leave that town with me. Where I wanted to go with that stake was Mexico. Hole up down there like I did after beating them here in this State. If she had just gone with me."

"How is that Mexico business?" Bowie said.

"I done a year down there. It's just like any place else though. If you haven't got no money it's no good."

"I don't imagine I'd like it down there. Some of them greasers might try to kick you around like fellows do them up here and I wouldn't stand for that."

"If you got the pesos to throw, you can get by down there. But you can't make no money down there and when my four hundred dollars went I had to get out."

"I don't savvy their lingo either and gettin' across that border would bother me."

"I never had to show a passport all the time I was down there and besides, you can buy one. Fifty pesos will get you anything you want in that Chili country. Them Laws down there are all hoss thieves."

"You savvy that lingo of theirs?"

"Seguro."

"Rattle me off something."

"En Mexico hay muchas señoritas con culas muy bonitas," Chicamaw said.

"You're another one. What did you say?"

"I said there was a lot of pretty gals in that country with prettier behinds."

"You look kind of like a Spick anyway. That's why you got by so good and then rattling off that stuff that way."

Chicamaw drank again. "I stayed on an old hacienda down there that was run by an old boy that used to be a thief himself. One of them revolution thieves. There was three more white guys on the place, all of us cooling off for something up here. I told you about Old Windy Hawkins."

"Who were the other two?"

"Banker from New Mexico and then the one we called Tangle Eyes. He was a deputy sheriff right out this line here close to El Paso."

"What did he do?"

"Killed a couple of farm boys. He just wasn't smart enough to make it. You remember when they had them big placards plastered up all over this state offering five thousand dollars reward for dead bank bandits?"

"Man, I was in Alky so long that I never knew nothing 'bout Out Here."

"They were doing it all right. This Tangle Eyes just planted a couple of old boys in front of a bank and let them have it. He just wasn't foxy enough."

"They don't still have that five-thousand dollar stuff in this State, do they?"

"Christ, no. The bankers had to stop it before they got everybody killed. The Laws were planting more people than there was bank robbers."

Spilled liquor wet the lines in Chicamaw's face, ran over his Adam's apple and down his neck. He put the bottle down and wiped his face on his shoulder. "You're in a good tough state, Boy. You didn't see that in the paper the other day. 'Bout five men dropping dead from heat prostration on that Bingham Prison farm. Heat, my hind foot. I know what killed them."

"I'm backing out of this just as soon as I get a little salted away," Bowie said. "I been intending to tell you boys."

Chicamaw lifted his left arm demonstratively and held his right hand up. "It's pretty tough when a man will take a hatchet and whack his arm off like this!"

"Goddamn, do they do that?"

"I saw four boys chop themselves in one week. One would whack the other and then that one would come down on the other one."

Bowie felt like his eyes were wired together.

"Them boys wanted to get off that farm pretty bad to do that, didn't they? And they just didn't want to get out of work. That's what they tell you in the Capital and them prison bosses say. There ain't a man in this State prison system that couldn't do the work they got. It's the way they work you and what they do to you."

"It don't sound good to me."

"Say it's cotton-picking time. All right. Maybe the cotton is five miles from the bunk house. Well, the building tenders rout you out at daybreak. Them are the little snitches that are doing a couple of years for busting a two-bit grocery and they give them saps and dirks and let them run over you. Anyway, they get you out and then the next thing you are going out in that field. Don't think you walk that five miles. You run it. Just as fast as that farm boss wants to lope his horse. And you do that back and forth three times a day. And if you fall out, it's spurs then and the bat or a barrel that night."

"That sure don't sound good to me."

"I've had them drop by me and they were as dead as door-nails. And one of them Bosses sitting up there on a horse with a double-barreled shotgun and he can't even read or write and saying: 'Old Thing, ain't you going to get up?' "

"Man," Bowie said.

"Yeah, they call you Old Thing. And if they get it in for you, you're not going to last. They'll say 'Reach down there, Old Thing, and pick up that piece of grass.' If you're not foxy and don't see that shotgun laying there in that grass, your pratt is mud because they want to go back and say you were trying to get to a gun."

"That sure don't sound worth a damn to me."

"I've heard that farm sound like a slaughter pen. Men squealing and begging like hogs. You don't last on that farm if you're any man at all. Unless you beat it. Then you either come off there a whining rat or still a man."

"I couldn't stand them doing me that way," Bowie said.

The dreggy contents of the fruit jar jostled as Chicamaw shook it around. He drank.

"No, I couldn't take that kind of stuff at all," Bowie said.

"Boy, I'm going up this road a long ways," Chicamaw said. "Plenty of people are going to know it. I ain't going to kill nobody. They're just going to kill themselves."

Bowie watched Chicamaw drain the jar. Now I know why he ain't got no toes on that right foot, he thought.

Chapter V

THEY had a furnished house in Zelton now all right, but they were as broke as bums. In MacMasters yesterday too, T-Dub had almost had a rumble and then he came over here and almost the same thing happened. While he was getting the coupe gassed up in MacMasters, a car of Laws drove right up alongside of him with guns sticking out all over. It just turned out that the Laws were looking for a couple of fellows that had made a Hole in the jail in the next town. Then in this town he draws up at a *Stop* sign and right there, looking him straight in the face, is a Law he has known since he was a kid. But that Law must not have recognized him.

"Naw, he didn't recognize you," Bowie said. He was lying on the cretonne-covered iron cot of the living-room. "You could have told it the way he acted right there."

"It's not anything to feel good about anyway," T-Dub said.

"We got a good Hole-up in this joint though," Bowie said.

"Seventy-five dollars is a lot of money for a dump like this,"

Chicamaw said. He sat slumped in the rocking-chair by the empty fireplace. His eyes were red-veined from yesterday's drinking.

"Things are always high in these oil towns," Bowie said. "This is a pretty good place when you take everything into consideration."

It was a five-room corner house, three blocks off Main Street. On the corner back of them was a machine shop, grinding day and night. Across the street was a fenced-in lot piled with drilling materials. On the opposite corner was a church tabernacle and across from it a two-story, barn-looking building that was a lodging house for oil-field workers. Moving cars kept sand and dust sifting through the window screens all the time and there was nearly always somebody walking on the street.

Right now, the three of them were waiting on Mattie, T-Dub's sister-in-law. She had gone up to the hamburger stand on the corner to get sandwiches and a milk bottle full of hot coffee. She was using her own money to feed them.

"I'm fed up on running around in these overalls like a damned Hoosier too," T-Dub said. "Now, Bowie, you look more like an oil-field guy in them khaki pants."

"I feel more like a hungry man than anything else," Bowie said.

"Quit crying, T-Dub," Chicamaw said. "I can get us some eatin' money from Old Windy over in MacMasters. I can give Mattie a note and it will be good for fifty bucks."

"Fifty dollars won't do us no good," T-Dub said. "It's going to take a couple of thousand. I'll be doggoned if I'm going to charge this bank here half-cocked. We need cars and a bunch of stuff."

"It takes money to make money all right," Bowie said.

"You know that little town we come through this morning," T-Dub said. "Morehead? The one that's got the bandstand in the middle of the street?"

"Yeah," Bowie said.

"There's a bank there that I robbed when I was a kid. Sawed me off a bar and crawled through and got fourteen dollars in pennies. I used to live in that little town."

Bowie grinned.

"What are you grinning about?" T-Dub said.

"You crawling through them bars and sacking up them pennies."

"I was a cutter then. I was getting me some bicycle money. It was the day after Christmas."

"What were you saying about Morehead?" Chicamaw said.

"I've got half a mind to charge that bank there. I just got a hunch. That bank will go for four or five thousand."

"And it might go for five hundred," Chicamaw said. "I swore one time that I never would fool with them two-bit banks again."

"Beggars can't be choosers. What do you think about it, Bowie?"

"Anything suits me. Whatever you-all say."

"Don't get me wrong, T-Dub," Chicamaw said. "If you boys want to charge a filling station I'm with you."

"When you hear me talking about banks you're not listening to me talk about my first one," T-Dub said.

The footsteps on the porch were like a man's and they listened. It was Mattie though. T-Dub went to the door and she came in. She was a big woman with hips like sacks of oats; the lines in her face were like the veins in dried corn-blades. She had a grease-slotted sack in her hand. "I thought they never were going to get these damned things cooked," she said.

"What's the matter, Mattie?" T-Dub said.

"Nothing." She put the sack on the fireplace shelf. Her toes knotted the leather of the loose black pumps. "I'm going to be checking it to you boys though in just a few minutes. I got to get back to my job."

"I sure hate to see you having to work as hard as you do, Mattie," T-Dub said. "I sure don't know what we would have done without you."

Bowie nodded.

"This is a cash on the barrel-head proposition to me," Mattie said. "I need some money."

"You're going to get it, girl," T-Dub said.

After Mattie left they started eating the hamburgers and T-Dub told them about her. She worked in a sandwich shop for a dollar a day. Showed you what a woman would do when she liked a man. His brother had been in two years and she had never missed a week without sending him money. One woman in ten thousand. He was going to see to it that she got hold of a good piece of money so she could buy a lawyer and spring that bud of his. He was going to stake them to a tourist camp too. Wasn't going to be any more need of that brother of his having to be a thief.

"This is not getting that Morehead business settled," Chicamaw said.

"I'm just waiting on you two," T-Dub said. "We can sack them gentlemen up right tomorrow. Rabbit that seven miles through MacMasters and then cool off at that wildcat. When it gets dark, come right back through that town, right on over here and tomorrow night I don't think we'll be setting here quite as busted."

"Call your shot, Bowie," Chicamaw said.

"I'm in," Bowie said. "I'm ready."

"It's settled," T-Dub said.

Chicamaw said some boys liked to rob a bank before it opened and others around ten-thirty in the morning and two o'clock, but any old time suited him.

T-Dub said that the bank in Morehead didn't have more than three or four working in it and they wouldn't have to count on handling more than the same number of customers if any at all. This bank here in this town though would be a man-sized job. Four men would be the best number to charge a bank like it. One man holding the car down outside and seeing to it that nobody came out; one holding down the lobby and keeping everybody in and the other two working the vault and cages and seeing to it that nobody kicked off any switches.

Bowie was lying on the cot again. I can rib myself up to do anything, he thought.

"Time you split money four ways though you haven't got enough to go around," Chicamaw said. "Three is plenty."

"I'm just telling you," T-Dub said. "These won't be the first banks I ever charged."

"I didn't mean anything," Chicamaw said.

"He didn't mean nothing," Bowie said. He sat up and

looked at the hearth, but the cigarette stubs on it were too short to snipe.

"The Outside man has the hardest job," T-Dub said. "Some of these ding-bats think the guy in the car has the snap. But he's the man that gets the rumbles first. The Inside is a snap. I never saw a banker yet that wouldn't fork over as soon as you throwed down on him. You can always figure that a man that's got sense enough to work in a bank has sense enough to act like a little man when you throw down on him."

"I've had to high-pressure a few of them," Chicamaw said.

"Only Hoosiers kill," T-Dub said.

"I don't believe you have to kill them," Bowie said.

"Them bankers will tell you to help yourself. It's insured. It's them billionaires up in New York that lose it. Them capitalists."

"I hope that Morehead bank will go for a nice piece," Bowie said.

"We'll get cigarette money anyway," Chicamaw said.

"Nossir, I've never robbed anybody in my life that couldn't afford to lose it," T-Dub said. "You couldn't hire me to rob a filling station or hamburger joint."

"I don't believe in that either," Bowie said. "Them boys in them filling stations don't make but two or three dollars a day and if they're robbed, they got to make it up. I'd just as soon beg as do that."

"I know one thing," Chicamaw said. "I'm going to be wearing me a fifteen-dollar Stetson and a sixty-dollar suit here pretty soon or it might be a black suit with some silk plush around me, but I'm sure not going to be wearing no overalls."

T-Dub went back to the kitchen and returned with three broom-straws. "The short man works the Outside," he said.

Bowie drew the short straw.

The others slept now. Bowie lay in the living-room's darkness, his elbow on the window-sill, his fingers scratching the screen. Five thousand, gentlemen, and I'm backing off.

The bed in the middle room creaked and Bowie listened. He smiled. That Indian, he thought.

Voices sounded in the yard outside and Bowie sat up, his hand extended toward the pump gun beside the cot. It was two men with dinner-pails cutting across the yard; going back to the machine-shop. Bowie lay back.

The next time I see that Little Soldier, he thought, I'll be driving a brand-new auto job and looking pretty good in a gray suit and red polka-dot tie and a flannel shirt with pearl buttons. I'll say to her: "I'm looking for that little girl that gave me a big lecture here a couple of years ago." She would look plenty surprised. He'd get a smile out of her though.

Who was that snoring? That old soldier. I got to be doing a little of that myself. One . . . two . . . three . . . four . . . five . . . six. . . .

Chapter VI

WITH its four blocks of filling stations and lunchrooms on the north side of the widened highway and then the intersecting, one-block main street, the town of Morehead had a business district shaped like a funnel. The funnel's mouth was corroded with low buildings of stone and wooden fronts. With Bowie driving the coupe, the three moved up it now toward the frame band-stand at the end of the block. It was ten-thirty o'clock.

The Farmers State Bank stood on the left corner near the band-stand. It was a one-story structure with two cement columns and barred windows. "There's our meat," Chicamaw said. T-Dub touched his forehead in a mock salute. "We'll be in to see you in a few minutes, gentlemen. Don't be impatient."

Bowie made a U turn around the band-stand and then drove, motor idling, past the bank, the Pressing Shop with its window display of bolted goods, the patent-medicine display of the Drug Store and then cut in to park diagonally in front of the Variety Store. In the Variety Store windows were women's underwear. To the left of it was a Meat Market and then a Grocery. Two farmer-looking men sat on cakes of salt lick in front of the Grocery. A youth in a red sweater with an M on it came out of the Pressing Shop and got in a truck.

T-Dub and then Chicamaw got out of the coupe. Chicamaw turned around, winked. "Ten dollars, the Sox beat the Giants this afternoon?" he said.

Bowie grinned. "Called."

The two moved up the street, the bagging seat of T-Dub's overalls wrinkling and Chicamaw's head bobbing on his long neck. They turned and entered the bank.

The bubble in Bowie's stomach broke and sprayed; he put the car in reverse, backed out and then moved down the street toward the highway.

The woman in the sedan ahead stopped parallel in front of the Post Office and Bowie turned out and passed her. That's the way I'll be parking in front of that bank in a minute, he thought. There were two men in broad-brimmed hats and boots standing on the corner in front of the Dry Goods Store. They did not look up. A dog, its ribs bulging, trotted across the street in front of Bowie toward the depot. There was a crated plow on the station's loading platform.

Bowie turned the second corner, passing the Lumber Yard. One block this way now and then another turn and he would be at the Bank again. That dream again last night? His Dad. He could hardly remember what his Dad looked like and yet he was as clear as himself in these dreams. Always the same thing happening. Him in that pool hall with his Dad and that other man getting ready to hit his Dad with the cue; him hollering and his Dad not hearing; him trying to shoot the gun and kill the man and the pistol breaking into pieces in his hand.

Bowie turned the last corner. Maybe that dream meant bad luck coming? If he counted to *thirteen* now with his fingers crossed, it would break the bad luck. *One . . . two . . . three . . . four. . . .*

Bowie stopped in front of the bank . . . *twelve . . . thirteen . . .* pulled the sawed-off shotgun up a little higher between his knees. Come on, Pals. Come on, you Old Soldier. Come on, you Indian. We got tall tracks to make. . . .

There were two more men standing now in front of the Grocery, one smoking a pipe with a curved stem. The pipe-smoker turned and looked up the street toward the Bank. All right, Square-John, that's a good way to get your eyes full and get in trouble. The man turned back.

T-Dub came out of the bank, the front of his overalls bulging! Chicamaw following, two cigar-boxes under his left arm. Bowie looked up and down the street, across to the other side. Nobody big-eyeing or smelling anything yet.

They got in the car and Bowie gunned the motor; Chicamaw slammed the door. The two men sitting on the salt cakes stood up and the others turned and looked.

Bowie swerved onto the highway, the left wheels groaning; the approaching oil truck stopped with a jerk. The driver shouted. Bowie pressed the accelerator harder; the *City Limits* dropped behind. The boy driving a cow with a stick turned his head and watched them go by.

"Anything behind us yet?" Bowie said.

"Naw," Chicamaw said. "Them guys are not going to get out of that Vault for a half-hour. They don't know the Civil War is over yet back there in that town."

T-Dub looked back. "Clear as a whistle."

"You-all do any good?" Bowie said.

"I think so," T-Dub said. He pulled a revolver from inside his overalls. "I picked me up a brand new Colt .45 here anyway. I'll will you that pearl-handled job, Bowie. Did you see me get it out of that till, Chicamaw?"

"Yeah, I saw you."

"Sacked up something else though, didn't you?" Bowie said.

"It went for three or four thousand, I think," T-Dub said.

Chicamaw turned back. "Naw, they don't know yet what it's all about back there."

A car zoomed over the rise ahead, hurtled toward them. It had a California license.

"Four thousand isn't bad, is it?" Bowie said.

"I don't say we got that much," T-Dub said.

"Man, you didn't expect us to stop and count it before we come out of there, did you?" Chicamaw said.

Bowie laughed.

The skyline of Zelton showed now: the fourteen-story hotel, the standpipe, the college buildings on the hill. "We're going to be holed up before they get out of that vault," T-Dub said. "Makes me half decide to go on to the house, but I want to save that place. We'll just go on to that wildcat."

Bowie turned the coupe off the highway and onto a dirt road this side of Zelton. They passed the Filteration Plant, the City Mule Barns, and then Bowie turned back East and presently they were on a paved, residential street. They crossed the town and cut back onto the highway by the Airport.

As they neared the turn-in to the old oil derrick, a car ahead of them approached and Bowie slowed. It was a big sedan with a negro driving and a man in the back seat smoking a cigar. After it was out of sight, Bowie turned the coupe onto the derrick road.

Chicamaw climbed the ladder of the derrick and started a lookout toward the highway. Bowie spread the big cotton-picking sack on the ground and T-Dub dumped the contents of the small canvas bag on it. The pile of currency, in rubber-banded packs of hundreds and twenties and tens and fives and ones, was as big as the crown of a cowboy Stetson. The two cigar boxes were spilling silver.

Chicamaw whistled and they looked up. "What's that stuff you boys are playing with down there?" he said.

"For Christ's sake," T-Dub said.

"Nose-wipin' paper, you damned Indian," Bowie said. "And there's ten bucks of it you'll never see. Them Giants have the Sox in a hole by now."

"Another ten says you're a liar."

"Accepted."

"Voices carry out here," T-Dub said. "You guys do your talking after while."

"Let's pipe down, Chicamaw," Bowie said.

T-Dub took four hundred and twenty-five dollars from the pile and snapped a rubber band around it. This represented the amount he had started out with and he put it in his shirt pocket. Bowie took a ten-dollar bill. "I'll take out six for Chicamaw," he said. "That's what he had."

Three piles of currency grew as T-Dub dealt out the bills like playing cards. Finally, it was divided and there was one thousand and twenty-five dollars apiece. The silver, it was decided, would just be left in the boxes and they would use it for general expenses like gasoline and beer and cigarettes. There were three or four hundred dollars of it.

Chicamaw descended the ladder and joined them.

"I just started telling Bowie here about that old banker back there," T-Dub said. "That old boy like to have never got it in his head that it was a stick-up."

"Never did put up his hands, did he?" Chicamaw said.

T-Dub laughed. "He never did. He was sitting at a desk there, Bowie, when we went in, just pecking away at an old Oliver typewriter and I had to almost kick the chair out from under him. 'Whatthehell?' he says. 'Whatdoyouthinkthisis?' I had to yank him up and knee him back into the Vault. I think we had the place half sacked before he ever caught on."

"All them others acted like little men," Chicamaw said. "They couldn't get in that Vault quick enough."

"No customers?" Bowie said.

"One," T-Dub said. "Didn't you take a sack off him, Chicamaw?"

"Yeah," said Chicamaw. "I got thirty or forty dollars here I think." He pulled a small money sack out of his hip pocket. "Naw, I don't have no kick coming about that little Bank, but we could have sacked up that Bank in Zelton just as easy. And had ten or twelve apiece. Isn't that right, T-Dub?"

"We'll get to them gentlemen," T-Dub said.

Long ranges of clouds, thick as beaten egg-whites, moved in the afternoon sky. Through the rifts, the dome was as clear as bluing water. The only sounds were the thrumming cars over on the highway and they would stop and listen to them pass. When they talked now, it was in quiet voices.

As soon as it got dark, it was decided, they would return to Zelton and then Bowie could take the coupe out to the edge of the town and burn it. Chicamaw would get a bus and go to El Paso and come back in a couple of days with two fast, light cars and some extra license plates. T-Dub would go over to MacMasters, get Mattie to rent a car and they would get at least two more houses. One in Gusherton and one in Clear Waters.

"We ought to have a sure-enough set-up here in two or three more days," Bowie said.

"Might be that kid sister of Mattie's will go along with me

and her to get them houses," T-Dub said. "You know, boys, I hadn't seen that little old girl since she was in diapers. Cute as a bug now. I want you two to meet her."

"What I'd like to have right now is something to eat," Chicamaw said. "You guys realize we haven't eaten nothing since them hamburgers last night."

"Funny, I'm not hungry," Bowie said. "What I could take on is a good tailor-made cigarette."

"I remember the last time I was cooling off in the country like this we had us a radio and we were gettin' a ball game," T-Dub said. "Chicamaw, maybe you'd better get radios put on them cars. Sure help to pass away the time when you're out like this."

Chapter VII

BUNDLE-LADEN Zelton people jostled and tripped and cut around Bowie in this Saturday-night shopping spree. He was downtown tonight just to stay away from that furnished house. Three nights now he had stayed in it alone and it was getting on his nerves. He had stayed in all morning and afternoon thinking that surely the boys would show up today, but Chicamaw was still somewhere out toward El Paso and T-Dub was rustling houses.

Tonight, Bowie had planned on going to a picture show, but there was nothing on at the two theaters except shoot-em-up cowboy stuff. Rain on that kind of show, he thought.

In front of the Drug Store with the window display of kodaks and photographs he paused now. There was a picture of a young couple with a baby; a hunter standing beside a car on the running board of which was an antlered deer; a bathing-suit girl in a canoe. Bowie peered closer. The gun in the hunter's hand was a .415 Winchester and the deer had six points.

Bowie went on. That Keechie Mobley would make a good picture, I'll bet.

Shaded lights behind the plate glass flushed the colors of

the women's things; the silk blouses, dresses, hose, under-things. Now in a little town like she had to live in, Keechie never saw a bunch of pretty things like this.

In the panel mirror of the Department Store entryway, Bowie looked at his reflection: the iron-gray suit, the broad-brimmed hat, the white handkerchief in his breast pocket. His right hip pocket bulged a little with the .38 T-Dub had given him. Just as soon as I get around to it, I'm going to get a holster and strap and wear it under my arm. Then I won't notice it any more than my hat. I look pretty good though. What was it old T-Dub said about him: "That Bowie looks more like a Law than he does a thief." And Chicamaw: "Like a country boy come to town." That Indian.

Bowie turned and went back up the street, past the 5 & 10, J. C. Penny's, and on the corner, The Guaranty State Bank. He turned it and then was on Front Street, a dim-lighted thoroughfare of small cafés and dollar-hotels. On the other side of the street was the Texas & Pacific Railroad lawn with its mulberry trees, the depot and the freight offices and plat-forms.

A negro in a porter's cap and white jacket sat on a stool in front of the hotel doorway. On the white globe above his head were the lighted letters: *Okeh Rooms.*

"Looking for a nice lady friend tonight, Boss?" the porter said.

"Hell no, you black bastard," Bowie said.

In front of the *New York Café*, on the corner, a policeman stood talking to a bareheaded man who had one foot on the bumper of an automobile at the curb. Bowie walked past them. You got the advantage of Laws all right. You can tell them, but they can't tell you. And the detectives and deputy sheriffs out here might just as well have uniforms, you can tell them so easy. All of them in cowboy boots and white hats and black suits and shoe-string ties. And say that flatfoot back there recognized him when he went past? All right, all that Law had was a pistol. And didn't he have one on too? One thing though, he had to get out in the country pretty soon and practise up with this .38. Get used to it.

Bowie turned toward the railroad lawn, going to the fur-nished house.

There were two new-looking automobiles in the driveway of the house and Bowie checked the impulse to break into a lope. That Indian is back just as sure as the dickens, he thought. The cars were Ford V-8's. One a black job with a trunk and the other was gun-metal colored, both sedans.

It was T-Dub who let Bowie in. He had on a new blue-serge suit and tan shoes.

"Chicamaw come in?" Bowie said.

T-Dub thumbed toward the sound of rushing water in the bathroom. "Taking a bath and gettin' drunk as a Lord. I think he bought up all the tequilla in Juarez."

"I begin to think you two had fell in somewhere," Bowie said. "How long you been here?"

"I got here a little after dark and he was here then." T-Dub went over and lay down on the cot. There was a pile of scattered newspapers beside it.

"I guess you read about Morehead," Bowie said. "Wasn't that a joke? Got one number right in that license. *Three*. And calling it a green coupe and the only thing green about that old Chevvy was the stripe around it."

"Them newspapers never get nothing right. You been casing this bank here any?"

"Every morning since you-all been gone. I went down yesterday morning before daybreak and I been inside of it three times. That Vault kicks off either at nine or maybe before because it's open when the doors open."

"Who goes in first?"

"Nigger. The porter. Around six o'clock. It's a bird's-nest on the ground to go in with him. And the nearest Law is up at the Depot right at that time watching that passenger come in."

"Don't sound half bad."

"How you been doing, T-Dub?"

"We got them houses all right. She went with us on both trips. Lula. That's Mattie's kid sister. I told you about her though."

"Gusherton and Clear Waters?"

"Yep. That Clear Waters place looks like a millionaire's dump. Lula sure liked it."

"Them cars out there look like old Chicamaw has been

doing his stuff. That was a job to tow that gun-metal job all the way in here."

T-Dub sat up. "You know I'd just as soon charge this bank here Monday as not. What do you say?"

"Tomorrow would suit me if it wasn't Sunday."

"I'm going to see the girls tomorrow," T-Dub said.

Chicamaw came out of the bathroom and into the living-room. He had on silk shorts and undershirt and his hair dripped water. The big veins of his biceps and forearms looked like pale earthworms.

"If it's not the old Country Boy himself?" he said.

"Hi, Chicamaw."

"Been teaching Sunday-school over in that tabernacle while we were gone?"

"I been asking for a job down at this nice little bank they got in this town."

"Old Bowie," Chicamaw said. "Believe anything anybody tells him." He looked at T-Dub and winked.

"Anybody except you," Bowie said.

Chicamaw laughed and his bare feet slapped the floor back toward the bedroom.

T-Dub picked up the newspaper again and Bowie went over and sat down in the rocker and lit a cigarette.

The flung newspaper rattled on the pile. "Every time I pick up a paper I see that damned little Squirt's name," T-Dub said. "If I ever run across him you going to see a guy get the damnedest behind-kicking a man ever got."

"Who's that, T-Dub?"

"Newspaper guy. He gave me the dirty end of the stick one time. I tried to make a Hole in this prison in this State one time and it went haywire and this Squirt comes to me and wants me to tell him all about it so he can write a big story for the magazine. Couple of the boys had gotten killed and I was shot right through the fleshy part here of my hip and it was all a mess. Everybody knew all about it anyway and this Squirt said if I would tell him the straight of it he would get it printed and split the money with me. I didn't even have cigarette money so I told him. You should have seen the way it come out in that magazine. I was the Big Shot, see. And I sent them two boys over that got killed first because I figured the guards would use up all their ammunition and then me and the other boy still down at the bottom of the ladder would have a clear way. Anybody knows that the Chair boys get the first break and that's why they went over first. Hell, I didn't go on up because the damned ladder had broke. One of them joint ladders you know. Then that Squirt getting it put in the magazine like that."

"Don't guess he ever sent you any money?"

T-Dub looked up and sneered.

Chicamaw came back in with a bottle of tequilla in his hand. He had on brown tweed trousers with pleats, a blue shirt and yellow tie. He offered the bottle and Bowie shook his head.

"For Christ's sake, come on and be human," he said.

Bowie took a drink.

"I ran into a pooloo in a sandwich stand close to Pecos that we knew up in Alky," Chicamaw said. "You guys remember that kid we called Satchel Pratt?"

Bowie and T-Dub nodded.

"He knew me right off and crawled all over that car and got to telling me how he knew where there was a good piece of money."

"Tin safe somewhere with thirty dollars in it," T-Dub said.

"I played him along. Told him I'd shove on and be back to the number he gave me right after dark and we would go and get together on that job he had."

"I remember that kid," Bowie said. "He played a banjo pretty good."

"I brought you something, boy, from the city," Chicamaw said. "I run into some good Colt .45's out there and you can throw that .38 job of yours away."

"Man, I'm glad to hear that."

"You got to promise me that you won't sleep with it under your pillow though."

"Now what's the joke?" Bowie said.

Chicamaw looked at T-Dub and winked. "All right," he said and pointed his finger at Bowie. "I'll bet that's the way you been sleeping at nights?"

"Yes."

Chicamaw looked at T-Dub and then back at Bowie. "That's just what I thought. Look here, man. Always sleep with your gun under the cover by your side. Then if anybody walks in on you, you got as much of a throw-down on them as they got on you. Just let 'em have it. But you sure can't do any reaching up and behind you . . . like *this*."

"I never thought of that before," Bowie said. "I'm sure glad you told me, Chicamaw."

T-Dub stood up. "What do you say we start talking about this bank here? Bowie is ready to go Monday, Chicamaw."

"You don't have to ask me if I'm ready. I'm always ready." He lifted the bottle and there was a gurgling sound.

"Boys, it's going to be my thirtieth," T-Dub said.

Chapter VIII

LAST night, T-Dub had drawn the short straw, but because he knew more about the Inside of a bank, it was decided Chicamaw would drive the black V-8 and Bowie would go Inside with T-Dub. They had gotten out of bed at four o'clock this morning, driven out to the Derrick Hole and left the gun-metal sedan. Now it was six o'clock and they sat parked in front of the Sears, Roebuck Company store next to the Guaranty State Bank. The empty street looked as wide as a river.

"If Bowie and me are not out of there by nine o'clock," T-Dub said, "you better be coming in after us, Chicamaw."

Chicamaw lifted his head in a laughing gesture.

Somewhere the sound of a street-sweeping machine whirred and threshed. Away down the street, in front of the Café, a man came out and got in a car. The slamming door echoed in the canyon of buildings. The car vanished.

"Here it comes, Boys," Bowie said. He pointed up the street. A negro in a gray rope sweater was approaching. Bowie and T-Dub got out of the car and stood beside it.

The negro was a middle-aged man with sideburns like steel wool. He stood there at the bank door, selecting a key on the ring. He inserted the key and grasped the knob.

"We're going in with you, Shine," T-Dub said. Bowie

pressed the gun's barrel firmly against the rope sweater and they went into the bank's clean, early-morning gloom. Bowie squatted down and looked under the slit of the drawn blind. Chicamaw was driving off.

The negro breathed like he had been running, his wrists sticking rigidly out of the frayed sweater cuffs. "I doesn't quite understand this," he said.

"Don't bother yourself, Shine," T-Dub said. "You're liable to wake up with somebody patting you in the face with a spade if you do."

Bowie started tying the negro's thumbs behind him with copper wire. "Mistah, I been porterin' heah fawh twenty yeahs. You can ask anybody in Zelton. Everybody heah knows old Ted. Right heah in this bank fawh twenty yeahs. When they had the old building. Yassah, I been . . ."

"That's enough, Shine," T-Dub said. "Now you'd like to be able to go to church again next Sunday, wouldn't you?"

"Yassah."

"Then you just answer the questions I'm going to ask you."

"Yassah. I never lied to nobody in mah life. You can ask anybody in Zelton about me."

The clock over the front door indicated 6:30. On both sides of the gray tile floor at the front of the bank were brown railings and inside of these were clean desks with lettered stands: *President . . . Vice-President . . . Vice-President. . . .* The bronze cages fenced the passageway of glass-topped tables back to the Vault. It was a big, broad door of aluminum and black colors. To the right was a passageway that led to the side-entrance door.

"What time does that big vault back there unlatch, Shine?" T-Dub said.

"Cap'n, that something I doesn't know about. Some of the big bosses don't even know that. Mistah Berger knows about it."

"What time does he come down?"

"He's the fust one. Li'l' before eight."

Bowie moved around. Through the slits of the Venetian blind at the side-entrance door he saw the closed, steel doors of the freight depot. An oil truck went past.

The clock clicked: 7:00.

More automobiles were sounding on the streets outside now. A switch engine whistled and then the intersection railroad signal began to dong. The exhaust of a bus popped, fluttered. Bowie read the hand-lettered football schedule on the wire stand by the front door.

The knob of the front door turned and the man smelling of hair tonic and shaving lotion came in. He was short and had a belly as round as the sides of a mare in foal.

"Mister Berger?" T-Dub said. He had an open pocket knife in his left hand.

The man stood there, his left hand extended in a paralyzed, door-closing movement. His head went up and down.

"Mister Berger, this is a stick-up, and if you want to stay a healthy man, and I think you do, you'll just co-operate."

"I see," Mister Berger said.

It was *7:15*.

The heavy doors of the freight depot creaked and groaned in opening. Box-cars bumped in the railroad yards. Automobile horns sounded.

7:45.

Through the blind slots of the side door, Bowie saw the black flannel coat, the silk-clad ankles of a woman. He turned and T-Dub, standing in front of the Vault with Mister Berger and Shine, nodded. Bowie opened the door.

The woman gasped like she had been pricked with a pin and Bowie put his hand over her mouth. She became limp in his arms. "Take it easy now, Lady," Bowie said. "Nobody is going to hurt you."

"Be calm, Miss Biggerstaff," Mister Berger said, "these men are not desperadoes."

"I never kill anybody," T-Dub said, "if they just do what I tell them to."

8:30.

Bowie peered through the blind slots. The black V-8 was parked there now, Chicamaw's head down over a spread newspaper on the steering wheel. A match worked in his mouth. That Indian.

Mister Berger and T-Dub were inside the Vault now. A cage door clicked and rattled. Bowie's toes squirmed in his shoes. Sack it, T-Dub. Dump it in. Just a minute, Chicamaw. . . .

Mister Berger came out; then T-Dub with the bulging laundry sack slung across his back.

"Ready?" T-Dub said.

"Ready," Bowie said.

"We're going to take you folks with us," T-Dub said. "There's a Ford just out that door there and you go out there and get in it and don't let me see any of you looking at anybody 'cause if you do you're liable to get somebody killed."

There were two men in striped overalls working on the loading platform across the street, but they did not stop. Mister Berger and Miss Biggerstaff and Shine got in the back; then Bowie. He told Shine to lay on the floor. T-Dub got in front with Chicamaw.

They moved off. The young fellow parking the coupe stared. He had on a tan suit and horn-rimmed glasses.

T-Dub turned around. "You know him?"

"One of the boys in the bank," Mister Berger said.

The speed indicator rose: past the Candy Factory . . . Produce Company . . . Cotton Compress . . . Nigger Town. . . . A farmer, high up on the cotton wagon, saluted. Chicamaw waved back.

They crossed the railroad tracks and then sped up the straight, dirt road toward the picket of telephone poles that marked the highway.

Miss Biggerstaff looked at Bowie. "What are you going to do with us?"

"Don't worry, Lady."

"I have done everything in the world I could, Men," Mister Berger said.

T-Dub turned around. "You folks just sit steady now. You have done all right and everything is okeh now."

Bowie could see the grinning lines on Chicamaw's cheek. He smiled too. The speedometer needle vibrated on *80*. Miss Biggerstaff shivered as if she were cold.

Holding to the top rung of the derrick ladder, Bowie saw the car leave the highway, its aluminum glittering like signal mirrors, and come onto this road. He whistled and below, T-Dub and Chicamaw picked up the corners of the spread cotton-picking sack with its piles of currency.

But the car was only turning around. Bowie whistled again and shook his head violently. The canvas was spread again.

Over in the black sedan, Mister Berger, Miss Biggerstaff and Shine sat, the feet of the men bound in copper wire. For three hours now, T-Dub had been dealing the bills and still he was wetting his fingers and going on. That's the prettiest sight I ever saw, Bowie thought. Bar none. He shifted his arm through the rung and grasped his belt. Bar none.

Chicamaw relieved Bowie on the lookout.

T-Dub grinned as Bowie approached. "Nossir, Bowie, that wasn't my first bank, but I never saw one go sweeter."

"I never saw a prettier sight then looking down here from up there," Bowie said.

Over in the black car, the glass rattled and Bowie saw Miss Biggerstaff rapping. "Go see what they want," T-Dub said.

Bowie came back. "It's the Lady. I think she wants to go to the bathroom. I think that's what she wants."

"She won't rabbit. Let her out."

"That Berger over there told me we got ten thousand dollars in securities here that's not worth anything to us and mean a lot to him."

"He's a damned liar. There's sixty thousand dollars' worth here, but he can have them back. They're no good to us."

At last the money was counted and divided. There was twenty-two thousand six hundred and seventy-five dollars apiece.

In the dusk, Chicamaw and Bowie tied Mister Berger and Shine to mesquites. Then Chicamaw went on up the road, out of sight, and presently they heard the motor of the gun-metal firing. It moved toward the hills and the Gusherton Highway.

Bowie drove the black car and T-Dub sat in the back with Miss Biggerstaff. "We're just going to take you up here a couple of miles, Lady," T-Dub said, "and then you can walk back and untie that gentleman friend of yours."

On the Gusherton Highway, Bowie and T-Dub got in the gun-metal with Chicamaw and left the flaming black car behind.

The house in the resort town of Clear Waters was an eight-room Spanish stucco with a patio, a three-car garage and big, sparrow-filled poplar trees in the parkways. It was a corner place and across from it was a four-story apartment house.

Bowie sat in the living-room now, soaking in its richness. There was a radio and a secretary and brocaded coverings on the divan and chairs. The lights on the rough plaster of the walls were shaped like candlesticks. Confession and Movie magazines littered the floor and the ashtrays were full of cigarette butts stained with lipstick. From the kitchen, where Mattie and Lula and T-Dub were cooking, came the smell of ham and eggs.

Chicamaw came in, his hair plastered and smelling of perfumed oil and indicated the room with a roll of his head. "Pretty good for some old boys that didn't have a pot or a window to throw it out three weeks ago, eh, Big Boy?"

"Pretty nice," Bowie said.

"You tied up with some fast company, didn't you, Boy?"

"I'll say."

Lula came in with T-Dub following. She was tall and had on a cotton house-dress and blue anklets. Her shaved legs had scratches on them and there was the tattoo of a red heart on the back of her left hand.

"Don't you think Lula and me would make a team," T-Dub said. They sat on the divan and T-Dub put his arm around her waist and began fingering the cloth over her stomach. "Last time I saw this little outfit she was just about up to my knees and now look at her."

"He's nuts," Lula said.

"I think you got him going, Lula," Bowie said.

Lula slapped T-Dub's hand away and reached in his coat pocket and brought out a package of cigarettes. She extended them toward Bowie and then Chicamaw. They shook their heads.

T-Dub held a match for her. "Yessir, this little girl is going to put a tattoo on her for me pretty soon." He winked at Bowie and then Chicamaw. "And it ain't going to be on her hand."

The smoke gushed from Lula's nostrils and she flecked the cigarette toward the ashtray. "I wouldn't be so sure about that now, Mister," she said. "And if I'm going up to that drug store before our midnight supper, you better be giving me a few nickels and let me get started."

Mattie came in. She had a dish towel tied over the black silk dress like an apron. "You boys come and get it. Was that Lula leaving, T-Dub?"

"We ought to wait until she gets back 'fore we eat," T-Dub said.

"Come on," Mattie said.

Their knives and forks scraped and slashed the eggs and ham. "I don't wonder that bud of mine isn't working his head off to get out with cooking like this, Mattie," T-Dub said.

"It's not cooking that's going to get him out," Mattie said.

Lula thrust the newspaper toward T-Dub. "It's all over the front page," she said. "All over it."

T-Dub pushed plates aside and spread the newspaper, and Chicamaw and Bowie bent over him.

ZELTON, Sept. 28—In one of the boldest bank hold-ups in West Texas history, three armed bandits this morning robbed the Guaranty State Bank here, kidnaped A. T. Berger, vice-president, his secretary, Miss Alma Biggerstaff, and escaped with what bank officials estimated at more than $100,000 in cash and securities.

Berger and Miss Biggerstaff with Ted Phillips, negro bank porter, also kidnaped by the trio, were picked up by passing motorists, 21 miles east of here at 8 o'clock tonight. Miss Biggerstaff was in a hysterical condition from the day of terror and imprisonment.

Working with the precision of master criminals, the robbers entered the bank before the doors opened this morning. Arriving bank employees, unable to get into the bank at 8 o'clock, sounded the alarm. William Pleasant, bank bookkeeper, saw a black, crowded sedan leave the bank's side entrance as he was getting ready to park, but did not realize its full significance until later.

Today's holdup followed within less than a week the $3,000 robbery of the Farmers State Bank at Morehead, adjoining community. Local authorities believe both crimes were committed by the same band.

One of the bandits, Police Chief Robert Blakely announced here tonight, has been positively identified as an escaped Oklahoma convict.

"Oh, oh," T-Dub said. "They got me identified."

"I don't care which one they got identified," Chicamaw

said, "they ain't going to have to guess long to know who was with you."

The food in Bowie's stomach felt like it was expanding.

A posse of more than two hundred police officers and citizens combed the country around here throughout the day in a fruitless search. At a called meeting this morning of the Chamber of Commerce, directors authorized the posting of a $100 reward for the capture, dead or alive, of any member of the gang.

"Now what did we do, boys?" Chicamaw said.

L. E. Sellers, a farmer living four miles east of town, reported that a loaded car passed him shortly after 8 o'clock this morning, traveling East at a high rate of speed.

The bandits were described as being well-dressed men around 30 years of age.

"If it had not been for the bravery of Mr. Berger," Miss Biggerstaff declared, "I am afraid we would not be alive to tell our stories. They threatened our lives almost every minute. Mister Berger talked to them coolly."

The two bank robberies in this vicinity this past week mark the first time in four years that a bank has been robbed in this section. The last one was at Stocton, 40 miles southwest of here, by the famous Trawler gang. Trawler was hanged by an enraged mob at Stocton last December after he killed a jailer in a desperate attempt to escape.

T-Dub pushed the newspaper aside. "Well, boys, that's the situation."

"They sure did put it all over the front page, didn't they?" Lula said.

"The next time, Sweetheart," T-Dub said, "you bring us some good news."

"Christ, let's finish eating," Chicamaw said.

Bowie lay on the ivory-inlaid bed, under the smooth sheet and silken comfort, in the feminine, mirror-paneled room where the perfume of powders and toilet waters still lingered. That blows me up, he thought. Yessir, that sure blows me up on going back to Alky.

Up in the living-room, Lula giggled and then there was T-Dub's rumbling laugh. The Mexican orchestra of the

Border radio station was playing *La Golondrina*, a background of guitars strumming plaintively.

Bowie moved and the .45 was cold against his naked thigh. Yessir, that sure blows me up. But what are you gripin' about, Man? You got twenty-two thousand dollars right under this bed.

Chapter IX

ON the afternoon of their third day in the Clear Waters Stucco, Chicamaw became staggering drunk and bumped around the house, his shirt tail hanging, and demanding who in the hell had hid his tequilla. Mattie and Lula threatened to leave and T-Dub became white-faced. Bowie finally got Chicamaw into the back bedroom. "Come on now, Chicamaw," he said, "and sleep a while. It'll be good for you."

"I'm not sleepy," Chicamaw said. "I'm drunk. I don't mind telling you I'm drunk. They ain't but two things I like to do and that's love and drink and there ain't enough women here to go around so I'm drinking. What do you think I left Alky for?"

"Don't talk so loud, Chicamaw."

"What do you think I left Alky for? To drink chicory coffee and look at art magazines?"

"Take it easy now, Pal."

"All right, old boy, old boy, old boy."

"You're scaring them girls."

"Let old Battle Axe leave."

"Snap out of it, Chicamaw."

"Old Country Boy is telling me what to do. You're just a big old farm boy, Bowie, but goddamit, you got something and I don't mind telling you, I can't figure it out. Let's you and me shell out of this place, Bowie. Go up to Oklahoma. Let's get us a bus and go to Dallas and get us a Packard and throw us a good one. You're going to Oklahoma with me, aren't you, Pal?"

"We ought to cool off here a few more days. There's still some heat out there."

"You going to Oklahoma with me, aren't you, Pal?"

"We'll talk about that later. What you want to do now is get yourself some sleep. You got to snap out of it, man. That real estate man was in here this morning taking an inventory and he big-eyed around plenty and that man that come up to the front door and said he was a census taker might just be nosying. There might be a little war around this place before you know it."

"You going to Oklahoma with me, aren't you, Pal?"

"We'll talk about that after you sleep a while. That and going to Mexico."

"Come on now, Bowie, wouldn't you like to go up to Oklahoma and see that little cousin of mine?"

"She's not interested in seeing me."

"That home town of mine is just forty miles from there and I want to see my folks, Bowie. I got to see them."

"I'd like to see Dee get three or four hundred dollars."

Chicamaw compressed his lips and closed his eyes and there was a whistling in his nostrils as he breathed. Bowie watched him for a little while and then bent down to unlace his shoe. Chicamaw's eyes opened. "You know why I want to go to Oklahoma?"

"Sure, boy. See your Old Man and Old Lady. And you want me to go along and stand on the corner with that pump gun of mine and see to it that nobody comes nosying around."

"That ain't all."

"You want to say hello to your folks."

"My folks know what I want and I got to take them the money to do it with. Them folks of mine haven't got a pot or a window to throw it out and I got to get them some money. Bowie, they ain't going to catch me floating around in no tank in them doctor schools if they ever get me. That's what they do to you if you can't pay the undertaker. They'll throw you in one of them tanks and carve on you."

"You must be drunk, boy, to talk that way."

"I want to be planted right. Goddamit, I'll give them every cent of it and I want to be planted right."

"I'll go get you a cold towel."

"Don't you leave me, boy."

T-Dub came in. His shaven face had a pink flush now and his hair was as white and soft as a baby's brush from the vinegar washing Lula had given it. He touched his forehead in a salute. "Feeling better, Chicamaw?"

"Who hid that tequilla, T-Dub?"

"Man, I don't know where it is."

"Tell that Battle Axe to rout it up."

"You're drunk, man, but you better start quieting down," T-Dub said.

"Old Foxy T-Dub," Chicamaw said. "Old Foxy."

Mattie came in, holding out a magazine. "Maybe this will sober him up some," she said.

It was a True Detective magazine and on the opened page were all their pictures: *Oklahoma Fugitives. $100 Reward.*

Bowie brushed it back. "He don't care about seeing that thing. Go burn that damned thing up."

T-Dub and Mattie left.

"Bowie, you going to Oklahoma with me?"

"If you'll go to sleep now I'll go. I don't mean that, boy. I'll go with you anyway."

"Then I'll go to Mexico with you, Bowie."

"That sure suits me."

Bowie lowered himself to the edge of the bed and after a little while, Chicamaw slept.

Bowie went up to the living-room and there were Mattie and Lula standing at the door, dressed up and bags around them. T-Dub was pale again. "The girls are going down to the Penitentiary to see my bud," he said. "I'm going to take them to the depot."

Bowie nodded.

"Your friend decided to quiet down?" Mattie said. The short fur jacket looked like she had another bag under it.

"He's all right," Bowie said.

"I was telling them that there's not a finer boy when he's sober," T-Dub said.

"He's all right," Bowie said.

"I hope we see you again soon, Bowie," Lula said. There was lipstick salve on her chin.

"Goodbye," Bowie said.

After T-Dub and the girls left, Bowie went back to the bedroom and looked at Chicamaw. He was snoring and had his mouth open. It was growing dark and Bowie stepped over and raised the blind a little. Then he sat down on the bench in front of the vanity.

I'll go on up there with him, he thought. There's nothing else for me to do and there's gettin' to be too many women around this joint. I'm ready to go to Mexico right now myself. If these boys want to rob that bank at Gusherton I'll help them, but I'm ready to clear out of this myself.

The breathing sounds in Chicamaw's throat sounded like air escaping from a flabby tire.

Mexico? Deer and wild turkey and cougars and bears even. A .414 Winchester would be the best for deer. A bear? Now that's something I'll have to do some figuring on when I get down there. Christ. If I was in Mexico with a .22 I would be satisfied. And just rabbits to hunt. Let me down there, man, and I'll run them rabbits down on foot.

The front door sounded and Bowie went up to the living-room. It was T-Dub. He went over and sat down on the divan and began flecking at bits of cigarette ash on the blue serge of his broad thighs. "I hated to see that little girl go," he said.

"You'll see her again," Bowie said.

"That Chicamaw back there has got it down all wrong," T-Dub said. "You can't make women a money-on-the-barrel-head proposition. Love 'em and leave 'em. It don't work when you meet somebody decent. He's nuts though."

"This business is no good for a girl," Bowie said. "That's what he means."

"Where would we have been if it hadn't been for Mattie?"

"I know it. It's a proposition."

T-Dub said that if Bowie and Chicamaw went to Oklahoma, he might go down to Houston and try and get Lula to go off with him on a little trip to Galveston or New Orleans. Mattie would come back and keep their houses held down. He had given her two thousand dollars to buy a car and have something to run around on.

Bowie said he and Chicamaw would come in and do their part on that two thousand.

In the distance, a siren sounded and they looked at each

other and listened. The sound grew nearer and then they heard the bells of the fire engine clanging and they relaxed.

"But I been thinking, Bowie, and you're not going to get three together like us again nor a set-up like we got now. In a couple of months if we just stay foxy we can have fifty thousand apiece and then will be the time to back off for keeps."

"If we're going to charge that bank at Gusherton I'm in favor of doing it and gettin' it over with."

T-Dub shook his head. "These banks out here are looking for trouble now. Look at what happened to those two kids day before yesterday. Trying to work right in our heat."

"You kill somebody though like they did and your heat really gets hot."

"They were Hoosiers."

Bowie began cleaning his finger-nails with a split match.

"What I want to do," T-Dub said, "is get me about fifty thousand salted away and invest it in one of the Big Syndicates and get it paid back to me two or three hundred dollars a month. I'd like to find me a doctor that's a thief like us and get him to saw off these finger-prints and I'd grow a beard about a foot long and rear back up in them Kentucky hills on that little farm and let the mistletoe hang on my coat tail for the rest of the world."

"I hate to stay cooped up like this in a house," Bowie said. "I'm like a mule though, I never know what I do want."

"You got to put up with things I don't care how you make your money. And you take a chance in anything. Take them aviators. I got a cousin that's in the army and he was writing my bud and telling him how he was soloing around up there. I'll bet that kid don't last as long as I do."

"I know I'm in this a lot deeper than I planned to be. I'm going to be like that Indian back there I guess. Go up this road as long as I can. Win, lose or draw."

"I made my mistake when I was a kid," T-Dub said. He lifted his leg and looked at the polished toe of the shoe critically. "But a kid can't see things. I should have made a lawyer or run a store or run for office and robbed people with my brain instead of a gun. But I never was cut out to work for any two or three dollars a day and have to kiss somebody's behind to get that."

"I don't guess I could have done anything else except what I have," Bowie said. "What will be, will be."

A little after midnight, Chicamaw's feet padded in the hallway and then he came into the lighted room, rubbing his nose and twisting his face. "Got a cigarette, anybody?" he said.

Bowie gave him a cigarette. Chicamaw went over and sat on the divan by T-Dub. The cigarette trembled in his hand and he began rubbing his ankles together and finally he reached down and scratched the left one. "What time is it gettin' to be?" he said.

"After twelve," Bowie said.

"What have I been doing around here?" Chicamaw said. "I feel like hell."

"You just been guzzling a little," T-Dub said. "The girls left."

"Did they?"

"They went down to see my bud."

Chicamaw scratched his other ankle and then his elbow.

"Bowie and me have been talking business," T-Dub said. "If you boys are going to Oklahoma, what do you say we let things rock for about a month and all of us meet up again in that house in Gusherton, say, November fifteenth?"

The cigarette fell out of Chicamaw's hand and he grunted as he picked it up. "Suits me."

"I'm in," Bowie said.

"November fifteenth in Gusherton then," T-Dub said. "Boys, if we sack them up over there it will be my thirty-first."

Chapter X

IT was cold this morning and the fallen leaves of the poplar-trees rustled and clattered on the sidewalk in the wind. Bowie carried Chicamaw's black Gladstone and his own brown strapped bag out to the gun-metal and put them in the back seat. In Dallas I'm going to buy myself an overcoat. Pretty good to know you got the old mazuma in your pockets to buy yourself a coat and anything else you might need. And I sure got it on me. Seven thousand in that bag; ten thousand in this coat pocket and these two pants pockets. And three thousand in silver in the trunk of this car.

Chicamaw came out with the guns in a blanket and then T-Dub with a black Gladstone. T-Dub's collar was turned up around his throat and he moved like his bones were on hinges. He said it was rheumatism.

"All you need is a good dose of Lula," Chicamaw said.

At the Sante Fe depot downtown, T-Dub got out, saluted and grinned and went on in. He was going to Houston.

On the road to Dallas, Bowie and Chicamaw talked about how they were going to do things there. They would register in at the biggest hotel, Bowie as *A. J. Peabody* and Chicamaw as *Frank Masters*, baseball players from Denver, Colorado. They would stay there all day, Chicamaw getting his car, and right after dark take out for Oklahoma.

"You better not go too strong on one of those big cars," Bowie said. "Get one of them big jobs and everybody will be big-eyeing you."

"That shows you what you know about it, boy. If I could get me a green Packard with red wheels and a calliope whistle I'd do it. Then they big-eye the car instead of you."

"After we give this car to Dee I think I'll get me another V-8," Bowie said.

The quiet of the thick-carpeted hotel room—*814*—was that of a bathroom and Bowie, alone now, soaked in it. A hotel is just about the safest place for a man, he thought. Say one of these hotel clerks thought he saw something? Well, he wouldn't be in any too big a hurry to call a bunch of Laws in. People staying in hotels wouldn't appreciate a little war busting in their faces. Then it was pretty hard for a man to get in a rank as long as he was throwing money. People taking your money just didn't run off and squawk. Men just weren't made that way. He took a sheaf of currency from his inside coat pocket and dropped it on the blue counterpane. "And, Brother, I got it to throw."

After bathing and shaving, Bowie went down and sat in the lobby. Everybody around him had on pressed suits and shined shoes and watch chains across their vests. They're not the kind of fellows that big-eye you, Bowie thought. It's these Hoosiers in these little filling stations that don't have anything else to do but chew tobacco and look in them damned detective magazines.

After a little while, he went to the street and started looking in the shop windows. In a mirror he studied his hat and decided that the brim was too broad. Too much like a cowboy. He went in the Department Store on the corner, and besides the new hat he bought a double-breasted blue overcoat, two handbags and a powder-blue suit with a belted back. I'll show that Indian a fancy thing or two in duds myself.

In the Jewelry Store, he bought an open-faced watch and chain and then a ladies' wrist watch with six diamonds on the band. That Little Soldier will open her eyes when I hand her this.

It was noon when he returned to *814* and Chicamaw had not showed up.

He tried on the powder-blue, but it was just too much of a go-to-hell suit for him. That Little Soldier would give him the laugh if he turned up in it. What am I ribbing myself up about that girl for? I'm just going to fool around here and make a donkey out of myself. That girl has other things to think about besides a damned thief like you, Man.

Now was the time, he decided, to send some money to Mama. Five of these one-hundred dollar bills with one of these pieces of hotel stationery around them and one of them envelopes. I wouldn't mind sending her five thousand if it wasn't for that no-good husband she's got. He'll get every damned bit of it. Now if it was that second husband she had it would be okeh. He was a pretty good fellow. Dumb, but I wouldn't mind helping him.

Old Jim and Red up there in Alky could sure stand a few bucks. Jim sure liked his sweet milk and them charging twenty cents a quart up there in that Prison when you could buy it in town for a nickel. And old Red wouldn't smoke nothing but tailor-mades. I'll get to you boys. I'll stop in one of these post-offices pretty soon and send you boys a hundred apiece. I've got to do some stopping in some of these towns pretty soon and get some of these dollar bills changed into twenties. Got enough of them things to pack a washtub. I'll just start shoving them through these bank windows, twenty and thirty at a time, and pretty soon I'll get rid of them.

Bowie pulled off his shoes and lay on the bed. *814*. Oh, oh. *Eight* plus *one* plus *four* equals *thirteen*. Aw, there's nothing to that. That's carrying it too far.

Mexico? Man, money will go a long ways down there. Three of them pesos for a dollar. Twenty thousand? Jesus Christ. That would be forty-five thousand pesos even after he took out for a car and the other expenses he would have while he stayed up here. Now if I go on through with it at Gusherton? Jesus Christ. I'll be a damned rich man. . . .

Bowie woke up with Chicamaw standing above him. "I thought I was going to have to pop my pistol to get you up. Man, you'd be a pushover." He smelled of liquor.

"What time is it?"

"If we're going to get out of here right after dark we better be gettin' in the saddle."

Bowie had the delicate, spraying feeling in his belly.

When Chicamaw, up there ahead of him in the new Auburn, held out his hand, Bowie slowed and then turned in to park alongside of him at the sandwich stand. It was a neon-lighted place with beer signs and a lettered board of sandwich prices. When the uniformed girl came out, Chicamaw said he wanted twelve bottles of beer to carry.

After the girl went back into the stand, Chicamaw pointed up the street toward the filling station on the left corner with the *Gas . . . 13 ¢* sign. "I run in that very station up there once and there was an old boy in there that sure big-eyed me. He had a wooden leg, I remember. I noticed him, see, out of the corner of my eye and finally he says to me: 'Boy, it ain't none of my business, but I know you.' I says to him: 'Brother, you just think you know me.' He says: 'You're Elmo Mobley as sure as hell, but after you leave here, I never have seen nobody that even looked like you.' "

"He really knew you, did he?"

"Sure he did. But I never did let on, see. He says to me: 'Boy, I just wish you had got this bank here 'fore it went busted and took my wad. I'd rather for a poor boy like you to have it than them goddamned bankers. Both of them bankers are out of prison now and still living swell on what they stole from me and about four or five hundred more folks here.'"

"I'll be doggoned. He was Real People."

"I gave him a ten and told him to keep the change."

"You run into Real People once in a while all right."

The girl returned with the bottles of beer in a sack and Chicamaw put them in his car. He said to Bowie: "If you're in such a big hurry, I'll just let you set the pace out of this town and I'm telling you, boy, you better stomp it or I'm liable to run over you."

"Okeh," Bowie said.

Bowie moved out the boulevard toward the Oklahoma Highway, the rear-vision mirror of his car reflecting the following lights of Chicamaw's automobile. I'm going to be in Keota in an hour and a half. This buggy is going to get stomped. He felt of the small hard bulge in his left vest pocket. Yes, the watch was still there. He pressed the accelerator harder.

The one-lamped car approached on the intersecting street ahead from the right, but there was a Stop Sign there and Bowie stepped back on the gas. The other car lunged right on across the Stop Sign and Bowie stomped brake and clutch, swerved, but the One-Lamp hit and then a bucket was shoved down over Bowie's head and tons of shattering glass were burying him. He thought: *This is liable to get me in trouble. . . .*

Thrown from the sprung door of his car, Bowie rose from the parquet grass, feeling like the figure in a slow-motion picture. He was on his feet now, a terrific weight on his back. Yonder was his car, the radiator caved in against a broken lamp-post and behind it was an old coupe, somebody inside of it groaning, its one lamp still burning.

Human forms moved like shadows about Bowie now. "Are you hurt, Friend?" a Shadow said. "No," Bowie said. He moved toward his car, dragging the weight that was like a plow. I got to get that stuff. . . . *I got to get that stuff. . . .*

It was a woman in the wrecked coupe: "Oh, my God. Oh, my God. Oh, my God. . . ."

Bowie reached his car, grasped at the handle with hands that felt like they had gone to sleep. He staggered with the push. "Get on over in my car, you damned boob," Chicamaw said.

Somewhere now there was a sound like a thousand trucks straining up a high hill in first gear. Them's not trucks, Man, Bowie thought. Sirens. His fingers groped at the emptiness of his right hip. Gun gone. That's the kind of luck I have, gentlemen. He moved across the street, through the working Shadows, dragging the Plow, toward Chicamaw's car.

He climbed into the front seat and then thrown bags were thumping in the rear. To hell with the rest, Chicamaw, boy. Come on. Everybody and his dog is coming. . . .

The flashlight was like a blow-torch in Bowie's face. The Voice behind it said: "What's your hurry, Buddy?"

"I'm in no hurry," Bowie said.

"I'm taking him to a doctor, Officer," Chicamaw said. Another bag thumped in the back. "He's bunged up pretty bad."

"I'm pretty bad bunged up," Bowie said. The flashlight clicked off and then he saw Officer, the bulging chin that was like a licked hog's knuckles. Another form in a black hat was with him.

"Where you from?" Officer said.

"Denver," Chicamaw said. "You fellows come on to the hospital, by God, if you want to ask questions."

"There's a woman over there hurt and from what I can hear you were traveling too fast," Officer said. "You get out of that car and come on with me. And you too, Buddy."

"Not this time, Friend," Chicamaw said.

Second Officer said: "Listen here, Bub, you going to get in jail yourself here 'fore you know it."

"Not this time, Friend. . . ." Shoes scraped and then the hoofs of a thousand horses were thundering on a tin roof above Bowie's head. Guns! Bowie reached toward the panel pocket: *This is liable to get me killed.*

Like a cut radio, the noise ended. Then Chicamaw was getting under the wheel; the motor roared like an airplane taking off and Shadows scattered in the street ahead of them like cotton-tail rabbits.

The car sliced the highway wind with the sound of simmering water. Chicamaw pressed the panel button and the illuminated speedometer, to Bowie, glowed through a mist. Chicamaw tapped and the instrument board was dark again. "You're bleeding like a stuck pig," he said.

"I'm all right."

"You better snap out of it."

"It was a Little War."

"They were men enough to start it. Let 'em be men enough to take it."

"It was an old one-light Jalope that got me. Come right out and got me good."

"I'm going to dump you at Dee's. There's plenty of heat behind us and I'm going to let you out and get on up the road and burn this car."

"It was a Little War. That old Jalope."

"You're not hurt bad, are you? You're bleeding like a stuck pig."

"I'm all right."

They whipped around the red tail-light of another car; then the twin glow of another.

I'm just sick at my stomach, Bowie thought. That's all. Why I used to get sick just from standing up when Mama was cuttin' my hair. Her name was Peabody then. No, that was the first man. It was Vines, the carpenter one, then. See, Chicamaw, that shows you I have snapped and my mind is clear. Vines was his name. Pain seized Bowie's back with the grip of a twisted monkey-wrench and his belly muscles became as rigid as a washboard.

"What the hell?" Chicamaw said.

"I'm all right."

Chicamaw ran the car under the darkened shed of Dee Mobley's filling station, got out and vanished behind it. Just let me lay down for an hour, Bowie thought, and then I'll feel just as good as ever.

Chicamaw came back with Dee and when Bowie got out, his legs felt like cooked macaroni and he sunk to his knees. "Ain't that funny?" he said. They carried him back to the Bunk.

"I put everything under the bed here," Chicamaw said.

"Thanks, Chicamaw," Bowie said.

The motor of Chicamaw's car roared and he was gone and then Dee Mobley gave Bowie a drink of whisky. It clawed his mouth and throat like fingernails.

Dee kept sitting down and getting up and moving around the room. Finally, he said: "You're not hurt bad, are you?"

"No," Bowie said.

"You see any use of me staying here?"

Bowie shook his head. "Not a bit, Dee."

"I don't know what kind of trouble you boys got in," Dee said, "but I don't see any use of me hanging around your heat. You're welcome to this place though, and if it wasn't for the fact that I'd be losing money I'd just as soon close it up and put a sign out there on the front door and go up to Tulsy. I could put plenty of grub in here and water and you could stay here as long as you wanted."

"Don't worry about the money."

"I got to worry about it, Bowie."

Bowie gave Dee ten fifty-dollar bills. "You better let your folks know to stay away from here."

"Nobody comes around here except Keechie and I'll give her some of this money and she can visit up in Muskogee or somewhere."

"You better do that."

The scraping branches of the pecan-tree against the Bunk's tin roof sounded like cat claws on a screen. I could be a lot worse off, Bowie, old boy, and don't you think different. I could be laying back yonder. You doggone whistling. I still got the money. The silver is gone, but to hell with that. That old Jalope. *814*. That was it. *Eight* plus *one* plus *four* equals *thirteen*. There you are; that was it. And if it hadn't been for that Chicamaw?

Chapter XI

DAWN oozed through the cracks of the closed Bunk door, the veins of the drawn window-blind, and pressed with leaden heaviness on Bowie's frozen soreness. The suit of winter underwear, Dee Mobley's, hung on the post of the bed like a scab. I will get up in a minute, Bowie thought, and light that stove. I'm chilled and that's what is wrong with me.

He touched his loosened front teeth with his tongue and heard them creak in their sockets. A car droned around the curve, thundered past the filling station and faded with the sound of a covey of quail in flight.

I'm going to get up. *One for the money, two for the show.* Now when I say *four to go*, I will get up. But what's the use of gettin' up? I've got all day. *One for the money . . .* Chicamaw won't be gone more than two days. He might show up right tonight. *One for the money . . .*

This might not really be happening, him lying here in this place and getting ready to get up. This was just his Spirit? His Real Self was back up that road. No, that was his Spirit too. His Real Self had got the Chair. I'm like a cat with nine lives. That's it. One of them in the Chair and one of them back yonder. Seven left. I'm going to go ding-batty if I keep lying here. *One for the money!* . . . A car was coming under the shed of this filling station. Bowie sat up, his right hand reaching for the floor. Man, you don't even have a gun. . . .

The knob turned and then the unarmed figure in the red sweater was standing there. It was Keechie. Bowie's face felt like it was encased in a cellophane mask and if he breathed his skin would crackle.

She closed the door and came toward him. "What's the matter with you?"

He breathed. "Accident."

She stood beside the bed. "What's the matter?"

He touched his mouth. "I guess you see my lips now. They're busted up pretty bad."

"Anything broke?"

He shook his head.

"Shot?"

"Just sprung my back a little."

She went over to the kerosene stove and then a match popped and the igniting wick sputtered. Bowie lowered himself back to the pillow. The pan of water rattled on top of the heater.

Two lines creased Keechie's face from her cheekbones to

the corners of her thin, dry lips. Her eyes were the color of powdered burnt sugar. "Hungry?" she said.

He shook his head. "Your Dad said you were going up to Muskogee or some place."

"Uh huh."

"I guess he left all right."

"Yes."

"I guess you better be careful about staying here, Keechie. I've been in a little trouble."

"You look like it."

The hot, wet towel melted the brittle casing on his face, softened his lips. Her fingers touched his face and he wanted to lick them. Just let her stay a little while. Just a little while. . . .

"I got money," he said. "On me and in that brown bag under this bed. Nineteen thousand dollars."

She straightened, cupping the towel in her hands, looked at him.

"I don't know why I said that."

"I'm glad you have it if that's what you want."

"That wasn't what I wanted to say. What I wanted to say was I don't guess it's best for you to be here."

"You need help."

"I just thought that I had this money and maybe you would like to take a trip or go some place. All girls like to go places."

"I don't know what other girls like to do."

"Now I didn't mean anything by that, Keechie. Now don't get me down wrong."

"I would do this for a dog," Keechie said. "If you will turn over and pull your shirt up I will put some liniment on your back."

She left at noon, but she was coming back. It would be after dark and she would bring plasters and cigarettes and something for him to gargle. She would leave the model-T and walk back out, telling her Aunt Mara that she was leaving town. She would sleep in the filling station at nights.

Bowie rested on the bed, his back and head propped against a quilt and pillow. It's all right, he thought. I've had more than my share of bad luck and I know it's going to be all right for two or three days.

The cotton underwear on the bed looked like the skin of a dead rabbit. Bowie got up, picked the rusty file from the window sill and scraped the garment to the floor. Then he kicked it under the bed.

Chapter XII

THEIR spoons tinkled in the peanut-butter glasses of soft-boiled eggs and crumbled crackers. Keechie sat on the edge at the foot of the bed, the golden glow of the oil heater's jagged crown caressing her face.

"It's about time you started eatin' something," Bowie said. "I never heard of anybody not eatin' any more than you do and not gettin' any more sleep. Just two or three hours a night. I never heard of it."

"I've gone three nights without sleeping and it doesn't bother me at all. I've done it all my life."

"You've fallen off some too since I saw you last and you better start sleepin' and eatin' more, young lady. Now me, I've got to have my eight and nine and ten hours at night or I'm just blowed up."

Their spoons scraped in the emptied glasses and they laughed.

"Don't you ever want to leave this town, Keechie?" Bowie said.

"Yes." She got up and took the glass out of his hand; placed it with her own on the table. Then she came back and sat down. She talked. Her voice was as soft as the reflection on the heater's dull brass.

Once, she said, an old couple drove into the filling station and she got acquainted with them. The man was paralyzed and they were touring the country for his health. They dropped her post-cards and talked about her coming to live with them and she would like to have gone, but then the cards stopped and finally one day she got a card from the woman saying the old man was dead.

"It makes it pretty hard on a girl when she doesn't have . . ."

"Have what?"

"A Mama."

Keechie shook her head. "It depends on the mother."

"I don't know what I would have done without mine. Never has bawled me out for a thing."

"My Aunt says my Mother is the reason why my Father drinks and goes on like he does, but that doesn't have a thing to do with it. He is no good and perhaps she was, but I can't see that she is any better."

Outside, there was a sound like the sirens in Texaco City and Bowie stiffened and the skin on his chin and throat stretched.

"What's the matter?" Keechie said. She got up.

It was only wind in the telephone wires over on the highway. "Nothing," Bowie said.

"Your back?"

He shook his head. "This old world is some old world, ain't it, Keechie?"

"Yes."

"Who's your fellow, Keechie?"

"Why do you ask that?"

"I just thought I would ask."

"Why?"

"It isn't any of my business. Most girls have fellows and I was just asking."

"I don't know what most girls have."

"I don't believe you like men folks, do you, Keechie?"

"They are as good as the women I have seen."

"I believe you are kinda down on people."

"I don't know."

"And you never have had a fellow?"

"No."

"Even just to go to church with or something like that?"

"No. Why, do you think I should have?"

"Why, no. I was just asking. That's your own business."

"I never did see any use of it." Keechie reached over him and picked up the pack of cigarettes on the window-sill. The breasts under the polo shirt stirred.

"I'll take one too," Bowie said. "You know I don't know what could have happened to that Chicamaw. I guess he is seeing his folks."

"You will get along a lot better if he stays away from you."

"Aw, Keechie, you just got that cousin of yours down wrong."

"I'm not kin to anybody."

"You're a Little Soldier, that's what you are."

"Why do you call me that?"

"Because you are. Isn't it all right?"

"Yes."

She went over to the table and picked up the granite coffee pot and looked inside of it. She put it down and then picked it back up.

"Keechie."

She turned, the coffee pot in her hand.

"You know I have been wanting to give you something ever since I been here and I'd like to give it to you now."

"What is it?"

"A little old watch."

She returned the pot to the table.

"Do you want it?"

"Do you want to give it to me?"

"Yes."

"Yes, I want it."

Chapter XIII

ON the fourth night, Chicamaw came, his eyes like a dog sick with distemper, his face the color of ham rind. Bowie's head quivered on his neck and he called, but Keechie left the Bunk without speaking to Chicamaw.

"You look like you been making it all right," Chicamaw said.

"I been all right."

"Well, I haven't been doing so well. I've throwed every cent I got."

"I'll swear, Chicamaw. What's been the trouble?"

Chicamaw said he had throwed it in a Tulsa hotel gambling. He did have a new car though and some guns. A tommy gun too. By god, he had a Big Papa out there now and he was as ready as anybody to start a Little War.

"You didn't see your folks?"

Chicamaw shook his head and began plucking at a hair in his nostril. "I didn't want to go around them as hot as I was, Bowie."

"Well, you're not broke, Chicamaw. I still got it, see, and you're welcome to what you need."

"Sure makes me anxious to get back with T-Dub in Gusherton and get me another piece of money. You going to feel like getting up in a few days and running these roads again?"

"I guess I could go right now."

"No, I wouldn't ask you to go now. If you'll let me have five thousand I'll go on over and see the folks. Make it six thousand. Will you do that?"

"Christ, yes, man."

"Can you beat me throwing that much though, Bowie? You know I'm a damned good poker player. They just took me to a cleaning. When I get to thinking about it, damned if I don't believe there was something crooked about it."

"Them big gamblers are thieves. You better stay away from them, boy."

"I guess you been reading the papers all right?"

"I haven't seen anything."

"Is that so?"

"I been just laying right here. You mean Texaco City?"

"Man, we're hot."

"Them Laws?"

"We're hotter than gun barrels, boy."

There was a scratching sound and Bowie looked toward the closed door expectantly, but it did not open. It was the pecan-tree touching the Bunk.

Chicamaw left the Bunk and returned quickly. Bowie had the brown bag on the bed and was taking money from it. Chicamaw put the two .45's on the bed.

"Sure glad to see them guns," Bowie said.

"Thanks for this loan," Chicamaw said. "You know I been

thinking about you, Bowie. You don't throw your money away and you don't get drunk. You're just a big old country boy, Bowie, but by God, I believe you're going to make it. You got something and I just can't figure it out."

"It didn't do me no good in Texaco City."

"Well, I guess I'll be shoving off, Bowie. Now if I get jumped and can't get back here in a couple of days or you have to rabbit from here, I'll see you in Gusherton. We sure can't let old T-Dub down."

"You be careful, Chicamaw. Go a little easier on the whiss, boy."

"Then if I don't see you here in a couple of days I'll see you in Gusherton?"

"What is it them Mexicans say when it's okeh?" Bowie said.

" 'Sta bien," Chicamaw said.

" 'Sta bien," Bowie said. "Man, I sure do want to get down there in that chili country some of these days. A man can't live like this always, Chicamaw. You know that."

"We'll make it down there, boy. Don't you worry."

Chapter XIV

IN the early mornings, when shadows crawled in a gray gloom and Bowie lay alone in the Bunk, he thought of First Officer, his hog-knuckle chin; the smothering bucket and shattering glass; the Chair, Spirits, Cats. The branches of the pecan-tree scratched the roof a hundred times and Keechie was never coming, he thought. For God's sake, man, *snap*. But at last she did come and then all that screwy Spirit stuff got out of his damned head.

In this evening's twilight, the polished peanut-butter glasses glowed with the delicacy of a blue flame. Bowie watched Keechie: the flipping cloth in her hands was like a blowing skirt and he seized her bare, strong fingers with his gaze. She had paint on her mouth tonight, but looking at her lips was like spying on her unclad through a keyhole.

She straightened the drying cloth on the back of the chair

and then picked up the kerosene can. "I'd better fill up your heater for tonight," she said.

"You ought to put a coat on," he said.

While she was gone, he planned what he would do in the morning when he woke up. He would not read the Sunday newspaper she had gotten him until in the morning. And then he would only look at the funny pages and the comics.

Keechie returned and filling the stove, she came to the bed. "I hope you get a good night's rest."

He played with the point of his shirt collar. "I hate to see you go."

"Do you?"

"I guess I've kinda got the blues tonight."

"I have done about everything I could around here, but I'm in no hurry. If you want me to stay——"

"Just a little while if you ain't in no hurry."

She lowered herself to the edge of the bed and crossed her legs. The sound of the tree now was like a gentle rain.

"I don't like to look behind," he said. "I try to just think of maybe the good things that will happen ahead. But I guess I know what is going to happen."

"No, you don't, Bowie. The things that you are afraid of most never happen. I'm a lot older than you in a lot of ways."

"I never have seen nothing like you before, Keechie. I know now what makes a fellow get him a little missus and swing a dinner pail."

"You mean that?"

"Yes."

She moved and he reached out and said: "Don't go."

"I'm not."

"My ears are ringing," he said.

She bent toward him and touched his face. He seized her then, brought her toward him. "Don't you go. Don't you go."

"I'm not, Bowie."

Strength swelled within him. I can snap her little body in my hands. I can break her little body in my grip. Her tight lips yielded until there was only softness and then her breath became as naked as her body. . . .

*

Frying bacon spluttered in the skillet on top of the oil heater and then it popped and Keechie jerked back and turned and smiled at Bowie.

"You better be careful, Little Girl," he said. She sure did look different. Where did he ever get the idea that she wasn't pretty? Those lines in her face. Where were they? And that little mouth was as soft and pretty.

"Wonder if you could take time out and come over here and give your Daddy a kiss?" he said.

She came over, the fork in her hand and bent down. "There's nothing sick about you," she said.

He kissed her. "I feel like a million bucks. I been thinking about getting up and running a half-mile before I eat."

"You just stay there. How do you want your eggs?"

"Any old way."

"How do you want them?"

"Any old way, honey. Over easy I guess. And hand me that newspaper over there while you don't have anything else to do."

She handed him the newspaper and he pointed at the three pale prongs of sunlight that lay on the splintered floor near the window. "Look, I believe the sun is going to shine today."

"I noticed the stars last night and I thought then that it might be clear today."

He began turning the pages and then he saw the thing that seized his eyes like a fish-hook:

TEXACO CITY, Texas, Oct. 6—Fingerprints found on the steering wheel of the wrecked, new automobile which the fugitive slayers of Plainclothesmen Vic Redford and Jake Hadman abandoned here last week, may lead to the identity of the killers, Chief of Detectives Musser revealed here today. The chief said his department was basing its hopes on this and also a revolver found nearby.

Redford and Hadman, veteran peace officers, were ruthlessly slain in a gun battle on Ector Boulevard while investigating an automobile crash. A woman received minor injuries in the collision.

"Are you very hungry this morning?" Keechie said.

The white of the paper glimmered like heat on the highway and Bowie jerked his eyes away. "I didn't understand what you said?"

"What's the matter, Bowie?"

"Nothing. Not a thing. I was just reading here."

"What are you reading?"

"Just something here."

Six suspects arrested here in connection with the case have been released. Two are still being questioned.

The abandoned automobile of the killers was purchased in El Paso, Texas, it was reported. Witnesses of the battle say that three and possibly four men were in the car that sped away after the shooting. One witness declared he saw a woman in the outlaw machine.

A police benefit here last night for the widows of the two slain officers netted $320.

Bowie took the warm plate with its eggs and bacon from Keechie's hand and put it on his lap. After a little while, he stuck the fork into the egg's yellow.

"What's the matter, Bowie?" She sat on the bed's edge with a plate on her knees.

"I don't want to hold nothing back from you, Keechie. I'm pretty deep in this business. I'm a lot deeper in it than I was when I was here before. I want you to know that."

"What is it?"

"I had some trouble back up the road. Two Laws killed."

Keechie placed her plate on the floor.

"You can see that I'm in it pretty deep now."

"Did you do it?"

"Them Laws?"

"Yes."

Bowie's head went up and down.

"You did not. You can't tell me that. I know who did it. Chicamaw. You can't conceal anything from me." She clutched his trouser cuff. "He did it."

"It don't make any difference who did it. And you got Chicamaw down all wrong. I wouldn't be sittin' here now if it wasn't for him."

"You did not do it, Bowie."

"I wouldn't tell you nothing but the straight. I got it on my back and there's no gettin' around it."

Keechie got up and the plate on the floor rattled and broke.

She looked down at it and for a moment her mouth twisted as if she were going to cry.

Bowie held up his plate. "Don't mind that. We can split this."

Keechie picked up the plate fragments and the spilled food. On the table was Bowie's untouched food.

"I'll just tell you the straight of it, Keechie. I'm not sorry. I'm not sorry for anything I ever did in this world. That when I was just a punk kid and they put the Chair on me don't count. But I'm not sorry for a one of these banks. The only regret I got is that I didn't get one hundred thousand instead of ten. I'm just a black sheep and there's no gettin' around it."

"The only thing black about you is your hair," Keechie said.

"You're a Little Soldier, Keechie. You're a Little Soldier from them toe-nails of yours up to your hair, but you can't get mixed up with me."

Keechie's face twisted like he had driven his fist into it. He grasped her arm. "Keechie, what's the matter?"

She shook her head.

He pulled her to him. "What's the matter, honey?"

"Didn't you mean that last night?"

"Mean what?"

"Bowie. You know what you said."

"Honey, I can't think of everything right now. What was it, honey? You come on now and tell me."

"You said you wished you had me."

"Sure I do. Godamighty, honey."

"What do you mean then? Getting too mixed up with you?"

"Don't you see how it is? When a man has them Laws after him and it's all in the papers they'll shoot you and ask questions afterwards. They'd just as soon shoot a woman down with him as not."

"Is that what you mean?"

"You see now, don't you, honey?"

"Does anybody else have any strings on you, Bowie? Anybody else?" She pulled away from his grasp.

"What do you mean?"

"Is there anybody else? A woman?"

"Oh, no, honey. Lord, no."

"I just wanted to know."

"How come you to ask a thing like that?"

"I'm in this pretty deep and I just wanted to know."

Bowie lay back against the pillow. "Keechie, come and lie down beside me a little while."

She got on the bed beside him.

"You like me, Keechie?"

"Yes."

"A whole lot?"

"Yes."

"Hundred bushels full?"

"Yes."

"Thousand bushels full?"

"Yes."

"A hundred thousand million trillion gillion bushels full?"

"Yes."

"Keechie, I love you." Her finger nails dug into the flesh of his throat.

There were sounds in the filling station and Keechie got out of bed and went across the darkened room to the door; Bowie following, in his underwear, a .45 in his right hand. Keechie peered through the cautiously opened crack of the door. After a long time she closed the door easily and Bowie stepped back. "It's my Aunt. Stealing some groceries."

Neither was sleepy now. They lay in bed, both their heads on the one pillow. "You know I been thinking, Keechie. This business of me staying here can't go on. I been here eight days now and Dee is going to be coming back pretty soon and this just can't go on now."

"Do you have anything in mind?"

"How would you like to go somewhere with me?"

"You want me to go?"

"You know doggone well I want you to go."

"What do you have in mind?"

"I'd like to get in a big city, Keechie. I mean like New Orleans or Louisville. Old T-Dub was always talking about them towns. In them big cities, people don't big-eye you so much and if you keep your nose clean, you can last as long as you want to."

"I guess so."

"I just don't know what's happened to that Chicamaw. That Indian can take care of himself though. He's probably gettin' everything fixed up at his folks'."

"We don't have to go around any of them, do we? Mister Masefeld and them?"

"No sir, honey. Not you. I should say not."

"I've been thinking some too, Bowie, and what I have had on my mind is what some people that used to live next door to my Aunt told me. Mister Carpenter and his wife and they had a girl my age named Agnes. Mister Carpenter had tuberculosis and they moved away down in Texas almost to the border in the Guadaloupe Hills. Agnes wrote and told me about it. They lived away out in the hills and wouldn't go to town for two months at a time and Agnes said that the only people they ever saw were some Mexican sheepherders and then a few sick people like Mister Carpenter. People chasing the cure, Agnes said they were."

"Close to Mexico, uh?"

"Bowie, I don't see why we couldn't go to a place like that and just live to ourselves and pretty soon people would forget all about Bowie Bowers and then finally there would just be the real Bowie Bowers."

"You know I hadn't thought of that. Them little towns though, Keechie, are bad. Everybody wants to know your business."

"We won't be in a town. We'll be away out and don't have to see anybody."

"You know I sure hadn't thought of that."

"That's where I would like to go."

"Man, we got the money to do it. Right here under this bed and in my breeches and coat yonder."

"I think that would be the best and just stay away from everybody you ever knew."

"How you and me going to get out of this place, Keechie? No car or nothing?"

"We can manage."

"Any trains stop here at night?"

"Two o'clock to Tulsy."

"We could get that train, by golly. You could walk about a half-block ahead of me and get a couple of tickets and I'll be hanging around and every once in a while we'll give each other a wink and then we'll sit in separate seats on the train and . . ."

"We'll sit together on the train."

"Sure, we can sit together on the train and then we'll get in Tulsy and I'll buy us a new V-8 and then we'll scat down to this Guadaloupe Hills country. Where is that place, Keechie?"

"I've looked at it on the map a hundred times. When Agnes was writing me I wanted to go down there. There's deer and wild turkey and squirrels and everything else, Agnes said."

"Man, I could knock me off a deer. I'll get me a .30-30 or a .415 Winchester and you and me will eat venison, kiddo. You just let me down there, Keechie, and I won't even need no gun. Just give me a rock."

"If we go down there, either you or me will suppose to be a lunger, you know, with t.b. Maybe both of us had better be. Now in renting a cabin or something we'll have to let on."

"I'll look like the best t.b. in the world."

"That's the thing for us to do. And you just forget everybody you ever knew."

"You'll have to get you some clothes in Tulsy, honey. How about a fur coat? To set that watch off I gave you?"

"We'll think about that later."

"I'll buy you a whole windowful of clothes. You can get anything you want. All you got to do is name it."

"We can't look like no millionaires. We're going to be sick people."

"Ah, you can get a few things. How you like them riding boots and pants, Keechie? Aw, I don't know though whether I'd like to see you in pants or not. You just get dresses. And plenty of them silk doodads. We'll get a couple of thermos jugs and keep them filled with soda pop and get some blankets and sun glasses and an extra can or two of gasoline and we'll split the breeze."

"When do you think we should go?"

"What time is it now?"

"It must be twelve."

"We can make it. Two hours. Let's get in the saddle, honey."

"Tonight, Bowie?"

"You doggone whistling. And honey we got the money to do it on too. Twenty thousand good old bucks. I mean fourteen. That's a lot of money, Keechie. You can say what you want to about money, Keechie, but by god, it talks."

"I guess so," Keechie said. "Well, let's start dressing."

Chapter XV

MESQUITE trees persisted even into this foothills country, but the Plains were far behind now. There were Spanish oaks and cedars and in the late afternoon this way the sage grass had a lavender flush. Away ahead, in the distance, a long range of sharp hills embroidered the horizon. Above the range, the sky was streaked with white, rigid panels as if the rain had crystallized and awaited a crack of lightning to unleash.

Keechie was driving and Bowie sat low in the seat, his hands deep in his pockets. She drove like Chicamaw, her left hand on the cross-bar and the other on the wheel; took the curves like they weren't there. In the holster under Bowie's left arm was a .45 and in the panel pocket another. There were four blankets in the back, a thermos jug of coffee, a sack of sandwiches, four cartons of tailor-made cigarettes. And Keechie had on hose that cost two dollars and shoes that cost ten and that military cravenette coat. It was her own fault that she didn't get the fur, but she looked like a Little Soldier in that coat and he had to hand it to her. And the way she had that little brown hat cocked over her eye. . . .

Down the road, beyond the Curve sign, the cement disappeared around the stone-studded bank; straight ahead, low, white barriers and space and blue sky. What if they just kept going straight and into that space and sky? They would keep going like a plane right over that valley. But cars don't fly.

What if they did go off? It would just mean that he and Kee-chie had drawn the poor cards. But what if they made it? It would mean Luck was riding with them for a long time to come. . . .

The wheels of the machine hung tenaciously on the curve and now they were on a long straight-away again. They ain't nothing going to stop us, Little Soldier.

"Light me a cigarette, Bowie."

"Yes, ma'am."

The dairy barn was white with green trimming and over its roof, white and black pigeons circled. On the porch of the house lay a big dog, its paws dangling over the edge. They passed an old sedan, its slender wheels wobbling, the top tattered and in pennants.

"Them old Jalopes," Bowie said. "They cause more accidents than anything else on the road. It's no crime to be poor, Keechie, but there ought to be a law against letting cars like that out on the highways."

They passed a Schoolhouse, two filling stations and on the porch of the General Store sat two men bent over a checker board. The black lettering on the highway board read: *San Antonio . . . 186.*

Down this highway, thirty miles more and then they would turn west on a dirt road. Out that road one hundred miles and they would be in them little hill towns, Antelope Center, Arbuckle. There they would start house hunting.

On the left was a cemetery with a half-dozen low tomb-stones and then an unpainted, box house. Farther down, at the wooden gate, two cows with swollen bags waited.

"You know anything about cows, Bowie? Do they ever have twins?"

"You got me there."

"I was just wondering."

"It looks like to me they could though. With that woman up in Canada doing what she did, it looks like to me a cow could do it."

"Those cows back there made me think of it."

"That woman up there in Canada, Keechie. That shows you nothing is impossible in this old world, doesn't it?"

"It sure does."

"And I was thinking back there. What is it you say we are doing? *Chasing the cure.* Well, what if we really did have t.b.? Well, I don't know but what I'd rather be a lot hotter than I am now than have something like that riding me. Don't you kind of feel that way about it?"

"I should say I do."

Bowie chose the big filling station with its stucco front and Keechie turned the car up the curving driveway. There was another car under the shed, a woman at the wheel, but it drove off as they stopped. The next time we gas up, Bowie thought, we'll be having us a home to go to. Just fifty miles more now and they would be in that town of Arbuckle.

The filling station attendant in the leather jacket said: "Yessir?"

"Fill 'er up and I got a couple of cans."

Keechie entered the Rest Room door and Bowie went over to the Coca Cola box and lifted the lid. The exhausts of stopping motorcycles popped and he turned. The two cops were coming right in here.

The Cops came toward the Coca Cola box and Bowie moved over. The tall cop was as brown as saddle leather and the short one had chapped, scaling lips. They had on gray uniforms and black Sam Browne belts. Their pistols were pearl-handled.

"What kind you want?" Tall Cop said.

"Coke," Short Cop said.

Their lips made drinking sounds on the mouths of the bottles.

"Got you a new one there, haven't you?" Tall Cop said.

"Yeah," Bowie said. "Them jobs over there can outrun it in reverse though, can't they?"

"They'll outrun that car all right."

"I guess them motorcycles there will outrun just about anything that gets on these roads, won't they?"

"Don't you think it, Mister," Short Cop said. "There's plenty of them out there I don't go after."

"You can tie them up in traffic sometimes," Tall Cop said.

"Ninety is about all I want to push that 'cycle over there of mine," Short Cop said, "and if anybody has anything that will do better than that I just check it to them."

Keechie came around the corner, stopped and then started smoothing the dress about her hips. Bowie winked and she went on to the car and got under the wheel.

"That all, Sir?" the Attendant said.

Bowie paid him.

They drove off and Bowie turned and reached toward the back seat. Tall Cop and Short Cop were sitting on top of the Coca Cola box.

"You didn't bat an eye, you doggone little dickens. Not an eye."

"What were you talking to them about?"

"Damned if I know."

"It looked like to me you were trying to make friends."

"They didn't know me from Adam's off ox, Keechie. Why, they're that way all over the country. How they going to know you? Look at a picture. Well, what's that?"

"I would stay away from them."

"Man, when they drove in that station though, I says to myself: 'Here's where a Little War starts.' "

"You better look behind."

Bowie looked back. The ribbon was clean. "Not a thing, honey. Nossir, you didn't bat an eye."

"I think maybe I had better start carrying that pistol in the pocket there, Bowie."

"Not that big gun, honey. That thing would jump clean out of your hands. I'll get you a little gun one of these days pretty soon though. Every woman ought to have a gun. I'm going to get you one. There's always some sonofabitch ready to get smart with a woman."

"I'm not afraid of that gun."

"Did you ever shoot a .45?"

"No, but I have a real strong grip. I could out-crack any of the girls in school on pecans. You remember that game. I won all the time."

"Yeah, I remember that game. What did we call it?"

"Hully gull."

"That's it. Yessir, Keechie, it just goes to show you how a

man don't have to jump from his shadow. I'll bet I could go right up to the Law over here in this town of Arbuckle and ask him if he knew of a furnished house and I'll bet he wouldn't know me from Adam's off ox."

"I will do the asking about the houses. I will go to the real estate office and do the asking."

"You going to tell them we're lungers, sure enough?"

"That is what we are down here for now, Bowie, and you want to remember it."

Bowie made a coughing sound and slapped his chest. "The bug is gettin' me down. How's it doing you, Little Lunger?"

"You'll make it, old Foot-in-the-Grave."

There were no furnished houses in the little town of Arbuckle or near it, the Real Estate Woman told Keechie, but over at Antelope Center, she said, forty miles farther West, the cottages of an old Sanitarium were being remodeled for tourists and sick people and deer hunters. Bowie and Keechie went to Antelope Center.

It was almost noon when they left the graveled highway, two miles west of Antelope Center, turned through an arched gate and started climbing the narrow, high-centered road. Through the cedars and frost-browned oaks, on the side of the Hill, stood a big gray building.

"Looks like a jail," Bowie said.

"It won't hurt to look," Keechie said.

The closed building was the old hospital, its cement the color of dead broomweed. Through the dust-filmed windows there were stacks of bare beds and piles of mattresses. Back of it and east, rows of small stucco cottages fenced it like a carpenter's tri-square. The cottages had glassed-in rooms and stone chimneys and there were lettered boards over the entrances: *Come Inn . . . Suits Us . . . Journey's Inn . . . Bella Vista.*

The man raking the weeds in front of the corner cottage in the V of the Square stopped, leaned on the handle and looked at their car. When Keechie got out, he dropped the rake and came toward them.

The man had on a khaki army shirt and a white cloth belt held his slick, blue serge trousers. He was middle-aged and

his teeth were broken and tobacco-stained. Yes, he had some
cottages. He was the caretaker out here. He had just fixed up
another cottage and it was twelve dollars and fifty cents a
month and that included water and electricity. It was the last
house at that end. Now he lived in that house on the corner,
and below him a School Teacher batched and next to him an
Auto Salesman with his wife and two children. They were the
only ones that lived out here now, but he hadn't got around
to fixing up any more cottages. They were fine people, the
folks that lived out here.

"You want to look at it, honey?" Keechie said.

"Yeah, I'd just as soon."

"You take that School Teacher feller yonder," the Caretaker
said, "he got him a hot plate from Sears, Roebuck and he's
just batching fine."

Bowie got out of the car.

The Caretaker thrust out his hand. "Lambert is my name,
young man. Old Bill Lambert. Traveled out of San Antonio
for thirty-five years, leather goods, saddles, grips and harness.
Had a lung collapse on me here a year ago and this air up
here, Son, is fine. What's your business, Son?"

Bowie removed his hand from the other's grip. "I'm a sick
man right now. Used to play ball."

"Son, you come to the right place. Not a healthier place in
the United States than right in here. Ball Player, uh? Well, we
got a School Teacher and two Salesmen and now we got a
Ball Player. Now that Salesman feller over yonder used to be
worth a right smart of money. Owned his own business right
yonder in Antelope and just went busted like any of us can
do. His wife didn't like it much out here at first, her being
used to gas and fancy things, but now she just likes it fine.
Your missus will like it too."

"Pretty quiet out here, I guess?" Bowie said.

"You won't get lonesome. Now that Salesman has got him
a radio and everybody out here is fine people."

"Used to be a lot of people out here, I guess?"

"I don't know all the history of this place. Now all this was
built right after the War, I think, and then it petered out and
then for a while it was a sort of tourist camp and I might just
as well tell you folks because I'm not the kind to hold nothing

back. This place got a pretty bad reputation with the folks in Antelope because here a couple of years back some bootleggers got out and people come out here and throwed wild parties. But that's not any more, son. Your wife will be just as safe here as any place in the world now."

"He has to stay awful quiet," Keechie said. "Let's go look at the place."

Bill Lambert walked ahead on the narrow sidewalk in front of the closed cottages, talking, spitting. "Now it's nothing swell, you know, but I'll fix it up just like you want it. There's one thing, I want to put you in some linoleum in the kitchen and if you ever have company and need an extra cot, why just let me know."

He stopped in front of the last cottage—*Welcome Inn*—and opened the scraping screen and inserted the key in the lock. The wooden floors inside creaked under their feet. In this front room there were a blackened, empty stone fireplace and an iron army cot covered with a yellowed counterpane. There were two hide-bottomed rocking-chairs and a rickety breakfast table. In the windowed sleeping-room there was a broad iron bed, a huge dresser with a smoky mirror and two straight dining-room chairs. The kitchen had a three-burner, grease-caked oil stove, a sink and an enamel-topped table. The bath had a shower and the toilet seat was split and part of it lay on the cement floor.

"Some strong lye soap and a mop and whitewash would help a lot around here," Keechie said. "Don't you think so, honey?"

Bowie grinned. "Don't you think the price though will about keep us busted?"

"Now I tell you, Mister . . ." Bill Lambert said. "What did you say your name was, Son?"

"Vines. V-i-n-e-s."

"Well, I tell you now, Mister Vines. It's just the best I can do. A bunch of millionaires own this out here and you know how they are. I been trying my best to fix these places up here and get some money to do it with because people just want things a little nicer for the money, but I tell you, it's just like gettin' blood out of a turnip to get something from one of these millionaires. Now you take Mister Philpott over there, he's the Salesman, they've fixed that place up over there just as pretty as a picture."

"There is a lot to do around here all right," Keechie said.

"I'll tell you what I'll do," Bill Lambert said. "I don't want to rush you folks, but if you decide to take it I'll throw in a half-cord of wood for nothing and tack that linoleum down the first thing this afternoon right after dinner."

"We must stay awfully quiet," Keechie said.

"Don't you worry about that, Mizzis Vines. Now you take here last month, it was the night of September fifteenth, there was a couple come out here and I thought I smelled liquor, but I didn't want to cause no trouble and I let them have the place although they just wanted it for two or three days. Well, before the night was over she was running around right in this house here, without anything on and kicking up as high as them trees and the blinds up to the ceiling and so I just politely told them we didn't want that going on around here. Now, Son, you want your wife protected and that is just the way I do out here. This is a place for respectable people and any time anybody runs around here kicking . . ."

"That's all right, Mister Lambert," Bowie said.

"Just one more thing now, Mister Vines, and then I'll let you go. Now you take Mizzis Philpott over there. One day she goes off and while she's gone her oil stove burns over and I busts in there and saves the whole place. They were mighty appreciative of that."

"I'm very satisfied," Bowie said.

"If we ever catch you in this house, you had better be putting out a fire," Keechie said.

Lambert laughed. "All right, Lady. All right. Now then I'll just leave you two together and let you decide."

Alone, Bowie and Keechie walked in the rooms. "Think it will do, Keechie?"

"I'm crazy about it."

"If I ever catch old Filthy MacNasty peepin' around here, I'll kick his hind-end clear off," Bowie said.

"He's harmless. Bowie, this is just the thing."

Bowie walked in the sleeping-room, Keechie following. "Some of them big, red Indian blankets would sure look pretty in here," he said. "And we'll get us a big radio to sit in yonder."

"I can go to town this afternoon and I'll buy enough groceries to last us three months," Keechie said.

"I forgot to ask old Filthy if there was really some deer around here," Bowie said.

Keechie sat on the edge of the bed and moved up and down on it experimentally. "Good springs and mattress, Bowie."

"I'm sold on it myself," Bowie said. "Go on out and pay Filthy a couple of months' rent and tell him I'll tack the damned linoleum down."

Chapter XVI

THERE was one hundred dollars' worth of bright-colored blankets on the big bed and the cot now, a radio that was as big as the fireplace in the living-room, two automatic shotguns and a rifle on the mantel and Keechie had a cigarette-case with a diamond in it. They had done a lot in four weeks. Old Filthy never did snoop around any more and just once had somebody come, Mrs. Philpott, the Salesman's wife, to borrow some sugar. Out here they never did see anybody except that little Philpott boy, Alvin, and then he was away down in the woods back of their place with a .22 rifle and that Spitz dog of his, Spots.

Bowie sat in front of the radio this evening, smoking the curved-stem pipe that Keechie liked, and thought how everything was looking pretty good. In that food-packed kitchen, Keechie was frying Irish potatoes the way he liked them, crisp and brown.

I don't care nothing about it myself, Bowie thought, but we can start taking in some picture shows down there in that town pretty soon. Girls like to get out and go places. And that Law down there? I got him spotted and he ain't never going to get close to me.

In the darkened living-room, the flames of the fireplace logs splashed on the ceiling and walls. Had he brought in the wood tonight? Yes. What time was it? *Seven-thirty.* Christ, that Mexican orchestra Keechie liked was on. Bowie switched the dial. This was the station all right, but now they were talking about them damned constipation crystals.

If they were jumped now and had to rabbit, this radio and everything would have to be left behind. Well, I'm no damned soda skeet making ten dollars a week. I'll buy another one. Five hundred-dollar one and two hundred dollars' worth of blankets and if we go busted I know where I can get plenty more.

He placed another log on the fire and sat back down. The prongs of light shadow-boxed now on the walls, hooking and jabbing frenziedly. The orchestra was playing and Bowie got up and went back to the kitchen. Keechie was standing in front of the oven with a cloth in her hand.

"Hear that piece?"

Keechie nodded. *"La Golondrina."*

"Always makes me kind of sad somehow. Makes me think of them boys."

"Why?"

"I don't know. I been thinking about Chicamaw though, Keechie. I don't know whether I did that boy right or not up there in Keota, Keechie. He might have been expecting me to wait for him there and I didn't leave him no note or nothing."

"How were you going to leave him a note?"

"I don't know."

"Well, quit worrying about it then."

"I was just thinking about them."

"You have somebody else to worry about now."

"We just all started out together and you can't keep from thinking about things like that."

Bowie went back to the living-room and sat down. The fire had lowered and its glow filtered the darkness like a luminous screen. A cowboy singer was yodeling now about the prairie.

I do have to meet them boys in Gusherton, Bowie thought. They never did let me down and I sure can't go back on them. Why, they would just wait and wait and wait on me and I wouldn't let them do that. She will understand. You will understand, won't you, honey?

The cowboy was singing *Nobody's Darling but Mine:*

> *Goodbye, Goodbye, Little Darling,*
> *I'm leaving this Old World behind.*
> *Oh promise me that you will never*
> *Be Nobody's Darling, but Mine. . . .*

Bowie cut the Voice off. I wish we could get more newspaper news over this and not that Mussolini and Africa and Congress and stuff like that. No news is good news though. If anything had happened to them boys, we would have heard about it.

Keechie called him. On the enameled table there were black-eyed peas, corn bread, fried potatoes, pineapple preserves and black coffee.

After supper, Bowie took the galvanized-iron tub of hot water off the stove and carried it into the living-room and lowered it to the floor in the hearth's glow. Keechie was going to take a bath.

He spread the bath mat and towels on the hearth around the tub and then looked around the room. The blinds were pulled close all right.

Standing, her naked thighs and legs glinted through the tub's rising vapors. She's sure filling out, Bowie thought. Now she raised her left arm and the soaped, dripping cloth in her right hand moved toward the shadowed pit. "I didn't know you were such a hairy little thing," he said.

Her arm came down. "Do you think I should shave?"

"I should say not. I like it. Don't you ever do it."

"I won't then. As long as I have you."

The whipping, drying towel covered and revealed and Bowie felt the heat of her burnished body glow in his eyes. He got up and picked up the white flannel pajamas off the radio. They smelled of clean soap. He handed them to her.

"Are you going to wash your feet tonight?" she said.

"Not tonight, honey. I washed them last night."

They lay under the warm, soft blankets now and Keechie's fingers played in the flannel over his chest. Outside, on the narrow cement walk, wind-kicked leaves scraped and scurried. In the daytime, he had watched the leaves leave the oak and they had twisted and spiraled to the ground like birds shot with an airgun.

She lay quietly now and he said softly: "Keechie?"

She half raised. "What is it, Bowie? Did you call me?"

"I thought you were asleep."

She peered at him hard. "What is it?"

"Nothing, honey. I didn't go to wake you up."

"What is it, Bowie?"

Distant, tiny, taut wires trilled in Bowie's ears. "I just been thinking."

"About what?"

"Just about things in general. Got to thinking about some of the boys up there in Alky. They come in there, Keechie, bragging about the women they got Outside waiting for them and after a little while they hush up and there's nothing more heard about it."

"I don't know anything about that."

"It doesn't make any difference, I don't suppose. I don't care what kind of a man you take. A doctor or a big college professor or any kind of a man and let him die and pretty soon his wife will be out running around with somebody else. These widows are just about as bad as any kind of a woman."

"I don't know about women like that."

"Some of these women bury a man and in no time at all pick right up with another. There's women, Keechie, that will take up with a dozen men in their lives. Just one right in after another."

"Those women didn't love."

"Well, I don't know about that now, Keechie. They are bound to have been pretty crazy about them and maybe they didn't love all of them, but they loved some of them."

"A woman just loves once."

"What makes a woman live with one man a while and then with another one and then just run around with four or five more?"

"They just don't love."

"They must like it, Keechie, or they wouldn't do it."

"I don't know why other women do things. Maybe they

are just looking and can't find anybody and then I guess some of them marry for a living."

"It just looks like to me that every woman will do it."

"I don't know what other women do."

"Now what would you do, Keechie, if I got in a little trouble somewhere and you and me might not be able to see each other again?"

Keechie did not say anything. The tiny wires were as loud as crickets now and they swarmed in Bowie's ears. "Didn't you hear me?"

"There wouldn't be anything for me after you were gone. There is no use to think about that."

"Keechie, look at all these other women. Maybe they don't the first year and maybe they go two or three or four years, but pretty soon you see them lettin' some man slobber all over them."

Keechie was quiet.

"Now what do you have to say to that, Keechie?"

"I guess a woman is kind of like a dog, Bowie. You take a good dog now and if his master dies that dog won't take food from anybody and he'll bite anybody that tries to pet him and if he goes on, he'll rustle his own food and a lot of times he will just die too."

"You know that's right?"

"A bad dog will eat out of anybody's hands and take things from anybody."

"That's those big thoroughbred dogs that cost a pile of money that do that I guess. Them are real dogs."

"Maybe they do. I never did see, I don't guess, a real thoroughbred. The dog I am thinking about was there in Keota. I don't know what he was. Nobody else I don't guess. Old Man Humphrey owned him and after he died I felt so sorry for that dog. But he wouldn't have anything to do with anybody and he wouldn't eat or drink and then he just died too."

"I'll be doggone, Keechie. You know that's right. It just goes to show you. You know, honey, you are the smartest little old thing I ever did see."

"I'm not smart."

"You're a Little Soldier that's what you are."

"You go to sleep now."

The ringing in Bowie's ears faded far, far away and his eyes grew heavy and he closed them. . . .

Chapter XVII

THE back yard of *Welcome Inn* had the width of an alley and then a fence of barbed wire and beyond that was ranch land, sage-grass and broomweed; far-reaching woods of green, pollen-blowing cedars and gray-trunked scrub-oaks. In it, long-horned, white-faced cattle grazed and sometimes one would come to their fence and nose in the rusty iron drum of burned cans and garbage. Once, Keechie had seen a doe and she called Bowie, but when he got to the back door, it was gone. Away to the south, beyond the woods, the Hills embossed the sky in a great, crawling circle. This evening, the sinking sun had flushed the horizon to a pretty pink like Keechie's underthings.

They sat now on the back steps of the cottage, Keechie in the coat of Bowie's gray suit. She was funny that way, always wearing something of his and even sleeping at nights in one of his shirts and he had paid fifteen dollars for that negligee and boudoir slippers.

Keechie pointed now and in the woods they saw the Philpott boy, Alvin, and the dog.

"I been kind of wanting to get out there with that kid some evening," Bowie said. "I never have seen him bringing back anything."

"He's having a good time though," Keechie said.

"Guess I just got too much else to think about." He tapped the bowl of his pipe on his palm and then slung the charred tobacco with a finger-spreading movement and wiped his hand across his thigh. The lining of his mouth felt thin and his tongue needle-pointed. I'll tell her after we go in, he thought. Only four days now and I got to be in Gusherton. That's all there is to it.

"Alvin yonder made me think of the little girl who used to live down on the corner from my Aunt. She died."

"Huh," Bowie said.

"She was awfully pretty. She used to say pieces in the church and her Mama fixed her up so pretty. It liked to have killed her Mama and I guess it was the reason that her Father went crazy. He was crazy before that, I would say though. He was a printer and he saved gold pieces. Every bit of money he saved he would go to the bank and get gold pieces. Go up in the front room at nights and sit at a table and count it and look at it. His wife told him that it was going to bring bad luck."

"And then the kid died?"

"And it took every bit of the gold he had saved to pay for the funeral."

Bowie started filling his pipe. "Chicamaw was telling me about that lawyer friend of his he knew down in Mexico. Hawkins. That lawyer didn't believe in this heaven or hell stuff and said that the only way a man lived on was through his children. That was as far as this After-Life business went."

"Is that why you would like to have children?"

He looked at her. "Why, I never said nothing about having children."

"I know it."

"Why, would you like to have a baby?"

"Some day, maybe."

"Some day is right."

She stood up on the step and pulled the coat about her throat. "I'm satisfied now."

The match snapped and he flipped it and felt in his pocket for another. "No, a baby wouldn't have very much business with us."

"Well, if it couldn't be with us, I'd rather for it to be just you and me."

It was getting dark. The storm-broken limb yonder on the big oak-tree was twisted about the trunk like a petrified snake.

Bowie got up, knocking the unlighted tobacco out on the heel of his shoe. "I been thinking about the boys, Keechie. I guess I'll have to see them in a few days."

"Why?"

"A little business. I promised them I would meet them on the fifteenth of this month."

"Why?"

"Just business. I'll just be gone a couple of days and be back here before you know it."

"What are you planning on?"

"I just promised them, Keechie. That's all."

"What are you planning on doing?"

"Now I want you to understand, Keechie, that I'm not looking for trouble any more. I'm going up there, but I don't have anything in mind except just not let them boys wait and depend on me. We got a bank picked there all right, but I'm not planning on robbing it."

Keechie turned and grasped the door-knob. "I'm going with you," she said. Then she went in the house.

He stood there alone. Up at the end of the row of cottages there was the sound of ax splitting wood. After a little while, he went in the house.

She lay on the bed in the darkness of the sleeping-room and he went over and sat on its edge. "No, you are not, Keechie," he said.

She did not say anything. She got up and went to the kitchen and he listened to the sound of water running in a glass. Presently, she came back.

"I said you weren't going," he said.

"I heard you."

"Well, quit running around when I'm talking to you."

She sat down on the bed beside him.

"Being in my heat is bad enough and you're certainly not going to get around three of us. I made up my mind about that a long time ago."

"All right, Bowie."

"Now let's get this straight. What do you mean all right?"

"I mean it will be all right."

"How are you going to be feeling when I come back?"

"All right."

"You are going to be here, aren't you?"

"Yes."

"And it is all right?"

Keechie got up and took her coat off, folded it and laid it

on the bed rail. "You are keeping your promise and when you get up there you are going to let them know you are through with all that kind of business?"

"After Gusherton, I'm through."

"You know that I expect that, Bowie?"

"I sure do."

"All right then."

Keechie went into the kitchen and Bowie heard the wick of the oil stove sputter and then the rattle of the kettle on the flames. He lay down on the bed. After a little while the water in the kettle began to simmer. It sounded like a whimpering baby.

Chapter XVIII

THE front door of the Gusherton house parted and there was the smell of cold bacon and raw onion and then in the crack of light was Lula's water-color face. The door opened farther and Bowie went in and now he was shaking T-Dub's rocklike hand.

"Where's Chicamaw?" Bowie said.

T-Dub nodded toward the rear of the house. "Sleeping one off."

"For God's sake don't wake him up," Lula said. She had on a green velvet dinner gown that reached her ankles, and was adjusting a gold earring in her lobe. "I will absolutely leave."

"He sure has been guzzlin' it, Bowie," T-Dub said. "I don't know what's going to become of that boy."

"He's sleeping, is he?" Bowie said.

"Don't you wake him up now," Lula said.

Bowie lowered himself to the studio couch, balancing his hat on his close-pressed knees. T-Dub looked tired: like the morning they had walked the railroad ties all night. "Take his hat, Lula," he said. "Boy, you act like you just dropped in to say hello."

"I've been traveling pretty long and fast today," Bowie said.

He watched Lula carry the hat and place it on the table by the door under the mirror.

"Where you been keeping yourself, Bowie?"

"Down south of here. Say, Chicamaw has been drinking a whole lot?"

"Oh, Christ, man. He brought an old bat in here last night that I'll swear to God he must have picked up in Nigger Town. Right in this house with Lula here."

"She was as drunk as he was and of all the goings-on," Lula said. "I told T. W. there that if you weren't here by nine o'clock tonight I was packing up and going to the hotel."

"She was too drunk to notice anything," T-Dub said. "That was one thing and as soon as he passed out I took her out and dumped her."

Lula had the other earring adjusted now and she smiled at Bowie. "We have something to show you and if you will just sit there I'll bring it right back."

"Okeh," Bowie said.

Lula disappeared in the back. "She has been prettying up for two hours just because you were coming, I think," T-Dub said.

"How you been gettin' along, T-Dub?"

"Just gettin' by. Chicamaw had to go over day before yesterday to MacMasters and get fifty dollars off that lawyer friend of his to buy us gasoline and something to eat."

"You don't mean you have throwed all that, do you?"

"I got a family on my back, Bowie. I sunk twelve thousand dollars in a tourist camp over in MacMasters for that bud of mine and Mattie."

"How is he?"

"We've had hard luck about him. The parole board turned him down. I think that next year, though, he'll make it."

"That's too bad. I guess poor old Mattie is still up in the air."

"Me and Lula have been having a pretty good time too. In that New Orleans. Money will just naturally get away from you fast down there."

"Chicamaw been with you?"

T-Dub shook his head. "I thought he was with you all the time and then I figured too that he wasn't. But I haven't seen him. He showed up here three nights ago it was. Drinking jake."

"I'll swear. I wish he would ease up on that drinking a little."

Lula came in. She had a roll of parchment-looking paper tied in a red ribbon and she looked at T-Dub now. "Do you want me to show it to him?"

T-Dub was grinning and his head went up and down.

Lula, smelling of fresh perfume, bent toward Bowie, unrolling the parchment and then spread it on his knees. It was a Marriage License.

"Did you two go and get hitched?"

T-Dub's head was still going up and down.

"Why, you got your right name on here, T-Dub," Bowie said.

"Just turned the initials around. W. T. Masefeld."

"That sure floors me," Bowie said. He handed the license back up to Lula.

"How are you and that little Oklahoma girl getting along?" T-Dub said.

Bowie's eyes quivered. "Who is that?"

"What's her name? Keechie. Keechie Mobley?"

"What do you know about her?"

"You remember, Bowie. I met her when we were all up there at Dee's place. I didn't know though that you two had teamed up until I begin to see that stuff in the papers."

Bowie's Adam's apple ached like it had been hit and he could not swallow. "What stuff is that?"

"Haven't you been seeing any of it?"

Bowie shook his head.

"I read something just last Sunday I think it was," Lula said. "Had her picture."

"Picture?" Bowie said.

"Why, hell, Bowie, I thought you knew all about that. That Dee Mobley up there claims you kidnaped her and I told Lula here that all that guy had done was yellowed up. Some Law got to pumping him and he just about let out that kind of a squawk. I told Lula here that that was the way it was. I knew damned well you wouldn't kidnap anybody. I mean a girl like that."

"And it's in the papers?" Bowie said.

"The last one was just last Sunday," Lula said. "It was a picture of her, I know, that she had taken when she was going to high school."

"Huh," Bowie said.

"It will die down, Bowie. I wouldn't let it worry me."

"It don't worry me."

Lula went over and sat crosswise on T-Dub's legs; he spread them and she lay against him and put her arm around his neck, the Marriage License roll in her left hand.

That means you and me have come to the parting of the ways, Little Soldier, Bowie thought. You can't be running with me no more.

T-Dub and Lula made a smacking sound as they kissed.

You can go on back up to Oklahoma and get everything squared up, Bowie thought. Let them think what they want. You have some money now, Little Soldier, and you can tell that old man of yours to go straight to Burning Hell.

"You go on back and pretty up some more, Sugar," T-Dub said. "Bowie and me want to talk a little business."

"Don't you go and get a headache now," Lula said.

I'd like to see some Law bother you while I'm gone, Bowie thought. Lay just one finger on you. I'll take care of myself, Brother Law, but you lay one finger on that girl and goddamn you, I'll get a machine gun and hunt *you* down!

Lula disappeared in the back of the house.

"This bank here is a bird's-nest on the ground," T-Dub said. "And it will go for fifty thousand or not a dime."

"I can use money," Bowie said. "A man never knows when he's going to need money and plenty of it in this business."

"You're not going to get three boys like us together every day," T-Dub said. "That is the way I look at it."

"And Chicamaw has been feeling pretty low?"

"Bowie, I think he would charge that bank tomorrow by himself if you and me both backed out."

"Well, he won't have to do it by himself."

They robbed the First National Bank of Gusherton at *10:01*

o'clock the following morning, Chicamaw looking like a man with galloping consumption and driving Bowie's car; T-Dub complaining of rheumatism. There were no rumbles and at *10:15* they were switching cars, setting a match to Bowie's machine, and at *10:30* Chicamaw drove T-Dub's car, T-Dub and Bowie crouched in the back, into the garage of their house at the edge of the city. Chicamaw went on in the house and fifteen minutes later T-Dub and then, after another interval, Bowie.

The bank went for only seventeen thousand dollars.

At noon, T-Dub fried bacon and eggs and made toast, but only Chicamaw ate. Bowie drank coffee.

That afternoon there was a football game on the radio and Bowie lost ten dollars to Chicamaw.

"You guys give me the jitters," Chicamaw said. "Why don't you say something?"

"You need a drink," T-Dub said.

"I need something to taper off on and just as soon as it gets dark I'm going to town and get it."

A little before dusk a car entered the driveway and they picked up guns, but it was only some damned bastard turning around to go back to town.

At dusk, T-Dub said he was going up to the first Drug Store and give Lula a ring at the Red Bonnet Hotel. "I might just go on down and pick her up and we'll shell out for New Orleans right tonight. You want to go down with me, either one of you?"

"I do," Chicamaw said.

"If you boys are going, I think I'll just go with you too," Bowie said. "You can just drop me off at the bus station. I got some business to attend to and I want to get it over with."

Chicamaw had his hat on his head. "Why don't you hang around with us some, Bowie? I believe you're getting stuck up or something."

"I'll see you boys pretty soon."

"You want to watch yourself on these busses," T-Dub said.

"When I get down the line a couple of hundred miles I'll hop off and get me a car," Bowie said.

T-Dub named the night club on Bourbon Street in New

Orleans and said he and Lula would be in it the night of December first.

"Okeh," Bowie said. "I guess you'll be there too, Chicamaw?"

"If I don't stump my toe," Chicamaw said.

The child in the shrunken coat slid off the Waiting Room bench, stood there, the drawers leg hanging, her hands behind her, looking at Bowie. He winked again. The child approached and when she got close, she thrust out her hand, palm up, fingers stretched.

"Oh, you want a nickel?" Bowie said.

The mother got up, a woman in a faded red coat with a cheap fur collar, and came toward them with her hands outstretched. "Is she bothering you?" she said.

"I should say not. Where are you going, Little Lady?"

"Grandpa's," Little Lady said. She extended the other hand now. "Why of all things, honey," the woman said.

Bowie placed the quarter on the child's palm and the fingers closed about it. "How about you sittin' up here by me a little while?" Bowie said. He patted the bench. The child looked at the coin and then up at her mother. The woman helped her up on the bench.

The hard heels of the Policeman scraped on the tile floor toward the ticket window and he talked for a moment with the clerk there and then turned and moved back toward the door. At the door, he stepped back and then aside and two girls in fur coats, carrying week-end bags entered, a man in a tweed topcoat following. The Policeman went on out and the girls and the tweed-coated man stood at the ticket window now.

Bowie carried Little Lady in his arms, and inside the crowded bus a bald-headed man in the third seat got up and gave Bowie and the Mother his seat.

The woman talked. The skin in the hollows of her eyes had the coloring of tobacco-stained cigarette paper. She said her husband was a barber and couldn't find work and she was going now to her father until things got better. The child was just getting over a bad cold.

Little Lady slept on Bowie's lap and now he shifted her a little so her head would not touch the hardness of the gun under his arm. The mother said she was hoping her husband had work by Christmas.

The finger-nails of Little Lady's limp fingers were black-rimmed and looked like paper. Keechie's nails were always clean and rounded short and pretty; not long and sharp like Lula's. The night before he left she had trimmed his toe-nails. All right now, Big Boy, don't start that stuff. . . . Now this woman here was having a tough time. She could stand a little piece of money and here he was with almost six thousand dollars on him.

The Mother was silent now, her head pressed back against the seat, eyes closed. Pasteboard showed through the paint of the purse on her lap.

What if he slipped a twenty in that purse? If he picked up that purse and she grabbed out and started yelling? It would win the fur-lined bathtub. It would bring him luck to get some money in that purse though. If he got five twenty-dollar bills in that purse and she didn't wake up it would break any jinx that was waiting up this road here. If he counted to thirteen and got five twenties in that purse there wouldn't anything stop him on this trip.

The woman was snoring now, the money in her purse.

A little after daybreak, Little Lady and her Mother left the bus and at eight o'clock, in San Angelo, Bowie got off and at ten o'clock he was driving south in the new automobile.

The clouds above the lowering sun looked like a picture of sea waves in the moonlight. A tiny flame was burning in Bowie's stomach. I've got to eat something. I haven't had anything to eat since. . . . Jesus Christ . . . I haven't eaten since day before yesterday. I'll be doggoned. I'm going to fool around and starve myself to death. Thinking about other things and here I am starving myself to death.

The sign read: *EATS*. Bowie drove into the broad parkway and stopped close to the screened door of the roadside lunch stand, a low, frame structure plastered with tin beer signs.

Bowie went in. There were a counter and five stools and a playing electric gramophone by a slot machine. A man in a white apron came from the back through the arched door and moved up inside the counter. The face of a woman peered through the kitchen slot.

"Soft boil me two and coffee," Bowie said. He straddled the first stool.

The man had a double chin, lumpy and soft-looking like the belly of a frog.

The gramophone was playing *El Rancho Grande.* Next to the cash register, held by the bottle of catsup and white mustard jar, was a folded newspaper. Bowie reached toward the newspaper and then brought his hand back. To hell with them damned newspapers.

The music ended and the machine made a clicking sound and was still. Frog Chin moved around the cash register and presently the coin slot jingled and then the machine was playing again: *El Rancho Grande.*

Bowie stirred the soft-boiled eggs and then broke crackers and dropped the crumbs into the glass. He got the salt and pepper and then picked up the newspaper. It was a San Antonio paper. He took a bite and then spread the front page:

GUSHERTON, Texas, Nov. 16—One bandit was dead here tonight, another wounded and the wife-accomplice of the slain desperado was in jail as a vengeful aftermath of the bold, $17,000 holdup of the First National Bank here this morning.

The dead bandit is T. W. (Tommy Gun) Masefeld, escaped Oklahoma convict and sought for two months in connection with a half-dozen bank robberies in West Texas. He was shot to death by officers as he sat in a car parked in front of the Red Bonnet Hotel. His companion, Elmo (Three-Toed) Mobley, badly wounded, was in the hospital here under heavy guard.

Bowie A. Bowers, fast-triggered killer and leader of the bank bandit gang, had still eluded late tonight the combing search of a posse that numbered more than 300 peace officers and outraged citizens.

Mrs. Lula Masefeld, reputed wife of the slain bandit, was captured a few minutes after the shooting and lodged in jail.

The downtown gun battle terrorized scores of pedestrians and sent motorists scurrying for safety. The officers beat their quarry to the draw and neither bandit was able to fire.

Ten thousand dollars of the First National Bank loot was recovered in the bullet-riddled automobile. Credit for the heavy blow against the gang was being given tonight to Hotel Detective Chris Lawton.

It was he who secured the tip that resulted in the laying of a trap for the bandit gang.

"What's the matter," Frog Chin said, "aren't them eggs all right?"

"Sure," Bowie said. He dipped the spoon into the glass.

At least three men and possibly two women participated in the sensational robbery here. Two bandits, identified as Bowie Bowers and Masefeld, entered the bank at 10 o'clock, forced a half-dozen bank workers and officials and a dozen customers into the vault at the points of six-shooters, rifled the safe and tills and escaped in the waiting car of confederates. Witnesses who saw the bandit machine speed away declared there was a woman in it.

Bowers, who escaped from the Oklahoma Penitentiary while serving a life term for murder, is wanted in connection with the murders of two Texaco City peace officers and a half-dozen bank robberies in Oklahoma, Kansas and Texas. Phantom-like, he has been seen traveling about the country in high-speed motor cars with a woman companion, said by Oklahoma authorities to be Keechie Mobley, cousin of the bandit wounded and captured here tonight.

"Those eggs done enough for you?"

"Fine," Bowie said. He took a bite and the food was like the man's phlegm in his mouth.

A woman is believed to have figured in Bowers' escape in Texaco City just as authorities here believe his disappearance here was abetted by a woman.

Mobley was suffering from wounds in the head and chest, but attending physicians declared he had a fighting chance to live. If he survives, however, he faces the electric chair. District Attorney Herbert Morton announced here tonight that he would ask the supreme penalty in the event Mobley went to trial.

"I loved Tommy more than anything in the world," pretty 19-year-old Lula Masefeld sobbed in her jail cell tonight. "He was the best thing in the world to . . ."

Bowie folded the newspaper and placed it back behind the bottle and jar. Then he got up and reached in his pocket before the cash register.

"It is getting so that you can't please anybody these days," Frog Chin said.

"I just wasn't hungry," Bowie said.

As he walked toward the car, his feet felt like clumps of prickly pear.

Chapter XIX

THE green-shaded lamp in the kitchen of *Welcome Inn* was burning, their signal that there had been no rumbles while he was gone, and now he closed the car door quietly and the leaves on the walk crackled under his moving shoes. He lifted on the knob so the door would not scrape and went in. Pale coals studded the mound of dark ashes in the fireplace and then he saw Keechie sitting on the end of the cot by the shadowy radio.

"I'm back," he said and he had the feeling that no sound had left his mouth and the words were melting in his hollow stomach. He strained: "I saw the light burning. You remembered all right."

"I did not know whether you were coming back or not," Keechie said.

He went over and stood on the hearth, clasping his hands behind him. Water dripped in the kitchen sink. "How has everything been?"

"All right."

The motor of a speeding car away over on the highway beat like a tom-tom.

"You want me to turn that light off in the kitchen?" Bowie said.

"If you want to."

"It doesn't matter. It really doesn't make any difference to me."

"I don't see that it makes any difference whether you came back here or not."

The heat at the base of his skull ignited and a film, like smoke, burned his eyes. "Oh, you mean about me, I guess?"

"Yes."

"Everything has happened pretty fast," he said. "Before you could say Jack Robinson, everything happened. You know about it?"

"Yes."

"About you?"

"Yes."

He moved toward her. "Doggone it, Keechie. I didn't mean for you to get mixed up in a business like this."

"Don't you worry about me."

He stopped.

"I will have to learn to take care of myself."

"All that old money is yours, Keechie. It will take care of you. Just don't go back around that . . . that old man of yours."

"I am not going back there. Don't worry about that."

"You will have to go back there, I guess. But don't you worry about that business. Them goddamned dingbats can't put nothing on you, nothing in this God's world."

"When did you start thinking about me?"

"Thinking about you?"

"You surely didn't think about me when you were gone?"

"Didn't think about you while I was gone?"

Keechie stood up. "You lied to me. *Lied.*"

"Why, Keechie." He moved toward her. "Why, you don't understand, Keechie."

"Don't you touch me." Her fists were clenched. "You took them. It was me or them and you knew it and you took them."

He lowered his hands. "I don't like to talk about them boys."

"They don't mean anything to me. They never did. You knew that. All right, you and me are through."

She was going toward the door now and he saw that she had on the cravenette coat and there was her two bags on the floor. "Where are you going?" he said.

"What does it matter to you?"

He reached her, bent and grasped the wrist of the hand reaching for the bag. She wrenched from him. "I told you not to touch me."

"You wait a minute," he said.

She stood there, making breathing sounds like her nostrils were stopped.

"You want to leave this way?" he said.

"Absolutely."

"Sore like this?"

"Whatever you want to call it."

His groin felt like it was emptying.

"Is that all?" Keechie said.

"You wait a minute."

"You won't stop me."

"No, I won't stop you, but you just wait a minute."

She stood there and now he turned and went over to the fireplace and looked at the smothering coals. He went into the kitchen and came back with crumpled papers and kindling and he scattered the ashes and placed them on the coals. The papers blazed and then he arranged sticks of wood on the flames.

"You don't have any business leaving this time of night," he said. "If anybody is going to leave this house, it's me."

"I'm not staying here."

"All right. Now I'm going to get it straight after a while. If you just have to go, all right. Now I'm going out this door here and I'm going to be gone on a long walk and if nothing will do you, but you have to go, there's a car out there and the keys are in it and you know where the money is."

"I don't want anything of yours."

"Don't be a damned fool." The knob grated with his wrench and he went out the door.

A bulbous crescent hung heavily in the bottom of the moon's slate-colored disk. Wind gushed in the trees with the sound of a distant river and the tops of the cedars, silhouetted against the cobalt and starlit heavens, whipped and threshed like tiny Christmas trees in a storm. He walked now on the gray woodcutters' road that twisted and slashed deep into the woods.

This is what you wanted, isn't it, Big Boy? It had to stop some time and what's the difference how it happened? You just keep going down this road and walk, by God, until these damned legs of yours come off. *Keechie in front of the oil heater in the Bunk, floor dust tatting the hem of her skirt.* All right now, don't start that stuff.

The wind's chill crawled under his trouser cuffs and down the neck of his collar and he turned up his lapels. I have plenty of things to do. Nothing in this old world will do you any more good, T-Dub, but, Chicamaw, you got a friend. Don't you think different for a minute, boy. You're just as liable as not to be running these roads again with me pretty soon and it's not going to be any year from now.

His shadow glided on the road beside him, stubby and slender. *Keechie picking cigarette butts off the floor to make him a smoke with a cigarette paper she had found.* Now lay off that stuff, goddamit. What difference does it make how it happened, just so it happened? Okeh. Okeh. Okeh. *Okeh!*

The broken tree stump yonder with its two short, outflung limbs looked like a man. Bowie pressed his hand against the gun's butt in the holster under his arm. Hell, I don't need a gun with one Law. Brave men. Heroes. Fifty of them to get one Thief, hundred, two hundred, three hundred. Big Shots. Heroes.

A plummeting meteor fragment streaked the heavens like the spark of a shaken log, vanished. That means you're gone, Little Soldier. That means you have left.

He left the woods now, moved across the clearing toward *Welcome Inn*, in a dawning mist that blew like sifted ashes. The car stood where he had left it. Christ, girl, you didn't leave this place walking? Now you didn't do *that*. Why, girl, you're liable to get in trouble. . . . Smoke was coming from the chimney.

She sat in front of the burning logs, smoking a cigarette, her coat off. "I couldn't leave," she said.

His neck was rigid, fixed; he could not move it.

"I couldn't leave," she repeated.

"I noticed the car out there," he said.

"There wasn't anything for me Out There," she said. "Nothing. *Nothing!*"

Bowie placed his hand on her shoulder, patted. "You ought to turn in."

"I guess so."

"That is what I would do."

After a little while, Keechie got up and moved toward the sleeping-room and he followed; stood in the doorway and watched her lie down on the bed. Then he went over and sat on the edge.

"I didn't want to leave you," Keechie said.

His head went up and down.

"You wouldn't have let me go, would you, Bowie?"

"No."

"Even if I had wanted to?"

"No."

"You would have made me stay?"

"Yes."

"I help you, don't I, Bowie?"

"Yes."

"A whole, whole lot?"

"Yes."

Keechie closed her eyes and presently she sucked in a deep breath through her mouth and nose, jerked convulsively and he placed his hands on her. She jerked again, easier though, and now her mouth was closed and she slept. Bowie took the gun out of his holster and placed it just under the edge of the bed, loosened his tie, unbuttoned his collar. Then he lay down beside her.

Chapter XX

KEECHIE said it looked like Santa Claus would have to come this year in a boat instead of a sleigh. It had rained for six days. In the daytime, the rain-shrouded woods and hills were merged with the sky and their cottage stood on a tiny island. They went to bed at night with the rain caressing their roof and awoke in the morning with it still beating a gentle, broken rhythm.

It was getting close to five o'clock this afternoon and any time now Alvin Philpott, the little boy, would be showing up with the San Antonio newspaper. Bowie had made a deal with him four weeks before, fifty cents a week, and every afternoon now, as Alvin came home from school, he brought a paper. They were going to get the boy something for Christmas. That was only four days off now.

"How would you like to have a little egg nogg for Christmas?" Keechie said. She stood there in the kitchen doorway, a sweet potato in one hand, a peeling knife in the other.

Bowie placed Keechie's polished oxford on the floor and picked up the other one. "Did you ever drink any of that?"

Keechie shook her head. "Maybe I did when I was little, I don't know. I just saw a recipe in the paper and I think nearly everybody drinks it around Christmas time. The eggs in it are good for you."

"If it's just the same to you," Bowie said, "we'll just get a quart of whisky and drink it straight. But no egg noggs for me. I got sick as a horse on it once and I swore to God in heaven that if I ever got over it, I would never drink no more egg nogg no more."

Keechie laughed and went back into the kitchen. They were going to have pork chops and candied sweet potatoes with marshmallows for supper.

Bowie rubbed the brown polish into Keechie's shoe. We'll do something Christmas all right, he thought. It won't be just like any other day. He had that Christmas present to his Mama off his mind now. One thousand dollars. He and Keechie had driven yesterday to San Antonio and mailed the envelope. There was one thing, though, he had to do pretty soon and that was get some money to that lawyer friend of Chicamaw's in MacMasters. Archibald J. Hawkins. He and Keechie would have to go back to San Antonio and attend to that. Two thousand dollars in an envelope to a lawyer? The guy might be dead and somebody else would get it? The thing to do was go in some bank in San Antonio and get a draft and send it to Hawkins. Lawyers knew better than to go south with a thief's money. That one in Tulsa had found that out. Now he could send Chicamaw a postal order for one hundred dollars. In the Christmas rush in them banks and post-offices in San Antonio, nobody would big-eye Keechie or him.

The screen rattled and Bowie got up and went to the door. It was Alvin. Water dripped from the boy's nose and he pulled the dry newspaper from underneath his soggy coat.

"You going to get wet, boy, if you ain't careful," Bowie said.

"It don't bother me," Alvin said.

After Alvin left, Bowie went back to the kitchen. "I know now what we will get that kid," he said. "A raincoat."

"That will be better than a shotgun," Keechie said.

There was nothing in the newspapers. There was enough in there day before yesterday, Bowie thought. Chicamaw was going to trial February fourth. That lawyer Hawkins sure had to have some money pretty soon because they would sure put the Chair on Chicamaw if he didn't get some money.

After supper, Keechie and Bowie played checkers. It was raining harder now, wind whistling in the window-screens and water splashing in the puddles under the eaves.

Bowie stacked the checkers in the box with the sliding top. "You know I been thinking, Keechie, about what you said the other day about it being easier for a woman to disguise than a man. I believe it's easier for a man when you get to thinking about it. A man can grow a beard and wear glasses and get his hair cut different."

"He can't use powder and paint though."

"He sure can. He can dress up like a woman and get by with it."

"I'd like to see you dressed up like a woman."

"Not me."

"And I'm not going to dress up like a man."

"I know it," Bowie said. "But you know, Keechie, there's men in this world though that go around all the time dressed up like women. They're no good."

"There was a woman in Keota that smoked cigars and acted just like a man," Keechie said.

"Them people are no good, Keechie. Absolutely. They're no good."

"There are more no-good people in this world than there are good ones," Keechie said. "A blind man can see that."

"Up there in Alky, Keechie, you never saw the like. You would never have thought so many no-good people could be gotten up all together at one time. That was one of the reasons why I just couldn't stand it there any longer. I don't know though, but what it's just about the same Out Here."

The window-screens whined and Bowie listened. Then he

put his finger in his ear and jiggled it. "Yessir, Keechie, I think you hit the nail on the head when you said that the only way to beat this game was just go off and pull the Hole in after you. Not have a single friend."

"You can't trust anybody, Bowie."

"I've always said that, honey. I wouldn't trust Jesus Christ if he come right in this door right this minute."

"You just have to depend on yourself in this world and nobody else," Keechie said.

Bowie got up and placed the box of checkers and the board on the mantel. He turned, placed his elbows on the mantel's edge and pushed his stomach out away from the heat. "But you know, Keechie, you never will see three boys like us together again. I think about that Chicamaw up there in that jail pulling through by himself and I'll bet he doesn't even have cigarette money."

"Nobody but a lawyer can help him now."

"I know it. That's what I have been thinking about. I'll bet that boy is beginning to think that he doesn't have a friend in this world."

"There is nothing you can do about it. Unless you want to get him some money."

"That will do it, Keechie. It will do it nine times out of ten in this world. That's what I have to do. Get him a lawyer lined up. And a good one."

"You don't have to go anywhere around him though?"

"What are you talking about? I should say not. No, all I have to do is to get some mazuma to a good lawyer and that will be all there is to it."

Keechie got up and went over to the wood box. She carried the stick to the fireplace and said: "Move over a little, Bowie."

Sparks popped under the dropped wood and Keechie stood there watching the flames lengthen. "Don't that rain sound good, Bowie?"

"What did you say, Keechie?"

"I said don't you like to hear that rain on the house?"

"Uh huh. I sure do. You bet I do."

"I like it," Keechie said.

The floor planks creaked as Bowie began moving about. "I

should have brought in more wood today," he said. "I guess this rain is just going to keep on forever."

On Christmas Eve morning, icicles hung from the eaves, but the day was breaking clear. The sun was going to shine. Bowie and Keechie lay in bed, talking now about how Alvin was going to act when they gave him the raincoat this afternoon. They had bought the raincoat in Antelope Center yesterday and also a half-dozen handkerchiefs that they were going to give Alvin to give to Filthy MacNasty.

"If we're going to go to San Antonio this morning and get back here by four o'clock, we got to be gettin' up and going," Bowie said. "We're not going to get any business done much less seeing a show at this rate."

"Well, I don't see nothing holding you down in this bed, Booie-Wooie," Keechie said.

"You usually get up before I do, don't you? What's got hold of your legs this morning? Can't you take them icicles this morning?"

"Sure. I was just waiting to see you show what a he-man you are. Why don't you get up and start the fire this morning?"

"Who, me?"

"I hope it's you and not somebody else I'm talking to."

"By God, I hope so too. Now let me see. All I got to do is just get up and sort of walk in there to that fireplace. All right, you win, Keechie-Weechie." Bowie swept back the covers, got out, tucked the blankets back under Keechie and trotted, barefooted, into the cold living-room.

In the kitchen, Bowie saw the flooded floor and then the burst pipe of the shower in the bathroom.

"I will go and get Filthy and tell him to phone a plumber," Keechie said.

"No, you just stay here," Bowie said. "I'll go."

It was ten o'clock when the rattling, banging Ford pick-up with the vise stopped in front of the cottage. Bowie, the mop in his hand, stood at the window and watched the plumber get out. The man had a head shaped like an Irish potato and an unlit cigar stub in the corner of his mouth.

"You the folks that are having a little trouble out here?" Plumber said.

Bowie thumbed toward the back. "Bathroom."

Plumber looked at Keechie standing by the bed.

"In the bathroom," Bowie said.

Plumber's smile was soggy. The cigar stub darkened against his draining face. "We been swamped," he said. "Freeze. Bathroom?"

Bowie pointed.

Plumber moved across the living-room and into the hallway toward the bath.

Bowie turned and looked at Keechie.

Keechie framed the question with soundless lips: What do you think?

Bowie's head went up and down.

Plumber came out of the hallway walking briskly toward the door. "Tools," he said.

They watched him through the window. He got in the pick-up, started the motor and then the machine moved off with a violent jerk.

Bowie pointed at Keechie's coat. "Get on out and start our car."

Mud-thickened water geysered from the puddles at the Gate and splattered on their windshield. Bowie pressed the wiper button and then turned onto the highway. The road extended ahead, gray and slick as phlegm; gravel rattled under the fenders.

"Light me a cigarette," Bowie said.

Keechie looked in the panel pocket. "We don't have a one, Bowie, not a one."

"Can you beat that?"

"We will get some."

"Can you beat that. Now that's what I call luck for you. You mean to say there's not a one there?"

"We will get some, Bowie."

"Now that's what I call luck."

Thunder rolled. It was like the hills around them had been undermined and were bumping around.

"I'm sure fed up on rain," Bowie said. "I'm sure fed up on it."

"Where are we going, Bowie?"

"MacMasters."

"MacMasters?"

"I'm going to see a lawyer there."

"MacMasters," Keechie repeated.

The highway stretched on like a long ribbon of wet funeral cloth; the rain-drunk weeds of the right-of-way rushing behind.

"Alvin won't get his raincoat," Keechie said. "It was laying there on the radio."

Bowie cleared his throat. "I been thinking. It's a good thing we gassed up yesterday and got them cans filled. What if we were just starting out with a couple of gallons like we had yesterday morning? By golly, we sure got some gas in this buggy."

"We're lucky," Keechie said.

Chapter XXI

THE house of J. Archibald Hawkins, the lawyer, was a straight, two-story house with a porch of warped planks and next to the First Christian Church. In the furniture-stuffed Front Room, there was a roll-desk, its top stacked with law books of tan and red cloth; a piano with two hymn-books on the rack and framed portraits on the shawl-scarfed top. The worn places in the carpet looked like burlap sacking and on the square of cracked linoleum by the broad, sliding door a gas-stove ejected long, curling flames.

When Hawkins smiled, his eyes became wrinkled pockets and his cheeks looked like balls wrapped in cellophane. His Sister, who lived with him, had gone to Amarillo to see her son and it had looked like he was going to spend Christmas night alone. "It appears though," he said, "that I have some pretty distinguished company."

Bowie, sitting there on the claw-carved, leather divan grinned, and Keechie looked down and covered the strip of house dress over her legs with the coat's skirt.

"Now about Chicamaw again, Judge?" Bowie said.

"We will get him fixed up," Hawkins said. He did not practice criminal law himself, he added, but he knew personally the members of the Law Firm in Gusherton who could do something with the case. It would take money though.

"How much?" Bowie said.

Hawkins smiled. "Just about all they decide a man has."

"Around how much?"

"I know this firm will not take a case for less than two thousand."

"Say three thousand?" Bowie said.

Hawkins nodded. "It is a pretty good newspaper case too."

"I'd like to see Chicamaw get some money too. Think you can manage it?"

"I can see him very easily."

"And I'll leave you five hundred for all this trouble."

"I can certainly use it."

Bowie crossed his leg and leaned forward with his elbow on his knee and chin in hand. "You know anything how that happened in Gusherton? Them boys gettin' in trouble, I mean?"

Hawkins nodded. "Yes, I know. That girl. What is her name? Masefeld's wife."

"Good lord," Bowie said. "Sure enough?"

"It was pure simple-mindedness. That hotel detective over there made some advances that were unwelcome to her and, instead of ignoring them, she made a scene. Complained to the Manager and said she had a husband and plenty of money. It seems this hotel detective got suspicious then sure enough and plugged in on her telephone. He got the tip that way."

"I'll swear," Bowie said.

"She is going to testify for the State in Chicamaw's trial."

"I'll swear."

Keechie said they had better be going.

Hawkins said that he had a big chicken back there in the oven and it would only take a half-hour for it to warm. Wouldn't they keep an old man company a little on Christmas night?

Bowie looked at Keechie. She consented.

The lawyer talked. There are more millionaires in this

country than in any other, he said, and at the same time more robbers and killers. Therein lay significance. Extremes in riches make extremes in crime. As long as a Social System permitted the acquisition of extreme riches, there would be equalizing crime and the Government and all law-enforcement organizations might as well fold their hands and accept it.

"The Rich," Hawkins said, "can't drive their big automobiles and flaunt bediamonded wives and expect every man just to simply look on admiringly. The sheep will do it and the sheep will even laud it and support it, but at the same time these sheep will feel something that they do not understand and demonstrate it and that is known as so-called glorification of the big criminal."

"I'm not proud of nothing I ever done," Bowie said.

Money interests fix the punishment for crime in this country, Hawkins said, and consequently there is no moral justice. A bum steals a pair of shoes from another and that is a great crime, but what will happen to the complaining bum at the police station? If that same thief pilfers fifteen cents from the telephone box of a big utility company, he can receive fifteen years, but if he snatches that amount from the cup of a blind beggar, he may get a twenty-dollar fine. . . .

Hawkins' stomach gurgled and Bowie looked down, saw the dried mud on the toe of his shoe and then looked at Keechie's shoes. There was mud on them too.

"Now you take the Stupid Sheep I was talking about a moment ago," Hawkins said, "just like this young fellow that lives right down here in a little two-room apartment across the corner from me. He drives a milk truck for a millionaire creamery man here and he works ten and twelve hours a day and he goes home at night and there is a baby that he has to help his wife with. His wife is sick. Still weak and unable to work from bearing that child. Now you take that boy. Is it strange that he doesn't feel what these newspapers yap about glorification of the criminal?"

"These newspapers never get nothing straight," Bowie said. "They got me working in towns that I have never even been inside of."

"There is nothing like a man hunt and trust the newspapers

to make an arena and ballyhoo the Kill. The Romans were not cruel. At least no more cruel than these newspapers that get their readers' tongues hanging out for the Kill. And just here last week the Chamber of Commerce gave the Creamery Millionaire a silver loving-trophy as being MacMasters' most useful citizen of the year. And the irony of it all is that you take that fourteen-dollar-a-week boy that is working for him and put him on a jury and some Prosecutor who wants his name in the newspapers more than anything else will have that boy thinking that red-hot spikes are too mild for a bank robber."

"I get a kick out of robbing banks," Bowie said. "I don't mind admittin' it."

Keechie touched the back of Bowie's hand. "It's getting pretty late."

"We'll go in a minute, honey."

"We have some chicken coming up," Hawkins said. "I bet you young folks think I am a long-winded old cuss."

"Go on," Bowie said. "I like to hear you."

"Speaking of crime," Hawkins said. His stomach gurgled. "There was a Consumptive that come down here from Detroit in an old rattletrap here a couple of months ago and he had two little dogs. That is all that man had and he moved in a little shack on the river down here close to town and then that ranchman, who lived across the river and is worth, I guess, fifty thousand dollars, killed those two dogs with a shotgun and there is not a law in this state that will punish that cold-blooded, low-down, degenerate murderer."

" 'Fraid he would get a cow bit, I guess?" Bowie said.

"That. But that man shoots dogs down like he would rattlesnakes."

"They caught a fellow in the town I used to live in," Keechie said, "throwing weenies with poison in them out to dogs. He was just driving around town doing it."

Bowie looked at her. "You never did tell me about that," he said.

"Prisons are simply pimples on a corrupt world," Hawkins said. "The great criminals, I mean the real enemies of man's welfare and peace and happiness, never go near a prison and the dead ones, out in these cemeteries, have the highest tomb-stones over their heads. Normal men with abnormal tendencies. Abnormal men with normal tendencies. My God. It is a wonder people do not smell, their minds are so rotten. Excuse me, young lady."

"Them capitalist fellows are thieves like us," Bowie said. "They rob widows and orphans."

"I do not fool myself one minute," Hawkins said. "I possess that. You take me, Bowers, and that five hundred you have given me. I am going to run for Justice of the Peace this spring. When an old broken-down lawyer gets old, Son, he runs for Justice of the Peace."

"You don't look old," Bowie said.

"Anyway I am going into this next election and I rather think I am going to have that Office. I will get a couple of constables, gun-toters, and these boys will go out and break up Negro dice games, raid petty little home-brew joints in Mexican town and take in some of these tourists that are exceeding the speed limit by a few miles. We will make good fees. Vultures are all we are."

"I guess a man has to make a living," Bowie said.

"In this system he is forced to be a criminal."

"I never robbed nobody that couldn't stand to lose it," Bowie said.

Hawkins looked at Keechie. "And whatever road a man takes there is always a woman that will follow him."

"If this man here will just get up and start," Keechie said, "I will follow him right now."

"Don't pay no attention to her, Judge," Bowie said.

The gurgling sounded in Hawkins' stomach again.

The strung, colored lights of this town's Main Street illuminated an empty, quiet thoroughfare. On the Court House lawn, a big, lighted Christmas tree glowed greens and reds and yellows. The sign at the edge of the town read: *New Orleans . . . 590 mi.*

"You think we will be there this time tomorrow night?" Keechie said.

"Uh huh. Keechie, I can just see that Indian's face when

them big lawyers start coming in his cell. He's sure going to know he's got a friend Out Here."

"You have done everything you could now."

Bowie turned his head toward her and grinned. "Say, did you hear Old Windy's guts growling?"

"I thought he was never going to stop talking."

"I never heard anything like it," Bowie said. "You could have heard it out in the street."

Chapter XXII

BOWIE and Keechie had the renting of a furnished house on their minds when they entered New Orleans, but it was late and they were so tired that they looked at an apartment and there were so many nice things about the very first one that they took it. The place—*The Colonial Apartments*—was a remodeled home and as big as an old West Texas court house. On an avenue of palm-fenced homes and big churches, this house was shadowed and darkened by spreading cotton-woods and hackberries, and crêpe myrtles screened the windows.

Mrs. Lufkin was the owner of *The Colonial Apartments*. She was a stout-bosomed woman with dyed black hair and smelled like a brewery. Mrs. Lufkin did not have much to do with the running of the apartments, leaving this to Rebecca, the little Negro woman with gold teeth. From Rebecca, Bowie and Keechie learned about the other occupants of the place: the Professor who taught in the University up the avenue; the Interne and his Nurse-Wife who were at the hospital most of the time; the four girls who lived in the two apartments up-stairs and were students in the University. Rebecca said Mrs. Lufkin bought whisky five gallons at a time and she prayed for her every night.

The ceiling of their living-room was so high that Keechie could not touch the plastered dome even when Bowie lifted her. There was a wide, high fireplace of polished granite and a log gas-heater. In a few days, when they made that one big shopping tour downtown, they would get a radio to put beside the library table and beaded parlor lamp. And a red-checkered cloth for the kitchen table, Keechie said.

The sleeping-room had a tiled floor and in it were wedged a bed and a clear-mirrored vanity. The kitchen was small too, but it would look a lot better, Bowie said, when that big pantry was filled with stuff to eat. The bathroom was as big as the kitchen and steaming water gushed from the *hot* tap. Now you can get all the baths you want, Bowie said, and when Keechie said she had been thinking about that, Bowie said he did not see how they had put up with it back in those Texas hills.

They would get a telephone put in, they decided, and any time there was drug-store buying or anything like that to do, they would have delivery boys bring it to their door. Rebecca had said that she went to the Grocery every morning and would be glad to get their things too. They would give her a few dollars a week, Bowie said, and that old black gal would break her neck for them. There would not be anybody to see except Rebecca and delivery boys and at nights they could duck in suburban picture shows.

The best thing about it all, Keechie said, was that no one in the world knew where they were. She lettered the slip that Bowie inserted in the slot of the mailbox in the lobby: *Mr. & Mrs. F. T. Haviland.*

When the trial of Chicamaw started back in Gusherton, Bowie waited in the kitchen every afternoon listening for the thump of the thrown newspaper on the back steps. There were three days of the trial and then on the fourth day, Bowie read in the Sunday-morning paper of its outcome. Chicamaw had beaten the Chair. He had drawn a pair of nines—ninety-nine years.

Bowie carried the newspaper back to Keechie who was still in bed this Sunday morning. "That boy beat them," Bowie said. "They're not going to kick any Switch off on him. It's right here in the paper, Keechie."

"I'm glad," Keechie said.

"Go ahead and read it, Keechie. Here it is, right here."

"Now you will feel a lot better," Keechie said.

"And don't think he is just sittin' up there in that jail with his brains sittin' too. And he won't have to kill anybody to beat that Pen either. Any day you want to kill somebody, Keechie, you can beat a Pen easy."

"That is none of your worry now."

"Go ahead and read it. I'll stir us up some breakfast. How about me cooking it up this morning? How about it?"

"All right."

By ten o'clock, sunlight was knifing through the crêpe myrtle and the raised windows, cutting bright squares on the living-room carpet and blue linoleum of the kitchen. This is one day I'm not going to stay cooped up, Bowie thought. We're going to get out. Keechie sat on the vanity bench with a curling iron in her hand. She had on the Chinese wrapper with the yellow and red dragon designs.

"Let's get out of this place today, Keechie. What do you say?"

"Where?"

"Don't make one bit of difference to me. Just so we go."

"Would you like to go walking in that Park up the avenue?"

"You're doggone whistling."

Keechie put the curling iron on the vanity and stood up. "I've always wanted to go through it in the daytime. I'll wear my gray flannel suit."

"I'll strut out in that double-breasted. Say, Little Soldier, you're getting as broad as I don't know what."

Keechie looked down her body, at her hips.

"You're puttin' on plenty," Bowie said.

"Don't you like it?"

"I should say I do. You could get as big as the side of a barn and I'd like it."

"Well, there's no danger of that."

The lower limbs of the big oak in the Park grew on the ground as if the task of going up was too much. The gray Spanish moss that fringed the boughs, Keechie said, was whiskers and showed how old the trees were. They circled the tree now and moved across the smooth fairway of the golf course, pausing near the fluttering pennant on the green, and then went on toward the lagoon. A couple passed ahead of them, a wire-haired terrier straining on a leash held by the woman. The man bent down now to tie a shoe-lace and then trotted to catch up.

"If I had a dog I would want one of them big police babies," Bowie said. "They're mean as hell."

Swans glided on the lagoon, the traced water smoothing behind them. Around the bend of water-dipping willows, a rowboat came, the oars splashing; three girls in it. The swans moved closer to the shore. On the boat were the letters *Nellie*. The girl rowing had on brown slacks and a white sweater. Bowie and Keechie lowered themselves to the grass of the bank's edge and watched the girls and the boat disappear around the bend below.

"What are you thinking about?" Keechie said.

"I had an aunt named Nell," Bowie said. "I was thinking about her."

"Your Daddy's sister?"

Bowie shook his head. "Mama's. We lived with her a while, I mean Grandma's, after my Dad got killed. It's funny that I got to thinking about her."

"What about her?"

"Oh, I don't know. She used to come on Sunday afternoons and bring a big old sack of red-hots and licorice drops and candy like that. You remember that kind of candy, don't you?"

Keechie nodded. She reached out and plucked a bit of grass from the silk of Bowie's socks.

"Makes me think of that boy I was running around with too then," Bowie said. "You know that kid, the last time I heard of him, was a big football player in Oklahoma University and he was just a cutter and a half. We were a pair now. His Dad was the County Treasurer in that town and why he was running around up back alleys and gettin' junk and sellin' it, I don't know. That boy had more devilment in him than anybody I ever did know. We got to going in vacant houses and tearing the plumbing out and selling the brass and lead. I remember one day we made eighty cents. We bought four of them nickel pies apiece. That kid always had money in his pockets. He would steal it out of his Dad's pants at nights."

Keechie plucked a blade of Bermuda grass and began chewing the white root.

"I don't know how come me to ever think of him, but he just knew about everything that was going on in that town. That's how come me to go out to them houses at the edge of town one day. The Red Light district. He said there was women out there who would give kids nickels and dimes if they just went out there and hung around the back door."

The hoofs of running horses sounded and then on the bridle path, on the other side of the lagoon and through the trees, they saw the bright jackets of the women riders.

"I saw her, but I don't think that she knows to this day that it was me. When the old woman in the House started hollering at us to get away, she come to the back door and I saw her."

"Saw who?" Keechie said.

Bowie looked at her. "My Aunt. I thought I told you."

"Oh," Keechie said.

"She didn't recognize me though."

Keechie leaned against Bowie's leg, picked another bit of dead grass and smoothed the silk.

The horsewomen were passing yonder again, posting.

"Ain't that a helluva way to ride?" Bowie said. "Bobbing your bottom up and down like that?"

"Uh huh."

Bowie indicated that golf green behind them with a twist of his head. "That's something else I never figured why anybody could get interested in. Batting that little old ball around and puttin' it in holes."

"Some people don't have anything else to do," Keechie said. "It wouldn't bother me though if they stood on their heads if they were having a good time."

"Me neither."

They walked now along the lagoon's bank toward the white dome of the Memorial Band-stand. Bowie stopped and pointed at the rat swimming in the water toward the little island of weeping willows. "I'll bet that rat has him a Hole over there," he said.

"I didn't know rats could swim," Keechie said.

"Them kind can. I know one kind that can't do anything but snitch. Them are yellow and have two legs."

"Oh," Keechie said. "Now I get you."

"I can tell you something else about some of these boys that are gettin' in trouble every day," Bowie said. "They like to see their names in the newspapers. Why, Keechie, there's guys that will put on acts and do anything just to get their names big in the newspapers."

"I had just as soon talk about something else," Keechie said.

"Just one more thing, Keechie. Have you been thinking about us not gettin' our names in the paper no more? There hasn't been hardly one thing since that damned plumber flushed us back yonder in them damned old rainy hills."

"Just don't do anything to get your name in the paper," Keechie said. "That is the thing."

"Say we got jumped here, Keechie. Now I know. There isn't a chance just as long as we keep our noses clean like we're doing. But just say we were. Where would you like to go?"

"I don't know."

"You know where I would like to go? Mexico. It takes somebody, though, that knows the ropes to get you across that border and situated good down there. Now you take Chicamaw, he knew the ropes down there from A to Z."

"Well, Chicamaw isn't here and he isn't going to be here."

"I know it. I was just telling you, honey."

The couple coming across the narrow rustic bridge were holding hands, and Bowie and Keechie stepped aside and gave them passageway. The girl had on a white silk dress and the black hair of the fellow grew long and curling down his neck. As they stepped off the bridge, the fellow put his arm around the girl supportingly.

Bowie and Keechie went on. "You can tell by looking at them they're not married," Bowie said.

"How can you tell?"

"I don't know. Just the way he was holding her hand as if she was going to fall off that bridge or something, I guess."

"Clever, aren't you?"

"I notice little things like that."

"Maybe she would have fallen off if he hadn't been helping her. Married or not married. A girl likes that anyway."

Bowie looked at her. "Say, do you want me to hold your hand like that?" He reached toward her. Keechie swept his hand down. "Just keep that to yourself," she said.

"Gollee, honey. What's come over you? What did I do?"

Keechie turned around. "Let's go home."

"Gollee, can you beat that. What have I done?"

Keechie started back and he caught up and walked alongside her again. Near the broad stone arch of the Park's exit, a bunch of boys, their shirt tails flapping, were playing with an indoor ball. Bowie asked Keechie to wait a minute and they stood there and watched the players a little while.

The sunshine was gone now and the air touched their bodies like cold feathers. The avenue would be quiet and then, with the spreading green of the green signal light down the thoroughfare, the gears of the waiting automobiles would grate and crash, and then they came, passing in rushing trains.

"I've been thinking about old T-Dub," Bowie said. "I guess that girl was just dumb. But you know they were like a couple of kids showing me that Marriage License."

"First I had heard about it," Keechie said.

"Didn't I ever tell you about that? Well, they were just like a couple of kids, dragging that License out and showing it all around."

"I guess it mattered to them."

Bowie looked at Keechie, a loosened curl moved on her upturned coat collar. "I guess it did," he said. "They were like a couple of kids."

A street-car crashed past, its trolley popping, a glued mass of humanity through its closed windows. At the intersection, Bowie touched Keechie's arm as they stepped down off the curb.

"Would you marry me, Keechie?"

She looked up at him, then ahead again. "I don't know whether I would or not."

"Now just what do you mean by that?"

"I can't see what difference some writing on a scrap of paper makes if that's what you are thinking about."

"I don't either. That's what I have been thinking. What

difference does a piece of red ribbon around some paper make? Besides, you're married to me already if you didn't know it."

Keechie looked up at him again. "Where do you get that?"

"It's the law, Keechie. Honest. If you introduce a woman three times in public as your wife, you're just as much married as if you had a Justice of the Peace and nine preachers to do it. Honest. That's the law and you can't get around it."

"I didn't know that."

"You take you and me now. All right, didn't Filthy MacNasty get it that way and Mrs. Lufkin up here and Rebecca and anybody that looks at that mail box? You can't get around it."

"I didn't know that."

"You can't get around it," Bowie said. "That's the law."

At the next crossing, he took her arm and held it the rest of the way home.

Chapter XXIII

FOR several days now Keechie had not been feeling well and this morning, after she smoked a cigarette, she felt sick at her stomach and had to lie down. Bowie rinsed towels under the cold tap in the kitchen and put them on her forehead.

It was only May, but the damp heat was like a jail cell in July. It clogged the nostrils and sweat streaked Bowie's cheeks from his sideburns. He said it was the heat that was making Keechie feel this way; that and the change of climate. The thing they had better do was go to town and duck in and see a doctor. Keechie said no, she had just been smoking too many cigarettes and everything would be all right in a day or so.

A little before noon, Keechie said sherbert appealed to her, pints and pints of it, orange or pineapple. Bowie said he would walk to the Drug Store and get it because it might take the delivery boy an hour to get here and he wanted her to have it while she was hungry.

On the newspaper rack in front of the Drug Store, there was a Noon Edition and Bowie picked it up and went on in. The Soda Clerk was at the table of two women and Bowie went on to the fountain, spread the newspaper and began to read the headlines.

Soda Clerk placed his hands, palms down, on the surface at the edge of the spread newspaper and Bowie looked up. "Dollar's worth of orange and pineapple sherbert," he said.

In this headline, the words *Prison Farm* swelled and Bowie began reading underneath it:

BINGHAM, Texas, May 29—Deputy Sheriff Oscar Dunning of Winkford County arrived here yesterday afternoon after a 650-mile trip with a bench warrant for the custody of Amos Ackerman, inmate of the Bingham Prison Farm, near here, but he was a half-hour too late to get his man alive. Ackerman, serving five years for assault with intent to kill, was shot to death by prison guards at 2:30 o'clock yesterday afternoon when he made a bold dash for freedom.

Deputy Dunning was planning on returning Ackerman to Winkford County to testify in a scheduled murder trial there.

Ackerman, a trusty and member of a chopping-cotton squad working two miles from the prison buildings, was sent back to get some tools and on the way made his ill-fated break. When he did not show up, a search was instituted and prison dogs led guards to a pile of brush just off the farm property. Ignoring the commands to halt, he was slain, prison officials stated.

The effort of Ackerman to escape, farm officials declared, was a lone attempt and not participated in by any other inmates. Extra precautions to prevent escapes were ordered by Farm Captain Fred Stammers today. There are several desperate criminals on the Farm now, including Elmo (Three-Toed) Mobley, bank robber, who arrived here last week from the State Penitentiary.

Outside, the sun stung Bowie's face like a shaving lotion and his knee-bones felt like dry sponges. He walked rapidly.

Water was gushing in the bathroom and Bowie went in there. In the filling tub, Keechie sat, her hair in a knot, water lapping the under-swell of her breasts.

"Feeling better, honey?" Bowie said.

"I'll say," Keechie said. There was the clean smell of soap and Keechie's body. Her long eyelashes clung to the wet skin. "What have you there in your hand?" she said.

"Paper."

The lathering soap in the washrag slowed. "What's the matter?"

"Nothing. Except they got him on a goddamned farm."

"Chicamaw?"

"Yes."

Keechie turned and looked at the gushing tap and then she bent and twisted it shut.

"You can't imagine what it is to be on one of those farms," Bowie said. "He won't last six months. They don't send you out to them farms unless they want to get rid of you. If you're any kind of a man you won't last, and by God, he's a man."

Keechie placed the soap and cloth on the rack and then pulled the stopper. The draining water began to swish and gurgle.

Bowie took the bath-mat off the basin and straightened it on the tile at the side of the tub. "It's cotton-chopping time now and you know what they do to them boys? Run 'em out there like horses and kick 'em with spurs and hit 'em with saps. They drop dead out in them fields, Keechie. Five of them in one day. It was in the papers."

"Well, you can't do anything about it."

Bowie helped her over the tub's rim, put the towel about her shoulders.

"Something could be done about it all right!" he said.

"For instance?"

"I mean if a man wanted to. I could go down there with one man to drive a car and take a machine gun and clean out that whole goddamned farm. Them dirty Laws and newspapers. Calling me a Number One this and a Number One that. I could set them sonsofbitches a real pace. If I wanted to hurt somebody, I wouldn't be sittin' here twiddling my thumbs."

Keechie spread the house dress about her waist and thighs. "You call this twiddling your thumbs?"

"Aw, honey, I don't mean you and me. I do tell you, though, one thing about you and me. We got to start getting out of this place here more. Get out and enjoy ourselves for a change. Go down to some of these night clubs in that French Quarter that we're all the time hearing over the radio and do a little drinking and have a good time."

"I think we can go out a little," Keechie said.

"That's what makes you feel bad in the mornings," Bowie said. "Staying cooped up like this all the time. It's not good for anybody."

"I think we can start going out some, but I don't see any use of drinking."

"We can drink beer."

"Beer, I guess, will be all right."

"You have to drink in those places. You couldn't go in one of those places and just sit there. You'd look like a I-don't-know-what."

"I'm going to get my feet dirty if you don't go in there and get my bedroom slippers," Keechie said. "In the bottom left-hand drawer."

Bowie came back with the slippers. They were red felt with black fur. "I just happened to think. I went out of that Drug Store without paying for that newspaper. I just paid for the sherbert. I'll bet them people over there think I tried to beat them out of it."

Bowie waited in their paralleled parked car under the shade of the French-balconied Second-Hand Store on Chartres Street. Keechie was up yonder in that big Department Store on Canal getting a dinner gown and sandals and a wrap. They were going to do this stepping out tonight in the right way.

Bowie turned now and looked at the wrapped boxes on the back seat. There was a white linen suit in the long box and a panama hat in the round one; white oxfords and baby-blue socks in the other. He was going to look like something himself tonight. He had a blue shirt and yellow tie like the combination Chicamaw had had.

The street on which he waited was the narrowest, craziest one he had ever seen. There were old chairs and stands and vases in front of the Antique Shop that didn't look worth ten cents a dozen and the window yonder was a crazy-quilt of oil paintings. On the corner was a bar: *Vieux Carre Haven*. A man stumbled out of the swinging doors and stood there, swaying uncertainly. He had on a white cotton shirt and faded blue-denim trousers.

If she stays much longer, Bowie thought, I'm going to duck

in that bar and get a beer. It takes a woman a lot longer to do things than a man. But he had fooled around and let that girl get down to where she didn't have a thing to wear. She might as well have had a shoe clerk or a flatfoot Law for a man. Not a fellow that had got himself almost thirty thousand dollars over in Texas in a couple of months.

The drunk was coming toward Bowie's car. His shirt was grass-stained and a tattoo showed through the torn sleeve. He grinned loosely: "You got a dime, Mack, for an old boy that sure needs a drink?"

"I'll give you a quarter to get that stinking breath out of my face," Bowie said. He put a half-dollar in the cupped hand.

"I just got out Stir this morning," Stink Breath said. "Thirty days I done."

"I don't give a damn," Bowie said. "Get on."

Stink Breath moved toward the bar, his hands spread like an exhausted wrestler, disappeared inside. Toward the waterfront, the whistle of a tugboat groaned.

Why couldn't a man get hold of some thief lawyer, Bowie thought, and get him to write out a Bench Warrant? Then get a Sheriff's badge and a big hat. He could go on one of them prison farms, show that and take any man off he wanted to. Them Farm Captains and Bosses couldn't see nothing but that Warrant.

A man in a beret and golf knickers stopped now in front of the window of oil paintings, shaded his forehead and pressed against the glass. He scratched his thigh.

It could be done all right, Bowie thought. Just go on that Farm like you owned it and flash your badge and be from one of those far western counties out by El Paso. Deputies and sheriffs were going on them farms every day and gettin' men.

Keechie was coming, stepping around other pedestrians, headed for the car. Bowie pushed out the door. "I begin to think you had fell in somewhere," he said.

"They are going to get the things out by five o'clock," Keechie said. "Sure good to be back here. All those women crowding around give me the creeps."

"Lady, could you spare a dime to a man that hasn't had a bite to eat?" It was Stink Breath, his face framed in the lowered window of the car.

"Get to hell away from here," Bowie said.

"Lady, if you can't spare anything but a nickel."

Bowie pushed the door on his side out with his foot. "Bowie," Keechie called. "Bowie!"

Bowie grasped Stink Breath's collar, kicked him in the seat. The collar ripped in his hands. He kicked again. "If you don't want to get your head stomped in this sidewalk, you get up this street, you bastard."

Stink Breath loped up the sidewalk. The man in the beret, the two men that stood now in the Second-Hand Store doorway, were laughing. Bowie grinned. "Bowie, get in here," Keechie said.

Bowie got in the car. "Something ought to be done about stew bums like that," he said.

"You ought to quit making a fool out of yourself," Keechie said.

They moved from the curb. "I'll bet he takes his next drink standing up," Bowie said.

Fastened couples churned to the beating music in a center of foaming light, but here among the tables and under the low ceiling, Bowie and Keechie sat in lavender darkness. The Mexican musicians on the palm-screened platform were playing *La Paloma*. Bowie beat on the gray tablecloth with his index finger. Now Keechie pressed a cigarette in the clay ashtray that was shaped like a sombrero. "You sure like Spanish music, don't you?" she said.

"That's one thing them Chilis can do."

"I like it too."

"I don't see anything to that dancing out there though, do you?"

"I never did care about dancing."

Bowie touched the frosted glass of beer. "Looks silly to me. Switching your tail around. Look at that gink out there, that four-eyed one, the one with the girl in the blue dress? . . . Don't he think he's a card now?"

Keechie lifted her glass, took a sip of the foamless beer and put it down. "You didn't think that when that Mexican girl was dancing," she said.

"What did I do?"

"You couldn't even find time to light my cigarette."

"I don't remember that. I'm talking about that kind of dancing out there now, honey."

The waiter came and picked up Bowie's emptied glass. His shirt front was a slick gray and the knuckles of his hand looked like a row of English walnuts. "Beer?" he said.

Bowie looked at Keechie. "Want to try something a little stronger? Whisky?"

Keechie shook her head.

"Two more beers," Bowie said. The knuckles moved away.

The orchestra was playing *La Cucaracha* now and the legs of the dancing couples were working faster and more heavily. Bowie beat on the beer glass with the ashtray. "You know, Keechie, I sure wouldn't mind going down to that country. Plenty of fellows have gone down there and liked it swell and you couldn't drag them back to this country."

"I don't know whether I would like living among a bunch of foreigners or not," Keechie said.

"I tell you a man that knows the ropes of that country. That Judge Hawkins. What that man doesn't know about that country isn't on the books."

"That man."

"I've heard you could live down there for a little or nothing. You and me could live like a couple of I-don't-know-whats down there on what we got salted away. In two or three years I'll bet I could get lined up with one of those big mining companies and where would we be then? I don't know but what that is a doggone good idea, Keechie?"

Keechie put her fingers around the glass, but did not pick it up. "It might be all right."

"Now I tell you an old boy that really knows it. Chicamaw. If he was here with us I'd be ready to start out tonight. Put that boy in the back seat of our car with a .30-30 and that Mexican army couldn't stop us from crossing that border. But if anybody knows the ropes, you can make it as easy as falling off a log."

Keechie got up and pulled her wrap off the back of the chair. "Let's go home," she said.

Bowie looked up at her. "Goodness me, honey. Why, I didn't think we was gettin' started good."

"I've had enough of this," Keechie said.

The music stopped. Bowie rose slowly. "Are you feeling bad again?"

"Yes," Keechie said.

Chairs scraped around them as the returning dancers started seating themselves. Bowie beckoned Knuckles.

Chapter XXIV

BOWIE picked up another ink-crusted pen off the table of crumbling blotters and tried the point. This one would write. A revolving door down the darkening corridor of the Post Office made a swishing, jolting sound and Bowie watched. It was a Negro in a porter's uniform, a bundle of papers and letters in his arms. The Negro's shoes crackled on the tile and echoed hollowly in the empty building. Bowie wrote:

Dear Mr. Hawkins:

Enclosed here is $200. I want you to get hold for me a Bench Warrant and get a seal and everything on it. Make it out for Elmo T. Mobley on the Bingham Prison Farm. Make it from Becus County and fix it up real proper and everything. Also I want a Sheriff badge.

A door swished again. The man in the straw hat and seersucker suit dropped the letter in the slot and presently the door bumped and Bowie was alone again.

I want you to please have these things ready and I may come in on you any time. So have them ready. Do it as soon as possible. Remember Xmas night. I am the same fellow.

Yours very truly,
Xmas Nite.

P. S. There will be another hundred for you when the goods are delivered. X. N.

Bowie sealed the envelope, pounded the flap with his closed hand and went over and dropped the letter in the slot.

On the sidewalk outside, he stopped and looked at the fresh, gold-painted lettering on the door of his car:

SUNSHINE CO. PRODUCTS
F. T. HAVILAND, AGENT

Around Lee Circle and then out St. Charles Avenue, Bowie drove. Chances are I never will see that Judge, he thought, but that letter will be just in case. I thought of it and I would just keep thinking about it if I didn't get the thing off my chest. This is just kind of like insurance, just looking ahead.

There was somebody in his apartment and Bowie brought his hand back from the knob and listened. Feet approached the door and then it opened. It was Mrs. Lufkin. Smelling of liquor and perfume. "Oh, how do you do, Mister Haviland?"

"All right." Through the doorway he saw Keechie sitting on the couch. She looked all right.

"Pretty warm weather we are having?" Mrs. Lufkin said.

"Too warm," Bowie said. He squeezed past Mrs. Lufkin and went inside.

"Well, goodbye," Mrs. Lufkin said.

"Goodbye," Keechie said.

Bowie closed the door. "What was that old souse doing in here?"

Keechie got up. "She wants us to move."

"Why?"

"It's nothing. She has a chance to rent it to some professor that wants it for a year and she said she knew we weren't permanent."

"You don't think she's smelled something?"

Keechie shook her head. "Oh, no."

"Well, what are we going to do?"

"There isn't anything to do, unless you want to pay her a lot of rent."

"I'll be damned if I do that. I'm ready to get out of this hot dump anyway. I can't see why anybody else would want it."

"There's plenty of places here."

"Sure. It don't worry me."

Keechie lowered herself back to the divan and lay down. "Did you get the sign on the car?"

"You ought to see it, honey. I got that fellow to do it that we saw that afternoon hanging around that Square, the one with the Jesus Christ beard. On both sides. We ought to have thought of that a long time ago."

"I thought you were never coming back."

He went over and sat down on the divan and jiggled the toe of her shoe. "It took him a pretty good while."

"Anything happen?"

"Not a thing."

After the supper of canned soup and crackers, Bowie and Keechie looked at road maps. This one here covered the whole United States and the regions were illustrated with bright-colored sketches: cattle in Texas, oil-wells in Oklahoma, shocks of wheat in Kansas.

"Doggoned if I know where to go," Bowie said.

"Looks like it would be easy with all this to pick from."

"Well, we don't have to leave New Orleans, you know."

"Oh, I'm fed up on this town, honey. It's just too doggone hot."

Keechie pointed at the Southwest Texas region. "Right in there somewhere is the place we lived."

"That's another place you couldn't drag me," Bowie said.

"Or any place else in Texas," Keechie said.

Bowie tapped the Gulf of Mexico. "You ever seen the ocean, Keechie?"

She shook her head.

"Me neither. I'm almost thirty years old and you know I never have seen the ocean. Can you beat that? Say, how would you like to live on the ocean?"

"Sounds pretty good to me."

Bowie folded the map. "We got plenty of time. It never pays to decide a thing too quick. We got a couple of weeks and by then we'll know exactly where we want to light out for."

"Sure," Keechie said.

Keechie whimpered in her sleep again and this time Bowie sat up and looked at her. In the moonlight that filtered through the crêpe myrtle and screen, he saw her mouth pucker like a child and she whimpered again. A mosquito sang with needle-like vibration in Bowie's ear and he waved his hand over Keechie's head. She was quiet now and he eased back, moving his hand over her head from time to time.

It's malaria, he thought. That's what it is. These god-damned mosquitoes.

Keechie sobbed out. It was a dry, throat-lodging cry. She turned over, her face toward the window and lay quiet. The mosquito sang, and he raised up and fanned furiously.

Back in the kitchen, the clock ticked, smothered now by the rush of a speeding car on the avenue; ticked again. She had bought that clock in Antelope Center and of all things to bring. She bought it the same day she got that big gunny sack of Irish potatoes. They had left it and there wasn't a fourth of them used.

Keechie made sounds now like she was losing her breath and he placed his hand on her shoulder and shook gently: "Keechie, Keechie. What's the matter, honey?"

She raised, her eyes wide open. "What is it?" she said. "Bowie?"

"You ain't feeling well, honey."

"What is it?"

"Are you hurtin'? Hurtin' any place, honey?"

Keechie let her head back on the pillow. "I'm all right."

"You must have been dreaming. Nightmare or something."

She did not say anything. An automobile horn sounded on the avenue, a street-car was coming.

"You been crying in your sleep, Keechie."

"I had a dream. I guess that was it."

"What was it?"

"Forget it. I'm all right."

The street-car grated in a stop in front of the house; ground and clicked on.

"Did you think you were falling off something? I've dreamed that. Gun breaking in my hand. I dreamed I couldn't make my Dad hear me a hundred times."

"I dreamed you had gone away," Keechie said.

"Me?"

"It's all right now. Go on and go to sleep. You're going to be worn out in the morning."

"Where did I go?"

"I don't know. You had just gone and I thought I was trying to find you. I couldn't find you."

"Well, there's no danger of me going any place without you."

"You went to town yesterday."

"That's different. I mean off any place. No, honey, it looks like you and me are going up the same road together."

"Up the same road?"

"It sure looks that way."

"Is that the way you want it, Bowie?"

"That's the way I want it, honey, but sometimes I think about you."

"That's the way I want it, Bowie, and you remember it."

Bowie slapped his hands together. "That damned mosquito been bothering you?"

"I hadn't noticed it," Keechie said.

"You sleepy?"

"No, I'm wide awake now."

This street-car rumbled on past and soon was a distant, fading hum.

"I been trying to figure out some place for us to go," Bowie said. "It's got me worried."

"There's plenty of places."

"You know, I have just about decided that we got to make Mexico. If only I knew the ins and outs of that damned country. I could kick myself for not pumping some fellows that had been down there. But there's nothing to this, Keechie. I'm not going to really feel good about us until we're plumb out of this country."

"We can go to Mexico."

"If I just knew the ropes about all that border down there and just knew one of them Thief officials down there that Chicamaw was telling me about. Now you take old Hawkins. I don't know but what it would be a good idea to go and see him."

"Not him," Keechie said.

"Why not?"

"There's plenty of other men that know about Mexico."

"Who?"

"I don't know, but there's plenty."

"But who?"

"There's plenty of men that know."

"But who, Keechie? That don't do no good. Just name me somebody that we could go to and he would give us all the lowdown that we got to have? I'm not any plain tourist, you know. I'm not the governor of this state, you know."

"Now don't get smart. What I am telling you is that you don't have any business back there in Texas. Or around anybody that knows you."

Bowie clutched at the air. "I'm going to get up and brain this mosquito in just about two seconds."

There was a little wind and stirred leaves of the crêpe myrtle sighed on the screen.

"Do you really want to go to Mexico, Bowie?"

"It's about all I know to do."

"Do you think Hawkins can really help?"

"I don't know of anybody else. I was just as sure you would take me up when I mentioned him about that. I even dropped him a line."

"When?"

"When I was getting that sign put on. That day."

"Yesterday, you mean?"

"Yes."

"Why didn't you tell me?"

"I just didn't. I'm telling you now."

"Did you write about Chicamaw?"

"Yes."

Keechie sat up.

"Now look here, Keechie. Now don't start that. Honey, I'm just worried to death." He sat up.

Keechie got off the bed. "You needn't say any more. That's all I want to know."

"Now look here, Keechie. Where you going?"

"What difference does that make?"

"Now look here, Keechie. Now come on, honey."

"Which is it, Bowie? Make up your mind right now. Once and forever. Which is it, Chicamaw or me?"

"It's you. If it wasn't you, I'd been down on that farm long before now and cleaning it from one end to the other gettin' him off. I know now how you feel about it, Keechie. I'm just learning. You been a Little Soldier to me and I'm going to play square with you."

Keechie shivered.

"As long, honey, as I'm any good to you, I'm going to stay with you. I'm telling you straight now, Keechie. I've had things on my mind and I don't mind admitting it to you, but they're all over. That's it, Keechie. The best I know how to tell you."

Keechie lowered herself to the edge of the bed. "Did you really want to see that lawyer about Mexico?"

"When we were talking while ago? . . . Yes, I did. I meant it."

Keechie picked up the edge of the twisted sheet and shook it with a flapping sound out over Bowie. Then she folded it back on her side of the bed and got under it.

"And you think the lawyer is the only one to see?" Keechie said.

"I leave it up to you, Keechie. It's all up to you."

"When do you want to go?"

"I leave that up to you."

"Tomorrow?"

"It suits me."

The clock was ticking again now in the kitchen. A truck passed on the narrow street by their window and presently there was the sound of milk bottles clattering in a tin rack. The moonlight was gone now and the sleeping-room was dark. Bowie raised up and listened to Keechie's even breathing. She was sleeping sound. He eased back, lay there a moment and then cautiously pulled up his foot and scratched the mosquito bite again.

Chapter XXV

THE moon had an eye-squinching brightness, radiating six splintered beams, broad as planks. It deepened the dark hollows of Keechie's eyes, shadowed the lines that slashed her face from cheek bones to tight lips. She sat there in their car, parked on the by-road just off the highway, her eyes closed, head resting on the back of the seat.

Bowie, standing on the ground with one foot on the running board, looked again toward the lights of MacMasters, as golden as oil lamps in the clear air. They had stopped here a little after sundown, deciding it was best to wait until ten o'clock or so and be sure that Hawkins would be at home.

"You feel any better, honey?" Bowie said.

"I want something ice-cold to drink," Keechie said. "I know I would feel a lot better if I had a cold soda pop."

"We'll get it when we gas up. The very first thing. I wish now we had stopped back up the road, but there was just so many Square Johns hanging around then."

"I can get along without it."

Bowie moved around the front of the car, got under the wheel. "We can go now," he said. "To hell with this waiting."

The neon sign on the left, at the city's edge, read: *Alamo Plaza Courts.* It burned in front of a filling station and behind that was a court of white frame cottages. On a bench under the shed of the station sat a man, an old fellow, licking a cone of ice cream. Bowie turned in and the old man rose.

"Fill it up," Bowie said. He went on to the big wooden ice-box.

The spring of the screen door whined and Bowie looked up. The woman coming out was Mattie. She was heavier; gold on her teeth. "Hi you do," she said.

"Okeh," Bowie said. He brought a bottle out of the icy water.

"Passing through?" Mattie said.

Bowie moved his head, indicating the old man holding the hose by the clicking pump.

"Papa," Mattie said.

"Just passing through," Bowie said.

Mattie looked at Keechie in the car, and Bowie jerked the bottle's cap and started back.

"Who is that?" Keechie said.

"T-Dub's sister-in-law." She took the bottle from his hand. "It's cold. She's Real People."

"I'll drink this when we get started."

"Go ahead and drink it, honey. I'll get plenty to carry."

Mattie lifted the ice-box top for Bowie. "How is everything around here?" he said.

"Okeh," Mattie said.

"How's the husband?"

"Still In There."

Bowie ran his hands over the bottles. "That's too bad."

"The cokes are at that end if that's what you are looking for," Mattie said.

"How's my heat around here?" Bowie said.

"You can find better places to run around in."

Papa hung the hose on the rack. "How's your oil?" he said. His voice squeaked like the broken note of a clarinet. "All right," Bowie said. He paid Mattie.

"Take care of yourself," Mattie said.

"Same to you," Bowie said.

The air on the boulevard was cool and clean. Out at its end was Hawkins' house.

"Aren't you going to drink that, honey?" Bowie said.

"Not now."

"What's the matter?"

"I'm afraid it might come up."

"Doggone, sugar."

"I think I had better lie down in the back. If I lie down a little while I think I will feel better."

Bowie drew alongside the curbing, stopped, got out and helped Keechie into the back. He took her coat, spread it over her feet, got back under the wheel and drove on.

There were four unoccupied automobiles parked in front of Hawkins' house. The church was dark.

"What are those cars, Bowie?" Keechie said.

"You just lay back down now, honey."

"I feel better. You think it's all right to go up there?"

"I'll be right back now before you can turn around. You just take it easy now."

The porch planks creaked and gave under Bowie's steps and then he knocked on the door. Under the half-raised blind he could see the trousered legs of men seated at a card table.

The door parted and there was a middle-aged woman in a black dress and white-lace collar.

"Judge in?"

"Why, yes. Won't you come in?"

"I'll just wait here."

The woman hesitated. "Who can I tell him?"

"Mister Knight. Mister Knight."

Bowie watched the legs through the window. The card table moved and then feet were coming to the door.

The porch globe showered light. Hawkins was in shirt sleeves and had a pipe in his right hand. He switched it quickly, reached and then the porch was dark again. "Wait a minute," he said. The door closed and Bowie backed down off the porch steps, his fingers grasping the butt of the gun under his arm.

The door opened again and Bowie went back up on the porch and took the extended envelope. It was heavy and he felt the badge's pin. "You busy?" he said.

Hawkins nodded toward the window. "Company," he whispered.

"I want to get some low down on Mexico."

Hawkins shook his head. "Can't help you there, son. That's the Sheriff in there."

"Okeh," Bowie said.

His heels clicked on the sidewalk toward the car. *I promised him another hundred, but to hell with him. He's just a little too busy. I don't need this damned stuff anyway. Where's Keechie?*

She lay face down in the bottom of the car, her left arm crooked like it was broken. "Keechie," he said. "Keechie." She was limp and heavy. "Keechie, honey. Baby. Keechie." Her teeth were clenched and he couldn't hear her breathing. He straightened her on the seat, got up in front and his hand shook on the knob above the grinding gears.

Papa pushed off the bench and approached. "Where's a vacant cabin?" Bowie said.

"Just about what kind of a price do you have in mind, Mister?"

"Any of 'em."

"We got some for a dollar and a half and some for . . ."

"Where's that woman that was around here?"

"You mean my darter? The girl that was . . ."

"Where is she?" Bowie started getting out of the car.

The screen's spring rasped and then Mattie came. "I got to have a place," Bowie said.

Mattie went around into the Court and Bowie followed her in the car. At the far, low end she pointed at the corner cabin and Bowie parked in front of it. Mattie went on in and turned on the light.

Bowie lowered Keechie to the bed, straightened the skirt down over her knees. Her face was drained, the lines deep. Mattie stood in the half-opened screen.

"I can't figure it out," Bowie said. He picked up a towel off the foot of the bed and went to the sink and turned on the water. "I can't figure it out. Go get a doctor, Mattie. Go on and get a doctor out here."

He started bathing Keechie's face. "Go on, Mattie. For Christ's sake." Mattie left.

He held the sopping towel under the running water again, went back and rubbed the back of her neck, pressed it under her collar on her chest. "Come on, Little Soldier. Show your old man you got it in you. You bet you got it in you. You bet you have . . ."

Her body quivered and then she sucked in with parted lips. "That's a girl. That's a girl." Her eyes opened and she moved her head from side to side and then suddenly looked at him. "Did you see him?" she said.

"Everything's swell, kiddo. Don't you worry about it one minute. Everything's swell."

"I'm glad." Her mouth twisted and she reached and clutched Bowie's hand. "Something is wrong with me, Bowie. I hate to tell you. I know it."

"Don't worry, honey. The doctor is coming. Don't you worry."

Keechie closed her eyes and Bowie took the dry towel and wiped her face. Then he took off her shoes. "I'm glad," she said. It was toneless, like she was talking in her sleep.

Bowie sat on the stone edge of the fish pond in the Court's center, watching the Doctor, a little man in a tan suit, through the half-raised blind of the cabin. I ought to have stayed in there. That Doctor's got sick people on his mind and not criminals. That Mattie.

The lights of a car brightened the yard. Papa came around and the car followed him, an old machine with packed running boards. It went on around to the row on the other side.

"I just can't get over it," Bowie said out loud.

The door of the cabin opened, laying a slab of light on the grass, and then Mattie was coming out. Bowie went to her. "What does he say?" he said.

"There's nothing wrong with her except she's pregnant," Mattie said. "I could have told you that."

"Who said it?"

"He did. Anybody could tell."

Bowie looked at the light from the half-raised blind. "I don't want to get mixed up any farther in this," Mattie said. "You're going to have to go on." Bowie did not answer. He moved toward the cabin; into the smell of licorice and paregoric.

The Doctor had a splotch of moustache over his mouth and sagging eyerims. "That is the only thing to do," he said. "Just keep her quiet and lying on her back and I think she will come out of it fine. But she cannot keep this up. I have given her something and that is going to keep her asleep quite a while. Rest is the thing."

Keechie's breasts were rising and falling in even breathing. "She sure is sleeping like she is awfully tired," Bowie said.

"That is the best thing," Doctor said. "Now I have put some medicine there on the table there and tomorrow, if she is still in pain, you can give it to her. She is likely to sleep a good while, and if she does awaken she more than likely will go right back to sleep again."

"She sure is sleeping."

"If you need me, call me," Doctor said.

"Sure, Doctor. Don't worry about that."

Bowie sat now on the chair by the sink in the cabin's darkness, watching Keechie's form, listening to her breathing. He got up now and touched her straightened arm, picked it up and put it on her breast; placed it back by her side. Then he left the cabin.

Mattie came out and walked around with him into the deep shadow of the station's side. "That girl can't be moved," Bowie said.

"I don't want anything happening around here," Mattie said. "I've done all I'm going to in this."

"If it's money that's holding you, don't worry about that."

"I don't want any of your money. All I want you to do is get off this place." The screen sounded and Mattie turned her head and started off.

"Hold it," Bowie said. Mattie stopped. "Now you listen to me," Bowie said. "You're a thief just like me and you ain't going to yellow on me when I'm asking you to lay off. She's not going to be moved, see, and if you or anybody else don't like it, it's just too goddamned bad."

Mattie walked on away.

Keechie had not moved. He lifted the blind, a square of moonlight baring her feet. He pulled the blind back down, took off her hose and placed the sheet over her legs.

The Court was quiet. In Bowie's ears, the cricket-ringing sounds were growing. That yellow Hawkins, he thought. The two-faced sonofabitch.

If only that Indian was here. Them white teeth. Little Soldier, it can't be got around. They got me in a rank now. The whole, lousy, yellow bunch.

Water dripped in the sink and he got up and tightened the tap.

We got to hole-up right pretty soon, girl. There ain't no *ifs* and *ands* about it. I have fooled around long enough.

You got Something Else to think about now, Little Soldier. Old Bowie is not so big in this picture now. But they can't put nothing on you, Keechie. They just can't do it. Don't you let them make you think it for a minute. Don't you let 'em.

The dropped match from his fingers rattled on the floor and he watched her. She did not move and he breathed again. But you're plumb out, honey. You're not going to be waking up until away in tomorrow.

If that Chicamaw was here, Keechie, we could beat them easy. He's the only friend we got in this world. You don't know it, Keechie, but I do, honey. He's the only one in this world that would help us. You and me are going up this road together and we got to find us a Hole and pull it in after us. 'Specially now. You can't run these roads much longer. That Mexico, Keechie. They ain't but one person in this world that can get us down there. Just one.

Somewhere in the night a dog bayed.

Say it worked, Keechie. Say I run that hundred and twenty miles over to that Farm from here, get there by seven o'clock this morning and spring that boy? You would be asleep, honey, and never know a thing about it. I would be back and you'd wake up and that Chicamaw would be with us and then I'd like to see somebody stop us. Honey, we'd be holed up in Mexico two days from now. Deep, Keechie. Pulled in after us.

The dog bayed again.

Well, say it didn't work, Keechie? Say it flopped? All right, Little Soldier, you got Somebody Else to think about now. Old Bowie stepped out don't mean so much. You don't have nobody to beat, Keechie. They can't hang a thing in this world on you. All you have ever done is just kind of run around with me. Say it flopped all right, Keechie? Well, there you are.

Bowie got up and buttoned his coat.

The high, net-wire fence was broken here by a wooden Arch: *Bingham Prison Camp*—and Bowie left the highway and turned his machine through it. Stone-bordered beds of flowers colored the sides of the gray road that led up there to the Buildings. There was the smell of sweet-peas.

There was the Office, a squat, brick building with an empty flagpole and behind it, long, barrack-looking buildings, stone foundations whitewashed, and barns.

A figure in the white sacking of a convict, on his knees and breaking clods around the rose bush with his hands, looked up as Bowie got out of his car. He lowered his head as Bowie passed on toward the Office porch, the two men in khaki uniforms sitting on a bench, cartridge belts around their waists, shotguns beside them.

"How do you do?" Bowie said.

The heads of the Guards moved. "Howdy . . . Hidy."

Bowie indicated the porch-shadowed door. "Captain Stammers in?"

The two nodded.

Bowie entered the smell of disinfectant, looked at the face framed in the top of the high, bookkeeper's desk, a Convict's; moved down the desk's length and stopped before the two men on the bench. The big one was dressed like the men on the porch, the other in blue serge trousers and white shirt. He got up.

"Captain Stammers?" Bowie said.

"That's me," the man said. He had thin black hair, parted in the middle, and held his left arm crooked as if it were in pain. He did not have a gun on. Bowie extended his hand. "I'm Sheriff Haviland, Becos County."

Captain Stammers pumped Bowie's hand. "Glad to know you, Sheriff. What can I do for you?"

The Guard on the bench got up and moved toward the door. "See you after while, Captain," he said.

"I want to see a boy you got on your place here," Bowie said. "Elmo Mobley."

"Yeah, we got him. Let me see now. He's in Boss Hebert's squad today I think. Now what is it we can do for you there?"

"I have a Bench Warrant, but I don't intend to take him." Bowie pulled the paper from his inside coat pocket and handed it to Stammers. "I just wanted to talk to him a little on this trip." The paper crackled as Stammers opened the Warrant:

THE STATE OF TEXAS

To the Honorable *Sheriff A. T. Haviland, Sheriff of Becos County,* Texas, GREETING;

On this *12 day of May A.D. 1935,* it appearing to the Court that there is now pending on the docket of this Court, a certain case entitled the STATE of Texas VS. *Elmo T. Mobley,* being our case *No. 754,* wherein said defendant is charged with the offense of murder,

Whereas, said case . . .

"You don't want to take him?" Stammers said. He started folding the paper.

"No, I just want to talk to him."

Stammers went over and picked the gray hat off the hook and turned and touched his left arm. "Neuritis, bad," he said.

"I've heard that it's bad," Bowie said.

On the porch, Stammers said to the three guards: "Watch that telephone, boys."

Bowie moved toward his car and Stammers followed. "We can just go in my car," Bowie said.

"Did you ever hear of anybody that found out anything to help it?" Stammers said.

"It just has to wear off, I hear," Bowie said.

Stammers pointed at the dirt road that twisted back of the building and toward the cotton-fields. Bowie moved onto it.

The cotton was fresh and green, the earth around it freshly hoed. "Mighty nice stand you got out here, Captain."

"Rain last week," Stammers said. He picked up his left hand and placed the elbow on his stomach. "Nice rain last week."

Puffs of dust rose from the chopping hoes of the working convicts yonder, fifteen or twenty men; two men on horses, shotguns in the cradles of their arms, watching. Faces of working men lifted and looked at the car, bent back again.

The horseman with the boots and jagged Spanish spurs approached. He was a heavy man with a billowing waist. There was a pistol on his belt; a rifle in the saddle scabbard.

"Mobley is in that bunch, isn't he?" Stammers said.

Spanish Spurs nodded. "Yessir."

"Bring him over here."

At the head of the squad, a figure raised, listened and then stepped out. He was coming now, the hoe in hand. Spanish Spurs spoke and Chicamaw threw the hoe down.

Chicamaw looked hard and well. He studied Bowie and then Stammers and then Bowie again.

"Get in this car, Mobley," Bowie said. "I want to talk to you a little while, boy. We'll go back up to your office, Captain."

"Sure."

Chicamaw sat in the front alongside Bowie; Stammers in the back. They were going now back up the road toward the Buildings. "You didn't stop by State and see the Warden, did you?" Stammers said.

"No, I went to Houston a different way. I'm stopping there on my way back though."

"Well, give the Warden my regards. You didn't go to the Convention this year, did you, Sheriff?"

"No, I didn't," Bowie said.

"You know I was a Sheriff for fourteen years. I'd like to have gone to that Convention this year."

Bowie nudged Chicamaw's thigh, indicated the panel pocket. Chicamaw pulled the ivory knob, grasped the pistol and turned on Stammers. "It's a break, Captain," he said. "Sit there."

"We're going right out through this gate up here, Captain," Bowie said. "Don't you let on to nobody in no way. You understand, don't you?"

"I understand."

The porch was empty. The Convict, working around the rose bush, looked up and then stood. Bowie passed the Office and the chaff of the road began peppering the fenders. He swerved up and onto the highway; opened the throttle wide.

"Well, boys, this is going to cost me," Stammers said.

"Don't let it get you down, Cap," Chicamaw said.

"It seems to me now that I had seen you before, Sheriff, but by God, I still don't know."

"Just forget it, Captain," Bowie said. "I guess you'll find out soon enough. How long do you think it will be before your boys back there figure something is wrong?"

"I wish I knew."

Chicamaw looked deeper in the car pocket, reached in it and explored with his hand.

"What you looking for?" Bowie said.

"Nothing," Chicamaw said.

"This is going to cost me, boys," Stammers said.

"Tell that to the Warden, Cap, " Chicamaw said.

"You been treated pretty good on that Farm, boy," Stammers said.

"Pipe down, Chicamaw," Bowie said. "For Christ's sake."

The highway sign read: *MacMasters . . . 68 mi.* At the off-road, Bowie turned and they drove along through the timber. After a half-mile, Bowie stopped and they all got out and crawled through the fence, and in the woods Bowie tied Stammers to a tree.

Heat glimmered from the highway's cement slabs. "Say they been pretty good to you back there?" Bowie asked.

"They don't use a bat or barrel any more," Chicamaw said. "Them big political boys stopped all that. They'd still do it, but they're afraid they'll lose them sixty-dollar jobs."

"That's something though."

Chicamaw turned and looked in the back of the car. "You're not going to tell me you didn't bring no pint along, are you?"

Bowie shook his head. "No liquor in this party, Chicamaw. I got some business that needs attending and it takes a clear head."

"I don't believe you're ever going to be human," Chicamaw said. "I tell you, man, I don't see how you do it. You get out here and run these roads and pull a thing like that back yonder and beat these Laws right and left, and, by God, Bowie, I don't see how in the hell you do it. You're just a big country boy and just chumpy as hell at times and yet you do it."

"What did you want to do, stay back yonder?"

"Me? Don't kid yourself. Not with that Texaco City trouble still up in the air. Man, I been thinking any day here they would come. You're the boy they want on that. Them fingerprints of yours sure played hell there. I was pretty foxy in that though. They got you tagged on that, but what they got on me for sure?"

"It's raised a lot of heat all right," Bowie said. "That trouble."

"You seem to beat it all right," Chicamaw said. "You just keep going right on."

"Just luck," Bowie said.

"That's it. Call it that. You're no more a criminal than that damned radiator cap there. And yet you do it. It rips my guts out. You're just a big Sunday-school chump and yet you can pull a thing like that back yonder and run these roads and make me look like thirty cents."

Bowie's head jerked. "You going crazy? What the hell is gettin' the matter with you?"

"It rips my guts out. Take you and on top of that a damned

little old girl that was never outside of a filling station and, by God, the papers don't do nothing but print about you all the time. Why, it makes me look like a damned penny slot machine . . ."

Bowie stopped at the side of the highway.

"What's the matter?" Chicamaw said. "What's this idea?"

Bowie got out of the car and walked around and pulled out Chicamaw's door. "Come on," he said. "You sonofabitch, come on."

"Good God, Bowie. What's got into you?"

"Get out."

Chicamaw got out.

"The only reason I'm not letting you have it right here," Bowie said, "is because there might be some dogs that will do it."

"Listen, Bowie. I want to go see my folks. I ain't never seen 'em, Bowie. Let me get that gun in the car."

"Get."

Chicamaw started running up the road.

A car with a blaring loudspeaker and bannered with lettering about a picture show was the only moving machine on the heat-stilled Square of MacMasters. The music was *Stars and Stripes Forever*. Bowie turned off the Square and moved out the highway that led to the Courts. Nossir, God, I never asked nothing from you before. Not a thing in this world. But just let me get up there the rest of the way now. And if it ain't asking too much, keep her still asleep. Just let her wake up and I'll be sittin' there. . . .

The driveway and yard of *Alamo Plaza Courts* were deserted. Bowie drove on down and parked parallel in front of the closed door and lowered blind.

She lay there on the bed, her eyes closed, still breathing, just as he had left her. He looked around. Nothing had been moved. Nothing. Thanks, God.

The afternoon heat pressed against the cabin, making the walls as hot as a dying stove. The roof's tar melted and smelled. Bowie stood above Keechie, flapping the wet towel. The little curls on her forehead trembled under the cooling air. Honey, you got to be waking up pretty soon and eating something. I mean real wide awake.

Dusk seeped into the room now, drying the sweat on Bowie's forehead, stiffening the hairs on his arms. Keechie stirred greater now, and he bent over. Her eyes opened. They were like petals submerged in tiny bowls of unchanged water.

"Bowie?" she said.

"Hello, sleepyhead."

"Bowie?"

"It's about time you were waking up."

"You wouldn't leave me, would you?"

"Me? You don't mean me. I should say not. Don't be silly now waking up."

"Bowie?"

"What, Keechie?"

"I mean it."

"God knows now too, Keechie. I mean it."

Keechie closed her eyes. He touched her. "Listen, Little Soldier, you got to get something inside that stomach of yours. How about a soda pop? Ice-cold to start things off?"

Keechie's head moved up and down on the pillow.

"Now let's see." Bowie stood erect and began rubbing his hands. "Just about what kind of flavor now would the little lady crave? Strawberry?"

Keechie nodded.

Bowie moved through the gloom to the door, pulled it back. *"Don't let a move out of you,"* the Voice said. It was like the swish of a missing blade. Cat with seven lives, Bowie thought. He whipped out his gun. Steampipes burst in his ears. *Seven.* He swirled in the bell of the roaring loudspeaker on the Square: *Stars and Stripes Forever.* Cat . . . *seven.* Things were wrinkling, folding gently, like paper dolls in a puff of cigarette smoke. *Strawberry . . .*

MacMasters, Texas, June 21—The crime-blazed trail of the Southwest's phantom desperado, Bowie Bowers, and his gun-packing girl companion, Keechie Mobley, was ended here early tonight in a battle with a sharp-shooting band of Rangers and peace officers who beat their covered quarry to the draw. The escaped convict, bank robber and quick-triggered killer, and his woman aide were trapped in the cabin of a tourist camp, one mile east of this city, and killed instantly in one burst of machine and rifle fire.

Stirred to a vengeful heat after Bowers' sensational liberation of his old pal, Elmo (Three-Toed) Mobley, from the Bingham Prison Farm early this morning, grim-faced officers swooped down on the camp. After the battle, Bowers lay sprawled in the doorway of the cabin, the girl inside on the floor. A gun was clutched in Bowers' hand, another near the hand of Keechie Mobley. Both were bullet-riddled, their deaths instantaneous.

A bag containing almost $10,000 in currency was recovered in the splintered cabin, also a quantity of what officers declared was narcotics.

The killings brought to a dramatic climax a search of more than a year for the desperado and his companion. Wanted in at least four states for murders, bank robberies, filling-station holdups, kidnapings of peace officers, Bowers had become one of the Southwest's most feared criminals.

This peaceful, thriving little city was stunned tonight by the news that it had harbored in its environs this pair. Knots of excited people thronged the streets tonight and crowds were viewing the bodies in a local undertaking parlor.

Tall, steel-eyed Ranger Captain Leflett refused to comment at length on the case, declaring that the owners of the tourist camp where the pair was slain, were unaware of the identity of their notorious guests. When he reported to his Chief in the State Capital, he declared simply: "Chief, we have got them."

Elmo Mobley, freed by Bowers earlier in the day when Captain Stammers was kidnaped, was captured by a farmer who became suspicious when he saw Mobley running in the road and then recognized the prison clothing.

Rewards totaling more than $1,000 will be distributed among the twenty picked officers who took part in the slayings.

Supplied a tip before daybreak this morning, local officers began acting quickly. Telephone and telegraph wires hummed to the State Capital and Penitentiary. An airplane brought Ranger Captain Leflett and four men.

At the State Penitentiary, according to news dispatches received here, Warden Joel Howard admitted to reporters, it is said, that the tip was furnished after a "deal" had been made for the liberation of an inmate in the prison there. "Bowers was a ruthless, cunning criminal," Warden Howard declared, "and we had to exert every resource to bring him down."

THE BIG CLOCK

by Kenneth Fearing

For Nan

Contents

George Stroud I 383

George Stroud II 387

George Stroud III 395

George Stroud IV 406

George Stroud V 414

Earl Janoth I 424

Earl Janoth II 428

Steve Hagen 437

George Stroud VI 444

George Stroud VII 450

Edward Orlin 457

George Stroud VIII 464

Earl Janoth III 476

Georgette Stroud 483

Emory Mafferson 488

George Stroud IX 493

Louise Patterson 497

George Stroud X 506

George Stroud XI 511

George Stroud I

I FIRST met Pauline Delos at one of those substantial parties Earl Janoth liked to give every two or three months, attended by members of the staff, his personal friends, private moguls, and public nobodies, all in haphazard rotation. It was at his home in the East Sixties. Although it was not exactly public, well over a hundred people came and went in the course of two or three hours.

Georgette was with me, and we were introduced at once to Edward Orlin of *Futureways*, and to others in the group who had the familiar mark upon them. Of Pauline Delos, I knew only the name. But although there could not have been anyone in the organization who hadn't heard a great deal about the lady, there were few who had actually seen her, and fewer still who had ever seen her on any occasion when Janoth was also present. She was tall, ice-blonde, and splendid. The eye saw nothing but innocence, to the instincts she was undiluted sex, the brain said here was a perfect hell.

"Earl was asking about you a moment ago," Orlin told me. "Wanted you to meet somebody."

"I was delayed. As a matter of fact, I've just finished a twenty-minute conversation with President McKinley."

Miss Delos looked mildly interested. "Who did you say?" she asked.

"William McKinley. Our twenty-fourth President."

"I know," she said, and smiled. A little. "You probably heard a lot of complaints."

A man I recognized as Emory Mafferson, a tiny little dark fellow who haunted one of the lower floors, *Futureways*, also, I think, spoke up.

"There's a guy with an iron face like McKinley's in the auditing department. If that's who you mean, you bet there were complaints."

"No. I was truly and literally detained in a conversation with Mr. McKinley. At the bar of the Silver Lining."

"He was," said Georgette. "I was, too."

"Yes. And there were no complaints at all. Quite the contrary. He's making out quite well, it seems." I had myself another Manhattan from a passing tray. "He's not under a contract, of course. But working steadily. In addition to being McKinley he's sometimes Justice Holmes, Thomas Edison, Andrew Carnegie, Henry Ward Beecher, or anyone important but dignified. He's been Washington, Lincoln, and Christopher Columbus more times than he can remember."

"I call him a very convenient friend to have," said Delos. "Who is he?"

"His earthly alias is Clyde Norbert Polhemus. For business purposes. I've known him for years, and he's promised to let me be his understudy."

"What's he done?" Orlin asked, with reluctance. "Sounds like he materialized a bunch of ghosts, and can't put them back."

"Radio," I said. "And he can put anyone anywhere."

And that was about all, the first time I met Pauline Delos. The rest of the late afternoon and early evening passed as always in this comfortable little palace, surrounded as it was by the big and little palaces of greater and lesser kingdoms than Janoth Enterprises. Old conversation in new faces. Georgette and I met and talked to the niece of a department store. Of course the niece wanted to conquer new territory. She would inherit several acres of the old territory, anyway. I met a titan in the world of mathematics; he had connected a number of adding machines into a single unit, and this super-calculator was the biggest in the world. It could solve equations unknown to and beyond the grasp of its inventor. I said: "That makes you better than Einstein. When you have your equipment with you."

He looked at me uneasily, and it occurred to me I was a little drunk.

"I'm afraid not. It was a purely mechanical problem, developed for special purposes only."

I told him he might not be the best mathematician on earth but he was certainly the fastest, and then I met a small legal cog in a major political engine. And next Janoth's latest invention in the way of social commentators. And others, all of them pretty damned important people, had they only known it. Some of them unaware they were gentlemen and scholars. Some of them tomorrow's famous fugitives from justice. A sizable sprinkling of lunatics, so plausible they had never been suspected and never would be. Memorable bankrupts of the future, the obscure suicides of ten or twenty years from now. Potentially fabulous murderers. The mothers or fathers of truly great people I would never know.

In short, the big clock was running as usual, and it was time to go home. Sometimes the hands of the clock actually raced, and at other times they hardly moved at all. But that made no difference to the big clock. The hands could move backward, and the time it told would be right just the same. It would still be running as usual, because all other watches have to be set by the big one, which is even more powerful than the calendar, and to which one automatically adjusts his entire life. Compared to this hook-up, the man with the adding machines was still counting on his fingers.

Anyway, it was time I collected Georgette and went home. I always go home. Always. I may sometimes detour, but eventually I get there. Home was 37.4 miles, according to the railroad timetable, but it could be 3,740 miles, and I would still make it. Earl Janoth had emerged from somewhere, and we said good-bye.

There was one thing I always saw, or thought I saw, in Janoth's big, pink, disorderly face, permanently fixed in a faint smile he had forgotten about long ago, his straight and innocent stare that didn't, any more, see the person in front of him at all. He wasn't adjusting himself to the big clock. He didn't even know there was a big clock. The large, gray, convoluted muscle in back of that childlike gaze was digesting something unknown to the ordinary world. That muscle with its long tendons had nearly fastened itself about a conclusion, a conclusion startlingly different from the hearty expression once forged upon the outward face, and left there, abandoned. Some day that conclusion would be reached, the muscle would strike. Probably it had, before. Surely it would, again.

He said how nice Georgette was looking, which was true, how she always reminded him of carnivals and Hallowe'en, the wildest baseball ever pitched in history, and there was as usual a real and extraordinary warmth in the voice, as though this were another, still a third personality.

"I'm sorry an old friend of mine, Major Conklin, had to leave early," he said to me. "He likes what we've been doing recently with *Crimeways*. I told him you were the psychic bloodhound leading us on to new interpretations, and he was interested."

"I'm sorry I missed him."

"Well, Larry recently took over a string of graveyard magazines, and he wants to do something with them. But I don't think a man with your practical experience and precision mentality could advise him. He needs a geomancer."

"It's been a pleasant evening, Earl."

"Hasn't it? Good night."

"Good night."

"Good night."

We made our way down the long room, past an atmospheric disturbance highly political, straight through a group of early settlers whom God would not help tomorrow morning, cautiously around a couple abruptly silent but smiling in helpless rage.

"Where now?" Georgette asked.

"A slight detour. Just for dinner. Then home, of course."

As we got our things, and I waited for Georgette, I saw Pauline Delos, with a party of four, disappearing into the night. Abandoning this planet. As casually as that. But my thought-waves told her to drop in again. Any time.

In the taxi, Georgette said: "George, what's a geomancer?"

"I don't know, George. Earl got it out of the fattest dictionary ever printed, wrote it on his cuff, and now the rest of us know why he's the boss. Remind me to look it up."

George Stroud II

ABOUT five weeks later I woke up on a January morning, with my head full of a letter Bob Aspenwell had written me from Haiti. I don't know why this letter came back to me the instant sleep began to go. I had received it days and days before. It was all about the warmth down there, the ease, and above all, the simplicity.

He said it was a Black Republic, and I was grinning in my sleep as I saw Bob and myself plotting a revolt of the whites determined not to be sold down the river into *Crimeways*. Then I really woke up.

Monday morning. On Marble Road. An important Monday.

Roy Cordette and I had scheduled a full staff conference for the April issue, one of those surprise packages good for everyone's ego and imagination. The big clock was running at a leisurely pace, and I was well abreast of it.

But that morning, in front of the mirror in the bathroom, I was certain a tuft of gray on the right temple had stolen at least another quarter-inch march. This renewed a familiar vision, beginning with mortality at one end of the scale, and ending in senile helplessness at the other.

Who's that pathetic, white-haired old guy clipping papers at the desk over there? asked a brisk young voice. But I quickly tuned it out and picked another one: *Who's that distinguished, white-haired, scholarly gentleman going into the directors' room?*

Don't you know who he is? That's George Stroud.

Who's he?

Well, it's a long story. He used to be general manager of this whole railroad. Railroad? Why not something with a farther future? *Airline. He saw this line through its first, pioneer stages. He might have been one of the biggest men in aviation today, only something went wrong. I don't know just what, except that it was a hell of a scandal. Stroud had to go before a Grand Jury, but it was so big it had to be hushed up, and he got off. After that, though, he was through. Now they let him put out the papers and cigars in the board room when there's a meeting. The rest of the time he fills the office inkwells and rearranges the travel leaflets.*

Why do they keep him on at all?

Well, some of the directors feel sentimental about the old fellow, and besides, he has a wife and daughter dependent on him. Hold that copy, boy. This is years and years from now. *Three children, no, I think it's four. Brilliant youngsters, and awfully brave about Stroud. Won't hear a word against him. They think he still runs the whole works around here. And did you ever see the wife? They're the most devoted old couple I ever saw.*

Drying my face, I stared into the glass. I made the dark, bland, somewhat inquisitive features go suddenly hard and still. I said:

"Look here, Roy, we've really got to do something." *About what?* "About getting ourselves some more money." I saw the vague wave of Roy Cordette's thin, long-fingered hand, and discerned his instant retreat into the land of elves, hobgoblins, and double-talk.

I thought, George, you went all over this with Hagen three months ago. There's no doubt about it, you and I are both crowding the limit. And then some.

"What is the limit, do you happen to know?"

The general level throughout the whole organization, I should say, wouldn't you?

"Not for me. I don't exactly crave my job, my contract, or this gilded cage full of gelded birds. I think it's high time we really had a showdown."

Go right ahead. My prayers go with you.

"I said *we*. In a way it involves your own contract as well as mine."

I know. Tell you what, George, why don't the three of us talk this over informally? You and Hagen and myself?

"A good idea." I reached for the phone. "When would be convenient?"

You mean today?

"Why not?"

Well, I'll be pretty busy this afternoon. But all right. If Steve isn't too busy around five.

"A quarter to six in the Silver Lining. After the third round.

You know, Jennett-Donohue are planning to add five or six new books. We'll just keep that in mind."

So I heard, but they're on a pretty low level, if you ask me. Besides, it's a year since that rumor went around.

A real voice shattered this imaginary scene.

"George, are you ever coming down? George has to take the school bus, you know."

I called back to Georgette that I was on my way and went back to the bedroom. And when we went into conference with Steve Hagen, then what? A vein began to beat in my forehead. For business purposes he and Janoth were one and the same person, except that in Hagen's slim and sultry form, restlessly through his veins, there flowed some new, freakish, molten virulence.

I combed my hair before the bedroom dresser, and that sprout of gray resumed its ordinary proportions. To hell with Hagen. Why not go to Janoth? Of course.

I laid the comb and brush down on the dresser top, leaned forward on an elbow, and breathed into the mirror: "Cut you the cards, Earl. Low man leaves town in twenty-four hours. High man takes the works."

I put on my tie, my coat, and went downstairs. Georgia looked up thoughtfully from the usual drift of cornflakes surrounding her place at the table. From beneath it came the soft, steady, thump, thump, thump of her feet marking time on a crossbar. A broad beam of sunlight poured in upon the table, drawn close to the window, highlighting the silverware, the percolator, the faces of Georgia and Georgette. Plates reflected more light from a sideboard against one wall, and above it my second favorite painting by Louise Patterson, framed in a strip of walnut, seemed to hang away up in the clouds over the sideboard, the room, and somehow over the house. Another picture by Patterson hung on the opposite wall, and there were two more upstairs.

Georgette's large, glowing, untamed features turned, and her sea-blue eyes swept me with surgical but kindly interest. I said good morning and kissed them both. Georgette called to Nellie that she could bring the eggs and waffles.

"Orange juice," I said, drinking mine. "These oranges just told me they came from Florida."

My daughter gave me a glance of startled faith. "I didn't hear anything," she said.

"You didn't? One of them said they all came from a big ranch near Jacksonville."

Georgia considered this and then waved her spoon, flatly discarding the whole idea. After a full twenty seconds of silence she seemed to remember something, and asked: "What man were you talking to?"

"Me? Man? When? Where?"

"Now. Upstairs. George said you were talking to a man. We heard."

"Oh."

Georgette's voice was neutral, but under the neutrality lay the zest of an innocent bystander waiting to see the first blood in a barroom debate.

"I thought you'd better do your own explaining," she said.

"Well, that man, George. That was me, practicing. Musicians have to do a lot of practicing before they play. Athletes have to train before they race, and actors rehearse before they act." I hurried past Georgette's pointed, unspoken agreement. "And I always run over a few words in the morning before I start talking. May I have the biscuits. Please?"

Georgia weighed this, and forgot about it. She said: "George said you'd tell me a story, George."

"I'll tell you a story, all right. It's about the lonely corn-flake." I had her attention now, to the maximum. "It seems that once there was a little girl."

"How old?"

"About five, I think. Or maybe it was seven."

"No, six."

"Six she was. So there was this package of cornflakes—"

"What was her name?"

"Cynthia. So these cornflakes, hundreds of them, they'd all grown up together in the same package, they'd played games and gone to school together, they were all fast friends. Then one day the package was opened and the whole lot were emptied into Cynthia's bowl. And she poured milk and cream and sugar in the bowl, and then she ate one of the flakes. And after a while, this cornflake down in Cynthia's stomach began to wonder when the rest of his friends were going to arrive.

But they never did. And the longer he waited, the lonelier he grew. You see, the rest of the cornflakes got only as far as the tablecloth, a lot of them landed on the floor, a few of them on Cynthia's forehead, and some behind her ears."

"And then what?"

"Well, that's all. After a while this cornflake got so lonely he just sat down and cried."

"Then what'd he do?"

"What could he do? Cynthia didn't know how to eat her cornflakes properly, or maybe she wasn't trying, so morning after morning the same thing happened. One cornflake found himself left all alone in Cynthia's stomach."

"Then what?"

"Well, he cried and carried on so bad that every morning she got a bellyache. And she couldn't think why because, after all, she really hadn't eaten anything."

"Then what'd she do?"

"She didn't like it, that's what she did."

Georgia started in on her soft-boiled eggs, which promised to go the way of the cereal. Presently she lowered the handle of the spoon to the table and rested her chin on the tip, brooding and thumping her feet on the crossbar. The coffee in my cup gently rippled, rippled with every thud.

"You always tell that story," she remembered. "Tell me another."

"There's one about the little girl—Cynthia, aged six—the same one—who also had a habit of kicking her feet against the table whenever she ate. Day after day, week in and week out, year after year, she kicked it and kicked it. Then one fine day the table said, 'I'm getting pretty tired of this,' and with that it pulled back its leg and whango, it booted Cynthia clear out of the window. Was she surprised."

This one was a complete success. Georgia's feet pounded in double time, and she upset what was left of her milk.

"Pull your punches, wonder boy," said Georgette, mopping up. A car honked outside the house and she polished Georgia's face with one expert wipe of the bib. "There's the bus, darling. Get your things on."

For about a minute a small meteor ran up and down and around the downstairs rooms, then disappeared, piping. Georgette came back, after a while, for her first cigarette and her second cup of coffee. She said, presently, looking at me through a thin band of smoke: "Would you like to go back to newspaper work, George?"

"God forbid. I never want to see another fire engine as long as I live. Not unless I'm riding on it, steering the back end of a hook-and-ladder truck. The fellow on the back end always steers just the opposite to the guy in the driver's seat. I think."

"That's what I mean."

"What do you mean?"

"You don't like *Crimeways*. You don't really like Janoth Enterprises at all. You'd like to steer in just the opposite direction to all of that."

"You're wrong. Quite wrong. I love that old merry-go-round."

Georgette hesitated, unsure of herself. I could feel the laborious steps her reasoning took before she reached a tentative, spoken conclusion: "I don't believe in square pegs in round holes. The price is too great. Don't you think so, George?" I tried to look puzzled. "I mean, well, really, it seems to me, when I think about it, sometimes, you were much happier, and so was I, when we had the roadhouse. Weren't we? For that matter, it was a lot more fun when you were a race-track detective. Heavens, even the all-night broadcasting job. It was crazy, but I liked it."

I finished my waffle, tracing the same circuit of memories I knew that she, too, was following. Timekeeper on a construction gang, race-track operative, tavern proprietor, newspaper legman, and then rewrite, advertising consultant, and finally—what? Now?

Of all these experiences I didn't know which filled me, in retrospect, with the greater pleasure or the more annoyance. And I knew it was a waste of time to raise such a question even in passing.

Time.

One runs like a mouse up the old, slow pendulum of the big clock, time, scurries around and across its huge hands, strays inside through the intricate wheels and balances and springs of the inner mechanism, searching among the cobwebbed mazes of this machine with all its false exits and dangerous blind alleys and steep runways, natural traps and artificial baits, hunting for the true opening and the real prize.

Then the clock strikes one and it is time to go, to run down the pendulum, to become again a prisoner making once more the same escape.

For of course the clock that measures out the seasons, all gain and loss, the air Georgia breathes, Georgette's strength, the figures shivering on the dials of my own inner instrument board, this gigantic watch that fixes order and establishes the pattern for chaos itself, it has never changed, it will never change, or be changed.

I found I had been looking at nothing. I said: "No. I'm the roundest peg you ever saw."

Georgette pinched out her cigarette, and asked: "Are you driving in?"

I thought of Roy and Hagen and the Silver Lining.

"No. And I may be home late. I'll call you."

"All right, I'll take you to the station. I may go in for a while myself, after lunch."

Finishing my coffee I sped through the headlines of the first three pages of the morning paper and found nothing new. A record-breaking bank robbery in St. Paul, but not for us. While Georgette gave instructions to Nellie I got into my coat and hat, took the car out of the garage, and honked. When Georgette came out I moved over and she took the wheel.

This morning, Marble Road was crisp but not cold, and very bright. Patches of snow from a recent storm still showed on the brown lawns and on the distant hills seen through the crooked black lace of the trees. Away from Marble Road, our community of rising executives, falling promoters, and immovable salesmen, we passed through the venerable but slightly weatherbeaten, huge square boxes of the original citizens. On the edge of the town behind Marble Road lay the bigger estates, scattered through the hills. Lots of gold in them, too. In about three more years, we would stake a claim of several acres there, ourselves.

"I hope I can find the right drapes this afternoon," said Georgette, casually. "Last week I didn't have time. I was in Doctor Dolson's office two solid hours."

"Yes?" Then I understood she had something to say. "How are you and Doc Dolson coming along?"

She spoke without taking her eyes from the road. "He says he thinks it would be all right."

"He thinks? What does that mean?"

"He's sure. As sure can be. Next time I should be all right."

"That's swell." I covered her hand on the wheel. "What have you been keeping it secret for?"

"Well. Do you feel the same?"

"Say, why do you think I've been paying Dolson? Yes. I do."

"I just wondered."

"Well, don't. When, did he say?"

"Any time."

We had reached the station and the 9:08 was just pulling in. I kissed her, one arm across her shoulders, the other arm groping for the handle of the door.

"Any time it is. Get ready not to slip on lots of icy sidewalks."

"Call me," she said, before I closed the door.

I nodded and made for the station. At the stand inside I took another paper and went straight on through. There was plenty of time. I could see an athlete still running, a block away.

The train ride, for me, always began with Business Opportunities, my favorite department in any newspaper, continued with the auction room news and a glance at the sports pages, insurance statistics, and then amusements. Finally, as the train burrowed underground, I prepared myself for the day by turning to the index and reading the gist of the news. If there was something there, I had it by the time the hundreds and thousands of us were intently journeying across the floor of the station's great ant heap, each of us knowing, in spite of the intricate patterns we wove, just where to go, just what to do.

And five minutes later, two blocks away, I arrived at the Janoth Building, looming like an eternal stone deity among a forest of its fellows. It seemed to prefer human sacrifices, of the flesh and of the spirit, over any other token of devotion. Daily, we freely made them.

I turned into the echoing lobby, making mine.

George Stroud III

JANOTH ENTERPRISES, filling the top nine floors of the Janoth Building, was by no means the largest of its kind in the United States. Jennett-Donohue formed a larger magazine syndicate; so did Beacon Publications, and Devers & Blair. Yet our organization had its special place, and was far from being the smallest among the many firms publishing fiction and news, covering political, business, and technical affairs.

Newsways was the largest and best-known magazine of our group, a weekly publication of general interest, with a circulation of not quite two million. That was on floor thirty-one. Above it, on the top floor of the building, were the business offices—the advertising, auditing, and circulation departments, with Earl's and Steve Hagen's private headquarters.

Commerce was a business weekly with a circulation of about a quarter of a million, far less than the actual reading public and the influence it had. Associated with it were the four-page daily bulletin, *Trade*, and the hourly wire service, *Commerce Index*. These occupied floor thirty.

The twenty-ninth floor housed a wide assortment of technical newspapers and magazines, most of them published monthly, ranging from *Sportland* to *The Frozen Age* (food products), *The Actuary* (vital statistics), *Frequency* (radio and television), and *Plastic Tomorrow*. There were eleven or twelve of these what's-coming-next and how-to-do-it publications on this floor, none with a large circulation, some of them holdovers from an inspired moment of Earl Janoth's, and possibly now forgotten by him.

The next two floors in descending order held the morgue, the library and general reference rooms, art and photo departments, a small but adequate first-aid room in frequent use, a rest room, the switchboards, and a reception room for general inquiries.

The brains of the organization were to be found, however, on floor twenty-six. It held *Crimeways*, with Roy Cordette as Associate Editor (Room 2618), myself as Executive Editor (2619), Sydney Kislak and Henry Wyckoff, Assistant Editors

(2617), and six staff writers in adjoining compartments. In theory we were the nation's police blotter, watchdogs of its purse and conscience, sometimes its morals, its table manners, or anything else that came into our heads. We were diagnosticians of crime; if the FBI had to go to press once a month, that would be us. If the constable of Twin Oaks, Nebraska, had to be a discerning social critic, if the National Council of Protestant Episcopal Bishops had to do a certain amount of legwork, that would be us, too. In short, we were the weather bureau of the national health, recorders of its past and present crimes, forecasters of those in the future. Or so, at one time or another, we had collectively said.

With us on the twenty-sixth floor, also, were four other magazines having similar set-ups: *Homeways* (more than just a journal of housekeeping), *Personalities* (not merely the outstanding success stories of the month), *Fashions* (human, not dress), and *The Sexes* (love affairs, marriages, divorces).

Finally, on the two floors below us, were the long-range research bureaus, the legal department, the organization's public relations staff, office supplies, personnel, and a new phenomena called *Futureways*, dedicated to planned social evolution, an undertaking that might emerge as a single volume, a new magazine, an after-dinner speech somewhere, or simply disappear suddenly leaving no trace at all. Edward Orlin and Emory Mafferson were both on its staff.

Such was the headquarters of Janoth Enterprises. Bureaus in twenty-one large cities at home and twenty-five abroad fed this nerve-center daily and hourly. It was served by roving correspondents and by master scientists, scholars, technicians in every quarter of the world. It was an empire of intelligence.

Any magazine of the organization could, if necessary, command the help and advice of any channel in it. Or of all of them. *Crimeways* very often did.

We had gone after the missing financier, Paul Isleman, and found him. That one could be credited to me. And we had exercised the legal department, the auditing bureau, and a dozen legmen from our own and other units to disentangle Isleman's involved frauds, while one of our best writers, Bert Finch, had taken a month to make the whole complicated business plain to the general public.

We had found the man who killed Mrs. Frank Sandler, beating the cops by three-tenths of a second. This one, also, could be credited to George Stroud. I had located the guy through our own morgue—with the aid of a staff thrown together for the job.

I went straight through my room into Roy's, stopping only to shed my hat and coat. They were all there in 2618, looking tired but dogged, and vaguely thoughtful. Nat Sperling, a huge, dark, awkward man, went on speaking in a monotonous voice, referring to his notes.

". . . On a farm about thirty miles outside Reading. The fellow used a shotgun, a revolver, and an ax."

Roy's remote, inquiring gaze flickered away from me back to Sperling. Patiently, he asked: "And?"

"And it was one of those gory, unbelievable massacres that just seem to happen every so often in those out-of-the-way places."

"We have a man in Reading," Roy meditated, out loud. "But what's the point?"

"The score this fellow made," said Nat. "Four people, an entire family. That's really big-scale homicide, no matter where it happens."

Roy sighed and offered a wisp of a comment. "Mere numbers mean nothing. Dozens of people are murdered every day."

"Not four at a clip, by the same man."

Sydney Kislak, perched on a broad window ledge in back of Elliot, sounded a brisk footnote: "Choice of weapons. Three different kinds."

"Well, what was it all about?" Roy equably pursued.

"Jealousy. The woman had promised to run away with the killer, at least he thought she had, and when she brushed him off instead, he shot her, her husband, then he took a gun and an ax to their two—"

Roy murmured absently: "In a thing like that, the big point to consider is the motive. Is it relevant to our book? Is it criminal? And it seems to me this bird just fell in love. It's true that something went wrong, but basically he was driven to his act by love. Now, unless you can show there is something inherently criminal or even anti-social in the mating instinct—" Roy slowly opened and closed the fingers of the hand on the desk before him. "But I think we ought to suggest it to Wheeler for *Sexes*. Or perhaps *Personalities*."

"*Fashions*," murmured Sydney.

Roy continued to look expectantly at Nat, across whose candid features had struggled a certain amount of reluctant admiration. He concentrated again on his notes, apparently decided to pass over two or three items, then resumed.

"There's a terrific bank robbery in St. Paul. Over half a million dollars, the biggest bag in history."

"The biggest without benefit of law," Henry Wyckoff amended. "That was last night, wasn't it?"

"Yesterday afternoon. I got the Minneapolis bureau on it, and we already know there was a gang of at least three people, maybe more, working on this single job for more than three years. The thing about this job is that the gang regularly incorporated themselves three years ago, paid income taxes, and paid themselves salaries amounting to $175,000 while they were laying their plans and making preparations for the hold-up. Their funds went through the bank they had in mind, and it's believed they had several full-dress rehearsals before yesterday, right on the spot. A couple of the guards had even been trained, innocently it's believed, to act as their extras. One of them got paid off with a bullet in the leg."

Nat stopped and Roy appeared to gaze through him, a pinch of a frown balancing itself delicately against the curiosity in his blue, tolerant eyes.

"Figures again," he delicately judged. "What is the difference whether it is a half million, half a thousand, or just half a dollar? Three years, three months, or three minutes? Three criminals, or three hundred? What makes it so significant that it must be featured by us?"

"The technical angle, don't you think?" suggested Wyckoff. "Staying within the law while they laid the groundwork. Those rehearsals. Working all that time right through the bank. When you think of it, Roy, why, no bank or business in the world is immune to a gang with sufficient patience, resources, and brains. Here's the last word in criminal technique, matching business methods against business methods.

Hell, give enough people enough time and enough money and brains, and eventually they could take Fort Knox."

"Exactly," said Roy. "And is that new? Attack catching up with defense, defense overtaking attack, that is the whole history of crime. We have covered the essential characteristics of this very story, in its various guises, many times before—too many. I can't see much in that for us. We'll give it two or three paragraphs in *Crime Wavelets*. 'Sober, hard-working thugs invest $175,000, three years of toil, to stage a bank robbery. Earn themselves a profit of $325,000, net.' At three men working for three years," he calculated, "that amounts to something over thirty-six thousand a year each. Yes. 'This modest wage, incommensurate with the daring and skill exercised, proves again that crime does not pay—enough.' About like that. Now, can't we get something on a little higher level? We still need three leading articles."

Nat Sperling had no further suggestions to make. I saw it was already 10:45, and with little or nothing done, an early lunch seemed an idle dream. Also, I would have to write off any hope for a conference today with Roy and Hagen. Tony Watson took the ball, speaking in abrupt, nervous rushes and occasionally halting altogether for a moment of pronounced anguish. It seemed to me his neurasthenia could have shown more improvement, if not a complete cure, for the four or five thousand dollars he had spent on psychoanalysis. Still, considering the hazards of our occupation, it could be that without those treatments Tony would today be speechless altogether.

"There's a bulletin by the Welfare Commission," he said, and after we waited for a while he went on, "to be published next month. But we can get copies. I've read it. It's about the criminal abortion racket. Pretty thorough. The commission spent three years investigating. They covered everything, from the small operators to the big, expensive, private s-sanatoriums. Who protects them, why and how. Total estimated number every year, amount of money the industry represents, figures on deaths and prosecutions. Medical effects, pro and con. Causes, results. It's a straight, exhaustive study of the subject. First of its kind. Official, I mean."

Long before Tony had finished, Roy's chin was down upon his chest, and at the close he was making swift notes.

"Do they reach any conclusions? Make any recommendations?" he asked.

"Well, the report gives a complex of causes. Economic reasons are the chief cause of interrupted pregnancies among married women, and among—"

"Never mind that. We'll have to reach our own conclusions. What do they say about old-age assistance?"

"What? Why, nothing, as I recall."

"Never mind, I think we have something. We'll take that bulletin and show what it really means. We'll start by giving the figures for social security survivor benefits. Funeral allowances, in particular, and make the obvious contrasts. Here, on the one hand, is what our government spends every year to bury the dead, while here, at the other end of the scale of life, is what the people spend to prevent birth. Get in touch with the Academy of Medicine and the College of Physicians and Surgeons for a short history of the practice of abortion, and take along a photographer. Maybe they have a collection of primitive and modern instruments. A few pictures ought to be very effective. A short discussion of ancient methods ought to be even more effective."

"Magic was one of them," Bert Finch told Tony.

"Fine," said Roy. "Don't fail to get that in, too. And you might get in touch with the Society of American Morticians for additional figures on what we spend for death, as contrasted with what is spent to prevent life. Call up a half a dozen department stores, ask for figures on what the average expectant mother spends on clothes and equipment up to the date of birth. And don't forget to bring in a good quotation or two from Jonathan Swift on Irish babies."

He looked at Tony, whose meager, freckled features seemed charged with reserve.

"That isn't exactly what I had in mind, Roy. I thought we'd simply dramatize the findings. The commission's findings."

Roy drew a line under the notes on his pad.

"That's what we will be doing, a take-out on the abortion racket. A round-up of the whole subject of inheritance and illegitimacy. But we will be examining it on a higher level, that's all. Just go ahead with the story now, and when the bulletin comes out we'll check through it and draw attention to the real implications of the general picture, at the same time pointing out the survey's omissions. But don't wait for the survey to be released. Can you have a rough draft in, say, two or three weeks?"

Tony Watson's strangled silence indicated that about two thousand dollars' worth of treatments had been shot to hell. Presently, though, he announced: "I can try."

The conference went on, like all those that had gone before, and, unless some tremendous miracle intervened, like many hundreds sure to follow.

Next month Nat Sperling's quadruple-slaying on a lonely farm would become a penthouse shooting in Chicago, Tony's bent for sociological research would produce new parole-board reports, novel insurance statistics, a far-reaching decision of the Supreme Court. Whatever the subject, it scarcely mattered. What did matter was our private and collective virtuosity.

Down the hall, in Sydney's office, there was a window out of which an almost forgotten associate editor had long ago jumped. I occasionally wondered whether he had done so after some conference such as this. Just picked up his notes and walked down the corridor to his own room, opened the window, and then stepped out.

But we were not insane.

We were not children exchanging solemn fantasies in some progressive nursery. Nor were the things we were doing here completely useless.

What we decided in this room, more than a million of our fellow-citizens would read three months from now, and what they read they would accept as final. They might not know they were doing so, they might even briefly dispute our decisions, but still they would follow the reasoning we presented, remember the phrases, the tone of authority, and in the end their crystallized judgments would be ours.

Where our own logic came from, of course, was still another matter. The moving impulse simply arrived, and we, on the face that the giant clock turned to the public, merely registered the correct hour of the standard time.

But being the measure by which so many lives were shaped and guided gave us, sometimes, strange delusions.

At five minutes to twelve, even the tentative schedule lined up for the April book was far too meager. Leon Temple and Roy were engaged in a rather aimless cross-discussion about a radio program that Leon construed as a profound conspiracy against reason, and therefore a cardinal crime, with Roy protesting the program was only a minor nuisance.

"It's on a pretty low level, and why should we give it free advertising?" he demanded. "Like inferior movies and books and plays, it's simply not on our map."

"And like confidence games, and counterfeit money," Leon jibed.

"I know, Leon, but after all—"

"But after all," I intervened, "it's noon, and we've come around to ultimate values, right on the dot."

Roy looked around, smiling. "Well, if you have something, don't let it spoil."

"I think maybe I have," I said. "A little idea that might do everyone a certain amount of good, ourselves included. It's about *Futureways*. We all know something of what they're doing downstairs."

"Those alchemists," said Roy. "Do they know, themselves?"

"I have a strong feeling they've lost their way with Funded Individuals," I began. "We could do a double service by featuring it ourselves, at the same time sending up a trial balloon for them."

I elaborated. In theory, Funded Individuals was something big. The substance of it was the capitalization of gifted people in their younger years for an amount sufficient to rear them under controlled conditions, educate them, and then provide for a substantial investment in some profitable enterprise through which the original indebtedness would be repaid. The original loan, floated as ordinary stocks or bonds, also paid life-insurance premiums guaranteeing the full amount of the issue, and a normal yearly dividend.

Not every one of these incorporated people—Funded Individuals was our registered name for the undertaking—would be uniformly successful, of course, however fortunate and talented he might originally be. But the Funded Individuals were operated as a pool, with a single directorship, and our figures had demonstrated that such a venture would ultimately show a tremendous overall profit.

It went without saying that the scheme would mean a great deal to those persons chosen for the pool. Each would be capitalized at something like one million dollars, from the age of seventeen.

I told the staff that the social implications of such a project, carried to its logical conclusions, meant the end of not only poverty, ignorance, disease, and maladjustment, but also inevitably of crime.

"We can suggest a new approach to the whole problem of crime," I concluded. "Crime is no more inherent in society than diphtheria, horse-cars, or black magic. We are accustomed to thinking that crime will cease only in some far-off Utopia. But the conditions for abolishing it are at hand—right now."

The idea was tailored for *Crimeways*, and the staff knew it. Roy said, cautiously: "Well, it does show a perspective of diminishing crime." His thin face was filled with a whole train of afterthoughts. "I see where it could be ours. But what about those people downstairs? And what about the thirty-second floor? It's their material, and they have their own ideas about what to do with it, haven't they?"

I said I didn't think so. Mafferson, Orlin, and half a dozen others downstairs in the research bureau known as *Futureways* had been working on Funded Individuals off and on for nearly a year, with no visible results as yet, and with slight probability there ever would be. I said: "The point is, they don't know whether they want to drop Funded Individuals, or what to do with it if they don't. I think Hagen would welcome any sort of a move. We can give the idea an abbreviated prevue."

" 'Crimeless Tomorrow,' " Roy improvised. " 'Research Shows Why. Finance Shows How.' " He thought for a moment. "But I don't see any pictures, George."

"Graphs."

We let it go at that. That afternoon I cleared the article with Hagen, in a three-minute phone call. Then I had a talk with Ed Orlin, who agreed that Emory Mafferson would be the right man to work with us, and presently Emory put in his appearance.

I knew him only casually. He was not much more than five feet high, and gave the illusion he was taller sitting than standing. He radiated a slight, steady aura of confusion.

After we checked over his new assignment he brought forward a personal matter.

"Say, George."

"Yes?"

"How are you fixed on the staff of *Crimeways*? After we line up Funded Individuals?"

"Why, do you want to join us?"

"Well, I damn near have to. Ed Orlin looked almost happy when he found I was being borrowed up here."

"Don't you get along with Ed?"

"We get along all right, sometimes. But I begin to think he's beginning to think I'm not the *Futureways* type. I know the signs. It's happened before, see."

"You write short stories, don't you?"

Emory appeared to grope for the truth. "Well."

"I understand. It's all right with me, Emory, if you want to come on here. What in hell, by the way, is the *Futureways* type?"

Emory's brown eyes swam around behind thick spectacles like two lost and lonely goldfish. The inner concentration was terrific. "First place, you've got to believe you're shaping something. Destiny, for example. And then you'd better not do anything to attract attention to yourself. It's fatal to come up with a new idea, for instance, and it's also fatal not to have any at all. See what I mean? And above all, it's dangerous to turn in a piece of finished copy. Everything has to be serious, and pending. Understand?"

"No. Just don't try to be the *Crimeways* type, that's all I ask."

We got Emory and Bert Finch teamed for the "Crimeless Tomorrow" feature, and at five o'clock I phoned Georgette to say I'd be home, after all, but Nellie told me Georgette had gone to her sister's in some emergency involving one of Ann's children. She would be home late, might not be home at all. I told Nellie I'd have supper in town.

It was five-thirty when I walked into the Silver Lining, alone. I had a drink and reviewed what I would have said to Roy and Steve Hagen, had they been present to listen. It did not sound as convincing as I had made it sound this morning. Yet there must be a way. I could do something, I had to, and I would.

The bar of the Silver Lining is only twenty feet from the nearest tables. Behind me, at one of them, I heard a woman's voice saying that she really must leave, and then another voice saying they would have to meet again soon. Half turning, I saw the first speaker depart, and then I saw the other woman. It was Pauline Delos. The face, the voice, and the figure registered all at once.

We looked at each other across half the width of the room, and before I had quite placed her I had smiled and nodded. So did she, and in much the same manner.

I picked up my drink and went to her table. Why not?

I said of course she didn't remember me, and she said of course she did.

I said could I buy her a drink. I could.

She was blonde as hell, wearing a lot of black.

"You're the friend of President McKinley," she told me. I admitted it. "And this was where you were talking to him. Is he here tonight?"

I looked all around the room.

I guess she meant Clyde Polhemus, but he wasn't here.

"Not tonight," I said. "How would you like to have dinner with me, instead?"

"I'd love it."

I think we had an apple-brandy sidecar to begin with. It did not seem this was only the second time we had met. All at once a whole lot of things were moving and mixing, as though they had always been there.

George Stroud IV

W E WERE in the Silver Lining for about an hour. We had dinner there, after Pauline made a phone call rearranging some previous plans.

Then we made the studio broadcast of *Rangers of the Sky;* the program itself was one of my favorites, but that was not the main attraction. We could have heard it anywhere, on any set. Quite aside from the appeal of the program, I was fascinated by the work of a new sound-effects man who, I believed, was laying the foundation for a whole new radio technique. This chap could run a sequence of dramatic sound, without voice or music, for as much as five minutes. Sustaining the suspense, and giving it a clear meaning, too. I explained to Pauline, who seemed puzzled but interested, that some day this fellow would do a whole fifteen- or thirty-minute program of sound and nothing but sound, without voice or music of course, a drama with no words, and then radio would have grown up.

After that Pauline made some more phone calls, rearranging some other plans, and I remembered Gil's bar on Third Avenue. It wasn't exactly a bar and it wasn't exactly a night club; perhaps it might have been called a small Coney Island, or just a dive. Or maybe Gil had the right name and description when he called it a museum.

I hadn't been there for a year or two, but when I had been, there was a game Gil played with his friends and customers, and to me it had always seemed completely worth while.

Although most of Gil's was an ordinary greased postage stamp for dancing to any kind of a band, with any kind of entertainment, there was one thing about it that was different. There was a thirty-foot bar, and on a deep shelf in back of it Gil had accumulated and laid out an inexhaustible quantity of junk—there is no other word for it—which he called his "personal museum." It was Gil's claim that everything in the world was there, somewhere, and that the article, whatever it was, had a history closely connected with his own life and doings. The game was to stump him, on one point or the other.

I never had, though all told I certainly had spent many happy hours trying to do so, and lots of money. At the same time, Gil's logic was sometimes strained and his tales not deeply imaginative. There was a recurrent rumor that every time Gil got stuck for something not in stock, he made it a point to go out and get its equivalent, thus keeping abreast of alert students of the game. Furthermore, his ripostes in the forenoon and early afternoon of the day were not on a par with the results achieved later on, when he was drunk.

"Anything?" Pauline asked, surveying the collection.

"Anything at all," I assured her.

We were seated at the bar, which was not very crowded, and Pauline was looking in mild astonishment at the deceptive forest of bric-a-brac facing us. There was even a regular bar mirror behind all that mountain of gadgets, as I knew from personal experience. Shrunken heads, franc notes, mark notes, confederate money, bayonets, flags, a piece of a totem pole, an airplane propeller, some mounted birds and butterflies, rocks and seashells, surgical instruments, postage stamps, ancient newspapers—wherever the eye wandered it saw some other incongruity and slipped rather dazedly on to still more.

Gil came up, beaming, and I saw he was in form. He knew me by sight only. He nodded, and I said: "Gil, the lady wants to play the game."

"Surely," he said. Gil was an affable fifty, I would have guessed, or maybe fifty-five. "What can I show you, Miss?"

I said, "Can you show us a couple of highballs, while she makes up her mind?"

He took our orders and turned to set them up.

"Anything at all?" Pauline asked me. "No matter how ridiculous?"

"Lady, those are Gil's personal memoirs. You wouldn't call a man's life ridiculous, would you?"

"What did he have to do with the assassination of Abraham Lincoln?"

She was looking at the headline of a yellowed, glass-encased newspaper announcing same. Of course, I had once wondered the same thing, and I told her: The paper was a family heirloom; Gil's grandfather had written the headline, when he worked for Horace Greeley.

"Simple," I pointed out. "And don't ask for lady's hats. He's got Cleopatra's turban back there, and half a dozen other moth-eaten relics that could pass for anything at all."

Gil slid our drinks before us, and gave Pauline his most professional smile.

"I want to see a steamroller," she said.

Gil's beam deepened and he went down the bar, returned with a black and jagged metal cylinder that had once served, if I properly remembered a wild evening, as Christopher Columbus' telescope—a relic certified by the Caribbean natives from whom Gil had personally secured it.

"I can't show you the whole steamroller, ma'am," Gil told Pauline. "Naturally, I haven't room here. Someday I'll have a bigger place, and then I can enlarge my personal museum. But this here is the safety valve from off a steamroller, this is. Go on," he pushed it at her. "It's a very clever arrangement. Look it over."

Pauline accepted the article, without bothering to look at it.

"And this is part of your personal museum?"

"The last time they paved Third Avenue," Gil assured her, "this here steamroller exploded right out in front there. The safety valve, which you have ahold of right there in your hand, came through the window like a bullet. Creased me. As a matter of fact, it left a scar. Look, I'll show you." I knew that scar, and he showed it again. That scar was Gil's biggest asset. "The valve off that steamroller was defective, as you can tell by looking at it. But, as long as it was right here anyway, why, I just left it up in back of the bar where it hit. It was one of the narrowest escapes I ever had."

"Me too," I said. "I was right here when it happened. What'll you have, Gil?"

"Why, I don't mind."

Gil turned and earnestly poured himself a drink, his honest reward for scoring. We lifted our glasses, and Gil jerked his gray, massive head just once. Then he went down the bar to an amateur customer who loudly demanded to see a pink elephant.

Gil patiently showed him the pink elephant, and courteously explained its role in his life.

"I like the museum," said Pauline. "But it must be terrible, sometimes, for Gil. He's seen everything, done everything, gone everywhere, known everyone. What's left for him?"

I muttered that history would be in the making tomorrow, the same as today, and we had another drink on that thought. And then Gil came back and Pauline had another experiment with his memories, and the three of us had another round. And then another.

At one o'clock we were both tired of Gil's life, and I began to think of my own.

I could always create a few more memories, myself. Why not?

There were many reasons why I should not. I weighed them all again, and I tried once more to explain somehow the thing that I knew I was about to do. But they all slipped away from me.

I conjured all sorts of very fancy explanations, besides the simple one, but either the plain or the fancy reasons were good enough; I was not particular on what grounds I behaved foolishly, and even dangerously.

Perhaps I was tired of doing, always, what I ought to do, wearier still of not doing the things that should not be done.

The attractions of the Delos woman multiplied themselves by ten, and then presently they were multiplying by the hundreds. We looked at each other, and that instant was like the white flash of a thrown switch when a new circuit is formed and then the current flows invisibly through another channel.

Why not? I knew the risks and the cost. And still, why not? Maybe the risks and the price were themselves at least some of the reasons why. The cost would be high; it would take some magnificent lying and acting; yet if I were willing to pay that price, why not? And the dangers would be greater still. Of them, I couldn't even begin to guess.

But it would be a very rousing thing to spend an evening with this blonde mystery that certainly ought to be solved. And if I didn't solve it now, I never would. Nobody ever would. It would be something lost forever.

"Well?" she said.

She was smiling, and I realized I had been having an imaginary argument with a shadow of George Stroud standing just in back of the blazing nimbus she had become. It was amazing. All that other Stroud seemed to be saying was: *Why not?* Whatever he meant, I couldn't imagine. Why not what?

I finished a drink I seemed to have in my hand, and said: "I'll have to make a phone call."

"Yes. So will I."

My own phone call was to a nearby semi-residential hotel. The manager had never failed me—I was putting his sons and daughters through school, wasn't I?—and he didn't fail me now. When I returned from the booth, I said: "Shall we go?"

"Let's. Is it far?"

"Not far," I said. "But it's nothing extravagant."

I had no idea, of course, where in that rather sad and partially respectable apartment-hotel we would find ourselves. Pauline took all this for granted, apparently. It gave me a second thought; and the second thought whisked itself away the moment it occurred. Then I hoped she wouldn't say anything about anyone or anything except ourselves.

I needn't have worried. She didn't.

These moments move fast, if they are going to move at all, and with no superfluous nonsense. If they don't move, they die.

Bert Sanders, the manager of the Lexington-Plaza, handed me a note when he gave me the key to a room on the fifth floor. The note said he positively must have the room by noon tomorrow, reservations had been made for it. The room itself, where I found my in-town valise, was all right, a sizable family vault I believed I had lived in once or twice before.

I was a little bit surprised and dismayed to see it was already three o'clock, as I brought out the half bottle of Scotch, the one dressing gown and single pair of slippers, the back number of *Crimeways*—how did that get here?—the three volumes of stories and poetry, the stack of handkerchiefs, pajamas, aspirin tablets comprising most of the contents of the valise. I said: "How would you like some Scotch?"

We both would. Service in the Lexington-Plaza perished at about ten o'clock, so we had our drinks with straight tap water. It was all right. The life we were now living seemed to quicken perceptibly.

I remembered to tell Pauline, lying on the floor with a pillow under her head and looking more magnificent than ever in my pajamas, that our home would no longer be ours after noon. She dreamily told me I needn't worry, it would be all right, and why didn't I go right on explaining about Louise Patterson and the more important trends in modern painting. I saw with some surprise I had a book open in my lap, but I had been talking about something else entirely. And now I couldn't remember what. I dropped the book, and lay down on the floor beside her.

"No more pictures," I said. "Let's solve the mystery."

"What mystery?"

"You."

"I'm a very average person, George. No riddle at all."

I believe I said, "You're the last, final, beautiful, beautiful, ultimate enigma. Maybe you can't be solved."

And I think I looked at our great big gorgeous bed, soft and deep and wide. But it seemed a thousand miles away. I decided it was just too far. But that was all right. It was better than all right. It was perfect. It was just plain perfect.

I found out again why we are on this earth. I think.

And then I woke up and saw myself in that big, wide bed, alone, with a great ringing and hammering and buzzing going on. The phone was closest, so I answered it, and a voice said: "I'm sorry, sir, but Mr. Sanders says you have no reservation for today."

I looked at my watch; 1:30.

"All right."

I believe I moaned and lay back and ate an aspirin tablet that somebody had thoughtfully laid on the table beside the bed, and then after a while I went to the door that was still pounding and buzzing. It was Bert Sanders.

"You all right?" he asked, looking more than a little worried. "You know, I told you I've reserved this suite."

"My God."

"Well, I hate to wake you up, but we have to—"

"All right."

"I don't know exactly when—"

"My God."

"If I'd thought—"

"All right. Where is she?"

"Who? Oh, well, about six o'clock this morning—"

"My God, never mind."

"I thought you'd want to sleep for a few hours, but—"

"All right." I found my trousers and my wallet and I somehow paid off Bert. "I'll be out of here in three minutes. Was there anything, by the way—?"

"Nothing, Mr. Stroud. It's just that this room—"

"Sure. Get my bag out of here, will you?"

He said he would, and after that I got dressed in a hurry, looking around the room for possible notes as I found a clean shirt, washed but did not attempt to shave, poured myself a fraction of an inch that seemed to be left in a bottle of Scotch somehow on hand.

Who was she?

Pauline Delos. Janoth's girl friend. Oh, God. What next?

Where did Georgette think I was? In town, on a job, but coming home a little late. All right. And then?

What was I supposed to be doing at the office today?

I couldn't remember anything important, and that was not so bad.

But about the major problems? Well, there was nothing I could do about them now, if I had been as stupid as all this. Nothing. Well, all right.

I combed my hair, brushed my teeth, put on my tie.

I could tell Georgette, at her sister's in Trenton, that I had to work until three in the morning and didn't want to phone. It would have awakened the whole household. Simple. It had always worked before. It would work this time. Had to.

I closed my valise, left it for Bert in the middle of the room, went downstairs to the barber shop in the lobby. There I got a quick shave, and after that I had a quicker breakfast, and then a split-second drink.

It was three o'clock in the afternoon when I got back to my desk, and there was no one around except Lucille, Roy's and my secretary, listlessly typing in the small room connecting our two offices. She did not appear curious, and I couldn't find any messages on my desk, either, just a lot of inter-office memos and names.

"Anyone phone me, Lucille?" I asked.

"Just those on your pad."

"My home didn't call? Nothing from my wife?"

"No."

So it was all right. So far. Thank God.

I went back to my desk and sat down and took three more aspirin tablets. It was an afternoon like any other afternoon, except for those nerves. But there should be nothing really the matter with them, either. I began to go through the routine items listed by Lucille. Everything was the same as it had always been. Everything was all right. I hadn't done anything. No one had.

George Stroud V

A ND ALL of that went off all right. And two months passed. And during those two months, Mafferson and I worked up the data and the groundwork for Funded Individuals, and we also worked up a take-out of bankruptcy for the May issue, and a detailed story about bought-and-sold orphans for the June book.

Then one evening, early in March, I had one of those moods. I reached for the phone, and from our confidential telephone service got the number I wanted. When the number answered I said: "Hello, Pauline. This is your attorney."

"Oh, yes," she said, after a second. "That one."

It was a spring day, I told her, as it was: the first. We fixed it to have cocktails at the Van Barth.

Georgette and Georgia were in Florida, returning in two days. Earl Janoth was in Washington, for at least a couple of hours, and possibly for a week. It was a Friday.

Before leaving that night I stepped into Roy's office and found him conferring with Emory Mafferson and Bert Finch. I gathered that Emory was filled with doubts regarding "Crimeless Tomorrow, Science Shows Why, Finance Shows How."

Emory said: "I can see, on paper, how Funded Individuals works out fine. I can see from the insurance rates and the business statistics that it works out for a few people who happen to be funded, but what I don't see is, what's going to happen if everyone belongs to the corporation pool? See what I'm driving at?"

Roy was being at his confident, patient, understanding best. "That's what it's supposed to lead to," he said. "And I think it's rather nice. Don't you?"

"Let me put it this way, Roy. If a person capitalized at a million dollars actually returns the original investment, plus a profit, then there's going to be a tremendous rush to incorporate still more individuals, for still more profit. And pretty soon, everyone will be in clover except the stockholders. What do they get out of the arrangement?"

Roy's patience took on palpable weight and shape. "Profit," he said.

"Sure, but what can they do with it? What have they got? Just some monetary gain. They don't, themselves, lead perfectly conditioned lives, with a big sum left over to invest in some new, paying enterprise. Seems to me the only people that get it in the neck with this scheme are the subscribers who make the whole thing possible."

Roy said: "You forget that after this has been in operation a few years, funded people will themselves be the first to reinvest their capital in the original pool, so that both groups are always interested parties of the same process."

I decided they were doing well enough without interference from me, and left.

In the bar of the Van Barth I met a beautiful stranger in a rather austere gray and black ensemble that looked like a tailored suit, but wasn't. I hadn't been waiting for more than ten minutes. After we settled on the drink she would have, Pauline said, rather seriously: "I shouldn't be here at all, you know. I have a feeling it's dangerous to know you."

"Me? Dangerous? Kittens a month old get belligerent when they see me coming. Open their eyes for the first time and sharpen up their claws, meowing in anticipation."

She smiled, without humor, and soberly repeated: "You're a dangerous person, George."

I didn't think this was the right note to strike, and so I struck another one. And pretty soon it was all right, and we had another drink, and then after a while we went to Lemoyne's for supper.

I had been living pretty much alone for the last three weeks, since Georgette and Georgia had gone to Florida, and I felt talkative. So I talked. I told her the one about what the whale said to the submarine, why the silents had been the Golden Age of the movies, why Lonny Trout was a fighter's fighter, and then I suggested that we drive up to Albany.

That is what we finally did. I experienced again the pleasure of driving up the heights of the only perfect river in the world, the river that never floods, never dries up, and yet never seems to be the same twice. Albany we reached, by stages, in about three hours.

I had always liked the city, too, which is not as common-place as it may look to the casual traveler, particularly when the legislature is in session. If there is anything Manhattan has overlooked, it settled here.

After registering under a name I dreamed up with some care and imagination, Mr. and Mrs. Andrew Phelps-Guyon, we went out and spent a couple of hours over food and drink, some entertainment and a few dances on a good, not crowded floor, at a damnably expensive night club. But it was an eve-ning with a definite touch of spring, snatched from the very teeth of the inner works, and exceedingly worth while.

We had breakfast at about noon, and shortly afterwards started a slow drive back to the city, by a different route. It was a different river we followed again, of course, and of course, I fell in love with it all over again; and of course, Pauline helped.

It was late Saturday afternoon when we reached the neigh-borhood of 58 East, Pauline's apartment building, so early she admitted she had time and lots of it. We went to Gil's. Pauline played the game for about three rounds. I thought Gil was stuck when she asked to see Poe's Raven, but he brought out a stuffed bluebird or something, well advanced in its last molt-ing, and explained it was Poe's original inspiration, personally presented to his close friend, Gil's great-grandfather. And then I remembered it was a long time, all of three months, since I'd explored Antique Row.

That is Third Avenue from about Sixtieth Street all the way down to Forty-second, or thereabouts; there may be bigger, better, more expensive and more authentic shops scattered elsewhere about the city, but the spirit of adventure and re-discovery is not in them, somehow. I once asked, on a tall evening in a Third Avenue shop, for the Pied Piper of Ham-lin's pipe. They happened to have it, too. I forget what I did with it, after I bought it for about ten dollars and took it first to the office, where it seemed to have lost its potency, and then home, where somebody broke it and then it disappeared. But it wasn't Third Avenue's fault if I hadn't known how to take care of it properly.

This afternoon Pauline and I dawdled over some not very interesting early New England bedwarmers, spinning wheels converted to floor and table lamps, and the usual commodes disguised as playchairs, bookshelves, and tea carts. All very sound and substantial stuff, reflecting more credit to the ingenuity of the twentieth century than to the imagination of the original craftsmen. It was interesting, some of it, but not exciting.

Then at about half-past seven, with some of the shops closing, we reached a little but simply jam-packed place on Fiftieth Street. Maybe I had been in here before, but I couldn't remember it and neither, seemingly, did the proprietor remember me.

I rummaged about for several minutes without his help, not seeing anything I may have missed before, but I had a fine time answering Pauline's questions. Then after a while somebody else came in and I became increasingly aware of the dialogue going forward at the front of the shop.

"Yes, I have," I heard the dealer say, with some surprise. "But I don't know if they're exactly the type you'd want. Hardly anyone asks for pictures in here, of course. I just put that picture in the window because it happened to be framed. Is that the one you wanted?"

"No. But you have some others, haven't you? Unframed. A friend of mine was in here a couple of weeks ago and said you had."

The customer was a big, monolithic brunette, sloppily dressed and with a face like an arrested cyclone.

"Yes, I have. They're not exactly in perfect condition."

"I don't care," she said. "May I see them?"

The dealer located a roll of canvases on an overhead shelf, and tugged them down. I had drifted down to the front of the shop by now, constituting myself a silent partner in the proceedings. The dealer handed the woman the entire roll, and I practically rested my chin on his left shoulder.

"Look them over," he told the woman.

He turned his head, frowning, and for a fraction of a moment one of his eyes loomed enormously, gazing into one of mine. Mine expressed polite curiosity.

"Where did you get these?" the customer asked.

She unrolled the sheaf of canvases, which were about four by five, some more and some less, and studied the one on top from her reverse viewpoint. It showed a Gloucester clipper under full sail, and it was just like all pictures of clippers, unusual only for a ring of dirt, like an enlarged coffee ring, that wreathed the vessel and several miles of the ocean. To say it was not exactly in perfect condition was plain perjury. The ring, I thought, was about the size of a barrelhead, and that would be about where it came from.

"They were part of a lot," the dealer guardedly told her. The big woman cut loose with a loud, ragged laugh. "Part of a lot of what?" she asked. "Material for an arson? Or is this some of that old WPA stuff they used to wrap up ten-cent store crockery?"

"I don't know where it came from. I told you it wasn't in the best of shape."

She thrust the one on top to the rear, exposing a large bowl of daisies. Nobody said anything at all, this time; I just closed my eyes for a couple of seconds and it went away.

The third canvas was an honest piece of work of the tenement-and-junkyard school; I placed it as of about fifteen years ago; I didn't recognize the signature, but it could have been painted by one of five or six hundred good, professional artists who had done the same scene a little better or a little worse.

"Pretty good," said the shop proprietor. "Colorful. It's real."

The tall, square brunette intently went on to the next one. It was another Gloucester clipper, this one going the other way. It had the same magnificent coffee ring that they all did. And the next one was a basket of kittens. "My Pets," I am sure the nice old lady who painted it had called this one. Anyway, the show was diversified. Clipper artists stuck to clippers, backyard painters did them by the miles, and the nice old lady had certainly done simply hundreds and hundreds of cats. Our gallery had them all.

"I'm afraid you haven't got anything here that would interest me," said the woman.

The man tacitly admitted it, and she resumed the show. Two more pictures passed without comment, and I saw there were only two or three more.

Then she turned up another one, methodically, and I suddenly stopped breathing. It was a Louise Patterson. There was no mistaking the subject, the treatment, the effect. The brothers and sisters of that picture hung on my walls in Marble Road. I had once paid nine hundred dollars for one of them, not much less for the others, all of which I had picked up at regular Patterson shows on Fifty-seventh Street.

The customer had already slipped a tentative finger in back of it to separate it from the next canvas and take it away, when I cleared my throat and casually remarked: "I rather like that."

She looked at me, not very amiably, swung the picture around and held it up before her, at arm's length; it curled at the edges where it wasn't frayed, and it had a few spots of something on it in addition to the trademark of the outsized coffee ring. It was in a frightful condition, no less.

"So do I," she flatly declared. "But it's in one hell of a shape. How much do you want for it?"

The question, ignoring me entirely, was fired at the dealer. "Why—"

"God, what a mess."

With her second shot she doubtless cut the dealer's intended price in half.

"I wouldn't know how to value it, exactly," he admitted. "But you can have it for ten dollars?"

It was the literal truth that I did not myself know what a Patterson would be worth, today, on the regular market. Nothing fabulous, I knew; but on the other hand, although Patterson hadn't exhibited for years, and for all I knew was dead, it did not seem possible her work had passed into complete eclipse. The things I had picked up for a few hundred had been bargains when I bought them, and later still the artist's canvases had brought much more, though only for a time.

I beamed at the woman. "I spoke first," I said to her, and then to the dealer: "I'll give you fifty for it."

The dealer, who should have stuck to refinished porch furniture, was clearly dazzled and also puzzled. I could tell the exact moment the great electric light went on in his soul: he had something, probably a Rembrandt.

"Well, I don't know," he said. "It's obviously a clever picture. Extremely sound. I was intending to have this lot appraised, when I had the time. This is the first time I've really looked at the lot, myself. I think—"

"It is not a Raphael, Rubens, or Corot," I assured him.

He leaned forward and looked more closely at the picture. The canvas showed two hands, one giving and the other receiving a coin. That was all. It conveyed the whole feeling, meaning, and drama of money. But the proprietor was unwrinkling the bottom right-hand corner of the canvas, where the signature would be rather legibly scrawled. I began to perspire.

"Pat something," he announced, studying it carefully, and the next moment he sounded disappointed. "Oh. Patterson, '32. I ought to know that name, but it's slipped my mind."

I let this transparent perjury die a natural death. The large brunette, built like an old-fashioned kitchen cabinet, didn't say anything either. But she didn't need to. She obviously didn't have fifty dollars. And I had to have that picture.

"It's a very superior work," the dealer began again. "When it's cleaned up, it'll be beautiful."

"I like it," I said. "For fifty bucks."

He said, stalling: "I imagine the fellow who painted it called the picture *Toil*. Something like that."

"I'd call it *Judas*," Pauline spoke up. "No, *The Temptation of Judas*."

"There's only one coin," said the dealer, seriously. "There would have to be thirty." Still stalling, he took the canvases and began to go through those we had not seen. A silo, with a cow in front of it. A nice thing with some children playing in the street. The beach at Coney Island. Depressed at stirring no further interest, he declared, "And that's all I have."

To the brunette, and smiling glassily, I said: "Why don't you take the *Grand Street Children*, for about five dollars? I'll take the *Judas*."

She unchained a whoop of laughter that was not, as far as I could make out, either friendly or hostile. It was just loud.

"No, thanks, I have enough children of my own."

"I'll buy you a frame, we'll fix it here, and you can take it home."

This produced another shriek, followed by a roar.

"Save it for your fifty-dollar masterpiece." This sounded derisive. I asked her, with a bite in it: "Don't you believe it's worth that?"

"A picture that is worth anything at all is certainly worth a lot more than that," she suddenly blazed. "Don't you think so? It is either worth ten dollars or a million times that much." Mentally I agreed with this perfectly reasonable attitude, but the shop proprietor looked as though he did, too. And I had to have that picture. It wasn't my fault I had only sixty odd dollars left after one of the most expensive week ends in history, instead of ten million. "But what do I know about paintings? Nothing. Don't let me interfere. Maybe sometime," there was another bloodcurdling laugh, "I'll have the right kind of wallpaper, and just the right space to match the *Grand Street Children*. Save it for me."

She went away, then, and in the quiet that came back to the little shop I firmly proved I would pay what I said I would and no more, and eventually we went away, too, and I had my prize.

Pauline still had some time, and we stopped in at the cocktail lounge of the Van Barth. I left the canvas in the car, but when we'd ordered our drinks Pauline asked me why on earth I'd bought it, and I described it again, trying to explain. She finally said she liked it well enough, but could not see there was anything extraordinarily powerful about it.

It became evident she was picture-blind. It wasn't her fault; many people are born that way; it is the same as being color-blind or tone-deaf. But I tried to explain what the work of Louise Patterson meant in terms of simplified abstractionism and fresh intensifications of color. Then I argued that the picture must have some feeling for her since she'd surely picked the right title for it.

"How do you know it's right?" she asked.

"I know it. I feel it. It's just what I saw in the picture myself."

On the spur of the moment I decided, and told her, that Judas must have been a born conformist, a naturally common-sense, rubber-stamp sort of fellow who rose far above himself when he became involved with a group of people who were hardly in society, let alone a profitable business.

"Heavens, you make him sound like a saint," Pauline said, smiling and frowning.

I told her very likely he was.

"A man like that, built to fall into line but finding himself always out of step, must have suffered twice the torments of the others. And eventually, the temptation was too much for him. Like many another saint, when he was tempted, he fell. But only briefly."

"Isn't that a little involved?"

"Anyway, it's the name of my picture," I said. "Thanks for your help."

We drank to that, but Pauline upset her cocktail.

I rescued her with my handkerchief for a hectic moment, then left her to finish the job while I called the waiter for more drinks, and he cleared the wet tabletop. After a while we had something to eat, and still more drinks, and a lot more talk.

It was quite dark when we came out of the lounge, and I drove the few blocks to 58 East. Pauline's apartment, which I had never been in, was in one of those austere and permanent pueblos of the Sixties. She asked me to stop away from the entrance, cool as she explained: "I don't think it would be wise for me to go in with a strange overnight bag. Accompanied."

The remark didn't say anything, but it gave me a momentarily uncomfortable measure of the small but nevertheless real risks we were running. I erased that idea and said nothing, but I ran past the building and parked half a block from the lighted, canopied entrance.

There I got out to hand her the light valise she had brought with her to Albany, and for a moment we paused.

"May I phone?" I asked.

"Of course. Please do. But we have to be—well—"

"Of course. It's been wonderful, Pauline. Just about altogether supreme."

She smiled and turned away.

Looking beyond her retreating shoulders I vaguely noticed a limousine pull in at the curb opposite the building's entrance. There was something familiar about the figure and carriage of the man who got out of it. He put his head back into the car to issue instructions to a chauffeur, then turned for a moment in my direction. I saw that it was Earl Janoth.

He noticed Pauline approaching, and I am certain that he looked past her and saw me. But I did not think he could have recognized me; the nearest street lamp was at my back.

And what if he had? He didn't own the woman.

He didn't own me, either.

I stepped into my car and started the motor, and I saw them disappearing together into the lighted entrance.

I didn't feel very happy about this unlucky circumstance, as I drove off, but on the other hand, I didn't see how any irreparable damage could have been done.

I drove back to Gil's. There, it was the usual raucous Saturday night. I had a whole lot of drinks, without much conversation, then I took the car around to my garage and caught the 1:45 for home. It was early, but I wanted to be clear-eyed when Georgette and Georgia got back from Florida in the afternoon. I would return by train, pick them up in the car, and drive them home.

I brought in my own bag, at Marble Road, and of course I didn't forget *The Temptation of St. Judas*. The picture I simply laid down on the dining room table. It would have to be cleaned, repaired, and framed.

I glanced at the Pattersons in the downstairs rooms and at the one upstairs in my study, before I went to bed. The *Temptation* was better than any of them.

It occurred to me that maybe I was becoming one of the outstanding Patterson collectors in the United States. Or anywhere.

But before I went to bed I unpacked my grip, put away the belongings it had contained, then put the grip away, too.

Earl Janoth I

Y GOD, I never had such an evening. I flatter myself that
I am never inurbane by impulse only, but these people,
supposedly friends of mine, were the limit, and I could have
strangled them one by one.

Ralph Beeman, my attorney for fifteen years, showed
damned little interest and less sympathy when the question of
the wire renewal for *Commerce Index* came up, or was deliberately brought up. The whole bunch of them quite openly
discussed the matter, as though I myself were some sort of
immaterial pneuma, not quite present at all, and as though I
might actually lose the franchise. Really, they weighed alternatives, when I did lose it.

"Ralph and I have something to say about that," I said,
heartily, but the mousey bastard didn't turn a hair. He was
just plain neutral.

"Oh, certainly. We'll renew no matter whom we have to
fight."

To me, it sounded as though he thought the fight was already lost. I gave him a sharp look, but he chose not to understand. It would have been well, had Steve been present.
He is immensely alert to such winds and undercurrents as I
felt, but could not measure, everywhere around me.

Ten of us were having dinner at John Wayne's, and since
he is a smooth but capable political leader, if we were discussing anything at all it should have been politics. But by
God, since I came into his home, a festering old incubus dat-
ing back at least a hundred years, we hadn't talked about anything except Janoth Enterprises, and what difficulties we were
having. But I wasn't having any difficulties. And I wasn't having any of this, either.

Then there was an awkward moment when Hamilton Carr
asked me how I had made out in Washington. I had just returned, and I had an uncomfortable feeling that he knew exactly everyone I had seen there and what I was about. Yet it
was really nothing. I had thought of broadening the corporate
basis of Janoth Enterprises, and my trip to Washington was

simply to obtain quick and reliable information on what procedure I might follow to achieve that end and fully observe all SEC regulations.

Ralph Beeman had gone down with me, had not said much while we were there, and I gave him another emphatic thought. But it couldn't be. Or were they all, in fact, in some kind of a conspiracy against me? Voyagers to new continents of reason have been caught offguard before.

But Hamilton Carr was no enemy; at least, I had never thought he was; he was simply my banking adviser. He had always known, to the last dime, what the paper issued by Janoth Enterprises was worth, and who held it. Tonight, he said: "You know, Jennett-Donohue still want either to buy or merge."

I gave him a huge laugh.

"Yes," I said. "So do I. What will they sell for?"

Carr smiled; it was icy dissent. God damn you, I thought, what's up?

There was a blasted foreign person present with a fearful English accent who went by the name of Lady Pearsall, or something equally insignificant, and she told me at great length what was wrong with my magazines. Everything was wrong with them, according to her. But it hadn't crossed her mind that I had gone far out of my way to obtain the very best writers and editors, the broadest and richest minds to be had. I had combed the newspapers, the magazines, the finest universities, and paid the highest salaries in the field, to hire what I knew were the finest bunch of journalists ever gathered together under one roof. She gobbled away extensively, her Adam's apple moving exactly like a scrawny turkey's, but to hear her tell it, I had found my writers in the hospitals, insane asylums, and penitentiaries.

I could smile at everything she had to say, but I didn't feel like smiling at what Carr and Beeman and finally a man by the name of Samuel Lydon had to say.

"You know," he told me, "there may not always be the same demand for superior presentation there has been in the past. I've been getting reports from the distributors." Anyone could. It was public knowledge. "I think you would like me to be quite candid with you, Mr. Janoth."

"Certainly."

"Well, the returns on some of your key magazines have shown strange fluctuations. Out of proportion to those of other publications, I mean." I placed him now. He was executive vice-president of a local distributing organization. "I wondered if there was any definitely known reason?"

This was either colossal ignorance or outrageous effrontery. *If I knew of definite reasons.* I looked at him, but didn't bother to reply.

"Maybe it's that astrology magazine of yours," said Geoffrey Balack, ineffectual, vicious, crude, and thoroughly counterfeit. He was some kind of a columnist. I had hired him once, but his work had not seemed too satisfactory, and when he left to take another job I had thought it was a fortunate change all round. Looking at him now, I couldn't remember whether he'd quit, or whether Steve had fired him. Or possibly I had. Offensively, now, he brushed a hand back over the rather thin hair on his head. "That's one I never understood at all. Why?"

I was still smiling, but it cost me an effort.

"I bought that little book, *Stars*, for its title alone. Today it has nothing to do with astrology. It is almost the sole authority in astrophysics."

"Popular?"

That didn't deserve a reply, either. This was what we had once considered a writer with insight and integrity. And good writers cost money, which I was more than glad to pay.

But they were growing more expensive all the time. Other publishing organizations, even though they were not in the same field at all, were always happy to raid our staff, though they rarely tampered with each others'. The advertising agencies, the motion pictures, radio, we were always losing our really good men elsewhere, at prices that were simply fantastic. A man we had found ourselves, and nursed along until we found just the right way to bring out the best and soundest that was in him, might then casually leave us to write trash for some perfume program, or speeches for a political amplifier. Contract or no contract, and at a figure it would be almost ruinous to the rest of the organization if we thought of meeting it.

Either that or they wanted to write books. Or went crazy. Although, God knows, most of them were born that way, and their association with us merely slowed up and postponed the inevitable process for a time.

Well. We still had the finest writers to be had, and the competition only kept us on our toes.

When it came to the point where Jennett-Donohue or Devers & Blair offered twenty-five thousand for a fifteen-thousand-dollar editor, we would go thirty thousand. If radio offered fifty thousand for a man we really had to keep, we'd go to sixty. And when Hollywood began raiding our copy boys and legmen for a million—well, all right. No use being morbid. But sometimes it's impossible not to be.

It was ten o'clock—the earliest moment possible—before I was able to leave. I had enough to worry about, without taking on any extra nonsense from this particular crowd.

It is all a matter of one's inherited nerves and glands. No matter how much one rationalizes, one has either a joyless, negative attitude toward everyone and everything, like these people, and it is purely a matter of the way in which the glands function, or one has a positive and constructive attitude. It is no great credit to me. But neither is it any credit to them.

In the car, I told Bill to drive me home, but halfway there I changed my mind. I told him to drive to Pauline's. Hell, she might even be there. Home was no place to go after an evening squandered among a bunch of imitation cynics, disappointed sentimentalists, and frustrated conspirators.

Without a word Bill spun the wheel and we turned the corner. It reminded me of the way he had always taken my orders, thirty years ago during the hottest part of a circulation war out West, then in the printer's strike upstate. That was why he was with me now. If he wouldn't talk even to me, after thirty odd years, he would never talk to anyone.

When we drew up in front of the place and I got out, I put my head in the window next to him and said: "Go on home, Bill. I'll take a taxi. I don't think I'll need you until tomorrow evening."

He looked at me but said nothing, and eased the car away from the curb.

Earl Janoth II

O N THE SIDEWALK I turned to go in, but as I turned, I caught sight of Pauline. She was leaving someone at the next corner. I couldn't see her face, but I recognized her profile, the way she stood and carried herself, and I recognized the hat she had recently helped to design, and the beige coat. As I stood there she started to walk toward me. The man with her I did not recognize at all, though I stared until he turned and stepped into a car, his face still in the shadows.

When Pauline reached me she was smiling and serene, a little warm and a little remote, deliberate as always. I said: "Hello, dear. This is fortunate."

She brushed away an invisible strand of hair, stopped beside me.

"I expected you'd be back yesterday," she said. "Did you have a nice trip, Earl?"

"Fine. Have a pleasant week end?"

"Marvelous. I went riding, swimming, read a grand book, and met some of the most interesting brand-new people."

We had moved into the building by now. I glanced down and saw that she carried an overnight bag.

I could hear though not see somebody moving behind the high screen that partitioned off the apartment switchboard and, as usual, there was no sign of anyone else. Perhaps this isolation was one of the reasons she had liked such a place in the beginning.

There was an automatic elevator, and now it was on the main floor. As I opened the door, then followed her in and pushed the button for five, I nodded toward the street.

"Was he one of them?"

"One of who? Oh, you mean the brand-new people. Yes."

The elevator stopped at five. The inner door slid noiselessly open, and Pauline herself pushed open the outer door. I followed her the dozen or so carpeted steps to 5A. Inside the small four-room apartment there was such silence and so much dead air it did not seem it could have been entered for days.

428

"What were you doing?" I asked.

"Well, first we went to a terrible place on Third Avenue by the name of Gil's. You'd love it. Personally, I thought it was a bore. But it's some kind of a combination between an old archeology foundation, and a saloon. The weirdest mixture. Then after that we went up and down the street shopping for antiques."

"What kind of antiques?"

"Any kind that we thought might be interesting. Finally, we bought a picture, that is, he did, in a shop about three blocks from here. An awful old thing that just came out of a dust-bin, it looked like, and he practically kidnapped it from another customer, some woman who bid for it, too. Nothing but a couple of hands, by an artist named Patterson."

"A couple of what?"

"Hands, darling. Just hands. It was a picture about Judas, as I understand it. Then after that we went to the Van Barth and had a few drinks, and he brought me home. That's where you came in. Satisfied?"

I watched her open the door of the small closet in the lobby and drop her bag inside of it, then close the door and turn to me again with her shining hair, deep eyes, and perfect, renaissance face.

"Sounds like an interesting afternoon," I said. "Who was this brand-new person?"

"Oh. Just a man. You don't know him. His name is George Chester, in advertising."

Maybe. And my name is George Agropolus. But I'd been around a lot longer than she had, or, for that matter, than her boy friend. I looked at her for a moment, without speaking, and she returned the look, a little too intently. I almost felt sorry for the new satellite she'd just left, whoever he was.

She poured us some brandy from a decanter beside the lounge, and across the top of her glass she crinkled her eyes in the intimate way supposed to fit the texture of any moment. I sipped my own, knowing again that everything in the world was ashes. Cold, and spent, and not quite worth the effort. It was a mood that Steve never had, a mood peculiarly my own. The question crossed my mind whether possibly others, too, experienced the same feeling, at least occasionally, but that could hardly be. I said: "At least, this time it's a man."

Sharply, she said: "Just what do you mean by that?"

"You know what I mean."

"Are you bringing up that thing again? Throwing Alice in my face?" Her voice had the sound of a wasp. Avenue Z was never far beneath the surface, with Pauline. "You never forget Alice, do you?"

I finished the brandy and reached for the decanter, poured myself another drink. Speaking with deliberate slowness, and politely, I said: "No. Do you?"

"Why, you goddamn imitation Napoleon, what in hell do you mean?"

I finished the brandy in one satisfying swallow.

"And you don't forget Joanna, do you?" I said, softly. "And that Berleth woman, and Jane, and that female refugee from Austria. And God knows who else. You can't forget any of them, can you, including the next one."

She seemed to choke, for a speechless moment, then she moved like a springing animal. Something, I believe it was an ashtray, went past my head and smashed against the wall, showering me with fine glass.

"You son of a bitch," she exploded. "You talk. You, of all people. *You*. That's priceless."

Mechanically, I reached for the decanter, splashed brandy into my glass. I fumbled for the stopper, trying to replace it. But I couldn't seem to connect.

"Yes?" I said.

She was on her feet, on the other side of the low table, her face a tangle of rage.

"What about you and Steve Hagen?"

I forgot about the stopper, and simply stared.

"What? What about me? And Steve?"

"Do you think I'm blind? Did I ever see you two together when you weren't camping?"

I felt sick and stunned, with something big and black gathering inside of me. Mechanically, I echoed her: "Camping? With Steve?"

"As if you weren't married to that guy, all your life. And as if I didn't know. Go on, you son of a bitch, try to act surprised."

It wasn't me, any more. It was some giant a hundred feet tall, moving me around, manipulating my hands and arms and even my voice. He straightened my legs, and I found myself standing. I could hardly speak. My voice was a sawtoothed whisper.

"You say this about Steve? The finest man that ever lived? And me?"

"Why, you poor, old carbon copy of that fairy gorilla. Are you so dumb you've lived this long without even knowing it?" Then she suddenly screamed: "Don't. Earl, don't."

I hit her over the head with the decanter and she stumbled back across the room. My voice said: "You can't talk like that. Not about us."

"Don't. Oh, God, Earl, don't. Earl. Earl. Earl."

I had kicked over the table between us, and I moved after her. I hit her again, and she kept talking with that awful voice of hers, and then I hit her twice more.

Then she was lying on the floor, quiet and a little twisted. I said: "There's a limit to this. A man can take just so much."

She didn't reply. She didn't move.

I stood above her for a long, long time. There was no sound at all, except the remote, muffled hum of traffic from the street below. The decanter was still in my hand, and I lifted it, looked at the bottom edge of it faintly smeared, and with a few strands of hair.

"Pauline."

She lay on her back, watching something far away that didn't move. She was pretending to be unconscious.

A fear struck deeper and deeper and deeper, as I stared at her beautiful, bright, slowly bleeding head. Her face had an expression like nothing on earth.

"Oh, God, Pauline. Get up."

I dropped the decanter and placed my hand inside her blouse, over the heart. Nothing. Her face did not change. There was no breath, no pulse, nothing. Only her warmth and faint perfume. I slowly stood up. She was gone.

So all of my life had led to this strange dream.

A darkness and a nausea flooded in upon me, in waves I had never known before. This, this carrion by-product had suddenly become the total of everything. Of everything there had been between us. Of everything I had ever done. This accident.

For it was an accident. God knows. A mad one.

I saw there were stains on my hands, and my shirt front. There were splotches on my trousers, my shoes, and as my eyes roved around the room I saw that there were even spots high on the wall near the lounge where I had first been sitting.

I needed something. Badly. Help and advice.

I moved into the bathroom and washed my hands, sponged my shirt. It came to me that I must be careful. Careful of everything. I closed the taps with my handkerchief. If her boy friend had been here, and left his own fingerprints. If others had. Anyone else. And many others had.

Back in the other room, where Pauline still lay on the carpet, unchanging, I remembered the decanter and the stopper to it. These I both wiped carefully, and the glass. Then I reached for the phone, and at the same time remembered the switchboard downstairs, and drew away.

I let myself out of the apartment, again using my handkerchief as a glove. Pauline had let us in. The final image of her own fingers would be on the knob, the key, the frame.

I listened for a long moment outside the door of 5A. There was no sound throughout the halls, and none from behind that closed door. I knew, with a renewed vertigo of grief and dread, there would never again be life within that apartment. Not for me.

Yet there had been, once, lots of it. All collapsed to the size of a few single moments that were now a deadly, unreal threat.

I moved quietly down the carpeted hall, and down the stairs. From the top of the first floor landing I could just see the partly bald, gray head of the man at the switchboard. He hadn't moved, and if he behaved as usual, he wouldn't.

I went quietly down the last flight of stairs and moved across the lobby carpet to the door. At the door, when I opened it, I looked back. No one was watching, there was no one in sight.

On the street, I walked for several blocks, then at a stand

on some corner I took a taxi. I gave the driver an address two blocks from the address I automatically knew I wanted. It was about a mile uptown.

When I got out and presently reached the building it was as quiet as it had been at Pauline's.

There was no automatic elevator, as there was at Pauline's, and I did not want to be seen, not in this condition. I walked up the four flights to the apartment. I rang, suddenly sure there would be no answer.

But there was.

Steve's kindly, wise, compact, slightly leathery face confronted me when the door swung open. He was in slippers and a dressing gown. When he saw me, he held the door wider, and I came in.

He said: "You look like hell. What is it?"

I walked past him and into his living room and sat down in a wide chair.

"I have no right to come here. But I didn't know where else to go."

He had followed me into his living room, and he asked, impassively: "What's the matter?"

"God. I don't know. Give me a drink."

Steve gave me a drink. When he said he would ring for some ice, I stopped him.

"Don't bring anyone else in on this," I said. "I've just killed someone."

"Yes?" He waited. "Who?"

"Pauline."

Steve looked at me hard, poured himself a drink, briefly sipped it, still watching me.

"Are you sure?"

This was insane. I suppressed a wild laugh. Instead, I told him, curtly: "I'm sure."

"All right," he said, slowly. "She had it coming to her. You should have killed her three years ago."

I gave him the longest look and the most thought I had ever given him. There was an edge of iron amusement in his locked face. I knew what was going on in his mind: *She was a tramp, why did you bother with her?* And I know what went on in my mind: *I am about the loneliest person in the world.*

"I came here, Steve," I said, "because this is just about my last stop. I face, well, everything. But I thought—hell, I don't know what I thought. But if there is anything I should do, well. I thought maybe you'd know what that would be."

"She deserved it," Steve quietly repeated. "She was a regular little comic."

"Steve, don't talk like that about Pauline. One of the warmest, most generous women who ever lived."

He finished his drink and casually put down the glass.

"Was she? Why did you kill her?"

"I don't know, I just don't know. From here I go to Ralph Beeman, and then to the cops, and then I guess to prison or even the chair." I finished my drink and put down the glass. "I'm sorry I disturbed you."

Steve gestured. "Don't be a fool," he said. "Forget that prison stuff. What about the organization? Do you know what will happen to it the second you get into serious trouble?"

I looked at my hands. They were clean, but they had undone me. And I knew what would happen to the organization the minute I wasn't there, or became involved in this kind of trouble.

"Yes," I said. "I know. But what can I do?"

"Do you want to fight, or do you want to quit? You aren't the first guy in the world that ever got into a jam. What are you going to do about it? Are you going to put up a battle, or are you going to fold up?"

"If there's any chance at all, I'll take it."

"I wouldn't even know you, if I thought you'd do anything else."

"And of course, it's not only the organization, big as that is. There's my own neck, besides. Naturally, I'd like to save it."

Steve was matter of fact. "Of course. Now, what happened?"

"I can't describe it. I hardly know."

"Try."

"That bitch. Oh, God, Pauline."

"Yes?"

"She said that I, she actually accused both of us, but it's

utterly fantastic. I had a few drinks and she must have had several. She said something about us. Can you take it?"

Steve was unmoved. "I know what she said. She would. And then?"

"That's all. I hit her over the head with something. A decanter. Maybe two or three times, maybe ten times. Yes, a decanter. I wiped my fingerprints off of it. She must have been insane, don't you think? To say a thing like that? She's a part-time Liz, Steve, did I ever tell you that?"

"You didn't have to."

"So I killed her. Before I even thought about it. God, I didn't intend anything like it, thirty seconds before. I don't understand it. And the organization is in trouble, real trouble. Did I tell you that?"

"You told me."

"I don't mean about this. I mean Carr and Wayne and—"

"You told me."

"Well, at dinner tonight I was sure of it. And now this. Oh, God."

"If you want to save the whole works you'll have to keep your head. And your nerve. Especially your nerve."

All at once, and for the first time in fifty years, my eyes were filled with tears. It was disgraceful. I could hardly see him. I said: "Don't worry about my nerve."

"That's talking," Steve said, evenly. "And now I want to hear the details. Who saw you go into this place, Pauline's apartment? Where was the doorman, the switchboard man? Who brought you there? Who took you away? I want to know every goddamn thing that happened, what she said to you and what you said to her. What she did and what you did. Where you were this evening, before you went to Pauline's. In the meantime, I'm going to lay out some clean clothes. You have bloodstains on your shirt and your trousers. I'll get rid of them. Meanwhile, go ahead."

"All right," I said, "I was having dinner at the Waynes'. And they couldn't seem to talk about anything else except what a hell of a mess Janoth Enterprises was getting into. God, how they loved my difficulties. They couldn't think or talk about anything else."

"Skip that," said Steve. "Come to the point."

I told him about leaving the Waynes', how Bill had driven me to Pauline's.

"We don't have to worry about Bill," said Steve.

"God," I interrupted. "Do you really think I can get away with this?"

"You told me you wiped your fingerprints off the decanter, didn't you? What else were you thinking of when you did it?"

"That was automatic."

Steve waved the argument away.

"Talk."

I told him the rest of it. How I saw this stranger, leaving Pauline, and how we got into a quarrel in her apartment, and what she had said to me, and what I had said to her, and then what happened, as well as I remembered it.

Finally, Steve said to me: "Well, it looks all right except for one thing."

"What?"

"The fellow who saw you go into the building with Pauline. Nobody else saw you go in. But he did. Who was he?"

"I tell you, I don't know."

"Did he recognize you?"

"I don't know."

"The one guy in the world who saw you go into Pauline's apartment, and you don't know who he was? You don't know whether he knew you, or recognized you?"

"No, no, no. Why, is that important?"

Steve gave me a fathomless glance. He slowly found a cigarette, slowly reached for a match, lit the cigarette. When he blew out the second drag of smoke, still slowly, and thoughtfully blew out the match, and then put the burned match away and exhaled his third lungful, deliberately, he turned and said: "You're damned right it is. I want to hear everything there is to know about that guy." He flicked some ashes into a tray. "Everything. You may not know it, but he's the key to our whole set-up. In fact, Earl, he spells the difference. Just about the whole difference."

Steve Hagen

W E WENT over that evening forward and backward. We put every second of it under a high-powered microscope. Before we finished I knew as much about what happened as though I had been there myself, and that was a lot more than Earl did. This jam was so typical of him that, after the first blow, nothing about it really surprised me.

It was also typical that his simple mind could not wholly grasp how much was at stake and how much he had jeopardized it. Typical, too, that he had no idea how to control the situation. Nor how fast we had to work. Nor how.

Pauline's maid would not return to the apartment until tomorrow evening. There was a good chance the body would not be discovered until then. Then, Earl would be the first person seriously investigated by the police, since his connection with her was common knowledge.

I would have to claim he was with me throughout the dangerous period, and it would have to stick. But Billy would back that.

After leaving the Waynes', Earl had come straight here. Driven by Billy. Then Billy was given the rest of the night off. That was all right, quite safe.

There would be every evidence of Earl's frequent, former visits to Pauline's apartment, but nothing to prove the last one. Even I had gone there once or twice. She had lots of visitors running in and out, both men and women. But I knew, from Earl's squeamish description, the injuries would rule out a woman.

The cover I had to provide for Earl would be given one hell of a going over. So would I. That couldn't be helped. It was my business, not only Earl's, and since he couldn't be trusted to protect our interests, I would have to do it myself.

Apparently it meant nothing to him, the prospect of going back to a string of garbage-can magazines edited from a due-bill office and paid for with promises, threats, rubber checks, or luck. He didn't even think about it. But I did. Earl's flair for capturing the mind of the reading public was far more

valuable than the stuff they cram into banks. Along with this
vision, though, he had a lot of whims, scruples, philosophical
foibles, a sense of humor that he sometimes used even with
me. These served some purpose at business conferences or
social gatherings, but not now.

If necessary, if the situation got too hot, if Earl just couldn't
take it, I might draw some of the fire myself. I could afford
to. One of our men, Emory Mafferson, had phoned me here
about the same time Earl was having his damned expensive
tantrum. And that alibi was real.

The immediate problem, no matter how I turned it over,
always came down to the big question mark of the stranger.
No other living person had seen Earl, knowing him to be Earl,
after he left that dinner party. For the tenth time, I asked:
"There was nothing at all familiar about that person you
saw?"

"Nothing. He was in a shadowy part of the street. With
the light behind him."

"And you have no idea whether he recognized you?"

"No. But I was standing in the light of the entranceway. If
he knew me, he recognized me."

Again I thought this over from every angle. "Or he may
sometime recognize you," I concluded. "When he sees your
face in the papers, as one of those being questioned. Maybe.
And maybe we can take care they aren't good pictures. But I
wish I had a line on that headache right now. Something to
go on when the story breaks. So that we can always be a jump
ahead of everyone, including the cops."

All I knew was that Pauline said the man's name was George
Chester. This might even be his true name, though knowing
Pauline, that seemed improbable, and the name was not listed
in any of the phone books of the five boroughs, nor in any of
the books of nearby suburbs. She said he was in advertising.
That could mean anything. Nearly everyone was.

They had gone to a place on Third Avenue called Gil's, and
for some reason it had seemed like an archeological foundation. This sounded authentic. The place could be located with
no difficulty.

They had stopped in at a Third Avenue antique shop, and
there the man had bought a picture, bidding for it against

some woman who apparently just walked in from the street, as they did. It would not be hard to locate the shop and get more out of the proprietor. The picture was of a couple of hands. Its title, or subject matter, was something about Judas. The artist's name was Patterson. The canvas looked as though it came out of a dustbin. Then they had gone to the cocktail lounge of the Van Barth. It should not be hard to get another line on our character there. He certainly had the picture with him. He may even have checked it.

But the antique shop seemed a surefire bet. There would have been the usual long, pointless talk about the picture. Even if the proprietor did not know either the man or the woman customer, he must have heard enough to offer new leads regarding the clown we wanted. The very fact he had gone into the place, then bought nothing except this thing, something that looked like it belonged in an incinerator, this already gave our bystander an individual profile. I said: "What kind of a person would do that, buy a mess like that in some hole-in-the-wall?"

"I don't know. Hell, I'd do it myself, if I felt like it."

"Well, I wouldn't feel like it. But there's another line. We can surely get a lead on the artist. We'll probably find a few clips in our own morgue. It's possible the man we are looking for is a great admirer of this artist, whoever he is. We can locate Patterson and get the history of this particular picture. Two hands. A cinch. There may be thousands, millions of these canvases around the city, but when you come right down to it, each of them has been seen by somebody besides the genius who painted it, and somebody would be certain to recognize it from a good description. After that, we can trace it along to the present owner."

Earl had by now come out of his first shock. He looked, acted, sounded, and thought more like his natural self. "How are we going to find this man, ahead of the police?" he asked.

"What have we got two thousand people for?"

"Yes, of course. But doesn't that mean—after all—isn't that spreading suspicion just that much farther?"

I had already thought of a way to put the organization in motion without connecting it at all with the death of Pauline.

"No. I know how to avoid that."

He thought that over for a while. Then he said: "Why should you do this? Why do you stick your neck out? This is serious."

I knew him so well I had known, almost to the word, he would say that.

"I've done it before, haven't I? And more."

"Yes. I know. But I have a hell of a way of rewarding friendship like that. I merely seem to exact more of it. More risks. More sacrifices."

"Don't worry about me. You're the one who's in danger."

"I hope you're not. But I think you will be, giving me an alibi, and leading the search for this unknown party."

"I won't be leading the search. We want somebody else to do that. I stay in the background." I knew that Earl himself would go right on being our biggest headache. I thought it would be better to take the first hurdle now. "In the first place, I want to disassociate you from this business as far as possible. Don't you agree that's wise?" He nodded, and I slowly added, as an afterthought, "Then, when our comedian is located, we want an entirely different set of people to deal with him."

Earl looked up from the thick, hairy knuckles of the fingers he seemed to be studying. His face had never, even when he was most shaken, lost its jovial appearance. I wondered whether he had seemed to be smiling when he killed the woman, but of course he had been.

The question forming in that slow, unearthly mind of his at last boiled up. "By the way. What happens when we do locate this person?"

"That all depends. When the story breaks, he may go straight to the police. In that case our alibi stands, and our line is this: He says he saw you on the scene. What was he doing there, himself? That makes him as hot as you are. We'll make him even warmer. We already know, for instance, that he spent a large part of the evening with Pauline."

Earl's round, large, staring eyes showed no understanding for a moment, then they came to life. "By God, Steve. I wonder—no. Of course you mean that only to threaten him off."

I said: "Put it this way. If the case goes to trial, and he persists in being a witness, that's the line we'll raise. Your own movements are accounted for, you were with me. But what was he doing there? What about this and that?—all the things we are going to find out about him long in advance. The case against you won't stand up."

Earl knew I had omitted something big, and in his mind he laboriously set out to find what it was. I waited while he thought it over, knowing he couldn't miss. Presently, he said: "All right. But if he doesn't go to the police the minute this breaks? Then what?"

I didn't want him to become even more hysterical, and if that were possible, I didn't want him to be even upset. I said, dispassionately: "If we find him first, we must play it safe."

"Well. What does that mean?"

Elaborately, I explained: "We could have him watched, of course. But we'd never know how much he actually did or did not realize, would we? And we certainly wouldn't know what he'd do next."

"Well? I can see that."

"Well. What is there to do with a man like that? He's a constant threat to your safety, your position in life, your place in the world. He's a ceaseless menace to your very life. Can you put up with an intolerable situation like that?"

Earl gave me a long, wondering, sick, almost frightened regard.

"I don't like that," he said, harshly. "There has already been one accident. I don't want another one. No. Not if I know what you mean."

"You know what I mean."

"No. I'm still a man."

"Are you? There are millions of dollars involved, all because of your uncontrollable temper and your God-forsaken stupidity. Yours, yours, not mine. Besides being an idiot, are you a coward, too?"

He floundered around for a cigar, got one, and with my help, finally got it going. Then, finally, he sounded a raw croak: "I won't see a man killed in cold blood." And as though he'd read my thoughts he added, "Nor take any part in it, either."

I said, reasonably: "I don't understand you. You know what kind of a world this is. You have always been a solid part of it. You know what anyone in Devers & Blair, Jennett-Donohue, Beacon, anyone above an M.E. in any of those houses would certainly do to you if he could reach out at night and safely push a button—"

"No. I wouldn't, myself. And I don't think they would, either."

He was wrong, of course, but there was no use arguing with a middle-aged child prodigy. I knew that by tomorrow he would see this thing in its true light.

"Well, it needn't come to that. That was just a suggestion. But why are you so worried? You and I have already seen these things happen, and we have helped to commit just about everything else for a lot less money. Why are you so sensitive now?"

He seemed to gag.

"Did we ever before go as far as this?"

"You were never in this spot before. Were you?" Now he looked really ghastly. He couldn't even speak. By God, he would have to be watched like a hawk and nursed every minute. "Let me ask you, Earl, are you ready to retire to a penitentiary and write your memoirs, for the sake of your morals? Or are you ready to grow up and be a man in a man's world, take your full responsibilities along with the rewards?" I liked Earl more than I had ever liked any person on earth except my mother, I really liked him, and I had to get both of us out of this at any cost. "No, we never went this far before. And we will never, if we use our heads, ever have to go this far again."

Earl absently drew at his cigar. "Death by poverty, famine, plague, war, I suppose that is on such a big scale the responsibility rests nowhere, although I personally have always fought against all of these things, in a number of magazines dedicated to wiping out each one of them, separately, and in some cases, in vehicles combating all of them together. But a personal death, the death of a definite individual. That is quite different."

He had reduced himself to the intellectual status of our own writers, a curious thing I had seen happen before. I risked it, and said: "We could take a chance on some simpler way, maybe. But there is more at stake than your private morals, personal philosophy, or individual life. The whole damned organization is at stake. If you're wiped out, so is that. When you go, the entire outfit goes. A flood of factory-manufactured nonsense swamps the market."

Earl stood up and paced slowly across the room. It was a long time before he answered me.

"I can be replaced, Steve. I'm just a cog. A good one, I know, but still only a cog."

This was better. This was more like it. I said, knowing him: "Yes, but when you break, a lot of others break, too. Whenever a big thing like this goes to pieces—and that is what could happen—a hell of a lot of innocent people, their plans, their homes, their dreams and aspirations, the future of their children, all of that can go to pieces with it. Myself, for instance."

He gave me one quick glance. But I had gambled that he was a sucker for the greatest good to the most people. And after a long, long while he spoke, and I knew that at heart he was really sound.

"Well, all right," he said. "I understand, Steve. I guess what has to be, has to be."

George Stroud VI

THE AWFULNESS of Monday morning is the world's great common denominator. To the millionaire and the coolie it is the same, because there can be nothing worse.

But I was only fifteen minutes behind the big clock when I sat down to breakfast, commenting that this morning's prunes had grown up very fast from the baby raisins in last night's cake. The table rhythmically shook and vibrated under Georgia's steadily drumming feet. It came to me again that a child drinking milk has the same vacant, contented expression of the well-fed cow who originally gave it. There is a real spiritual kinship there.

It was a fine sunny morning, like real spring, spring for keeps. I was beginning my second cup of coffee, and planning this year's gardening, when Georgette said: "George, have you looked at the paper? There's a dreadful story about a woman we met, I think. At Janoth's."

She waited while I picked up the paper. I didn't have to search. Pauline Delos had been found murdered. It was the leading story on page one.

Not understanding it, and not believing it, I read the headlines twice. But the picture was of Pauline.

The story said her body had been discovered at about noon on Sunday, and her death had been fixed at around ten o'clock on the night before, Saturday. I had left her at about that hour.

"Isn't that the same one?" Georgette asked.

"Yes," I said. "Yes."

She had been beaten to death with a heavy glass decanter. No arrest had been made. Her immediate friends were being questioned; Earl Janoth was one of them, the story went, but the publisher had not seen her for a number of days. He himself had spent the evening dining with acquaintances, and after dinner had spent several hours discussing business matters with an associate.

"A horrible story, isn't it?" said Georgette.

"Yes."

"Aren't you going to finish your coffee? George?"

"Yes?"

"You'd better finish your coffee, and then I'll drive you to the station."

"Yes. All right."

"Is something the matter?"

"No, of course not."

"Well, heavens. Don't look so grim."

I smiled.

"By the way," she went on. "I didn't tell you I liked that new picture you brought home. The one of the two hands. But it's in terrible condition, isn't it?"

"Yes, it is."

"It's another Patterson, isn't it?"

A hundred alarm bells were steadily ringing inside of me.

"Well, perhaps."

"Pity's sake, George, you don't have to be so monosyllabic, do you? Can't you say anything but 'yes,' 'no,' 'perhaps'? Is something the matter?"

"No. Nothing's the matter."

"Where did you get this new canvas?"

"Why, I just picked it up."

I knew quite well I had seen Earl entering that building at ten o'clock on Saturday evening. She was alive when they passed into it. He now claimed he had not seen her for several days. Why? There could be only one answer.

But had he recognized me?

Whether he had or not, where did I stand? To become involved would bring me at once into the fullest and fiercest kind of spotlight. And that meant, to begin with, wrecking Georgette, Georgia, my home, my life.

It would also place me on the scene of the murder. That I did not like at all. Nothing would cover Janoth better.

Yet he almost surely knew someone had at least seen him there. Or did he imagine no one had?

"George?"

"Yes?"

"I asked you if you knew much about this Pauline Delos?"

"Very little."

"Goodness. You certainly aren't very talkative this morning."

I smiled again, swallowed the rest of my coffee, and said: "It is a ghastly business, isn't it?"

Somehow Georgia got packed off to school, and somehow I got down to the station. On the train going into town I read every newspaper, virtually memorizing what was known of the death, but gathering no real additional information.

At the office I went straight to my own room, and the moment I got there my secretary told me Steve Hagen had called and asked that I see him as soon as I got in.

I went at once to the thirty-second floor.

Hagen was a hard, dark little man whose soul had been hit by lightning, which he'd liked. His mother was a bank vault, and his father an International Business Machine. I knew he was almost as loyal to Janoth as to himself.

After we said hello and made about one casual remark, he said he would like me to undertake a special assignment.

"Anything you have on the fire downstairs at the moment," he said, "let it go. This is more important. Have you anything special, at this moment?"

"Nothing." Then because it could not be avoided, plausibly, I said: "By the way, I've just read about the Pauline Delos business. It's pretty damn awful. Have you any idea—?"

Steve's confirmation was short and cold. "Yes, it's bad. I have no idea about it."

"I suppose Earl is, well—"

"He is. But I don't really know any more about it than you do."

He looked around the top of his desk and located some notes. He raked them together, looked them over, and then turned again to me. He paused, in a way that indicated we were now about to go to work.

"We have a job on our hands, not hard but delicate, and it seems you are about the very best man on the staff to direct it." I looked at him, waiting, and he went on. "In essence, the job is this: We want to locate somebody unknown to us. Really, it's a missing person job." He waited again, and when I said nothing, he asked: "Would that be all right with you?"

"Of course. Who is it?"

"We don't know."

"Well?"

He ruffled his notes.

"The person we want went into some Third Avenue bar and grill by the name of Gil's last Saturday afternoon. He was accompanied by a rather striking blonde, also unidentified. They later went to a Third Avenue antique shop. In fact, several of them. But in one of them he bought a picture called *Judas*, or something to that effect. He bought the picture from the dealer, overbidding another customer, a woman who also wanted to buy it. The picture was by an artist named Patterson. According to the morgue," Steve Hagen pushed across a thin heavy-paper envelope from our own files, "this Louise Patterson was fairly well known ten or twelve years ago. You can read up on all that for yourself. But the picture bought by the man we want depicted two hands, I believe, and was in rather bad condition. I don't know what he paid for it. Later, he and the woman with him went to the cocktail lounge of the Van Barth for a few drinks. It is possible he checked the picture there, or he may have had it right with him."

No, I hadn't. I'd left it in the car. Steve stopped, and looked at me. My tongue felt like sandpaper. I asked: "Why do you want this man?"

Steve clasped his hands in back of his neck and gazed off into space, through the wide blank windows of the thirty-second floor. From where we sat, we could see about a hundred miles of New York and New Jersey countryside.

When he again turned to me he was a good self-portrait of candor. Even his voice was a good phonographic reproduction of the slightly confidential friend.

"Frankly, we don't know ourselves."

This went over me like a cold wind.

"You must have some idea. Otherwise, why bother?"

"Yes, we have an idea. But it's nothing definite. We think our party is an important figure, in fact a vital one, in a business and political conspiracy that has reached simply colossal proportions. Our subject is not necessarily a big fellow in his own right, but we have reason to believe he's the payoff man between an industrial syndicate and a political machine, the one man who really knows the entire set-up. We believe we can crack the whole situation, when we find him."

So Earl had gone straight to Hagen. Hagen would then be the business associate who provided the alibi. But what did they want with George Stroud?

It was plain Earl knew he had been seen, and afraid he had been recognized. I could imagine how he would feel.

"Pretty vague, Steve," I said. "Can't you give me more?"

"No. You're right, it is vague. Our information is based entirely on rumors and tips and certain, well, striking coincidences. When we locate our man, then we'll have something definite for the first time."

"What's in it? A story for *Crimeways*?"

Hagen appeared to give that question a good deal of thought. He said, finally, and with apparent reluctance: "I don't think so. I don't know right now what our angle will be when we have it. We might want to give it a big play in one of our books, eventually. Or we might decide to use it in some entirely different way. That's up in the air."

I began to have the shadowy outline of a theory. I tested it.

"Who else is in on this? Should we co-operate with anyone? The cops, for instance?"

Cautiously, and with regret, Steve told me: "Absolutely not. This is our story, exclusively. It must stay that way. You will have to go to other agencies for information, naturally. But you get it only, you don't give it. Is that perfectly clear?"

It was beginning to be. "Quite clear."

"Now, do you think you can knock together a staff, just as large as you want, and locate this person? The only additional information I have is that his name may be George Chester, and he's of average build and height, weight one-forty to one-eighty. It's possible he's in advertising. But your best lead is this place called Gil's, the shop where he bought the picture, and the bar of the Van Barth. And that picture, perhaps the artist. I have a feeling the picture alone might give us the break."

"It shouldn't be impossible," I said.

"We want this guy in a hurry. Can you do it?"

If I didn't, someone else would. It would have to be me. "I've done it before."

"Yes. That's why you're elected."

"What do I do when I find this person?"

"Nothing." Steve's voice was pleasant, but emphatic. "Just let me know his name, and where he can be found. That's all."

It was like leaning over the ledge of one of these thirty-second floor windows and looking down into the street below. I always had to take just one more look.

"What happens when we locate him? What's the next step?"

"Just leave that to me." Hagen stared at me, coldly and levelly, and I stared back. I saw, in those eyes, there was no room for doubt at all. Janoth knew the danger he was in, Hagen knew it, and for Hagen there was literally no limit. None. Furthermore, this little stick of dynamite was intelligent, and he had his own ways, his private means.

"Now, this assignment has the right-of-way over everything, George. You can raid any magazine, use any bureau, any editor or correspondent, all the resources we have. And you're in charge."

I stood up and scooped together the notes I had taken. The squeeze felt tangible as a vise. My personal life would be destroyed if I ran to the cops. Death if Hagen and his special friends caught up with me.

"All right, Steve," I said. "I take it I have absolute carte blanche."

"You have. Expense, personnel, everything." He waved toward the windows overlooking about ten million people. "Our man is somewhere out there. It's a simple job. Get him."

I looked out of the windows myself. There was a lot of territory out there. A nation within a nation. If I picked the right kind of a staff, twisted the investigation where I could, jammed it where I had to, pushed it hard where it was safe, it might be a very, very, very long time before they found George Stroud.

George Stroud VII

I HATED to interrupt work on the coming issues of our own book, and so I decided to draw upon all the others, when needed, as evenly as possible.

But I determined to work Roy into it. Bert Finch, Tony, Nat, Sydney, and the rest of them would never miss either of us. And although I liked Roy personally, I could also count upon him to throw a most complicated monkey-wrench into the simplest mechanism. Leon Temple, too, seemed safe enough. And Edward Orlin of *Futureways*, a plodding, rather wooden esthete, precisely unfitted for the present job. He would be working for George Stroud, in the finest sense.

I told Roy about the new assignment, explained its urgency, and then I put it up to him. I simply had to have someone in charge at the office, constantly. This might be, very likely would be, a round-the-clock job. That meant there would have to be another man to share the responsibility.

Roy was distantly interested, and even impressed. "This takes precedence over everything?"

I nodded.

"All right. I'm in. Where do we start?"

"Let me line up the legmen first. Then we'll see."

Fifteen minutes later I had the nucleus of the staff gathered in my office. In addition to Roy and Leon, there were seven men and two women drawn from other magazines and departments. Edward Orlin, rather huge and dark and fat; Phillip Best of *Newsways*, a small, acrid, wire-haired encyclopedia. The two women, Louella Metcalf and Janet Clark, were included if we needed feminine reserves. Louella, drawn from *The Sexes*, was a tiny, earnest, appealing creature, the most persistent and transparent liar I have ever known. Janet was a very simple, eager, large-boned brunette whose last assignment had been with *Homeways*; she did every job about four times over, eventually doing it very well. Don Klausmeyer of *Personalities* and Mike Felch of *Fashions* had also been conscripted, and one man each from *Commerce*, *Sportland*, and the auditing department. They would do for a convincing start.

From now on, everything would have to look good. Better than good. Perfect. I gave them a crisp, businesslike explanation.

"You are being asked to take on a unique and rather strange job," I said. "It has to be done quickly, and as quietly as possible. I know you can do it.

"We have been given a blank check as far as the resources of the organization are concerned. If you need help on your particular assignment, help of any sort, you can have it. If it's a routine matter, simply go to the department that can give it. If it's something special, come either to me, or to Roy, here, who will be in charge of the work whenever for some reason I have to be elsewhere myself.

"We are looking for somebody. We don't know much about this person, who he is, where he lives. We don't even know his name. His name may be George Chester, but that is doubtful. It is possible he is in the advertising business, and that will be your job, Harry." I said this to Harry Slater, the fellow from *Commerce.* "You will comb the advertising agencies, clubs, if necessary the advertising departments of first the metropolitan newspapers and magazines, then those farther out. If you have to go that far, you will need a dozen or so more men to help you. You are in complete charge of that line of investigation." Harry's inquiries were safe, and they could also be impressive. I added: "Take as many people as you need. Cross-check with us regularly, for the additional information about our man that will be steadily coming in from all the other avenues we will be exploring at the same time. And that applies to all of you.

"We not only don't know this man's right name or where he lives—and that will be your job, Alvin." This was Alvin Dealey, from the auditing department. "Check all real estate registers in this area, all tax records, public utilities, and all phone books of cities within, say, three or four hundred miles, for George Chester, and any other names we give you. Take as many researchers as you need.

"Now, as I said, we not only don't know this man's name or whereabouts, but we haven't even got any kind of a physical description of him. Just that he is of average height, say five nine to eleven, and average build. Probably between one-forty and one-eighty.

"But there are a few facts we have to go upon. He is an habitué of a place on Third Avenue called Gil's. Here is a description of the place." I gave it, but stayed strictly within the memo as given by Steve Hagen. "This man was in that place, wherever it is, last Saturday afternoon. At that time he was there with a woman we know to be a good-looking blonde. Probably he goes there regularly. That will be your job, Ed. You will find this restaurant, night club, saloon, or whatever it is, and when you do you will stay there until our man comes into it." Ed Orlin's swarthy and rather flabby face betrayed, just for an instant, amazement and incipient distaste.

"On the same evening our subject went into an antique shop, also on Third Avenue. He went into several, but there is one in particular we want, which shouldn't be hard to find. You will find it, Phil. Because the fellow we are looking for bought a picture, unframed, while he was in the place, and he bought it after outbidding another customer, a woman." I did not elaborate by a hairsbreadth beyond Steve's written memo. "The canvas was by an artist named Louise Patterson, it depicted two hands, was in bad condition, and the name of it, or the subject matter, had something to do with Judas. The dealer is certain to remember the incident. You can get an accurate description of our man from him. Perhaps he knows him, and can give us his actual identity.

"Don, here is our file on this Louise Patterson. There is a possibility that this picture can be traced from the artist to the dealer and from him to our unknown. Look up Patterson, or if she's dead, look up her friends. Somebody will remember that canvas, what became of it, may even know who has it now. Find out." I had suddenly the sick and horrid realization I would have to destroy that picture. "Perhaps the man we are looking for is an art collector, even a Patterson enthusiast.

"Leon, I want you and Janet to go to the bar of the Van Barth, where this same blonde went with this same person, on the same evening. At that time he had the picture, and perhaps he checked it. Find out. Question the bartenders, the checkroom attendants for all they can give you regarding the man, and then I guess you'd better stay right there and wait for him to turn up, since he's probably a regular there, as well as Gil's. You may have to be around for several days and if so you will have to be relieved by Louella and Dick Englund."

Leon and Janet looked as though they might not care to be relieved, while Louella and Dick perceptibly brightened. It was almost a pleasure to dispense such largesse. I wished them many a pleasant hour while they awaited my arrival.

"That is about all I have to give you now," I concluded. "Do you all understand your immediate assignments?" Apparently, the lieutenants in charge of the hunt for George Stroud all did, for none of them said anything. "Well, are there any questions?"

Edward Orlin had one. "Why are we looking for this man?"

"All I know about that," I said, "is the fact that he is the intermediary figure in one of the biggest political-industrial steals in history. That is, he is the connecting link, and we need him to establish the fact of this conspiracy. Our man is the payoff man."

Ed Orlin took this information and seemed to retire behind a wall of thought to eat and digest it. Alvin Dealey earnestly asked: "How far can we go in drawing upon the police for information?"

"You can draw upon them, but you are not to tell them anything at all," I said, flatly. "This is our story, in the first place, and we intend to keep it ours. In the second place, I told you there is a political tie-up here. The police machinery we go to may be all right at one end, ours, but we don't know and we have no control over the other end of that machine. Is that clear?"

Alvin nodded. And then the shrewd, rather womanish voice of Phillip Best cut in. "All of these circumstances you have given us concern last Saturday," he said. "That was the night Pauline Delos was killed. Everyone knows what that means. Is there any connection?"

"Not as far as I know, Phil," I said. "This is purely a big-time business scandal that Hagen himself and a few others have been digging into for some time past. Now, it's due to break." I paused for a moment, to let this very thin logic take what hold it could. "As far as I understand it, Earl intends to go through with this story, regardless of the ghastly business last Saturday night."

Phil's small gray eyes bored through his rimless glasses. "I just thought, it's quite a coincidence," he said. I let that pass without even looking at it, and he added: "Am I to make inquiries about the woman who was with the man?"

"You will all have to do that." I had no doubt of what they would discover. Yet even delay seemed in my favor, and I strongly reminded them, "But we are not looking for the woman, or any other outside person. It is the man we want, and only the man."

I let my eyes move slowly over them, estimating their reactions. As far as I could see, they accepted the story. More important, they seemed to give credit to my counterfeit assurance and determination.

"All right," I said. "If there are no more questions, suppose you intellectual tramps get the hell out of here and go to work." As they got up, reviewing the notes they had taken, and stuffed them into their pockets, I added, "And don't fail to report back, either in person or by phone. Soon, and often. Either to Roy or myself."

When they had all gone, except Roy, he got up from his chair beside me at the desk. He walked around in front of it, then crossed to the wall facing it, hands thrust into his pockets. He leaned against the wall, staring at the carpet. Presently, he said: "This is a crazy affair. I can't help feeling that Phil somehow hit the nail on the head. There is a curious connection there, I'm certain, the fact that all of this happened last Saturday."

I waited, with a face made perfectly blank.

"I don't mean it has any connection with that frightful business about Pauline Delos," he went on, thoughtfully. "Of course it hasn't. That would be a little too obvious. But I can't help thinking that something, I don't know what, something happened last week on Friday or Saturday, perhaps while Janoth was in Washington, or certainly a few days before, or even last night, Sunday, that would really explain why we are looking for this mysterious, art-collecting stranger at this moment, and in such a hurry. Don't you think so?"

"Sounds logical," I said.

"Damn right it's logical. It seems to me, we would do well to comb the outstanding news items of the last two weeks, particularly the last five or six days, and see what there is that might concern Janoth. This Jennett-Donohue proposition, for instance. Perhaps they are actually planning to add those new books in our field. That would seriously bother Earl, don't you think?"

Roy was all right. He was doing his level best.

"You may be right. And again it may be something else, far deeper, not quite so apparent. Suppose you follow up that general line? But at the same time, I can't do anything except work from the facts supplied to me."

Actually, I was at work upon a hazy plan that seemed a second line of defense, should it come to that. It amounted to a counterattack. The problem, if the situation got really bad, was this: How to place Janoth at the scene of the killing, through some third, independent witness, or through evidence not related to myself. Somewhere in that fatal detour his car had been noted, he himself had been seen and marked. If I had to fight fire with fire, somehow, surely he could be connected.

But it would never come to that. The gears being shifted, the wheels beginning to move in this hunt for me were big and smooth and infinitely powered, but they were also blind. Blind, clumsy, and unreasoning. "No, you have to work with the data you've been given," Roy admitted. "But I think it would be a good idea if I did follow up my hunch. I'll see if we haven't missed something in recent political developments."

At the same time that I gave him silent encouragement, I became aware of the picture above his head on the wall against which he leaned. It was as though it had suddenly screamed.

Of course. I had forgotten I had placed that Patterson there, two years ago. I had bought it at the Lewis Galleries, the profiles of two faces, showing only the brow, eyes, nose, lips, and chin of each. They confronted each other, distinctly Pattersonian. One of them showed an avaricious, the other a skeptical leer. I believe she had called it *Study in Fury*.

It was such a familiar landmark in my office that to take it away, now, would be fatal. But as I looked at it and then looked away I really began to understand the danger in which I stood. It would have to stay there, though at any moment someone might make a connection. And there must be none, none at all, however slight.

"Yes," I told Roy, automatically, feeling the after-shock in fine points of perspiration all over me. "Why not do that? We may have missed something significant in business changes, as well as politics."

"I think it might simplify matters," he said, and moved away from the wall on which the picture hung. "Janoth was in Washington this week end, remember. Personally, I think there's a tie-up between that and this rush order we've been given."

Thoughtfully, Roy moved away from the wall, crossed the thickly carpeted floor, disappeared through the door leading to his own office.

When he had gone I sat for a long moment, staring at that thing on the wall. I had always liked it before.

But no. It had to stay there.

Edward Orlin

GIL'S TAVERN looked like just a dive on the outside, and also on the inside. Too bad I couldn't have been assigned to the Van Barth. Well, it couldn't be helped.

It was in the phone book, and not far off, so that part of it was all right. I walked there in twenty minutes.

I took along a copy of *War and Peace*, which I was rereading, and on the way I saw a new issue of *The Creative Quarterly*, which I bought.

It was a little after one o'clock when I got there, time for lunch, so I had it. The food was awful. But it would go on the expense account, and after I'd eaten I got out my notebook and put it down. Lunch, $1.50. Taxi, $1.00. I thought for a minute, wondering what Stroud would do if he ever came to a dive like this, then I added: Four highballs, $2.00.

After I'd finished my coffee and a slab of pie at least three days old I looked around. It was something dug up by an archeological expedition, all right. There was sawdust in the corners, and a big wreath on the wall in back of me, celebrating a recent banquet, I suppose: CONGRATULATIONS TO OUR PAL.

Then I saw the bar at the end of the long room. It was incredible. It looked as though a whole junkyard had been scooped up and dumped there. I saw wheels, swords, shovels, tin cans, bits of paper, flags, pictures, literally hundreds upon hundreds of things, just things.

After I paid for the 85¢ lunch, a gyp, and already I had indigestion, I picked up my Tolstoy and *The Creative Quarterly* and walked down to the bar.

The nearer I came to it the more things I saw, simply thousands of them. I sat down and noticed there was a big fellow about fifty years old, with staring, preoccupied eyes, in back of it. He came down the bar, and I saw that his eyes were looking at me but didn't quite focus. They were like dim electric lights in an empty room. His voice was a wordless grunt.

"A beer," I said. I noticed that he spilled some of it when

he put the glass down in front of me. His face really seemed almost ferocious. It was very strange, but none of my business. I had work to do. "Say, what've you got in back of the bar there? Looks like an explosion in a five-and-ten-cent store."

He didn't say anything for a couple of seconds, just looked me over, and now he seemed really sore about something.

"My personal museum," he said, shortly.

So that was what the memo meant. I was in the right place, no doubt about it.

"Quite a collection," I said. "Buy you a drink?"

He had a bottle on the bar by the time I finished speaking. Scotch, and one of the best brands, too. Well, it was a necessary part of the assignment. Made no difference to me; it went on the expense account.

He dropped the first jigger he picked up, left it where it fell, and only finally managed to fill the second one. But he didn't seem drunk. Just nervous.

"Luck," he said. He lifted the glass and the whisky was all gone, in five seconds, less than five seconds, almost in a flash. When he put down the jigger and picked up the bill I laid on the bar he noisily smacked his lips. "First of the day," he said. "That's always the best. Except for the last."

I sipped my beer, and when he laid down the change, he was charging 75¢ for his own Scotch, I said: "So that's your personal museum. What's in it?"

He turned and looked at it and he sounded much better. "Everything. You name it and I've got it. What's more, it's an experience what happened to me or my family."

"Sort of a petrified autobiography, is that it?"

"No, just my personal museum. I been around the world six times, and my folks before me been all over it. Farther than that. Name me one thing I haven't got in that museum, and the drinks are on me."

It was fantastic. I didn't see how I'd ever get any information out of this fellow. He was an idiot.

"All right," I said, humoring him. "Show me a locomotive."

He muttered something that sounded like, "Locomotive? Now, where did that locomotive get to." Then he reached away over in back of a football helmet, a stuffed bird, a bowl heaped to the brim with foreign coins, and a lot of odds and ends I couldn't even see, and when he turned around he laid a toy railroad engine on the bar. "This here locomotive," he confided, slapping it affectionately and leaning toward me, "was the only toy of mine what got saved out of the famous Third Avenue fire next to the carbarns fifty years ago. Saved it myself. I was six years old. They had nine roasts."

I finished my beer and stared at him, not sure whether he was trying to kid me or whether he was not only half drunk but completely out of his mind besides. If it was supposed to be humor, it was certainly corny, the incredibly childish slapstick stuff that leaves me cold. Why couldn't I have gotten the Van Barth, where I could at least read in peace and comfort, without having to interview a schizophrenic, probably homicidal.

"That's fine," I said.

"Still runs, too," he assured me, and gave the key a twist, put the toy down on the bar, and let it run a few feet. It stopped when it bumped into *The Creative Review*. He actually sounded proud. "See? Still runs."

God, this was simply unbelievable. I might as well be back in the office.

The lunatic gravely put the toy back behind the bar, where I heard its spring motor expend itself, and when he turned around he wordlessly filled up our glasses again, mine with beer and his with Scotch. I was still more surprised when he tossed off his drink, then returned and absently paused in front of me, appearing to wait. For God's sake, did this fellow expect a free drink with every round? Not that it mattered. He had to be humored, I suppose. After I'd paid, and by now he seemed actually friendly, he asked: "Yes, sir. That's one of the best private museums in New York. Anything else you'd care to see?"

"You haven't got a crystal ball, have you?"

"Well, now, as it happens, I have." He brought out a big glass marble from a pile of rubbish surmounted by a crucifix and a shrunken head. "Funny how everybody wants to see that locomotive, or sometimes it's the airplane or the steamroller, and usually they ask to see the crystal ball. Now this here little globe I picked up in Calcutta. I went to a Hindu gypsy what told fortunes, and he seen in the glass that I was in danger of drowning. So I jumped the ship I was on and went on the beach awhile, and not two days passed before that boat went down with all hands. So I says to myself, Holy Smoke, how long's this been going on? I never put much stock in that stuff before, see? So I went back to this fellow, and I says, I'd like to have that there gadget. And he says, in his own language of course, this been in his family for generations after generations and he can't part with it."

This juvenile nonsense went on and on. My God, I thought it would never stop. And I had to look as though I were interested. Finally it got so boring I couldn't stand any more of it. I said: "Well, I wish you'd look into that globe and see if you can locate a friend of mine for me."

"That's a funny thing. When I finally paid the two thousand rupees he wanted, and I took it back to my hotel, I couldn't make the damn thing work. And never could since."

"Never mind," I said. "Have another drink." He put the marble away and drew another beer and poured himself another Scotch. I couldn't see how a fellow like this stayed in business for more than a week.

Before he could put his drink away I went on: "A friend of mine I haven't seen for years comes in here sometimes, and I wonder if you know him. I'd like to see him again. Maybe you know what would be a good time to find him here."

The man's eyes went absolutely blank.

"What's his name?"

"George Chester."

"George Chester." He stared at the far end of the room, apparently thinking, and a little of the mask fell away from him. "That name I don't know. Mostly, I don't know their names, anyway. What's he look like?"

"Oh, medium height and build," I said. "A mutual acquaintance told me he saw him in here late last Saturday afternoon. With a good-looking blonde."

He threw the shot of whisky into his mouth and I don't believe the glass even touched his lips. Didn't this fellow ever take a chaser? He frowned and paused.

"I think I know who you mean. Clean-cut, brown-haired fellow?"

"I guess you could call him that."

"I remember that blonde. She was something for the books. She wanted to see the raven that fellow wrote about, nevermore quoth he. So I let her have a look at it. Yes, they were in here a couple of nights ago, but he don't come around here very often. Four or five years ago he was in here lots, almost every night. Smart, too. Many's the time I used to show him my museum, until me and some hacker had to pick him up and carry him out. One night he wouldn't go home at all, he wanted to sleep right inside the museum. 'Book me the royal suite on your ocean liner, Gil,' he kept saying. We got him home all right. But that was several years ago." He looked at me with sharp interest. "Friend of yours?"

I nodded. "We used to work for the same advertising agency."

He puzzled some more. "I don't think he did then," he decided. "He worked for some newspaper, and before that he and his wife used to run a joint upstate, the same as mine. No museum, of course. Seems to me his name might have been George Chester, at that. I had to garage his car once or twice when he had too much. But he gradually stopped coming in. I don't think he was here more than twice in the last three or four months. But he might come in any time, you never can tell. Very intelligent fellow. What they call eccentric."

"Maybe I could reach him through the blonde."

"Maybe."

"Who is she, do you know?"

This time his whole face went blank. "No idea, sir."

He moved up the bar to serve some customers who had just entered, and I opened *The Creative Review*. There was a promising revaluation of Henry James I would have to read, though I knew the inevitable shortcomings of the man who wrote it. A long article on Tibetan dance ritual that looked quite good.

I finished my beer and went to a phone booth. I called the office and asked for Stroud, but got Cordette instead.

"Where's Stroud?" I asked.

"Out. Who's this?"

"Ed Orlin. I'm at Gil's Tavern."

"Found it, did you? Get the right one?"

"It's the right one, no question. And what a dive."

"Pick up anything?"

"Our man was here last Saturday, all right, and with the blonde."

"Fine. Let's have it."

"There isn't much. The bartender isn't sure of his name, because the guy doesn't come in here any more." I let that sink in, for a moment. I certainly hoped to get called off this drab saloon and that boring imbecile behind the bar. "But he thinks his name may actually be George Chester. He has been described by the bartender, who is either a half-wit or an out-right lunatic himself, as very intelligent and eccentric. Believe me, Chester is probably just the opposite."

"Why?"

"It's that kind of a place. Eccentric, yes, but only a moron would come into a dump like this and spend hours talking to the fellow that runs this menagerie."

"Go on."

"The physical description we have does not seem far wrong, but there's nothing to add to it, except that he's brown-haired and clean-cut."

"All right. What else? Any line on the blonde?"

"Nothing."

"That certainly isn't much, is it?"

"Well, wait. Our man is unquestionably a dipsomaniac. Four or five years ago he was in here every night and had to be sent home in a taxi. At that time he was a newspaperman, the bartender believes, and he never heard of him as working for an advertising concern. And before he was a newspaper-man he ran a tavern somewhere upstate, with his wife."

"A drunk. Formerly, with his wife, a tavern proprietor. Probably a newspaperman, eccentric, clean-cut in appearance. It isn't much, but it's something. Is that all?"

"That's all. And our baby hasn't been in here more than twice in the last eight or ten months. So what should I do? Come back to the office?"

There was a pause, and I had a moment of hope.

"I think not, Ed. He was in there two days ago, he might not wait so long before he returns. And you can work on the bartender some more. Psychoanalyze him for more details. Have a few drinks with him."

Oh, my God.

"Listen, this fellow is a human blotter."

"All right, get drunk with him, if you have to. But not too drunk. Try some of the other customers. Anyway, stick around until we call you back, or send a relief. What's the address and the phone number?"

I gave them to him.

"All right, Ed. And if you get anything more, call us at once. Remember, this is a hurry-up job."

I hoped so. I went back to the bar, already a little dizzy on the beers. It would be impossible to concentrate on the magazine, which demanded an absolutely clear head. One of the customers was roaring at the bartender, "All right, admit you ain't got it. I ask you, show me a *mot de passe* out of that famous museum, so-called."

"No double-talk allowed. You want to see something, you got to ask for it in plain language."

"That is plain language. Plain, ordinary French. Admit it, and give us a beer. You just ain't got one."

"All right, all right, I'll give you a beer. But what is this here thing? How do you spell it? Only don't ask for nothing in French again. Not in here, see?"

Well, there was a newspaper at the end of the bar, thank God. This morning's, but it could kill a couple of hours.

George Stroud VIII

WHEN they all cleared out of my office on their various assignments, I called in Emory Mafferson. His plump face was in perpetual mourning, his brain was a seething chaos, his brown eyes seemed always trying to escape from behind those heavy glasses, and I don't believe he could see more than ten feet in front of him, but somewhere in Emory I felt there was a solid newspaperman and a lyric investigator.

"How are you coming along with Funded Individuals?" I asked him.

"All right. I've explained it all to Bert, and we're finishing the article together."

"Sure Bert understands it?"

Emory's face took a turn for the worse.

"As well as I do," he finally said. "Maybe better. You know, I can't help feeling there's something sound in back of that idea. It's a new, revolutionary vision in the field of social security."

"Well, what's troubling you?"

"How can you have a revolution without a revolution?"

"Just leave that to Bert Finch. He has your *Futureways* notes, and he can interpret the data as far as you've gone with it. Suppose you let Bert carry on alone from here?"

Emory sighed.

If I understood him, many an afternoon supposedly spent in scholarly research at the library or interviewing some in-surance expert had found him instead at Belmont, the Yankee Stadium, possibly home in bed.

"All good things have to come to an end sometime, Emory."

"I suppose so."

I came abruptly to the point. "Right now I have got to work on a special, outside job. At the same time, one of the most sensational murders of the year has occurred, and be-yond a doubt it will assume even greater proportions and sometime *Crimeways* will want a big story about it."

"Delos?"

I nodded.

"And I don't want *Crimeways* left at the post. You wanted to go on our regular staff. This can start you off. Suppose you go down to Center Street, Homicide Bureau, and pick up everything you can, as and when it happens. The minute you've got it, phone it to me. I'll be busy with this other assignment, but I want to be up-to-date on the Delos story, every phase of it."

Emory looked more stunned and haggard than ever. Those brown goldfish eyes swam three times around the bowl of his glasses.

"God, you don't expect me to break this thing alone, do you?"

"Of course not. If we wanted to break it, we'd give it a big play, thirty or forty legmen. I just want all the facts ready when the case is broken, by the cops. All you have to do is keep in close touch with developments. And report back to me, and only me, regularly. Got it?"

Emory looked relieved, and said he understood. He got up to go. My private detective force wasn't much bigger standing than sitting, and looked even less impressive.

"What have you got for me to go on?" he asked.

"Nothing. Just what you have, no more."

"Will this be all right with Bert?"

I said I'd arrange that, and sent him on his way. After he'd gone I sat and looked at that Patterson *Study in Fury* on the opposite wall, facing me, and did nothing but think.

The signature was quite visible, and even moving the canvas downward into the lower part of the frame would not obscure it. I did not believe it possible, but there might, also, be others in the Janoth organization who would recognize a Patterson simply from the style.

I could not remove that picture. Even if I changed it for another, the change would be noticed by someone. Maybe not by Roy, the writers, or the reporters, but by someone. Lucille or one of the other girls, somebody else's secretary, some research worker.

If only that picture weren't there. And above all, if only I had never brought home *The Temptation of St. Judas.*

Because Georgette had seen the new picture.

Hagen was certain whoever had bought it could be traced through it. If he thought it necessary, he would insist upon a far more intensive search for it than the one I had, as a safe-guard, assigned Don Klausmeyer to undertake. I knew Don would never trace it clear through from the artist to the dealer, let alone to me. But Hagen might at any moment take independent steps; I could think of some, myself, that would be dangerous.

I had better destroy the *Temptation.*

If somebody did his job too well, if Hagen went to work on his own, if some real information got to him before I could short-circuit it, that thing would nail me cold. I must get rid of it.

I put on my hat and went into Roy's office, with two half-formed ideas, to destroy that picture now and to find a means of locating Earl Janoth at 58 East through other witnesses. I could trust no one but myself with either of these jobs.

"I'm going out on a lead, Roy," I told him. "Take over for a while. And by the way, I've assigned somebody to follow the Delos murder. We'll want to handle it in an early issue, don't you think?" He nodded thoughtfully. "I've assigned Mafferson."

He nodded again, dryly and remotely. "I believe Janoth will want it followed, at least," he said. "By the way, I'm having the usual missing-person index prepared."

This was a crisscross of the data that came in, as rapidly as it came, simplified for easy reference. I had myself, at one time or another, helped to simplify it.

Over my shoulder I said, briskly: "That's the stuff."

I went out to the elevators, rode down and crossed the street to the garage. I decided to get the car, drive out to Marble Road and burn up that business right now.

In the garage, I met Earl Janoth's chauffeur, Billy, coming out of it. He had just brought in Janoth's car. I had ridden in it perhaps a dozen times, and now he nodded, impassively pleasant.

"Hello, Mr. Stroud."

"Hello, Billy."

We passed each other, and I felt suddenly cold and aware. There were two people Janoth trusted without limit, Steve

Hagen and Billy, his physical shadow. When and if the missing unknown was located, Billy would be the errand boy sent to execute the final decision. He would be the man. He didn't know it, but I knew it.

Inside the garage an attendant was polishing Janoth's already shining Cadillac. I walked up to him, memorizing the car's license. Somebody else, somewhere, had seen it that night, and Earl, I hoped, and seen them where they were not supposed to be.

"Want your car, Mr. Stroud?"

I said hello and told him I did. I had often stopped for a minute or two with this particular attendant, talking about baseball, horses, whisky, or women.

"Got a little errand to do this afternoon," I said, and then gave him a narrow smile. "I'll bet this bus is giving you plenty of trouble."

I got a knowing grin in return.

"Not exactly trouble," he confided. "But the cops have been giving it a going over. Us too. Was it cleaned since Saturday night? How long was it out Saturday night? Did I notice the gas, the mileage, anything peculiar? Hell, we guys never pay any attention to things like that. Except, of course, we know it wasn't washed, and it wasn't even gassed."

He called to another attendant to bring down my car, and while I waited for it, I asked: "I suppose the cops third degree'd the chauffeur?"

"Sure. A couple of them tackled him again a few minutes ago. But the driver's got nothing to worry about. Neither has Mr. Janoth. They drove to a dinner somewhere and then they drove straight to some other place. Your friend Mr. Hagen's. It checks okay with us. They never garage this car here nights or week ends, so what would we know about it? But I don't mind cops. Only, I don't like that driver. Nothing I could say, exactly. Just, well."

He looked at me and I gave him an invisible signal in return and then my car was brought down.

I got into it and drove off, toward Marble Road. But I hadn't gone more than three blocks before I began to think it all over again, and this time in a different mood.

Why should I destroy that picture? I liked it. It was mine.

Who was the better man, Janoth or myself? I voted for my-self. Why should I sacrifice my own property just because of him? Who was he? Only another medium-sized wheel in the big clock.

The big clock didn't like pictures, much. I did. This partic-ular picture it had tossed into the dustbin. I had saved it from oblivion, myself. Why should I throw it back?

There were lots of good pictures that were prevented from being painted at all. If they couldn't be aborted, or lost, then somebody like me was despatched to destroy them.

Just as Billy would be sent to destroy me. And why should I play ball in a deadly set-up like that?

What would it get me to conform?

Newsways, Commerce, Crimeways, Personalities, The Sexes, Fashions, Futureways, the whole organization was full and overrunning with frustrated ex-artists, scientists, farmers, writ-ers, explorers, poets, lawyers, doctors, musicians, all of whom spent their lives conforming, instead. And conforming to what? To a sort of overgrown, aimless, haphazard stenciling apparatus that kept them running to psychoanalysts, sent them to insane asylums, gave them high blood pressure, stom-ach ulcers, killed them off with cerebral hemorrhages and heart failure, sometimes suicide. Why should I pay still more tribute to this fatal machine? It would be easier and simpler to get squashed stripping its gears than to be crushed helping it along.

To hell with the big gadget. I was a dilettante by profession. A pretty good one, I had always thought. I decided to stay in that business.

I turned down a side street and drove toward 58 East. I could make a compromise. That picture could be put out of circulation, for the present. But it would really be a waste of time to destroy it. That would mean only a brief reprieve, at best. Its destruction was simply not worth the effort.

And I could beat the machine. The super-clock would go on forever, it was too massive to be stopped. But it had no brains, and I did. I could escape from it. Let Janoth, Hagen, and Billy perish in its wheels. They loved it. They liked to suffer. I didn't.

I drove past 58 East, and began to follow the course the

other car must have taken going away. Either Janoth had dismissed Billy when he arrived, and returned by taxi, or he had ordered Billy to come back later. In any case, Janoth had dined at the Waynes', according to all accounts, and then, as I knew, he had come to 58 East, and then of course he must have gone directly to Hagen's.

I followed the logical route to Hagen's. I saw two nearby cabstands. Janoth must have used one of them if he had returned by taxi, unless he had found a cruising cab somewhere between the two. He certainly would not have been so stupid as to pick one up near 58 East.

The farthest cabstand was the likeliest. I could begin there, with a photograph of Janoth, then try the nearer, and if necessary I could even check the bigger operators for cruisers picking up fares in the neighborhood on that evening. But that was a tall order for one man to cover.

From Hagen's, timing the drive, I went to the Waynes', then turned around and drove slowly back to 58 East. The route Earl must have followed took about thirty minutes. Allowing another thirty minutes for the fight to develop, that meant Earl was covering up about one hour. This checked with the facts known to me.

Perhaps he had stopped somewhere along the way, but if so, no likely place presented itself.

That gave me only two possible leads, a cab by which Earl may have made his getaway, or possibly some attendant at Pauline's or Hagen's.

It was pretty slim. But something.

I drove back to the office, garaged the car again, and went up to 2619. There was no one there, and no memos. I went straight on into 2618.

Roy, Leon Temple, and Janet Clark were there.

"Any luck?" Roy asked me.

"I don't know," I said.

"Well, we're starting to get some reports." Roy nodded with interest toward the cross-reference chart laid out on a big blackboard covering half of one wall. "Ed Orlin phoned a while ago. He located Gil's with no trouble and definitely placed the man and the woman there. Interesting stuff. I think we're getting somewhere."

"Fine," I said.

I went over to the board, topped with the caption: *X.*

In the column headed: "Names, Aliases," I read: *George Chester?*

Under "Appearance" it said: *Brown-haired, clean-cut, average height and build.*

I thought, thank you, Ed.

"Frequents": *Antique shops, Van Barth, Gil's. At one time frequented Gil's almost nightly.*

It was true, I had.

"Background": *Advertising? Newspapers? Formerly operated an upstate tavern-resort.*

Too close.

"Habits": *Collects pictures.*

"Character": *Eccentric, impractical. A pronounced drunk.*

This last heading was something that had been added by Roy in the Isleman and Sandler jobs. He imagined he had invented it, and valued it accordingly.

I said, standing beside the word-portrait of myself: "We seem to be getting somewhere."

"That isn't all," Roy told me. "Leon and Janet have just returned from the Van Barth with more. We were discussing it, before putting it on the board."

He looked at Leon, and Leon gave his information in neat, precise, third-person language.

"That's right," he said. "First of all it was established that Chester was in the lounge on Saturday night. He did not check the Judas picture he bought, but he was overheard talking about it with the woman accompanying him. And the woman with him was Pauline Delos."

I registered surprise.

"Are you sure?"

"No doubt about it, George. She was recognized by the waiter, the bartender, and the checkroom girl, from the pictures of her published in today's papers. Delos was in there Saturday night, with a man answering to the description on the board, and they were talking about a picture called *Judas* something-or-other. There can be no doubt about it." He looked at me for a long moment, in which I said nothing, then he finally asked: "I feel that's significant, don't you?

Doesn't this alter the whole character of the assignment we are on? Personally, I think it does. Somebody raised the very same question this morning, and now it looks as though he had been right."

I said: "That's logical. Do the police know Delos was in there Saturday night?"

"Of course. Everyone in the place promptly told them."

"Do the police know we are looking for the man with her?"

"No. But they are certainly looking for him, now. We didn't say anything, because we thought this was exclusive with us. But what should we do about it? We're looking for George Chester, and yet this Delos tie-up is terrific, seems to me."

I nodded, and lifted Roy's phone.

"Right," I said. When I had Steve Hagen I barked into the receiver: "Steve? Listen. The woman with our man was Pauline Delos."

The other end of the wire went dead for five, ten, fifteen, twenty seconds.

"Hello, Steve? Are you there? This is George Stroud. We have discovered that the woman who was with the person we want was Pauline Delos. Does this mean something?"

I looked at Roy, Janet, and Leon. They seemed merely expectant, with no second thoughts apparent in their faces. At the other end of the wire I heard what I thought was a faint sigh from Steve Hagen.

"Nothing in particular," he said, carefully. "I knew that she saw this go-between. Perhaps I should have told you. But the fact that she was with him that night does not concern the matter we have in hand. What we want, and what we've got to have, is the name and whereabouts of the man himself. Delos is a blind alley, as far as our investigation is concerned. The murder is one story. This is a different, unrelated one. Is that plain?"

I said I understood him perfectly, and after I broke the connection I repeated the explanation almost verbatim to the three people in the room.

Roy was complacent.

"Yes," he said. "But I said all along this was an issue related to some recent crisis, and now we know damn well it is."

He rose and went over to the blackboard, picked up some

chalk. I watched him as he wrote under "Associates": *Pauline Delos*. Where the line crossed "Antique shops," "Gil's," "Van Barth" he repeated the name. Then he began to add a new column.

"At the same time, Leon and Janet brought in something more tangible," he went on. "Tell George about it."

Leon's small and measured voice resumed the report. "When they left the cocktail lounge of the Van Barth, our subject forgot something and left it behind him."

Nothing about me moved except my lips.

"Yes?"

Leon nodded toward Roy's desk and his eyes indicated an envelope. I seemed to float toward it, wondering whether this had all been an extravagant, cold-blooded farce they had put together with Hagen, whether I had actually mislaid or forgotten something that gave me away altogether. But the envelope was blank.

"A handkerchief," I heard Leon say, as from a great distance. "It can probably be traced, because it's obviously expensive, and it has what I believe is an old laundry mark."

Of course. She had borrowed it. When she spilled her cocktail I had used it, then given it to her. And it had been left there.

I turned the envelope over and shook the handkerchief from the unsealed flap. Yes. I could even see, faintly, the old stain.

"I wouldn't touch it, George," said Leon. "We may be able to raise a few fingerprints. It's a very fine, smooth fabric."

So I had to do that. I picked up the handkerchief and unfolded it. And laid it down and spread it out, very carefully and cautiously.

"I imagine it already has plenty," I said. "The waitress's, the cashier's, yours, one more set won't matter." I inspected the familiar square of linen with grave attention. It was one of a lot I had bought at Blanton's & Dent's, about a year ago. And there was the faint, blurred, but recoverable laundry mark on a bit of the hem, several months old, for it must have been put there when I last spent a week in the city and sent some of my things to a midtown laundry. "Yes, I imagine this can be traced."

I refolded the handkerchief, stuffed it back into the envelope. I could now account for the presence of my own fingerprints, but I knew I could not save the handkerchief itself from the mill.

I handed the envelope to Leon.

"Do you want to take this to Sacher & Roberts?" That was the big commercial laboratory we used for such work. "Whatever they find, we'll put another team on it. I suppose Dick and Louella relieved you at the Van Barth?"

"Oh, sure. Our man comes in there once or twice a week, they said."

"We've got the fellow covered at this place called Gil's, and at the Van Barth," Roy pointed out. "He'll come back, and then we've got him."

I nodded, rather thoughtfully. I said: "Certainly. He'll return to one place or the other. Then that will be that."

I don't know how that conference broke up. I think Leon went on to Sacher & Roberts. I believe I left Roy making additional entries on the big progress-board. I told him to eat and get some rest when he'd finished, I would be leaving around seven.

If they actually brought out prints on that handkerchief, we would all have to volunteer our own, mine with the rest. That in itself I had taken care of. But for a long, long time in my own office I sat trying to remember whether my fingerprints could be found anywhere on Pauline's overnight bag. Such a duplication could not be explained away. Hardly.

I forced myself to relive that last day with Pauline. No. I had not touched that grip anywhere except on the handle, and Pauline's final touches had certainly smudged them all out.

Sometime in the afternoon I took a call from Don Klausmeyer.

"Oh, yes, Don," I said. "Any luck with Patterson?"

Don's slow, malicious, pedantic voice told me: "I had a little trouble, but I found her. I've been talking to her for about an hour, going over old catalogues of her shows, looking at her fifth-rate pictures, and trying to keep her four kids out of my hair."

"Okay. Shoot."

"I have turned up one very significant fact. Louise Patterson was the customer who bid, unsuccessfully, for her own picture in the dealer's shop that night. A friend saw her canvas there, told her about it, and it was Patterson's hope that she could buy it back for herself. God knows why."

"I see. Anything else?"

"Do you understand? It was Patterson herself, in the shop that night."

"I get it. And?"

"And she described the man who bought the picture, at great length. Are you ready to take it?"

"Let's have it."

"This is Patterson speaking. Quote. He was a smug, self-satisfied, smart-alecky bastard just like ten million other rubber-stamp sub-executives. He had brown hair, brown eyes, high cheekbones, symmetrical and lean features. His face looked as though he scrubbed and shaved it five times a day. He weighed between one sixty and one sixty-five. Gray tweed suit, dark blue hat and necktie. He knows pictures, says she, and is certainly familiar with the works of L. Patterson, which he doubtless collects, but only for their snob-appeal. Personally, I think the dame overestimates herself. She admits she's been forgotten for the last ten years. But to go on. Our man is a good deal of an exhibitionist. He imagines he is Superman and that is what he plays at being. The woman with him was beautiful if you like Lesbians in standard, Park Avenue models. Unquote. Got it?"

"Yes."

"Does it help?"

"Some," I said.

"I've been poking around the studio-loft she lives in—God what a paradise for rats and termites—looking at acres and acres of pictures. Artistically she's impossible." How would Don know? "But they reminded me of something I'm sure I've seen somewhere very recently. If I can only remember what it is, maybe I'll have another lead."

He laughed and I echoed him, but I was staring straight at *Study in Fury* on the wall opposite me.

"Maybe you will, but don't worry about it. I'll see you tomorrow."

When he hung up I stared at that picture, without really seeing it, for a long five minutes. Then I took my scribbled notes and went into Roy's empty office and duly entered Don's report on the chart. By now it was crystallizing into a very unpleasant definition of myself indeed. And after that, I took three good, recent photographs of Earl Janoth out of the morgue.

A little past seven o'clock Roy returned. We arranged about relieving each other on the following day and then I went out, feeling I'd had about all I could stand for the time being. But I still had work to do.

At the cabstand I had that afternoon selected as the likeliest, I got my first real break. A good one. A driver identified Janoth as a passenger he'd ridden a little after ten o'clock last Saturday night. The driver was positive. He knew when he'd picked him up, and where, and where he'd put him down. A block from Hagen's.

I knew this might save my neck, as a last desperate resort. But it would not necessarily save my home.

It was around midnight when I reached Marble Road. Georgia and Georgette were asleep.

I found *The Temptation of St. Judas* where I had left it, in a closet downstairs, and in twenty minutes I had it concealed in back of another canvas.

It could be discovered, and easily, if they ever really caught up with me. But if anyone ever got this far, I was finished anyway.

Earl Janoth III

FIVE DAYS after Steve first organized the search we had enough material concerning that damned phantom to write a long biography of him. We had dates, addresses, his background, a complete verbal description of him, X-rays of every last thought, emotion, and impulse he'd ever had. I knew that blundering weak fool better than his own mother. If I shut my eyes I could actually see him standing in front of me, an imbecilic wisp of a smile on his too good-looking face, I could hear his smooth, studied, disarming voice uttering those round, banal whimsicalities he apparently loved, I could almost reach out and touch him, this horrid wraith who had stumbled into my life from nowhere to bring about Pauline's death and my possible ruin.

Yet we didn't have the man himself. We had nothing.

"Candidly, I think you are holding something back," said George Stroud. He was talking to Steve. I had insisted on being present, though not directly participating, when we re-examined the paralysis that seemed to grip our plans. "And I think that thing, whatever it may be, is the one solid fact we need to wrap up the whole business."

"Stick to the facts," said Steve. "Your imagination is running away with you."

"I think not."

We were in Steve's office, Steve behind his desk, myself a little to one side of it, Stroud facing Steve. The room was filled with sunlight, but to me it looked dim, like the bottom of a pool of water. I don't believe I'd slept more than two hours a night in the last week.

The damned wolves were closing in on me. I'd been questioned by dozens of detectives and members of the district attorney's staff three, four, and sometimes five times a day, every day. At first they'd been polite. Now they weren't bothering much with that any more.

And Wayne knew it. Carr knew it. They all knew it. It was a secret only to the general public. In the downtown district and on Forty-second Street it was open knowledge. Nobody, conspicuously, had phoned or come near me for days. The more tightly the official gang closed in on me, the farther my own crowd drew away. The more they isolated me, the easier it became for the police. I could handle one pack of wolves, but not two.

There was no real evidence against me. Not yet. But neither was there any prospect that the pressure to get it would be relaxed.

I could stand that. But we had to find that damned will-o'-the-wisp, and find him before anyone else did. He was the one serious threat I faced. If the police got to him first, as at any moment they might, and eventually would, I knew exactly what he would say, and what would happen.

It didn't make sense. We had this mountain of data, and yet we were, for all practical purposes, right where we had started.

"All right, let's stick to the facts," Stroud told Steve. "You say this man is the key figure in a political-industrial deal. But we haven't turned up one single political connection, and no business connections worth mentioning. Why not? I say, because there aren't any."

Steve told him sharply: "There are. You simply haven't dug deeply enough to get them. I'm holding nothing back except rumors and suspicions. They'd do you no good at all. In fact, they'd simply throw you off."

Stroud's voice was soft and rather pleasant, but it carried a lot of emphasis.

"I couldn't be thrown off more than I was, when you knew Delos was right in the middle of the situation, but you somehow forgot to tell me so."

This senseless bickering would get us nowhere. I had to intervene.

"What is your own opinion, George?" I asked him. "How do you account for the fact we seem to be going around in circles? It isn't like you to be held up so long on a simple thing like this. What is your honest theory about this business?"

Stroud turned and gave me a long, keen regard. He was what I had always classified as one of those hyper-perceptive people, not good at action but fine at pure logic and theory.

He was the sort who could solve a bridge-hand at a glance, down to the last play, but in a simple business deal he would be helpless. The cold fighter's and gambler's nerve that Steve had was completely lacking in him, and he would consider it something foreign or inhuman, if indeed he understood it at all.

After five days of the present job Stroud showed the strain. That was a good thing, because he had to understand this was not merely a routine story.

"Yes, I have a theory," he told me. "I believe the Delos murder and the man we want are so closely connected they are identical. I am forced to reject Steve's idea that one is only accidentally related to the other."

I nodded. It was inevitable, of course. We hadn't selected Stroud to lead the investigation because of his good looks, fancy imagination, or vanity, which was colossal.

I glanced at Steve, trusting he would go on from there more sensibly.

"I follow your reasoning, George," he said. "And I think you are right. But here is something you've overlooked, and we now have to consider. We know that Pauline had knowledge of this big combination. She helped to fill in the background, fragmentary as it is, of the whole thing. She would naturally follow it up if she could. Suppose she did just that? Suppose somebody caught her doing it? And got to her first. Have you thought of that?"

Stroud paused, remote and deliberate. He was just a little too keen for this.

"If this deal is for such high stakes, and if the other parties have already gone the limit," he said, and stopped for an even longer pause, "then we're in rough company. Our man is either in Mexico and still going south, or he has already been disposed of altogether, in such a way he will never again be found."

"That can't be," Steve told him, sharply. "Here's why. A man like this, eccentric, with a wide and varied circle of acquaintances, married and with at least one child, a responsible position somewhere, would leave a pretty big hole if he suddenly dropped out of circulation. Yet you've been in close touch with the Missing Persons Bureau—since when?"

"Tuesday morning."

"Tuesday. And no one like our man has been reported. His disappearance would certainly leak out somewhere, somehow. It hasn't, and that means he's still around." Stroud nodded, cautiously, and Steve went swiftly to another point. "Now let's look at some of these other leads a little more closely. You're still checking the list of upstate liquor licenses suspended or not renewed with the Board?"

Stroud passed a handkerchief across his perspiring face.

"Yes, but that's a tall order. There are hundreds." Stroud looked down for a moment of abstraction at the handkerchief, then he folded the cloth with great deliberation and thrust it slowly and carefully away. "The list is being fed straight to me. If I get anything, you'll know at once."

It was a strange thing to say. Of course we would.

"You've seen the story *Newsways* ran about this Patterson woman?" Steve asked, and Stroud said he had. "It's too early for results. But our spread is going to put that woman on the map. Somebody is certain to recognize and remember that *Judas* picture from our description of it. Our evaluation of it as 'priceless' is sure to locate it. It's my hunch the picture alone will nail our man to the wall."

Stroud smiled faintly, but said nothing, and then they went on to other lines of investigation involving tax lists, advertising agencies, newspapers, fingerprints on a handkerchief, all of them ending in so much fog and vapor. At length, I heard Steve saying: "Now those bars, art galleries, and so on."

"All covered."

"Exactly. And why hasn't our man shown, by now? To me, that's fantastic. No one suddenly abandons his habitual routine of life. Not without some good reason."

"I've already suggested he has either left the country, or been killed," said Stroud. "Here are some more versions of the same general theory. He may have killed Delos, himself, and in that case he's naturally not making himself conspicuous. Or he knows that he's in fast company, knows the score, and he's gone to ground, right where he is, so that the same thing won't happen to him."

I carefully looked away from Steve, and also away from

Stroud. In a curious way Stroud's conclusion was almost perfect. The room was momentarily too quiet.

"You think he may believe himself to be in danger?" Steve presently asked.

"He knows somebody is playing for keeps. Why wouldn't he be worried?"

"And he's keeping pretty well under cover." Steve appeared to be groping toward something. He stared absently at Stroud. "At least, he stays away from all the places where he always went before." Steve was silent for a moment, then he asked: "How many people in the organization, George, know about this particular job?"

Stroud seemed not to understand him.

"Our own?"

"Right here at Janoth Enterprises. How many, at a guess?"

Stroud displayed a thin smile. "Well, with fifty-three people now working on this assignment, I'd say everyone knows about it. The entire two thousand."

"Yes," Steve admitted. "I guess so."

"Why?"

"Nothing. For a second I thought I had something." Steve came back into himself, leaned aggressively forward. "All right, I guess that reports on everything. And it's still nothing."

"Do you think I've missed a bet anywhere?" Stroud demanded.

"Just bear down on it, that's all."

"I shall. Now that we've decided the killing and our particular baby are identical twins, there are a lot more lines we can follow."

"What lines?"

Stroud got up to go. He put a cigarette in his mouth, reflected before lighting it.

"For one thing, I'll have some men cover all the cabstands in the neighborhood of Pauline Delos' apartment. On the night of her death, and a few minutes after it, somebody took a taxi away from that vicinity, and he couldn't help being rather noticeable." He lit his cigarette, drew deeply, casually exhaled. "The driver will remember, and tell us all about him."

My eyes went to Steve, and stayed there. I knew he understood, because he did not, even for a second, glance in my direction.

"I don't follow that, George," he said, in a dead-level voice.

"It's quite simple. Our subject took Pauline to Gil's, to a number of antique shops, and to the Van Barth. Why wouldn't he take her home? Of course he did. Our timing checks with the police timing. He took her home and then he had to leave. No matter what happened there, no matter who killed her, no matter what he saw or what he knew, he had to leave. The first and most obvious line to follow is that he left in a taxi."

I was forced to say, "Perhaps he had his own car."

"Perhaps he did."

"He may have walked," said Steve. "Or taken a bus."

"That's true. But we can't afford to pass up the fact he may have done none of those things. He may have taken a cab. We'll just put a bet on that and hope for the best." Stroud had never lacked confidence in himself, and now it was engraved all over him. He moved toward the door. Standing there, he added, finally: "It's my hunch we'll discover he did take a cab, we'll locate the driver, find out where he went, and that will close our whole assignment."

There was a long and complete silence after he had gone, with Steve intently staring at the door that closed behind him. I thought I was reading his mind. "Yes. You're right."

"About what?"

"We'll close the assignment, all right. We're going to call the whole job off."

"No, we're not. Why should we? I was thinking of something else. About Stroud. I don't like that bastard."

"It's the same thing. I don't want Stroud looking for that taxi."

There was a smoldering anger in Steve that seemed to feed itself, perceptibly mounting.

"That's nothing. You'll never be tied to that. Our staff is good, but not that good. What worries me is what's holding us up? Why is it the only smart idea Stroud can dream up is one we don't like? He's cutting corners somewhere—but where?"

"Pull him off the job. Right now. Before he sends another

team out looking for that driver. I hate the way his mind works."

Steve's eyes were shining like an animal's, and as insensate. "We can't drop the inquiry, and there's no point in replacing Stroud. We have to go through with it, and Stroud has to deliver the goods. He has to do it a damn sight quicker, that's all. We started with an inside track, but that advantage we're losing, now, every hour."

I thought of hunters stalking big game, and while they did so, the game closed in on its own prey, and with the circle eventually completing itself, unknown disaster drew near to the hunters. It was a thing ordained. I said: "You don't know the whole situation. There have been a number of informal, really secret board meetings recently, and that dinner last Saturday—"

Steve interrupted, still watching me. "Yes. You told me."

"Well, if this business goes the wrong way, or even drags itself out, that's all they'll need to take some kind of overt action. I'm certain they've been discussing it these last four or five days. If that should happen—well, that's even worse than this."

Steve seemed not to hear. He looked out at me, and upon the whole of life, deeply and steadily as a bronze, inhumanized idol. Surprisingly, he asked: "You haven't been sleeping much, have you?"

"Not since it happened."

He nodded, spoke with persuasive but impersonal finality. "You're going to a hospital. You've got a strep throat. Forget about everything. Doc Reiner is sending you to bed for a couple of days. With no visitors. Except me."

Georgette Stroud

I HADN'T seen George when he came home last night. He had worked late, even though it had been Sunday. For that matter, I hadn't seen him any evening during the past week. It was nothing unusual for him to work late, either here or at the office. Some evenings he did not return at all.

But this Monday morning I knew something was different. It was not just another long and tough assignment, though that is what he said it was.

When he came down to breakfast I saw what I had only been feeling, but without knowing it. Now I knew something was altogether unusual, and I forced myself to search for it.

He kissed Georgia and myself and sat down. Always, when he started breakfast, he said something about the first dish he happened to see. Now he began with his grapefruit, and said nothing.

"Tell me a story, George," Georgia presently demanded, as though a perfectly novel idea had just occurred to her.

"Story? Story? What's a story, anyway? Never heard of it."

That was all right, though a little mechanical.

"Go on. George said you would. She promised."

"All right, I'll tell you a story. It's about a little girl named Sophia."

"How old?"

"Six."

Again there was that wrong note. She always had to coax him before he gave her right age.

"So what did she do?"

"Well, this is really about Sophia and her very best friend, another little girl."

"And what was her name?"

"Sonia, as it happens."

"How old?"

"Six."

"So what did they do?"

I saw, for the first time, he must have lost a lot of weight. And when he talked to me, he was not there at all. Normally, he wrapped himself in clouds of confetti, but anyone who knew him at all understood exactly what he meant and just where he could be found. But now he really, really wasn't there. His light evasions weren't light. They were actual evasions. The clouds of confetti were steel doors.

It crossed my mind he had been like this two years ago, during the affair I knew he had with Elizabeth Stoltz. That one I was certain about. And there had been others before that, I had believed then, and more than ever believed now.

A wave of utter unreality swept over me. And I recognized the mood, too well, like the first twinges of a recurrent ailment. It was too hideous to be real. That, that was what made it finally so hideous.

"Well, Sophia never saw her friend Sonia except at certain times. Only when Sophia climbed up on a chair and looked into the mirror to wash her face or comb her hair. Whenever she did that she always found Sonia, of all people, there ahead of her."

"So what did they do then?"

"So then they had long, long talks. 'What's the idea, always getting in my way?' Sophia would ask. 'You go away from here, Sonia, and leave me alone.' "

"So what did Sonia say?"

"Well, that's the strangest thing of all. Sonia never said a word. Not one word. But whatever Sophia did in front of the looking glass, Sonia copied her. Even when Sophia stuck out her tongue and called Sonia an old copycat."

"Then what happened?"

"This went on for a long time, and Sophia was pretty mad, believe me." Yes, George, Sophia was pretty damn mad. Just how many years, George, did it go on? "But she thought it over, and one day she told Sonia, 'If you don't stop getting in my way every time I come to the mirror, Sonia, why, I'll never get out of your way, either.' "

"So then what?"

"That's just what Sophia did. Every time Sonia, the little girl who never talked, came to the mirror to comb her hair, so did Sophia. And everything Sonia did, Sophia copied her right back."

No. I don't think so. I think they both did something else. They simply went away from each other.

It can't be. I can't go through that horror again.

What is the matter with him? Is he insane? I can't fall over that terrible cliff again.

Can he ever change and grow up? He's been all right since the Stoltz girl. I thought that would be the last, because she had to be the last. There is a limit beyond which nerves cannot be bruised and torn, and still live. If that is what it is, I cannot endure it again.

Is he quite sane? He can't be, to be so blind.

"I have a best friend," Georgia announced.

"I should hope so."

"A new one."

"What do you and your best friend do?"

"We play games. But sometimes she steals my crayons. Her name's Pauline."

"I see. And then what happens?"

It was too pat, like something rehearsed and coming out of a machine, a radio or a phonograph.

The horn of the school bus sounded and Georgia jumped up. I dabbed at her face with my napkin, then followed her into the hall where she rushed for her school bag, contents one drawing pad, one picture book, and the last time I looked into it, a handful of loose beads, some forgotten peanuts, the broken top of a fountain pen.

I stood there for a moment after I kissed her good-bye and she ran down the walk. Perhaps I was wrong.

I had to be wrong. I would be wrong. Until I was forced to be otherwise.

On my way back to the breakfast room I saw the last issue of *Newsways*, and remembered something. I brought it with me.

"George," I said, "you forgot to bring home a *Newsways*."

He went on with his eggs and coffee and said, absently: "It slipped my mind. I'll bring one home tonight without fail. And *Personalities*, just off."

"Never mind the *Newsways*, I bought one yesterday." He looked at me and saw the magazine, and for just an instant there was something strange and drawn in his face I had never seen before, then it was gone so quickly I wasn't sure it had been there at all. "There's something in it I meant to ask you about. Did you read the article about Louise Patterson?"

"Yes, I read it."

"It's grand, isn't it? It's just what you've been saying for years." I quoted a sentence from the article. " 'Homunculus grows to monstrous size, with all the force of a major explosion, by grace of a new talent suddenly shooting meteorlike across the otherwise turgid skies of the contemporary art world. Louise Patterson may view her models through a microscope, but the brush she wields is Gargantuan.' "

"Yes, it's grand. But it is not what I've been saying for years."

"Anyway, they recognize her talent. Don't be so critical, just because they use different words than you would. At least they admit she's a great painter, don't they?"

"That they do."

Something was away off key. The words were meant to be lightly skeptical, but the tone of his voice was simply flat.

"For heaven's sake, George, don't pretend you aren't pleased. You must have seven or eight Pattersons, and now they're all terribly valuable."

"Priceless. I believe that's the *Newsways* term for them." He dropped his napkin and stood up. "I'll have to run. I think I'll drive in as usual, unless you need the car."

"No, of course not. But wait, George. Here's one thing more." I found another paragraph in the same article, and read from it. " 'This week interest of the art world centered in the whereabouts of Patterson's lost masterpiece, her famed *Judas*, admittedly the most highly prized canvas of all among the priceless works that have come from the studio of this artist. Depicting two huge hands exchanging a coin, a consummate study in flaming yellow, red, and tawny brown, this composition was widely known some years ago, then it quietly dropped from view.' And so on."

I looked up from the magazine. George said: "Neat but not gaudy. They make it sound like a rainbow at midnight."

"That's not what I'm driving at. Would you know anything about that picture?"

"Why should I?"

"Didn't I see an unframed picture you brought home, about a week ago, something like that?"

"You sure did, Georgie-porgie. A copy of it."

"Oh, well. What became of it?"

George winked at me, but there was nothing warm in back of it. There was nothing at all. Just something blank.

"Took it to the office, of course. Where do you think those plumbers got such an accurate description of the original?" He patted my shoulder and gave me a quick kiss. "I'll have to step on it. I'll call you this afternoon."

When he'd gone, and I heard the car go down the driveway, I put down the magazine and slowly got up. I went out to Nellie in the kitchen, knowing how it feels to be old, really old.

Emory Mafferson

I'D NEVER known Stroud very well until recently, and for that matter I didn't know him now. Consequently, I couldn't guess how, or whether, he fitted the Janoth pattern.

When he told me not to be the *Crimeways* type, that meant nothing. This was standard counsel on all of our publications, and for all I knew, Stroud was merely another of the many keen, self-centered, ambitious people in the organization who moved from office to office, from alliance to alliance, from one ethical or political fashion to another, never with any real interest in life except to get more money next year than this, and always more than his colleagues did.

Yet I had a feeling Stroud was not that simple. All I knew about him, in fact, was that he considered himself pretty smooth, seemed to value his own wit, and never bought anything we manufactured here.

Neither did I. Until now.

Leon Temple was in Stroud's office when I came in late that Monday morning, asking Stroud to O.K. an order for some money he swore he had to have for this new, hysterical assignment nearly everyone except myself seemed to be working on. From what I gathered, Temple did nothing but loaf around the cocktail lounge of the Van Barth with a nice little wisp of a thing by the name of Janet Clark. Roaming around the office and trying to figure the best approach to Stroud, I felt like an outsider. They were having one long, happy party, while I spent my days in the ancient Homicide Bureau or the crumbling ruins of the District Attorney's office.

When Stroud signed the order for cash and Leon Temple had gone, I went over and lifted myself to the window ledge in back of his desk. He swung his chair around and in the cross-light I saw what I had not noticed before, that the man's face was lined and hard.

"Anything new, Emory?" he asked.

"Well. Yes. Largely routine stuff. But I wanted to talk about something else."

"Shoot."

"Do you know about the strange thing that happened a week ago last Saturday night?"

"The night of the murder?"

"Yes. But this is about Funded Individuals. I met Fred Steichel, M.E. of Jennett-Donohue, that night. Do you know him?"

"I've met him. But I don't know what you are referring to."

"Well, I know Fred pretty well. His wife and mine were classmates, and still see a lot of each other. We met at a dinner, and there was quite a party afterwards. Fred got drunk, and he began to tell me all about Funded Individuals. In fact, he knew as much about it as I did."

Stroud showed no great concern. "No reason why he shouldn't. It isn't a profound secret. Anything like that gets around."

"Sure, in a general way. But this was different. Fred's all right when he's sober, but he's obnoxious when he's drunk, and that night he was deliberately trying to make himself about as unpleasant as possible. It amused him to recite our computations, quote the conclusions we'd reached, and even repeat some of the angles we'd tried out for a while and then abandoned. The point is, he had the exact figures, the precise steps we'd taken, and he had, for instance, a lot of the phrases I'd personally used in my reports. Not just generally correct, but absolutely verbatim. In other words, there was a leak somewhere, and he'd seen the actual research, the reports, and the findings."

"And then?"

"Well, I got pretty sore. It's one thing that Jennett-Donohue hears rumors about what we're doing, but it's another thing if they have access to supposedly confidential records. I mean, what the hell? I just didn't like the way Fred talked about Funded Individuals. As though it's a dead pigeon. According to him, I was wasting my time. It was only a matter of weeks or days before the whole scheme would be shelved. So the more I thought it over, the less I liked it. He didn't get that data just by accident, and his cockiness wasn't based entirely on a few drinks."

Stroud nodded.

"I see. And you thought it's something we ought to know about."

"I did, and I do. I don't pretend to understand it, but it's my baby, I invested a lot of work in it, and it's something more than the run-of-the-mill mirages we put together around here. It fascinates me. There's something about it almost real." Stroud was at least listening with interest, if not agreement, and I pressed the argument. "It's not just another inspirational arrow shot into the air. This is a cash-and-carry business. And the minute you know there can be a society in which every individual has an actual monetary value of one million dollars, and he's returning dividends on himself, you also know that nobody is going to shoot, starve, or ruin that perfectly sound investment."

Stroud gave me a faint, understanding, but wintry smile.

"I know," he said. "All right, I'll tell Hagen or Earl about this peculiar seepage of our confidential material."

"But that's the point, I already did. That was the strange thing about that Saturday night. I phoned you first, and I couldn't reach you, then I phoned Hagen. He was in, and he agreed with me that it was damn important. He said he would take it up with Earl, and he wanted to see me the first thing Monday morning. Then I didn't hear another word from him."

Stroud leaned back in his chair, studying me, and plainly puzzled. "You called Hagen that night?"

"I had to let somebody know."

"Of course. What time did you call?"

"Almost immediately. I told Steichel I would, and the bastard just laughed."

"Yes, but what time?"

"Well, about ten-thirty. Why?"

"And you talked only to Hagen? You didn't talk to Earl, did you?"

"I didn't talk to him, no. But he must have been there at the time I called. That's where he was that night, you know."

Stroud looked away from me, frowning.

"Yes, I know," he said, in a very tired, distant voice. "But exactly what did Hagen say, do you recall?"

"Not exactly. He told me he would take it up with Earl.

That's a double-check on Earl's whereabouts, isn't it? And Hagen said he would see me Monday morning. But on Monday morning I didn't hear from him, I haven't heard from him since, and I began to wonder what happened. I thought maybe he'd relayed the whole matter to you."

"No, I'm sorry, he didn't. But I'll follow it up, of course. I quite agree with you, it's important. And with Hagen." I saw again that wintry smile, this time subzero. "A human life valued at a million paper dollars would make something of a story, wouldn't it? Don't worry, Emory, your dreamchild will not be lost."

He was one of those magnetic bastards I have always admired and liked, and of course envied and hated, and I found myself, stupidly, believing him. I knew it couldn't be true, but I actually believed he was genuinely interested in protecting Funded Individuals, and would find a way, somehow, to give it a full hearing and then, in the end, contrive for it a big, actual trial. I smiled, digging some notes out of my pocket, and said: "Well, that's all I wanted to talk about. Now, here's the latest dope the cops have on the Delos murder. I already told you they know she was out of town from late Friday until the following Saturday afternoon." Stroud gave a half nod, and concentrated his attention. I went on: "Yesterday they found out where she was. She was in Albany, with a man. There was a book of matches found in her apartment, from a night club in Albany that doesn't circulate its matches from coast to coast, only there on the spot, and in the course of a routine check-up with Albany hotels, they found that's where she actually was. Got it?"

He nodded, briefly, waiting and remote and again hard. I said: "The cops know all about this job you're doing here, by the way, and they're convinced the man you are looking for and the man who was with Delos last Friday and Saturday in Albany is one and the same person. Does that help or hinder you any?"

He said: "Go on."

"That's about all. They are sending a man up there this afternoon or tomorrow morning, with a lot of photographs which he will check with the night club, the hotel, and elsewhere. I told you they had the Delos woman's address book.

Well, this morning they let me look at it. They've been round-ing up pictures of every man mentioned on this extensive list of hers, and most likely the guy that was with her in Albany is one of them. Do you follow me?"

"I follow you."

"They know from the general description of this man, as they got it over the phone from the personnel of the hotel and the club up there, that he most definitely was not Janoth. At the hotel, they were registered as Mr. and Mrs. Andrew Phelps-Guyon, a phoney if there ever was one. Does the name mean anything to you?"

"No."

"Your name was in the woman's address book, by the way."

"Yes," he said. "I knew Pauline Delos."

"Well, that's all."

Stroud seemed to be considering the information I had given him.

"That's fine, Emory," he said, and flashed me a quick, heat-less smile. "By the way, is the department looking for a pho-tograph of me?"

"No. They've already got one. Something you once turned in for a license or a passport. The man they are sending up-state has quite a collection. He has fifty or sixty photographs."

"I see."

"I can go along to Albany with this fellow, if you like," I said. "If he doesn't accomplish anything else, I imagine he'll be able to identify the man you've been hunting for, your-self."

"I'm sure he will," he said. "But don't bother. I think that can be done better right here."

George Stroud IX

THE TWO LINES of investigation, the organization's and the official one, drew steadily together like invisible pincers. I could feel them closing.

I told myself it was just a tool, a vast machine, and the machine was blind. But I had not fully realized its crushing weight and power. That was insane. The machine cannot be challenged. It both creates and blots out, doing each with glacial impersonality. It measures people in the same way that it measures money, and the growth of trees, the life-span of mosquitoes and morals, the advance of time. And when the hour strikes, on the big clock, that is indeed the hour, the day, the correct time. When it says a man is right, he is right, and when it finds him wrong, he is through, with no appeal. It is as deaf as it is blind.

Of course, I had asked for this.

I returned to the office from a lunch I could not remember having tasted. It had been intended as an interlude to plan for new eventualities and new avenues of escape.

The Janoth Building, covering half of a block, looked into space with five hundred sightless eyes as I turned again, of my own free will, and delivered myself once more to its stone intestines. The interior of this giant God was spick and span, restfully lighted, filled with the continuous echo of many feet. A visitor would have thought it nice.

Waiting for me, on my desk, I found the list of nonrenewed licenses for out-of-town taverns, for six years ago. I knew this was the one that would have my own name. That would have to be taken care of later. Right now, I could do nothing but stuff it into the bottom drawer of my desk.

I went into Roy's room and asked him: "Starved?"

"Considerably, considerably."

"The St. Bernards have arrived." He slowly stood up, rolled down the sleeves of his shirt. "Sorry if I kept you waiting. Any developments?"

"Not that I know of, but Hagen wants to see you. Maybe I'd better postpone lunch until you've talked with him."

"All right. But I don't think I'll keep you waiting."

I went upstairs. These conferences had daily become longer, more frequent, and more bitter. It was cold comfort to have a clear understanding of the abyss that Hagen and Janoth, particularly Janoth, saw before them.

For the hundredth time I asked myself why Earl had done this thing. What could possibly have happened on that night, in that apartment? God, what a price to pay. But it had happened. And I recognized that I wasn't really thinking of Janoth, at all, but of myself.

When I stepped into Hagen's office he handed me a note, an envelope, and a photograph.

"This just came in," he said. "We're giving the picture a half-page cut in *Newsways*, with a follow-up story."

The note and the envelope were on the stationery of a Fifty-seventh Street gallery. The photograph, a good, clear 4×6, displayed one wall of a Louise Patterson exhibition, with five of her canvases clearly reproduced. The note, from the dealer, simply declared the photograph had been taken at a show nine years ago, and was, as far as known, the only authentic facsimile of the picture mentioned by *Newsways* as lost.

There could be no mistaking the two hands of my *Judas.* It was right in the middle. The dealer duly pointed out, however, that its original proper title was simply: *Study in Fundamentals.*

The canvas at the extreme right, though I recognized none of the others, was the *Study in Fury* that hung on my wall downstairs.

"This seems to answer the description," I said.

"Beyond any doubt. When we run that, quoting the dealer, I'm certain we'll uncover the actual picture." Maybe. It was still concealed behind another canvas on Marble Road. But I knew that if Georgette saw the follow-up, and she would, my story of finding a copy of it would not hold. For the photograph would be reproduced as the only known authentic facsimile. "But I hope to God we have the whole thing cleaned up long before then." I tensed as he looked at the photograph again, certain he would recognize the *Fury*. But he didn't. He laid it down, regarded me with a stare made out of acid. "George, what in hell's wrong? This has drifted along more than a week."

"It took us three weeks to find Isleman," I said.

"We're not looking for a man missing several months. We're looking for somebody that vanished a week ago, leaving a trail a mile wide. Something's the matter. What is it?" But, without waiting for an answer, he discarded the question, and began to check off our current leads. "How about those lapsed licenses?"

I said they were still coming in, and I was cross-checking them as fast as they were received. Methodically, then, we went over all the ground we had covered before. By now it was hash. I'd done a good job making it so.

Before leaving I asked about Earl, and learned he was out of the hospital, after two days. And that was all I learned.

I returned to my office about an hour after I had come upstairs. When I walked in I found Roy, Leon Temple, and Phil Best. It was apparent, the second I stepped into the room, there had been a break.

"We've got him," said Leon.

His small and usually colorless face was all lit up. I knew I would never breathe again.

"Where is he?"

"Right here. He came into this building just a little while ago."

"Who is he?"

"We don't know yet. But we've got him." I waited, watching him, and he explained: "I slipped some cash to the staff of the Van Barth, let them know there'd be some more, and they've all been looking around this district in their free hours. One of the porters picked him up and followed him here."

I nodded, feeling as though I'd been kicked in the stomach.

"Nice work," I said. "Where is this porter now?"

"Downstairs. When he phoned me, I told him to watch the elevators and follow the guy if he came out. He hasn't. Now Phil's bringing over the antique dealer, Eddy is bringing a waitress from Gil's, and then we'll have all six banks of elevators completely covered. I've told the special cops what to do when our man tries to leave. They'll grab him and make him identify himself from his first birthday up to now."

"Yes," I said. "I guess that's that." It was as though they had treed an animal, and that, in fact, was just the case. I was the animal. I said: "That's smart stuff, Leon. You used your head."

"Dick and Mike are down on the main floor, helping the fellow from the Van Barth. In about two minutes we'll have every door and exit covered, too."

I suddenly reached for my coat, but didn't go through with it. I couldn't, now, it was too late. Instead, I pulled out some cigarettes, moved around in back of my desk and sat down.

"You're certain it's the right man?" I asked.

But of course there was no question. I had been seen on my way back from lunch. And followed.

"The porter is positive."

"All right," I said. The phone rang and mechanically I answered it. It was Dick, reporting that they now had the elevators fully covered. In addition to the porter, a night bartender at the Van Barth, Gil's waitress, and the dealer had all arrived. "All right," I said again. "Stay with it. You know what to do."

Methodically, Phil Best explained, in his shrewish voice, what was unmistakably plain.

"If he doesn't come out during the afternoon, we're sure to pick him up at five-thirty, when the building empties." I nodded, but my stunned and scattered thoughts were beginning to pull themselves together. "It'll be jammed, as usual, but we can have every inch of the main floor covered."

"He's in the bag," I said. "We can't miss. I'm going to stay right here until we get him. I'll send out for supper, and if necessary I'll sleep upstairs in the restroom on the twenty-seventh floor. Personally, I'm not going to leave this office until we've got it all sewed up. How about the rest of you?"

I wasn't listening to what they replied.

Even Roy would know that if a man came into a building, and didn't go out, he must logically still be inside of it. And this inescapable conclusion must eventually be followed by one and only one logical course of action.

Sooner or later my staff must go through the building, floor by floor and office by office, looking for the only man in it who never went home.

It wouldn't take long, when they did that. The only question was, who would be the first to make the suggestion.

Louise Patterson

THIS TIME when I answered the doorbell, which had been ringing steadily for the last four days, I found that tall, thin, romantic squirt, Mr. Klausmeyer, from that awful magazine. It was his third visit, but I didn't mind. He was such a polite, dignified worm, much stuffier than anyone I'd ever met before, he gave my apartment a crazy atmosphere of respectability or something.

"I hope I'm not disturbing you, Mrs. Patterson," he said, making the same mistake he'd made before.

"MISS Patterson," I shrieked, laughing. "You are, but come in. Haven't you caught your murderer yet?"

"We aren't looking for any murderer, Miss Patterson. I have told you the—"

"Save that for *Hokum Fact's* regular subscribers," I said. "Sit down."

He carefully circled around the four children, where the two younger ones, Pete's and Mike's, were helping the older pair, Ralph's, as they sawed and hammered away at some boards and boxes and wheels, building a wagon, or maybe it was some new kind of scooter. Mr. Klausmeyer carefully hitched up his pants, he would, before sitting down in the big leather chair that had once been a rocker.

"You have us confused with *True Facts*," he firmly corrected me. "That's another outfit altogether, not in the same field with any of our publications. I'm with Janoth Enterprises. Until recently I was on the staff of *Personalities*." With wonderful irony he added, "I'm sure you've heard of it. Perhaps you've even read it. But right now I'm working on a special—"

"I know, Mr. Klausmeyer. You wrote that article about me in *Newsways Bunk*." He looked so mad that if he hadn't come because of his job I'm sure he would have gotten up and gone like a bat out of hell. "Never mind," I said, simply whooping. "I enjoyed it, Mr. Klausmeyer. Really I did. And I appreciated it, too, even if you did get it all cockeyed, and I know you didn't really mean any of those nice things you tried to say about me. I know you're just looking for that murderer. Would you like some muscatel? It's all I have."

I dragged out what was left of a gallon of muscatel and found one of my few remaining good tumblers. It was almost clean.

"No, thank you," he said. "About that article, Miss Patterson—"

"Not even a little?"

"No, really. But regarding the article—"

"It isn't very good," I admitted. "I mean the wine," I explained, then I realized I was simply bellowing, and felt aghast. Mr. Klausmeyer hadn't done anything to me, he looked like the sensitive type who takes everything personally, and the least I could do was to refrain from insulting him. I made up my mind to act exactly like an artist should. I poured myself a glass of the muscatel and urged him, quite gently, "I do wish you'd join me."

"No, thanks. Miss Patterson, I didn't write that article in *Newsways.*"

"Oh, you didn't?"

"No."

"Well, I thought it was a perfectly wonderful story." It came to me that I'd said the wrong thing again, and I simply howled. "I mean, within limits. Please, Mr. Klausmeyer, don't mind me. I'm not used to having my pictures labeled 'costly.' Or was it 'invaluable'? The one the murderer bought for fifty bucks."

Mr. Klausmeyer was mad, I could see, and probably I was boring him besides. I swore I would keep my mouth shut and act reasonably for at least fifteen minutes, no matter what he said, and no matter how I felt. Fifteen minutes. That's not so long.

"I merely supplied some of the information," Mr. Klausmeyer carefully explained. "For instance, I supplied the *Newsways* writer with the description of the *Judas* picture, exactly as you gave it to me."

The son of a bitch.

"God damn it all," I screamed, "where do you get that *Judas* stuff? I told you the name of the picture was *Study in Fundamentals.* What in hell do you mean by giving my own picture some fancy title I never thought of at all? How do you dare, you horrible little worm, how do you dare to throw your idiocy all over my work?"

I looked at him through a haze of rage. He was another picture burner. I could tell it just by looking at his white, stuffy face. Another one of those decent, respectable maniacs who'd like nothing better than to take a butcher knife and slash canvases, slop them with paint, burn them. By God, he looked exactly like Pete. No, Pete's way had been to use them to cover up broken window panes, plug up draughts, and stop leaks in the ceiling. He was more the official type. His method would be to bury them in an authorized warehouse somewhere, destroy the records, and let them stay there forever.

I drank off the muscatel, poured myself some more, and tried to listen to him.

"I did use your own title, I assure you, but there must have been a slip somewhere in the writing and editing. That will be corrected in a story *Newsways* is now running, with a photograph of the *Study in Fundamentals.*"

"I know you, you damned arsonist." His large gray eyes bugged out just the way Ralph's had when he showed me the pile of scraps and ashes and charred fragments, all that was left of five years' work, heaped up in the fireplace. How proud he'd been. You really amount to something, I guess, if you know how to destroy something new and creative. "What do you want now?" I demanded. "Why do you come here?"

I saw that Mr. Klausmeyer was quite pale. I guess if he hadn't been a tame caterpillar doing an errand for *Anything But the News* he would have picked up Elroy's scout hatchet and taken a swing at me.

"We've located the man who bought your picture, Miss Patterson," he said, with great control. "We believe we know where he is, and he'll be found at any moment. We wish you'd come to the office, so that you can identify him. Of course, we'll pay you for your time and trouble. We'll give you a hundred dollars if you can help us. Will you?"

"So you've found the murderer," I said.

With emphatic weariness, Mr. Klausmeyer repeated: "We are not looking for a murderer, Miss Patterson. I assure you, we want this man in some altogether different connection."

"Crap," I said.

"I beg your pardon?"

"Nonsense. Detectives have been around here, asking me the same questions you have. You are both looking for the same man, the one who bought my picture, and murdered that Delos woman. What do you think I am? Apparently you think I'm a complete dope."

"No," Mr. Klausmeyer told me, strongly. "Anything but that. Will you come back to the office with me?"

A hundred dollars was a hundred dollars.

"I don't know why I should help to catch a man with brains enough to like my *Study in Fundamentals.* I haven't got so many admirers I can afford to let any of them go to the electric chair."

Mr. Klausmeyer's face showed that he fully agreed, and it pained him that he couldn't say so.

"But perhaps we can help you reclaim your picture. You wanted to buy it back, didn't you?"

"No. I didn't want to buy it back, I just didn't want it to rot in that black hole of Calcutta."

And I knew no one would ever see that picture again. It was already at the bottom of the East River. The murderer would have to do away with it to save his own hide. He would get rid of anything that connected him with the dead woman.

Yet one more noble little angel of destruction.

I realized this, feeling mad and yet somehow cold. It was no use telling myself that I didn't care. The canvas was not one of my best. And yet I did care. It was hard enough to paint the things, without trying to defend them afterwards from self-appointed censors and jealous lovers and microscopic deities. Like Mr. Klausmeyer.

"All right," I said. "I'll go. But only for the hundred dollars."

Mr. Klausmeyer rose like something popping out of a box. God, he was elegant. When he died they wouldn't have to embalm him. The fluid already ran in his veins.

"Certainly," he said, warmly.

I looked around and found my best hat on the top shelf of the bookcases. Edith, who was four—she was Mike's—scolded me for taking away her bird's nest. I explained the nest would be back in place before nightfall. Leaving, I put the whole trading-post in charge of Ralph junior until further notice. He looked up, and I think he even heard me. Anyway, he understood.

In a taxi, on the way to his office, Mr. Klausmeyer tried to be friendly.

"Splendid children," he told me. "Very bright and healthy. I don't believe you told me much about your husband?"

"I've never been married," I said, again shrieking with laughter, against my will. God, I would learn how to act refined, beginning tomorrow, if it was the last thing I ever did. "They're all LOVE children, Mr. Klausmeyer." He sat so straight and earnest and looking so sophisticated I had to postpone my graduation from kindergarten for at least another minute. And then I had that awful sinking sensation, knowing I'd behaved like a perfect fool. As of course I was. Nobody knew that better than I did. But Mr. Klausmeyer was so perfect, I wondered if he could possibly know it. Probably not. Perfect people never understand much about anything.

"Excuse me, Mr. Klausmeyer, if I confide in you. I've never done it before. There's something about you *Factways* people that seems to invite all kinds of confidences."

I suppose this lie was just too transparent, for he said nothing at all, and a moment later we were getting out of the cab, Mr. Klausmeyer looking just too pleased and preoccupied for words because he would soon be rid of me. God damn him. If I'd been dressed when he arrived, if I'd really wanted to make an impression, I could have had him under my thumb in five seconds. But who wanted to have an angleworm under her thumb?

I was drunk and sedate for the whole three minutes it took us to enter the building and ride up in the elevator. Dignity was a game two could play at. But after I'd used up mine, and we got out of the elevator, I asked: "Just what am I supposed to do, Mr. Klausmeyer? Besides collect a hundred dollars?"

Of course, without meaning to, I'd cut loose with another raucous laugh.

"Don't worry about your hundred dollars," he said, shortly. "The man who bought your picture is somewhere in this building. It is just a question of time, until we locate him. All you have to do is identify him when we do locate him."

I was suddenly awfully sick of Mr. Klausmeyer, the detectives who'd been questioning me, and the whole insane affair. What business was it of mine, all of this? I had just one business in life, to paint pictures. If other people got pleasure out of destroying them, let them; perhaps that was the way they expressed their own creative instincts. They probably referred to the best ones they suppressed or ruined as their outstanding masterpieces.

It was a black thought, and I knew it was not in the right perspective. As Mr. Klausmeyer put his hand on the knob of an office door, and pushed it open, I said: "You must be a dreadfully cynical and sophisticated person, Mr. Klausmeyer. Don't you ever long for a breath of good, clean, wholesome, natural fresh air?"

He gave me a polite, but emotional glare.

"I've always avoided being cynical," he said. "Up until now."

We entered a room filled with a lot of other office angleworms.

"How many children have you got, Mr. Klausmeyer?" I asked, intending to speak in a low voice, but evidently I was yelling, because a lot of people turned around and looked at us.

"Two," he whispered, but it sounded like he was swearing. Then he put on a smile and brought me forward. But as I crossed the room, and looked around it, my attention was abruptly centered upon a picture on the wall. It was one of mine. *Study in Fury.* It was amazing. I could hardly believe it. "George," Mr. Klausmeyer was saying, "this is Miss Patterson, the artist." It was beautifully framed, too. "Miss Patterson, this is George Stroud, who has charge of our investigation. She's agreed to stay here until we have the man we want. She can give us some help, I believe."

A good-looking angleworm got up in back of a desk and came forward and shook hands with me.

"Miss Patterson," he said. "This is an unexpected pleasure."

I looked at him, and started to bellow, but lost my breath. Something was quite mad. It was the murderer, the very same man who bought the picture in the Third Avenue junkshop.

"How d'you do?" I said. I turned to Mr. Klausmeyer, but Mr. Klausmeyer just looked tired and relieved. I stared back at Mr. Stroud. "Well," I said, uncertainly, "what can I do for you?"

For the fraction of a second we looked at each other with complete realization. I knew who he was, and he knew that I knew. But I couldn't understand it, and I hesitated.

This ordinary, bland, rather debonair and inconsequential person had killed that Delos woman? It didn't seem possible. Where would he get the nerve? What would he know about the terrible, intense moments of life? I must be mistaken. I must have misunderstood the whole situation. But it was the same man. There was no doubt about it.

His eyes were like craters, and I saw that their sockets were hard and drawn and icy cold, in spite of the easy smile he showed. I knew this, and at the same time I knew no one else in the room was capable of knowing it, because they were all like poor Mr. Klausmeyer, perfect.

"It's very kind of you to help us," he said. "I imagine Don explained what we're doing."

"Yes." My knees were suddenly trembling. This was away over my head, all of it. "I know everything, Mr. Stroud. I really do."

"I don't doubt it," he said. "I'm sure you do."

Why didn't somebody do something to break this afternoon nightmare? Of course it was a nightmare. Why didn't somebody admit it was all a stupid joke? What fantastic lie would this Stroud person invent, plausible as all hell, if I chose to identify him here and now?

I gave an automatic, raucous laugh, yanked my hand away from his, and said: "Anyway, I'm glad somebody likes my *Study in Fury*."

"Yes, I like it very much," said the murderer.

"It's yours?" I squeaked.

"Of course. I like all of your work."

There were about five people in the office, though it

seemed more like fifty, and now they all turned to look at the *Fury*. Mr. Klausmeyer said: "I'll be damned. It really is Miss Patterson's picture. Why didn't you tell us, George?"

He shrugged.

"Tell you what? What is there to tell? I liked it, bought it, and there it is. It's been there for a couple of years."

Mr. Klausmeyer looked at the Stroud person with renewed interest, while the rest of them gaped at me as though for the first time convinced I was an artist.

"Would you care for a drink, Miss Patterson?" the murderer invited me. He was actually smiling. But I saw it was not a smile, only the desperate imitation of one.

I swallowed once, with a mouth that was harsh and dry, then I couldn't help the feeble, half-measure of a roar that came out of me. Even as I laughed, I knew I wasn't laughing. It was plain hysteria.

"Where in hell's my *Study in Fundamentals*?" I demanded. "The one your lousy magazine calls *Judas*."

Stroud was very still and white. The others were only blank. Mr. Klausmeyer said, to Stroud: "I told her we'd try to get the picture back for her." To me, he patiently explained, "I didn't say we had it, Miss Patterson. I meant that we'd automatically find the picture when we found the man."

"Will you?" I said, looking hard at Stroud. "I think more likely it's been destroyed."

Something moved in that rigid face of his, fixed in its casual, counterfeit smile.

"No," he said, at last. "I don't think so, Miss Patterson. I have reason to believe your picture is quite safe." He turned back to his desk and lifted the phone. Holding it, he gave me a hard, uncompromising stare it was impossible for me to misconstrue. "It will be recovered," he told me. "Provided everything else goes off all right. Do you fully understand?"

"Yes," I said. God damn him. He was actually blackmailing me. It was me who should be blackmailing him. In fact, I would. "It damn well better be safe. I understand it's worth thousands and thousands of dollars."

He nodded.

"We think so. Now, what would you like to drink?"

"She likes muscatel," said Mr. Klausmeyer.

"Rye," I yelled. What did I care why he killed her? If the *Fury* was safe, probably the *Fundamentals* was safe, too, and it actually was worth a lot of money—now. And if it wasn't safe, I could always talk up later. Besides, he really did collect my pictures. "Not just one. A whole lot. Order a dozen."

It would take something to stay in the same room with a murderer. And at the same time remember that dignity paid, at least in public.

George Stroud X

SOMETIME very early I woke on a couch I'd had moved into my office, put on my shoes and necktie, the only clothing I'd removed, and in a mental cloud moved over to my desk.

My watch said a few minutes after eight. Today was the day. I still didn't know how I would meet it. But I knew it was the day. The police would finish the check-up in Albany. Somebody would think of combing the building.

Yesterday should have been the day, and why it wasn't, I would never really know. When that Patterson woman walked in here I should have been through. I knew why she hadn't identified me, the fact that I had not destroyed her picture, and my threat that I still would, if she opened her mouth. Artists are curious. I shuddered when I thought how close I'd come, actually, to getting rid of that canvas. She could still make trouble, any time she felt like it, and maybe she would. She was erratic enough. At about eight in the evening she'd packed herself off. But she might be back. At any moment, for any reason, she might change her mind.

Nobody answered when I pressed the button for a copy boy, and at last I phoned the drugstore downstairs. Eventually I got my sandwich and my quart of black coffee. In Roy's office, Harry Slater and Alvin Dealey were keeping the death watch.

Shortly before nine the rest of the staff began to come in. Leon Temple arrived, and then Roy, Englund, and Don and Eddy reached the office almost simultaneously.

"Why don't you go home?" Roy asked me. "There's nothing you can do now, is there?"

I shook my head. "I'm staying."

"You want to be in at the finish?"

"Right. How's everything downstairs?"

Leon Temple said: "Tighter than a drum. Phil Best has just spelled Mike. We've got the whole night side of the Van Barth down there, and some more special cops. I don't understand it."

This was it. I felt it coming. "What don't you understand?" I asked.

"Why that guy hasn't come out. What the hell. He's here, but where is he?"

"Maybe he left before we threw a line around the place," I said.

"Not a chance."

"He may have simply walked in one door and out the other," I argued. "Perhaps he knew he was being followed."

"No," said Leon. "That porter followed him right to the elevator. He took an express. He could be anywhere above the eighteenth floor. For all we know, he's somewhere up here in our own organization."

"What can we do about it?" Englund asked.

"He'll show," I said.

"I thought time was essential, George," Roy reminded me.

"It is."

"It occurs to me," said Leon, "if he doesn't show—" So it was going to be Leon Temple. I looked at him and waited. "We could take those eyewitnesses, with the building police, and some of our own men, and go through the whole place from top to bottom. We could cover every office. That would settle it. It would take a couple of hours, but we'd know."

I had to appear to consider the idea. It already looked bad that I hadn't suggested it myself. I nodded, and said: "You have something."

"Well, shall we do it?"

If I knew where those eyewitnesses were, if I could be informed of their progress from floor to floor and from suite to suite, there might still be a way. No game is over until the whistle blows.

"Get started," I said. "You handle this, Leon. And I want you to keep me informed of every move. Let me know what floor you start on, which direction you're working, and where you're going next."

"O.K.," he said. "First, we'll get witnesses and cops on every floor above eighteen. They'll cover the stairs, the elevators, and I'll have them be careful to watch people moving from office to office, the mail-chutes, johns, closets—everything." I nodded, but didn't speak. "I think that would be right, don't you?"

God, what a price. Here was the bill, and it had to be paid. Of course this was whining, but I knew no man on earth ever watched his whole life go to bits and pieces, carrying with it the lives of those close to him also down into ashes, without a silent protest. The man who really accepts his fate, really bows without a quiver to the big gamble he has made and lost, that is a lie, a myth. There is no such man, there never has been, never will be.

"All right," I said. "Keep me informed."

"I'd like to take Dick and Eddy and Don. And some more, as soon as they come in."

"Take them."

"And I think those witnesses should be encouraged."

"Pay them. I'll give you a voucher." I signed my name to a cashier's form, leaving the amount blank, and tossed it to Leon. "Good hunting," I said, and I think I created a brief smile.

Pretty soon the office was empty, and then Leon called to say they were going through the eighteenth floor, with all exits closed and all down-elevators being stopped for inspection. There was just one way to go. Up.

I had a half-formed idea that there might be some safety in the very heart of the enemy's territory, Steve's or Earl's offices on the thirty-second floor, and I was trying to hit upon a way to work it when the phone rang and it was Steve himself. His voice was blurred and strained, and somehow bewildered, as he asked me to come up there at once.

In Hagen's office I found, besides Steve, Earl Janoth and our chief attorney, Ralph Beeman, with John Wayne, the organization's biggest stockholder, and four other editors. And then I saw Fred Steichel, M.E. of Jennett-Donohue. All of them looked stunned and slightly embarrassed. Except Steichel, who seemed apologetic, and Earl, who radiated more than his customary assurance. He came forward and heartily shook my hand, and I saw that the self-confidence was, instead, nervous tension mounting to near hysteria.

"George," he said. "This makes me very glad." I don't

think he really saw me, though, and I don't believe he saw, actually saw, anyone else in the room as he turned and went on, "I see no reason why we should wait. What I have to say now can be drawn up and issued to the entire staff later, expressing my regret that I could not have the pleasure of speaking to each and every one of them personally." I sat down and looked at the fascinated faces around me. They sensed, as I did, the one and only thing that could be impending. "As you may know, there have been certain differences on our controlling board, as to the editorial policies of Janoth publications. I have consistently worked and fought for free, flexible, creative journalism, not only as I saw it, but as every last member of the staff saw it. I want to say now I think this policy was correct, and I am proud of our record, proud that I have enlisted the services of so much talent." He paused to look at Hagen, who looked at no one as he stonily concentrated upon a scramble of lines and circles on the pad before him. "But the controlling board does not agree that my policies have been for the best interests of the organization. And the recent tragedy, of which you are all aware, has increased the opposition's mistrust of my leadership. Under the circumstances, I cannot blame them. Rather than jeopardize the future of the entire venture, I have consented to step aside, and to permit a merger with the firm of Jennett-Donohue. I hope you will all keep alive the spirit of the old organization in the new one. I hope you will give to Mr. Steichel, your new managing editor, the same loyalty you gave to Steve and myself."

Then the attorney, Beeman, took up the same theme and elaborated upon it, and then Wayne began to talk about Earl's step as being temporary, and that everyone looked to his early return. He was still speaking when the door opened and Leon Temple stepped inside. I went over to him.

"We've drawn a blank so far," he told me. "But just to be sure, I think we should go through both Janoth's and Hagen's offices."

In the second that the door opened and shut, I saw a knot of people in the corridor, a porter from Gil's and a waiter from the Van Barth among them.

"Drop it," I said. "The assignment is killed."

Leon's gaze went slowly around the room, absorbing a scene that might have been posed in some historical museum. His eyes came back to me, and I nodded.

"You mean, send them all away?"

"Send them away. We are having a big change. It is the same as Pompeii."

Back in the room I heard Wayne say to Hagen: "—either the Paris bureau, or the Vienna bureau. I imagine you can have either one, if you want it."

"I'll think it over," Hagen told him.

"The organization comes ahead of everything," Earl was too jovially and confidently reiterating. It was both ghastly and yet heroic. "Whatever happens, that must go on. It is bigger than I am, bigger than any one of us. I won't see it injured or even endangered."

Our new managing editor, Steichel, was the only person who seemed to be on the sidelines. I went over to him.

"Well?" I said.

"I know you want more money," he told me. "But what else do you want?"

I could see he would be no improvement at all. I said: "Emory Mafferson."

I thought that would catch him off balance, and it did.

"What? You actually want Mafferson?"

"We want to bring out Funded Individuals. In cartoon strips. We'll dramatize it in pictures." Doubt and suspicion were still there, in Steichel's eyes, but interest began to kindle. "Nobody reads, any more," I went on. "Pictorial presentation, that's the whole future. Let Emory go ahead with Funded Individuals in a new five-color book on slick paper."

Grudgingly, he said: "I'll have to think that one over. We'll see."

George Stroud XI

T HE REST of that day went by like a motion picture running wild, sometimes too fast, and again too slow.

I called up Georgette, and made a date to meet her for dinner that evening at the Van Barth. She sounded extra gay, though I couldn't imagine why. I was the only member of the family who knew what it meant to go all the way through life and come out of it alive.

I explained that the last assignment was over, and then she put Georgia on the wire. The conversation proceeded like this:

"Hello? Hello? Is that you, George? This is George."

"Hello, George. This is George."

"Hello."

"Hello."

"Hello? Hello?"

"All right, now we've said hello."

"Hello, George, you have to tell me a story. What's her name?"

"Claudia. And she's at least fifteen years old."

"Six."

"Sixteen."

"Six. Hello? Hello?"

"Hello. Yes, she's six. And here's what she did. One day she started to pick at a loose thread in her handkerchief, and it began to come away, and pretty soon she'd picked her handkerchief until all of it disappeared and before she knew it she was pulling away at some yarn in her sweater, and then her dress, and she kept pulling and pulling and before long she got tangled up with some hair on her head and after that she still kept pulling and pretty soon poor Claudia was just a heap of yarn lying on the floor."

"So then what did she do? Hello?"

"So then she just lay there on the floor and looked up at the chair where she'd been sitting, only of course it was empty by now. And she said, 'Where am I?' "

Success. I got an unbelieving spray of laughter.

"So then what did I do? Hello? Hello?"

"Then you did nothing," I said. "Except you were always careful after that not to pull out any loose threads. Not too far."

"Hello? Is that all?"

"That's all for now."

"Good-bye. Hello?"

"We said hello. Now we're saying good-bye."

"Good-bye, good-bye, good-bye, good-bye."

After that I phoned an agency and got a couple of tickets for a show that evening. And then, on an impulse, I phoned the art dealer who had sent us the photograph of the Louise Patterson exhibit. I told him who I was, and asked: "How much are Pattersons actually worth?"

"That all depends," he said. "Do you want to buy, or have you got one you want to sell?"

"Both. I want a rough evaluation."

"Well. Frankly, nobody knows. I suppose you're referring to that recent article in your *Newsways*?"

"More or less."

"Well. That was an exaggeration, of course. And the market on somebody like Patterson is always fluctuating. But I'd say anything of hers would average two or three thousand. I happen to have a number of canvases of hers, exceptional things, you could buy for around that figure."

"What would the *Judas* bring? I mean the one with the hands. You sent us a photograph of it."

"Well, that's different. It's received a lot of publicity, and I suppose that would be worth a little more. But, unfortunately, I haven't got the picture itself. It is really lost, apparently."

"It isn't lost," I said. "I have it. How much is it worth?"

There was a perceptible wait.

"You actually have it?"

"I have."

"You understand, Mr.—"

"Stroud. George Stroud."

"You understand, Mr. Stroud, I don't buy pictures myself. I simply exhibit pictures, and take a commission from the sales made through my gallery. But if you really have that *Judas* I believe it can be sold for anywhere between five and ten thousand dollars."

I thanked him and dropped the phone.

The big clock ran everywhere, overlooked no one, omitted no one, forgot nothing, remembered nothing, knew nothing. Was nothing, I would have liked to add, but I knew better. It was just about everything. Everything there is.

That afternoon Louise Patterson came roaring into the office, more than a little drunk. I had been expecting her. She wanted to talk to me, and I packed us both off to Gil's.

When we were lined up at the bar at Gil's she said: "What about that picture of mine. What have you done with it?"

"Nothing. I have it at my home. Why should I have done anything with it?"

"You know why," she thundered. "Because it proves you killed Pauline Delos."

Three customers looked around with some interest. So then I had to explain to her that I hadn't, and in guarded language, suppressing most of the details, I outlined the police theory of the case. When I had finished, she said, disappointedly: "So you're really not a murderer, after all?"

"No. I'm sorry."

A cyclone of laughter issued from her. For a moment she couldn't catch her breath. I thought she'd fall off her chair.

"I'm sorry, too, Mr. Stroud. I was being so brave yesterday afternoon in your office, you have no idea. God, what I won't do to save those pictures of mine. The more I saw you the more sinister you looked. Come to think of it, you really are sinister. Aren't you?"

She was quite a woman. I liked her more and more. Yesterday she'd looked like something out of an album, but today she'd evidently taken some pains to put herself together. She was big, and dark, and alive.

Gil ranged down the bar in front of us.

"Evening," he said to both of us, then to me, "Say, a friend of yours was hanging around here for the last week or so, looking for you. He sure wanted to see you. Bad. But he ain't here now. A whole lot of people been looking for you."

"I know," I said. "I've seen them all. Give us a couple of rye highballs, and let the lady play the game."

Then for a while Gil and the Patterson woman worked away
at it. She started by asking for a balloon, which was easy, the
only toy Gil had saved from the old fire next to the carbarns,
and ended by asking for a Raphael, also quite simple, a postcard he'd mailed to his wife from Italy, on a long voyage.

Something like eight drinks later Patterson remembered
something, as I'd known she sooner or later would.

"George, there's something I don't understand. Why did
they want me to identify you? What was the idea?"

She was more than a little drunk, and I gravely told her:
"They wanted to find out who had that picture of yours. It
was believed lost. Remember? And it's priceless. Remember
that? And naturally, our organization wanted to trace it
down."

She stared for a moment of semi-belief, then exploded into
another storm of laughter.

"Double-talk. I want the truth. Where's my picture? I want
it back. I could have it back the minute you were found, according to Mr. Klausmeyer." The memory of Don seemed to
touch off another wave of deafening hilarity. "That angleworm. To hell with him. Well, where is it?"

"Louise," I said.

"It's worth a lot of money, it belongs to me, and I want
it. When are you going to give it to me?"

"Louise."

"You're a double-talker. I can spot a guy like you a hundred
miles away. You've got a wife, no children, and a house you
haven't paid for. Tonight you're slumming, and tomorrow
you'll be bragging all over the commuter's special that you
know a real artist, the famous Louise Patterson." She
slammed a fist on the bar. Gil came back to us and phleg-
matically assembled two more drinks. "But to hell with all
that. I want my *Study in Fundamentals*. It was promised to
me, and it's worth a lot of money. Where is it?"

"You can't have it," I said, bluntly. "It's mine."

She glared, and snarled.

"You bastard, I think you mean it."

"Certainly I mean it. After all, it is mine. I paid for it, didn't
I? And it means something to me. That picture is a part of
my life. I like it. I want it. I need it."

She was, all at once, moderately amiable.

"Why?"

"Because that particular picture gave me an education. It is continuing to give me an education. Maybe, sometime, it will put me through college." I looked at my watch. If I could get to the Van Barth in ten minutes, I would be approximately on time. "But I'll make a deal with you. I've got that *Fury* in the office, and four other things of yours at home. You can have them all, instead of the *Temptation of St. Judas*, which is not for sale at any price. Not to anyone."

She asked me, wistfully: "Do you really like it so much?"

I didn't have time to explain, and so I simply said: "Yes."

This shut her up, and I somehow got her out of the place. In front of Gil's I put her into a cab, and paid the driver, and gave him her address.

I caught the next taxi that passed. I knew I'd be a few minutes late at the Van Barth. But it didn't seem to matter so much.

The big, silent, invisible clock was moving along as usual. But it had forgotten all about me. Tonight it was looking for someone else. Its arms and levers and steel springs were wound up and poised in search of some other person in the same blind, impersonal way it had been reaching for me on the night before. And it had missed me, somehow. That time. But I had no doubt it would get around to me again. Inevitably. Soon.

I made sure that my notebook was stowed away in an inside pocket. It had Louise's address, and her phone number. I would never call her, of course. It was enough, to be scorched by one serious, near-disaster. All the same, it was a nice, interesting number to have.

My taxi slowed and stopped for a red light. I looked out of the window and saw a newspaper headline on a corner stand.

EARL JANOTH, OUSTED PUBLISHER,
PLUNGES TO DEATH.

NIGHTMARE ALLEY

by William Lindsay Gresham

To
Joy Davidman

Contents

CARD ONE   *The Fool* 523

CARD TWO   *The Magician* 529

CARD THREE   *The High Priestess* 547

CARD FOUR   *The World.* 566

CARD FIVE   *The Empress* 601

CARD SIX   *Resurrection of the Dead* . . . 608

CARD SEVEN   *The Emperor.* 623

CARD EIGHT   *The Sun* 634

CARD NINE   *The Hierophant.* 647

CARD TEN   *The Moon* 659

CARD ELEVEN   *The Lovers* 671

CARD TWELVE   *The Star* 684

CARD THIRTEEN   *The Chariot* 701

CARD FOURTEEN   *The Tower.* 728

CARD FIFTEEN   *Justice* 748

CARD SIXTEEN   *The Devil* 755

CARD SEVENTEEN   *The Hermit* 758

CARD EIGHTEEN   *Time* 765

CARD NINETEEN   *The Wheel of Fortune.* 767

CARD TWENTY   *Death* 777

CARD TWENTY-ONE   *Strength* 783

CARD TWENTY-TWO   *The Hanged Man* 791

Madame Sosostris, famous clairvoyante,
Had a bad cold, nevertheless
Is known to be the wisest woman in Europe,
With a wicked pack of cards. Here, said she,
Is your card, the drowned Phoenician Sailor,
(Those are pearls that were his eyes. Look!)
Here is Belladonna, the Lady of the Rocks,
The lady of situations.
Here is the man with three staves, and here the Wheel,
And here is the one-eyed merchant, and this card,
Which is blank, is something he carries on his back,
Which I am forbidden to see. I do not find
The Hanged Man. Fear death by water . . .
                                        —*The Waste Land*

For at Cumae I saw with my own eyes the Sibyl hanging in a bottle.
And when the boys asked her, "What do you want, Sibyl?" she answered, "I want to die."
                                        —*The Satyricon*

The Fool

who walks in motley, with his eyes closed,
over a precipice at the end of the world.

STAN CARLISLE stood well back from the entrance of the canvas enclosure, under the blaze of a naked light bulb, and watched the geek.

This geek was a thin man who wore a suit of long underwear dyed chocolate brown. The wig was black and looked like a mop, and the brown greasepaint on the emaciated face was streaked and smeared with the heat and rubbed off around the mouth.

At present the geek was leaning against the wall of the pen, while around him a few—pathetically few—snakes lay in loose coils, feeling the hot summer night and sullenly uneasy in the glare. One slim little king snake was trying to climb up the wall of the enclosure and was falling back.

Stan liked snakes; the disgust he felt was for them, at their having to be penned up with such a specimen of man. Outside the talker was working up to his climax. Stan turned his neat blond head toward the entrance.

". . . where did he come from? God only knows. He was found on an uninhabited island five hundred miles off the coast of Florida. My friends, in this enclosure you will see one of the unexplained mysteries of the universe. Is he man or is he beast? You will see him living in his natural habitat among the most venomous rep-tiles that the world provides. Why, he fondles those serpents as a mother would fondle her babes. He neither eats nor drinks but lives entirely on the atmosphere. And we're going to feed him one more time! There will be a slight additional charge for this attraction but it's not a dollar, it's not a quarter—it's a cold, thin dime, ten pennies, two nickels, the tenth part of a dollar. Hurry, hurry, hurry!"

Stan shifted over to the rear of the canvas pen.

The geek scrabbled under a burlap bag and found something. There was the wheet of a cork being drawn and a couple of rattling swallows and a gasp.

The "marks" surged in—young fellows in straw hats with their coats over their arms, here and there a fat woman with beady eyes. Why does that kind always have beady eyes, Stan wondered. The gaunt woman with the anemic little girl who had been promised she would see everything in the show. The drunk. It was like a kaleidoscope—the design always changing, the particles always the same.

Clem Hoately, owner of the Ten-in-One show and its lecturer, made his way through the crowd. He fished a flask of water from his pocket, took a swig to rinse his throat, and spat it on the ground. Then he mounted the step. His voice was suddenly low and conversational, and it seemed to sober the audience.

"Folks, I must ask ya to remember that this exhibit is being presented solely in the interests of science and education. This creature which you see before ya . . ."

A woman looked down and for the first time spied the little king snake, still frantically trying to climb out of the pit. She drew in her breath shrilly between her teeth.

". . . this creature has been examined by the foremost scientists of Europe and America and pronounced a man. That is to say: he has two arms, two legs, a head and a body, like a man. But under that head of hair there is the brain of a beast. See how he feels more at home with the rep-tiles of the jungle than with humankind."

The geek had picked up a black snake, holding it close behind the head so it couldn't snap at him, and was rocking it in his arms like a baby, muttering sounds.

The talker waited while the crowd rubbered.

"You may well ask how he associates with poisonous serpents without harm. Why, my friends, their poison has no effect whatsoever upon him. But if he were to sink his teeth in my hand nothing on God's green earth could save me."

The geek gave a growl, blinking stupidly up into the light from the bare bulb. Stan noticed that at one corner of his mouth there was a glint from a gold tooth.

"But now, ladies and gentlemen, when I told you that this creature was more beast than man I was not asking you to take my word for it. Stan—" He turned to the young man, whose brilliant blue eyes had not a trace of revelation in them. "Stan, we're going to feed him one more time for this audience alone. Hand me the basket."

Stanton Carlisle reached down, gripped a small covered market basket by the handle, and boosted it over the heads of the crowd. They fell back, jamming and pushing. Clem Hoately, the talker, laughed with a touch of weariness. "It's all right, folks; nothing you haven't seen before. No, I reckon you all know what this is." From the basket he drew a half-grown leghorn pullet, complaining. Then he held it up so they could see it. With one hand he motioned for silence.

The necks craned down.

The geek had leaned forward on all fours, his mouth hanging open vacantly. Suddenly the talker threw the pullet into the pit with a whirl of feathers.

The geek moved toward it, shaking his black cotton mop of wig. He grabbed for the chicken, but it spread its stumpy wings in a frenzy of self-preservation and dodged. He crawled after it.

For the first time the paint-smeared face of the geek showed some life. His bloodshot eyes were nearly closed. Stan saw his lips shape words without sound. The words were, "You son of a bitch."

Gently the youth eased himself out of the crowd, which was

straining, looking down. He walked stiffly around to the entrance, his hands in his pockets.

From the pit came a panicky clucking and cackling and the crowd drew its breath. The drunk beat his grimy straw hat on the rail. "Get 'at ole shicken, boy! Go get 'at ole shicken!"

Then a woman screamed and began to leap up and down jerkily; the crowd moaned in an old language, pressing their bodies tighter against the board walls of the pit and stretching. The cackling had been cut off short, and there was a click of teeth and a grunt of someone working hard.

Stan shoved his hands deeper in his pockets. He moved through the flap entrance back into the main ring of the Ten-in-One show, crossed it to the gate and stood looking out on the carnival midway. When his hands came from his pockets one of them held a shiny half-dollar. He reached for it with his other hand and it vanished. Then with a secret, inner smile of contempt and triumph, he felt along the edge of his white flannel trousers and produced the coin.

Against the summer night the ferris wheel lights winked with the gaiety of rhinestones, the calliope's blast sounded as if the very steam pipes were tired.

"Christ a-mighty, it's hot, huh, kid?"

Clem Hoately, the talker, stood beside Stan, wiping the sweat from the band of his panama with a handkerchief. "Say, Stan, run over and get me a bottle of lemon soda from the juice joint. Here's a dime; get yourself one too."

When Stan came back with the cold bottles, Hoately tilted his gratefully. "Jesus, my throat's sore as a bull's ass in fly time."

Stan drank the pop slowly. "Mr. Hoately?"

"Yeah, what?"

"How do you ever get a guy to geek? Or is this the only one? I mean, is a guy born that way—liking to bite the heads off chickens?"

Clem slowly closed one eye. "Let me tell you something, kid. In the carny you don't ask nothing. And you'll get told no lies."

"Okay. But did you just happen to find this fellow—doing—doing this somewhere behind a barn, and work up the act?"

Clem pushed back his hat. "I like you, kid. I like you a lot. And just for that I'm going to give you a treat. I'm *not* going to give you a boot in the ass, get it? That's the treat."

Stan grinned, his cool, bright blue eyes never leaving the older man's face. Suddenly Hoately dropped his voice.

"Just because I'm your pal I ain't going to crap you up. You want to know where geeks came from. Well, listen—you don't find 'em. You *make* 'em."

He let this sink in, but Stanton Carlisle never moved a muscle. "Okay. But how?"

Hoately grabbed the youth by the shirt front and drew him nearer. "Listen, kid. Do I have to draw you a damn blueprint? You pick up a guy and he ain't a geek—he's a drunk. A bottle-a-day booze fool. So you tell him like this: 'I got a little job for you. It's a temporary job. We got to get a new geek. So until we do you'll put on the geek outfit and fake it.' You tell him, 'You don't have to do nothing. You'll have a razor blade in your hand and when you pick up the chicken you give it a nick with the blade and then make like you're drinking the blood. Same with rats. The marks don't know no different.' "

Hoately ran his eye up and down the midway, sizing up the crowd. He turned back to Stan. "Well, he does this for a week and you see to it that he gets his bottle regular and a place to sleep it off in. He likes this fine. This is what he thinks is heaven. So after a week you say to him like this, you say, 'Well, I got to get me a real geek. You're through.' He scares up at this because nothing scares a real rummy like the chance of a dry spell and getting the horrors. He says, 'What's the matter? Ain't I doing okay?' So you say, 'Like crap you're doing okay. You can't draw no crowd faking a geek. Turn in your outfit. You're through.' Then you walk away. He comes following you, begging for another chance and you say, 'Okay. But after tonight out you go.' But you give him his bottle.

"That night you drag out the lecture and lay it on thick. All the while you're talking he's thinking about sobering up and getting the crawling shakes. You give him time to think it over, while you're talking. Then throw in the chicken. He'll geek."

The crowd was coming out of the geek show, gray and

listless and silent except for the drunk. Stan watched them with a strange, sweet, faraway smile on his face. It was the smile of a prisoner who has found a file in a pie.

The Magician

who holds toward heaven the wand of fire
and points with his other hand toward earth.

I F YOU'LL step right over this way, folks, I want to call your attention to the attraction now appearing on the first platform. Ladies and gentlemen, you are about to witness one of the most spectacular performances of physical strenth the world has ever seen. Now some of you young fellows in the crowd look pretty husky but I want to tell you, gents, the man you are about to see makes the ordinary blacksmith or athalete look like a babe in arms. The power of an African gorilla in the body of a Greek god. Ladies and gents, Herculo, the world's most perfect man."

Bruno Hertz: If only once she would over here look while I have the robe off I would be glad to drop dead that minute. *Um Gotteswillen*, I would cut my heart out and hand it to her on a plate. Cannot she ever see that? I cannot get up courage to hold her hand in the kinema. Why has a man always to feel over some woman like this? I cannot even tell Zeena how crazy I am for her because then Zeena would try to put us together and then I would feel a *dummkopf* from not knowing how to say to her. Molly—a beautiful *Amerikanische* name. She will never love me. I know it in my heart. But I can tear to pieces any of the wolves in the show such as would hurt that girl. If one of them would try, then maybe Molly could see it. Perhaps then she could guess the way I feel and would give me one word for me to remember always. To remember, back in Wien.

". . . right over here, folks. Will you step in a little closer? On account of this exhibit ain't the biggest thing you ever seen; how about it, Major? Ladies and gentlemen, I now present for your edification and amusement Major Mosquito, the tiniest human being on record. Twenty inches, twenty pounds, and twenty years—and he's got plenty of big ideas for his age. Any of you girls would like to date him after the show, see me and I'll fix ya up. The Major will now entertain you with a little specialty number of his own, singing and tap-dancing to that grand old number, 'Sweet Rosie O'Grady.' Take it away, Major."

Kenneth Horsefield: If I lit a match and held it right close under that big ape's nose I wonder if I'd see the hairs in his nose-holes catch fire. Christ, what an ape! I'd like to have him tied up with his mouth propped open and then I'd sit back smoking my cigar and shoot his teeth out one after another. Apes. They're all apes. Especially the women with their big moon faces. I'd like to sink a hammer in 'em and watch 'em splash like pumpkins. Their great, greasy red mouths open like tunnels. Grease and filth, all of them.

Christ, there it goes. That same crack. The one woman makes it to the other behind her hand. If I see that same hand come up and that same routine once more I'll yell the goddamned place down. A million dames and always the same goddamned crack behind the same goddamned hand and the other one always champing on gum. Some day I'll blast 'em. I don't keep that equalizer in my trunk to play Boy Scout with. And that's the dame I'll blast. I'd of done it before now. Only they'd laugh at seeing me hold the butt with one hand and work the trigger with the other.

*

Joe Plasky: "Thank you, professor. Ladies and gents, I am known as the Half-man Acrobat. As you can see, my legs are both here but they're not much good to me. Infantile paralysis when I was a kid—they just naturally never growed. So I just made up my mind to tie 'em in a knot like this and forget about 'em and go on about my business. This is the way I get upstairs. Up on the hands. Steady. Here we go with a hop, skip, and a jump. Turn around and down we go, easy as pie. Thank you, folks.

"Now here's another little number I worked out by myself. Sometimes in a crowded trolley car I don't have room enough to stand on both hands. So up we go. Steady. And I stand on one! Thank you very much.

"Now then, for my next number I'm going to do something that no other acrobat in the world has ever attempted. A full somersault from a handstand back onto the hands. Are we all set? Let's go. It's a good trick—if I do it. Maybe some of you folks in the front row had better move back a couple steps. Don't bother. I'm just kidding. I've never missed yet, as you can see, for I'm still in the land of the living. All right, here we go—up—and *over!* Thank you very much, folks.

"And now if you'll just step right in close I'm going to give away a few little souvenirs. Naturally, I can't get rich giving away merchandise, but I'll do my best. I have here a little booklet full of old songs, recitations, jokes, wheezes, and parlor games. And I'm not going to charge you a dollar for it, nor even a half, but a cold, thin dime. That's all it costs, folks, a dime for a full evening of fun and fancy. And with it I'm going to give away, as a special inducement at this performance only, this little paper shimmy-dancer. Hold a match behind the paper: you see her shadow; and this is how you make her shake.

"You want one? Thank you, bud. Here you are, folks—brimful of assorted poems, dramatic readings, and witty sayings by the world's wisest men. And only a dime. . . ."

Sis wrote me the kids are both down with whooping cough. I'll send them a box of paints to help keep them quiet. Kids love paints. I'll send them some crayons, too.

*

"Sailor Martin, the living picture gallery. Ladies and gents, this young man that you see before you went to sea at an early age. He was shipwrecked on a tropical island which had only one other inhabitant—an old seafaring man, who had been there most of his life—a castaway. All he had managed to save from the wreck of his ship was a tattoo outfit. To pass the time he taught Sailor Martin the art and he practiced on himself. Most of the patterns you see are his own work. Turn around, Sailor. On his back, a replica of that world-famous painting, the Rock of Ages. On his chest—turn around, Sailor—the Battleship *Maine*, blowing up in Havana Harbor. Now if any of you young fellows in the audience would like an anchor, American flag, or sweetheart's initials worked on your arm in three beautiful colors, step right up to the platform and see the Sailor. No sissies need apply."

Francis Xavier Martin: Boy, that brunette working the electric-chair act is a beaut. Have I got what would make her happy and moan for more! Only Bruno would land on me like a ton of tomcats. I wonder if I'll hear from that redhead in Waterville. God, I can get one on thinking about her yet. What a shape—and knowing right where to put it, too. But this brunette kid, Molly, is the nuts. What a pair of bubbies! High and pointed—and that ain't no cupform either, brother; that's God.

I wish to Christ that kraut Bruno would bust a blood vessel some day, bending them horseshoes. Goddamn, that Molly kid's got legs like a racehorse. Maybe I could give her one jump and then blow the show. Jesus, it would be worth it, to get into that.

"Over here, folks, right over here. On this platform you see one of the most amazing little ladies the wide world has ever known. And right beside her we have an exact replica of the electric chair at Sing Sing prison. . . ."

Mary Margaret Cahill: Don't forget to smile; Dad always said that. Golly, I wish Dad was here. If I could only look out there and see him grinning up at me everything would be hunky dory. Time to drop the robe and give them an eyeful. Dad, honey, watch over me. . . .

Dad taught Molly all kinds of wonderful things while she was growing up and they were fun, too. For instance, how to walk out of a hotel in a dignified manner with two of your best dresses wrapped around you under the dress you had on. They had to do that once in Los Angeles and Molly got all of her clothes out. Only they nearly caught Dad and he had to talk fast. Dad was wonderful at talking fast and whenever he got in a tight place Molly would go all squirmy inside with thrill and fun because she knew her dad could always wiggle out just when the others thought he was cornered. Dad was wonderful.

Dad always knew nice people. The men were sometimes soused a little but the ladies that Dad knew were always beautiful and they usually had red hair. They were always wonderful to Molly and they taught her to put on lipstick when she was eleven. The first time she put it on by herself she got on too much and Dad burst out laughing loud and said she looked like something from a crib house—and jail bait at that.

The lady that Dad was friendly with at the time—her name was Alyse—shushed Dad and said, "Come over here, darling. Alyse'll show you. Let's take this off and start over. The idea is to keep people from knowing that you have any makeup on at all—especially at your age. Now watch." She looked at Molly's face carefully and said, "This is where you start. And don't let anybody talk you into putting rouge on anywhere else. You have a square face and the idea is to soften it and make it look round." She showed Molly just how to do it and then took it all off and made her do it herself.

Molly wanted Dad to help her but he said it wasn't his business—getting it off was more in his line, especially on the collars of shirts. Molly felt awful, having to do it all by herself because she was afraid she wouldn't do it right and finally she cried a little and then Dad took her on his lap and Alyse showed her again and after that it was all right and she always used makeup, only people didn't know about it. "My, Mr. Cahill—what a lovely child! Isn't she the picture of health!

Such lovely rosy cheeks!" Then Dad would say, "Indeed, ma'am, lots of milk and early to bed." Then he would wink at Molly because she didn't like milk and Dad said beer was just as good for you and she didn't like beer very much but it was always nice and cold and besides you got pretzels with it and everything. Also Dad said it was a shame to go to bed early and miss everything when you could sleep late the next day and catch up—unless you had to be at the track for an early workout, to hold the clock on a horse, and then it was better to stay up and go to bed later.

Only, when Dad had made a real killing at the track he always got lit and when he got lit he always tried to send her off to bed just when everything was going swell and because other people in the crowd were always trying to get her to take some, Molly never cared for liquor. Once, in a hotel where they were stopping, there was a girl got terribly drunk and began to take her clothes off and they had to put her to bed in the room next to Molly's. There were a lot of men going in and coming out all night and the next day the cops came and arrested the girl, and Molly heard people talking about it and somebody said later that they let the girl go but she had to go to the hospital because she had been hurt inside someway. Molly couldn't bear the thought of getting drunk after that because anything might happen to you and you shouldn't let anything happen to you with a man unless you were in love with him. That was what everybody said and people who made love but weren't really in love were called tramps. Molly knew several ladies who were tramps and she asked Dad one time why they were tramps and that's what he said: that they'd let anybody hug and kiss them either for presents or money. You shouldn't do that unless the guy was a swell guy and not likely to cross you up or take a powder on you if you were going to have a baby. Dad said you should never let anybody make love to you if you couldn't use his toothbrush, too. He said that was a safe rule and if you followed that you couldn't go wrong.

Molly could use Dad's toothbrush and often did, because one of their brushes was always getting left behind in the hotel or sometimes Dad needed one to clean his white shoes with.

Molly used to wake up before Dad and sometimes she

would run in and hop into his bed and then he would grunt and make funny snorey noises—only they sounded all funny and horrible—and then he would make believe he thought there was a woodchuck in the bed and he would blame the hotel people for letting woodchucks run around in their joint and then he would find out it was Molly and no woodchuck and he would kiss her and tell her to hurry up and get dressed and then go down and get him a racing form at the cigar stand.

One morning Molly ran in and there was a lady in bed with Dad. She was a very pretty lady and she had no nightie on and neither did Dad. Molly knew what had happened: Dad had been lit the night before and had forgotten to put on his pajamas and the girl had been lit and he had brought her up to their rooms to sleep on account of she was too tight to go home and he had intended to have her sleep with Molly but they had just fallen asleep first. Molly lifted the sheet up real, real careful and then she found out how she would look when she got big.

Then Molly got dressed and went down and got the racing form on the cuff and came back and they were still asleep, only the lady had snuggled in closer to Dad. Molly stood quiet in a corner a long time and kept still, hoping they would wake up and find her and she would run at them and go "Woo!" and scare them. Only the lady made a low noise like a moan and Daddy opened one eye and then put his arms around her. She opened her eyes and said, "Hello, sugar," all slow and sleepy, and then Dad started kissing her and she woke up after a while and started to kiss back. Finally Dad got on top of the lady and began to bounce up and down in the bed and Molly thought that was so funny that she burst out laughing and the lady screamed and said, "Get that kid out of here."

Dad was wonderful. He looked over his shoulder in one of his funny ways and said, "Molly, how would you like to sit in the lobby for about half an hour and pick me a couple of winners out of that racing form? I have to give Queenie here her exercise. You don't want to startle her and make her sprain a tendon." Dad kept still until Molly had gone but when she was outside the door she could hear the bed moving and she wondered if this lady could use Dad's toothbrush and she hoped she wouldn't because Molly wouldn't want to use it afterwards. It would make her sick to use it.

When Molly was fifteen one of the exercise boys at the stable asked her to come up in the hay loft and she went and he grabbed her and started kissing her and she didn't like him enough to kiss him and besides it was all of a sudden and she started wrestling with him and then she called, "Dad! Dad!" because the boy was touching her and Dad came bouncing up into the loft and he hit the boy so hard he fell down on the hay as if he was dead, only he wasn't. Dad put his arm around Molly and said, "You all right, baby?" And Dad kissed her and held her close to him for a minute and then he said, "You got to watch yourself, kidlet. This world's full of wolves. This punk won't bother you no more. Only watch yourself." And Molly smiled and said:

"I couldn't have used his toothbrush anyhow." Then Dad grinned and rapped her easy under the chin with his fist. Molly wasn't scared any more only she never strayed very far from Dad or from other girls. It was awful that had to happen because she could never feel right around the stables any more, and couldn't talk to the exercise boys and the jockeys any more in the old way and even when she did they were always looking at her breasts and that made her feel all weak and scarey inside somehow even when they were polite enough.

She was glad she was beginning to have breasts, though, and she got used to boys looking at them. She used to pull the neck of her nightie down and make like the ladies in evening dresses and once Dad bought her an evening dress. It was beautiful and one way you looked at it it was light rose and the other way it was gold and it came down off the shoulders and was cut low and it was wonderful. Only that was the year Centerboard ran out of the money and Dad had the bankroll on him to show and they had to sell everything they had to get a grubstake. That was when they went back to Louisville. That was the last year.

Dad got a job with an old friend who ran a gambling place down by the river, and Dad was his manager and wore a tuxedo all the time.

Things were going fine after a while and as soon as Dad

squared up some of his tabs he registered Molly at a dancing school and she started to learn acrobatic and tap. She had a wonderful time, showing him the steps as she learned them. Dad could dance a lot of softshoe himself and he never had a lesson. He said he just had Irish feet. Also he wanted her to take music lessons and sing, only she never could sing—she took after Mother that way. When the school gave a recital Molly did a Hawaiian number with a real hula skirt somebody had sent Dad from Honolulu and her hair falling over her shoulders like a black cloud and flowers in her hair and dark makeup and everybody applauded and some of the boys whistled and that made Dad mad because he thought they were getting fresh but Molly loved it because Dad was out there and as long as he was there she didn't care what happened.

She was sixteen and all grown up when things went to smash. Some fellows from Chicago had come down and there was trouble at the place where Dad worked. Molly never did find out what it was, only a couple of big men came to the house one night about two o'clock and Molly knew they were cops and she went all weak, thinking Dad had done something and they wanted him but he had always told her that the way to deal with cops was to smile at them, act dumb, and give them an Irish name.

One said, "You Denny Cahill's daughter?" Molly said yes. He said, "I got some mighty tough news for you, kid. It's about your dad." That was when Molly felt her feet slip on glass, like the world had suddenly tilted and it was slippery glass and she was falling off it into the dark and would fall and fall forever because there was no end to the place where she was falling.

She just stood there and she said, "Tell me."

The cop said, "Your dad's been hurt, girlie. He's hurt real bad." He wasn't like a shamus now; he was more like the sort of man who might have a daughter himself. She went up close to him because she was afraid of falling.

She said, "Is Dad dead?" and he nodded and put his arm around her and she didn't remember anything more for a while, only she was in the hospital when she came to and somehow she was all groggy and sleepy and she thought she had been hurt and kept asking for Dad and a cross nurse said she had better keep quiet and then she remembered and Dad was dead and she started to scream and it was like laughing, only it felt horrible and she couldn't stop and then they came and stuck her arm with a hype gun and she went out again and it was that way for a couple of times and finally she could stop crying and they told her she would have to get out because other people needed the bed.

Molly's grandfather, "Judge" Kincaid, said she could live with him and her aunt if she would take a business course and get a job in a year and Molly tried but she couldn't ever get it into her head somehow, although she could remember past performances of horses swell. The Judge had a funny way of looking at her and several times he seemed about to get friendly and then he would chill up. Molly tried being nice to him and calling him Granddad but he didn't like that and once, just to see what would happen, she ran up to him when he came in and threw her arms around his neck. He got terribly mad that time and told her aunt to get her out of the house, he wouldn't stand having her around.

It was terrible without Dad to tell her things and talk to and Molly wished she had died along with Dad. Finally she got a scholarship to the dancing school and she worked part time there with the young kids and Miss La Verne, who ran the school, let her stay with her. Miss La Verne was very nice at first and so was her boy friend, Charlie, who was a funny-looking man, kind of fat, who used to sit and look at Molly and he reminded her of a frog, the way he used to spread his fingers out on his knees, pointing in, and pop his eyes.

Then Miss La Verne got cross and said Molly better get a job, but Molly didn't quite know how to begin and finally Miss La Verne said, "If I get you a job will you stick with it?" Molly promised.

It was a job with a carny. There was a Hawaiian dance show, what they called a kooch show—two other girls and Molly. The fellow who ran it and did the talking was called Doc Abernathy. Molly didn't like him a bit and he was always trying to make the girls. Only Jeannette, one of the dancers, and Doc were steady and Jeannette was crazy-mad jealous of the other two. Doc used to devil her by horsing around with them.

Molly always liked Zeena, who ran the mental act in the Ten-in-One show across the midway. Zeena was awfully nice and she knew more about life and people than anybody Molly had ever met except Dad. Zeena had Molly bunk in with her, when she stayed in hotels, for company, because Zeena's husband slept in the tent to watch the props, he said. Really it was because he was a souse and he couldn't make love to Zeena any more. Zeena and Molly got to be real good friends and Molly didn't wish she was dead any more.

Then Jeannette got nastier and nastier about Doc's paying so much attention to Molly and she wouldn't believe that Molly didn't encourage him. The other girl told her, "With a chassis like that Cahill kid's got you don't have to do no encouraging." But Jeannette thought Molly was a stinker. One day Doc whispered something to her about Molly and Jeannette started for her looking like a wild animal with her lips pulled back over her teeth. She smacked Molly in the face and before Molly knew what was going on she had pulled off her shoe and was swinging at her, beating her in the face with it. Doc came rushing over and he and Jeannette had a terrible battle. She was cursing and screaming and Doc told her to shut up or he would smash her in the tits. Molly ran out and went over to the Ten-in-One and the boss fired Doc out of the carny and the kooch show went back to New York.

"Fifteen thousand volts of electricity pass through her body without hurting a hair of the little lady's head. Ladies and gentlemen, Mamzelle Electra, the girl who, like Ajax of Holy Writ, defies the lightning. . . ."

Glory be to God, I hope nothing happens to that wiring. I want Dad. God, how I want him here. I've got to remember to smile. . . .

"Stand over here, Teddy, and hold onto Ma's hand. So's you won't git tromped on and kin see. That there's a 'lectric chair, same's they got in the penitentiary. No, they ain't going to hurt the lady none, leastways I hope not. See? They strap her in that chair—only there's something about her body that don't take 'lectricity. Same's rain rolls right off the old

gander's back. Don't be scared, Teddy. Ain't nothing going
to happen to her. See how the 'lectricity makes her hair stand
out stiff? Lightning'll do the same thing I heard tell. There.
See? She's holding a 'lectric bulb in one hand and grabbing
the wire with the other. See the bulb light? That means the
'lectricity is passing right through her 'thout hurting her
none. I wisht your pa was that way with 'lectricity. He got a
powerful bad burn last winter, time the wires blowed down
and he was helping Jim Harness get his road cleared. Come
along, Teddy. That's all they're going to do over here."

Now I can get up. Sailor Martin's looking at me again. I
can't keep saying no to him every time he asks me to go out
with him. But he can always think faster than I can. Only I
mustn't let him, ever. I mustn't be a tramp; I don't want it
this way, the first time. Dad . . .

Stanton Carlisle: The great Stanton stood up and smiled, running his glance over the field of upturned faces. He took a
deep breath. "Well, folks, first of all I'm going to show you
how to make money. Is there anybody in the crowd who's
willing to trust me with the loan of a dollar bill? You'll get it
back—if you can run fast. Thanks, bud. Now then—nothing
in either hand, nothing up the sleeves."

Showing his hands empty, save for the borrowed bill, Stan
gave a hitch to his sleeves. In the folds of his left sleeve was
a roll of bills which he acquired deftly. "Now then, one dollar— Wait a minute, bud. Are you sure you gave me only one?
You're sure. Maybe that's all you got with you, eh? But here
are two—one and two. Count 'em. It's a good trick, especially
along toward the end of the week."

Which one will smile at the oldest gag? One out of every
five. Remember that. One in five is a born chump.

He produced the bills one after another, until he had a
green fan of them. He returned the bill to the lad. In doing
so he turned his left side from the crowd, got a metal cup in
his hand. It hung by an elastic from his left hip.

"Now then, out of nowhere they came. Let's see what happens to them when we roll them up. One, two, three, four,
five, six. All present and accounted for. Into a roll—" He

placed the bills in his left hand, slipping them into the vanisher. "Blow on the hand—" The vanisher, released, thudded softly against his hip under his coat. "Lo and behold! Gone!"

There was a scattering of applause, as if they were a little ashamed of it. The chumps.

"Where did they go? You know, day after day I stand here—wondering just where they do go!" That's Thurston's gag. By God, I'm going to use it until I see one face—just one—in this bunch of rubes that gets the point. They never do. But that dollar bill production goes over. Poverty-struck bastards—they all wish they could do it. Make money out of the air. Only that's not the way I make mine. But it's better than real estate. My old man and his deals. Church vestryman on Sundays, con man the rest of the week. Frig him, the Bible-spouting bastard.

"Now then, if I can have your attention for a moment. I have here a bunch of steel rings. Each and every one of them a separate, solid hoop of steel. I have one, two, three-four, five, sixseveneight. Right? Now I take two. Tap 'em. Joined together! Would you take these, madam, and tell me if you can find any joints or signs of an opening? No? Thank you. All solid. And again, two separate rings. Go! Joined!"

Better speed it up, they're getting restless. This is the life, though. Everyone looking at you. How does he do it? Gosh, that's slick. Trying to figure it out. It's magic to them, all right. This is the life. While they're watching and listening you can tell 'em anything. They believe you. You're a magician. Pass solid rings through each other. Pull dollars out of the air. Magic. You're top man—while you keep talking.

"And now, folks, eight separate and distinct rings; yet by a magic word they fly together and are joined inextricably into a solid mass. There you are! I thank you for your kind attention. Now I have here a little booklet that's worth its weight in gold. Here is a collection of magic tricks that you can do—an hour's performance before your club, lodge, or church gathering or in your own parlor. An hour's practice—a lifetime of fun, magic, and mystery. This book formerly sold for a dollar, but for today I'm going to let you have it for two bits—a quarter of a dollar. Let's hurry it up, folks, because I know you all want to see and hear Madam Zeena, the seeress, and her act does not go on until everyone who wants one of these great books gets one. Thank you, sir. And you. Any more? Right.

"Now then, folks, don't go 'way. The next complete show will not start for twenty minutes. I call your attention to the next platform. Madam Zeena—miracle woman of the ages. She sees, she knows, she tells you the innermost secrets of your past, your present, and your future. Madam Zeena!"

Stan jumped down lightly from his own small platform and pushed through the crowd to a miniature stage draped in maroon velvet. A woman had stepped out from between the curtains. The crowd flowed over and stood waiting, looking up at her, some of the faces absently chewing, hands cupping popcorn into mouths.

The woman was tall, dressed in flowing white with astrological symbols embroidered on the hem of her robe. A cascade of brassy blond hair fell down her back and a band of gilt leather studded with glass jewels was around her forehead. When she raised her arms the loose sleeves fell back. She had large bones, but her arms were white and capable-looking, with a spattering of freckles. Her eyes were blue, her face round, and her mouth a shade too small, so that she looked a trifle like an elaborate doll. Her voice was low-pitched with a hearty ring to it.

"Step right up, folks, and don't be bashful. If there's any of you that want to ask me a question Mr. Stanton is now passing among you with little cards and envelopes. Write your question on the card; be careful not to let anybody else see what you write, because that's your business. I don't want anybody asking me about somebody else's business. Just let's all mind our own and we'll stay out of trouble. When you've written your question, sign your initials to the card or write your name as a token of good faith. Then give the sealed envelope to Mr. Stanton. You'll see what I'm going to do next.

"Meantime, while we're waiting for you to write your questions, I'm going to start right in. It isn't necessary for you to write anything, but that helps you to fix it firmly in mind and keeps your mind from wandering off it, same as if you want to remember somebody's name you just met it helps to jot it down. Isn't that so?"

One out of every five heads nodded, entranced, and the rest looked on, some with dull eyes, but most of them with questions written on their faces.

Questions? They've all got questions, Stan thought, passing out cards and envelopes. Who hasn't? Answer their questions and you can have them, body and soul. Or just about. "Yes, madam, you can ask her anything. The questions are held in strictest confidence. No one will know but yourself."

"First of all," Zeena began, "there's a lady worried about her mother. She's asking me mentally, 'Is mother going to get better?' Isn't that so? Where is that lady?"

Timidly a hand went up. Zeena pounced on it. "Well, madam, I'd say your mother has had a lot of hard work in her life and she's had a lot of trouble, mostly about money. But there's something else in there that I don't see quite clear yet." Stan looked at the woman who had raised her hand. Farmer's wife. Sunday best, ten years out of style. Zeena could go to town on this one—a natural.

"I'd say, ma'am, that what your mother needs is a good long rest. Mind, I'm not saying how she's going to get it—what with taxes and sickness in the family and doctor's bills piling up. I know how it is because I've had my share of troubles, same as all of us, until I learned how to govern my life by the stars. But I think if you and your brothers—no, you have a couple of sisters, though, haven't you? One sister? Well, if you and your sister can work out some way to let her get a couple weeks' rest I think her health ought to improve mighty quick. But you just keep following a doctor's orders. That is, you better get her to a doctor. I don't think them patent medicines will do her much good. You got to get her to a doctor. Maybe he'll take a few bushels of potatoes or a shoat as part of the bill. Anyhow, I think she'll be all right if you have plenty of faith. If you'll see me right after the demonstration, maybe I can tell you more. And you want to watch the stars and make sure you don't do anything at the wrong time of the month.

"I see now that Mr. Stanton has got a good handful of questions, so if he'll bring them right up here on the stage we'll continue with the readings."

Stan pushed through the crowd to a curtained door on one

side of the little proscenium. He passed through. Inside there was a flight of rough board steps leading to the stage. It was dark and smelled of cheap whisky. Under the steps there was a square window opening into the low, boxlike compartment beneath the stage. At the window a bleary, unshaven face blinked out over a spotlessly clean white shirt. One hand held out a bunch of envelopes. Without a word Stan handed the man the envelopes he had collected, received the dummy batch, and in a second was onstage with them. Zeena moved forward a little table containing a metal bowl and a dark bottle.

"We'll ask the gentleman to drop all the questions into this bowl. Now then, people ask me if I have spirit aid in doing what I do. I always tell them that the only spirits I control are the ones in this bottle—spirits of alcohol. I'm going to pour a little on your questions and drop a match into the bowl. Now you can see them burning, and that's the last of them. So anybody who was afraid someone would find out what he wrote or that I was going to handle his question can just forget it. I've never touched them. I don't have to because I get an impression right away."

Stan had backed to one corner of the stage and stood watching the audience quietly as they strained their necks upward, hanging on every word of the seeress. In the floor, which was a few inches above their eye level, was a square hole. Zeena stroked her forehead, covering her eyes with her hand. At the opening appeared a pad of paper, a grimy thumb holding it, on which was scrawled in crayon, "What to do with wagon? J. E. Giles."

Zeena looked up, folding her arms with decision. "I get an impression— It's a little cloudy still but it's getting clearer. I get the initials *J* . . . *E* . . . *G*. I believe it's a gentleman. Is that right? Will the person who has those initials raise his hand, please?"

An old farmer lifted a finger as gnarled as a grapevine. "Here, ma'am."

"Ah, there you are. Thank you, Mr. *Giles*. The name *is* Giles, isn't it?"

The crowd sucked in its breath. "I thought so. Now then, Mr. Giles, you have a problem, isn't that right?" The old man's head wagged solemnly. Stan noted the deep creases in his red neck. Old sodbuster. Sunday clothes. White shirt, black tie. What he wears at funerals. Tie already tied—he hooks it onto his collar button. Blue serge suit—Sears, Roebuck or a clothing store in town.

"Let me see," Zeena went on, her hand straying to her forehead again. "I see— Wait. I see green trees and rolling land. It's plowed land. Fenced in."

The old man's jaw hung open, his eyes frowning with concentration, trying not to miss a single word.

"Yes, green trees. Probably willow trees near a crick. And I see something under those trees. A— It's a wagon."

Watching, Stan saw him nod, rapt.

"An old, blue-bodied wagon under those trees."

"By God, ma'am, it's right there this minute."

"I thought so. Now you have a problem on your mind. You are thinking of some decision you have to make connected with that wagon, isn't that so? You are thinking about what to do with the wagon. Now, Mr. Giles, I would like to give you a piece of advice: don't sell that old blue-bodied wagon."

The old man shook his head sternly. "No, ma'am, I won't. Don't belong to me!"

There was a snicker in the crowd. One young fellow laughed out loud. Zeena drowned him out with a full-throated laugh of her own. She rallied, "Just what I wanted to find out, my friend. Folks, here we have an honest man and that's the only sort I want to do any business with. Sure, he wouldn't think of selling what wasn't his, and I'm mighty glad to hear it. But let me ask you just one question, Mr. Giles. Is there anything the matter with that wagon?"

"Spring's broke under the seat," he muttered, frowning.

"Well, I get an impression that you are wondering whether to get that spring fixed before you return the wagon or whether to return it with the spring broken and say nothing about it. Is that it?"

"That's it, ma'am!" The old farmer looked around him triumphantly. He was vindicated.

"Well, I'd say you had just better let your conscience be your guide in that matter. I would be inclined to talk it over with the man you borrowed it from and find out if the spring was weak when he loaned it to you. You ought to be able to work it out all right."

Stan quietly left the stage and crept down the steps behind the draperies. He squeezed under the steps and came out beneath the stage. Dead grass and the light coming through chinks in the box walls, with the floor over his head. It was hot, and the reek of whisky made the air sweetly sick.

Pete sat at a card table under the stage trap. Before him were envelopes Stan had passed him on his way up to the seeress; he was snipping the ends off with scissors, his hands shaking. When he saw Stan he grinned shamefacedly.

Above them Zeena had wound up the "readings" and gone into her pitch: "Now then, folks, if you really want to know how the stars affect your life, you don't have to pay a dollar, nor even a half; I have here a set of astrological readings, all worked out for each and every one of you. Let me know your date of birth and you get a forecast of future events complete with character reading, vocational guidance, lucky numbers, lucky days of the week, and the phases of the moon most conducive to your prosperity and success. I've only a limited amount of time, folks, so let's not delay. They're only a quarter, first come, first served and while they last, because I'm getting low."

Stan slipped out of the sweatbox, quietly parted the curtains, stepped into the comparatively cooler air of the main tent, and sauntered over toward the soft drink stand.

Magic is all right, but if only I knew human nature like Zeena. She has the kind of magic that ought to take anybody right to the top. It's a convincer—that act of hers. Yet nobody can do it, cold. It takes years to get that kind of smooth talk, and she's never stumped. I'll have to try and pump her and get wised up. She's a smart dame, all right. Too bad she's tied to a rumdum like Pete who can't even get his rhubarb up any more; so everybody says. She isn't a bad-looking dame, even if she is a little old.

Wait a minute, wait a minute. Maybe here's where we start to climb. . . .

The High Priestess

Queen of borrowed light who guards
a shrine between the pillars Night and Day.

BEYOND the flowing windshield the taillight of the truck ahead wavered ruby red in the darkness. The windshield wiper's tock-tock-tock was hypnotic. Sitting between the two women, Stan remembered the attic at home on a rainy day—private, shut off from prying eyes, close, steamy, intimate.

Molly sat next to the door on his right, leaning her head against the glass. Her raincoat rustled when she crossed her legs. In the driver's seat Zeena bent forward, peering between the swipes of the wiper, following blindly the truck that held the snake box and the gear for the geek show, Bruno's weights, and Martin's baggage with the tattoo outfit. The geek, with his bottle, had crawled into a little cavern made by the piled gear and folded canvas.

In her own headlights, when the procession stopped at a crossing, Zeena could see Bruno's chunky form in a slicker swing from the cab and plod around to the back to look at the gear and make sure the weights were fast. Then he came over and stepped on the running board. Zeena cranked down the window on her side. "Hi, Dutchy—wet enough for you?"

"Joost about," he said softly. "How is things back here? How is Pete?"

"Right in back of us here having a snooze on the drapes. You reckon we'll try putting up in this weather?"

Bruno shook his head. His attention crept past Zeena and Stan, and for a moment his eyes lingered sadly on Molly, who had not turned her head.

"I joost want to make sure everything is okay." He turned back into the rain, crossing the streaming beam of the headlights and vanishing in the dark. The truck ahead began to move; Zeena shifted gears.

"He's a fine boy," she said at last. "Molly, you ought to give Bruno a chance."

Molly said, "No, thanks. I'm doing okay. No, thanks."

"Go on—you're a big girl now. Time you was having some fun in this world. Bruno could treat you right, by the looks of him. When I was a kid I had a beau that was a lumberjack—he was built along the lines of Bruno. And oh, boy!"

As if suddenly aware that her thigh was pressed close to Stan's, Molly squeezed farther into the corner. "No, thanks. I'm having fun now."

Zeena sighed gustily. "Take your time, kid. Maybe you just ain't met the right fella. And Stan here ought to be ashamed of himself. Why, me and Pete was married when I was seventeen. Pete wasn't much older'n Stan. How old are you, Stan?"

"Twenty-one," Stan said, keeping his voice low.

Approaching a curve, Zeena braced herself. Stan could feel the muscles of her thigh tighten as she worked the wheel. "Them was the days. Pete was working a crystal act in vaudeville. God, he was handsome. In a soup and fish he looked about two feet taller than in his street clothes. He wore a little black beard and a turban. I was working in the hotel when he checked in and I was that green I asked him when I brought in the towels if he'd tell my fortune. I'd never had my fortune told. He looked in my hand and told me something very exciting was going to happen to me involving a tall, dark man. I got the giggles. It was only because he was so good-looking.

I wasn't bashful around men. Never was. I couldn't have kept that hotel job a minute if I had been. But the best I'd been hoping for was to hook some gambler or race-track man—hoping he would help me get on the stage."

Suddenly Molly spoke. "My dad was a race-track man. He knew a lot about horses. He didn't die broke."

"Well, now," Zeena said, taking her eyes from the point of ruby light ahead long enough to send Molly a warm look in the darkness. "What d'you know. Oh, the gamblers was the great sheiks in my day. Any gal who could knock herself off a gambling man was doing something. We started when we were fourteen or fifteen. Lordy, that was fifteen years ago! Seems like yesterday some ways and like a million years in others. But the gamblers were the heartbreakers. Say, honey—I'll bet your dad was handsome, eh? Girls generally take after their fathers."

"You bet he was handsome. Daddy was the best-looking man I ever saw. I always said I'd never get married until I found a man as good-looking as Daddy—and as sweet. He was grand."

"Umm. Tall, dark, and handsome. Guess that lets you out, Stan. I don't mean about being tall. You're tall enough. But Molly likes 'em dark."

"I could get some hair dye," Stan said.

"Nope. Nope, never do. That might fool the public, Goldy Locks, but it would never fool a wife. Less'n you wanted to dye all over." She threw back her head and laughed. Stan found himself laughing too, and even Molly joined in.

"Nope," Zeena went on, "Pete was a real brunette all over; and, boy, could he love. We got married second season I traveled with him. He had me doing the back-of-the-house steal with the envelopes at first, in an usherette's uniform. Then we worked out a two-person act. He worked the stage, with his crystal, and I worked the audience. We used a word code at first and he used to ring in that part of the act as a stall while another girl was copying out the questions backstage. I'd go out and have people give me articles and Pete would look into his crystal and describe them. When we started we only used about ten different things and it was simple, but half the time I would get mixed up and then Pete would do some tall ad-libbing. But I learned. You should of seen our act when we were working the Keith time. By God, we could practically send a telegram word by word, and nobody could tumble, it was that natural, what we said."

"Why didn't you stay in vaudeville?" Stan asked intently. Suddenly he knew he had said the wrong thing; but there was no way to recall it, so he kept quiet.

Zeena paid close attention to her driving for a moment and then she rallied. "Pete's nerve began to go back on him." She turned and looked back into the rear of the van at the curled, sleeping figure, covered with a raincoat. Then she went on, dropping her voice. "He began muffing the code and he always needed a few shots before going on. Booze and mentalism don't mix. But we do as well in the carny, figuring up the net at the end of the year. And we don't have to cut no dash—living in swell hotels and all that. Horoscopes are easy to pitch and cost you about twenty-five a thousand. And we can take it easy in the winter. Pete don't drink much then. We got a shack down in Florida and he likes it down there. I do a little tea-leaf reading and one winter I worked a mitt camp in Miami. Palmistry always goes good in a town like Miami."

"I like Miami," Molly said softly. "Dad and I used to go there for the races at Hialeah and Tropical Park. It's a grand place."

"Any place is grand, long as you got the old do-re-mi in the grouch bag," Zeena said. "Say, this must be it. They're turning. I can tell you I ain't going to sleep in the truck tonight. Little Zeena's going to get her a room with a bathtub if they got any in this town. What say, kid?"

"Anything suits me," Molly said. "I'd love to have a hot bath."

Stan had a vision of what Molly would look like in the bathtub. Her body would be milk-white and long-limbed there in the water and a black triangle of shadow and her breasts with rosy tips. He would stand looking down at her and then bend over and she would reach soapy arms up but she would have to be someone else and he would have to be someone else, he thought savagely, because he had never managed to do it yet and always something held him back or the girl seemed to freeze up or suddenly he didn't want her any more once it was within reach and besides there was never the time or the place was wrong and besides it took a lot of dough and a car and all kinds of stuff and then they would expect you to marry them right away and they would probably get a kid the first thing. . . .

"Here we are, chillun," Zeena said.

The rain had slackened to a drizzle. In the lights of head-lamps the roughnecks were busy tearing canvas from the trucks. Stan threw his slicker over his shoulders, went around to open the rear doors of the truck. He crawled in and gently shook Pete by the ankle. "Pete, wake up. We're here. We've got to put up."

"Oh, lemme sleep five minutes more."

"Come on, Pete. Zeena says to give us a hand putting up."

He suddenly threw off the raincoat which covered him and sat up shivering. "Just a minute, kid. Be right with you." He crawled stiffly from the truck and stood shaking, tall and stooped, in the cool night air. From one pocket he drew a bottle, offering it to Stan, who shook his head. Pete took a pull, then another, and corked the bottle. Then he drew the cork out, finished it, and heaved it into the night. "Dead soldier."

The floodlights were up and the carny boss had laid out the midway with his marking stakes. Stan shouldered planks that fitted together to make Zeena's stage and drew one bundle of them from the van.

The top of the Ten-in-One was going up. Stan gave a hand on the hoist, while watery dawn showed over the trees and in houses on the edge of the fair grounds lights began to snap on in bedrooms, then in kitchens.

In the growing lavender of daybreak the carny took shape. Booths sprang up, the cookhouse sent the perfume of coffee along the dripping air. Stan paused, his shirt stuck to him with sweat, a comfortable glow in the muscles of his arms and back. And his old man had wanted him to go into real estate!

Inside the Ten-in-One tent Stan and Pete set up the stage for the mental act. They got the curtains hung, moved the bridge table and a chair under the stage, and stowed away the cartons of horoscopes.

Zeena returned. In the watery gold light of morning lines showed around her eyes, but she held herself as straight as a tent pole. "Got me a whole damn bridal suite—two rooms and bawth. C'mon over, both of you, and have a good soak."

Pete needed a shave, and his gaunt, angular face seemed stretched tighter over his bones. "I'd like to, sugar. Only I got to do a few little chores first in town. I'll see you later on."

"It's 28 Locust Lane. You got enough dough?"

"You might let me have a couple of dollars from the treasury."

"Okay, honey. But get some coffee into you first. Promise Zeena you'll have breakfast."

Pete took the money and put it carefully away in a billfold. "I shall probably have a small glass of iced orange juice, two three-minute eggs, melba toast and coffee," he said, his voice suddenly vibrant. Then he seemed to fade. He took out the billfold and looked in it. "Must make sure I got my money safe," he said in an off-key, strangely childish tone. He started off across the lot toward a shack at the edge of the village. Zeena watched him go.

"I'll bet that joint is a blind pig," she said to Stan. "Pete's sure a real clairvoyant when it comes to locating hidden treasure—long as it gurgles when you shake it. Well, you coming back and clean up? Look at you! Your shirt's sticking to you with sweat!"

As they walked, Stan breathed in the morning. Mist hung over the hills beyond the town, and from a slope rising from the other side of the road came the gentle tonk of a cowbell. Stan stopped and stretched his arms.

Zeena stopped too. "Never get nothing like this working the two-a-day. Honest, you know, Stan, I'd get homesick just to hear a cow moo."

The sun, breaking through, sparkled in wagon ruts still deep with rain. Stan took her arm to help her across the puddles. Under the warm, smooth rubber of the raincoat he pressed the soft bulge of her breast. He could feel the heat steaming up over his face where the cool wind struck it.

"You're awful nice to have around, Stan. You know that?"

He stopped walking. They were out of sight of the carnival grounds. Zeena was smiling at something inside herself. Awkwardly his arm went around her and he kissed her. It was lots different from kissing high-school girls. The warm, intimate searching of her mouth left him weak and dizzy. They broke apart and Stan said, "Wow."

Zeena let her hand stay for an instant pressed against his cheek; then she turned and they walked on, hand in hand.

"Where's Molly?" he asked after a while.

"Pounding her ear. I talked the old gal that has the house into giving us the two rooms for the price of one. While I was waiting for her to put up her husband's lunch I took a quick peek in the family Bible and got all their birth dates down pat. I told her right off that she was Aries—March 29th. Then I gave her a reading that just set her back on her heels. We got a real nice room. Always pays to keep your eyes open, I always say. The kid had her a good soak and hit the hay. She'll be pounding her ear. She's a fine kid, if she could only grow up some and stop yelping for her daddy every time she has a hangnail. But she'll get over it, I reckon. Wait till you see the size of these rooms."

The room reminded Stan of home. The old house on Linden Street and the big brass bedstead in his parents' room, where it was all tumbled and smelling of perfume on Mother's pillow and of hair restorer on his father's side.

Zeena threw off her raincoat, rolled a newspaper into a tight bar, tied it with string in the middle and hung the coat up on a hook in the closet. She pulled off her shoes and stretched out on the bed, reaching her arms wide. Then she drew out her hairpins and the brassy hair which had been in a neat double roll around her head fell in pigtails. Swiftly she unbraided them and let the hair flow around her on the pillow.

Stan said, "I guess I'd better get that bath. I'll see if there's any hot water left. He hung his coat and vest on a chairback. When he looked up he saw that Zeena had her eyes on him. Her lids were partly closed. One arm was bent under her head and she was smiling, a sweet, possessive smile.

He came over to her and sat beside her on the edge of the bed. Zeena covered his hand with hers and suddenly he bent and kissed her. This time there was no need for them to stop and they didn't. Her hand slid inside his shirt and felt the smooth warmth of his back tenderly.

"Wait, honey. Not yet. Kiss me some more."

"What if Molly should wake up?"

"She won't. She's young. You couldn't wake that kid up. Don't worry about things, honey. Just take it easy and slow."

All the things Stan had imagined himself saying and doing at such a time did not fit. It was thrilling and dangerous and his heart beat so hard he felt it would choke him.

"Take all your things off, honey, and hang 'em on the chair, neat."

Stan wondered that he didn't feel in the least ashamed now that this was it. Zeena stripped off her stockings, unhooked her dress and drew it leisurely over her head. Her slip followed.

At last she lay back, her bent arm under her head, and beckoned him to come to her. "Now then, Stan honey, you can let yourself go."

"It's getting late."

"Sure is. You got to get your bath and get back. Folks'll think Zeena's gone and seduced you."

"They'd be right."

"Damned if they wouldn't." She raised herself on her elbows and let her hair fall down on each side of his face and kissed him lightly. "Get along with you. Skat, now."

"Can't. You're holding me pinned down."

"Try'n get away."

"Can't. Too heavy."

"See'f you can wiggle loose."

There was a knock at the door, a gentle, timid tapping. Zeena threw her hair out of her eyes. Stan started but she laid one finger on his lips. She swung off the bed gracefully and pulled Stan up by one hand. Then she handed him his trousers, underwear, and socks and pushed him into the bathroom.

Behind the bathroom door Stan crouched, his ear to the panel, his heart hammering with alarm. He heard Zeena get her robe out of a bag and take her time about answering the tap. Then the hall door opened. Pete's voice.

"Sorry t'wake you, sugar. Only—" His voice sounded thicker. "Only, had little shopping to do. I sorta forgot 'bout getting breakfast."

There was the snap of a pocketbook opening. "Here's a buck, honey. Now make sure it's breakfast."

"Cross my heart, hope die."

Stan heard Zeena's bare feet approach the bathroom. "Stan," she called, "hurry up in there. I want to get some sleep. Get out of that tub and fall into your pants." To Pete she said, "The kid's had a hard night, tearing down and putting up in all that rain. I expect he's fallen asleep in the tub. Maybe you better not wait for him."

The door closed. Stan straightened up. She had never turned a hair, lying to Pete about him being in the bathtub. It comes natural in women, he thought. That's the way they all do when they have guts enough. That's the way they would all like to do. He found himself trembling. Quietly he drew a tub of hot water.

When it was half full he lay in it and closed his eyes. Well, now he knew. This was what all the love-nest murderers killed over and what people got married to get. This was why men left home and why women got themselves dirty reputations. This was the big secret. Now I know. But there's nothing disappointing about the feeling. It's okay.

He let his hands trail in the hot water and splashed little ripples over his chest. He opened his eyes. Drawing his hand out of the steamy warmth he gazed at it a moment and then carefully took from the back of it a hair that gleamed brassy-gold, like a tiny, crinkled wire. Zeena was a natural blonde.

The weeks went by. The Ackerman-Zorbaugh Monster Shows crawled from town to town, the outline of the sky's edge around the fair grounds changing but the sea of up-turned faces always the same.

The first season is always the best and the worst for a carny. Stan's muscles hardened and his fingers developed great sure-ty, his voice greater volume. He put a couple of coin sleights in the act that he would never have had the nerve to try in public before.

Zeena taught him many things, some of them about magic.

"Misdirection is the whole works, honey. You don't need no fancy production boxes and trap doors and trick tables. I've always let on that a man that will spend his time learning misdirection can just reach in his pocket and put something in a hat and then go ahead and take it out again and everybody will sit back and gasp, wondering where it came from."

"Did you ever do magic?" he asked her.

Zeena laughed. "Not on your sweet life. There's very few girls goes in for magic. And that's the reason. A gal spends all her time learning how to attract attention to herself. Then in magic she has to unlearn all that and learn how to get the audience to look at something else. Strain's too great. The dolls can never make it. I couldn't. I've always stuck to the mental business. It don't hurt anybody—makes plenty of friends for you wherever you go. Folks are always crazy to have their fortunes told, and what the hell— You cheer 'em up, give 'em something to wish and hope for. That's all the preacher does every Sunday. Not much different, being a fortuneteller and a preacher, way I look at it. Everybody hopes for the best and fears the worst and the worst is generally what happens but that don't stop us from hoping. When you stop hoping you're in a bad way."

Stan nodded. "Has Pete stopped hoping?"

Zeena was silent and her childish blue eyes were bright. "Sometimes I think he has. Pete's scared of something—I think he got good and scared of himself a long time ago. That's what made him such a wiz as a crystal-reader—for a few years. He wished like all get out that he really could read the future in the ball. And when he was up there in front of them he really believed he was doing it. And then all of a sudden he began to see that there wasn't no magic anywhere to lean on and he had nobody to lean on in the end but himself—not me, not his friends, not Lady Luck—just himself. And he was scared he would let himself down."

"So he did?"

"Yeah. He did."

"What's going to happen to him?"

Zeena bristled. "Nothing's going to happen to him. He is a sweet man, down deep. Long as he lasts I'll stick to him. If it hadn't been for Pete I'd of probably ended up in a crib house. Now I got a nice trade that'll always be in demand as long as there's a soul in the world worried about where next month's rent is coming from. I can always get along. And take Pete right along with me."

Across the tent the talker, Clem Hoately, had mounted the platform of Major Mosquito and started his lecture. The Major drew back one tiny foot and aimed a kick with deadly accuracy at Hoately's shin. It made the talker stammer for a moment. The midget was snarling like an angry kitten.

"The Major is a nasty little guy," Stan said.

"Sure he is. How'd you like to be shut up in a kid's body that way? With the marks all yawping at you. It's different in our racket. We're up head and shoulders above the marks. We're better'n they are and they know it. But the Major's a freak born."

"How about Sailor Martin? He's a made freak."

Zeena snorted. "He's just a pecker carrying a man around with it. He started by having a lot of anchors and nude women tattooed on his arms to show the girls how tough he was or something. Then he got that battleship put on his chest and he was off. He was like a funny paper, with his shirt off, and he figured he might as well make his skin work for him. If he was ever in the Navy, I was born in a convent."

"He doesn't seem to be making much time with your Electric Chair pal."

Zeena's eyes flashed. "He better not. That kid's not going to get it until she runs into some guy that'll treat her right. I'll see to that. I'd beat the be-Jesus out of any snot-nose that went monkeying around Molly."

"You and who else?"

"Me and Bruno."

Evansburg, Morristown, Linklater, Cooley Mills, Ocheke-tawney, Bale City, Boeotia, Sanders Falls, Newbridge.

Coming: Ackerman-Zorbaugh Monster Shows. Auspices Tall Cedars of Zion, Caldwell Community Chest, Pioneer Daughters of Clay County, Kallakie Volunteer Fire Department, Loyal Order of Bison.

Dust when it was dry. Mud when it was rainy. Swearing, steaming, sweating, scheming, bribing, bellowing, cheating, the carny went its way. It came like a pillar of fire by night, bringing excitement and new things into the drowsy towns—lights and noise and the chance to win an Indian blanket, to ride on the ferris wheel, to see the wild man who fondles those rep-tiles as a mother would fondle her babes. Then it vanished in the night, leaving the trodden grass of the field and the debris of popcorn boxes and rusting tin ice-cream spoons to show where it had been.

Stan was surprised, and gnawed by frustration. He had had Zeena—but how few chances ever came his way for him to have her again. She was the wise one, who knew all the ropes of the carny and everywhere else. She knew. And yet, in the tight world of the carnival, she could find very few opportunities to do what her eyes told Stan a dozen times a day that she would take pleasure in doing.

Pete was always there, always hanging around, apologetic, crestfallen, hands trembling, perfumed with bootleg, always a reminder of what he had been.

Zeena would beg off from a rendezvous with Stan to sew a button on Pete's shirt. Stan couldn't understand it; the more he thought about it the more confused and bitter he got. Zeena was using him to satisfy herself, he kept repeating. Then the thought struck him that maybe Zeena played a game of make-believe with him, and actually saw over his shoulder a shadow of Pete as he had been—handsome and straight and wearing his little black beard.

The thought would strike him right in the middle of his act and his patter would turn into a snarl.

One day Clem Hoately was waiting beside the platform when he came down after the last show. "Whatever's eating you, kid, you better turn it off while you're on the box. If you can't be a trouper, pack up your junk and beat it. Magicians come two for a nickel."

Stan had acquired enough carny to reach over, take a half dollar from Hoately's lapel, and vanish it in his other hand before walking away. But the call-down by the older man burnt into him. No woman or man his own age could drive the gall into his system like that. It took an old bastard, particularly when the stubble on his face looked silvery like fungus growing on a corpse. The bastard.

Stan went to sleep that night on his cot in the Ten-in-One tent with fantasies of slowly roasting Hoately over a fire, inquisition fashion.

Next day, just as they were about to open, Hoately stopped by his platform while Stan was opening a carton of pitch books.

"Keep them half-dollar tricks in the act, son. They got a nice flash. The marks love it."

Stan grinned and said, "You bet." When the first tip came wandering in he gave them all he had. His sale of the magic books almost doubled. He was on top of the world all day. But then came night.

By night Zeena's body plagued his dreams and he lay under the blanket, worn out and with his eyes burning for sleep, thinking back and having her over and over in memory.

Then he waited until closing one night. He stepped back of the curtains on her miniature stage. Zeena had taken off the white silk robe and was putting her hair up, her shoulders white and round and tantalizing over her slip. He took her roughly in his arms and kissed her and she pushed him away. "You beat it out of here. I got to get dressed."

"All right. You mean we're washed up?" he said.

Her face softened and she laid her palm gently against his cheek. "Got to learn to call your shots, honey. We ain't married folks. We got to be careful. Only one person I'm married to and that's Pete. You're a sweet boy and I'm fond as all hell of you. Maybe a little too fond of you. But we got to have some sense. Now you be good. We'll get together one of these days—or nights. And we'll have fun. That's a promise. I'll lay it on the line just as soon as ever we can."

"I wish I could believe it."

She slid her cool arms around his neck and gave him the promise between his lips, warm, sweet, and searching. His heart began to pound.

"Tonight?"

"We'll see."

"Make it tonight."

She shook her head. "I got to make Pete write some letters. He can't if he gets too loaded and he's got some that need answering. You can't let your friends down in show business. You find that out when you get on your uppers and have to hit 'em for a loan. Maybe tomorrow night."

Stan turned away, rebellious and savage, feeling as if the whole surface of his mind had been rubbed the wrong way. He hated Zeena and her Pete.

On his way over to the cookhouse for his supper he passed Pete. Pete was sober and shaky and profane. Zeena would have hidden his bottle in view of the letter-writing session. His eyes had begun to pop.

"Got a spare dollar on you, kid?" Pete whispered.

Zeena came up behind them. "You two boys stay right here and have your supper," she said, pushing them toward the cookhouse. "I've got to find a drugstore in this burg that keeps open late. Nothing like a girl's being careful of her beauty, huh? I'll be right back, honey," she said to Pete, fastening a loose button of his shirt. "We got to catch up on our correspondence."

Stan ate quickly, but Pete pushed the food around, wiped his mouth on the back of his hand, and wiped his hand carefully with his napkin.

He crushed the napkin into a hard, paper wad and aimed it at the cook's back with a curse.

"You got a spare fin, kid?"

"No. Let's get on back to the tent. You got the new Billboard to read. Zeena left it under the stage."

They walked back in silence.

Stan put up his cot and watched the Ten-in-One settle down for the night. Under the astrology stage a single light burned, winking through the cracks of the boards. Inside Pete was sitting at the table, trying to read the Billboard and going over and over the same paragraph.

Why couldn't Zeena have let him accompany her to the store, Stan asked himself. Then, on the way, maybe they could have warmed up and she would have forgotten about Pete and writing letters.

Zeena had slipped the bottle under the seat of Major Mosquito's chair. Stan jumped down from his own platform and crossed the tent softly. The Major's tiny cot was just above his head; he could hear above him the quick breathing which sounded soprano. His hand found the bottle, drew it out.

There was only an inch or two left in it. Stan turned back and crept up the steps of Zeena's theater. A few moments later he came down and squeezed into the understage compartment. The bottle, more than half full now, was in his hand.

"How about a drink, Pete?"

"Glory be to God!" The flask was nearly snatched from his hand. Pete jerked the cork, holding it out to Stan automatically. The next instant he had it in his mouth and his Adam's apple was working. He drained it and handed it back. "God almighty. A friend in need as the saying goes. I'm afraid I didn't leave much for you, Stan."

"That's all right. I don't care for any right now."

Pete shook his head and seemed to pull himself together. "You're a good kid, Stan. You got a fine act. Don't let anything ever keep you out of the big time. You can go places, Stan, if you don't get bogged down. You should have seen us when we were on top. Used to pack 'em in. They'd sit through four other acts just to see us. Boy, I can remember all the times we had our names on the marquee in letters a foot high—top billing—everywhere we went. We had plenty fun, too.

"But you— Why, kid, the greatest names in the business started right where you are now. You're the luckiest kid in the world. You got a good front—you're a damn good-looking kid and I wouldn't crap you up. You can talk. You can do sleights. You got everything. Great magician someday. Only don't let the carny . . ." His eyes were glazing over. He stopped speaking and sat rigid.

"Why don't you turn out the light and take it easy until Zeena gets back?" Stan suggested.

A grunt was his only answer. Then the man stood up and threw back his shoulders. "Kid, you should have seen us when we played the Keith time!"

Good God, is this idiot never going to pass out, Stan thought. Beyond the wooden walls of the understage compartment and the canvas of the tent was the sound of a car's engine starting, the whirr of the starter rising through the night as the nameless driver pressed it. The motor caught and Stan heard the gears.

"You know, kid—" Pete drew himself up until his head nearly touched the boards of the ceiling. The alcohol seemed to stiffen his back. His chin came up commandingly. "Stan, lad like you could be a great mentalist. Study human nature!" He took a long, last pull at the bottle and finished it. Barely swaying, he opened his eyes wide and swallowed.

"Here—chord from the orchestra, amber spot—and I'm on. Make my spiel, give 'em one laugh, plenty mystery. Then I jump right into the reading. Here's m'crystal." He focused his eyes on the empty whisky bottle and Stan watched him with an uneasy twinge. Pete seemed to be coming alive. His eyes became hot and intent.

Then his voice altered and took on depth and power. He passed his left hand slowly over the bottle's surface. "Since the dawn of history," he began, his words booming in the wooden box-room, "mankind has sought to see behind the veil which hides him from tomorrow. And through the ages certain men have gazed into the polished crystal and seen. Is it some property of the crystal itself? Or does the gazer use it merely to turn his eyes inward? Who can tell? But visions come. Slowly, shifting their form, visions come . . ."

Stan found himself watching the empty bottle in which a single pale drop slanted across the bottom. He could not take his eyes away, so contagious was the other's absorption.

"Wait! The shifting shapes begin to clear. I see fields of grass and rolling hills. And a boy—a boy is running on bare feet through the fields. A dog is with him."

Too swiftly for his wary mind to check him, Stan whispered the words, "Yes. Gyp."

Pete's eyes burned down into the glass. "Happiness then . . . but for a little while. Now dark mists . . . sorrow. I see people moving . . . one man stands out . . . evil . . . the boy hates him. Death and the wish of death . . ."

Stan moved like an explosion. He snatched for the bottle; it slipped and fell to the ground. He kicked it into a corner, his breath coming quick and rapid.

Pete stood for a moment, gazing at his empty hand, then dropped his arm. His shoulders sagged. He crumpled into the folding chair, resting his elbows on the card table. When he raised his face to Stan the eyes were glazed, the mouth slack. "I didn't mean nothing, boy. You ain't mad at me, are ya? Just fooling around. Stock reading—fits everybody. Only you got to dress it up." His tongue had thickened and he paused, his head drooping, then snapping up again. "Everybody had some trouble. Somebody they wanted to kill. Usually for a boy it's the old man. What's childhood? Happy one minute, heartbroke the next. Every boy had a dog. Or neighbor's dog—"

His head fell forward on his forearms. "Just old drunk. Just lush. Lord . . . Zeena be mad. Don't you let on, son, you gimme that little drink. She be mad at you, too." He began to cry softly.

Stan felt his stomach heave with disgust. He turned without a word and left the steaming compartment. In comparison, the air of the Ten-in-One tent, darkened now and still, felt cool.

It seemed as if half the night had worn away before Zeena did come back. Stan met her, talking in whispers so as not to disturb the others in the tent, now snoring heavily in their bunks.

"Where's Pete?"

"Passed out."

"Where'd he get it?"

"I—I don't know. He was over by the geek's layout."

"God damn it, Stan, I told you to watch him. Oh, well, I'm tuckered out myself. Might as well let him sleep it off. Tomorrow's another day."

"Zeena."

"What is it, honey?"

"Let me walk you home."

"It ain't far and I don't want you getting ideas. The landlady of this dump has a face like a snapping turtle. We don't want to start no trouble in this burg. We've had enough trouble with the wheels pretty near getting shut down for gambling. This is bluenose."

They had left the tent and the darkened midway stretched out ahead of them, light still streaming from the cookhouse. "I'll walk you over," Stan said. There was a leaden feeling in his chest and he fought to throw it off. He laced his fingers in hers and she did not draw her hand away.

In the shadow of the first trees on the edge of the lot they stopped and kissed and Zeena clung to him. "Gosh, honey, I've missed you something awful. I guess I need more loving than I thought. But not in the room. That old battle-ax is on the prowl."

Stan took her arm and started along the road. The moon had set. They passed a field on a little rise and then the road dipped between clay banks with fields above road level. "Let's go up there," Stan whispered.

They climbed the bank and spread their coats out on the grass.

Stan reached the Ten-in-One tent just before light. He crept into his bunk and was out like a shot. Then something was chirping in his ear and tugging at his shoulder. A voice like a fiddle's E string was cutting through the layers of fatigue and the void which was in him from having emptied his nerves.

"Kid, wake up! Wake up, you big lump!" The shrill piping got louder.

Stan growled and opened his eyes. The tent was tawny gold with sun on the outside of it above him. The pestiferous force at his shoulder was Major Mosquito, his blond hair carefully dampened and brushed over his bulging baby forehead.

"Stan, get up! Pete's dead!"

"What?"

Stan shot off the bunk and felt for his shoes. "What happened to him?"

"Just croaked—the stinking old rum-pot. Got into that bottle of wood alcohol Zeena keeps to burn the phoney questions. It was all gone or pretty near. And Pete's dead as a herring. His mouth's hanging open like the Mammoth Cave. Come on, take a look. I kicked him in the ribs a dozen times and he never moved. Come and look at him."

Without speaking Stan laced up his shoes, carefully, correctly, taking great pains with them. He kept fighting back the thought that wouldn't stay out of his mind. Then it broke over him like a thunder storm: They'll hang me. They'll hang

me. They'll hang me. Only I didn't mean it. I only wanted
to pass him out. I didn't know it was wood— They'll hang
me. I didn't mean it. They'll—"

He leaped from the platform and pressed through the knot
of show people around the seeress's stage. Zeena stepped out
and stood facing them, tall and straight and dry-eyed.

"He's gone all right. He was a good guy and a swell
trouper. I told him that alky was bad. Only last night I hid
his bottle on him—" She stopped and suddenly ducked back
through the curtains.

Stan turned and pushed through the crowd. He walked out
of the tent into the early sun and kept on to the edge of the
grounds where the telephone poles beside the road carried
their looping strands off into the distance.

His foot clinked against something bright and he picked up
a burned-out electric bulb which lay in the ashes of a long-
dead fire. It was iridescent and smoky inside, dark as a crystal
ball on a piece of black velvet. Stan kept it in his hand, looking
for a rock or a fence post. His diaphragm seemed to be pressing up around his lungs and keeping him from drawing his
breath. On one of the telephone poles was a streaked election
poster, carrying the gaunt face of the candidate, white hair
falling dankly over one eyebrow, lines of craft and rapacity
around the mouth that the photographer couldn't quite hide.

"Elect MACKINSEN for SHERIFF. HONEST—INCOR-
RUPTIBLE—FEARLESS."

Stan drew back his arm and let the bulb fly. "You son-of-
a-bitch whoremonger!" Slowly, as if by the very intensity of
his attention he had slowed down time itself, the bulb struck
the printed face and shattered, the sparkling fragments sailing
high in the air and glittering as they fell.

As if an abscess inside him had broken, Stan could breathe
again and the knot of fear loosened. He could never fear again
with the same agony. He knew it. It would never come again
as bad as that. His mind, clear as the bright air around him,
took over, and he began to think.

The World

Within a circling garland a girl dances;
the beasts of the Apocalypse look on.

SINCE MORNING, Stan's brain had been full of whirring wheels, grinding away at every possible answer. Where were you when he was over by the geek? On my platform, setting up my cot. What did you do then? Practiced a new move with cards. What move? Front-and-back-hand palm. Where did he go? Under the stage, I guess. You were watching him? Only that he didn't go outside. Where were you when Zeena came back? At the entrance waiting for her. . . .

Now the crowd was thinning out. Outside the stars had misted over and there was a flash of lightning behind the trees. At eleven Hoately stopped the bally. The last marks left and the inhabitants of the Ten-in-One smoked while they dressed. At last they gathered with sober faces around Hoately. Only Major Mosquito seemed unaffected. He started to whistle gaily, someone told him to pipe down.

When the last one was ready they filed out and got into cars. Stan rode with Hoately, the Major, Bruno, and Sailor

Martin toward the center of town where the undertaker's parlor was located.

"Lucky break the funeral happened on a slow night," the Sailor said. No one answered him.

Then Major Mosquito chirruped, "O death, where is thy sting? O grave, where is thy victory?" He spat. "Why do they have to crap it up with all that stuff? Why can't they just shovel 'em under and let 'em start falling apart?"

"You shut up!" Bruno said thickly. "You talk too much for little fellow."

"Go frig a rubber duck."

"Tough on Zeena," Bruno said to the others. "She is fine woman."

Clem Hoately, driving with one hand carelessly on the wheel, said, "That rum-pot ain't going to be missed by nobody. Not even Zeena after a while. But it makes you take a good think for yourself. I remember that guy when he was big stuff. I ain't touched a drop in over a year now and I ain't going to, either. Seen too much of it."

"Who's going to work the act with Zeena?" Stan asked after a time. "She going to change her act? She could handle the questions herself and work one ahead."

Hoately scratched his head with his free hand. "That ain't too good nowadays. She don't have to change the act. You could work the undercover part. I'll take the house collection. We'll throw the Electric Girl between your spot and Zeena's, give you time to slip in and get set."

"Suits me."

He said it, Stan kept repeating. It wasn't my idea. The Major and Bruno heard him. He said it.

The street was empty and the light from the funeral parlor made a golden wedge on the sidewalk. Behind them the other car drew up. Old Maguire, the Ten-in-One's ticket seller and grinder, got out, then Molly; then Joe Plasky swung himself out on his hands and crossed the sidewalk. He reminded Stan of a frog, moving deliberately.

Zeena met them at the door. She was wearing a new black outfit, a dress with enormous flowers worked on it in jet. "Come on in, folks. I—I got Pete all laid out handsome. I just phoned a reverend and he's coming over. I thought it was

nicer to get a reverend if we could, even if Pete wasn't no
church man."

They went inside. Joe Plasky fumbled in his pocket and held
an envelope up to Zeena. "The boys chipped in for a stone,
Zeena. They knew you didn't need the dough but they
wanted to do something. I wrote the Billboard this afternoon.
They'll carry a box. I just said, 'Mourned by his many friends
in show business.'"

She bent down and kissed him. "That's—that's damn sweet
of you all. I guess we better get into the chapel. This looks
like the reverend coming."

They took their places on folding chairs. The clergyman was
a meek, dull little old man, looking sleepy. Embarrassed, too,
Stan figured. As if carny folks were not quite human—like
they had all left their pants off only he was too polite to let
on he noticed.

He put on his glasses. ". . . we brought nothing into this
world and it is certain we can carry nothing out. The Lord
gave, and the Lord hath taken . . ."

Stan, sitting beside Zeena, tried to concentrate on the
words and guess what the reverend was going to say next.
Anything to keep from thinking. It's not my fault he's
dead. I didn't mean to kill him. I killed him. There it starts
again and all day I wasn't feeling anything and I thought I'd
lost it.

"Lord, let me know my end, and the number of my days;
that I may be certified how long I have to live . . ."

Pete never knew his end. Pete died happy. I did him a favor.
He had been dying for years. He was afraid of living and he
was trying to ease himself out only I had to go and kill him.
I didn't kill him. He killed himself. Sooner or later he would
have taken a chance on that wood alky. I only helped him a
little. Christ, will I have to think about this damn thing the
rest of my life?

Stan slowly turned his head and looked at the others. Molly
was sitting with the Major between her and Bruno. In the
back row Clem Hoately had his eyes shut. Joe Plasky's face
held the shadow of a smile that was too deeply cut into it ever
to vanish completely. It was the sort of smile Lazarus must

have had afterwards, Stan thought. Sailor Martin had one eye closed.

The sight of the Sailor rushed Stan back to normal. He had done that a hundred times himself, sitting beside his father on the hard pew, watching his mother in a white surplice there in the choir stall with the other ladies. There's a blind spot in your eye and if you shut one eye and then let the gaze of the other travel in a straight line to one side of the preacher's head there will be a point where his head seems to disappear and he seems to be standing there preaching without any head.

Stan looked at Zeena beside him. Her mind was far away somewhere. The reverend speeded up.

"Man that is born of woman hath but a short time to live, and is full of misery. He cometh up and is cut down, like a flower; he fleeth as it were a shadow, and never continueth in one stay. In the midst of life we are in death . . ."

Behind them Major Mosquito heaved a sharp sigh and wriggled, the chair creaking. Bruno said, "Shoosh!"

When they got to the Lord's Prayer Stan found his voice with relief. Zeena must hear it. If she heard it she couldn't suspect him of having anything to do with— Stan lowered his voice and the words came automatically. She mustn't ever think—and yet she had looked at him sharp when he had said Pete was hanging around the geek. She mustn't think. Only he mustn't overplay it. God damn it, this was the time for misdirection if ever there was one. ". . . *for thine is the kingdom, the power and the glory for ever and ever.*"

"Amen."

The undertaker was silently brisk. He removed the coffin lid and set it noiselessly behind the casket. Zeena brought her handkerchief up to her face and turned away. They formed a line and passed by.

Clem Hoately came first, his furrowed face showing nothing. Then Bruno, holding Major Mosquito on his forearm so he could look down and see. Molly came next and Sailor Martin fell in behind her, moving close. Then old Maguire, his cap crushed in his hand. Joe Plasky hopped across the floor, pushing one of the folding chairs. When it came his turn to view the remains he moved the chair into place by the head of the coffin and swung himself up on the seat. He looked down and the smile was still around the corners of his eyes although his mouth was sober. Without thinking he made the sign of the cross.

Stan swallowed hard. It was his turn and there was no way of getting out of it. Joe had hopped to the floor and pushed the chair against the wall; Stan shoved both hands deep into his pockets and approached the casket. He had never seen a corpse; the skin of his scalp prickled at the thought.

He drew his breath and forced himself to look.

It seemed at first like a wax figure in a dress suit. One hand rested easily on the white waistcoat, the other was by the side. It held a round, clear glass ball. The face was rosy—the undertaker had filled out the drawn cheeks and painted the skin until it glowed with a waxen counterfeit of life. But there was something else that hit Stan like a blow between the ribs. Carefully fashioned of crêpe hair and stuck to the chin was a lifelike, neatly trimmed, little black beard.

"For the last demonstration Mamzelle Electra will perform a feat never attempted since Ben Franklin harnessed the lightning with his kite string. Holding the two filaments of a carbon arc light, she will allow the death-dealing current to pass through her body. . . ."

Stan quietly slipped into the compartment below the stage of Zeena, the Woman Who Knows. It no longer smelled of whisky. Stan had installed a piece of canvas as a ground sheet and had cut ventilation scrolls in the sides of the boxlike little room. Over the bridge table and on three sides of it he had erected a cardboard shield so he could open the envelopes and copy the questions on the pad by the light of a flashlight.

The rustle of feet surging around the stage outside, then Zeena's voice in her opening spiel. Stan took a bundle of dummy questions—blank cards in small envelopes—and stood by the window where Hoately would pass behind the curtains.

They parted at the side of the stage; Hoately's hand appeared. Quickly Stan took the collected questions and placed the dummy batch in the hand which vanished upward. Stan heard the creak of feet on the boards above him. He sat down at the table, switched on the shaded flashlight bulb, squared up the pack of envelopes and cut the ends from them with one snip of the scissors. Moving quickly, he shook out the cards and arranged them before him on the table.

Question: "Where is my son?" Handwriting old-fashioned. Woman over sixty, he judged. A good one to open with—the signature was clear and spelled out in full—Mrs. Anna Briggs Sharpley. Stan looked for two more complete names. One was signed to a wiseacre question which he put aside. He reached for the black crayon and the pad, wrote, "Where son?" printed the name swiftly but plainly, and held the pad up to the hole in the stage at Zeena's feet.

"I get the impression of the initial *S*. Is there a Mrs. Sharpley?"

Stan found himself listening to the answers as if they held a revelation.

"You think of your boy as still a little fellow, the way you knew him when he used to come asking you for a piece of bread with sugar on it. . . ."

Where the hell did Zeena get all that stuff from? She was no more telepathic than that kid, Molly, was electricity proof. The Electric Chair act was gaffed like everything in the carny. But Zeena—

"My dear lady, you must remember that he's a man grown now and probably has children of his own to worry about. You want him to write to you. Isn't that so?"

It was uncanny how Zeena could fish out things just by watching the person's face. Stan got a sudden thrust of cold fear. Of all the people in the world for him to hide anything from, it had to be a mind reader. He laughed a little in spite of his anxiety. But there was something which pulled him toward Zeena more strongly than his fear that she would find out and make him a murderer. How do you get to know so much that you can tell people what they are thinking about just by looking at them? Maybe you had to be born with the gift.

"Is Clarissa here? Clarissa, hold up your hand. That's a good girl. Now Clarissa wants to know if the young fellow she's been going around with is the right one for her to marry. Well, Clarissa, I may disappoint you but I have to speak the truth. You wouldn't want me to tell you no fibs. I don't think this boy is the one for you to marry. Mind, he may be and I don't doubt that he's a mighty fine young man. But something tells me that when the right young fellow comes along you won't ask me, you won't ask anybody—you'll just up and marry him."

That question had come up before and Zeena nearly always answered it the same way. The thought struck Stan that it was not genius after all. Zeena knew people. But people were a lot alike. What you told one you could tell nine out of ten. And there was one out of five that would believe everything you told them and would say yes to anything when you asked them if it was correct because they were the kind of marks that can't say no. Good God, Zeena is working for peanuts! Somewhere in this racket there is a gold mine!

Stan picked up another card and wrote on the pad: "Advise important domestic step, Emma." By God, if she can answer that one she must be a mind reader. He held it up to the trap and listened.

Zeena pattered on for a moment, thinking to herself and then her voice lifted and her heel knocked gently. Stan took down the pad and knew that this would be the blow-off question and he could relax. After this one she would go into the pitch.

"I have time for just one more question. And this is a question that I'm not going to ask anybody to acknowledge. There's a lady here whose first name begins with *E*. I'm not going to tell her full name because it's a very personal question. But I'm going to ask Emma to think about what she is trying to tell me mentally."

Stan switched off the flashlight, crept out of the understage compartment and tiptoed up the stairs behind the side curtains. Parting them carefully with his fingers he placed his eye to the crack. The marks' faces were a mass of pale circles below him. But at the mention of the name "Emma" he saw one face—a pale, haggard woman who looked forty but might be thirty. The lips parted and the eyes answered for an instant. Then the lips were pressed tight in resignation.

Zeena lowered her voice. "Emma, you have a serious problem. And it concerns somebody very near and dear to you. Or somebody who used to be very near and dear, isn't that right?" Stan saw the woman's head nod involuntarily.

"You are contemplating a serious step—whether to leave this person. And I think he's your husband." The woman bit her under lip. Her eyes grew moist quickly. That kind cries at the drop of a hat, Stan thought. If only she had a million bucks instead of a greasy quarter.

"Now there are two lines of vibration working about this problem. One of them concerns another woman." The tension left the woman's face and a sullen frown of disappointment drew over it. Zeena changed her tack. "But now the impressions get stronger and I can see that while there may have been some woman in the past, right now the problem is something else. I see cards . . . playing cards falling on a table . . . but no, it isn't your husband who's playing. It's the place . . . I get it now, clear as daylight. It's the back room of a saloon."

A sob came from the woman, and people twisted their heads this way and that; but Emma was watching the seeress, unmindful of the others.

"My dear friend, you have a mighty heavy cross to bear. I know all about it and don't you think I don't. But the step that confronts you now is a problem with a good many sides. If your husband was running around with other women and didn't love you that would be one thing. But I get a very strong impression that he does love you—in spite of everything. Oh, I know he acts nasty-mean sometimes but you just ask yourself if any of the blame is yours. Because here's one thing you must never forget: a man drinks because he's unhappy. Isn't anything about liquor that makes a man bad. A man that's happy can take a drink with the boys on Saturday night and come home with his pay safe in his pocket. But when a man's miserable about something he takes a drink to forget it and one isn't enough and he takes another snort and pretty soon the week's pay is all gone and he gets home and sobers up and then his wife starts in on him and he's more miserable than he was before and then his first thought is to go get drunk again and it runs around and around in a circle."

Zeena had forgotten the other customers, she had forgotten the pitch. She was talking out of herself. The marks knew it and were hanging on every word, fascinated.

"Before you take that step," she went on, suddenly coming back to the show, "you want to be sure that you've done all you can to make that man happy. Maybe you can't learn what's bothering him. Maybe he don't quite know himself. But try to find it. Because if you leave him you'll have to find some way to take care of yourself and the kids anyhow. Well, why not start in tonight? If he comes home drunk put him to bed. Try talking to him friendly. When a man's drunk he's a lot like a kid. Well, treat him like a son and don't go jumping on him. Tomorrow morning let him know that you understand and mother him up a little. Because if that man loves you—" Zeena paused for breath and then rushed on. "If that man loves you it don't matter whether he makes a living or not. It don't matter if he stays sober or not. If you've got a man that really loves you, you hang on to him like grim death for better or worse." There was a catch in her voice and for a long moment silence hung in the air over the waiting crowd. "Hang on—because you'll never regret it as much as you'll regret sending him away and now folks if you really want to know how the stars affect your life you don't have to pay five dollars or even one dollar I have here a set of astrological readings all worked out for each and every one of you let me know your date of birth and you get a forecast of future events complete with character reading, vocational guidance, lucky numbers. . . ."

For the long haul the Ackerman-Zorbaugh Monster Shows took to the railroad. Trucks loaded on flatcars, the carnies themselves loaded into old coaches, the train boomed on through darkness—tearing past solitary jerk towns, past sidings of dark freight empties, over trestles, over bridges where the rivers lay coiling their luminous way through the star-shadowed countryside.

In the baggage car, among piles of canvas and gear, a light burned high up on the wall. A large packing case with auger holes bored in its sides to admit air, stood in the middle of a cleared space. From inside it came intermittent scrapings. At one end of the car the geek lay on a pile of canvas, his ragged, overalled knees drawn up to his chin.

Around the snake box men made the air gray with smoke.

"I'm staying." Major Mosquito's voice had the insistence of a cricket's.

Sailor Martin screwed up the left side of his face against the smoke of his cigarette and dealt.

"I'm in," Stan said. He had a Jack in the hole. The highest card showing was a ten in the Sailor's hand.

"I'm with you," Joe Plasky said, the Lazarus smile never changing.

Behind Joe sat the hulk of Bruno, his shoulders rounding under his coat. He watched intently, his mouth dropping open as he concentrated on Joe's hand.

"I'm in, too," Martin said. He dealt. Stan got another Jack and pushed in three blues.

"Going to cost you to string along," he said casually.

Martin had dealt himself another ten. "I'll string along."

Major Mosquito, his baby head close to the boxtop, stole another glance at his hole card. "Nuts!"

"Guess it's between you gents," Joe said placidly. Bruno, from behind him, said, "Ja. Let them fight it out. We take it easy this time."

Martin dealt. Two little ones fell between them. Stan threw more blues in. Martin met him and raised him two more.

"I'll see you."

The Sailor threw over his hole card. A ten. He reached for the pot.

Stan smiled and counted his chips. At a sound from the Major all of them jumped. "Hey!" It was like a long-drawn fiddle scrape.

"What's eating you, Big Noise?" Martin asked, grinning.

"Lemme see them tens!" The Major reached toward the center of the snake box with his infant's hand and drew the cards toward him. He examined the backs.

Bruno got up and moved over behind the midget. He picked up one of the cards and held it at an angle toward the light.

"What's eating you guys?" Martin said.

"Daub!" Major Mosquito wailed, taking his cigarette from

the edge of the box and puffing it rapidly. "The cards are marked with daub. They're smeared to act like readers. You can see it if you know where to look."

Martin took one and examined it. "Damn! You're right."

"They're your cards," the Major went on in his accusing falsetto.

Martin bristled. "What d'ya mean, my cards? Somebody left 'em around the cookhouse. If I hadn't thought to bring 'em we wouldn't have had no game."

Stan took the deck and riffled them under his thumb. Then he riffled again, throwing cards face down on the table. When he reversed them they were all high ones, picture cards and tens. "That's daub, all right," he said. "Let's get a new deck."

"You're the card worker," Martin said aggressively. "What do you know about this? Daub is stuff you smear on the other fellow's cards during the game."

"I know enough not to use it," Stan said easily. "I don't deal. I never deal. And if I wanted to work any angles I'd stack them on the pick up until I got the pair I wanted on top the deck, undercut and injog the top card of the top half, shuffle off eight, outjog and shuffle off. Then I'd undercut to the outjog—"

"Let's get a new deck," Joe Plasky said. "We won't any of us get rich arguing about how the cards got marked. Who's got a deck?"

They sat silent, the expansion joints of the rails clicking by beneath them. Then Stan said, "Zeena has a deck of fortune-telling cards we can play with. I'll get them."

Martin took the marked deck, stepped to the partly open door and sent the cards flying into the wind. "Maybe a new deck will change my luck," he said. "I been going bust every hand except the last one."

The car shook and pounded on through the dark. Behind the open door they could see the dark hills and a sliver of moon setting behind them with a scattering of stars.

Stan returned and with him came Zeena. Her black dress was relieved by a corsage of imitation gardenias, her hair caught up on top of her head with a random collection of blond hairpins.

"Howdy, gents. Thought I'd take a hand myself if I wouldn't be intruding. Sure gets deadly back in that coach. I reckon I've read every movie magazine in the outfit by this time." She opened her purse and placed a deck of cards on the box. "Now you boys let me see your hands. All clean? 'Cause I don't want you smooching up these cards and getting 'em dirty. They're hard enough to get hold of."

Stan took the deck carefully and fanned them. The faces were an odd conglomeration of pictures. One showed a dead man, his back skewered with ten swords. Another had a picture of three women in ancient robes, each holding a cup. A hand reaching out of a cloud, on another, held a club from which green leaves sprouted.

"What do you call these things, Zeena?" he asked.

"That's the Tarot," she said impressively. "Oldest kind of cards in the world. They go all the way back to Egypt, some say. And they're sure a wonder for giving private readings. Every time I have something to decide or don't know which way to turn I run them over for myself. I always get some kind of an answer that makes sense. But you can play poker with 'em. They got four suits: wands are diamonds, cups are hearts, swords are clubs, and coins are spades. This bunch of pictures here—that's the Great Arcana. They're just for fortunetelling. But there's one of 'em—if I can find it—we can use for a joker. Here it is." She threw it out and placed the others back in her purse.

Stan picked up the joker. At first he couldn't figure out which end was the top. It showed a young man suspended head down by one foot from a T-shaped cross, but the cross was of living wood, putting out green shoots. The youth's hands were tied behind his back. A halo of golden light shone about his head and on reversing the card Stan saw that his expression was one of peace—like that of a man raised from the dead. Like Joe Plasky's smile. The name of the card was printed in old-fashioned script at the bottom. *The Hanged Man.*

"Holy Christ, if these damn things don't change my luck, nothing will," the Sailor said.

Zeena took a pile of chips from Joe Plasky, ante'd, then

shuffled and dealt the hole cards face down. She lifted hers a
trifle and frowned. The game picked up. Stan had an eight of
cups in the hole and dropped out. Never stay in unless you
have a Jack or better in the hole and drop out when better
than a Jack shows on the board. Unless you've got the difference.

Zeena's frown deepened. The battle was between her, Sailor
Martin, and the Major. Then the Sailor dropped out. The
Major's hand showed three Knights. He called. Zeena held a
flush in coins.

"Ain't you the bluffer," the Major piped savagely. "Frowning like you had nothing and you sitting on top a flush."

Zeena shook her head. "I wasn't meaning to bluff, even. It
was the hole card I was frowning at—the ace of coins, what
they call pentacles. I always read that 'Injury by a trusted
friend.'"

Stan uncrossed his legs and said, "Maybe the snakes have
something to do with it. They're scraping around under the
lid here like they were uncomfortable."

Major Mosquito spat on the floor, then poked his finger in
one of the auger holes. He withdrew it, chirruping. From the
hole flicked a forked thread of pink. The Major drew his lips
back from his tiny teeth and quickly touched the lighted ember of his cigarette to the tongue. It flashed back into the box
and there was the frenzied scraping of coils twisting and whipping inside.

"Jesus!" Martin said. "You shouldn't of done that, you
little stinker. Them damn things'll get mad."

The Major threw back his head. "Ho, ho, ho, ho! Next
time I'll do it to you—I'll make a hit on the Battleship
Maine."

Stan stood up. "I've had enough, gents. Don't let me break
up the game, though."

Balancing against the rock of the train, he pushed through
the piled canvas to the platform of the next coach. His left
hand slid under the edge of his vest and unpinned a tiny metal
box the size and shape of a five-cent piece. He let his hand
drop and the container fell between the cars. It had left a dark
smudge on his finger. Why do I have to frig around with all
this chickenshit stuff? I didn't want their dimes. I wanted to

see if I could take them. Jesus, the only thing you can depend on is your brains!

In the coach, under the dimmed lights, the crowd of carnival performers and concessioners sprawled, huddled, heads on each others' shoulders; some had stretched themselves on newspapers in the aisles. In the corner of a seat Molly slept, her lips slightly parted, her head against the glass of the black window.

How helpless they all looked in the ugliness of sleep. A third of life spent unconscious and corpselike. And some, the great majority, stumbled through their waking hours scarcely more awake, helpless in the face of destiny. They stumbled down a dark alley toward their deaths. They sent exploring feelers into the light and met fire and writhed back again into the darkness of their blind groping.

At the touch of a hand on his shoulder Stan jerked around. It was Zeena. She stood with her feet apart, braced easily against the train's rhythm. "Stan, honey, we don't want to let what's happened get us down. God knows, I felt bad about Pete. And I guess you did too. Everybody did. But this don't stop us from living. And I been wondering . . . you still like me, don't you, Stan?"

"Sure—sure I do, Zeena. Only I thought—"

"That's right, honey. The funeral and all. But I can't keep up mourning for Pete forever. My mother, now—she'd of been grieving around for a year but what I say is, it's soon enough we'll all be pushing 'em up. We got to get some fun. Tell you what. When we land at the next burg, let's us ditch the others and have a party."

Stan slid his arm around her and kissed her. In the swaying, plunging gait of the train their teeth clicked and they broke apart, laughing a little. Her hand smoothed his cheek. "I've missed you like all hell, honey." She buried her face in the hollow of his throat.

Over her shoulder Stan looked into the car of sleepers. Their faces had changed, had lost their hideousness. The girl Molly had waked up and was eating a chocolate bar. There was a smudge of chocolate over her chin. Zeena suspected nothing.

Stan raised his left hand and examined it. On the ball of the ring finger was a dark streak. Daub. He touched his tongue to it and then gripped Zeena's shoulder, wiping the stain on the black dress.

They broke apart and pushed down the aisle to a pile of suitcases where they managed to sit. In her ear Stan said, "Zeena, how does a two-person code work? I mean a good one—the kind you and Pete used to work." Audiences in evening clothes. Top billing. The Big Time.

Zeena leaned close, her voice suddenly husky. "Wait till we get to the burg. I can't think about nothing except you right now, honey. I'll tell you some time. Anything you want to know. But now I want to think about what's coming between the sheets." She caught one of his fingers and gave it a squeeze.

In the baggage coach Major Mosquito turned over his hole card. "Three deuces of swords showing and one wild one in the hole makes four of a kind. Ha, ha, ha, ha. *The Hanged Man!*"

When Stan woke up it was still dark. The electric sign which had been flaring on and off with blinding regularity, spelling out the name of Ayres' Department Store, was quiet at last and the smeared windowpane was dark. Something had wakened him. The mattress was hard and sagging; against his back he felt the warmth of Zeena's body.

Silently the bed shook and Stan's throat tightened with a reflex of fear at the unknown and the darkness until he felt the shake again and then a muffled gasp. Zeena was crying.

Stan turned over and slid his arm around her and cupped her breast with his hand. She had to be babied when she got this way.

"Stan, honey—"

"What's the matter, baby?"

Zeena turned heavily and pressed a damp cheek against his bare chest. "Just got to thinking about Pete."

There was nothing to say to this so Stan tightened his arms around her and kept quiet.

"You know, today I was going through some of the stuff in the little tin trunk—Pete's stuff. His old press books and old letters and all kinds of stuff. And I found the notebook he used to keep. The one he had the start of our code in. Pete invented that code himself and we were the only people that ever knew it. Pete was offered a thousand dollars for it by Allah Kismet—that was Syl Rappolo. He was one of the biggest crystal-workers in the country. But Pete just laughed at him. That old book was just like a part of Pete. He had such nice handwriting in them days . . ."

Stan said nothing but turned her face up and began kissing her. He was fully awake now and could feel the pulse jumping in his throat. He mustn't seem too eager. Better love her up first, all the way if he could do it again.

He found that he could.

It was Zeena's turn to keep quiet. Finally Stan said, "What are we going to do about your act?"

Her voice was suddenly crisp. "What about the act?"

"I thought maybe you were thinking of changing it."

"What for? Ain't we taking in more on the pitch than ever? Look, honey, if you feel you ought to be cut in for a bigger percentage don't be bashful—"

"I'm not talking about that," he interrupted her. "In this damn state nobody can write. Every time I stick a card and a pencil under the nose of some mark he says, 'You write it for me.' If I could remember all that stuff I could let 'em keep the cards in their pockets."

Zeena stretched leisurely, the bed creaking under her. "Don't you worry about Zeena, honey. When they can't write their names they're even more receptive to the answers. Why, I could quit the question-answering part of the act and just get up there and spiel away and then go into the pitch and still turn 'em."

A thrill of alarm raced along Stan's nerves at the thought of Zeena's being able to do without him before he could do without her. "But I mean, couldn't we work a code act? You could still do it, couldn't you?"

She chuckled. "Listen, schniggle-fritz, I can do it in my sleep. But it takes a hell of a lot of work to get all them lists and things learned. And the season's more than half over."

"I could learn it."

She thought for a while and then she said, "It's all right

with me, honey. It's all down in Pete's book. Only don't you lose that book or Zeena'll cut your ears off."

"You have it here?"

"Wait a minute. Where's the fire? Sure I've got it here. You'll see it. Don't go getting sizzle-britches."

More silence. At last Stan sat up and swung his feet to the floor. "I better get back to that pantry they rented me for a room. We don't want the townies here to get any more ideas than they've got already." He snapped on the light and began to put on his clothes. In the garish light overhead Zeena looked haggard and battered like a worn wax doll. She had the sheet pulled over her middle but her breasts sagged over it. Her hair was in two brassy braids and the ends were uneven and spiky. Stan put on his shirt and knotted his tie. He slipped on his jacket.

"You're a funny fella."

"Why?"

"Getting all dressed up to walk thirty feet down the hall of a fleabag like this at four in the morning."

Somehow Stan felt this to be a reflection on his courage. His face grew warm. "Nothing like doing things right."

Zeena yawned cavernously. "Guess you're right, kiddo. See you in the morning. And thanks for the party."

He made no move to turn out the light. "Zeena, that notebook— Could I see it?"

She threw off the sheet, got up and squatted to snap open the suitcase. Does a woman always look more naked after you've had her, Stan wondered. Zeena rummaged in the bag and drew out a canvas-covered book marked "Ledger."

"Now run along, honey. Or come back to bed. Make up your mind."

Stan tucked the book under his arm and switched off the light. He felt his way to the door and with caution turned back the bolt. Yellow light from the hall sliced over the patchy wallpaper as he opened the door.

There was a whisper from the bed. "Stan—"

"What is it?"

"Come kiss your old pal good night."

He stepped over, kissed her cheek and left without another word, closing the door softly behind him.

The lock of his own door sounded like a rifle shot.

He looked each way along the hall but nothing stirred.

Inside, he tore off his clothes, went to the washbowl and washed and then threw himself down on the bed, propping the book on his bare stomach.

The first pages were taken up with figures and notations:

"Evansport. July 20th. Books—$33.00 taken in. Paid—Plants at $2—$6.00. Plants: Mrs. Jerome Hotchkiss. Leonard Keely, Josiah Boos. All okay. Old spook workers. Boos looks like deacon. Can act a little. Worked the found ring in the coat lining . . ."

"Spook workers" must refer to the local confederates employed by traveling mediums. Swiftly Stan flipped the pages. More expenses: "F. T. rap squared. Chief Pellett. $50." That would be an arrest on a charge of fortune telling.

Stan felt like Ali Baba in the cavern of riches left by the Forty Thieves.

Impatiently he turned to the back of the book. On the last page was a heading: "Common Questions." Beneath it was a list, with figures:

"Is my husband true to me? 56, 29, 18, 42.

"Will mother get well? 18, 3, 7, 12.

"Who poisoned our dog? 3, 2, 3, 0, 3." Beside this was the notation, "Not a big item but a steady. Every audience. Can pull as cold reading during stall part of act."

The figures, then, were a record of the number of similar questions collected from the same audience. The question "Is my wife faithful?" had only about a third the number of entries as the one about the husband.

"The chumps," Stan whispered. "Either too bashful to ask or too dumb to suspect." But they were anxious to find out, all of them. As if jazzing wasn't what they all want, the goddamned hypocrites. They all want it. Only nobody else must have it. He turned the page.

"There is a recurring pattern followed by the questions asked. For every unusual question there will be fifty that you have had before. Human nature is the same everywhere. All have the same troubles. They are worried. Can control anybody by finding out what he's afraid of. Works with question-answering act. Think out things most people are afraid of and hit them right where they live. Health, Wealth, Love. And Travel and Success. They're all afraid of ill health, of poverty, of boredom, of failure. Fear is the key to human nature. They're afraid. . . ."

Stan looked past the pages to the garish wallpaper and through it into the world. The geek was made by fear. He was afraid of sobering up and getting the horrors. But what made him a drunk? Fear. Find out what they are afraid of and sell it back to them. That's the key. The key! He had known it when Clem Hoately had told him how geeks are made. But here was Pete saying the same thing:

Health. Wealth. Love. Travel. Success. "A few have to do with domestic troubles, in-laws, kids, pets. And so on. A few wisenheimers but you can ditch them easily enough. Idea: combine question-answering act with code act. Make list of questions, hook up with code numbers. Answer vague at first, working toward definite. If can see face of spectator and tell when hitting."

On the following pages was a neatly numbered list of questions. There were exactly a hundred. Number One was "Is my husband true to me?" Number Two was "Will I get a job soon?"

Outside the front of Ayres' Department Store had turned rosy-red with the coming sun. Stan paid it no heed. The sun slid up, the sound of wagon tires on concrete told of the awakening city. At ten o'clock there was a tap on the door. Stan shook himself. "Yes?"

Zeena's voice. "Wake up, sleepy head. Rise and shine."

He unlocked the door and let her in.

"What you got the light on for?" She turned it out, then saw the book. "Lord's sake, kid, ain't you been to bed at all?"

Stan rubbed his eyes and stood up. "Ask me a number. Any number up to a hundred."

"Fifty-five."

"Will my mother-in-law always live with us?"

Zeena sat down beside him and ran her fingers through his hair. "You know what I think, kid? I think you're a mind reader."

The carny turned south and the pines began to line sandy

roads. Cicadas drummed the late summer air and the crowds of white people were gaunter, their faces filled with desolation, their lips often stained with snuff.

Everywhere the shining, dark faces of the South's other nation caught the highlights from the sun. They stood in quiet wonder, watching the carny put up in the smoky morning light. In the Ten-in-One they stood always on the fringe of the crowd, an invisible cordon holding them in place. When one of the whites turned away sharply and jostled them the words "Scuse me," fell from them like pennies balanced on their shoulders.

Stan had never been this far south and something in the air made him uneasy. This was dark and bloody land where hidden war traveled like a million earthworms under the sod.

The speech fascinated him. His ear caught the rhythm of it and he noted their idioms and worked some of them into his patter. He had found the reason behind the peculiar, drawling language of the old carny hands—it was a composite of all the sprawling regions of the country. A language which sounded Southern to Southerners, Western to Westerners. It was the talk of the soil and its drawl covered the agility of the brains that poured it out. It was a soothing, illiterate, earthy language.

The carny changed its tempo. The outside talkers spoke more slowly.

Zeena cut the price of her horoscopes to a dime each but sold "John the Conqueror Root" along with them for fifteen cents. This was a dried mass of twisting roots which was supposed to attract good fortune when carried in a bag around the neck. Zeena got them by the gross from an occult mail-order house in Chicago.

Stan's pitch of the magic books took a sudden drop and Zeena knew the answer. "These folks down here don't know nothing about sleight-of-hand, honey. Half of 'em figure you're doing real magic. Well, you got to have something superstitious to pitch."

Stan ordered a gross of paper-backed books, "One Thousand and One Dreams Interpreted." He threw in as a free gift a brass lucky coin stamped with the Seal of Love from the Seventh Book of Moses, said to attract the love of others and lead to the confusion of enemies. His pitch picked up in fine style. He learned to roll three of the lucky coins over his fingers at once. The tumbling, glittering cascade of metal seemed to fascinate the marks, and the dream books went fast.

He had learned the verbal code for questions not a day too soon, for the people couldn't write or were too shy to try.

"*Will* you *kindly* answer this lady's question *at once*?" Stan had cued the question, "Is my daughter all right?"

Zeena's voice had taken on a deeper southern twang. "Well, now, I get the impression that the lady is worried about someone near and dear to her, someone she hasn't heard from in a long time, am I right? Strikes me it's a young lady— It's your daughter you're thinking of, isn't it? Of course. And you want to know if she's well and happy and if you'll see her again soon. Well, I believe you will get some news of her through a third person before the month is out. . . ."

There was one question that came up so often that Stan worked out a silent signal for it. He would simply jerk his head in Zeena's direction. The first time he used it the question had come to him from a man—massive and loose-jointed with clear eyes smoldering in a handsome ebony face. "Am I ever going to make a trip?"

Zeena picked it up. "Man over there is wondering about something that's going to happen to him and I want to say right here and now that I believe you're going to get your wish. And I think it has something to do with travel. You want to make a trip somewheres. Isn't that so? Well, I see some troubles on the road and I see a crowd of people—men, they are, asking a lot of questions. But I see the journey completed after a while, not as soon as you want to make it but after a while. And there's a job waiting for you at the end of it. Job with good pay. It's somewhere to the north of here; I'm positive of that."

It was sure-fire. All of 'em want North, Stan thought. It was the dark alley, all over again. With a light at the end of it. Ever since he was a kid Stan had had the dream. He was running down a dark alley, the buildings vacant and black and menacing on either side. Far down at the end of it a light burned; but there was something behind him, close behind him, getting closer until he woke up trembling and never reached the light. They have it too—a nightmare alley. The North isn't the end. The light will only move further on. And the fear close behind them. White and black, it made no difference. The geek and his bottle, staving off the clutch of the thing that came following after.

In the hot sun of noon the cold breath could strike your neck. In having a woman her arms were a barrier. But after she had fallen asleep the walls of the alley closed in on your own sleep and the footsteps followed.

Now the very country simmered with violence, and Stan looked enviously at the sculptured muscles of Bruno Hertz. It wasn't worth the time and backbreaking effort it took to get that way. There must be an easier way. Some sort of jujitsu system where a man could use his brains and his agility. The Ackerman-Zorbaugh Monster Shows had never had a "Hey-rube" since Stan had been with them, but the thought of one ate at his peace of mind like a maggot. What would he do in a mob fight? What would they do to him?

Then Sailor Martin nearly precipitated one.

It was a steaming day of late summer. The South had turned out: hollow-eyed women with children in their arms and clinging to their skirts, lantern-jawed men, deadly quiet.

Clem Hoately had mounted the platform where Bruno sat quietly fanning himself with a palm-leaf fan. "If you'll step right this way, folks, I want to call your attention to one of the miracle men of all time—Herculo, the strongest man alive."

Stan looked back to the rear of the tent. In the corner by the geek's enclosure Sailor Martin had a couple of local youths engrossed in the strap on the barrelhead. He took a leather strap, folded it in the middle, then coiled it on the top of a nail keg. He placed his own finger in one of the two loops in the center and pulled the strap. His finger had picked the real loop in the strap. Then he bet one of the marks he couldn't pick the real loop. The mark bet and won and the Sailor handed him a silver dollar.

Zeena drew the curtains of the little stage and came out at the side. She drew a handkerchief from her bosom and touched her temples with it. "Whew, ain't it a scorcher to-

day?" She followed Stan's glance to the rear of the tent. "The
Sailor better go easy. Hoately don't like anybody to case the
marks on the side this far south. Can't blame him. Too likely
to start a rumpus. I say, if you can't make a living with your
pitch you don't belong in no decent Ten-in-One. I could pick
up plenty of honest dollars if I wanted to give special private
readings and remove evil influences and all that stuff. But that
just leads to trouble."

She stopped speaking and her hand tightened on Stan's
arm. "Stan, honey, you better take a walk over there and see
what's going on."

Stan made no move to go. On the platform he was king;
the marks in their anonymous mass were below him and his
voice held them, but down on their level, jammed in among
their milling, collective weight, he felt smothered.

Suddenly one of the youths drew back his foot and kicked
over the nail keg on which Martin had wound the strap with
the elusive loop. The Sailor's voice was raised just a fraction
above conversational level and he seemed to be speaking to
the mark when he said, clearly and coolly, "Hey, rube!"

"Go on, Stan. Hurry. Don't let 'em get started."

As if he had a pistol pointed at his back, Stan marched
across the tent to the spot where trouble was simmering.
From the corner of his eye he saw Joe Plasky hop on his hands
down the steps behind his own platform and swing his way
toward the corner. He would not be alone, at least.

Plasky got there first. "Hello, gents. I'm one of the owners
of the show. Everything all right?"

"Like hell it is," blustered one of the marks. A young
farmer, Stan judged. "This here tattooed son-of-a-bitch got
five dollars of my money by faking. I seen this here strap swindle afore. I aims to get my money back."

"If there's any doubt in your mind about the fairness of
any game of chance in the show I'm sure the Sailor here will
return your original bet. We're all here to have a good time,
mister, and we don't want any hard feelings."

The other mark spoke up. He was a tall, raw-boned sodbuster with a mouth which chronically hung open, showing
long yellow teeth. "I seen this here trick afore, too, mister.
Cain't fool me. Cain't nobody pick out that loop, way this

feller unwinds it. A feller showed me how it works one time. It's a gahdamned swindle."

Joe Plasky's smile was broader than ever. He reached in the pocket of his shirt and drew out a roll of bills and took off a five. He held it up to the farmer. "Here's the money out of my own pocket, son. If you can't afford to lose you can't afford to bet. I'm just returning your bet because we want everybody to have a good time and no hard feelings. Now you boys better mosey along."

The youth shoved the five into the pocket of his pants and the two of them slouched out. Plasky turned to the Sailor. His smile was still there, but a hard, steady light shone in his eyes. "You dumb bastard! This is a tough town. The whole damn state is tough. And you haven't any more sense than to start a Hey-rube. For Christ's sake watch your step! Now give me the five."

Sailor Martin spat between his teeth into the dust. "I won that fin and I could of handled them two jakes. Who elected you Little Tin Jesus around here?"

Plasky put his fingers in his mouth and whistled a single blast. The tip around the last platform was on its way out and Hoately turned back. Joe waved his hand in an arc and Hoately signaled back and let the canvas drop to close the front entrance. Outside old Maguire began to grind, trying to gather a tip and hold them until the show was opened again.

Bruno dropped lightly from his platform and strode over. Stan felt Zeena beside him. Major Mosquito was running back on his infant's legs, shrilling something incoherent.

Joe Plasky said evenly, "Sailor, you been leaving a trail of busted hearts and busted cherries all along the route. Now you're going to hand me that fin and pack up your gear. You're quitting the show. Hoately will back me up."

Stan's knees were weak. Zeena's hand was on his arm, her fingers gripping it. Would he be expected to take on the Sailor? Joe was a cripple, Bruno a superman. Stan was broader and heavier than the Sailor but the thought of a fight sickened him. He never felt that fists were good enough. He would have carried a gun except that it was a lot of trouble and he was afraid of killing with it.

Martin eyed the group. Bruno stood quietly in the background. "I don't fight no cripples, polack. And I don't owe you no five." The Sailor's lips were pale, his eyes hot.

The half-man acrobat reached up and took him by the hand, gripping the fingers together and bending them so that the tattooed man quickly sank to his knees. "Hey, leggo, you bastard!"

Silently and with his face a blank, Plasky crossed his forearms. He let go of Martin's hand and seized the collar of his robe in both fists. Then he levered his wrists together, forcing the backs of his hands into the Sailor's throat. Martin was caught in a human vise. His mouth dropped. He clawed frantically at the crossed arms of the half-man but the more he tugged, the tighter they crushed him. His eyes began to bulge and his hair fell over them.

Major Mosquito was leaping up and down, making fighting motions and shadowboxing. "Kill him! Kill him! Kill him! Choke him till he's dead! Kill the big ape!" He rushed in and began hammering the Sailor's staring face with tiny fists. Bruno picked him up, wriggling, and held him at arm's length by the collar of his jacket.

Joe began to shake the tattoo artist, gently at first and then harder. The calm deadliness of that ingenious and unbreakable hold filled Stan with terror and wild joy.

Clem Hoately came running up. "Okay, Joe. Guess he's educated. Let's break it up. We got a good tip waiting."

Joe smiled his smile of one raised from the dead. He released Sailor, who sat up rubbing his throat and breathing hard. Plasky reached into the pocket of the robe and found a wad of bills, took out a five and put the rest back.

Hoately picked the Sailor up and stood him on his feet. "You knock off, Martin. I'll pay you up to the end of the month. Pack up your stuff and leave whenever you want to."

When Martin was able to speak his voice was a hoarse whisper. "Okay. I'm on my way. I can take my needles into any barber shop and make more dough than in this crummy layout. But watch out, all of you."

Middle evening and a good crowd. Beyond the canvas and the gaudily painted banners Hoately's voice was raspy.

"Hi, look! Hi, look! Hi, look! Right this way for the monster aggregation of nature's mistakes, novelty entertainments, and the world-renowned museum of freaks, marvels, and curiosities. Featuring Mamzelle Electra, the little lady who defies the lightning."

Stan looked across at Molly Cahill. When she held the sputtering arc points together she always flinched; the last day or two, whenever he saw it, a little thrill leaped up his spine. Now she bent over and placed her compact behind the electric chair. Bending stretched her sequinned trunks tight over her buttocks.

It's funny how you can see a girl every day for months and yet not see her, Stan thought. Then something will happen—like the way Molly's mouth presses together when she holds the arc points and the fire starts to fly. Then you see her all different.

He dragged his glance away from the girl. Across the tent the massive chest of Bruno Hertz shone pink with sweat as he flexed the muscles of his upper arms, rippling under the pink skin, and the crowd rubbered.

Molly was sitting demurely in a bentwood chair beside the heavy, square menace with its coiled wires, its straps and its chilling suggestion of death which was as phoney as everything else in the carny. She was studying a green racing form. Absorbed, she reached down and scratched one ankle and Stan felt the ripple go up his back again.

Molly's eyes were on the racing sheet but she had stopped looking at it and was looking through it, her mind in the dream she always dreamed.

There was a man in it and his face was always in shadow. He was taller than she and his voice was low and intense and his hands were brown and powerful. They walked slowly, drinking in the summer reflected from every grass blade, shining from every pebble in fields singing with summer. An old rail fence and beyond it a field rising like a wave, a pasture where the eyes of daisies looked up at a sky so blue it made you ache.

His face was shadowy still, as his arms stole about her. She pressed her hands against the hardness of his chest, but his mouth found hers. She tried to turn her head away; but then his fingers were caressing her hair, his kisses falling upon the hollow of her throat while his other hand found her breast . . .

"Over here, folks, right over here. On this platform we have a little lady who is one of the marvels and mysteries of the age—Mamzelle Electra!"

Stan came up the steps behind Joe Plasky's platform and sat on the edge of it. "How they going?"

Joe smiled and went on assembling the novelties in his joke books, slipping the free gifts between the pages. "Can't complain. Good crowd tonight, ain't it?"

Stan shifted his seat. "I wonder if the Sailor will try to do us any dirt?"

Joe swung himself closer on his calloused knuckles and said, "Can't tell. But I don't think so. After all, he is carny. He's a louse, too. But we just want to keep our eyes open. I don't think he'll try to call me in spades—not after he's felt the *nami juji*."

Stan frowned. "Felt what?"

"*Nami juji*. That's the Jap name for it—that crosshanded choke I slipped on him. That takes some of the starch out of 'em."

The blond head was alert. "Joe, that was terrific, what you did. How in hell did you ever learn that?"

"Jap showed me. We had a Jap juggler when I was with the Keyhoe Shows. It's easy enough to do. He taught me a lot of ju-jit stuff only that's one of the best."

Stan moved closer. "Show me how you do it."

Plasky reached over and slid his right hand up Stan's right coat lapel until he was grasping the collar at the side of Stan's throat. He crossed his left arm over his right and gripped the left side of the collar. Suddenly Stan felt his throat caught in an iron wedge. It loosened immediately; Plasky dropped his hands and smiled. Stan's knees were trembling.

"Let me see if I can do it." He gripped Plasky's black turtle-neck sweater with one hand.

"Higher up, Stan. You got to grab it right opposite the big artery in the neck—here." He shifted the younger man's hand slightly. "Now cross your forearms and grab the other side. Right. Now then, bend your wrists and force the backs of your hands into my neck. That cuts off the blood from the brain."

Stan felt a surge of power along his arms. He did not know that his lips had drawn back over his teeth. Plasky slapped his arm quickly and he let go.

"Christ a-mighty, kid, you want to be careful with that! If you leave it on just a mite too long you'll have a corpse on your hands. And you got to practice getting it quick. It's a little hard to slip on but once you've got it the other fella can't break it—unless he knows the real Jap stuff."

Both men looked up as Maguire, the ticket seller, hurried toward them.

"She-ess-oo flee-ess-eyes!" He ducked past them to where Hoately stood on the Electric Girl's platform.

Plasky's smile widened as it always did in the face of trouble. "Shoo flies, kid. Cops. Just take it easy and you'll be all right. Herc's where Hoately will have to do some real talking. And the fixer will have to earn his pay. I been expecting they'd slough the whole joint one of these days."

"What happens to us?" Stan's mouth had gone dry.

"Nothing, kid, if everybody keeps his head. Never argue with a cop. That's what you pay a mouthpiece for. Treat 'em polite and yes 'em to death and send for a mouthpiece. Hell, Stan, you got a lot to learn yet about the carny."

A whistle sounded from the entrance. Stan's head spun toward it.

A big, white-haired man with a badge pinned to his denim shirt stood there. His hat was pushed back and he had his thumbs hooked in his belt. A holster containing a heavy revolver hung from a looser belt on a slant. Hoately raised his voice, grinning down at the marks below Molly's platform.

"That will conclude our performance for the time being, folks. Now I guess you're all kind of dry and could stand a nice cold drink so I call your attention to the stand directly across the midway where you can get all the nice cold soda pop you can drink. That's all for now, folks. Come back tomorrow night and we'll have a few surprises for you—things you didn't see tonight."

The marks obediently began to drift out of the tent and

Hoately approached the law. "What can I do for you, Chief? My name's Hoately and I'm owner of this attraction. You're welcome to inspect every inch of it and I'll give you all the cooperation you want. We've got no girl shows and no games of skill or chance."

The old man's hard little colorless eyes rested on Hoately as they would on a spider in the corner of a backhouse. "Stand here."

"You're the boss."

The old man's gaze flickered over the Ten-in-One tent. He pointed to the geek's enclosure. "What you got in there?"

"Snake charmer," Hoately said casually. "Want to see him?"

"That ain't what I heard. I heard you got an obscene and illegal performance going on here with cruelty to dumb animals. I got a complaint registered this evening."

The showman pulled out a bag of tobacco and papers and began to build a cigarette. His left hand made a quick twist, and the cigarette took form. He licked the paper with his tongue and struck a match. "Why don't you stay as my guest and view the entire performance, Chief? We'd be glad—"

The wide mouth tightened. "I got orders from the marshal to close down the show. And arrest anybody I see fit. I'm arresting you and—" He slid his eyes over the performers: Bruno placid in his blue robe, Joe Plasky smilingly assembling his pitch items, Stan making a half dollar vanish and reappear, Molly still sitting in the Electric Chair, the sequins of her skimpy bodice winking as her breasts rose and fell. She was smiling tautly. "And I'm taking that woman there—indecent exposure. We got decent women in this town. And we got daughters; growin' girls. We don't allow no naked women paradin' around and makin' exposes of 'emselves. The rest of you stay right here in case we need you. All right, you two, come along. Put a coat on that girl first. She ain't decent enough to come down to the lockup thataway."

Stan noticed that the stubble on the deputy marshal's chin was white—like a white fungus on a dead man, he thought savagely. Molly's eyes were enormous.

Hoately cleared his throat and took a deep breath. "Looky

here, Chief, that girl's never had no complaints. She's got to wear a costume like that on account of she handles electric wires and ordinary cloth might catch fire and . . ."

The deputy reached out one hand and gripped Hoately by the shirt. "Shut up. And don't try offering me any bribes, neither. I ain't none o' your thievin' northern police, kissin' the priest's toe on Sundays and raking in the graft hell-bent for election six days a week. I'm a church deacon and I aim to keep this a clean town if I have to run every Jezebel out of it on a fence rail."

His tiny eyes were fastened on Molly's bare thighs. He raised his glance ever so slightly to take in her shoulders and the crease between her breasts. The eyes grew hot and the slack mouth raised at the corners. Beside the Electric Girl's platform he noticed a neat young man with corn-yellow hair saying something to the girl who nodded and then darted her attention back to the deputy.

The law lumbered over, dragging Hoately with him. "Young lady, git off that contraption." He reached up a red-knuckled hand toward Molly. Stan was on the other side of the platform feeling for the switch. There was an ominous buzzing and crackling: Molly's black hair stood straight up like a halo around her head. She brought her finger tips together. Blue fire flowed between them. The deputy stopped, stony. The girl reached out, and sparks jumped in a flashing stream from her fingers to the deputy's. With a shout he drew back, releasing Hoately. The buzz of the static generator stopped and a voice drew his attention; it was the blond youth.

"You can see the reason, Marshal, for the metal costume the young lady is forced to wear. The electricity would ignite any ordinary fabric and only by wearing the briefest of covering can she avoid bursting into flame. Thousands of volts of electricity cover her body like a sheath. Pardon me, Marshal, but there seem to be several dollar bills coming out of your pocket."

In spite of himself, the deputy followed Stan's pointing finger. He saw nothing. Stan reached out and one after another five folded dollar bills appeared from the pocket of the denim shirt. He made them into a little roll and pressed them into the old man's hand. "Another minute and you'd have lost your money, Marshal."

The deputy's eyes were half shut with disbelief and hostile suspicion; but he shoved the cash into his shirt pocket.

Stan went on, "And I see that you have bought your wife a little present of a few silk handkerchiefs." From the cartridge belt Stan slowly drew out a bright green silk, then another of purple. "These are very pretty. I'm sure your wife will like them. And here's a pure white one—for your daughter. She's about nineteen now, isn't she, Marshal?"

"How'd you know I got a daughter?"

Stan rolled the silks into a ball and they vanished. His face was serious, the blue eyes grave. "I know many things, Marshal. I don't know exactly how I know them but there's nothing supernatural about it, I am sure. My family was Scotch and the Scotch are often gifted with powers that the old folks used to call 'second sight.' "

The white head with its coarse, red face, nodded involuntarily.

"For instance," Stan went on, "I can see that you have carried a pocket piece or curio of some kind for nearly twenty years. Probably a foreign coin."

One great hand made a motion toward the pants pocket. Stan felt his own pulse racing with triumph. Two more hits and he'd have him.

"Several times you have lost that luck-piece but you've found it again every time; and it means a lot to you, you don't exactly know why. I'd say that you should always carry it."

The deputy's eyes had lost some of their flint.

From the tail of his eye Stan saw that the Electric Chair above them was empty; Molly had disappeared. So had everyone else except Hoately who stood slightly to the rear of the deputy, nodding his head wisely at every word of the magician's.

"Now this isn't any of my business, Marshal, because I know you are a man who is fully capable of handling his own affairs and just about anything else that is liable to come along. But my Scotch blood is working right this minute and it tells me that there is one thing in your life that is worrying you and it's something you find it difficult to handle. Because all your strength and your courage and your authority in the town seem to be of no avail. It seems to slip through your grasp like water—"

"Wait a minute, young fella. What are you talkin' 'bout?"

"As I said, it's absolutely none of my business. And you are a man in the prime of life and old enough to be my father and by rights you should be the one to give me good advice and not the other way round. But in this case I may be able to do you a good turn. I sense that there are antagonistic influences surrounding you. Someone near to you is jealous of you and your ability. And while part of this extends to your work as a peace officer and your duties in upholding the law, there is another part of it that has to do with your church . . ."

The face had changed. The savage lines had ironed out and now it was simply the face of an old man, weary and bewildered. Stan hurried on, panicky for fear the tenuous spell would break, but excited at his own power. If I can't read a Bible-spouting, whoremongering, big-knuckled hypocrite of a church deacon, he told himself, I'm a feeblo. The old son-of-a-bitch.

Stan's eyes misted over as if they had turned inward. His voice grew intimate. "There is someone you love very dearly. Yet there is an obstacle in the way of your love. You feel hemmed-in and trapped by it. And through it all I seem to hear a woman's voice, a sweet voice, singing. It's singing a beautiful old hymn. Wait a moment. It's 'Jesus, Savior, Pilot Me.' "

The deputy's mouth was open, his big chest was lifting and falling with his breath.

"I see a Sunday morning in a peaceful, beautiful little church. A church into which you have put your energy and your labor. You have labored hard in the Lord's vineyard and your labor has borne fruit in the love of a woman. But I see her eyes filled with tears and somehow your own heart is touched by them . . ."

Christ, how far do I dare go with this? Stan thought behind the running patter of his words.

"But I feel that all will come out well for you. Because you have strength. And you'll get more. The Lord will give you strength. And there are malicious tongues about you, ready to do you an injury. And to do this fine woman an injury if they can. Because they are like whited sepulchers which appear beautiful outward but are full of dead men's bones and all uncleanness and . . ."

The deacon's eyes were hot again but this time not at Stan. There was a hunted look in them too as the youth bore down:

"And the spirit of our Lord and Savior, Jesus Christ, has shined upon them but in vain, because they see as through a glass, darkly, and the darkness is nothing but a reflection of their own blackness and sin and hypocrisy and envy. But deep inside yourself you will find the power to combat them. And defeat them. And you will do it with the help of the God you believe in and worship.

"And while I feel the spirit talking to me straight out, like a father to his son, I must tell you that there's a matter of some money coming to you that will cause you some disappointment and delay but you will get it. I can see that the people in this town have been pretty blind in the past but something in the near future will occur which will wake them up and make them realize that you are a more valuable man than they ever would admit. There's a surprise for you—about this time next year or a little later, say around November. Something you've had your heart set on for a long time but it will come true if you follow the hunches you get and don't let anybody talk you out of obeying your own good judgment which has never let you down yet—whenever you've given it a free rein."

Hoately had evaporated. Stan turned and began to move slowly toward the gate. The midway outside was buzzing with little groups of talk. The entire carny had been sloughed and the deputies had chased the townies off the lot. Stan walked slowly, talking still in a soft, inward voice. The old man followed beside him, his eyes staring straight ahead.

"I'm very glad to have met you, Marshal. Because I expect to be back here again some day and I'd like to see if my Scotch blood had been telling me true, as I'm sure it has. I'm sure you don't mind a young fellow like myself presuming to tell you these things, because, after all, I'm not pretending to advise you. I know you've lived a lot longer than I and have more knowledge of the ways of the world than I could ever have. But when I first set eyes on you I thought to myself, 'Here's a man and a servant of the law who is troubled deep in his mind,' and then I saw that you had no reason to be because things are going to turn out just the way you want them to, only there will be a little delay . . ."

How the hell shall I finish this off, Stan wondered. I can talk myself right back into the soup if I don't quit.

They reached the entrance and Stan paused. The deputy's red, hard face turned toward him; the silence seemed to pour over Stan and smother him. This was the pay-off, and his heart sank. There was nothing more to be said now. This was where action started. Stan felt out of his depth. Then he suddenly knew the business that would work, if anything would. He turned away from the old man. Making his face look as spiritual as possible, he raised one hand and rested it easily in a gesture of peace and confidence against the looped canvas. It was a period at the end of the sentence.

The deputy let out a long, whistling breath, hooked his thumbs in his belt, and stood looking out on the darkening midway. Then he turned back to Stan and his voice was just an ordinary old man's voice. "Young fella, I wisht I'd met you a long time ago. Tell the others to go easy in this town because we aim to keep it clean. But, by God, when—if I'm ever elected marshal you ain't got nothing to worry about, long as you have a good, clean show. Good night, son."

He plodded away slowly, his shoulders squared against the dark, authority slapping his thigh on a belt heavy with cartridges.

Stan's collar was tight with the blood pounding beneath it. His head was as light as if he had a fever.

The world is mine, God damn it! The world is mine! I've got 'em across the barrel and I can shake them loose from whatever I want. The geek has his whisky. The rest of them drink something else: they drink promises. They drink hope. And I've got it to hand them. I'm running over with it. I can

get anything I want. If I could hand this old fart a cold reading and get away with it I could do it to a senator! I could
do it to a governor!

Then he remembered where he had told her to hide.

In the black space where the trucks were parked, Zeena's
van was behind the others, dark and silent. He opened the
cab door softly and crept in, his blood hammering.

"Molly!"

"Yes, Stan." The whisper came from the black cavern behind the seat.

"It's okay, kid. I stalled him. He's gone."

"Oh, Stan, gee, you're great. You're great."

Stan crawled back over the seat and his hand touched a soft,
hot shoulder. It was trembling. His arm went about it.
"Molly!"

Lips found his. He crushed her back on a pile of blankets.

"Stan, you won't let anything happen to me—will you?"

"Certainly not. Nothing's ever going to happen to you
while I'm around."

"Oh, Stan, you're so much like my dad."

The hooks which held the sequinned bodice came open in
his shaking fingers. The girl's high, pointed breasts were
smooth under his hands, and his tongue entered her lips.

"Don't hurt me, Stan, honey. Don't." His collar choked
him, the blood hammering in his throat. "Oh. Stan—hurt me,
hurt me, hurt me—"

The Empress

*who sits on Venus' couch amid the
ripening grain and rivers of the earth.*

THE NIGHT was quiet at last, with only the katydids. The
ferris wheel stood as gaunt as a skeleton against the stars;
the cookhouse lights were lonely in the dark.

Stan stepped down into the grass beside the van and held
his hand up to help Molly. Her palm was hot and damp. When
she stood beside him she clung to him for a moment and
pressed her forehead against his cheek. They were almost the
same height. Her hair smelled sweet and tickled his lips. He
shook his head impatiently.

"Stan, honey, you do love me—don't you?"

"Sure I do, baby."

"And you won't tell a soul. Promise me you won't tell.
Because I never let any man do it to me before, honest."

"Are you sure?" Stan thrilled at his power over her. He
wanted to hear her voice with fear in it.

"Yes, honey. Yes. Honest. You hurt me something terrible
at first. You know—"

"Yes."

"Darling, if I'd ever done it before you wouldn't have hurt me. Only I'm glad you hurt me, honey, I'm glad. Because you were the first."

The air was chilly; she began to shiver. Stan slipped off his jacket and put it around her shoulders. "Gee, you're good to me, Stan."

"I'll always be."

"Always?" Molly stopped and turned to face him, resting both hands on his forearm. "What do you mean, Stan?"

"Just always."

"You mean until the season's over and we all split up?" Her voice held a deeper question.

Stan had decided. In his mind he saw the blaze of the foots, with himself standing there straight. In command. Molly was in the audience in an evening gown, walking slowly down the aisle. The marks—the audience—craned their necks to look at her. She was an eyeful. The placards at each side of the stage said simply, STANTON. The big time.

"Molly, you like show business, don't you?"

"Why, sure, Stan. Daddy always wanted to see me in show business."

"Well, what I mean is— Well, let's head for the big time. Together."

Her arm slid around his waist and they walked on again, slowly. "Darling, that's wonderful. I was hoping you'd say that to me."

"I mean it. Together we can get right to the top. You've got the class and the shape. I mean, you're beautiful and we can work up a two-person code act that'll knock 'em dead."

Molly's arm tightened around him. "Stan, that's what I always wanted. Daddy would be awful proud of us. I know he would. He'd be crazy about you, Stan. The way you can talk your way out of a tight place. That's what he admired most in anybody. That and not double-crossing a pal, ever. Daddy said he wanted on his tombstone, 'Here lies Denny Cahill. He never crossed up a pal.' "

"Did he get it?"

"No. My grandfather wouldn't hear of it. The stone just says, 'Dennis Cahill' and under it the dates when he was born and when he passed away. Only one night, just before I left Louisville, I went out and wrote it below the dates with chalk. I'll bet some of the chalk is still there."

They had reached the Ten-in-One. Inside a single bulb glowed. Stan peered in. "All clear, kid. Get into your things. I wonder where the others are?"

While Molly was dressing behind the curtains of Zeena's stage Stan walked over to the cookhouse and found the cook cleaning coffee urns. "Where's the bunch?"

"Scattered. The bulls run in a couple of fellows on the wheels and games. They even sloughed the cat rack. The fixer'll get 'em sprung tomorrow. And I'll have to put on a tub of water so they can boil up and get the crumbs out of their clothes. Want a cup o' java?"

"No, thanks. I want to find my bunch. Got any idea where they went?"

The cook wiped his hands and lit a cigarette. "Hoately's gone up the road to a lunch wagon or something. Roadside joint. You can't miss it. He said he didn't want to hang around the lot tonight. Can't blame him. Seems somebody put in a beef to the cops about the geek show you fellows got. And about the wheels. Way I heard it, that tattooed guy used to be in the Ten-in-One and had the run-in with Plasky was in town shooting off his mouth."

"Sailor Martin?"

"That's the son-of-a-bitch. What I heard, he worked on the townies and got them to beef to the cops. Can you imagine a carny doing that? Somebody ought to stick a butcher knife up his rear end and kick the handle off."

Stan heard a low whistle from outside and said good night to the cook. Molly was standing in the shadow of the Ten-in-One, looking prim and neat in a dark suit and a white silk blouse. He took her arm and they set off down the road.

It was a chicken-dinner shack; from inside came voices and laughs. He pushed open the screen door.

At a table with a red-checkered tablecloth the bunch was gathered. Pints of whisky stood among plates of chicken bones. Hoately was talking:

". . . and the minute I heard the kid go into that jerk-'em-to-Jesus routine I knowed we was all set. I want to tell you, it was something to watch. That old buzzard's trap was hanging open a mile—lapping up every word the kid handed him."

He paused and let out a whoop at the sight of Stan and Molly.

The others helloed; Zeena bustled up and put her arms around Molly and kissed her. "Sakes alive, honey, I'm glad to see you. You come over and sit down right by Zeena. Where on earth did you skedaddle to? We knew they didn't pinch you or Stan because Clem hung around and watched. But I was looking all over for you."

"I hid in the van," Molly said. She looked down at her purse and ran her finger over the clasp.

"And Stan!" Zeena enveloped him in a hug and kissed him warmly on the mouth. "Stan, boy, you sure done noble. I always knew you were a mentalist. Imagine that—giving a cold reading to a cop and getting away with it! Oh, I just love you."

The rasping, fiddle voice of Major Mosquito cut through. "Come on over and have a drink. Hoately's treat. Come on over. I'm getting stinko."

They took their seats, and a gangling youth with spiky hair brought in two more plates of chicken. "Watch them bottles, folks. Town's hell on enforcement."

Stan and Molly sat together. Suddenly they were ravenous and dug into the chicken.

Joe Plasky said, "Nice going, kid. You kept your head. You're real carny, and no mistake."

Bruno said nothing. He had been about to start on his fourth plate of chicken but now it lay in front of him, neglected. Molly caught Stan's hand and squeezed it under the tablecloth. They exchanged a quick look.

Zeena poured herself a drink and took it in two swallows. "Liquor's terrible, Clem. It's that bad, I nearly left some—as the Scotch fella says."

Clem Hoately was picking his teeth with a sharpened match. "Short notice. I asked one of the deputies—young fellow who looked okay—where I could pick up a pint. He sent me to his brother-in-law. Town's all right if you case it careful. We won't have no trouble after tonight. That old son-of-a-bitch that sloughed us was the toughest they got. We'll open tomorrow night and pack 'em in. Best advertising in the world."

Molly looked startled. "I—I shouldn't think it would be safe."

Hoately grinned. "You can wear riding boots and breeches. That'll be all right. You got the shape to look good in 'em. Don't worry about it."

Zeena took a chicken bone from her mouth and said, "I think we all ought to give Stan a great big hand. We might have got into a peck of trouble if it hadn't been for him. I always say, there's nothing like the second sight. Anybody who can give a good reading'll never starve. Only, gosh"— she turned to face Stan—"I never knew you could spout the Bible, the way Clem's been telling us." She paused, chewing, and then went on, "Stan, 'fess up. Were you ever really a preacher?"

He shook his head, hard lines at the corners of his mouth. "That was my old man's idea once—to make me one. Only I couldn't see it. Then he wanted me to go into real estate. But that's too slow a turn. I wanted magic. But the old gent was a great hand at quoting scripture. I guess a lot of it rubbed off onto me."

Major Mosquito, holding a tumbler in both hands, lifted it. "Here's to the Great Stanton, purveyor of fun, magic, mystery and bullshit! He's a jolly good fellow, he's a jolly good . . ."

Bruno Hertz said, "You shut up. You talk too much for little fellow." His sad steer's eyes were on Molly. Suddenly he blurted out, "Molly, you and Stan going to get married?"

The room got as quiet as if a needle had been lifted off a record. Molly choked and Zeena slapped her on the back. Her face was red when she answered, "Why—what makes you think—"

Bruno, bold and desperate, stumbled on. "You and Stan been together! You going to get married?"

Stan looked up and met the strongman's gaze levelly. "As a matter of fact, Molly and I are going to head for vaudeville. We've got it all figured out. In the two-a-day nobody's going to run her in for wearing skimpies."

Zeena set down her glass. "Why—why, I think that's just splendid. Clem, did you hear? They're going to try the two-a-day. I think it's perfectly fine. I think it's great." She crushed Molly in another hug. Then she reached out and rumpled Stan's hair. "Stan,—ain't—ain't you the foxy one! And you all the time—making out like you never—never knew the child was on the face of the earth." She dumped more whisky in her glass and said, "All right, folks, here's a toast to the bride and groom. Long life and may all your troubles be little ones—eh, Molly?"

Hoately lifted his coffee cup. Major Mosquito said, "Hoo-ray! Let me hide under the bed, the first night. I'll be quiet. Just let me—"

Bruno Hertz poured a small drink for himself and gazed at Molly over the glass. *"Prosit, Liebchen."* Under his breath he muttered, "Better wish luck. You going to need luck. Maybe some day you going to need—"

Joe Plasky's Lazarus smile was like a lamp. "All the best, kids. Glad to see it. I'll give you a letter to a couple of booking agents in New York."

Zeena cleared the plates and glasses from before her with an unsteady sweep. She reached into her purse and drew out a pack of cards. "Here you are, kids. Now's a good time to see what the Tarot has for you. The Tarot's always got an answer." She shuffled. "Go ahead, honey. Cut 'em. Let's see what you cut."

Molly cut the cards and Zeena grabbed them and turned them over. "Well, what d'you know—The Empress! That's her, honey. See, she's sitting on a couch and it's got the sign of Venus on it. That's for love. And she's got stars in her hair. That's for all the good things your husband's going to give you."

Major Mosquito squeaked with laughter, and Bruno hissed at him to keep quiet.

"The Empress is a good fortune card in love, honey. Couldn't be better 'cause it means you'll get what you want most." She shuffled again and held them up to Stan, who had stood up and moved in behind Molly's chair. Molly had taken his hand and was holding it near her cheek.

"Go on, Stan. You cut 'em, see what comes out."

Stan released Molly's hand. In the stacked cards, the edge of one showed darker than the others from handling and Stan cut to it without thinking, turning his half of the deck face up.

Major Mosquito let out a squall. Zeena knocked over the bottle and Hoately caught it before it had gurgled away. Bruno's stolid face was alight with something like triumph. Molly looked puzzled and Stan laughed. The midget across the table was beating the cloth with a spoon and crying out in an ecstasy of drunken glee:

"Ha! Ha! Ha! Ha! *The Hanged Man!*"

Resurrection of the Dead

*At the call of an angel with fiery wings, graves
open, coffins burst, and the dead are naked.*

". . . I CAN SEE, madam, that there are many persons surrounding you who are envious of your happiness, your culture, your good fortune and—yes, I must be frank—your
good looks. I would advise you, madam, to go your own way,
doing those things which you know down deep in your heart
of hearts is right. And I am sure your husband, who sits beside
you in the theater now, will agree with me. There is no
weapon you can use against malicious envy except the confidence in your way of life as the moral and righteous one, no
matter what the envious say. And it is one of these, madam,
and I believe you know of whom I am speaking, who has
poisoned your dog."

The applause was slow in starting. They were baffled; they
were awe-struck. Then it began from the back of the theater
and traveled forward, the people whose questions had been
whispered to Molly and whose questions he had answered,
clapping last. It was a storm of sound. And Stan, hearing it

through the heavy drop curtain, breathed it in like mountain air.

The curtains parted for his second bow. He took it, bowing slowly from the waist and then he extended his hand and Molly swept from the wings where she had arrived by the door backstage behind the boxes. They bowed together, hand in hand, and then the curtains cut down again and they moved off through the wings and up the concrete stairs that led to the dressing rooms.

Stan opened the dressing-room door, stood aside for Molly to go in, then followed and shut the door. He sat for a moment on the wicker couch, then whipped off his white tie and unbuttoned the neckband of his stiff shirt and lit a cigarette.

Molly had stepped out of the skin-tight evening gown she wore and hung it on a hanger. She stood for a moment without a stitch on, scratching her ribs under the arms. Then she slipped on a robe, caught up her hair in a knot and began to dab cold cream on her face.

Finally Stan spoke. "Two nights running is too much."

Her hand stopped, pressed against her chin. Her head was turned away from him. "I'm sorry, Stan. I guess I was tired."

He got up and moved over, looking down at her. "After five years you still fluff it. My God, what do you use for brains anyway? What's eighty-eight?"

Her wide, smoky-gray eyes were brilliant with tears. "Stan, I—I'll have to think about it. When you come at me all of a sudden that way I have to think. I—just have to think," she finished lamely.

He went on, his voice cool. "Eighty-eight!"

"Organization!" she said, smiling quickly. "Shall I join some club, fraternity, or organization? Of course. I hadn't forgotten it, Stan. Honest, honey."

He went over to the couch and lay back on it. "You'll say it backwards and forwards a hundred times before you go to sleep tonight. Right?"

"Sure, Stan."

She brightened, relieved that the tension had passed. The towel came away from her face pink from the makeup. Molly patted powder on her forehead, started to put on her street lipstick. Stan took off his shirt and threw a robe around his shoulders. With a few practiced swipes he cold-creamed his face, frowning at his reflection. The blue eyes had grown frosty. There were lines, faint ones, at the corners of his mouth. They had always been there when he smiled but now he noticed for the first time that they stayed there when his face was relaxed. Time was passing over his head.

Molly was fastening the snaps of her skirt. "Glory be, but I'm tired. I don't want to go anywhere tonight but to bed. I could sleep for a week."

Stan sat gazing at his image in the mirror, made hard by the lights blazing around the edge. He was like a stranger to himself. He wondered what went on behind that familiar face, the square jaw, the corn-yellow hair. It was a mystery, even to himself. For the first time in months he thought of Gyp and could see him clearly through the mist of years, bounding through fields grown lush with neglected weeds of late summer.

"Good boy," he muttered. "Good old boy."

"What was it, honey?" Molly was sitting on the wicker couch reading a movie magazine while she waited for him to dress.

"Nothing, kid," he said over his shoulder. "Just mumbling in my beard."

Who poisoned our dog? People around you who envy you. Number fourteen. One: Will. Four: Tell. *Will* you *tell* this lady what she is thinking about?

Stan shook his head and rubbed his face evenly with the towel. He hung up his suit of tails and stepped into his tweed trousers. He ran a comb through his hair and knotted his tie.

Outside the snow was falling lightly, lingering on the dark surface of the dirty window of the dressing room.

At the stage door the winter met them with an icy breath. They found a cab and got in and Molly slipped her arm through his and rested her cheek against his shoulder and stayed that way.

"Here y'are, buddy. Hotel Plymouth."

Stan handed the driver a dollar and helped Molly out.

They passed through the revolving door into the drowsy heat of the lobby and Stan stopped by the cigar counter for cigarettes. He lifted his eyes to the desk and then he stopped and Molly, turning back to see if he was coming, hurried up. She put her hand on his arm. "Stan, darling—what's the matter with you? God, you look terrible. Are you sick, honey? Answer me. Are you sick? You're not mad at me, are you, Stan?"

Abruptly he turned away and strode out of the lobby into the wind and the winter night. The cold air felt good and his face and neck needed the cold. He turned to the girl. "Molly, don't ask any questions. I just saw somebody I'm trying to duck. Go upstairs and pack our stuff. We're checking out. Got any dough? Well, square up the bill and have the bellhop bring the stuff out."

Without asking any more questions she nodded and went in.

When she came down the woman at the desk, the night clerk, smiled up at her from a detective story. "Will you make up my bill, please? Mr. and Mrs. Stanton Carlisle."

The woman smiled again. She was white-haired and Molly wondered why so many white-haired women insist on bright lipstick. It makes them look like such crows, she thought. If I ever get white-haired I'll never wear anything darker than Passion Flower. Yet this woman had been quite a chick in her day, Molly decided. And she had lived. There was something about her that made you think she had been in show business. But then lots of good-looking people had when they were young and that really didn't mean a thing. It was managing to stay in show business and stay at the top that counted. Never getting to be a has-been and washed-up. That was the worst thing, to be washed-up. Only you had to save a pile of money while you were in the chips. And what with staying at the best places and buying dinners and drinks for managers and newspapermen and people they never seemed to get much ahead at the end of a season on the road. That is, the more the act was worth, the more it seemed to take to sell it.

"That will be eighteen dollars and eighty-five cents," the woman said. She looked searchingly at Molly. "Is—is your husband coming back to the hotel?"

Molly thought fast. "No. As a matter of fact, he's already waiting for me further downtown. We have to make a train."

The woman's face was not smiling any more. It had a

hunted, hopeful look which was, at the same time, strangely hungry. Molly didn't like it a blessed bit. She paid and went out.

Stan was pacing up and down savagely. A cab was standing by the curb with its meter ticking. They put the bags in and rode off.

All hotels are the same place, Molly thought later, lying beside Stan in the partial darkness. Why do they always have street lights outside the windows and car lines in the street and elevators in the wall right beside your head and people upstairs who bang things? But anyhow it was better than never getting around or seeing anything.

Watching Stan undress had stirred her and made her remember so many good times and she had hoped he would feel like it even if they were both as tired as dogs. He had been so cross lately and they always seemed to be tired when they went to bed. With a little flare of panic she wondered if she were losing her looks or something. Stan could be so wonderful. It made her go all wriggly and scarey inside to think about it. God, it was worth waiting for—when he really wanted a party. But then she remembered something else and she began saying to herself, "Eighty-eight—organization. Shall I join some club, union, fraternity, or organization? Shall I join some club, union, fraternity, or organization?" She repeated it three times before she fell asleep with her lips slightly open and her cheek on one palm, her black hair tumbled over the pillow.

Stan reached out and felt around on the bedside table for the cigarettes. He found one and his match flared. Below them a late car whined into hearing from the distance, the steel rails carrying the sound. But he let it slip from his mind.

A memory was coming back. A day when he was eleven years old.

It was like other days of early summer. It began with a rattle of locusts in the trees outside the bedroom window. Stan Carlisle opened his eyes, and the sun was shining hotly.

Gyp sat on the chair beside the bed, whining gently deep in his throat and touching the boy's arm with one paw.

Stan reached out lazily and rubbed the mongrel's head

while the dog writhed in delight. In a moment he had leaped onto the bed joyfully wagging all over. Then Stan was fully awake and remembered. He pushed Gyp off and began brushing violently at the streaks of dried clay left on the sheets by the dog's paws. Mother always got mad when Gyp Jumped Up.

Stan stole to the door, but the door to his parents' room across the hall was still closed. He tiptoed back and idly pulled on his underwear and the corduroy knickers. He stuffed a paper-backed book inside his shirt and laced up his shoes.

Down in the yard he could see the garage doors open. Dad had left for the office.

Stan went downstairs. Being careful not to make any noise he got a bottle of milk from the ice box, a loaf of bread and a jar of jelly. Gyp got bread and milk in a saucer on the floor.

While Stan sat in the early morning stillness of the empty kitchen, cutting off slices of bread and loading them with jelly, he read the catalog:

". . . a real professional outfit, suitable for theater, club, or social gathering. An hour's performance complete. With beautiful cloth-bound instruction book. Direct from us or at your toy or novelty dealer's. $15.00."

After his eighth slice of bread and jelly he put the remains of his breakfast away and went out on the back porch with the catalog. The sun was growing hotter. The brightness of the summer morning filled him with a pleasant sadness, as if at the thought of something noble and magic which had happened long ago in the days of knights and lonely towers.

Upstairs he heard the sharp rap of small heels on the floor and then the roar of water in the bathtub. Mother had gotten up early.

Stan hurried upstairs. Above the rush of the water he could make out his mother's voice, singing in a hard, glittering soprano, "Oh, my laddie, my laddie, I luve the kent you carry. I luve your very bonnet with the silver buckle on it . . ."

He was disturbed and resentful of the song. Usually she sang it after he had been sent up to bed, when the parlor was full of people and Mark Humphries, the big dark man who taught singing, was playing the accompaniment while Dad sat in the dining room, smoking a cigar and talking in low tones about deals with one of his own friends. It was part of the grown-up world with its secrets, its baffling changes from good temper to bad without warning. Stan hated it.

He stepped into the bedroom that always smelled of perfume. The shining brass bedstead was glittering big and important in the bar of sunlight through the blind. The bed was rumpled.

Stan went over and buried his face in the pillow that smelled faintly of perfume, drawing in his breath through it again and again. The other pillow smelled of hair tonic.

He knelt beside the bed, thinking of Elaine and Lancelot—how she came floating down on a boat and Lancelot stood by the bank looking at her and being sorry she was dead.

The rush of water in the bathroom had given way to splashing and snatches of singing. Then the chung of the stopper and the water gurgling out.

Beyond the window, with its shades making the room cool and dark, a cicada's note sounded, starting easy and getting loud and dying away, sign of hot weather coming.

Stan took one more breath of the pillow, pushing it around his face to shut out sound and everything except its yielding softness and its sweetness.

There was a sharp click from the latch of the bathroom door. The boy frantically smoothed out the pillow; he tore around the big brass bed and out into the hall and across to his own room.

Downstairs he heard Jennie's slow step on the back porch and the creak of the kitchen chair as she slumped her weight into it to rest before she took off her hat and her good dress. It was the day for Jennie to do the wash.

Stan heard his mother come out of the bathroom; then he heard the bedroom door close. He crept out into the hall and paused beside it.

Inside there was a pat of bare feet on the floor and the catch of the bedroom door quietly slipped on. Grownups were always locking themselves in places. Stan got a sudden shiver of mystery and elation. It started in his lower back and rippled up between his shoulder blades.

Through the closed door came the soft clink of a perfume

bottle being set down on the dressing table and then there was the scrape of chair legs. The chair creaked ever so little; it scraped the floor again; the bottle clinked as the stopper was put in.

When she came out she would be dressed up and ready to go downtown and she would have a lot of jobs for him to do while she was gone—like cleaning up the closet in his room or cutting the grass on the terrace.

He moved stealthily along the hall and eased open the door to the attic stairs, closed it behind him gently and went up. He knew the creaky steps and skipped them. The attic was hot and heavy with the smell of wood and old silk.

Stan stretched out on an iron bed covered with a silk patchwork quilt. It was made of strips of silk sewn in squares, different colors on each side and a single square of black silk in the center of each. Grandma Stanton made it the winter before she died.

The boy lay face down. The sounds of the house filtered up to him from far away. The whining scrape of Gyp, banished to the back porch. Jennie in the cellar and the chug of the new washing machine. The brisk clatter of Mother's door opening and the tap of her high heels on the stairs. She called his name once sharply and then called something down to Jennie.

Jennie's voice came out the cellar window, mournful and rich. "Yes, Mis' Carlisle. If I see him I tell him."

For a moment Stan was afraid Mother would go out the back door and that Gyp would Jump Up and make her cross and then she would start talking about getting rid of him. But she went out the front door instead. Stan heard the mail box rattle. Then she went down the steps.

He leaped up and ran over to the attic window where he could see the front lawn through the maple tops below him.

Mother was walking quickly away toward the car line.

She would be going downtown to Mr. Humphries for her singing lesson. And she would not be back for a long time. Once she paused before the glass signboard on the lawn of the church. It told what Dr. Parkman would preach about next Sunday, but it was so black, and with the glass in front of it, it was like looking into a mirror. Mother stopped, as if reading about next Sunday's sermon; turning her head first one way and then another, she pulled her hat a little more forward and touched her hair.

She went on then, walking slower. The boy watched her until she was out of sight.

On every hilltop and rise Stan turned and gazed back across the fields. He could spy the roof of his own house rising among the bright green of the maples.

The sun beat down.

The air was sweet with the smell of summer grasses. Gyp bounded through the hummocks, chasing away almost out of sight and bouncing back again.

Stan climbed a fence, crossed a pasture, and then mounted a stone wall, boosting Gyp over. On the other side of the wall the fields were thicker with brush and little oak bushes and pines and beyond it the woods began.

When he stepped into their dark coolness he felt again that involuntary shudder, which was part pleasure and part apprehension, rise between his shoulder blades. The woods were a place to kill enemies in. You fought them with a battle-ax and you were naked and nobody dared say anything about it because you had the ax always hanging from your wrist by a piece of leather. Then there was an old castle deep in the forest. It had green moss in the cracks between the stones and there was a moat around it full of water and it stood there deep and still as death and from the castle there was never a sound or a sign of life.

Stan trod softly now and held his breath, listening to the green silence. The leaves were tender under his feet. He stepped over a fallen tree and then looked up through the branches to where the sun made them bright.

He began to dream. He and Lady Cynthia rode through the forest. Cynthia was Mother's name, only Lady Cynthia was not like Mother except that she looked like her. She was just a beautiful lady on a white palfrey and the bridle was set with gems and jewels that winked in the dappled light through the branches. Stan was in armor and his hair was long and cut straight across and his face was tanned dark and with no freckles. His horse was a powerful charger as black as midnight. That was its name—Midnight. He and Lady Cynthia had come to the forest to seek an adventure, for in the forest was a powerful old magician.

Stan came out on a long-disused timber road where he slipped out of the dream, for he remembered that they had been here on the picnic. That was the time they had come out with Mr. and Mrs. Morris and Mark Humphries had driven Mother and Dad and Stan in his car with the top down. They brought the food in baskets.

Sudden anger rose up in him when he thought how his dad had had to spoil the day by having a fuss with Mother about something. He had spoken in low tones but then Mother had said, "Stan and I are going for a walk all by ourselves, aren't we, Stan?" She was smiling at the others the way she did when something was wrong. Stan had felt that delicious shudder go up between his shoulders.

That was the time they found the Glade.

It was a deep cleft in a ridge and you would never know it was there unless you stumbled on it. He had been back since but on that day Mother had been there and all of a sudden, as if she had felt the magic of the place, she had knelt and kissed him. He remembered the perfume she had on. She had held him off at arm's length and she was really smiling this time, as if at something deep inside herself, and she said, "Don't tell anybody. This place is a secret just between us."

He had been happy all the way back to the others.

That night when they were back home and he was in bed, the sound of his father's voice, rasping and rumbling through the walls, had made him sick with rebellion. What did he have to always be fussing with Mother for? Then the thought of the Glade, and of how she looked when she kissed him, made him wriggle with delight.

But the next day it was all gone and she spoke sharp to him about everything and kept finding jobs for him to do.

Stan started down the loggers' road. In a damp spot he stooped and then knelt like a tracker examining a spoor. The spot was fed by a trickle of spring. Across it were the tracks of auto tires, their clear and sacrilegious imprints just beginning to fill with water.

Stan hated them—the grownups were everywhere. He hated their voices most of all.

Cautiously he crossed the road, calling Gyp to him to keep him from rustling through the brush. He held the dog's collar and went on, taking care not to tread on any dead twigs. The Glade had to be approached with the reverence of silence. He climbed the last bank on his hands and knees and then on looking over the crest he froze.

Voices were coming from the Glade.

He peered further over. Two people were lying on an Indian blanket and with a hot rush Stan knew that one was a man and the other was a woman and this was what men and women did secretly together that everybody stopped talking about when he came around, only some grownups never talked about it at all. Curiosity leaped inside of him at the thought of spying on them when they didn't know he was there. He was seeing it all—all of it—the thing that made babies grow inside of women. He could hardly breathe.

The woman's face was hidden by the man's shoulder, and only her hands could be seen pressing against his back. After a while they were still. Stan wondered if they were dead—if they ever died doing it and if it hurt them but they had to do it even so.

At last they stirred and the man rolled over on his back. The woman sat up, holding her hands to her hair. Her laughter rang up the side of the Glade, a little harsh but still silvery.

Stan's fingers tightened on the grass hummock under his hand. Then he spun around, dragging Gyp by the collar, and stumbled, sliding and bumping, down the slope to the road. He ran with his breath scorching his throat, his eyes burning with tears. He ran all the way back and then went up in the attic and lay on the iron bed and tried to cry, but then he couldn't.

He heard Mother come in after a while. The light outside began to darken and shadows got longer.

Then he heard the car drive up. Dad got out. Stan could tell by the way he slammed the car door that he was mad. Downstairs he heard his father's voice, rasping through the floors, and his mother's raised, the way she spoke when she was exasperated.

Stan came downstairs, one step at a time, listening.

His father's voice came from the living room. ". . . I don't care for any more of your lies. I tell you, Mrs. Carpenter saw the two of you turning up the road into Mills' Woods. She recognized you and she saw Mark and she recognized the car."

Mother's tone was brittle. "Charles, I should think you would have a little more—*pride*, shall we say?—than to take the word of anyone as malicious and as common as your *friend*, Mrs. Carpenter."

Dad was hammering on the mantelpiece with his fist; Stan could hear the metal thing that covered the fireplace rattle. "New York hats! A nigger to clean up the house! Washing machines! Music lessons! After all I've given you, you turn around and hand me something like this. You! I ought to horsewhip that snake-in-the-grass within an inch of his life!"

Mother spoke slowly. "I rather think Mark Humphries can take care of himself. In fact, I should dearly love to see you walk right up to him on the street and tell him the things you've been saying to me. Because he would tell you that you are a liar. And you would get just what you're asking for; just what you're asking for. Besides that, Charles, you have a filthy mind. You mustn't judge others by yourself, dear. After all, it is quite possible for a person with some breeding to enjoy an hour's motoring in friendship and nothing more. But I realize that if you and—Clara Carpenter, shall we say? . . ."

Dad let out a noise that was something like a roar and something like a sob. "By the Eternal, I've sworn never to take the Lord's name in vain, but you're enough to try the patience of a saint. God *damn* you! D'you hear? *God damn you and all*—"

Stan had reached the ground floor and stood with his fingers running up and down the newel post of the stairs, looking in through the wide double doors of the living room. Mother was sitting very straight on the sofa without leaning back. Dad was standing by the mantel, one hand in his pocket and the other beating against the wood. When he looked up and saw Stan he stopped short.

Stan wanted to turn and run out the front door but his father's eyes kept him fastened to the floor. Mother turned her head and saw him and smiled.

The telephone rang then.

Dad started and plunged down the hall to answer it, his savage "Hello!" bursting like a firecracker in the narrow hallway.

Stan moved painfully, like walking through molasses. He crossed the room and came near his mother whose smile had hardened and grown sick-looking. She whispered, "Stan, Dad is upset because I went riding with Mr. Humphries. We wanted to take you riding with us but Jennie said you weren't here. But—Stan—let's make believe you did go with us. You'll go next time. I think it would make Dad feel better if he thought you were along."

From the hall his father's voice thundered, "By the Eternal, why did the fool have to be told in the first place? I was against telling him. It's the Council's business to vote on the committee's recommendation. We had it in the bag, sewed up tight. Now every idiot in town will know just where the streets will be cut and that property will shoot sky-high by tomorrow morning. . . ."

As Mother leaned close to Stan he smelled the perfume she had on her hair. She always put it on when she went downtown to take her singing lesson. Stan felt cold inside and empty. Even when she kissed him. "Whose boy are you, Stan? You're Mother's boy, aren't you, dear?"

He nodded and walked clumsily to the double doors. Dad was coming back. He took Stan roughly by the shoulder and shoved him toward the front door. "Run along, now. Your mother and I are talking."

Mother was beside them. "Let him stay, Charles. Why don't you ask Stanton what—what he did this afternoon?"

Dad stood looking at her with his mouth shut tight. He still had Stan by the shoulder. Slowly he turned his head. "Stan, what's your mother talking about?"

Stan swallowed. He hated that slack mouth and the stubble of pale yellow on the chin that came out when Dad hadn't shaved for several hours. Mark Humphries did a trick with four little wads of newspaper and a hat and had showed Stan how to do it. And he used to ask riddles.

Stan said, "We went riding with Mr. Humphries in his automobile." Over his father's arm, still holding him, Stan saw

Mother's face make a little motion at him as if she were kissing the air.

Dad went on, his voice quiet and dangerous. "Where did you go with Mr. Humphries, son?"

Stan's tongue felt thick. Mother's face had gotten white, even her mouth. "We—we went out where we had the picnic that time."

Dad's fingers loosened and Stan turned and ran out into the falling dusk. He heard the front door close behind him.

Someone switched on the living-room lamp. After a while Dad came out, got in his car and went downtown. Mother had left some cold meat and bread and butter on the kitchen table and Stan ate it alone, reading the catalog. Only it had lost its flavor and there seemed to be something terribly sad about the blue willow-pattern plate and the old knife and fork. Gyp whined under the table. Stan handed him all his own meat and got some jelly and ate it on the bread. Mother was upstairs in the spare bedroom with the door locked.

The next day Mother got breakfast for him. He said nothing and neither did she. But she wasn't a grownup any more. Or he wasn't a kid any more. There were no more grownups. They lied when they got scared, just like anybody. Everybody was alike only some were bigger. He ate very little and wiped his mouth and said, "Excuse me," politely. Mother didn't ask him to do any jobs. She didn't say anything at all.

He tied Gyp up to the kennel and set out for the woods where the old loggers' road cut into them. He moved in a dream and the shine of the sun seemed to hold back its warmth. At the top of the Glade he paused and then slid doggedly down its slope. Around him the trees rose straight and innocent in the sun and the sound of a woodpecker came whirring through them. The grass was crushed in one place; close by Stan found a handkerchief with "C" embroidered in a corner.

He looked at it with a crawling kind of fascination and then scooped out a hole in the earth and buried it.

When he got back he kept catching himself thinking about things as if nothing had happened, then stopping and the wave of desolation would sweep over him.

Mother was in her room when he came upstairs.

But something was lying big and square on his bed. He raced in.

There it was. The "Number 3" set—Marvello Magic. A full hour's entertainment, suitable for stage, club, or social gathering, $15.00. Its cover was gay with a picture of Mephistopheles making cards rise from a glass goblet. On the side of the box was a paper sticker which read, "Myers' Toy and Novelty Mart" and the address downtown. The corners of the box were shiny with imitation metal bindings, printed on the paper.

Stan knelt beside the bed, gazing at it. Then he threw his arms around it and beat his forehead against one of the sharp corners until the blood came.

Outside the trolley had approached and slid under the hotel window, groaning its lonely way through the night. Stan was trembling. He threw back the covers, switched on the bed light and stumbled into the bathroom. From his fitted case he took a vial and shook a white tablet into his hand. He found the tooth glass, swallowed the tablet with a gulp of tepid water.

When he got back in bed it was several minutes before the sedative began to work and he felt the peaceful grogginess stealing up to his brain.

"Christ, why did I have to go thinking of that?" he said aloud. "After all these years, why did I have to see her? And Christmas only a week off."

The Emperor

*carved on his throne the name of power
and on his scepter the sign of power.*

"STAN, honey, I'm scared."

He slowed the car and bent to look at the road signs. Sherwood Park—8 miles. "We're nearly there. What are you scared of? Because these people have a lot of jack? Whistle the eight bars of our opener and you'll snap out of it."

"I've tried that, Stan. Only—gosh, it's silly. But how'll I know which fork to grab? The way they lay out these fancy dinners looks like Tiffany's window."

The Great Stanton turned off the highway. Late light of summer evening lay over the sky; his headlights threw back the pale undersides of leaves as the roadster sped up the lane. On either side elms stood in columns of dignity.

"Nothing to it. Watch the old dame at the head of the table. Just stall until she dives in and she'll cue you on the hardware. My mother's folks had barrels of jack once. The old lady knew her way around. That's what she used to tell my old man whenever they went anywhere."

The house rose out of the dusk behind a sweep of lawn as big as a golf course. At the door a Negro butler with tiny brass buttons said, "Let me rest your coat and hat, sir."

"My name is Stanton. Stanton the Mentalist."

"Oh. Mis' Harrington say to show you right upstairs. She say you be wanting to have dinner upstairs, sir."

Stan and Molly followed him. Through an archway they could see women in evening dresses. A man in a dinner jacket stood with his back to a dark, enormous fireplace. He held a cocktail glass, gripping it by the foot instead of the stem.

The room was on the top floor, rear; the ceiling slanted.

"Dinner'll be served right soon, sir. Anything you want, just pick up that phone and push button eight on the box. That's butler's pantry."

When he had closed the door Stan locked it. "Relax, kid," he said wryly, "we're eating private. Let's get loaded first and try out the batteries."

He opened their traveling bags; Molly drew her dress over her head and hung it in a closet. From one of the bags she shook out a black net evening gown laden with sequins. "Hold the wires, honey, so they won't catch in my hair."

Expertly Stan eased the dress over her head. It was high-cut in the back with a ruff. He took a curved metal band attached to a flat earphone and slipped it over her head while the girl held her hair forward. When she threw it back the hair covered her ears so that the compact headset was completely hidden. Stan reached into the low V of the neck, found a miniature plug, and connected the headset. From his own suitcase he took his tails and began to stud a dress shirt.

"Go slow on that makeup, kid. Remember—you're not working behind foots now. And don't do any bumps or grinds while you're supposed to be hypnotized."

Standing in his underwear, he put on a linen vest with pockets like a hunting jacket's. They bulged with flat flashlight batteries. A wire dangled; strapping it to his leg in three places, he carried it down and drew on a black silk sock, feeding the wire through a tiny hole. His shoe followed, then the wire plugged into a socket at the side of the shoe. Finally he put on his shirt. Moistening his fingers, he rubbed them on a handkerchief, took from a wax paper envelope a spotless white tie, and tied it, frowning in the mirror of the dresser. In his coat a spider web of fine wire was sewed into the lining as an aerial; another plug connected it with the hidden vest which held the transmitter.

The Great Stanton adjusted his suspenders, then buttoned his waistcoat; he gave his hair a touch with the brushes and handed Molly a whiskbroom so that she could dust his shoulders for him.

"Gee, honey, you look handsome."

"Consider yourself kissed good and hard. I don't want to get smeared up. For God's sake take some of that lipstick off."

Under the toes of his left foot was the reassuring bulge of the contact key. Stan reached under his white vest and threw an invisible switch. He walked across the floor. "Get any buzz?"

"Not yet."

"Now." He pressed hard with his toes inside his shoe; but Molly made no sign. "God damn! If I'd been able to get a line on who was going to be at this shindig I'd have worked a straight crystal routine. There's too many things to come loose in this damn wireless gimmick." He ran his hands over the girl's dress, checking. Then he said, "Hold up your hair." The headset plug had slipped out. Stan spread its minute prongs with the point of a nail file and rasped them bright with irritable strokes. He connected it and Molly rearranged her hair.

On the other side of the room he again pressed with his left toes.

"I've got it, honey. Nice and clear. Now walk and see if it buzzes when you don't want it to."

Stan paced back and forth, keeping his weight off his toes, and Molly said she couldn't hear a thing, only when he wiggled his toes and made the contact.

"Okay. Now I'm in another room. What are the tests?"

"A card, a color, and a state."

"Right. What's this?"

Molly closed her eyes. From the earphone came a faint buzz three times—spades. Then a long buzz and three short ones—five plus three is eight. "Eight of spades."

"Right."

A tap from the door made Stan hiss for her to keep quiet.

"Dinner is served, sir. Mis' Harrington send her respects. She'll let you know on the phone when it's time for you all to come down. Better let me open up this bottle now, sir; we's powerful busy downstairs." He eased the cork out, his polished fingers dark against the napkin.

Stan felt in his pocket for a quarter and caught himself just in time. The butler bowed out.

"Gee, lookit, Stan! Champagne!"

"One glass for you, Cahill. We're working. If you load up on that stuff you'll be calling the old girl 'dearie.'"

"Aw, Stan."

He poured, put a few drops in his own glass, then carried the bottle into the bathroom and emptied the rest, bubbling gaily, down the drain of the washbowl.

From the rear Mrs. Bradburn Harrington looked like a little girl, but, Christ, what a crow when you see her head-on, Stan thought. She tapped a brass gong until the babble died. "Now I have a real treat for us. Mr. Stanton, whom I'm sure many of us have seen in the theater, will show us some wonderful things. I don't know just what they're going to do so I'll let Mr. Stanton tell you all about it himself."

Stan stood in the hall beside Molly. He took a deep breath and smoothed down his hair with both hands. The butler suddenly appeared beside him, holding a silver plate. On it was a slip of paper, folded. "Mis' Harrington tell me to give you this, sir."

Stan took it, unfolded it deftly with one hand, and read it at a single glance. He crushed it and swept it into his pocket, his face darkening. Molly whispered, "What's the matter, hon? What's happened?"

"Nothing!" he spat out savagely. "It's in the bag."

From the drawing room Mrs. Harrington's voice continued, ". . . and it will all be very exciting, I'm sure. May I present Mr. Stanton."

Stan drew a breath and walked in. He bowed to the hostess, again to the guests. "Ladies and gentlemen, what we are about to do may have many explanations. I shall offer none. In the realm of the human mind science has hardly scratched the surface. Most of its mysteries lie hidden from us yet. But down through the years certain people have had unusual gifts. I take no credit for mine." This time his bow was hardly more than a lowering of the eyes. This audience was the top. This was class. With a momentary shock Stan recognized a famous novelist, tall, slightly stooped, half bald. One of the season's debutantes, who had already made the papers with an affair involving a titled émigré, sat primly holding a highball on her knee, her white dress so low-cut that Stan fancied he could see the aureoles of her nipples.

"My family was Scotch originally, and the Scotch are said to possess strange faculties." The gray head of a stern-faced old judge nodded. "My ancestors used to call it 'second sight.' I shall call it simply—mentalism. It is a well-known fact that the minds of two people can establish a closer communication than words. A *rapport*. I discovered such a person several years ago. Ladies and gentlemen, allow me to present my assistant, Miss Cahill."

Molly swept in smiling, with her long stride, and rested her hand lightly on Stan's bent forearm. The debutante turned to a young man sitting on the arm of her chair. "Friend of yours, Diggie?" He closed her lips with his hand, staring fascinated at Molly.

Her eyes were half closed, her lips slightly parted. The old judge quietly took off his reading glasses.

"If I may trouble you, I should like to have Miss Cahill recline on that sofa."

There was a scurry of people finding other seats and a man snickered. Stan led Molly to the sofa and arranged a pillow behind her. She lifted her feet and he tucked the folds of the sequinned gown up from the floor. Reaching into his waist-coat pocket he drew out a ball of rock crystal the size of a marble and held it above the level of her eyes. "Concentrate."

The room was still at last.

"Your eyelids are growing heavy. Heavy. Heavy. You cannot lift them. You are falling asleep. Sleep. Sleep . . ."

Molly let her breath out in a long sigh and the lines about her mouth relaxed. Stan picked up her hand and laid it in her lap. She was limp. He turned to the company: "I have placed her in deep hypnosis. It is the only way I know by which telepathy can be made sure. I shall now pass among you, and I shall ask you to show me a number of objects, such as jewels, theater tickets, anything you wish."

He turned back to the reclining girl. "Miss Cahill, I shall touch a number of objects in this room. As I touch them you are to describe them. Is that clear?"

Dreamily she nodded. Her voice was a whisper. "Yes. Objects. Describe . . ."

Stan crossed the room and the old judge held out a gold fountain pen. Stan took it, focused his attention on it, his eyes widening. His back was to Molly and her head was turned toward the back of the sofa. She could see nothing. But her voice came as from a distance, just clear enough for them to hear if they listened hard. "A pen. A fountain pen. Gold. And something's . . . engraved. *A . . . G . . . K.*"

There was a ripple of applause, which Stan stopped with a lifted hand.

The hostess pointed to the spray of little brown orchids she wore as a corsage. Molly's voice went on, far away. "Flowers . . . beautiful flowers . . . they're . . . they're . . . or . . . orchids, I think."

The crowd sucked in its breath.

The debutante with the scarlet lips and the low-cut dress beckoned to Stan. When he drew near she reached into the pocket of the young man beside her and took out a gold mesh vanity case. Throwing open the cover, she held it so that only Stan could see what it contained. He frowned and she giggled up at him. "Go on, Mister Mindreader. Read my mind."

Stan stood motionless. He took a deep breath and by straining it against his throat forced the color to rise in his face.

"Look. He blushes too," said the girl.

The Great Stanton never moved but Molly's voice went on. "Something . . . something . . . do I have to tell what it is?"

Over his shoulder Stan said softly, "No, never mind it."

The girl snapped the bag shut and replaced it in the man's pocket. "You win, brother. You win." She gulped down the rest of her drink.

The Great Stanton bowed. "Lest I be accused of using trickery and signaling Miss Cahill, I should like a committee to follow me from the room for a few moments. Five or six persons will do nicely. And I shall ask someone here to take a slip of paper and record what Miss Cahill says while I am out of the room."

The hostess volunteered, and three couples followed Stan across the hall and into the library. When they were inside he closed the door. Something touched his hand; it was cold and made him jump. The guests laughed. Beside him stood a harlequin Great Dane, gazing up with eyes that held mastery in their steadiness and an odd loneliness too. The dog nudged Stan's leg with his paw and the mentalist began to scratch him idly behind the ears while he spoke to the others.

"I should like one of you now to choose some card in a pack of fifty-two."

"Deuce of clubs."

"Fine. Remember it. Now will someone select a color?"

"Chartreuse."

"That's a little difficult to visualize, but we'll try. Now will one of the ladies think of a state—any state in the union."

"That's easy," the girl spoke with a drawl. "There's only one state worth thinking about—Alabama."

"Alabama. Excellent. But would you care to change your mind?"

"No, indeedy. It's Alabama for sure."

Stanton bowed. "Shall we join the others?"

He held the door for them and they filed out. Stan knelt and laid his cheek against that of the Great Dane. "Hello, beautiful. Bet you wish you were my dog, don't you?"

The Dane whined softly.

"Don't let 'em get you down, boy. Bite 'em in their fat asses."

He rose, brushed his lapel, and strolled back to the lights and the voices.

Molly still lay on the couch, looking like a sleeping princess waiting for the kiss of a deliverer. The room was in a hubbub.

"The deuce of clubs! And the color—they picked chartreuse and she couldn't decide whether it was yellow or green! Isn't it amazing! And Alabama!"

"How would you like to have him for a husband, darling? Someone I know would have to scoot back to Cannes."

"Miraculous. Nothing short of miraculous."

Stan sat beside Molly, took one of her hands in his and said, "Wake up! Come now, wake up!"

She sat up, passing the back of her hand over her eyes. "Why—what's happened? Oh! Was I all right?"

"You were splendid," he said, looking into her eyes. "Every test was perfect."

"Oh, I'm so glad."

Still holding her hand, he drew her to her feet. They walked to the door, turned and bowed slightly and passed through it, applause clattering behind them.

"Stan, don't we stay for the party? I mean, the rest of it?"

"Shut up!"

"But—Stan—"

"I said shut up! I'll tell you later. Beat it upstairs. I'll be up in a little while and we'll get to hell out of here."

Obediently she went, pressing her lips together, fighting back an impulse to cry. This was nothing more than any other show; she had hoped there would be a party afterwards and dancing and more champagne.

Stan crossed over to the library, and the dog met him, jumping up. Heedless of his starched shirt bosom, Stan let him. "You know a pal, don't you, boy."

"Mr. Stanton—"

It was the old man who looked like a judge.

"I couldn't let you go without telling you how miraculous your work is."

"Thank you."

"I mean it, my boy. I'm afraid you don't realize what you've stumbled onto here. This goes deeper than you realize."

"I have no explanation for it," Stan said abruptly, still scratching the dog behind the ears.

"But I think I know your secret."

Silence. Stan could feel the blood surging up over his face. Good Christ, another amateur magician, he thought, raging. I've got to ditch him. But I've got to get him on my side, first. At last he said, smiling, "Perhaps you have the solution. A few persons of unusual intelligence and scientific knowledge might be able to guess at the main principle."

The old man nodded sagely. "I've guessed it, my boy. I've guessed it. This is no code act."

Stan's smile was intimate and his eyes danced with fellowship. God, here it comes. But I'll handle him somehow.

"Yes, my boy. I know. And I don't blame you for keeping your secret. It's the young lady."

"Yes?"

The judge lowered his voice. "I know it isn't telepathy. You have *spirit aid*!"

Stan felt like shouting. Instead he closed his eyes, the shadow of a smile passing over his mouth.

"They don't understand, my boy. I know why you have to present it as second sight. They're not ready to receive the glorious truth of survival. But our day will come, my boy. It will come. Develop your gift—the young lady's mediumship. Cherish it, for it is a fragile blossom. But what a soul-stirring thing it is! Oh, to think of it—this precious gift of mediumship, this golden bridge between us and those who have joined the ranks of the liberated, there to dwell on ever-ascending planes of spiritual life—"

The door opened and both men turned. It was Molly. "Oh. I'm sorry. I didn't know you were busy. Say, Stan—"

"Miss Cahill, I should like you to meet Judge Kimball. It *is* Judge Kimball, I am certain of it, although I do not recall ever having seen your photograph."

The old man nodded, smiling as if he and Stan shared a secret. He patted Molly's hand. "A great gift, my dear child, a great gift."

"Yeah, it's a gift all right, Judge. Well, I guess I'll be going back upstairs."

Stan took both her hands in his and shook them. "You were splendid tonight, my dear. Splendid. Now run along and I'll join you shortly. You had better lie down and rest for a few minutes."

When he released her Molly said, "Oops," and looked at her left hand; but Stan urged her toward the door, closing it gently behind her. He turned back to the judge.

"I'll confess, Judge. But"—he tilted his head toward the room across the hall—"they wouldn't understand. That is why I dropped in here for a moment. Someone here does understand." He looked down at the dog. "Don't you, boy?"

The Dane whined softly and crept closer.

"You know, Judge, they can sense things that are beyond all human perception. They can see and hear presences about us which we can never detect." Stan had moved toward a reading lamp beside an armchair. "For instance, I received a very faint but clear impression just now that someone from the Other Side is in the room. I am sure it is a young girl, that she is trying to get through to us. But I can tell nothing more about her; I cannot see her. If only our handsome friend here could talk he might be able to tell us."

The dog was staring into a dark corner of the book-lined room. He growled questioningly. Then, while the old man watched, fascinated, the Dane leaped up and shot into the corner, standing there alert and quiet, looking upward.

The mentalist slid his hand unobtrusively into his trousers pocket. "They know, sir. They can see. And now—I bid you good evening."

The house had grown full of unseen presences for the old judge; in thinking of some who might be near him now, his eyes grew wet. Slowly, elegantly, his shoulders straight, the Great Stanton ascended the stairs with the tread of an emperor, and the judge watched him go. A wonderful young man.

In the room with the tilted ceiling Molly was lying on the bed in her brassière and panties, smoking a cigarette. She sat up, hugging her knees. "Stan, for crying out loud, tell me why you got so mad at me when I wanted to stay for the party! Other private bookings we always stay and have fun and I don't get lit on three champagnes, honest I don't, honey. You think I don't know how to behave!"

He shoved his hands into his pockets, pulled out a slip of paper and crushed it, then flung it into a corner of the room. He spoke in a savage whisper. "For Christ's sake, don't go turning on the tears until we get out of here. I said *no* because it wasn't the spot for it. We gave 'em just enough. Always leave 'em wanting more. We built ourselves up and I didn't see any sense in knocking it all down again. For Christ's sake, we gave 'em a goddamned miracle! They'll be talking about it the rest of their lives. And they'll make it better every time they tell it. And what do we get for it? Three hundred lousy bucks and get treated like an extra darky they hired to pass the booze around. This is the big time, all right. Get your name in lights a foot high and then come out to one of these joints and what do they hand you—a dinner on a plate like a hobo at a back door."

He was breathing heavily, his face red and his throat working. "I'll sweat it out of them. By Christ, that old guy downstairs gave me the angle. I'll shake 'em loose from a pile of dough before I'm done. I'll have 'em begging me to stay a week. I'll have 'em wondering why I take my meals in my room. And it'll be because they're not fit to eat with—the bastards. I've been crazy not to think of this angle before, but from now on I know the racket. I've given 'em mentalism and they treat it like a dog walking on his hind legs. Okay. They're asking for it. Here it comes."

He stopped and looked down at the staring girl, whose face was chalky around the lips. "You did okay, kid." He smiled with one corner of his mouth. "Here's your ring, baby. I needed it for a gag."

Frowning still, Molly slipped the diamond back on her finger and watched the tiny specks of light from it spatter the dark corner of the sloping ceiling.

Stan carefully unhooked the wires and got out of his clothes. He went into the bathroom and Molly heard the bolt slammed shut.

You never could tell why Stan did anything. Here he was, madder than a wet hen, and he wouldn't say why and besides she wouldn't have pulled any boners; she'd just have smiled and kept her voice low and made believe she was tired from being hypnotized. She hadn't muffled any signals. What was eating him?

She got up and retrieved the crumpled slip from the corner. That was when it all started, when the colored waiter handed it to Stan just before they went on. Her fingers shook as she opened it.

"Kindly do not mingle with the guests."

The Sun

*On a white horse the sun child, with flame
for hair, carries the banner of life.*

I'M NOT going to put on the light. Because we're not going to argue all night again. I tell you, there's not a god-damned bit of difference between it and mentalism. It's nothing but our old act dressed up so it will lay 'em in the aisles. And for real."

"Honey, I don't like it."

"In God's name, what's the matter with it?"

"Well, what if there are—what if people do come back? I mean, well, they mightn't like it. I can't explain it. I'm scared."

"Listen, baby. I been over this a hundred times. If anybody's going to come back they're not going to get steamed up because we fake a little. We'll be doing the marks a favor; we'll make 'em plenty happy. After all, suppose you thought you could really speak to your dad, now. Wouldn't that make you happy?"

"Oh, God, I wish I could. Maybe it's because I've wished so hard for just that and hoped that maybe someday I could."

"I know, kid. I know how it is. Maybe there's something in it after all. I don't know. But I've met half a dozen spook workers in the past year and they're hustlers, every one of them. I tell you, it's just show business. The crowd believes we can read minds. All right. They believe it when I tell them that 'the lawsuit's going to come out okay.' Isn't it better to give them something to hope for? What does a regular preacher do every Sunday? Only all he does is promise. We'll do more than promise. We'll give 'em proof!"

"I—honey, I just can't."

"But you don't have to *do* anything! I'll handle all the effects. All you have to do is get into a cabinet and go to sleep if you want to. Leave everything else to me."

"But s'pose we got caught? I can't help it; I think it's mean. Remember how I told you once, the night you—you asked me to team up with you—about how I chalked on Daddy's tombstone 'He never crossed up a pal?' I was scared to death out there in that cemetery, and I was scared every minute until I touched Daddy's headstone, and then I started to cry and I said his name over and over, just as if he could hear me, and then somehow I felt like he really could. I was certain he could."

"All right. I thought you were his daughter. I thought you had guts enough to turn a trick that would get you the kind of life he'd want you to have. Give us a few years in this dodge and just one big job and then we can knock off. Stop jackassing all around the country and settle down. We'll—we'll get married. And have a house. And a couple of dogs. We'll—have a kid."

"Don't fib, honey."

"I mean it. Don't you think I want a kid? But it takes dough. A wad of dough. Then it'll be Florida in the winter and the kid sitting between us in the grandstand when the barrier goes up and they streak out, fighting for the rail. That's the kind of life I want and I've got my angles worked out, every one of them. Got my ordination certificate today. Baby, you're in bed with a full-blown preacher. I bet you never thought you'd bed down with a reverend! Last week I had a tailor make me an outfit—black broadcloth. I got a turn-around collar and everything. I can put on a pair of black gloves and a black hood and work in a red light like a dark-room lamp—and nobody can see a thing. I've even got cloth buttons so they won't reflect light. I tell you, it's a perfect setup. Don't you know a spook worker never takes a real rap? If anybody grabs, the chumps rally around him and start alibiing their heads off. Do you think I'm a feeblo to go monkeying around with scientific committees or any other wise guys that are likely to upset the works? Pick your crowd and you can sell 'em anything. And all *you* have to do is sit there with the old ladies admiring you and thanking you afterward for all the comfort you've brought 'em. But if you are yellow I can do it alone. You can go back to the carny and find yourself another kooch show and start all over."

"No, honey. I didn't mean—"

"Well, I do mean. I mean just that. One way is the big dough and plenty of class and a kid and clothes that will make you look like a million bucks. The other way is the carny, doing bumps and grinds and waggling your fanny for a bunch of rubes for a few more years. And then what? You know what. Make up your mind."

"Just let me think about it. Please, honey."

"You've thought about it. Don't make me do anything I don't want to do. Look, baby, I love you. You know that. No, don't pull away. Keep quiet. I said I love you. I want a kid by you. Get it? Put your other arm around me. It's like old times, eh, kid? There. Like it? Sure you do. This is heaven, kid. Don't break it up."

"Oh, honey, honey, honey."

"That's better. And you will do it? Say you will. Say yes, baby."

"Yes. Yes—I'll do anything."

In the old gray stone house near Riverside Drive, Addie Peabody (Mrs. Chisholm W.) answered the door herself. She had given Pearl the evening off and Pearl had gone willingly enough, in view of what was coming.

The first to arrive were Mr. and Mrs. Simmons, and Mrs. Peabody shooed them into the parlor. "Honestly, I was just dying for somebody to talk to, I thought the afternoon would never go by, I'd have gone to the matinee but I just knew I couldn't sit through one, I'd be so excited about tonight, they say this new medium is simply grand—and so young, too. They say she hasn't a speck of background, she's so spontaneous and natural, she used to be a show girl I hear but it really doesn't matter, it's one of the strangest things how the gift strikes people in all walks of life and it's so often among humble people. I'm sure none of us will ever develop full power although they do say the Reverend Carlisle is simply wonderful at developmental sittings. I have a friend who's been developing with him for nearly a year now and she has noticed some amazing phenomena in her own home when not a soul was there but herself. She's simply mad about Mr. Carlisle, he's so sincere and sympathetic."

In twos and threes the rest of the company gathered. Mr. Simmons made one or two little jokes just to liven things up, but they were all in good taste and not offensive, because, after all, you should approach a séance with joy in your heart and all the people have to be attuned or the phenomena are likely to be scarce and very disappointing.

The bell rang a steady, insistent note, full of command. Mrs. Peabody hurried out, taking a quick look in the hall mirror and straightening her girdle before she opened the door. Outside, the light above the door fell on the heads of two people, the first a tall, dramatic-looking woman in her late twenties, rather flashily dressed. But Mrs. Peabody's glance slid over her and came to rest on the man.

The Rev. Stanton Carlisle was about thirty-five. He was holding his black hat and the lamplight made his hair glisten golden—just like the sun, she thought. He made her think of Apollo.

Mrs. Peabody noticed in her first swift glance that he was dressed in street clericals with a black vest and a turn-about collar. He was the first spiritualist minister she had ever seen who wore clericals but he was so distinguished-looking that it didn't seem a bit ostentatious; anybody would have taken him for an Episcopalian.

"Oh, Mr. Carlisle, I just knew it was you. I got a distinct impression the minute you rang the bell."

"I am sure we shall establish an excellent vibrational harmony, Mrs. Peabody. May I present our medium, Mary Margaret Cahill."

Inside, Mrs. Peabody introduced them to the others. She served tea and it was so English—just like having the vicar over, she thought. Miss Cahill was a sweet-looking girl, and after all some people can't help being born on the wrong side of the tracks. She probably did the best she could with what she had to start with. Even if she did look a little cheap she was beautiful and had an odd, haggard expression about her mouth that touched Mrs. Peabody's heart. Mediumship takes so much out of them—we owe them such a tremendous debt.

Mr. Carlisle was charming and there was something about his voice that stirred you, as if he were speaking just to you even when he addressed the others. He was so understanding.

Finally Mrs. Peabody stood up. "Shall I play something? I always say there's nothing like having an old-fashioned family organ. They're so sweet-toned and so much nicer than a piano." She sat at the console and struck a gentle chord. She would have to get the pedal levers oiled; the left one squeaked a little. The first piece she turned to was "The Old Rugged Cross" and one by one the company picked it up, Mr. Simmons coming in with a really fine baritone.

The Rev. Carlisle cleared his throat. "Mrs. Peabody, I wonder if you recall that splendid old hymn, 'On the Other Side of Jordan.' It was a favorite of my sainted mother's, and I should dearly love to hear it now."

"Indeed I do. At least, it's in the hymnal."

Mr. Simmons volunteered to lead, standing by the organ, with the others humming:

> On the other side of Jordan
> In the sweet fields of Eden
> Where the Tree of Life is blooming
> There is rest for me.
>> There is rest for the weary,
>> There is rest for the weary,
>> On the other side of Jordan
>> There is rest for me.

Mrs. Peabody's eyes were wet when the hymn was finished,

and she knew that this was the psychological moment. She sat silently on the bench and then closed her eyes and let her fingers find the chords. Everyone sang it softly.

> *Shall we gather by the river,*
> *The beautiful, the beautiful river.*
> *Yes, we shall gather by the river*
> *That flows by the throne of God.*

She played the "Amen" chords softly, drawing them out, and then turned to the Rev. Carlisle. His eyes were closed; he sat upright and austere with his hands resting on the knees of his black broadcloth trousers. When he spoke he kept his eyes closed.

"Our hostess has provided us with a fine cabinet. The niche between the organ and the wall will serve beautifully. And, I believe, there are hangings which can be lowered. Let us all compose ourselves with humble hearts, silently, and in the presence of God who hath hid these things from the wise and prudent and hast revealed them unto babes.

"I call upon the Spirit of Eternal Light, whom some call God the Father and some call the Holy Ghost; who, some believe, came among the earth-bound as our Lord and Savior, Jesus the Christ; who spoke to Gautama under the Bo tree and gave him enlightenment, whose praise was taught by the last of India's great saints, Sri Ramakrishna. Marvel not at what we shall attempt, for the hour is coming in which all that are in the graves shall hear his voice and shall come forth. Many of them that sleep in the dust of the earth shall awake, but some who did evil in their days upon the earth shall be reborn and remain among the earth-bound for yet another existence. No spirit who has ever returned speaks to us of hell fire but rather of rebirth and another chance. And when a man has done much evil he does not descend into a pit of eternal torment but wanders between the worlds, neither earth-bound nor liberated; for the Lord, being full of compassion, forgives their iniquity. He remembers that they were but flesh, a wind that passeth away and cometh not again until the prayers and faith of liberated and earth-bound alike cause their absorption into the Universal Soul of God, who is in all things and from which everything is made that was made. We ask that the Great Giver of Love enter our hearts and make us to become as little children, for without innocence we cannot admit those presences who draw near about us now, anxious to speak to us and make their nearness known. For it is written: 'He bowed the heavens also, and came down: and darkness was under his feet. And he rode upon a cherub, and did fly: yea, he did fly upon the wings of the wind.' Amen."

He opened his eyes and Mrs. Peabody thought she had never seen eyes as blue or with a glance so resembling an eagle's. Spiritual power flowed out of him; you could just feel it.

The spiritualist continued, "Let Mrs. Simmons sit nearest to the cabinet on the far side. Mrs. Peabody on the other side, before the organ which she plays so beautifully. I shall sit here, next to her. Mr. Simmons next to his wife."

An armchair was carried into the niche for Miss Cahill who sat tautly, her knees close together, her hands clenched. The Rev. Carlisle stepped into the niche.

"Are you sure you feel equal to it this evening, my dear?"

Miss Cahill smiled bravely up at him and nodded.

"Very well. You are among friends. No one here will break the circle. There are no skeptics to endanger your life by suddenly flooding you with light. No one will move from his chair when it is dangerous to the vibration lines. Any ectoplasmic emanations from your body will be carefully observed but not touched so you have nothing to fear. Are you perfectly comfortable?"

"Yes. Comfortable. Fine."

"Very well. Do you want music?"

Miss Cahill shook her head. "No. I feel so—so sleepy."

"Relax, my dear friend."

She closed her eyes.

Mrs. Peabody tiptoed about and extinguished all the lamps except one. "Shall I close the cabinet curtains?"

Carlisle shook his head. "Let us first have her with us. Without anything between us. Let us form the circle."

Silently they took their places. Minutes crept by; a chair creaked and outside a car passed. Behind the velvet drapes which shut off the street light it sounded out of key and impertinent. The Rev. Carlisle seemed in a trance himself.

Knock!

Everyone gasped and then smiled and nodded.

Knock!

Carlisle spoke. "Ramakrishna?"

Three sharp raps answered him.

"Our dear teacher—our loving *guru* who has never left us in spirit—we greet you in the love of God, which you imparted so divinely while you were earth-bound. Will you speak to us now through the lips of our dear medium, Mary Cahill?"

Miss Cahill stirred in her chair and her head drew back. Her lips opened and her voice came softly, as from a great distance:

"The body of man is a soul-city containing the palace of the heart which contains, in turn, the lotus of the soul. Within its blossom are heaven and earth contained, are fire and water, sun and moon, and lightning and stars."

Her voice came, monotonous, as if it were a transmitter of the words of another. "He, whose vision is clouded by the veils of maya, will ask of that city, 'What is left of it when old age covers it and scatters it; when it falls to pieces?' To which the enlightened one replies, 'In the old age of the body the soul ages not; by the death of the body it is not slain.' There is a wind that blows between the worlds, strewing the lotus petals to the stars."

She stopped and let out her breath in a long sigh, pressing her hands against the chair arms and then letting them drop into her lap.

"Our guide has spoken," Carlisle said gently. "We may expect a great deal tonight, I am sure."

Miss Cahill opened her eyes, then jumped from the chair and began to walk about the room, touching the furniture and the walls with the tips of her fingers. She turned to the Rev. Carlisle. "D'you mind if I get into something more comfortable?"

The reverend nodded. "My friends, it has always been my aim to present tests of mediumship under such conditions that the slightest suspicion of fraud is impossible. We must face it: there are fraudulent mediums who prey on the noblest and purest emotions known to man. And I insist that the gifts of Mary Cahill be removed from the category of ordinary mediumship. She is able, at an expense to her strength it is true, to work in a faint light. I should like a number of the ladies here tonight to accompany her when she changes her clothes and make sure that there is no chance of fraud or trickery, that nothing is concealed. I know that you do not for one moment harbor such thoughts, but to spread the gospel of Spiritualism we must be able to say to the world—and to our most hostile critics—I *saw*. And under test conditions."

Mrs. Peabody and Mrs. Simmons rose and Miss Cahill smiled to them and waited. Carlisle opened a small valise, drawing out a robe of white watered silk and a pair of white slippers. He handed these to the medium and the ladies filed out.

Mrs. Peabody led the way up to her own bedroom. "Here you are, dear. Just change your things in here. We'll be waiting downstairs."

Miss Cahill shook her head. "Mr. Carlisle wants you to stay. I don't mind a bit." The ladies sat down, tongue-tied with embarrassment. The medium slowly drew off her dress and slip. She rolled down her stockings neatly and placed them beside her shoes. When she stood completely stripped before them, leisurely shaking out the robe, a sadness gripped Mrs. Peabody, deep and nameless. She saw the naked woman, unashamed there in the frilly celibacy of her own bedroom, and a lump rose in her throat. Miss Cahill was so beautiful and it was all so innocent, her standing there with her mind, or certainly part of her mind, far away still in that mysterious land where it went voyaging. It was with regret and a feeling she had had as a little girl when the last curtain descended on a play, that she watched Miss Cahill finally draw the robe about her and tie the cord loosely. She stepped into the slippers and smiled at them; and Mrs. Peabody got up, straightening her dress.

"My dear, it is so good of you to come to us. We appreciate it so."

She led the way downstairs.

In the living room all the lights were extinguished, save for a single oil lamp with a shade of ruby-red glass which the clergyman had brought with him. It gave just enough light for each person to see the faces of the others.

The Rev. Carlisle took the medium by the hand and led her to the armchair in the niche. "Let us try first without closing the curtains."

They formed the circle, waiting patiently, devoutly. Mary Cahill's eyes were closed. She moaned and slumped lower in the chair, twisting so that her head rested against its back. A low whimper came from deep within her, and she twisted again and began to breathe heavily. The cord of the white robe loosened, the fringed ends fell to the carpet. Then her body suddenly arched itself and the robe fell open.

With a swift intake of breath the sitters leaned forward.

"Mrs. Peabody, do you mind?" The reverend's voice was like a benediction.

She hurried over, feeling the warmth in her face, and closed the robe, tying the cord firmly. She couldn't resist giving the girl's hand an affectionate little pat, but the medium seemed unconscious.

When she had regained her chair she looked over at the Rev. Carlisle. He sat upright, eyes closed, his hands motionless on his knees. In the dim red glow of the lamp his face, above the severe collar, seemed to hang in mid-air; his hands to float as motionless as if they were made of papier-mâché. Save for the indistinct circle of faces the only other thing visible in the room was the medium in her white robe. Her hair was part of the darkness.

Slowly and gently spirit sounds began. Gentle raps, then louder knocks. Something set the glass prisms of the chandelier tinkling, and their musical voices continued for several minutes, as if a ghostly hand were playing with them—as a child might play with them if it could float to the ceiling.

Mrs. Simmons spoke first, in a hushed, awed voice. "I see a light."

It was there. A soft, greenish spark hovered near the floor beside Mrs. Peabody and then vanished. Mrs. Peabody felt a breeze—the psychic breeze of which Sir Oliver Lodge had written. Then, moving high in the air across the room, was another light. She tilted her eyeglasses a trifle to bring it into sharper focus. It was a hand with the forefinger raised as if toward heaven. It vanished.

The shadows now seemed to flit with lights but some, she

knew, were in her own eyes. The next time, however, they all saw it. Floating near the floor, in front of the medium, was a glowing mass which seemed to unwind from nowhere. It took form and rose before her and for a moment obscured her face.

It grew brighter and Mrs. Peabody made out the features of a young girl. "Caroline! *Carol*, darling—is it you?"

The whisper was gentle and caressing. "Mother. Mother. Mother."

It was gone. Mrs. Peabody took off her glasses and wiped her eyes. At last Caroline had come through to her. The perfect image of the child! They seem to stay the age when they pass over. That would make Caroline still sixteen, bless her heart. "Carol—don't leave! Don't go, darling! Come back!"

Darkness. The oil lamp sputtered, the flame died down and pitch black enfolded them. But Mrs. Peabody did not notice it. Her eyes were tight shut against the tears.

The Rev. Carlisle spoke. "Will someone turn on the lights?"

Orange glow leaped out brilliantly, showing the reverend still sitting with his hands on his knees. He rose now and went to the medium; with a handkerchief he wiped the corners of her eyes and her lips. She opened her eyes and got to her feet swaying, saying nothing.

The spiritualist steadied her arm and then she smiled once at the company. "Let me go upstairs," she said breathlessly.

When she was gone they crowded around the Rev. Stanton Carlisle, pressing his hand and all talking at once from the release of the tension.

"My dear friends, this is not our last evening. I see many more in the future. We shall indeed explore the Other Side together. Now I must go as soon as Miss Cahill is ready. We must look after our medium, you know. I will go up to her now and I shall ask all of you to remain here and not to say good-bye. She has been under tremendous strain. Let us leave quietly."

He smiled his blessing on them and closed the door softly behind him. On the hall table was a blue envelope, "To our dear medium as a token of our appreciation." Inside was Mrs. Peabody's check for seventy dollars.

"Ten bucks apiece," Stan said under his breath and crushed

the envelope in his fingers. "Hang on to your hat, lady; you ain't seen nothing yet."

Upstairs he entered Mrs. Peabody's room and shut the door. Molly was dressed and combing her hair.

"Well, kid, we laid 'em in the aisles. And with the light on every minute and the medium visible. The robe business was terrific. Jesus, what misdirection! They couldn't have pried their eyes away even if they'd known what I was doing."

From under his clerical vest he drew two papier-mâché replicas of a man's hands and two black mittens. From a large flat pocket inside his coat came a piece of black cardboard on which was pasted a picture of a movie actress cut from a magazine cover and touched up with luminous paint. From his sleeve he took a telescopic reaching-rod made of blue steel. Bundling all the props into the white robe he stuffed them into the valise which he had brought upstairs. Then he lifted his shoe, pulled a luminous-headed thumbtack from the instep, tossed it in, and shut the bag.

"You all set, kid? You better endorse this before I forget it. It's only seventy skins, but, baby, we're just starting. I got it fixed so we can slip downstairs and out without a lot of congratulations and crap. Baby, next time we really turn the heat on the old gal."

Molly's lip was trembling. "Stan, Mrs. Peabody's awful sweet. I—I can't go on with this sort of stuff. I just can't. She wants to speak to her daughter so bad and all you could do was whisper at her a little."

The Rev. Stanton Carlisle was an ordained spiritualist minister. He had started by sending two dollars and an affidavit, saying that he had produced spirit messages, to the United Spiritual League, and had received a medium's certificate. To get his Minister's certificate he had sent five dollars and had been interviewed by an ordained minister who turned his rostrum over to Candidate Carlisle for a few minutes one Thursday night. Messages were forthcoming and the new minister of the spiritualist gospel was sworn in. He was now entitled to perform marriages, conduct services, and bury the dead. He threw back his head and laughed silently.

"Don't worry, kid. She'll hear from her daughter. And in

something louder than a whisper. And she'll see her too. This routine with the lights on and the medium in view all the time was just the convincer. The next time we work with this bunch we'll work in a regular dark séance or a curtain over the cabinet. And do you know who's going to give Mrs. Peabody the big thrill of talking to her daughter? See if you can guess."

"No. Not me, Stan. I couldn't."

He was suddenly steely. "You don't want me to let on to all those nice old folks down there that I have been deceived by a fraudulent medium, do you, sugar? You've got 'em eating out of your hand, my little kooch dancer. And when the time comes—you're going to be one ghost that talks. Come on, kid. Let's beat it out of here. The sooner I ditch this bag of props the rosier life will get. You think you're the only one in this show that ever gets the shakes?"

The guests stayed late for a buffet supper. Mrs. Peabody had rallied from the shock of recognizing her daughter and was fully launched in praise of the new medium and her mentor, the Rev. Stanton Carlisle. "You know, I got a definite psychic flash the moment that man touched the doorbell, the very moment. And when I opened the door there he was with the light shining on his hair—just like a halo in the sun, it was a perfect halo effect. He's like Apollo, I said to myself. Those were the very words."

When the other sitters had gone Addie Peabody was too excited to sleep. At last she drew on a housecoat and came downstairs, feeling constantly the unseen presence of Caroline beside her. At the organ she let her hands fall on the keyboard in chords, and they sounded so spiritual and inspired. There was certainly a new quality about her playing. Then from beneath her fingers a melody took shape and she played with her eyes closed, from memory:

> *On the other side of Jordan*
> *In the sweet fields of Eden,*
> *Where the Tree of Life is blooming*
> *There is rest for me.*

The Hierophant

They kneel before the high priest,
wearer of the triple crown and bearer of the keys.

THE FACE floated in air, unearthly in its greenish radiance, but it was the face of a girl and when it spoke Addie could see the lips move. Once the eyes opened, heartbreakingly dark and empty. Then the glowing lids closed again; the voice came:

"Mother . . . I love you. I want you to know."

Addie swallowed hard and tried to control her throat. "I know, darling. Carol, baby—"

"You may call me Caroline . . . now. It was the name you gave me. You must have loved it once. I was so foolish to want a different name. I understand so many things now."

The voice grew fainter as the face receded in the darkness. Then its glow changed and diminished until it was a pool of light near the floor. It vanished.

The voice whispered again, this time amplified by the metal trumpet which had been placed in the cabinet with the medium. "Mother . . . I have to go back. Be careful. . . . There are bad forces here, too. All of us are not good. Some are evil. I feel them all around me. Evil forces . . . Mother . . . good-bye."

The trumpet clanged against the music rack of the organ and tumbled to the floor. It rolled against the leg of Addie's chair and stopped. Groping for it, she picked it up eagerly but it was silent and chill except at the narrow end where it was warm as if from Caroline's lips.

The raps which had disturbed them on the last two evenings now began and jumped from the walls, the organ, her own chair back, the floor, everywhere. They rapped in the mocking cadences and ridiculous rhythms that spiteful children use to torment a teacher.

A vase crashed from the mantelpiece and shattered on the tiles of the hearth. Addie screamed.

The tones of the Rev. Carlisle came from the darkness near her. "Let us have patience. I call upon the presence which has come here unbidden to listen to me. We are not hostile to you. We wish you no harm. We are here to help you attain liberation by prayer, if you can only listen."

A mocking rap on the back of his own chair answered him.

Mrs. Peabody felt the trumpet snatched from her hands. It clanged on the ceiling above her head and then a voice came from it and the rappings and rustlings stopped. The voice was low and vibrant and deeply accented.

"The way to God lies through the Yoga of Love." It was the control spirit, Ramakrishna. "You little, mischievous ones of the baser planes, listen to our words of love and grow in spirit. Do not plague us nor our medium nor the sweet spirit of the girl who has visited her mother and was driven away by you. Listen to the love in our hearts which are as mountain streams pouring out their love to the distant sea which is the great heart of God. *Hari Aum!*"

With the fall of the trumpet to the floor the room became still.

At the door, while he was saying good night, the Rev. Carlisle took Addie's hand firmly between his own. "We must have faith, Mrs. Peabody. Poltergeist disturbances are not infrequent phenomena. Sometimes it is possible for us, and our liberated dear ones, to overcome them by prayer. I shall pray. Your little girl, Caroline, may not be able to aid us very much but I am sure she will try—from her side of the River. And now, take courage. I will be near you even after I have gone. Remember that."

Addie closed the front door with dread of the vast, empty house behind and above her. If only she could get a girl to live in. But Pearl had left and then the Norwegian couple and after them old Mrs. Riordan. It was impossible. And Mr. Carlisle had said it would do no good to go to a hotel; the elementals attached themselves to people and not to houses and that would be horrible. In a hotel before the maids and the bellboys and everybody.

Besides, this had been Caroline's home when they all had been alive—*in earth life*, she corrected herself. They had bought this house when Caroline was three. Just before Christmas it was. And she had had her Christmas tree in the niche where Miss Cahill always sat at the séances. Addie took a chiffon handkerchief from her belt and blew her nose. It was awful that all this had to start just when Caroline had begun to come through so wonderfully.

The armchair was still in the niche and Addie sat down in it gingerly. That corner was really Miss Cahill's now; she had sanctified it by her sacrifices and her suffering just to enable Caroline to speak to them and appear in full form. Addie sank deeper into the chair, trying to reason away the feeling that somehow this wasn't *her* home any more. She tried thinking back to Caroline's third Christmas and the gifts. There was a little wooden telephone, she remembered, and Caroline had spent all Christmas Day "calling up" people.

Now the house wasn't like home any longer—it belonged to a terrifying stranger. A stupid, jealous boor of a spirit that broke things and rapped on windowpanes until Addie thought she would lose her mind. It was everywhere; there was no escaping it. Even when she went shopping or took in a movie she seemed to feel things crawling under her skin. She had tried to tell herself it was just nerves but Mr. Carlisle had once mentioned a case he had helped to exorcise—where the poltergeist actually haunted a man's skin. And now she was positive of it. She broke into a fit of sobbing which made her sides ache. But it was a relief. You just couldn't feel any more miserable and that was a relief in a way.

The house was silent but on the long journey upstairs she felt herself watched. It was not by anything that had eyes, just an evil intelligence that *saw* without any eyes.

Addie Peabody braided her hair hastily and threw some water on her face, rubbing it a couple of times with a towel.

In bed, she tried to read one of the books the Rev. Carlisle had given her on Ramakrishna and the Yoga of Love but the words jumbled up and she found herself reading the same sentence over and over, hoping that the raps would not start again. They were only taps on her windowpane and the first time they came she had run to the window and opened it, thinking boys were throwing pebbles. But no one was there; the rooming houses across the street were all dark and asleep with their windows as black as caverns and the dingy lace curtains of one or two blowing out on the night wind. That was nearly a week ago.

Tap!

Addie jumped and looked at the bed-table clock. Ten minutes after one. She turned off the reading light and left on the night lamp in its opaque shade with the light glowing through the delicate cut-out letters: "God is Love."

Tap!

Addie switched on the light and looked at the clock. One-twenty. She gripped the leather traveling clock in her hands, straining her eyes until she could see the minute hand actually moving, slowly and inevitably, like life itself going by. She put the clock down and clutched the spread tightly with both hands and waited. It was one-thirty. Maybe it wouldn't come again. Oh, please, God, I have faith; indeed I do. Don't let it—

Tap!

She threw on her robe and hurried downstairs, snapping on the lights as she went. Then the emptiness of the illumined house made her flesh creep. She put out the upstairs lights by the hall switch and the blackness up the staircase seemed to smother her.

In the kitchen Addie filled a kettle, spilling water down her sleeve, and set it on the stove for tea. A crash from the pantry made her grab the robe together at her throat.

"Dear—" She addressed the air, hoping, willing to make it hear her. "I don't know who you are, dear, but you must be a little boy. A mischievous little boy. I—I wouldn't want to punish you, dear. God—God is love."

A crash from the cellar shook the floor under her feet. She was too frightened to go down to see but she knew that the big shovel by the furnace had fallen over. Then, through the still house, standing with its lights on in the midst of the sleeping city, she heard another sound from below, a sound which made her cover her ears and run back upstairs leaving the kettle humming on the stove.

From the cellar had come the metallic rasp of the coal shovel, creeping over the concrete in little jumps as if it had sprouted legs like a crab. An inch at a time. Scrape. Scrape.

This time she picked up the telephone and managed to dial a number. The voice which answered was muffled and indistinct but it was like a warm shawl thrown over her shoulders.

"I am sorry to hear it, Mrs. Peabody. I shall start an intensive meditation at once, spending the night in mental prayer, holding the thought. I don't believe that the phenomena will trouble you further. Or, at least, not tonight."

Addie fell asleep as soon as she got back in bed. She had made herself a cup of tea, and once she fancied she heard a sound from the cellar but even if she had she would not have been afraid, for the Rev. Carlisle was with her now, in spirit. If only she could persuade him to stay over for a few days at the house. She must ask him again.

The old gray stone house was dark and as silent as its neighbors. A milkman, driving on his lonely route, saw a man in a dark overcoat pulling what looked like a length of heavy fish-line out of a cellar window. He wondered if he oughtn't to tell the cops but the guy was probably a wack. There were a lot of 'em in this territory.

Light was beginning to show at the window when Molly Cahill turned over and found Stan slipping into bed beside her. She buried her face in the hollow of his throat for a moment and then turned back and fell asleep. You can always smell perfume on them if they've been with another woman. That was what people said.

Addie Peabody got up late and called the Rev. Carlisle but there was no answer. She had the oddest feeling that the ringing she heard in her own telephone also came from one of the rooming houses across the street but she put it down to her nerves. Anyhow, nobody answered.

A little later when she opened the medicine cabinet to get the toothpaste one of those big brown roaches, about three inches long, was in there and flew out at her. She was sure the poltergeist had put it in there just to devil her.

And at breakfast the milk tasted like garlic and that she knew was the poltergeist because they always sour milk or make the cows' milk taste of garlic. And it was certified milk from the best company. She dressed hurriedly and went out. In the beauty parlor the chatter of Miss Greenspan and the heat of the dryer were restful and reassuring. Addie treated herself to a facial and a manicure, and felt better. She did some shopping and saw part of a movie before she got so restless she had to leave.

It was late afternoon when she returned. She had hardly taken off her things when she smelled smoke. For a moment she was paralyzed, not knowing whether to go and find out what was burning or call the fire department and she stood between the two ideas for several seconds while the smell got stronger. Then she saw that something was burning in the umbrella stand in the hall—evil-smelling and smoky. It wasn't doing any damage, just smoking and Addie carried the brass stand out in the back yard. The odor was like old-fashioned phosphorous matches. That was why the ancients always said the Evil One appeared in a burst of fire and brimstone—poltergeist fires smelled like phosphorus.

Minute by minute the evening drew on. The fire had set all her nerves on edge again; she had always been deathly afraid of fires. And then the raps started at the windows and even on the fanlight above the front door.

What a relief it was when she heard the doorbell ring and knew it was Mr. Carlisle and Miss Cahill. The Simmonses were not coming tonight, and with a little guilty pang Addie thought of it with elation—she would have Mr. Carlisle all to herself. That always seemed to get the best results. It was hard to get good results with so many different sets of vibrations even though the Simmonses were just as dear and devoted as any spiritualists she had ever known.

Miss Cahill seemed even more tired and run-down-looking than ever and Addie insisted on giving her a hot Ovaltine before the séance but it didn't seem to strengthen her any. The lines about her mouth grew deeper if anything.

After she had played "On the Other Side of Jordan" Mr. Carlisle asked her if Caroline had a favorite hymn. She had to answer truthfully that Caroline was not a religious child. She sang hymns in Sunday school, of course, but she never sang any around the house.

"Mrs. Peabody, what *did* she sing about the house? That is, what songs of a serious nature? An old love song perhaps?"

Addie thought back. It was amazing what she could re- member when Mr. Carlisle was there; it was like being nearer to Caroline just to talk with him. And now she remembered. "Hark, hark, the lark at heaven's gate sings!" She turned and played it, gently at first and then more strongly until it filled the room and a metal dish vibrated in sympathy. She played it over and over, hearing Caroline's thin but true-pitched young voice through the blast of the organ. Her legs ached with pumping before she stopped.

Mr. Carlisle had already extinguished all the lights and drawn the curtain before the cabinet. She took her place in the straight-backed chair beside him and he turned out the last light and let the dark flow around them.

Addie started when she heard the trumpet clink as it was levitated. Then from a great distance came a shrill, sweet pip- ing—like a shepherd playing on reeds. ". . . And Phoebus 'gins arise, His steeds to water at those springs . . ."

A cool breeze fanned her face and then a touch of some- thing material stroked her hair. From the dark, where she knew the cabinet to be, came a speck of greenish light. It trembled and leaped like a ball on a fountain, growing in size until it stopped and unfolded like an opening flower. Then it grew larger and took shape, seeming to draw a veil from before its face. It was Caroline, standing in the air a few inches above the floor.

The green light that was her face grew brighter until Addie could see her eyebrows, her mouth and her eyelids. The eyes opened, their dark, cavernous blankness wrenched her heart.

"Caroline—baby, speak to me. Are you happy? Are you all right, baby?"

The lips parted. "Mother . . . I . . . must confess something."

"Darling, there isn't anything to confess. Sometimes I did scold you, but I didn't— Please forgive me."

"No . . . I must confess. I am not . . . not altogether liberated. I had selfish thoughts. I had mean thoughts. About you. About other people. They keep me on a low plane . . . where the lower influences can reach me and make trouble for me. Mother . . . help me."

Addie had risen from her chair. She stumbled toward the materialized form but the hand of the Rev. Carlisle caught her wrist quickly. She hardly noticed. "Caroline, baby! Anything—tell me what to do!"

"This house . . . evil things have entered it. They have taken it away from us. Take me away."

"Darling—but how?"

"Go far away. Go where it is warm. To California."

"Yes. Yes, darling. Tell Mother."

"This house . . . ask Mr. Carlisle to take it for his church. Let us never live here any more. Take me to California. For if you go I will go with you. I will come to you there. And we will be happy. Only when this house is a church can I be happy. Please, Mother."

"Oh, baby, of course. Anything. Why didn't you ask me before?"

The form was growing dim. It sank, wavering, and the light went out.

The pair in the cab was the usual stuff: gab, gab, gab. Jesus, what a laugh!—"they lived happy ever afterwards." The hackie slid between a bus and a sedan, grazing the car and making the driver mutter in alarm.

"G'wan, ya dumb son-of-a-bitch," he yelled back.

The couple were at it again and he listened in, for laughs.

"I tell you, we've got our foot in the door. Don't you see, baby, this is where it starts? With this house, I can gimmick it up from cellar to attic. I can give 'em the second coming of Christ if I want to. And you were swell, baby, just swell."

"Stan, take your hands off me."

"What's eating you? Get hold of yourself, kid. How about a drink before you hit the hay?"

"I said take your hands off me! I can't stand it! I can't stand it! Let me out of this cab! I'll walk. Do you hear? Let me out!"

"Baby, you better calm down."

"I won't. I won't go up there with you. Don't touch me."

"Hey, driver, let us out. Right here at the corner. Anywhere."

The cabbie took a quick look in his rear vision mirror. Before he got control of the wheel he had nearly piled the boat up against a light pole. Holy gees, the dame's face was glowing bright green right inside his own cab!

From Ed Wolfehope's column, "The Hardened Artery":

". . . She is a widow who owned a fine old mansion in the Seventies near the Drive. Her only child died years ago and she lived on in the house because of memories. Recently a pair of spook workers 'materialized' the daughter and she told her mother to give them the house and move to the West Coast. No one knows how much they took the widow for in cash first. But she left on her journey beaming and rosy—kissed both crooks at the train gate. And they put guys in jail for welching on alimony! . . ."

From "The Trumpet Voice":

"To the Editor:

"A friend of mine recently sent me a piece from a Broadway columnist, which is one lie from beginning to end about me and the Reverend Stanton Carlisle. I want to say it could not have been a practical joker with an air pistol who made the raps on my window. I kept my eyes open the whole time. And anybody who knows anything about Psychic Phenomena knows all about poltergeist fires.

"Miss Cahill and the Reverend Carlisle are two of the dearest people I have ever been privileged to meet and I can testify that all the séances they conducted were under the strictest test conditions and no decent person could even have dreamed of fraud. At the very first séance I recognized my dear daughter Caroline who 'died' when she was sixteen, just a few days before her high school commencement. She came back again and again in the other sittings and I could almost have touched her dear golden hair, worn in the very style she wore it when she passed over. I have a photograph of her taken for her high school yearbook which shows her hair worn this way and it was something no one but I could have possibly known of.

"The Reverend Carlisle never said one word asking for my house. It was Caroline who told me to give it to him and in fact I had a hard time to persuade him to take it and Caroline had to come back and beg him before he would give in. And I am happy to say that here in California, under the guidance of the Rev. Hallie Gwynne, Caroline is with me almost daily. She is not as young as she was in New York and I know that means she is reflecting my own spiritual growth. . . ."

Sun beat on the striped awnings while six floors below them Manhattan's streets wriggled in the rising heat from the pavement. Molly came out of the kitchenette with three fresh cans of cold beer and Joe Plasky, sitting on the overstuffed sofa with his legs tied in a knot before him, reached up his calloused hand for the beer and smiled. "Sure seems funny—us loafing in midseason. But that's Hobart for you—too many mitts in the till. Show gets attached right in the middle of the season."

Zeena filled an armchair beside the window, fanning herself gently with a copy of *Variety*. She had slipped off her girdle and was wearing an old kimono of Molly's, which hardly met in the middle. "Whew! Ain't it a scorcher? You know, this is the first summer I've ever been in New York. I don't envy you all here. It ain't quite this bad in Indiana. Say, Molly"— she finished the last swallow of beer and wiped her mouth with the back of her hand—"if they ever get this mess straightened out, why don't you come out with us and finish the season? You say Stan is working this new act of his solo."

Molly sat down next to Joe and stretched out her long legs; then she curled them under her and lit a cigarette, the match shaking just a little. She was wearing an old pair of rehearsal rompers; she still looked like a kid in them, Zeena noticed a little sadly.

Molly said, "Stan's awfully busy at the church. The folks are crazy about him. He gives reading services every night. I used to help him with those but he says a straight one-ahead routine is good enough. Then he has development classes every afternoon. I—I just take it easy."

Zeena set down the empty can on the floor and took the full one which Molly had put on the window sill. "Lambie-pie, you need a good time. Why don't you get yourself slicked up and come out with us? We'll get you a date. Say, I know a swell boy with Hobart Shows this season—an inside talker. Let's hire a car and get him and have dinner up the line some-wheres. He's a swell dancer and Joe don't mind sitting out a couple, do you, snooks?"

Joe Plasky's smile, turned on Zeena, deepened; his eyes grew softer. "Swell idea. I'll call him now."

Molly said quickly, "No, please don't bother. I'm really fine. I don't feel like going anywhere in this heat. Really, I'm okay." She looked at the little leather traveling clock on the mantel, which Addie Peabody had given her. Then she switched on the radio. As the tubes warmed, the voice came through clearer. It was a familiar voice but richer and deeper than Zeena had ever heard it before.

". . . therefore, my beloved friends, you can see that our claims for evidence of survival are attested to and are based on proof. Men of the caliber of Sir Oliver Lodge, Sir Arthur Conan Doyle, Camille Flammarion, and Sir William Crookes did not give their lives to a dream, to a chimera, to a delusion. No, my unseen friends of the radio audience, the glorious proofs of survival lie about us on every hand.

"We at the Church of the Heavenly Message rest content and secure in our faith. And it is with the deepest gratitude that I thank them, the splendid men and women of our con-gregation, for their generosity, which has enabled me to bring you this Sunday afternoon message for so many weeks.

"Some persons think of the 'new religion of Spiritualism' as a closed sect. They ask me, 'Can I believe in the power of our dear ones to return and still not be untrue to the faith of my fathers?' My dearly beloved, the doors of Spiritual Truth are open to all—it is something to cherish close to your heart *within* the church of your own faith. Whatever your creed it will serve simply to strengthen it, whether you are accustomed to worship God in meeting house, cathedral, or synagogue. Or whether you are one of the many who say 'I do not know' and then proceed to worship unconsciously under the leafy arches of the Creator's great Church of the Out of Doors, with, for your choir, only the clear, sweet notes of the song sparrow, the whirr of the locust among the boughs.

"No, my dear friends, the truth of survival is open to all. It is cool, pure water which will gush from the forbidding rock of reality at the touch of a staff—your own willingness to believe the evidence of your own eyes, of your own God-given senses. It is we, of the faith of survival, who can say with joy and *certainty* in our heart of hearts, 'O death, where is thy sting? O grave, where is thy victory?' "

Joe Plasky's smile was now a faint, muscular imprint on his face; nothing more. He leaned across Molly and gently switched off the radio. "Got a deck of cards, kid?" he asked her, his face lighting up again. "I mean a deck of your own cards—the kind your dad would have played with. The kind that read from only one side."

The Moon

Beneath her cold light howl the dog and the wolf.
And creeping things crawl out of slime.

IN THE black alley with a light at the end, the footsteps followed, drawing closer; they followed, and then the heart-stopping panic as something gripped his shoulder.

". . . in about another fifteen minutes. You asked me to wake you, sir." It was the porter shaking him.

Stan sat up as though a rope had jerked him, his pulse still hammering. In the early light he sat watching the fields whip by, trying to catch his breath, to shake off the nightmare.

The town looked smaller, the streets narrower and cheaper, the buildings dingier. There were new electric signs, dark now in the growing dawn, but the horse chestnuts in the square looked just the same. The earth doesn't age as fast as the things man makes. The courthouse cupola was greener with time and the walls were darker gray.

Stanton Carlisle walked slowly across the square and into the Mansion House, where Old Man Woods was asleep on

the leather couch behind the key rack. Knocking on the
counter brought him out, blinking. He didn't recognize the
man with the arrogant shoulders, the cold blue eyes; as the
Rev. Carlisle signed the register he wondered if anyone at all
would recognize him. It was nearly seventeen years.

From the best room, looking out on Courthouse Square,
Stan watched the town wake up. He had the bellboy bring
up a tray of bacon and eggs, and he ate slowly, looking out
on the square.

Marston's Drug Store was open; a boy came out and emptied a pail of gray water into the gutter. Stan wondered if it
was the same pail after all these years—his first job, during
high school vacation. This kid hadn't been born then.

He had come back, after all. He could spend the day loafing
around town, looking at the old places, and catch the night
train out and never go near the old man at all.

Pouring himself a second cup of coffee, the Rev. Carlisle
looked at his face in the polished surface of the silver pot.
Hair thinner at the temples, giving him a "widow's peak" that
everyone said made him look distinguished. Face fuller around
the jaw. Broader shoulders, with imported tweed to cover
them. Pink shirt, with cuff links made from old opal earrings.
Black knitted tie. All they could remember would be a kid in
khaki pants and leather jacket who had waited behind the
water tank for an open freight-car door.

Seventeen years. Stan had come a long way without looking
back.

What difference did it make to him whether the old man
lived or died, married or suffered or burst a blood vessel? Why
was he here at all?

"I'll give it the once over and then highball out of here
tonight," he said, drawing on his topcoat. Picking up his hat
and gloves he took the stairs, ancient black woodwork with
hollows worn in the marble steps. On the porch of the Mansion House he paused to take a cigarette from his case, cupping the flame of his lighter against the October wind.

Horse-chestnut leaves were a golden rain in the early sun,
falling on the turf of the park where the fountain had been
turned off for the winter. In its center a stained bronze boy

smiled up under his bronze umbrella at the shower which wasn't falling.

Stan followed the south side of the park and turned up Main Street. Myers' Toy and Novelty Mart had taken in the shop next to it and expanded. In the window were construction kits for airplanes with rubber-band motors. Mechanical tractors. A playsuit of what looked like long red underwear, with a toy rocket-pistol. A new generation of toys.

Leffert's Kandy Kitchen was closed but the taffy still lay golden in metal trays in the window with almonds pressed in it to form flower-petal designs. Christmas was the time for Leffert's taffy, not autumn. Except the autumn when they had beaten Childers Prep; he had taken a bag of it to the game.

The wind whirled down the street, making store signs creak above him. The autumns were colder than they used to be, but the snow of winter wasn't as deep.

On the edge of town Stan looked out across rolling country. A farmhouse had stood on the ridge once. Must have burned down or been pulled down. Dark against the sky Mills' Woods lay over the rise, too far to walk; and what was the use of going through all that again. She was probably dead by now. It didn't matter. And the old man was dying.

Stan wondered if he could get a bus out of town before the night train left. Or he might load up with magazines and go to the hotel and read. It was well past noon but there was a lot of the day left.

Then a side street led him down familiar ways; here and there a lot stood empty, with a gaping cellar where a house had been.

He didn't realize he had walked so far when the sight of the school brought him up short. In a country of square, brick boxes some long-dead genius on a school board had made them build this high school differently: gray stone with casement windows, like a prep school or an English college. The lawn was still green, the ivy over the archway scarlet with the old year.

It was a cool June evening and Stan wore a blue coat with white pants; a white carnation in his lapel. Sitting on the platform he watched the audience while the speaker droned on.

His father was out there, about ten rows back. And alone. Couples everywhere else, only his father, it seemed, was alone.

". . . and to Stanton Carlisle, the Edwin Booth Memorial medal for excellence in dramatic reading."

He was before them now but applause didn't register; he couldn't hear it. The excitement under his ribs was pleasant. The power of the eyes upon him lifted him out of the black emptiness in which he had been sunk all evening. Then, as he turned, he suddenly heard the applause and saw his father, beaming, smashing his palms together, shooting quick looks left and right, enjoying the applause of the others.

"Taxi!" Stan saw the old limousine lumbering toward him and flagged it. The driver was Abe Younghusband, who didn't recognize him until he gave the address.

"Oh, say, you must be Charlie Carlisle's boy, ain't you? Ain't seen you around for some time."

"Sixteen—nearly seventeen years."

"That a fact? Well, guess there's lots of improvements since you left. Say, I heard you're a preacher now. That ain't true, is it?"

"Sort of half and half. More of a lecturer."

They turned off the car tracks, down the familiar street with the maples scarlet in the rays of the afternoon sun.

"I always figured you'd go on the stage. I still remember that show you put on at the Odd Fellows' Hall, time you borrowed Chief Donegan's watch and made believe you was smashing the hell out of it. His face was sure something to see. But I guess you got kind of tired of that stuff after a while. My boy's a great one on tricks. Always sending away for stuff. Well, here we are. I hear Charlie's pretty shaky these days. I hear he's turned worse during the last week."

The house looked tiny and run to seed. A wooden staircase had been built up one side of it, and a door cut into the attic floor. The yard was scuffed, with bare patches; the maples that used to shelter the house had been cut down. Where Gyp's kennel had stood there was still a rectangle in the ground. The earth forgets slowly.

The woman who answered the door was white-haired and stout, the lines about her mouth petulant. It was Clara Carpenter; but what a tub she had turned into!

"How do you do. Mrs. Carpenter?"

"Mrs. *Carlisle*. Oh." Her face lost some of its caution. "You must be Stan Carlisle. Come right in. Your dad's been asking me a dozen times an hour when you were coming." She lowered her voice. "He's not a bit well, and I can't make him stay in bed. Maybe you can persuade him to take it easy, a little. It's his heart, you know." She called upstairs, "Charlie, somebody to see you." To Stan she said, "I guess you know your way upstairs. The big bedroom. I'll be up directly."

The stairs, the newel post, the two ridiculous spouted urns on the mantelpiece, seen through the double doors. The metal fireplace covering. The wallpaper was different, and the upper hall looked different some way, but he didn't stop to find out why.

The old man was seated in a chair by the window, with a knitted afghan over his knees; seamed face, scrawny neck. His eyes looked frightened and sullen.

"Stanton?" Charlie Carlisle moved with difficulty, hands gripping the chair arms. "Stanton, come over here and let me take a good look. Gosh, you—you don't look so very different, son. Only you've filled out a lot. You're—you're looking all right, son."

Stan tried to throw his shoulders back. But a weight was pressing them, a deadly weight that made his knees tremble. The life seemed to be leaking out of him, flowing into the carpet under his feet. He took a chair on the other side of the window and leaned back in it, drawing his breath, trying to fight off the crushing weariness.

"I didn't know you'd married Clara," Stan said at last, getting a cigarette out and lighting it. He offered one to his father, who shook his head.

"Doctor's got me cut down to one cigar a day. Yes, I kept bachelor's hall for quite a spell after you left. I—I always figured I'd hear from you, boy, and then I'd tell you. Clara's a fine girl. Ever hear from your mother?"

The words had a hard time coming out, his lips were so tired. "No. Never did."

"I'm not surprised. Guess she didn't find us exciting enough. What do they call it now—glamour? That's what Cynthia wanted. Glamour. Well, if she found it I don't reckon

she's got much of it now." The mouth came down in creases
of bitterness. "But tell me what you been doing, Stan. I said
to Clara, sure he'll come. I said, we had our differences, and
I guess he's been busy, making his own way. I said, I know
he'll come if I tell him I'm in bad shape. Feel a lot better
today, though. I told the doctor I'd be back at the office in
a month. Feel a lot better. What's this I hear you're a minister
of the gospel, Stan? Clara heard you on the radio one day, she
said. That's how we knew where to send that telegram."

The Rev. Carlisle uncrossed his legs and knocked the ashes
from his cigarette into a jardiniere holding a fern. "I'm more
of a lecturer. But I do have a Minister's certificate."

The elder Carlisle's face brightened. "Son, I'm gladder to
hear that from you, and believe it, than any other news I've
heard in a month of Sundays. You work your way through
seminary? Why, son, I wanted you to go. I was willing to lay
out cold cash to pay your way. You know that. Only you
couldn't see it at the time. Always fooling with that magic
nonsense. I'm glad you finally got that out of your system. It
was your mother put those ideas in your head, Stan, buying
you that box of tricks. I haven't forgotten it. But I don't even
know your denomination."

The Rev. Carlisle closed his eyes. His voice sounded flat and
toneless in his own ears. "It's not a big or a rich church, Dad.
The United Spiritual League. It's devoted to preaching the
gospel that the soul survives earthly death, and that those of
us who still are earth-bound can receive intelligence—from
those who have passed over to the higher spheres."

"You mean you're a spiritualist? You believe the dead come
back?"

Stan forced a smile, his eyes wandering up to the ceiling
where cracks made the outline of an old man's face. The sun
was slanting through the window now and night was coming
but not fast enough. He came back with a start.

"I'm not going to try converting you, Dad. I am secure in
my faith. Many others share my views, but I am no prose-
lytizer."

His father was silent for a time, swallowing uneasily. His
head seemed to nod back and forth a fraction of an inch as
he sat, a quick, rhythmic, involuntary nod of weakness. "Well,

everybody to his own faith. I don't hold with spiritualism much. But if you're convinced, that's all that matters. Real estate is all shot, here in this town, son. If I was younger I'd pull out. Town's dying. I been trying to get the Civic Betterment Committee to put on a little campaign—make it a good, open-shop town and no nonsense. Attract industry. But they don't listen. Property values way down— Oh, here's Clara. Reckon it's most suppertime. We been talking so much."

"I'll wash up and be right down," Stan said. The load of weariness— There was a place where he might leave it, where it might slip from him like a weight cut from his neck.

In the hall he turned left and his hand was reaching for the knob when, with a cold flash, he realized that he was facing a smooth, papered wall. The attic door was not there! Looking down, he saw a single step at the bottom of the wall. So that was it—the stairs outside. It was an apartment now, cut off from the rest of the house. Strangers living in it, under the slope of the roof, around the brick chimney. The iron bed, the silk patchwork, smell of camphor and silk and lumber and the tight mesh of maple leaves below, seen through the narrow windows where you could make out the signboard on the lawn of the church. The house was dying, too.

Stan closed the bathroom door and locked it. The same taps on the washbowl anyhow, even though the walls were painted a different color. And the odd mix-up of tiles in the floor, where he used to find half-tiles and try to count them. The old-fashioned tub on its high legs; marble-topped commode with its old-fashioned mahogany drawers; shaving stand with its circular cabinet and a mirror on a swivel, where Dad kept his shaving brush, his mug and his soap, his hones.

Stan wondered if the water still made the sharp sucking gurgle in the tub when the stopper was pulled out—as it did when his mother had finished splashing and singing to herself. He recalled the day when he had fallen out of the tree, and Mother had picked him up in her arms and carried him upstairs, bleeding all down the front of her dress. She hadn't minded the dress getting messed up. He had made leggings of corrugated cardboard, like explorers wear in the jungle. One of them had been bloody; after the doctor had sewed up the cut in his forehead Mother undressed him, taking the cardboard leggings off carefully. She had put them on the marble top of the commode. They stayed there for a long time, until the blood stains became black. Jennie finally threw them out—said they gave her the jimjams.

If only they could all have stayed together a few more years. If Mother had not minded the town. If Dad had always been as weak and as friendly as he was now that he was dying. If only he could have been dying for twenty years, Stan might have loved him. Now there was nothing but the old things, and they were going past him and would soon be gone.

He drew his breath and tried again to strain his shoulders back. *I mustn't forget to ask the old man about the church and how to go about selling it when it's time to pull out.* But the Church of the Heavenly Message seemed too far away to matter, now. The old man was slipping into that dark hole where you fall and fall forever because there's no bottom to it. *We are all creeping to its edge, some slowly, some, like the old man, balanced on the brink. And then what? Like the rush of wind past a bullet, probably, forever and ever.* Gyp was dead all these years. Even the memories of him were dead and forgotten except in one mind. And when that was gone Gyp would be forgotten entirely. *When the old man was dead and under ground Stan could forgive it.*

Gyp never knew what hit him. They said the vet just put chloroform on a rag and dropped it in the box.

But that end of rope, tied to the leg of the workbench in the garage—it had been cut when Stan came home from school. *Why did they tie Gyp up in there if they wanted to get rid of him? There was no they. Only he.* Gyp had a chain on his kennel. *Why the rope?*

Oh, Christ, let me get to hell out of here. But the voice that had said "son" held him. The house was swallowing him. And they had sealed up the attic door; there was no way. All the years had dropped off, tearing with them his poise, so carefully built up tone by tone. They had taken his cleverness, his smile, his hypnotic glance, leaving him powerless and trapped inside the walls of old familiarity.

He had come back because Dad was dying and Mother was gone and the maples were cut down, the square still visible where Gyp's kennel had stood, and the shaving stand on its smooth pillar of wood, still in the same place and still smooth under his hand, smelling sweetly of shaving soap.

The strop.

It hung from the brass hook where it had always hung. It was smooth, black with handling and with oil, shining.

The garage at night with the moonlight making bars of silver across the floor, silvering the workbench, sparkling on the bar of the vise and on the lidless coffee cans of nails and bolts. Shining blue and cold on the concrete floor. And the shadows hiding dread and shame.

"Take down your pants."

That was to add to the shame: nakedness.

Stan fumbled with the belt of his knickers, stalling for split seconds.

"Hurry up. I said drop 'em."

His knickers bound his feet about the ankles. He couldn't run. He had to take it. "Now bend over." A hand on his shoulder pushed him into the patch of moonlight, where his nakedness could show. Stan saw the shadow of the strop rise and braced himself. The pain split its way up to his brain in waves and he bit his lip, his breath catching at the bottom of his lungs. He pushed his knuckles in his mouth so they wouldn't hear him next door. The moonlight was a fuzzy blur of tears; and the strop, when it struck the roundness of his bare flesh, made a sound that got to his brain before the stab of pain—and the rope's end, tied to the leg of the workbench there in the smell of oil and gasoline on the day when the sun went out.

Downstairs Charlie Carlisle fidgeted with his napkin, pushing himself back in the chair by bracing his hands against its polished arms. "Confound it, Clara, what d'you s'pose the boy's doing up there? Oh, there you are, son. Sit right down."

When Charlie raised his glance to the man who entered the dining room he caught his old, quick breath at something he saw. It was Stan, much as he had appeared a few minutes before. Maybe with his face fresh-washed and his hair damped down a little. But in the set of the shoulders was something strange. And when old Charlie met his son's eyes they were a sharper blue than any he had ever seen before; as hard as a frozen pond.

The Great Stanton pulled back a chair and sat down swiftly and gracefully, opening his napkin with a single snap. Mrs. Carlisle brought in a platter of chicken. When rice and gravy arrived Charlie said, "Sit down, Clara. Quit running in and out. Stan'll pronounce the blessing."

The Rev. Carlisle ran his hands once over his hair and took a deep breath. His voice came resonantly:

"Almighty God, our heavenly father, we thank Thee from the bottom of our hearts for what we are about to receive. We come to Thee steeped in sin and corruption, our hearts black with guilt, knowing that in the river of Thy forgiveness they will be washed as white as snow."

His father had slid one heavily veined hand over his eyes.

"He who watches the sparrow's fall will hold us in the hollow of his hand to the end of our days, on earth and beyond."

Clara was frowning in bewilderment or worrying about the chicken getting cold.

". . . in the name of thy son, our Lord and Savior, Jesus Christ, we ask it. Amen."

The old man said "Amen" and then grinned weakly at his wife. "No matter what denomination, Clara, it's a proud day when we can have a son saying grace and him a preacher. Pass Stan the rice."

Clara was not one to eat in silence. She began a brief history of the community during the past sixteen years, full of hot summers, hard winters, deaths, births, weddings, and disasters.

Stan ate quickly and took a second helping of everything. At last he slid his plate away from him and lit a cigarette. He looked at Clara Carpenter Carlisle for a long minute; the penetrating blue glance made her conscious of the old apron over her good dress.

"My dear friend, have you ever thought that these persons whom you have mourned as dead will never die?"

Under that brilliant stare she began to simper and found it difficult to control her hands. "Why, Stan, I—I've always *believed*. But I think it's one of those things you just have to feel. I never paid much attention. I took it for granted, about heaven."

The Rev. Carlisle wiped his lips with his napkin and took a swallow of water. "I have seen magnificent proofs that the spirit does not lie fallow until the Day of Judgment. The spirits of the liberated are around us every moment. How often have we said, in anguish, 'If only I could speak to him again. And feel the touch of his hand.' "

Both the older Carlisles looked embarrassed, eyed one another and then each took a sip of coffee.

Stan's mellow voice rolled on. "Yes. And the glorious truth is that it can be done. The spirits of the liberated are around us even now, as we speak." His eyes were still on Clara; he dropped his voice. "I feel one presence beside me now, distinctly. Insistently. Trying to get through."

On his father's face was the suggestion of a sly grin.

"It is one who loved me in its earth existence. But it is not human."

They stared at him.

"A small spirit, a humble presence. But brimming with devotion and loyalty. I believe it is the spirit of my old dog, Gyp." Charles Carlisle had slumped forward, his arms before him on the tablecloth, but now he sat up straighter, the bitter lines around his mouth deeper and more biting.

"Son, you don't believe that! That's blasphemous! You can't mean it—about a dog having a soul same as a man."

Stan smiled. "As I said before, I shall not try to convert you, Dad. Only the ones who have passed over into spirit life can do that. But I have communicated with Gyp—not in words, naturally, since Gyp did not speak in words. Yet this house is full of his presence. He has spoken to me, trying to tell me something." Watching his father keenly, Stan noticed a little flash of alarm on the wrecked face. He covered his eyes with his hand, watching his father's hands on the cloth before him, and bore in:

"Something about his last day on earth. I remember you told me, when I came home from school, that you had had a veterinary chloroform Gyp. But there's some contradiction, here. I get another impression . . ."

A pulse was beginning to pound in the shrunken wrist.

"Gyp has been trying to tell me something . . . wait a minute . . . the garage!"

His father's hands clenched into fists and then released the tablecloth, which they had seized.

"That's it . . . I see it clearly before me. Gyp is tied to the leg of the workbench in the garage. I see something rising and falling . . . in anger . . . faster and faster."

The clatter of a fork on the floor made Stan look up. The old man's face was ashy; he kept shaking his head, trying to speak. "No. No, son. Don't."

"That was the day—the day Mother left. With Mark Humphries. You came home and found her note. Gyp got in your way—you had to vent your temper on something. If I'd been home you'd have licked me. But Gyp got it. He died."

Old Carlisle had heaved to his feet, one hand clawing at his shirt collar. Stan turned, swaying a little, and walked stiffly through the doors into the living room, across it to the hall. When he took down his hat and coat his arms felt numb and heavy. One last glimpse of Clara shaking capsules from a bottle and holding a glass of water; the old man swallowing painfully.

The moon brightened concrete steps leading down the terrace where the grass was ragged. Stan's legs felt stiff as he descended to the street where the arching maples closed over him, moonlight showering through their leaves now black with night. A sound came from the house he had left, an old man weakly crying.

In a patch of silver the Rev. Carlisle stopped and raised his face to the full moon, where it hung desolately, agonizingly bright—a dead thing, watching the dying earth.

The Lovers

They stand between the Eden trees; winged Love hovers over-
head while Knowledge lies in serpent coils upon the ground.

WHEN Molly woke up the third time, Stan was dressing. She looked at the clock: four thirty. "Where you
going?"

"Out."

She didn't question him, but lay awake watching. His
movements were so jumpy lately you didn't dare speak to him
for fear he would bite your head off. Lately he had been sleeping worse and worse, and Molly worried about him taking so
many sleeping pills all the time. They didn't have any more
effect on him, it seemed, and his temper got worse and he
looked like hell. She began to cry softly and Stan stopped in
the middle of buttoning his shirt and came over.

"Now what?"

"Nothing. Nothing. I'm all right."

"What's eating you, kid?"

"Stan—" Molly sat up, holding the covers in front of her
for warmth. "Stan, let's quit and go back to the old act."

He went on buttoning. "Where we going to book it? On street corners? Vaudeville's a dead pigeon. I know what I'm doing. One live John and we're set."

She drew the covers up tighter. "Honey, you look like hell. Why don't you go see a doctor? I—I mean give you something for your nerves or something. Honest, I'm worried sick you're going to have a nervous breakdown or something."

He rubbed his eyes. "I'm going out for a walk."

"It's snowing."

"I've got to get out, do you hear? I'm going down to the church and look over the props. I've got an idea I want to try out. Go back to sleep."

It was no use. He would just keep going until he dropped and Molly prayed it wouldn't happen some time in the middle of a reading—or of a séance, where it would blow up the whole works. If anybody made trouble the cops would nail her along with Stan and in the shape Stan was in he couldn't talk his way out of a jam no matter how bad it was. Molly was worried sick and took half a sleeping pill herself when he had gone.

It was too early to go out and get a racing form, and all the magazines were old, and nothing was on the radio except platter programs, and they made her feel so lonesome—records being dedicated to the boys in Ed's Diner out on the turnpike. She wished she was in the diner with the truck drivers having a few laughs.

Stan let himself into the old Peabody house. He was glad he had banked the furnace the night before; down in the cellar he threw in more coal. Soon the fire was roaring and he stood with the heat on his face, watching blue flames feel their way up through the black coal.

After a moment he sighed, shook himself, and unlocked an old metal cabinet which had once held paint and varnish. Inside was a phonograph turntable which he switched on, placing a pickup arm into position above the aluminum record. Then he went upstairs.

The vast room which had been a parlor and a dining room before he knocked the partition out, was still chilly. Stan turned on the lamps. The bridge chairs sat in empty rows, waiting for something to happen to him—something to go wrong. Walking over to a lamp with a dead bulb, he snapped the switch, gave the amplifying tubes a minute to warm up, then crossed to the desk, where the trumpet usually lay at the developmental classes and trumpet séances.

Near the organ his foot, from long habit, found the loosened board beneath the carpet, and he put his weight on it. Ghostly, with the sound of a voice through a metal tube, came the deep tones of Ramakrishna, his spirit guide. "*Hari Aum.* Greetings, my beloved *chelas*, my disciples of earth life. You who have gathered here tonight." The voice stopped; Stan felt a crawling fear flowing over his scalp. The wiring must have broken again. And there was no time to rip it out. Or was it the loudspeaker? Or the motor? He ran down to the cellar; but the disc was still revolving. It must be in the amplifying unit. There was no time to fix it. The séance was scheduled for that evening. He could always blame it on conditions; a séance without phenomena was common enough for all mediums. But Mrs. Prescott was bringing two trusted friends, both social register. He had looked up all the dope on them and the recording was ready. They might not come back. They might be the ones who would bring in the live John he was waiting for.

Stan took off his coat and put on an old smock; he checked the tubes, the wiring. Then he went back upstairs and began to pry the panel loose. The loudspeaker connections were tight enough. Where was the break? And there was no time, no time, no time. He thought of a dozen stalls to tell a radio repairman, and threw them all out. Once he let anyone know the house was wired he was sunk. He thought of getting a repairman from Newark or somewhere. But there was no one he could trust.

Loneliness came over him, like an avalanche of snow. He was alone. Where he had always wanted to be. You can only trust yourself. There's a rat buried deep in everybody and they'll rat on you if they get pushed far enough. Every new face that showed up at the séances now seemed charged with suspicion and malice and sly knowledge. Could there be a cabal forming against him in the church?

Frantically he switched on the phonograph again and

stepped on the board. *"Hari Aum.* Greetings, my beloved *chelas*, my disciples of earth life . . ." It wasn't broken! The last time he must have shifted his weight unconsciously off the loose board that closed the circuit. He stopped it now with a chilling fear that the next words the voice, his own voice, would say would not be words he had recorded on aluminum—the record would turn on him with a malevolent life of its own.

In the silence the house was closing in. The walls had not moved, nor the ceiling; not when he looked straight at them. He ran his hands over his hair once and took a deep breath. Hum the first eight bars of our opener. But it was no use.

Outside, across backyards, a dog barked.

"Gyp!"

His own voice startled him. Then he began to laugh.

He laughed as he walked into the hall, laughing up the stairs and in and out of bedrooms, now chastely bare. In the dark-séance room he snapped on the light. Blank white walls. Still laughing and chuckling he snapped the light off and felt for the panel in the baseboard where he kept the projector.

He aimed it at the wall; and there it was, jumping up and down crazily as his hand shook with laughing—the hazy image of an old woman. He twisted a knob and she vanished. Another twist and a baby appeared in a halo of golden mist, jumping crazily as his hand shook with laughing. "Dance, you little bastard," his voice thundered against the close walls.

He twisted the hand projector until the baby floated upside down, and he roared with laughter. He fell to the floor, laughing, and aimed the beam at the ceiling, watching the baby fly up the angle of the wall and come to rest overhead, still smiling mistily. Laughing and strangling, Stan began to beat the projector against the floor; something snapped, and the light went out.

He crawled to his feet and couldn't find the door and stopped laughing then, feeling his way around and around. He counted nine corners. He began to shout and then he found it and let himself out, dripping with sweat.

In his office the day was breaking gray through the Venetian blinds. The desk light wouldn't come on and he seized it and jerked it out of the wall plug and tossed it into a corner. The blinds got tangled with the cord; he gathered them in his arms and wrenched; the whole business came down on top of him and he fought his way free of them. At last the card index.

R. R. R. God damn it. Who had stolen the R's? Raphaelson, Randolph, Regan—here it was. *Woman psychologist, mentioned by Mrs. Tallentyre. Said to be interested in the occult. Has recommended that her patients take yoga exercises.* But the phone number, Jesus God, it wasn't there. Only her name—Dr. Lilith Ritter. Try the phone book. R. R. R.

The voice that answered the telephone was cool, low-pitched, and competent. "Yes?"

"My name is Carlisle. I've been having trouble sleeping—"

The voice interrupted. "Why not consult your physician? I am not a doctor of medicine, Mr. Carlisle."

"I've been taking pills, but they don't seem to help. I've been working too hard, they tell me. I want to see you."

There was silence for a long moment; then the cool voice said, "I can see you the day after tomorrow at eleven in the morning."

"Not before then?"

"Not before then."

Stan beat his fist once against the desk top, squeezing his eyes shut. Then he said, "Very well, Dr. Ritter. At eleven o'clock—Tuesday."

Whatever she might look like, the dame had a wonderful voice. And he must have pulled her out of a sound sleep. But Tuesday— What was he supposed to do until then, chew the rug?

The house grew warmer. Stan went over and pressed his forehead against the chill of the windowpane. Down in the street a girl in a fur coat and no stockings was walking an Irish setter. Stan's eyes followed the curve of the bare legs, wondering if she had on anything under the fur coat. Some of them run out that way—naked under their furs—to buy cigarettes or club soda or a douche bag.

Back in the flat Molly would be lying sprawled across the bed with her hair caught up on top of her head with a single pin. She would be wearing the black chiffon negligee but she might as well have on a calico wrapper. There was no one to look at her.

The Irish-setter girl turned, tugging at the leash, and the fur coat swung open, showing a pink slip. With a growl of frustration Stan twisted away from the window. He sat down at the desk and pulled out his appointment book. Message service that evening at eight-thirty. Monday morning, developmental class in trance mediumship and the Science of Cosmic Breath. God, what a herd of hippos. The Science of Cosmic Breath: in through the left nostril, on a count of four. Retain breath for count of sixteen. Exhale through the right nostril to count of eight. Measure the counts by repeating *Hari Aum, Hari Aum.*

Monday afternoon, lecture on the Esoteric Significance of the Tarot Symbols.

Stan took the Tarot deck from the side drawer and slowly his fingers began remembering; the front-and-back-hand palm, making the cards vanish in the air and drawing them out from under his knee. He paused at one card and laid it before him, holding his head in his hands, studying it. The Lovers. They were naked, standing in Eden with the snake down on the ground all ready to wise them up. Over their heads was the angel-form, its wings extended above the trees of Life and Knowledge. *Where the Tree of Life is blooming, there is rest for me.*

The lovers were naked. A wave of prickling crawled up over his scalp out of nowhere and, as he watched, the rounded hips and belly of the woman seemed to rotate. Jesus, if this is what I wanted I could have stayed with the Ten-in-One and been talker for the kooch show! There's a guy that always gets plenty.

He swept the cards to the floor and drew the telephone toward him, dialing. This time the voice said, "Yes, sir. I'll see if Mrs. Tallentyre's in."

She was in to the Rev. Carlisle.

"Mrs. Tallentyre, I spent most of last night in meditation. And from my meditation I drew a thought. I shall have to seek three days of silence. Unfortunately I cannot go to the Himalayas, but I think the Catskills will serve. You understand, I'm sure. I would appreciate it if you will take charge of the service tonight and notify class members that I have been called away. Just say that I have gone in search of the Silence. I shall return, without fail, on the third day."

That was that. Now lock up. Lock the office door—time to clean up all the havoc later. Leave the appointment book downstairs on the hall table. Mrs. Tallentyre had a key to the outside door. Leave the inner door unlocked.

He put on his coat and a few minutes later was hurrying through the soft snow.

"Gee, honey, I'm glad you come back! Are you okay?"

"Yeah. Sure. How many times do I have to tell you I can take care of myself?"

"Want a couple of eggs? I'm starved. Let me fix you a couple. The coffee's all ready."

Stan stood in the kitchen door watching her. She was wearing the black chiffon negligee; against the early winter light from the window she might as well not have had on a stitch. Whoever figured out dames' clothes knew his onions. What made her seem so far away and long ago? The one dame who wouldn't cross him up. And the shape was still something you usually see behind footlights or in magazines.

Stan ran his hands once over his hair and said, "Come here." They stood watching each other for a moment, and he saw her take a deep breath. Then she turned off the gas under the skillet and ran over and threw her arms around his neck.

It was like kissing the back of your own hand but he picked her up in his arms and carried her into the bedroom. She clung to him and slid her hand under his shirt and he drew the chiffon open and started to kiss her shoulder but it was no use.

And now she was crying, looking up at him reproachfully as he threw on his jacket.

"Sorry, kid. I've got to get away. I'll be back Tuesday. I've—I've got to breathe."

When he had thrown some stuff in a keyster and locked it and hurried out Molly pulled the covers over her, still crying, and drew up her knees. After a while she got up and put on a robe and fried herself an egg. She didn't seem to be able to

get enough salt on it, and in the middle of breakfast she suddenly took the plate and slammed it on the floor of the
kitchen.

"Oh, God damn it, what's eating him? How can I know
how to give him a party if I don't know what's the matter?"

After a while she got dressed and went out to have her hair
washed and set. First she went around to the barber shop and
saw Mickey, and he handed her sixteen dollars. The horse had
paid off at seven to one.

With the wheels clicking past under him, Stan felt a little
better. The Palisades had fingers of snow pointing up their
slopes, and the river was rough with broken ice, where gulls
sailed and settled. He read, sketchily, in Ouspensky's *A New
Model of the Universe*, looking for tag lines he could pull out
and use, jotting notes in the margin for a possible class in
fourth dimensional immortality. Immortality was what they
wanted. If they thought they could find it in the fourth dimension he would show them how. Who the hell knew what
the fourth dimension was, anyway? Chumps. Johns.

A girl was having trouble getting her valise down from the
rack and Stan leaped up to help her. Getting off at Pough-
keepsie. His hand touched hers on the valise handle and he
felt blood rising over his face. The kid was luscious; his eyes
followed her as she walked primly down the car, carrying the
bag before her. He crossed the train and watched her, out on
the platform.

When he got to Albany he took a cab to the hotel, stopping
off to buy a fifth of Scotch undercover from a saloon.

The room was good-sized and cleaner than most.

"You ain't been through lately, Mr. Charles. Territory been
changed?"

Stan nodded, throwing his hat on the bed and getting out
of his overcoat. "Bring some club soda. And plenty of ice."

The boy took a five and winked. "Like some company? We
got swell gals in town—new since you was here last. I know
a little blonde that's got everything. And I mean everything."

Stan lay down on the other bed and lit a cigarette, folding
his hands behind his head. "Brunette."

"You're the boss."

He smoked when the boy had gone. In the ceiling cracks he could make out the profile of an old man. Then there was a tap on the door—the soda and ice. The boy scraped the collodion seal from the Scotch bottle.

Quiet again. In the empty, impersonal wilderness of the hotel Stan listened to noises coming up from the street. The whir of the elevator, stopping at his floor; footsteps soft in the corridor. He swung off the bed.

The girl was short and dark. She had on a tan polo coat and no hat, but there was an artificial gardenia pinned in her hair over one ear.

She came in, her nose and cheeks rosy from the cold, and said, "Howdy, sport! Annie sent me. Say—how'd ya know I drink Scotch?"

"I read minds."

"Gee, you musta." She poured two fingers' into a glass and offered it to Stan, who shook his head.

"On the wagon. But don't let that stop you."

"Okay, sport. Here's lead in your pencil." When she finished it she poured herself another and then said, "You better give me the fin now before I forget it."

Stan handed her a ten-dollar bill and she said, "Gee, thanks. Say, would you happen to have two fives?"

Silence. She broke it. "Lookit—radio in every room! That's something new for this dump. Say, let's listen to Charlie McCarthy. D'you mind?"

Stan was looking at her spindly legs. As she hung the polo coat carefully in the closet he saw that her breasts were tiny. She was wearing a Sloppy Joe sweater and a skirt. They used to look like whores. Now they look like college girls. They all want to look like college girls. Why don't they go to college, then? They wouldn't be any different from the others. You'd never notice them. Christ, what a crazy way to run a world.

She was having a good time listening to the radio gags, and the whisky had warmed her. Taking off her shoes, she curled her feet under her. Then motioning Stan to throw her a cigarette, she stripped off her stockings and warmed her feet with her hands, giving him a flash at the same time.

When the program was over she turned the radio down a little and stood up, stretching. She drew off her sweater carefully, so as not to disturb the gardenia, and spread it over the chair back. She was thin, with sharp shoulder blades; her collar bones stood out starkly. When she dropped her skirt it was a little better but not too good. On one thigh, evenly spaced, were four bruises, the size of a big man's fingers.

She stood smoking, wearing nothing but the imitation gardenia and Stan let his eyes go back to the old man's face in the ceiling.

Tear-ass out of town, ride for hours, hotel, buy liquor, and for this. He sighed, stood up and slipped off his jacket and vest.

The girl was humming a tune to herself and now she did a soft-shoe dance step, her hands held up by her face, and spun around, then sang the chorus of the song that was coming over the loudspeaker. Her voice was husky and pleasant with power under control.

"You sing, too?" Stan asked dryly.

"Oh, sure. I only party to fill in. I sing with a band sometimes. I'm studying the voice." She threw back her head and vocalized five notes. "Ah . . . ah . . . AH . . . ah . . . ah."

The Great Stanton stopped with his shirt half off, staring. Then he seized the girl and threw her on the bed.

"Hey, look out, honey, not so fast! Hey, for Christ's sake, be careful!"

He twisted his hand in her hair. The girl's white, waxy face stared up at him, fearful and stretched tight. "Take it easy, honey. Don't. Listen, Ed McLaren, the house dick, is a pal of mine. Now go easy—Ed'll beat the hell out of any guy that did that."

The radio kept on. ". . . bringing you the music of Phil Requete and his Swingstars direct from the Zodiac Room of the Hotel Teneriffe. And now our charming vocalist, Jessyca Fortune, steps up to the mike with an old-fashioned look in her eye, as she sings—and swings—that lovely old number of the ever popular Bobbie Burns, 'Oh, Whistle and I'll Come to You, My Lad.'"

Ice in the river, piled against the piers of boat clubs, a dark channel in the middle. And always the click of the rail joints underneath. North south east west—cold spring heat fall—

love lust tire leave—wed fight leave hate—sleep wake eat sleep —child boy man corpse—touch kiss tongue breast—strip grip press jet—wash dress pay leave—north south east west . . .

Stan felt the prickle crawl up over his scalp again. The old house was waiting for him and the fat ones with pince-nez and false teeth; this woman doc probably was one of them, for all the music of voice and cool, slow speech. What could she do for him? What could anybody do for him? For anybody? They were all trapped, all running down the alley toward the light.

The nameplate said, "Dr. Lilith Ritter, Consulting Psychologist. Walk In."

The waiting room was small, decorated in pale gray and rose. Beyond the casement window snow was falling softly in huge flakes. On the window sill was a cactus in a rose-colored dish, a cactus with long white hair like an old man. The sight of it ran along Stan's nerves like a thousand ants. He put down his coat and hat and then quickly looked behind a picture of sea shells drawn in pastel. No dictaphone. What was he afraid of? But that would have been a beautiful place to plant a bug if you wanted to work the waiting room gab angle when the doc's secretary came in.

Did she have a secretary? If he could make the dame he might get a line on this woman doc or whatever she was, find out how much overboard she was on occult stuff. He might swap developmental lessons for whatever she gave her patients—some kind of advice. Or did she interpret dreams or something? He lit a cigarette and it burned his finger as he knocked the ashes off. In reaching down to pick it up he knocked down an ashtray. He got on his hands and knees to pick up the butts and that was where he was when the cool voice said, "Come in."

Stan looked up. This dame wasn't fat, she wasn't tall, she wasn't old. Her pale hair was straight and she wore it drawn into a smooth roll on the nape of her neck. It glinted like green gold. A slight woman, no age except young, with enormous gray eyes that slanted a little.

Stan picked up the ashtray and put it on the edge of a table.

It fell off again but he didn't notice. He was staring at the woman who stood holding the door open into another room. He weaved to his feet, lurching as he came near her. Then he caught a whiff of perfume. The gray eyes seemed as big as saucers, like the eyes of a kitten when you hold its nose touching yours. He looked at the small mouth, the full lower lip, carefully tinted but not painted. She said nothing. As he started to push past her he seemed to fall; he found his arm around her and held on knowing that he was a fool, knowing something terrible would strike him dead, knowing he wanted to cry, to empty his bladder, to scream, to go to sleep, wondering as he tightened his arms around her. . . .

Stan lay sprawling on the floor. She had twisted his shoulders, turning him until his back was toward her, and then planted one neat foot at the back of his knee. Now she knelt beside him on the carpet, gripping his right hand in both of hers, forcing it in toward the wrist and keeping him flat by the threatened pain of the taut tendons. Her expression had not changed.

She said, "The Rev. Stanton Carlisle, I believe. Pastor of the Church of the Heavenly Message, lecturer on Tarot symbolism and yogic breathing, a producer of ghosts with cheesecloth—or maybe you use a little magic lantern. Now if I let you up will you promise to be co-operative?"

Stan had thrown one arm over his eyes and he felt the tears slipping down his face into his ears. He managed to say, "Promise."

The deft hands released his and he sat up, hiding his face with his palms, thinking of a pillow that had been slept on and perfumed, with shame washing back and forth over him, the light too strong for his eyes, and the tears that wouldn't stop running. Something in his throat seemed to be strangling him from inside.

"Here—drink this."

"What—what is it?"

"Just a little brandy."

"Never drink it."

"I'm telling you to drink it. Quickly."

He felt blindly for the glass, held his breath and drank, coughing as it burned his throat.

"Now get up and sit over here in this chair. Open your eyes and look at me."

Dr. Lilith Ritter was regarding him from across a wide mahogany desk. She went on, "I thought I'd be hearing from you, Carlisle. You were never cut out to run a spook racket solo."

The Star

*shines down upon a naked girl who, between land
and sea, pours mysterious waters from her urns.*

LIE BACK on the couch."
   "I don't know what to talk about."
   "You say that every time. What are you thinking about?"
   "You."
   "What about me?"
   "Wishing you sat where I could see you. I want to look at you."
   "When you lie down on the couch, just before you lean back, you run your hands over your hair. Why do you do that?"
   "That's my get-set."
   "Explain."
   "Every vaudeville actor has some business: something he does in the wings just before he goes on."
   "Why do you do that?"
   "I've always done it. I used to have a cowlick when I was

a kid and my mother would always be telling me to slick it down."

"Is that the only reason?"

"What difference does it make?"

"Think about it. Did you ever know anybody who did that—anybody else in vaudeville?"

"No. Let's talk about something else."

"What are you thinking about now?"

"Pianos."

"Go on."

"Pianos. People playing pianos. For other people to sing. My mother singing. When she sang my old man would go in the dining room and whisper all the time to one of his pals. The rest would be in the living room listening to my mother."

"She played the piano herself?"

"No. Mark played. Mark Humphries. He'd sit down and look up at her as if he was seeing right through her clothes. He'd run his hands once over his hair—"

"Yes?"

"But it's crazy! Why would I want to swipe a piece of business from that guy? After she'd run off with him I used to lie awake nights thinking up ways to kill him."

"I think you admired him."

"It was the dames that admired him. He was a great big guy with a rumbling voice. The dames were crazy over him."

"Did this Humphries drink?"

"Sure. Now and then."

"Did your father drink?"

"Hell, no. He was White Ribbon."

"The first day you were here I offered you a glass of brandy to help you get hold of yourself. You said you never drank it."

"God damn it, don't twist everything around to making it look as if I wanted to be like my old man. Or Humphries either. I hated them—both of 'em."

"But you wouldn't take a drink."

"That was something else."

"What?"

"None of your—I—it's something I can't tell you."

"I'm being paid to listen. Take your time. You'll tell me."

"The stuff smelled like wood alcohol to me. Not any more but the first time."

"Did you ever drink wood alcohol?"

"Christ, no, it was Pete."

"Pete who?"

"I never knew his last name. It was in Burleigh, Mississippi. We had a guy in the carny named Pete. A lush. One night he tanked up on wood alky and kicked off."

"Did he have a deep voice?"

"Yes. How did you know?"

"Never mind. What was he to you?"

"Nothing. That is—"

"What are you thinking about?"

"Damn it, quit deviling me."

"Take your time."

"He—he was married to Zeena, who ran the horoscope pitch. I was—I was—I was screwing her on the side I wanted to find out how she and Pete had done their vaude mental act and I wanted a woman and I made up to her and Pete was always hanging around I gave him the alky to pass him out I didn't know it was wood or I'd forgotten it he died I was afraid they'd pin it on me but it blew over. That's all. Are you satisfied?"

"Go on."

"That's all. I was scared of that murder rap for a long time but then it blew over. Zeena never suspected anything. And then Molly and I teamed up and quit the carny and it all seemed like a bad dream. Only I never forgot it."

"But you felt so guilty that you would never drink."

"For God's sake—you can't do mentalism and drink! You've got to be on your toes every minute."

"Let's get back to Humphries. Before he ran away with your mother you preferred him to your father?"

"Do we have to go over that again? Sure. Who wouldn't? But not after—"

"Go on."

"I caught him—"

"You caught him making love to your mother? Is that it?"

"In the Glade. We'd found it, together. Then I went there.

And I saw it. I tell you, I saw it. All of it. Everything they did. I wanted to kill my old man. He drove her to Humphries, I thought. I wanted—I wanted—"

"Yes."

"I wanted them to take me with them! But she didn't, God damn her, she left me with the old son-of-a-bitch to rot in his goddamned hick town. I wanted to go away with her and see something and maybe get into show business. Humphries had been in show business. But I was left there to rot with that Bible-spouting old bastard."

"So you became a Spiritualist minister."

"I'm a hustler, God damn it. Do you understand that, you frozen-faced bitch? I'm on the make. Nothing matters in this goddamned lunatic asylum of a world but dough. When you get that you're the boss. If you don't have it you're the end man on the daisy chain. I'm going to get it if I have to bust every bone in my head doing it. I'm going to milk it out of those chumps and take them for the gold in their teeth before I'm through. You don't dare yell copper on me because if you spilled anything about me all your other Johns would get the wind up their necks and you wouldn't have any more at twenty-five bucks a crack. You've got enough stuff in that bastard tin file cabinet to blow 'em all up. I know what you've got in there—society dames with the clap, bankers that take it up the ass, actresses that live on hop, people with idiot kids. You've got it all down. If I had that stuff I'd give 'em cold readings that would have 'em crawling on their knees to me. And you sit there out of this world with that dead-pan face and listen to the chumps puking their guts out day after day for peanuts. If I knew that much I'd stop when I'd made a million bucks and not a minute sooner. You're a chump too, blondie. They're all Johns. They're asking for it. Well, I'm here to give it out. And if anybody was to get the big mouth and sing to the cops about me I'd tell a couple of guys I know. They wouldn't fall for your jujit stuff."

"I've been shouted at before, Mr. Carlisle. But you don't really know any gangsters. You'd be afraid of them. Just as you're afraid of me. You're full of rage, aren't you? You feel you hate me, don't you? You'd like to come off that couch and strike me, wouldn't you?—but you can't. You're quite helpless with me. I'm one person you can't outguess. You can't fool me with cheesecloth ghosts; you can't impress me with fake yoga. You're just as helpless with me as you felt seeing your mother run away with another man when you wanted to go with her. I think you went with her. You ran away, didn't you? You went into show business, didn't you? And when you start your act you run your hands over your hair, just like Humphries. He was a big, strong, attractive man, Humphries. I think you have become Humphries—in your mind."

"But he—he—"

"Just so. I think you wanted your mother in the same way."

"God damn your soul, that's—"

"Lie back on the couch."

"I could kill you—"

"Lie back on the couch."

"I could— Mother. Mother. Mother."

He was on his knees, one hand beating at his eyes. He crawled to her and threw his head in her lap, burrowing in. Dr. Lilith Ritter, gazing down at the disheveled corn-colored hair, smiled slightly. She let one hand rest on his head, running her fingers gently over his hair, patting his head reassuringly as he sobbed and gasped, rooting in her lap with his lips. Then, with her other hand, she reached for the pad on the desk and wrote in shorthand: "Burleigh, Mississippi."

In the spring darkness the obelisk stood black against the sky. There were no clouds and only a single star. No, a planet; Venus, winking as if signaling Earth in a cosmic code that the worlds used among themselves. He moved his head a fraction, until the cold, brilliant planet seemed to rest on the bronze tip of the stone shaft. The lights of a car, winding through the park, sprayed for a moment across the stone and the hieroglyphics leaped out in shadow. Cartouches with their names, the boasts of the dead, invocations to dead gods, prayers to the shining, fateful river which rose in mystery and found the sea through many mouths, flowing north through the ancient land. Was it mysterious when it still lived? he wondered. Before the Arabs took it over and the chumps started measuring the tunnel of the Great Pyramid in inches to see what would happen in the world.

The spring wind stirred her hair and trailed a loose wisp of it across his face. He pressed her cheek against his and with his other hand pointed to the planet, flashing at the stone needle's point. She nodded, keeping silence; and he felt the helpless wonder sweep over him again, the impotence at touching her, the supplication. Twice she had given it to him. She had given it as she might give him a glass of brandy, watching his reactions. Beyond that elfin face, the steady eyes, there was something breathing, something that was fed blood from a tiny heart beating under pointed breasts. But it was cobweb under the fingers. Cobweb in the woods that touches the face and disappears under the fingers.

The hot taste of need rose in his mouth and turned sour with inner turmoil and the jar of forbidding recollection. Then he drew away from her and turned to look at her face. As the wind quickened he saw her perfectly molded nostrils quiver, scenting spring as an animal tastes the wind. Was she an animal? Was all the mystery nothing more than that? Was she merely a sleek, golden kitten that unsheathed its claws when it had played enough and wanted solitude? But the brain that was always at work, always clicking away behind the eyes—no animal had such an organ; or was it the mark of a superanimal, a new species, something to be seen on earth in a few more centuries? Had nature sent out a feeling tentacle from the past, groping blindly into the present with a single specimen of what mankind was to be a thousand years hence?

The brain held him; it dosed him with grains of wild joy, measured out in milligrams of words, the turn of her mouth corner, one single, lustful flash from the gray eyes before the scales of secrecy came over them again. The brain seemed always present, always hooked to his own by an invisible gold wire, thinner than spider's silk. It sent its charges into his mind and punished him with a chilling wave of cold reproof. It would let him writhe in helpless misery and then, just before the breaking point, would send the warm current through to jerk him back to life and drag him, tumbling over and over through space, to the height of a snow mountain where he could see all the plains of the earth spread out before him, and all the power of the cities and the ways of men. All were his, could be his, would be his, unless the golden thread broke and sent him roaring into the dark chasm of fear again.

The wind had grown colder; they stood up. He lit cigarettes and gave her one and they passed on, circling the obelisk, walking slowly past the blank, unfinished wall of the Museum's back, along the edge of the park where the busses trailed their lonely lights away uptown.

He took her hand in his and slid it into the pocket of his topcoat, and for a moment, as they walked, it was warm and a little moist, almost yielding, almost, to the mind's tongue, sweet-salty, yielding, musky; then in an instant it changed, it chilled, it became the hand of a dead woman in his pocket, as cold as the hand he once molded of rubber and stretched on the end of his reaching rod, icy from a rubber sack of cracked ice in his pocket, straight into the face of a believer's skeptical husband.

Now the loneliness grew inside him, like a cancer, like a worm of a thousand branches, running down his nerves, creeping under his scalp, tying two arms together and squeezing his brain in a noose, pushing into his loins and twisting them until they ached with need and not-having, with wanting and not-daring, with thrust into air, with hand-gripping futility—orgasm and swift-flooding shame, hostile in its own right, ashamed of shame.

They stopped walking and he moved toward a backless bench under the trees which were putting out the first shoots of green in the street lamp's glow, delicate, heartbreakingly new, the old spring which would bring the green softly, gently, like a young girl, into the earth's air long after they and the fatal, coursing city, were gone. They would be gone forever, he thought, looking down into her face which was now as empty as a ball of crystal reflecting only the window light.

The rush, the rocketing plunge of the years to death, seized hold of him and he gripped her, pressing her to him in a fierce clutch after life. She let him hold her and he heard himself moaning a little under his breath as he rubbed his cheek against the smooth hair. Then she broke away, reached up and brushed his lips with hers and began to walk again. He fell in behind her for a few steps, then came abreast of her and took her hand once more. This time it was firm, muscular, determined. It closed on his own fingers for a single reassuring instant, then broke away and she thrust her hands into the pockets of her coat and strode on, the smoke of her cigarette whirling back over her shoulder like a sweet-smelling scarf in the wind.

When she walked she placed her feet parallel, as if she were walking a crack in the sidewalk. In spite of high heels the ankles above them never wavered. She wore gunmetal stockings, and her shoes had buckles of cut steel.

Two ragged little boys, gleeful at being out after midnight, came bounding toward them, chasing each other back and forth across the walk by the wall where the trees leaned over. One of them pushed the other, screaming dirty words, and the one pushed caromed toward Lilith. Turning like a cat released in mid-air, she spun out of his path and the boy sprawled to the cinders, his hands slipping along, grinding cinders into the palms. He sat up and as Stan turned to watch, he suddenly sprang at his companion with his fists. Kids always play alike. Roughhouse around until one gets hurt and then the fight starts. A couple of socks and they quit and the next minute are friends again. Oh, Christ, why do you have to grow up into a life like this one? Why do you ever have to want women, want power, make money, make love, keep up a front, sell the act, suck around some booking agent, get gypped on the check—?

It was late and the lights were fewer. Around them the town's roar had softened to a hum. And spring was coming with poplar trees standing slim and innocent around a glade with the grass hummocks under one's hands—can't I ever forget it? His eyes blurred and he felt his mouth tighten.

The next moment Lilith's hand was through his arm, pressing it, turning him across the avenue to the apartment house where she lived, where she worked her own special brand of magic, where she had her locked files full of stuff. Where she told people what they had to do during the next day when they wanted a drink, when they wanted to break something, when they wanted to kill themselves with sleeping tablets, when they wanted to bugger the parlor maid or whatever they wanted to do that they had become so afraid of doing that they would pay her twenty-five dollars an hour to tell them either why it was all right to do it or go on doing it or think about doing it or how they could stop doing it or stop wanting to do it or stop thinking about doing it or do something else that was almost as good or something which was bad but would make you feel better or just something to do to be able to do something.

At her door they stopped and she turned to him, smiling serenely, telling him in that smile that he wasn't coming in tonight, that she didn't need him, didn't want him tonight, didn't want his mouth on her, didn't want him to kneel beside her, kissing her, didn't want anything of him except the knowledge that when she wanted him in the night and wanted his mouth on her and wanted him kneeling beside her, kissing her, she would have him doing all those things to her as she wanted them done and just when she wanted them done and just how she wanted them done to her because she had only what she wanted from anybody and she had let him do those things to her because she had wanted them done to her not because he could do them better than anyone else although he didn't know if there was anybody else and didn't want to know and it didn't matter and she could have him any time she wanted those things done to her because that was the way she was and she was to be obeyed in all things because she held in her hand the golden thread which carried the current of life into him and she held behind her eyes the rheostat that fixed the current and she could starve him and dry him up and kill him by freezing if she wanted to and this was where he had gotten himself only it didn't matter because as long as one end of the golden wire was embedded in his brain he could breathe and live and move and become as great as she wanted since she sent the current along the wire for him to become great with and live with and even make love to Molly with when Molly begged him to tell her if he didn't want her any more so she might get some man before she looked like an old hay-burner and her insides were too tight for her ever to have a kid.

All these things he saw in the full lower lip, the sharp cheek-bones and chin, the enormous eyes of gray that looked like ink now in the dark of the vestibule. He was about to ask her something else and he wet his lips with his tongue. She caught his thought, nodded, and he stood there, three steps below her with his hand holding his hat, looking up at her and needing and then she gave him what he was begging for, her lips for a full, warm, soft, sweet, moist moment and her little tongue between his like the words, "Good night" formed of soft moisture. Then she had gone and there he was for another day, another week, another month, willing to do anything she said, as long as she would not break the golden wire and now he had her permission, which she had pulled out of his mind, and he hurried off to take advantage of it before she changed her mind and sent him refusal, chilling along the invisible wire embedded in his brain, that would stop his hand six inches from his lips.

Three doors down was a little cocktail bar with a glass sign over it that was illumined some way from inside and said "BAR." Stan hurried in. The murals jagged crazily this way and that up the three-toned wall and a radio was playing softly where the bar man nodded on a stool at one end of the bar. Stan laid a dollar on the polished wood.

"Hennessy, Three Star."

" 'Inside, above the din and fray, We heard the loud musicians play The "Treues Liebes Herz" of Strauss—' "

"What's that?"

"It's from *The Harlot's House*. Shall we go in?"

They were walking down a side street in the early summer twilight; ahead of them Lexington Avenue was gaudy with neon. In the basement of an old brownstone was a window painted in primary blues and reds; above it a sign, "Double Eagle Kretchma." Gypsy music was filtering out on the heated air.

"It looks like a joint to me."

"I like joints—when I'm in the mood for dirt. Let's go in."

It was dark with a few couples sliding around on the little dance floor. A sad fat man with blue jowls, wearing a Russian blouse of dark green silk, greasy at the cuffs, came toward them and took them to a booth. "You wish drinks, good Manhattan? Good Martini?"

"Do you have any real vodka?" Lilith was tapping a cigarette.

"Good vodka. You, sir?"

Stan said, "Hennessy, Three Star, and plain water."

When the drinks came he offered the waiter a bill but it was waved away. "Later. Later. Have good time first. Then comes the payment—the bad news, huh? Have good time—always have to pay for everything in the end." He leaned across the table, whispering, "This vodka—it's not worth what you pay for it. Why you want to come here anyhow? You want card reading?"

Lilith looked at Stan and laughed. "Let's."

From the shadows in the back of the room a woman stepped out and waddled toward them, her bright red skirt swishing as her hips rolled. She had a green scarf around her head, a curved nose, loose thin lips and a deep, greasy crease between her breasts which seemed ready to burst from her soiled white blouse at any moment. When she wedged herself into the booth beside Stan her round hip was hot and burning against his thigh.

"You cut the cards, lady; we see what you cut, please. Ah, see! Good sign! This card called The Star. You see this girl—she got one foot on land, one foot on water; she pour wine out on land and water. That is good sign, lucky in love, lady. I see man with light hair going to ask you to marry him. Some trouble at first but it come out all right."

She turned up a card. "This one here—Hermit card. Old man with star in lantern. You search for something, no? Something you lose, no? Ring? Paper with writing on it?"

Against Lilith's blank, cold face the gypsy's questions bounded back. She turned another card. "Here is Wheel of Life. You going to live long time with not much sickness. Maybe some stomach trouble later on and some trouble with nervous sickness but everything pass off all right."

Lilith took a puff of her cigarette and looked at Stan. He pulled two bills from his wallet and held them to the gypsy. "That'll do, sister. Scram."

"Thank you, mister. But lots more fortune in cards. Tell lots of thing about what going to happen. Bad luck, maybe; you see how to keep it away."

"Go on, sister. Beat it."

She shoved the bills into her pocket along with the Tarot deck and heaved out of the booth without looking back.

"She'll probably put the hex on us now," Stan said. "Christ, what corn. Why the hell did I ever leave the carny? I could be top man in the mitt camp right now and tucking ten grand in the sock at the end of every season."

"You don't want to, darling." Lilith sipped her vodka. "Do you think I'd be sitting here with you if your only ambition was to be top man in a—what did you call it?"

"Mitt camp." He grinned weakly. "You're right, doctor. Besides I'd probably have pulled the switch once too often and gotten jugged." He answered her frown. "The switch is what the gypsies call *okana borra*—the great trick. You have the chump tie a buck up in his hanky. He sleeps on it and in the morning he has two bucks and comes running back with all his savings out of the teapot. Then when he wakes up next time he has nothing in the hank but a stack of paper and he comes back looking for the gypsy."

"You know such fascinating bits of folklore, Mr. Carlisle. And you think you could ever be happy using those very keen, crafty brains of yours to cheat some ignorant farmer? Even if you did make ten thousand a year and loaf all winter?"

He finished the brandy and signaled the waiter for a refill. "And when it rains you read mitts with your feet in a puddle and a river down the back of your neck. I'll stick to Mrs. Peabody's house—it's got a better roof on it."

Lilith's eyes had narrowed. "I meant to speak to you, Stan, when we got a chance. There are two women who will be introduced to your congregation, not directly through me, naturally, but they'll get there. One of them is a Mrs. Barker. She's interested in yoga; she wants to go to India but I told her not to uproot her life at this stage. She needs something to occupy her time. I think your Cosmic Breath would be just about right."

Stan had taken a slip of paper from his pocket and was writing. "What's her first name?"

"Give me that paper." She put it in the ashtray and touched her lighter to it. "Stan, I've told you not to write down anything. I don't want to have to remind you again. You talk very glibly about making a million with your brains and yet you continue to act as naïve as a carnival grifter."

He downed the drink desperately and found another in its place and finished that one as quickly.

Lilith went on. "The name is Lucinda Barker. There's nothing else you need to know."

There was silence for a minute, Stan sullenly rattling the ice in the chaser glass.

"The other woman is named Grace McCandless. She's single, forty-five years old. Kept house for her father until he died three years ago. She's gone through Theosophy and come out the other side. She wants proof of survival."

"Give—can you tell me something about the old man?"

"He was Culbert McCandless, an artist. You can look him up with the art dealers probably."

"Look, Lilith, give me just one 'test.' I know you're afraid I'll louse it up and they'll think back to you. But you've got to trust me. After all, lady, I've been in this racket all my life."

"Well, stop apologizing and listen. McCandless went to bed with his daughter—once. She was sixteen. They never did it again but they were never separated. Now that's all you'll get. I'm the only person in the world who knows this, Stan. And if your foot slips I shall have to protect myself. You know what I mean."

"Yeah. Yeah, pal. Let's get out of here. I can't stand the bum air."

Above them the summer leaves cut off the glow of the city in the night sky. By the obelisk they paused for a moment and then Lilith took the lead and they passed it. The back of the Museum seemed to leer at him, full of unspoken threats with doom straining at its leash in the shadows.

When she came out of the bathroom her hands gleamed white against the black silk robe as she tied the cord. On her feet were tiny black slippers. Lilith sat at the desk by the bedroom window and from its side compartment took a case containing several flat drawers, labeled "Sapphires," "Cat's Eyes," "Opals," "Moss Agates."

She said, without looking at him, "The notes wouldn't do

you the slightest bit of good, Stan. They're all in my own shorthand."

"What do you mean?"

Her glance, raised to his for the first time, was calm and benevolent. "While I was in the bathroom you went into my office and tried out the key you had made for my file cabinet. I saw it on the dressing table after you had taken off your clothes. Now it's not there. You've hidden it. But I recognized the notches. You took the impression from my key the last time you went to bed with me, didn't you?"

He said nothing but smoked quickly; the ember of his cigarette became long and pointed and angry red.

"I was going to send you home, Stan, but I think you need a little lesson in manners. And I need my toenails fixed. You can help me with the polish. It's in the drawer of the bed table. Bring it over here."

Dully he stamped out his cigarette, spilling some of the embers and quickly sweeping them back into the tray. He took the kit of nail polish and went over to her, feeling the air against his naked flesh cold and hostile. He threw his shirt over his shoulders and sat down on the carpet at her feet.

Lilith had taken the drawer marked sapphires from its little cabinet and was lifting the stones with a pair of jeweler's forceps, holding them in the light of the desk lamp. Without looking at him she shook one foot free of its slipper and placed it on his bare knee. "This is very good for you, darling. Occupational therapy."

The Great Stanton twisted cotton on the end of an orangewood stick and dipped it into the bottle of polish remover. It smelled acrid and sharply chemical as he swabbed one tiny toenail with it, taking off the chipped polish evenly. Once he paused to kiss the slender foot at the instep but Lilith was absorbed in her tray of gems. Growing bolder, he drew aside the black silk and kissed her thigh. This time she turned and pulled the robe primly over her knees, giving him a glance of amused tolerance. "You've had enough sinfulness for one evening, Mr. Carlisle. Be careful not to spill polish on the rug. You wouldn't want me to rub your nose in it and then throw you out the back door by the scruff of your neck, would you, darling?"

Bracing his hand against the curved instep he began to paint her nails. The rose-colored enamel spread evenly and he thought of the workbench out in the garage and its paint cans. Painting a scooter he had made out of boxes and old baby-carriage wheels. Mother said, "That's beautiful, Stanton. I have several kitchen chairs you can paint for me." The old man had been saving that paint for something. That meant another licking.

"Stan, for heaven's sake, be more careful! You hurt me with the orange stick."

He had finished the first foot and started on the other without knowing it.

"What would you do for a shoeshine if you didn't have me around?" He was startled at the amount of hostility in his own voice.

Lilith laid down a sapphire, narrowing her eyes. "I might have another friend of mine do them. Possibly someone who could take me to the theater, who didn't have to be so afraid of being seen with me. Someone who wouldn't have to sneak in and out."

He set down the bottle of polish remover. "Lilith, wait until we make a killing. One big-time believer—" But he didn't sound convinced himself; his voice died. "I—I want to be seen with you, Lilith. I—I didn't think up this setup. You were the one who told me to hang on to Molly. If I went back to the carny—"

"Stanton Carlisle. Pastor of the Church of the Heavenly Message. I didn't think you could be jealous. I didn't think you had that much of a heart, Stan. I thought all you cared about was money. And power. And more money."

He stood up, throwing off the shirt, his hands clenched. "Go on, pal. You can tell me about as many other guys as you want. This is fifty-fifty. I'm not jealous if another guy shakes hands with you. How's that so different from—the other thing?"

She watched him through eyes almost closed. "Not so very different. No. Not different at all. I shook hands regularly with the old judge—the one who set me up in practice when I was a court psychiatrist on a city salary. All cats have gray paws in the dark, you know, Stan. And I can vaguely recall, when I was sixteen, how five boys in our neighborhood waited for me one evening as I was coming home from night school. They took me into a vacant lot and shook hands with me one after the other. I think each came back twice."

He had turned as she spoke, his mouth hanging open idiotically, his hair falling over his face. He lurched over to the dressing table with its wing mirrors, gaped at his image, his eyes ravaged. Then in a spatter of desperate groping he seized the nail scissors and gouged at his forehead with them.

The stab of pain was followed instantly by a tearing sensation in his right wrist and he saw that Lilith stood beside him, levering his hand behind his shoulder until he dropped the scissors. She had not forgotten to pull up her robe and held it bunched under one arm to keep it from brushing her toes with their wet enamel.

"Put a drop of iodine on it, Stan," she said crisply. "And don't try drinking the bottle. There's not enough in it to do more than make you sick."

He let the cold water roar past his face and then tore at his hair with the rich, soft towel. His forehead wasn't bleeding any more.

"Stan, darling—"

"Yeah. Coming."

"You never do anything by halves, do you, lover? So few men have the courage to do what they really want to do. If you'll come in here and fuss over me a little more—I love to be fussed over, darling—I'll tell you a bedtime story, strictly for adults."

He was putting on his clothes. When he was dressed he pulled up a hassock and said, "Give me your foot."

Smiling, Lilith put the gems away and leaned back, stretching her arms luxuriously, watching him with the sweetest of proprietary smiles.

"That's lovely, darling. Much more accurately than I could do it. Now about the bedtime story—for I've decided to risk it and ask you to stay over with me. You can, darling. Just this once. Well, I know a man—don't be silly, darling, he's a patient. Well, he started as a patient and later became a friend—

but not like you, darling. He's a very shrewd, capable man and he might do us both a lot of good. He's interested in psychic phenomena."

Stan looked up at her, holding her foot in both his hands. "How's he fixed for dough?"

"Very well-heeled as you would put it, darling. He lost a sweetheart when he was in college and he has been weighed down with guilt from it ever since. She died from an abortion. Well, at first I thought I'd have to pass him along to one of my tame Freudians—he seemed likely to get out of hand with me. But then he became interested in the psychic. His company makes electric motors. You'll recognize the name—Ezra Grindle."

The Chariot

holds a conqueror. Sphinxes draw him.
They turn in opposite directions to rend him apart.

G RINDLE, EZRA, industrialist, b. Bright's Falls, N. Y. Jan.
3, 1878, s. Matthias Z. and Charlotte (Banks). Brewster
Academy and Columbia U. grad. 1900 engineering. m. Eileen
Ernst 1918, d. 1927. Joined sales staff, Hobbes Chem. and Dye,
1901, head of Chi. office 1905; installed plants Rio de Janeiro,
Manila, Melbourne 1908–10; export mgr. 1912. Dollar-a-year
man, Washington, D. C. 1917–18. Amer. Utilities, gen. mgr.
1919, v.p. 1921. Founded Grindle Refrigeration 1924, Manitou
Casting and Die 1926 (subsidiary), in 1928 merged five com-
panies to form Grindle Sheet Metal and Stamping. Founded
Grindle Electric Motor Corp. 1929, pres. and chairman of
board. Author: The Challenge of Organized Labor, 1921; Ex-
pediting Production: a Scientific Guide, 1928; Psychology in
Factory Management (with R. W. Gilchrist) 1934. Clubs:
Iroquois, Gotham Athletic, Engineering Club of Westchester
County. Hobbies: billiards, fishing.

From *The Roll Call*—1896, Brewster Academy:

EZRA GRINDLE ("Spunk") Major: Math. Activities: chess club, math club, manager of baseball 3 years, business manager of *The Roll Call* 2 years. College: Columbia. Ambition: to own a yacht. Quotation: "By magic numbers and persuasive sound"—Congreve.

When the red-haired kid looked up he saw a man standing by the counter. The clerical collar, the dead-black suit, the panama with a black band, snapped him to life.

"My son, I wonder if you would be so kind as to help me on a little matter?" He slipped a breviary back into his pocket.

"Sure, Father. What can I do for you, Father?"

"My son, I am preparing a sermon on the sin of destroying life before birth. I wonder if you could find me some of the clippings which have appeared in your newspaper, recounting the deaths of unfortunate young women who have been led to take the lives of their unborn infants. Not the most recent accounts, you understand—of these there are so many. I want to see some of the older accounts. Proving that this sin was rampant even in our parents' time."

The kid's forehead was pulled up with the pain of thought. "Gee, Father, I'm afraid I don't getcha."

The smooth voice lowered a little. "Abortions, my son. Look under A-B."

The kid blushed and pounded away importantly. He came back with an old envelope. ABORTION, DEATHS—1900–10.

The man in the clerical collar riffled through them quickly. 1900: MOTHER OF TWO DIES FROM ILLEGAL OPERATION. SOCIETY GIRL . . . HUSBAND ADMITS . . . DEATH PACT . . .

DEATH OF A WORKING GIRL
BY ELIZABETH McCORD

Last night in Morningside Hospital a slender young girl with raven tresses covering her pillow turned her face to the wall when a youth fought his way into the ward where she lay on the brink of death. She would not look upon him, would not speak to him although he begged and implored her forgiveness. And in the end he slunk away, eluding Officer Mulcahy who had been stationed in the hospital to watch for just such an appearance of the man responsible for the girl's condition and untimely death. He did not escape, however, before a keen-eyed little probationer nurse had noted the initials E.G. on his watch fob.

Somewhere in our great city tonight a coward crouches and trembles, expecting at any moment the heavy hand of the law to descend on his shoulder, his soul seared (let us hope) by the unforgiving gesture of the innocent girl whose life he destroyed by his callous self-interest and criminal insistence.

This girl—tall, brunette and lovely in the first bloom of youth—is but one of many. . . .

The man in black clucked his tongue. "Yes—even in our parents' time. Just as I thought. The sin of destroying a little life before it has been born or received Holy Baptism."

He stuffed the clippings back into the envelope and beamed his thanks on the kid with red hair.

In Grand Central the good father picked up a suitcase from the check room. In a dressing cubicle he changed into a linen suit, a white shirt, and a striped blue tie.

Out on Madison Avenue he stopped, grinning, as he turned the pages of a worn breviary. The edges were crinkled from rain; and on the fly leaf was written in faded, Spencerian script, "Fr. Nikola Tosti" and a date. The blond man tossed it into a trash can. In his pocket was a clipping, the work of a sob sister thirty years ago. *May 29, 1900.*

The morgue office of Morningside Hospital was a room in the basement inhabited by Jerry, the night attendant, a shelf of ancient ledgers, and a scarred wreck of a desk. There were two kitchen chairs for visitors, a radio, an electric fan for hot nights and an electric heater for cold ones. The fan was going now.

A visitor in soiled gray slacks and a sport shirt looked up as Jerry came back into the room.

"I borrowed a couple of shot glasses from the night nurse on West One—the little number with the gams. These glasses got markings on 'em but don't let that stop us. Fill 'em up.

Say, brother, it's a break we got together over in Julio's and you had this bottle. I hadn't had a chance to wet the whistle all evening. I was dying for a few shots."

His new friend pushed a straw skimmer further back on his head and filled the medicine glasses with applejack.

"Here's lead in the old pencil, huh?" Jerry killed his drink and held out the glass.

Blondy filled it again and sipped his brandy. "Gets kind of dull, nights, eh?"

"Not so bad. I listen to the platter programs. You get some good records on them programs. And I do lots of crossword puzzles. Say, some nights they don't give you a minute's peace around here—stiffs coming down every ten minutes. That's mostly in the winter and in the very hot spells—old folks. We try not to get 'em in here when they're ready to put their checks back in the rack but you can't keep 'em out when a doctor says 'In she goes.' Then we got the death entered on our books and the city's books. It don't look good. Thanks, don't care if I do."

"And you got to keep 'em entered in all these books? That would drive me nuts." The blond man put his feet on the desk and looked up at the shelf full of ledgers.

"Naa. Only in the current book—here, on the desk. Them books go all the way back to when the hospital started. I don't know why they keep 'em out here. Only once in a while the Medical Examiner's office comes nosing around, wanting to look up something away back, and I dust 'em off. This ain't a bad job at all. Plenty of time on your hands. Say—I better not have any more right now. We got an old battle-ax, the night supervisor. She might come down and give me hell. Claim I was showing up drunk. I never showed up drunk on the job yet. And she never comes down after three o'clock. It ain't bad."

Cool blue eyes had picked out a volume marked *1900*.

Jerry rattled on. "Say, y'know that actress, Doree Evarts—the one that did the Dutch night before last in the hotel across the way? They couldn't save her. This evening, 'bout eight o'clock, I got a call to collect one from West Five—that's private. It was her. I got her in the icebox now. Wanna see her?"

The stranger set down his glass. His face was white but he said, "Sure thing. I ain't never seen a dead stripper. Boy, oh, boy, but I seen her when she was alive. She used to flash 'em."

The morgue man said, "Come on. I'll introduce you."

In the corridor were icebox doors in three tiers. Jerry went down the line, unlatched one and pulled out a tray. On it lay a form covered by a cheap cotton sheet which he drew back with a flourish.

Doree Evarts had cut her wrists. What lay on the galvanized tray was like a dummy, eyes half open, golden hair damp and matted. The nostrils and mouth were plugged with cotton.

There were the breasts Doree had snapped by their nipples under the amber spotlight, the belly which rotated for the crowd of smoke-packed old men and pimply kids, the long legs which spread in the final bump as she made her exit. Her nail polish was chipped and broken off; a tag with her name on it was tied to one thumb; her wrists were bandaged.

"Good-looking tomato—once." Jerry pulled up the sheet, slid in the drawer and slammed the door. They went back to the office and the visitor knocked off two quick brandies.

Doree had found the end of the alley. What had she been running from that made her slice at her veins? Nightmare coming closer. What force inside her head, under the taffy-colored hair, pushed her into this?

The dank office swam in the heat of the brandy as Jerry's voice clattered on. "You get lotsa laughs some nights. One time—last winter it was—we had a real heavy night. I mean a real night. They was conking out like flies, I'm telling you. Lotsa old folks. Every five, ten minutes the phone'd ring: 'Jerry, come on up, we got another one.' I'm telling you, I didn't get a minute's peace all night. Finally I got the bottom row of boxes filled and then the second row. Now, I didn't want to go sticking 'em up in that top row—I'd have to get two ladders and two other guys to help me lift 'em. Well, what would you do? Sure. I doubled 'em up. Well, along about four o'clock the old battle-ax phones down and asks me where such-and-such a stiff is and I tell her—it was a dame. Then she asks about a guy and I look up the book and I tell her. Well, I'd shoved 'em into the same box. What the hell—they was dead people! She blows up and you shoulda heard her."

Good Christ, was this guy never going to shut up and get out for a minute? Just one minute would be enough. On the shelf over Jerry's head. *1900.*

"She was raising hell. She says, 'Jerry'—you shoulda heard her; you wouldn't believe it—'Jerry, I think you might have the decency'—those was her very words—'I think you might have the decency not to put men and women together in the same refrigerator compartment!' Can you beat that? I says to her, I says, 'Miss Leary, do you mean to insinuate that I should go encouraging homo-sex-uality amongst these corpses?'" Jerry leaned back in his swivel chair, slapping his thigh, and his companion laughed until tears came, getting the tightness worked out of his nerves.

"Oh, you shoulda heard her rave then! Wait a minute—there's the phone." He listened, then said, "Right away, keed," and pushed back his chair. "Got a customer. Be right back. Gimme a shot before I go."

His hard heels rang off down the corridor. The elevator stopped, opened, closed, and hummed as it went up.

1900. May 28th. Age: 95, 80, 73, 19 . . . 19 . . . Doris Mae Cadle. Diagnosis: septicemia. Admitted—hell, where was she from? No origin. Name, age, diagnosis. The only young one on the 28th and on the page before and after it. The elevator was coming down and he shoved the ledger back in its place.

Jerry stood in the doorway, swaying slightly, his face glistening. "Wanna give me a hand? A fat one! Jesus!"

"No. She ain't lived here in my time. 'Course, I only took over the house eight years ago. Mis' Meriwether had the house before me. She's been in the Home for the Blind ever since. Cataracts, you know."

A soft, cultured voice said: "Mrs. Meriwether, I hate to bother you with what is, after all, only a hobby of mine. I am a genealogist, you see. I am looking up the branches of my mother's family—the Cadles. And in an old city directory I noted that someone by that name lived at the house which you ran as a rooming house about thirty-five years ago. Of course, I don't expect you to remember."

"Young man, I certainly do remember. A fine girl she was,

Doris Cadle. Remember it like it was yesterday. Some kind of blood poisoning. Took her to the hospital. Too late. Died. Buried in Potter's Field. I didn't know where her folks was. I would have put up the money to get her a plot only I didn't have it. I tried to get up a purse but none of my roomers could make it up."

"She was one of the Cadles of New Jersey?"

"Might a been. Only, as I recall, she come from Tewkes-bury, Pennsylvania."

"Tell me, Mrs. Meriwether, are you related to the Meri-wethers of Massachusetts?"

"Well, now, young man, that's right interesting. I had a grandmother come from Massachusetts. On my father's side she was. Now, if you're interested in the Meriwethers—"

"Mrs. Cadle, I thought I had all the data I needed but there are a couple of other questions I'd like to ask for the government records." The dark suit, the brief case, the horn-rimmed glasses over a polka-dot bow tie, all spoke of the servant of government.

"Come in. I been tryin' to find Dorrie's pitcher. Ain't seen it sence I showed it to you a while ago."

"Doris Mae. That was your second child, I believe. But you put the picture back in the Bible, Mrs. Cadle."

His voice sounded dry and bored. He must get awful tired, pestering folks this way all day and every day.

"Let's look again. Here—here it is. You just didn't look far enough. Did I ask you the date of your daughter's graduation from high school?"

"Never graddiated. She took a business course and run off to New York City and we never seen her no more."

"Thank you. You said your husband worked in the mines from the age of thirteen. How many accidents did he have in that time? That is, accidents that caused him to lose one or more days from work?"

"Oh, Lord, I can sure tell you about them! I mind one time just after we was married . . ."

The collector of vital statistics walked slowly toward the town's single trolley line. In his brief case was a roll of film recording both sides of a postcard. One was a cheap photograph of a young girl, taken at Coney Island. She was sitting in a prop rowboat named *Sea Breeze*, and holding an oar. Behind her was a painted lighthouse. On the message side was written in precise, characterless handwriting:

Dear Mom and all,
    I am sending this from Coney Island. It's like the biggest fair you ever saw. A boy named Spunk took me. Isn't that a silly nickname? I had my picture taken as you can see. Tell Pop and all I wish I was with you and hug little Jennie for me. Will write soon.

                                        Fondly,
                                        DORRIE

Conversation flattened out to an eager rustle as the Rev. Carlisle entered the room and walked to the lectern in the glass alcove, where ferns and palms caught the summer sun in a tumult of green. The rest of the room was cool and dark, with drawn hangings before the street windows.

He opened the Bible with the gold-plated clasps, ran his hands once over his hair, then gazed straight out above the heads of the congregation which had assembled in the Church of the Heavenly Message.

"My text this morning is from Ephesians Five, verses eight and nine: *'For ye were sometimes darkness, but now are ye light in the Lord: walk as children of light: for the fruit of the Spirit is in all goodness and righteousness and truth . . .'*"

Mrs. Prescott was late, damn her. Or was it the mark who was holding up the works? He must be the kind of bastard that always comes late—thinks the world will hold the curtain waiting for him.

Blue eyes lifted from the page and smiled their blessing on the faces before them. About twenty in the house with a few odd husbands dragged along; and a couple of male believers.

"Dearly beloved, on this day of summer, with God's glorious sunlight illuminating the world, we find an object lesson in its brilliance . . ."

Where was Tallentyre? She was supposed to ride herd on Prescott and the mark.

". . . for we, who once walked in darkness of fear and ignorance and doubt, find our path through the earth-plane made bright and shining by the surety of our faith."

At the other end of the shadowy room the front door opened and closed. In the dim light two stout women in flowered print dresses came in—Tallentyre and Prescott. Son-of-a-bitch! Did the chump back out at the last minute? With a flash of anxiety Stan wondered if somebody might have wised him up.

Then in the doorway a man appeared, big, in a light gray flannel suit, holding a panama in his hand. A black silhouette in the gentle glow cast by the fanlight. The spread of shoulder spoke of arrogant ownership. The man was an owner—land, buildings, acres, machines. And men. Two round, owl-like saucers of light winked from the dark head—the light of the conservatory reflected from rimless glasses as he turned his head, whispering to Prescott. Then he sat down in the back row, pulling out one of the bridge chairs to make room for his legs.

The Rev. Carlisle drew breath and fixed his eyes on the gold-embossed Bible before him.

"My dear friends, let me tell you a story. There was a man who had been in the Great War. One dark night he was sent scouting into No Man's Land with one of his buddies—a star shell rose from the enemy trenches and illuminated the field. Well might he have prayed at that moment with David, *'Hide me from my deadly enemies who compass me about.'* The man of whom I speak dashed for the security of a shell hole, pushing his companion aside, while the machine guns of the Germans began to fill the field with death."

Ezra Grindle was fanning himself idly with his panama.

"The soldier who was left without cover fell, mortally wounded. And before the baleful glare of the star shell died, the other soldier, crouching in the shell crater, saw his companion's eyes fixed on him in a mute look of scorn and accusation.

"My dear friends, years passed. The survivor became a pillar of society—married, a father, respected in his community. But always, deep in his soul, was the memory of that dying boy's face—the eyes—accusing him!"

The panama was motionless.

"This man recently became interested in Spiritual Truth. He began to attend the church of a medium who is a dear friend of mine in a city out west. He unburdened his heart to the medium. And when they finally established contact with the 'buddy' whose earth life was lost through his cowardice, what do you suppose were the first words the friend in spirit uttered to that guilt-ridden man? They were, 'You are forgiven.'

"Picture to yourselves, my friends, the unutterable joy which rose in that man's tortured heart when the crushing weight of guilt was lifted from him and for the first time in all those years he was a free man—drinking in the sun and the soft wind and the bird song of dawn and eventide."

Grindle was leaning forward, one hand on the back of the chair in front of him. Mrs. Prescott whispered something in his ear; but he was deaf to it. He seemed caught and held by the voice of the man behind the lectern, a man in white linen with a black clerical vest, whose hair, in the shaft of summer sun, was as golden as his voice.

"My dear friends, there is no need for *God* to forgive us. How can we sin against the wind which blows across the fields of ripening grain, how can we injure the soft scent of lilacs in the spring twilight, the deep blue of an autumn sky or the eternal glory of the stars on a winter's night? No, no, my friends. We can sin only against mankind. And man, in his next mansion of the soul, says to us tenderly, lovingly, 'You are forgiven, beloved. When you join us you will know. Until then, go with our love, rejoice in our forgiveness, take strength from us who live forever in the shadow of his hand.' "

The tears had mounted to the clergyman's eyes and now, in the light of the alcove, they glistened faintly on his cheeks as he stopped speaking, standing erect with the bearing of an emperor in his chariot.

"Let us pray."

At the back of the room a man who had spent his life ruining competitors, bribing congressmen, breaking strikes, arming vigilantes, cheating stockholders, and endowing homes for unwed mothers, covered his eyes with his hand.

"Reverend, they tell me you bring voices out of trumpets."

"I have *heard* voices from trumpets. I don't bring them.

They come. Mediumship is either a natural gift or it is acquired by devotion, by study, and by patience."

The cigars had cost Stan twenty dollars; but he pushed the box across the desk easily and took one himself, holding his lighter for the tycoon. The Venetian blinds were drawn, the windows open, and the fan whirring comfortably.

Grindle inhaled the cigar twice, let the smoke trickle from his nostrils, approved it, and settled farther back in his chair.

As if suddenly remembering an appointment, the spiritualist said, "Excuse me," and jotted notes on a calendar pad. He let Grindle smoke on while he made a telephone call, then turned back to him, smiling, waiting.

"I don't care about trumpet phenomena in *your* house. I want to see it in *my* house."

The clergyman's face was stern. "Mr. Grindle, spirit phenomena are not a performance. They are a religious experience. We cannot say where and when they will appear. They are no respecters of houses. Those who have passed over may reveal themselves in the humble cottage of the laborer and ignore completely the homes of wealth, of culture, and of education."

The big man nodded. "I follow you there, Carlisle. In one of your sermons you said something about Spiritualism being the only faith that offers *proof* of survival. I remember you said that the command 'Show me' is the watchword of American business. Well, you hit the nail right on the head that time. I'm just asking to be shown, that's all. That's fair enough."

The minister's smile was unworldly and benign. "I am at your service if I can strengthen your resolve to find out more for yourself."

They smoked, Grindle eyeing the spiritualist, Carlisle seemingly deep in meditation.

At the left of Grindle's chair stood a teakwood coffee table, a relic of the Peabody furnishings. On it sat a small Chinese gong of brass. The silence grew heavy and the industrialist seemed to be trying to force the other man to break it first; but neither broke it. The little gong suddenly spoke—a clear, challenging note.

Grindle snatched it from the table, turning it upside down

and examining it. Then he picked up the table and knocked the top with his knuckles. When he looked up again he found the Rev. Carlisle smiling at him.

"You may have the gong—and the table, Mr. Grindle. It never before has rung by an exudation of psychic power— what we call the odylic force—as it did just now. Someone must be trying to get through to you. But it is difficult—your innate skepticism is the barrier."

On the big man's face Stan could read the conflict—the fear of being deceived against the desire to see marvels and be forgiven by Doris Mae Cadle, 19, septicemia, May 28, 1900: *But I tell you, Dorrie, if we get married now it will smash everything, everything.*

Grindle leaned forward, poking the air with the two fingers which gripped his cigar. "Reverend, out in my Jersey plant I've got an apothecary's scale delicate enough to weigh a human hair—just one human hair! It's in a glass case. You make that scale move and I'll give your church ten thousand dollars!"

The Rev. Carlisle shook his head. "I'm not interested in money, Mr. Grindle. You may be rich. Perhaps I am too—in a different way." He stood up but Grindle stayed where he was. "If you wish to arrange a séance in your own home or anywhere else, I can try to help you. But I should warn you— the place does not matter. *What matters is the spiritual environment.*" He had been speaking slowly, as if weighing something in his mind, but the last sentence was snapped out as if he had come to a decision.

"But God damn it—pardon me, Reverened—but I know all this! You'll get full co-operation from me. I've got an open mind, Carlisle. An open mind. And the men I'll pick for our committee will have open minds too—or they'll hear from me later. When can you come?"

"In three weeks I shall have a free evening."

"No good. In three weeks I'll have to be up in Quebec. And I've got this bee in my bonnet. I want to find out once and for all, Carlisle. Show me one tiny speck of incontrovertible evidence and I'll listen to anything else you have to say. Can't you consider this an emergency and come out to the plant tonight?" Stan had moved toward the door and Grindle followed him. "Mr. Grindle, I believe you are a sincere seeker."

They descended the carpeted stairs and stood for a moment at the front door. "Then you'll come, Reverend? Tonight?"

Carlisle bowed.

"That's splendid. I'll send the car for you at six. Will that be all right? Or how about coming out earlier and having dinner at the plant? We all eat in the same cafeteria, right with the men. Democratic. But the food's good."

"I shall not want anything very heavy, thank you. I'll have a bite before six."

"Right. The car will pick you up here at the church." Grindle smiled for the first time. It was a chilly smile, tight around the eyes, but was probably his best attempt. Stan looked at the big man closely.

Hair thin and sandy. Forehead domed and spattered with freckles. A large rectangle of a face with unobtrusive, petulant features set in the center of it. Habitual lines about the mouth as if etched there by gas pains, or by constantly smelling a faintly foul odor. Voice peevish and high-pitched, bluster on the surface, fear underneath. Afraid somebody will get a dime away from him or a dime's worth of power. Waistline kept in by golf and a rowing machine. Maybe with shoulder braces to lean against when troubles try to make him stoop like one of his bookkeepers. Hands large, fingers covered with reddish fur. A big, irritable, unsatisfied, guilt-driven, purse-proud, publicity-inflamed dummy—stuffed with thousand dollar bills.

The hand which the Rev. Carlisle raised as a parting gesture was like a benediction—in the best possible taste.

When Stan got back to the apartment it was two o'clock in the afternoon. Molly was still asleep. He jerked the sheet off her and began tickling her in the ribs. She woke up cross and laughing. "Stan, stop it! Oh—oh, honey, it must be good news! What is it?"

"It's the live One, kid. He's nibbling at last. Séance tonight out at his joint in Jersey. If it goes over we're set! If not, we're in the soup. Now go out and get me a kitten."

"A what? Stan, you feeling okay?"

"Sure, sure, sure. Fall into some clothes and go out and

find me a delicatessen store that has a kitten. Bring it back with you. Never mind if you have to swipe it."

When she had gone he eased the eraser from the end of a pencil, wedged the pencil in the jamb of a door and bored into the shaft with a hand drill. Then he pushed the eraser back and put the pencil in his pocket.

The kitten was a little tiger tom about three months old.

"Damn, it couldn't be a white one!"

"But, honey, I didn't know what you wanted with it."

"Never mind, kid. You did okay." He shut himself and the kitten up in the bathroom for half an hour. Then he came out and said to Molly, "Here. Now you can take him back."

"Take him back? But I promised the man I'd give him a good home. Aw, Stan, I thought we could keep him." She was winking back tears.

"Okay, okay, kid. Keep him. Do anything you want with him. If this deal goes over I'll buy you a pedigreed panther."

He hurried back to the church, and Molly set a saucer of milk on the floor and watched the kitten lap it up. She decided to call him Buster.

"Here's where the Grindle property starts, sir," said the chauffeur. They had rolled through Manhattan, under the river with the tunnel walls gleaming, past the smoke of North Jersey and across a desolation of salt marshes. Ahead of them, over a flat waste of cinders and struggling marsh grass, the smokestack and long, glass-roofed buildings of the Grindle Electric Motor Corporation rose glittering in the last sunlight.

The car slowed down at a gate in a barbed fence around the top of which ran wire held by insulators.

The private cop on duty at the gate nodded to the chauffeur and said, "Go right in, Mr. Carlisle. Report at Gatehouse Number Five."

They drove down a gravel road and came to another wire fence and Gatehouse Number Five. "Have to go in and register, sir," said the chauffeur.

Inside the concrete shack a man in a gray military shirt, a Sam Browne belt and a dark blue cap, was sitting at a desk. He was reading a tabloid; when he looked up Stan read his life history from the face: Thrown off some small city police force for excessive brutality; or caught in a shakedown and sent up—the face bore the marks of the squad room and the prison, one on top of the other.

"Carlisle? Waiting for you. Sign this card." It projected from a machine like a cash register. Stan signed. Then the cop said, "Pull the card out." Stan grasped its waxed surface and pulled. "Watch out—don't tear it. Better use both hands."

The Rev. Carlisle used both hands. But what was it all about? He handed the card to Thickneck, then realized that he had left them a record of his fingerprints on its waxed surface.

"Now step inside here and I'll go through the regulations."

It was a small dressing room.

"Take off your coat and hand it to me."

"May I ask what this is for?"

"Orders of Mr. Anderson, Head of Plant Security."

"Does Mr. Grindle know about this?"

"Search me, Reverend; you can ask him. Now give me your coat. Anderson is tightening up on regulations lately."

"But what are you searching for?"

Stumpy fingers felt in pockets and along seams. "Sabotage, Reverend. Nothing personal. The next guy might be a senator, but we'd have to frisk him." The examination included the Rev. Carlisle's shoes, his hatband and the contents of his wallet. As the cop was returning the vest a pencil fell out; he picked it up and handed it to the clergyman who stuck it in his pocket. On his way out Stan gave the cop a cigar. It was immediately locked up in the green metal desk, and the Great Stanton wondered if it was later tagged, "Bribe offered by the Rev. Stanton Carlisle. Exhibit A."

At the door of the plant a thin, quick-moving man of thirty-odd with black patent-leather hair stepped out and introduced himself. "My name's Anderson, Mr. Carlisle. Head of Plant Security." The left lapel of his blue serge suit bulged ever so slightly. "The committee is waiting for you."

Elevators. Corridors. Plaster walls pale green. A white spot painted on the floor in all the corners. "They'll never spit in a corner painted white." The hum of machines and the clank of yard engines outside. Then one glass-paneled door opening on a passage walled with oak. Carpets on the floor. The reception room belonged in an advertising agency; it was a sudden burst of smooth, tawny leather and chrome.

"This way, Mr. Carlisle."

Anderson went ahead, holding open doors. The directors' room was a long one with a glass roof but no windows. The table down its center must have been built there; certainly it could never be taken out now.

Grindle was shaking his hand and presenting him to the others: Dr. Downes, plant physician; Mr. Elrood of the legal staff; Dr. Gilchrist, the industrial psychologist, also on the plant staff; Professor Dennison, who taught philosophy at Grindle College; Mr. Prescott ("You know Mrs. Prescott, I believe, through the church.") and Mr. Roy, both directors of the company. With Anderson and Grindle they made eight—Daniel Douglas Home's traditional number for a séance. Grindle knew more than he let on. But didn't his kind always?

At the far end of the table—it seemed a city block away— stood a rectangular glass case a foot high; inside it was an apothecary's precision balance, a cross arm with two circular pans suspended from it by chains.

Grindle was saying, "Would you care to freshen up a little? I have an apartment right off this room where I stay when I'm working late."

It was furnished much like Lilith's waiting room. Stan shut the bathroom door and washed sweat from his palms. "If I get away with it this time," he whispered to the mirror, "it's the Great Stanton and no mistake. Talk about your Princeton audiences . . ."

One last look around the drawing room revealed a flowing cloud of blue fur, out of which shone eyes of bright yellow as the cat streamed down from a chair and floated along the floor toward him. Stan's forehead smoothed out. "Come to papa, baby. Now it's in the bag."

When he joined the committee he was carrying the cat in his arms and Grindle smiled his tight, unpracticed smile. "I see you've made friends with Beauty. But won't she disturb you?"

"On the contrary. I'd like to have her stay. And now, per- haps you gentlemen will tell me what this interesting apparatus is and how it works." He dropped the cat gently to the carpet, where she tapped his leg once with her paw, demanding to be taken up again, then crawled under the table to sulk.

The head of Plant Security stood with his hand resting on top of the glass. "This is a precision balance, Mr. Carlisle. An apothecary's scale. The indicator in the center of the bar registers the slightest pressure on either of the two pans. I had one of our boys rig up a set of electrical contacts under the pans so that if either one is depressed—by so much as the weight of a hair—this electric bulb in the corner of the case flashes on. The thing is self-contained; flashlight batteries in the case supply current. The balance has been set level and in this room there are no vibrations to disturb it. I watched it for an hour this afternoon and the light never flashed. To turn on that light some force must depress one of the pans of the balance. Is that clear?"

The Rev. Carlisle smiled spiritually. "May I inspect it?"

Anderson glanced at Grindle, who nodded. The private police chief opened the doors of the case and hovered close. "Don't touch anything, Reverend."

"I'm afraid I don't understand much about electricity. But you're sure that this lighting device hasn't interfered with the free movement of the scale? What are these copper strips?" He pointed to them with the end of a pencil from which the eraser was missing, indicating two narrow metal strips leading from under the pans of the balance to insulated connections behind it.

"They're contact points. Two on each side. If either pan moves it touches these points, closes the circuit and the light goes on." Anderson swiftly shut the glass doors and latched them.

The Rev. Carlisle was not listening. His face had grown blank. Moving as if in a dream, he returned to the far end of the room and slipped down into the chair at the end of the table, thirty feet from the mechanism in its glass house.

Without speaking, Grindle motioned the others to their places—Anderson on Stan's left, Grindle taking a chair on his right, the rest on either side. The precision balance had half the long table to itself.

The Rev. Carlisle closed his eyes, folded his arms, and

placed his head upon them as if trying to catch a nap. His breathing deepened, jerky and rasping. Once he stirred and muttered something incoherent.

"He's gone into a trance?"

The boss must have shut the speaker up with a look.

Silence grew. Then Grindle scratched a match to light a cigar and several others took courage and smoked. The room was in semi-darkness and the tension of the waiting men piled up.

The medium had been searched at the gate. Their eyes had been on him every second since he arrived. He had never touched the instrument—Anderson had been watching him for the slightest move. They had all been warned to look out for threads, or for attempts to tilt the massive table. Mr. Roy had quietly slipped from his chair and was sitting on the floor, watching the medium's feet beneath the table even though they were thirty feet from the balance. The scale was enclosed in glass; Anderson had latched the doors. And this medium claimed to be able to move solids without touching them! They waited.

On his right Stan could feel the great man, his attention frozen on the rectangular glass frame. They waited. Time was with the spiritualist. This was a better break than he had ever dreamed of. First the cat showing up, then this magnificent nerve-racking stall for the committee. Would it work after all?

He heard Grindle whisper, "Beauty—Beauty, come here!"

Stan raised his head, moaning a little, and from under one eyelid saw that the cat had wriggled from Grindle's lap and now stood gazing into the balance case.

A gasp ran around the waiting circle. The light had snapped on, burning clear and ruby-red, a tiny bulb, Christmas-tree size, in an upright socket in one corner.

Stan moaned again, his hands closing into fists. The light went out; his fists relaxed.

Grindle cut short the buzzing whispers by a snap of his fingers.

Another wait. Stan's breath came heavier. He felt the saliva in his mouth thickening; his tongue was dry, the saliva like cotton; he forced it out over his lower lip. This was one time when he didn't have to fake the foam.

The light flared again and the medium's breathing became a whistling, agonizing battle.

Off again. Stan let out a sigh.

Silence. Time ticking by on someone's wrist watch. At the foot of the table the Persian looked back, frowning, at Grindle, saying in cat talk, "Let me get into that glass box."

The light again. This time it stayed on. Anderson slid from his seat while Stan's heart pounded but Grindle motioned him back and he compromised by standing in his place. From under folded arms Stan could see Anderson's lean hand, the nails softly polished, braced against the mahogany as he bent forward. The light went out.

This time the medium trembled and threw himself back in his chair, his head lolling. Thickly he said, "Open the case. Let the air into it! Take the cover off and examine the apparatus. Hurry!"

Anderson was already there. The Rev. Carlisle crumpled down in his chair, eyes closed, the foam thick on his lower lip and chin.

Through slit lids he could see Anderson and the psychologist taking the balance from its box. Beauty had stood close by and now was tapping with her paw at the metal contacts on the floor of the case. Grindle picked her up, squirming, and shut her up in the apartment.

Then Stan felt something touch his lips; he let his eyelids flick open. The doctor was standing over him, holding a bit of sterile gauze which he dropped into a flat glass culture dish, putting it back in his pocket. Go ahead, you goddamned wisenheimer townie, analyze it for soap! I could give you a good specimen right in the eye.

Now Grindle had Stan by the arm and was leading him toward the apartment. Over his shoulder he said, "Good evening, gentlemen. You may go."

With Grindle alone Stan began to recover. The industrialist offered him brandy and he drank it slowly. Beauty stared at him from hot, yellow eyes.

"I'll have the car take you back to New York, Mr. Carlisle, as soon as you feel up to traveling."

"Oh, thank you so much. I—I feel a little shaky. Did any phenomena occur?"

"The light in the cabinet went on three times." Behind the rimless glasses Grindle's gray, small eyes almost flashed. "That's proof enough for me, Mr. Carlisle. I shan't drag you all the way out here again. I told you I'm a hard-headed man. I needed proof. Well—" His voice broke with a tiny shading of emotion which habitual restraint could not hide. "I've seen something tonight that cannot possibly be explained by fraud or trickery. The conditions were absolutely air-tight. Some force inside the case depressed the pans of that balance and if anybody ever talks to me about magnets I'll laugh right in his face. The instrument is made of brass. This plant is miles from city vibrations—it's rooted in concrete. There were no threads. You never came near the thing; never touched it. . . ."

Grindle was pacing the carpet, smoking furiously, his face flushed.

The Rev. Carlisle finished his brandy and stretched out an affectionate hand to the Persian cat. Safe! This was the money-bags mountain and he stood, not on the top of it, but in sight of the top. He rose at last, rubbing his eyes wearily. The great man had been talking.

". . . ten thousand dollars. I told you I'd do it and I mean what I say. The check will reach you."

"Please, Mr. Grindle, let's not talk about money. If I have given you proof—"

"Well, you have. You have, man! Let me—"

"The church can always use donations, Mr. Grindle. You can take care of that through Mrs. Prescott. I know she will be pleased. A fine, devoted woman. But for me it is enough to know that some little corner of the glorious truth has been revealed."

Beauty, lolling in the most comfortable chair in the room, suddenly started up and began to scratch her chin with her hind foot. Stan eased Grindle away toward the door. As it closed behind them he saw Beauty biting industriously at the fur over her ribs.

On the steps of the plant its owner paused. From his pocket he took out two envelopes, held them to the light and handed one to Stan. "Here—might as well give you this now, Carlisle.

I was going to send it to Mrs. Prescott as you suggested, but you can save me the trouble. This other we won't need." He tore the envelope and its contents to bits.

"I don't understand, Mr. Grindle."

The smile broke out again with a glitter of white teeth. "It was a warrant for your arrest—in case you tried any fraudulent methods of producing phenomena. It wasn't my idea, Mr. Carlisle. I have to take advice once in a while, you know, from some of the boys who look after my interests."

Stan was erect and the blue eyes were hard. "That warrant was signed by a judge?"

"I presume so."

"And on what grounds was I supposed to be arrested—if you or one of your employees thought he detected trickery?"

"Why, with conspiracy with intent to defraud."

"And how would I have defrauded you, Mr. Grindle? Out of taxi fare from New York?"

The big man frowned. "You understand, I had nothing to do with it. Mr. Anderson—"

"You may tell Mr. Anderson," said the Rev. Carlisle tautly, "that I would be quite capable of suing for false arrest. I have never taken a penny for exercising gifts of mediumship. I never shall. Good night, sir."

He got into the waiting car and said coldly to the driver, "Just to the railroad station—don't drive me all the way in to New York."

Grindle stood gaping after him, then turned and went back to the plant.

Anderson was a good lad, devoted, devoted. Couldn't ask for more loyalty. But God damn it, he didn't understand. He just didn't understand the deeper, the spiritual things of life. Well, from now on Andy would be told to keep his nose out of psychic research.

The others had left the directors' room but Anderson was still there. He was attacking the end of the conference table with mighty heaves, trying to make the light flash.

"Give it up, Andy," the Chief said acidly. "On home. Go on."

"I'll find out how he did it! He did something."

"Andy, you can't find it in your soul anywhere to admit that it might have been an odylic force that you can't see or feel or measure?"

"Nuts, Chief. I know a hustler when I see one."

"I said go home, Andy."

"You're the boss."

As he was leaving Grindle called to him: "And fire the woman you had taking care of Beauty's coat. It's a disgrace—she's been neglected."

Anderson's voice was smoldering but weary. "What is it now, Chief?"

"It's disgusting—Beauty's coat is swarming with fleas."

"Okay, Chief. She gets the gate tomorrow." He walked quickly from the plant, found his car in the parking lot and rammed in the ignition key irritably. That goddamned phoney reverend. He would be just the one to weasel inside the Chief. And the Chief would protect him. But how in the jumping blue blazes of merry hell did he ever turn that light on and off inside the case? Odylic force, balls!

"Is that your odylic force, Reverend?"

"Yeah. That's it, babe. Like it?"

She chuckled, warm and enfolding, beneath him in the dark of the bedroom.

"Wait, lover. Let's rest."

They rested. Stan said, "He's going overboard, all right. He's not so tough—just another chump."

"Go easy with him, Stan."

"I'm easy. Every test a little stronger until he's fattened up for the full-form stuff. There's only one thing—"

"Molly?"

"Yeah, Molly. That dame's going to give us a lot of trouble."

"She can be handled."

"Yeah. But it wears you out, handling. Lilith, I'm sick of the dame. She's like a rock around my neck."

"Patience, darling. There's no one else."

They lay silent for a time, seeing each other with their finger tips and with their mouths.

"Lilith—"

"What, lover?"

"What does that guy really want? I've beaten him over the head with 'forgiveness' but I get only half a response. He doesn't gobble it. There's something else. Okay. We bring back the dead dame. She tells him he's forgiven and everything's jake. But where do we go from there?"

Dr. Lilith Ritter, at the moment in a very unethical but satisfying position in relation to one of her patients, laughed deep in her throat.

"What does he want to *do*? With his first love? Don't be so naïve, lover. He wants to do this . . . and this . . ."

"But—no; that's no good. Not with Molly. She'll never—"

"Oh, yes, she will."

"Lilith, I know that dame. She never stepped out of line once in all the years we been teamed up. I can't sell her on jazzing the chump."

"Yes, you can, darling."

"Christ's sake, *how?*"

The warm mouth closed his and he forgot Molly and the con game which kept him in a torment of scheming. Through their pressed lips Lilith murmured, "I'll tell you when the time comes."

The psychic lamp, provided by the Rev. Carlisle, shed no light except through a single dark-red disc in the center of its tin slide. The medium, dressed in a black silk robe, black silk pajamas and slippers, lay back in an armchair on one side of the billiard-room doorway. Grindle, in his shirtsleeves, sat opposite him, the lamp on a coffee table at his side. Dark curtains covered the door and a faint breeze tugged at them. Carlisle had raised one window in the inner room a few inches for ventilation. It was not open far enough for a man to stick his head through and it had been sealed. Grindle had pressed his signet ring into the hot wax. The other windows were sealed shut. There was a fifteen foot drop to the lawn outside, which sloped down to the river.

Beyond the darkened billiard room the two men waited. The medium's head was thrown back. His left wrist was fastened to Grindle's right by a long strand of copper wire, and he had poured salt water on their wrists.

The heel of the reverend's slipper was pressed tight against the leg of his chair.

Rap!

It seemed to come from the table bearing the red lantern.

Rap!

"Is there one in spirit life speaking?" The medium's words were a hoarse whisper.

Rap! Rap! Rap!

"We greet you. Are conditions favorable? May we turn up the lamp a little?"

Three more raps answered him. Grindle leaned over and raised the lamp's wick until a warning rap commanded him to stop. His big face was intent and ill at ease, but Stan detected no craft or outright skepticism. He was interested, moving in the right direction.

They waited. More silence. Then from beyond the dark draperies of the doorway came another knock—a hollow, musical sound, as if something had struck the window. Grindle started from his chair but the warning, upraised hand of the spiritualist stopped him. Carlisle's breathing came fast now, and heavy, and he seemed to lose consciousness.

The "sitter" began to sweat. Did he imagine a tingling discharge of current at his wrist where the wire was bound?

Another sound, a distinct click, from the billiard room. Then a whole chorus of clicks which he made out to be billiard balls, knocking against one another, sometimes in rhythm, as if they were dancing.

Sweat began to roll from the industrialist's forehead. It was a hot night, but not that hot. His shirt was sticking to his chest and his hands were dripping.

The ghostly billiard game went on; then a white ivory ball rolled out from under the curtains and hit the table-leg between him and the medium.

Carlisle stirred uneasily and a voice came from his stiff lips: "*Hari Aum!* Greetings, newcomer to the Life of Spiritual Truth. Greetings, our new *chela*. Believe not blindly. Believe the proof of the mind given you by the senses. They cannot give you the Truth but they point the Path. Trust my disciple, Stanton Carlisle. He is an instrument on which spiritual forces play as a lover plays his *sitar* beneath the window of his beloved. Greetings, Ezra. A friend has come to you from Spirit Life. *Hari Aum!*"

The resonant, accented chanting broke off. Grindle snapped his attention from the lips of the medium to the curtains before the darkened room. The clicks of billiard balls now sounded closer, as if they were rolling and knocking on the floor just beyond the curtains. He stared, his lips drawn back from his dentures, his breath whistling. A white ball rolled slowly from under the curtains and stopped six inches inside the room where they sat. The red cue ball followed it. Click!

While he watched, the hairs on the back of the big man's neck raised, the skin drew tight over his temples. For in the dim, ruby light a tiny hand felt its way out from under the curtains, groped delicately for the red ball, found it, and rolled it after the white one. Click! And the hand was gone.

With an unconscious shout Grindle leaped up and threw himself after the vanishing hand, only to spin around and claw at the curtains of the doorway to keep himself from falling. For his right wrist was firmly secured by copper wire to the wrist of the medium who was now groaning and gasping, his eyes half open and rolled up, until the whites looked as stark as the eyes of a blind beggar.

Then Grindle felt the room beyond them to be empty and still. He stood, fighting for breath, making no further attempt to enter.

The medium drew a long breath and opened his eyes. "We can remove the wire now. Were there any phenomena of note?"

Grindle nodded, still watching the doorway. "Get me out of this harness, Reverend! I want a look in there."

Stan helped unwind the wire and said, "One favor, Mr. Grindle—I wonder if you could get me a glass of brandy?"

His host poured him one and knocked off two straight ones himself. "All set?"

He drew the curtains and snapped the wall switch.

A reassuring glow fell from the hanging lamp above the billiard table. Stan's hand on his arm restrained him from entering.

"Careful, Mr. Grindle. Remember our test precautions."

The floor had been thickly sprinkled with talcum powder. Now it bore traces, and as Grindle knelt to examine them he saw with a chill that they were the unmistakable bare footprints of a small child.

He rose, wiping his face with a wad of handkerchief. The room had been the scene of grotesque activity. Cues had been taken from their racks and thrust into the open mouths of stuffed sailfish on the wall. The cue chalk had been thrown down and smashed. And everywhere were the tiny footprints.

Carlisle stood in the doorway for a moment, then turned back and sank into his chair and covered his eyes with his hand as if he were very tired.

At last the light in the billiard room snapped off and Grindle stood beside him, pale, breathing heavily. He poured himself another brandy and gave one to the medium.

Ezra Grindle was shaken as no stock-market crash or sudden South American peace treaty could have shaken him. For with a crumb of cue chalk a message had been written on the green felt of the billiard table. It held the answer to a vast, secret, shameful ache inside him—a canker which had festered all these years. Not a soul in the world could know of its existence but himself—a name he had not spoken in thirty-five years. It held the key to an old wrong which he would willingly give a million hard-earned dollars to square with his conscience. A million? Every cent he owned!

The message was in a characterless, copybook hand:

Spunk darling,
We tried to come to you but the force was not strong enough. Maybe next time. I so wanted you to see our boy.
DORRIE

He drew the doors together and locked them. He raised his hand for the bell rope, then dropped it, and poured himself another brandy.

At his side stood the tall, silken figure in black, his face compassionate.

"Let us pray together—not for them, Ezra, but for the living, that the scales may fall from their eyes. . . ."

The train to New York was not due for half an hour and

Mrs. Oakes, who had been visiting her daughter-in-law, had read the time table all wrong; now she would have to wait.

On the station platform she walked up and down to relieve her impatience. Then, on a bench, she saw a little figure stretched out, its head pillowed on its arms. Her heart was touched. She shook him gently by the shoulder. "What's the matter, little man? Are you lost? Were you supposed to meet mamma or papa here at the station?"

The sleeper sat up with a snarl. He was the size of a child; but was dressed in a striped suit and a pink shirt with a miniature necktie. And under his button nose was a mustache!

The mustachioed baby pulled a cigarette from his pocket and raked a kitchen match on the seat of his trousers. He lit the cigarette and was about to snap away the match when he grinned up at her from his evil, old baby face, thrust one hand into his coat and drew out a postcard, holding the match so she could see it.

Mrs. Oakes thought she would have a stroke. She tried to run away, but she couldn't. Then the train came and the horrible little creature swung aboard, winking at her.

The Tower

rises from earth to heaven but
avenging lightning finds its walls.

B EYOND the garden wall a row of poplars rustled in the
night wind. The moon had not risen; in the gentle darkness the voice was a monotonous, musical ripple, as soothing
as the splash of a fountain.

"Your mind is quiet . . . a lamp in a sheltered corner where
the flame does not flicker. Your body is relaxed. Your heart is
at peace. Your mind is perfectly clear but at ease. Nothing
troubles you. Your mind is a still, calm pool without a ripple . . ."

The big man had a white scarf knotted around his neck and
tucked into his tweed jacket. He let his hands lie easily on the
arms of the deck chair; his legs in tawny flannel trousers were
propped on the footrest.

Beside him the spiritualist in black was all but invisible
under the starlight.

"Close your eyes. When you open them again, stare straight
at the garden wall and tell me what you see."

"It's faint—" Grindle's voice was flaccid and dreamy. All the bite had gone out of it.

"Yes?"

"It's growing clearer. It's a city. A golden city. Towers. Domes. A beautiful city—and now it's gone."

The Rev. Carlisle slipped back into his pocket a "Patent Ghost Thrower, complete with batteries and lenses, to hold 16 millimeter film, $7.98" from a spiritualists' supply house in Chicago.

"You have seen it—the City of Spiritual Light. My control spirit, Ramakrishna, has directed us to build it. It will be patterned after a similar city—which few outsiders have ever seen—in the mountains of Nepal. I myself was permitted to see it under Ramakrishna's guidance. I was teleported physically to the spot. I was leaving the church one snowy night last winter when I felt Ramakrishna near me."

The tycoon's head was nodding belief.

"I was walking through the snow when suddenly the street vanished; it became a stony mountain path. I felt light as air but my feet seemed heavy. That was the altitude. Then, stretching below me in a little valley, I saw the City—just as you have described your vision of it a few moments ago. And I knew that it had been revealed to me for a purpose. Once this realization dawned on me the mountains, the rugged outline of bare peaks and glaciers, softened. They seemed to close in and I was back on the doorstep of the Church of the Heavenly Message. But there, stretching away up the sidewalk, were my own tracks of a few minutes before! A few yards farther on they *stopped. I had dematerialized when I reached that spot.*"

Grindle said, "A wonderful experience. I've heard of such experiences. The holy men of Tibet claim to have them. But I never thought I'd ever meet a man who had reached such psychic heights." His voice was humble and old and a little foolish. Then he started up from his chair.

A vague light had drifted past on the garden wall. It had the shape of a young girl.

The medium said, "You must relax. No tension. All receptivity—all love."

Grindle settled back.

The sky clouded over; the darkness deepened. This time he did not stir but said hopefully, "I—I think I see something, out there by the sundial. Something moving—a spot of light."

It was true. By the shadows at the base of the sundial was a spot of greenish light. Expanding slowly, it moved toward them, a cloud of glowing vapor taking form.

This time the industrialist sat up in spite of Stan's reproving hand on his wrist.

The apparition drifted closer until they could see that it was a girl, dressed in shining garments which floated about her like a mist. Her dark hair was bound by a tiara in which seven bright jewels shone by their own cold light. She seemed to move a few inches above the ground, drifting toward them down a breath of night wind.

The believer's voice had become a feeble, despairing whisper. "Dorrie— Could it be Dorrie?"

"My dear . . ." The materialized form spoke in a voice which seemed part of the garden and the night. "It's Dorrie. But only for a moment. I can't stay . . . it's hard . . . hard to come back, darling."

The Rev. Carlisle's hand tightened on the older man's arm; but the clergyman himself seemed to have passed into a deep trance.

The ghostly figure was fading. It receded, lost outline, sank into a single dot of green glow and then vanished.

"Dorrie—Dorrie—come back. Please come back. Please—" He was on his knees now by the sundial, where the light had disappeared. His broad stern in the tawny slacks was toward Stan, who could have planted a kick right in the middle of it.

Grindle knelt for several seconds, then got to his feet heavily and dropped back into the deck chair, covering his face with his hands.

Beside him the Rev. Carlisle stirred and sat up. "Was there a full materialization? I 'went under' very rapidly. I could feel the force leaving me as the light grew. What happened?"

"I—I saw an old friend."

Molly was so happy she could cry. It had been a long time since they'd had anything like a holiday together. Stan had been acting so screwy she was afraid he was living on Queer Street. And then, all of a sudden, these three days—just driving anywhere, stopping at chicken-dinner shacks and roadhouses. Dancing and, in the daytime, going for a swim wherever a lake looked good. It was heaven; she got sad thinking about going back to the flat and starting all over again, doing nothing, just waiting for Stan to come home or something.

Stan was still awfully jumpy and sometimes you'd talk to him and he'd seem to be listening and then he'd say, "What was that, kid?" and you'd have to go through it all over again. But it was great to be getting around like this.

Stan looked nice in a bathing suit. That was something to be thankful for. Some guys were sweet guys but too skinny or with a pot. Stan was just right. She guessed they were both just right by the way other fellows ran their eyes over her chassis when she stepped out on a diving board. What hippos some girls her own age turned out to be!

The Great Stanton pulled himself out of the water and lay beside her on the float. They had the lake all to themselves except for some kids at the other end. He sat looking down at her and then leaned over and kissed her. Molly threw her arms around him. "Oh, honey, don't ever let anything bust us up, honey! All I want is you, Stan."

He slid his arm under her head. "Baby, how'd you like to do this every day in the year? Huh? Well, if this deal goes over we're set. And every day is Christmas."

Molly had a cold, sinking feeling inside her. He had said that so many times. Once it was "Get the house away from old Mrs. Peabody." Always something. She didn't really believe it any more.

He felt her go limp. "Molly! Molly! look at me! Honest to God, this is the thing I've been building toward ever since I started in this racket. I've run myself almost into the nut college building the guy. My foot's never slipped yet. And if you think that guy is easy to handle—"

She pressed her face against his chest and began to cry. "Stan, why do we have to be this way? He seemed like a nice sort of old guy—from what I could tell in the dark up there. I felt like an awful heel, honest. I don't mind taking some

guy that thinks he's wise and is trying to be a cheater himself—"

He held her tighter. "Molly, we're in this deeper than you
have any idea. That guy has millions. He has a whole private
army. You ought to see that joint in Jersey. It's like a fort. If
we step on the flypaper from now on they'll turn that bunch
of private cops loose on us like a pack of bloodhounds. They'll
find us no matter where we scram to. We've got to go into it
all the way. I've put him in touch with his girl that died when
he was a kid in college. He wants to make it up to her somehow. Money doesn't mean anything to that guy. He's willing
to give anything—just to get square with his conscience. He's
overboard on the spook dodge. He's letting his business run
itself. He's living on Dream Street."

Stan had straightened the girl until she sat on the edge of
the float, her feet in the cool water. He took both her hands.
"Baby, from now on it depends on you. Whether every day
is Christmas and I can get my nerves back in shape and act
like a human being—or whether the wolves start howling for
our blood."

Molly's eyes were big now and Stan bored in.

"Now, look. This is what we've got to do."

When she had heard it she sat for a moment with her hair
falling over her face, looking down at her bare thighs and the
bright yellow of the bathing suit. She ran her hands slowly
from her crotch down to her knees. They felt cold and the
water was cold around her feet; she raised them and drew
them up, leaning her head on her knees, not looking at the
man beside her.

"That's how it is, kid. I'll make it up to you. Honest to
God, baby. Don't you see—this is the only thing that can put
us back together again?"

Suddenly she stood up, throwing her hair back. Her fingers
trembled as she drew on her cap. Then, without looking at
him, she dived from the float and set out for the dock. Stan
was churning the water with his legs, trying to overtake her.
She reached the dock and raced up the ladder with him close
behind. When they got to the cabin he bolted the door.

Molly whipped off her cap and shook out her hair. Then
she slipped the bathing suit down and left it on the floor in a

sodden pile, stepping out of it. Stan watched her, his heart thumping with anxiety. Now.

She said, "Stan, take a good look. Make believe you never saw me undressed before. I mean it. Now then, tell me, if I— if I—do it—will I look any different? To you?"

He kissed her so hard that her lip began to bleed.

Lilith opened the door for him and they went into her office. She sat behind the desk, where the contents of a tray of star sapphires lay spread out on a square of black velvet. She tumbled them back into the tray and swung out the false drawer fronts on the right-hand side of the desk, revealing the steel door of a safe. She put the gems away and spun the dial twice, then closed the panel and took a cigarette from the box on her desk.

Stan held his lighter. "She's hooked."

"The virtuous Molly?"

"Sure. It took some selling but she'll play ball. Now let's lay out the moves from here on in. I planted the City of Spiritual Light with him just before the first full-form job in the garden up at his place. Next séance, we'll start warming him up to the idea of kicking in some dough."

Stan had brought with him a portfolio. He drew the tapes and opened it, laying an architect's drawing before the woman who claimed to be a psychiatrist.

A bird's-eye view of a dream city, clustered about a central tower which rose from the desert amid a circling park of palms.

"Very pretty, Reverend."

"There's more." He lifted out the drawing. Beneath it was a Geodetic Survey map of an Arizona county. Drawn in red ink and carefully lettered was the location of the City.

Lilith nodded. "And this is the spot where you are going to take off into thin air? That's very well thought out, darling." She frowned, looking at the map. "Where are you going to hide the second car?"

"I'm going to leave it somewhere in this jerk town, marked over here."

"No good, darling. It must be hidden out of town—somewhere in the desert. Let's go through it again. You go out by train; you buy a car in Texas and drive into this town of Peñas, where you put it in a garage. Then you hire a car in Peñas. You drive your new car outside the town and park it. You walk back, pick up the hired car, go to your own car, tow it to the spot near the site of the City and hide it well and drive back to Peñas in the hired car. You come back here by train. Correct?"

"Right. Then when we get ready to blow I drive out there, telling him to follow me in a day or two. I drive my car out to the site of the City and just off the highway. I get out, walk a hundred yards straight into the sand, then backtrack to the car, and from there follow the rock to the highway; hike on up the highway and pull out the new car. And drive like hell back east. And I've disappeared in the middle of the desert. He'll come along, following this map, and find the car. He'll follow the footprints—and blam! Gone! And me carrying all that dough. Ain't it a shame?"

She laughed softly at him over her cigarette. "It's complicated, Stan. But you'll probably be able to get away with it. I believe you could make a living selling spiritualism to other mediums."

"Say!" He leaned forward, his eyes narrow, thinking quickly; then he relaxed and shook his head. "No go. It's peanuts—they never have any real dough. Industry is the only place where dough is any more."

She looked back at the idealized drawing of the City of Spiritual Light. "There's one thing, Stan, that I wish you'd tell me."

"Sure, baby."

"How *did* you move that precision balance out at his factory?"

The Rev. Carlisle laughed. It was something he very seldom did; but now he laughed in a high key and was still bubbling when he spoke. "I'll tell you, doctor, as soon as we've got the chump cleaned. It's a promise."

"Very well. It was probably something ridiculous."

Stan changed the subject. "I'll get busy this week and rent a shack jammed right up next to his estate."

Dr. Lilith was filing a thumbnail. "Don't be so dramatic, darling. Yonkers is good enough. I agree that it should be in

Westchester. The City of Light location will spread any hue and cry out in the southwest. But I don't think there will be any hue and cry. However, he may take the matter up with this Mr. Anderson. Don't forget that he has some very shrewd men working for him. Mr. Anderson would try to outthink you. He knows he is dealing with an ingenious man. He would start his hunt for you on his own hook, and it would begin at the country place and fan out from there. No. Yonkers is neither here nor there." She dropped the nail file back into the drawer. "How are you going to brush off the faithful Penelope?"

"Molly?" Stan was pacing the room, his hands in his pockets. "I'll give her a couple of grand and tell her to meet me some place in Florida. All she needs is a few bucks and a race track to keep her happy. She'll be in a daze as long as the dough holds out. If she wins a little she'll forget the day of the month and everything else. When she's broke she can go back to the carny and work the Ten-in-One. Or get a job as a hat check somewhere. She won't starve."

Lilith stood up and came over to him, stretching tailored gray arms up around his neck and giving him her mouth.

They swayed for a moment and Stan rubbed his cheek against the smooth hair. Then she pushed him away. "Run along, Reverend. I've a patient due in five minutes."

When Grindle got to the church he found the Rev. Carlisle in his study upstairs. On the desk, spread out under the lamp, were letters with currency clipped to them. Stan picked up one which held a ten-dollar bill and read aloud: " 'I know the wonderful future which the City holds for us all in the line of a pooling of our spiritual forces. What a joy it will be when our friends and loved ones in spirit life can be with us as often as we wish. God bless you, Stanton Carlisle.' Well, the rest of it is of no consequence." He smiled at the ten-spot. "It's very touching, Ezra, some of the letters. Many of them are from uneducated people—yet their faith is so pure and unselfish. The City will be a dream come true. They should thank Ramakrishna, though, for everything I do is done with the hand of that great spiritual leader on my shoulder."

Grindle sat staring at the ember of his cigar. "I'll do my

share, Stanton. I'm pretty well fixed. I'll do what I can. This idea of pooling all the spiritual power in one spot makes sense to me. Same as any business merger. But my part isn't easy: I've built such a wall around myself that I can't get out any more. They're all devoted, loyal people. None better. But they won't understand. I'll have to think of some way . . ."

While the turntable revolved Stan leaned over the machine with a clothesbrush, keeping the blank record clear of acetate threads cut by the recording needle. Suddenly he raised the needle arm, tore the record from the turntable and slung it into a corner. "God damn it, kid, you've got to sound *wistful*. The dame and the old guy can be together forever, frigging like rabbits, only he's got to help the church build this City. Now take it again. And get in there and *sell* it."

Molly was almost crying. She turned back the pages of her script and leaned closer to the mike, watching Stan put on a new record blank.

I can't *act*. Oh, golly, I've got to try!

She started to cry, forcing the words out between catches of her breath, struggling through it and winking so she could still read the script. Toward the end she was crying so hard she couldn't see it at all and ad-libbed the rest. She was waiting any minute for Stan to blow up and bawl her out, but he let it ride.

When she was through he raised the recording arm. "That's the stuff, kid—plenty of emotion. Let's listen to it."

The playback sounded awful, Molly thought. All full of weepy noises and gasps. But Stan was grinning. He nodded to her and when he had heard it all he said, "That's the stuff, kid. That'll shake him loose. You wait and see. You think that sounds corny? Forget it. The chump's overboard. I could roll up my pants legs, throw a sheet over me, and he'd take me for his long lost love. But we're going to need one circus to nail him to the cross."

Moonlight struck through fern leaves in the conservatory; the rest of the church was in darkness. The minutes slid by— twenty of them by Stan's luminous-dial watch. He shifted his feet and found the floor board by the organ.

A tinkle came from the trumpet lying on the lectern, across the Bible. Grindle leaned forward, clenching his fists.

The trumpet stirred, then floated in air, moonlight winking from its aluminum surface. The chump moaned, cupping one hand behind his ear so as not to miss a single syllable. But the voice came thin and clear, a little metallic.

"Spunk darling . . . this is Dorrie. I know you haven't forgotten us, Spunk. I hope to materialize enough for you to touch me soon. It's wonderful . . . that you are with us in building the City. We can be together there, darling. Really together. We will be. Believe that. I'm so glad that you are working with us at last. And don't worry about Andy and the rest. Many of them will come to accept the truth of survival in time. Don't try to convince them now. And don't alarm them: you have some securities—some bonds—that they don't know about. That is the way out, dear. And let no one know how much you give, for all must feel that the City is their very own. Give your part to Stanton, bless him. And don't forget, darling . . . next time I come to you . . . I shall come as a bride."

It was late when Stan pressed the buzzer outside the apartment. Lilith opened the door, frowning. "I don't like your coming here so much, Stan. Somebody might see you."

He said nothing but hurried in and threw his brief case on her desk, tugging at the straps. Lilith closed the Venetian blinds a little tighter.

From the case he dug a helter-skelter of papers, the faked letters with currency still attached, which Lilith gathered up, pulling off the cash. She emptied them into the fireplace and put a match to them.

Stan was feverishly smoothing out bills and arranging them in stacks. "The convincer boodle did the trick, babe. I took every cent I had in the sock—eleven grand." He patted the piles of bills. "Jesus, what blood I've sweat to get it in this goddamned racket! But here's the payoff."

In two legal-sized brown envelopes were thick oblong packets. He drew them out and broke confining strips of paper. "There it is, baby. How many people ever see that much cash in all their lives? *One hundred and fifty thousand!* Look at it!

Look at it! And the McCoy. I never saw *one* five-yard note before. God almighty, we're lousy with 'em!"

The doctor was amused. "We'd better put them away, darling. That's a lot of money for one person to carry in his pocket. You might spend it foolishly."

While Stan gathered the crumpled bills of the convincer into a wad and slipped a rubber band around them Lilith assembled the "take" and placed it carefully back in the brown envelopes, sealing them. She swung open the dummy drawers of the desk and when she dialed the combination Stan automatically tried to get a peek but her shoulder was in the way. Lilith put the money away and spun the dial.

When she stood up the Rev. Carlisle was staring into the polished mahogany of the desktop, his face flushed. "Wounds of God! A hundred and fifty grand!"

She handed him a double brandy and poured one for herself. He took the glass from her hand and set it on the bookcase. Then he slid his arms around her roughly. "Baby, baby— God, this high class layout had me dizzy but I get it good and clear now. Baby, you're nothing but a *gonif* and I love you. We're a couple of hustlers, a pair of big-time thieves. How does it feel?"

He was grinning down at her, squeezing her ribs until they hurt. She took his wrists and loosened them a little, closing her eyes and raising her face to him. "You're wonderful, darling, the way you read my mind."

Dr. Lilith Ritter did not go to bed right away. After Carlisle had gone she sat smoking and drawing careful parallel lines on a scratch pad. Once she turned back to the file cabinet behind her and took out a folder identified only by a number. It contained a chart on graph paper, an idea with which she often played, an emotional barometric chart, marked with dates, showing a jagged rise and fall. It was an emotional diagram of Stanton Carlisle. She did not trust it entirely; but the curve had reached a high point, and on four other occasions such peaks had been followed by sudden drops into depression, instability, and black despair. Finally she put the folder away, undressed, and drew a tub of hot water into which she threw pine bath salts.

She lay in the water reading the financial section of the evening paper. Grindle Motors was off two points; it would go still lower before it started to rise again. Lilith's smile, as she tossed the paper to the floor and snuggled deeper in the comforting, scented warmth, was the smile of a well-fed kitten.

With a twist of triumphant glee her mind drew pictures of her two sisters as she had seen them last: Mina, spare and virginal, still proud of a Phi Beta key after all these years of beating Latin into the heads of brats. And Gretel—still looking like a wax angel off a *Tannenbaum*, with half a lung left to breathe with and a positive Wassermann.

Old Fritz Ritter had kept a State Street saloon called "The Dutchman's." His daughter Lille smiled. "I must be part Swedish," she said softly to a bar of pink soap, molded in the form of a lotus. "The middle way."

For two days Ezra Grindle had dropped from sight. His legal staff, his chauffeur-bodyguard, and his private chief of police, Melvin Anderson, had conferred again and again as to where the boss might be, without getting anywhere. Anderson knew little about the Old Man's activities lately and was afraid to stick a tail on him for fear he would find out about it. The Chief was cagy as hell. The lawyers learned that Grindle had not touched his checking accounts. Nothing, at least, had cleared. But he had been into one of his safe-deposit boxes. It was difficult to find out what securities the Chief had liquidated or how much. And where was he? He had left word: "I shall be away on business."

The lawyers went over the will. If he had made a new one they would have drawn it. All his faithful employees were remembered, and the rest was distributed to his pet colleges, medical foundations, and homes for unwed mothers. They would just have to wait.

In a tiny bedroom, lit only by a skylight, on the top floor of the Church of the Heavenly Message, the great man sat with his glasses off and his dentures in a glass of water beside him. He was wearing the yellow robe of a Tibetan lama. On the pale green wall of his cell was painted in Sanskrit the word *Aum*, symbol of man's eternal quest for spiritual At-One-ness with the All Soul of the Universe.

At intervals Grindle meditated on spiritual things but often he simply daydreamed in the cool quiet. The dreams took him back to the campus, and her lips when he kissed her for the first time. She wanted to see his college and he was showing her the buildings which stood there in the night, illumined, important. Afterward they strolled in Morningside Park, and he kissed her again. That was the first time she let him touch her breast . . .

He went over every detail. It was amazing what meditation could do. He remembered things he had forgotten for years. Only Dorrie's face eluded him; he could not bring it back. He could recall the pattern of her skirt, that day at Coney Island, but not her face.

With the pleasure of pressing a sore tooth, he brought back the evening, walking on the Drive, when she told him what she had been afraid of; and now it was true. It seemed that no time had passed at all. His frantic inquiries for a doctor. He had exams the very time she was supposed to go; she went by herself. Afterwards, up in the room, she seemed all right, only shaky and depressed. What a hellish week that was! He had to put her out of his mind until exams were through. Then the next night—they told him she was in the hospital and he ran all the way over there and they wouldn't let him in. And when he did get in Dorrie wouldn't speak to him. It went around and around in his head—like a Tibetan prayer wheel. But it was slowing down. Soon it would stop and they would be Joined in Spirit.

The skylight had grown a darker blue. The Rev. Carlisle brought him a light supper and gave him further Spiritual Instruction. When the night had come there was a tap at the door and Carlisle entered, carrying with both hands a votive candle in a cup of ruby-red glass. "Let us go to the chapel."

Grindle had never seen that room before. A large divan was piled with silk cushions and in an alcove was a couch covered with black velvet for the medium. The entire room was hung in folds of dark drapery. If there were any windows they were covered.

The clergyman led his disciple to the divan; taking his hand he pressed him back against the cushions. "You are at peace. Rest, rest."

Grindle felt foggy and vague. The bowl of jasmine tea which he had been given for supper had seemed bitter. Now his head was swimming lightly and reality retreated to arm's length.

The medium placed the votive candle in a sconce on the far wall; its flickering light deepened the shadows of that dead-black room and, on looking down, the bridegroom could barely make out the form of his own hands. His eyesight blurred.

Carlisle was chanting something which sounded like Sanskrit, then a brief prayer in English which reminded Grindle of the marriage service; but somehow the words refused to fit together in his mind.

In the alcove the medium lay back on the couch and the black curtains flowed together by their own power. Or was it the medium's odylic force?

They waited.

From far away, from hundreds of miles it seemed, came the sound of wind, a great rushing of wind or the beating of giant wings. Then it died and there arose the soft, tinkling notes of a *sitar.*

Suddenly from the alcove which served as a cabinet came the trumpet voice of the control spirit, Ramakrishna, last of India's saints, greatest of *bhakti* yogis, preacher of the love of God.

"*Hari Aum!* Greetings, my beloved new disciple. Prepare your mind for its juncture with the Spirit. On the seashore of endless worlds, as children meet, you will join for an instant the Life of Spirit. Love has made smooth your path—for all Love is but the Love of God. *Aum.*"

Ghostly music began again. From the curtains before the alcove a light flashed, then a sinuous coil of glowing vapor poured from between them, lying in a pool of mist close to the floor. It swelled and seemed to foam from the cabinet in a cascade. Its brilliance grew, until on looking down Grindle could see his own figure illumined by the cold flaming brilliance of the light. It rose now and pulsated, glowing bright and then dimming slightly. The air was filled with a mighty rhythm, like the heart of a titan, roaring and rushing.

The pool of luminous matter began to take form. It swayed as a cocoon might sway from a moth's emerging. It became a cocoon, holding something dark in its center. Then it split and drew back toward the cabinet, revealing the form of a girl, lying on a bed of light, but illumined only by the stuff around her. She was naked, her head resting on one bent arm.

Grindle sank to his knees. "Dorrie—Dorrie—"

She opened her eyes, sat up and then rose, modestly drawing a film of glowing mist over her body. The old man groped forward awkwardly on his knees, reaching up to her. As he drew near, the luminous cloud fell back and vanished. The girl stood, white and tall, in the flicker of the votive candle across the room; and as she gazed down at him her hair fell over her face.

"Dorrie—my pet—my honey love—my bride . . ."

He picked her up in his arms, overjoyed at the complete materialization, at the lifelike smoothness of her body—she was so heartbreakingly earthly.

Inside the cabinet the Rev. Carlisle was busy packing yards of luminous-painted China silk back into the hem of the curtains. Once he put his eye to the opening and his lips drew back over his teeth. Why did people look so filthy and ridiculous to anyone watching? Christ!

The second time in his life he had seen it. Filth.

The bride and bridegroom were motionless now.

It was up to Molly to break away and get back to the cabinet. Stan turned the switch and the rhythmic, pounding heartbeat filled the room, growing louder. He tossed one end of the luminous silk through the curtains.

The quiet forms on the divan stirred, and Stan could see the big man burrowing his face between Molly's breasts. "No—Dorrie—my own, my precious—I can't let you go! Take me with you, Dorrie—I don't want earth life without you . . ."

She struggled out of his arms; but the bridegroom seized her around the waist, rubbing his forehead against her belly.

Stan grabbed the aluminum trumpet. "Ezra—my beloved disciple—have courage. She must return to us. The force is growing weaker. In the City—"

"No! Dorrie—I must—I—once more . . ."

This time another voice answered him. It was not a spiritual voice. It was the voice of a panicky showgirl who has more than she can handle. "Hey, quit it, for God's sake! Stan! Stan! *Stan!*"

Oh, bleeding wounds of Christ, the dumb, stupid bitch!

The Rev. Carlisle tore the curtains apart. Molly was twisting and kicking; the old man was like one possessed. In his pent-up soul the dam had broken, and the sedative Stan had loaded into his tea had worn off.

Grindle clutched the squirming girl until she was jerked from his hands.

"Stan! For God's sake *get me out of here! Get me out!*"

Grindle stood paralyzed. For in the dim, red, flickering light he saw the face of his spiritual mentor, the Rev. Stanton Carlisle; it was snarling. Then a fist came up and landed on the chin of the spirit bride. She dropped to the floor, knees gaping obscenely.

Now the hideous face was shouting at Grindle himself. "You goddamned hypocrite! Forgiveness? All you wanted was a piece of ass!" Knuckles smashed his cheekbone and Grindle bounced back on the divan.

His brain had stopped working. He lay looking stupidly at the red, jumping light. A door opened somewhere and somebody ran out. He stared at the leaping red flame, not thinking, not living, just watching. He heard something stir near him but couldn't turn his head. He heard sounds of crying and somebody say "Oh, good God," and then the faltering slap of bare feet and a girl's voice sobbing and a fumbling for a door and a door opening and staying open against a hallway where there was a dim yellow light but it all made no sense to Ezra Grindle and he preferred to watch the little flame in its ruby-red glass cup flickering and dancing up and down. He lay there a long time.

Below him the front door slammed once. But it didn't seem to matter what happened. He groaned and turned his head.

One arm—his left one—numb. And all one side of his face frozen. He sat up and stared about him. This dark room—there had been a girl's body. Dorrie's. She was a bride. It was his wedding. The Rev. Carlisle—

Slowly he remembered things in little snatches. But was it the Rev. Carlisle who hit Dorrie? Or was it an evil spirit impersonating him?

Grindle stood up, having trouble balancing. Then he shuffled over to the door. One leg was numb. He was in the hallway of a house. There was a room upstairs.

He held onto the banister and took a step but he fell against the wall and sank to his knees. He crawled, step by step, dragging his left leg, which felt wooden and dead. He had to get upstairs for some reason—his clothes were upstairs—but everybody had gone—dematerialized.

He found the cell with the green walls and hauled himself to his feet, his breath whistling. What had happened? His clothes were still in the closet. Have to put them on. There was a wedding. There was a bride. Dorrie. They had been together, just as Stan had foretold. Stanton— Where was he? Why had Stanton left him this way?

Grindle was annoyed with Stanton. He struggled to get his trousers on and his shirt. Have to sit down and rest. Dorrie was there in spirit. Who else could it be but Dorrie, his Dorrie, come back again? Had she lived after all? And come back to him? A dream—?

But they had gone.

Glasses. Wallet. Keys. Cigar case.

He limped back into the hall. Stairs again, a mile of them going steeply down. Hold on. Have to hold on tight. Andy! Where was Andy and why had he let him get caught this way in a house with so many stairs and what had hurt his leg? With a sudden surge of anger Grindle wondered if he had been kidnapped. Shot? Slugged over the head? There were desperate men who might—*the mob rule grows ever more menacing, even as we sit here tonight, gentlemen, enjoying our cigars and our . . .* That was from a speech.

And the door to that black room open.

Grindle felt as if twenty years had fallen over him like a blanket. Twenty more years. He stood looking into the dark. There was a cabinet over there, and a single splash of green light still lay on the floor.

"Stanton! Dorrie! Stanton, where are you!"

Halfway across the room he stumbled and crawled the rest

of the way to the pool of light. But it wasn't moist and musky, like Dorrie. It felt like fabric.

"Stanton!"

Grindle struck a match and found a wall switch. The light revealed that the patch of luminous vapor was a piece of white silk sticking out from the bottom hem of the black curtains in the alcove.

But Stanton had struck Dorrie!

He drew aside the curtains. There was the couch, all right. Maybe Stanton had fallen behind it when the evil presence— this was Thursday? I've missed the board meeting. They would hold it without me; too important. I should have been there, to act as a sea anchor on Graingerford. But Russell would be there. Dependable man. But could Russell convince them by himself of the soundness of the colored-labor policy? The competition was doing it—it was a natural. Graingerford be damned.

On the floor by the couch lay a control box with several switches on its bakelite panel. Grindle turned one.

Above him began the faint, ghostly music of a *sitar*. Another turn of the switch and it stopped.

He sat on the medium's couch for a moment, holding the box on his knees, the wire trailing from it underneath the black velvet cover toward the wall. A second switch produced the cosmic heartbeat and the rushing wind. Another— *"Hari Aum!"*

At the sound of Ramakrishna's voice he snapped it off. The click of the switch seemed to turn on his own reason. In one jagged, searing flash he saw everything. The long build-up, the psychic aura, the barrage of suggestion, the manufactured miracles.

Dorrie— But how, in heaven's name, did that sanctimonious devil find out about Dorrie? I've never spoken her name all these years—not even to Dr. Ritter. Even the doctor doesn't know about Dorrie or how she died.

The villain must be genuinely psychic. Or some debased telepathic power. A fearful thought—such a black heart and such uncanny powers. Maybe Dr. Ritter can explain it.

Downstairs. Got to get downstairs. Telephone. In that devil's office—

He made it.

"Andy? I'm perfectly all right—just can't talk very plain. Something's the matter with one side of my face. Probably neuralgia. Andy, for the Lord's sake, stop fussing. I tell you I'm all right. It doesn't matter where I am. Now keep quiet and listen. Get Dr. Samuels. Get him out of bed and have him up home when I get there. I'll be there in two hours. I want a checkup. Yes, this evening. What time is it? Get Russell up there too. I've got to find out what happened at the meeting this morning."

The voice at the other end of the wire was frantic. Grindle listened for a time and then said, "Never mind, Andy. I've just been—away."

"One question, Chief. Are you with that spirit preacher?"

The Chief's voice grew clearer. "Andy—I forbid you ever to mention that man's name to me again! That's an order. You and everyone else in the organization. Is that clear? And I forbid anyone to ask me where I've been. I know what I'm doing. This is final."

"Okay, Chief. The curtain is down."

He made two more calls. One was for a cab and the other was to Dr. Lilith Ritter. There was one chamber in his brain that wasn't functioning yet. He didn't dare open it until he was safely in Dr. Ritter's office.

Molly had not stopped for clothes. She pulled on her shoes, threw a coat around her, grabbed her purse, and ran from that awful house. She ran all the way home.

In the flat Buster miaowed to her, but she gave him a quick pat. "Not now, sugar. Mamma has to scram. Oh, my God!"

She heaved a suitcase onto the bed and threw into it everything small and valuable she could see. Still crying in little bubbling starts, she drew on the first panties and bra that came out of a drawer; she got into the first dress she touched in the closet, shut the keyster, and put Buster in a big paper bag.

"Oh, my God, I've got to hurry." Play dumb and give them an Irish name. "I've got to hurry, somewhere. Stan—oh, damn you, damn you, damn you, I *don't* feel dirty! He was just as clean as you, you damn cheap hustler. Oh—Daddy—"

The hotel people were nice about Buster. She expected cops any minute but nothing happened. And the address she found in the *Billboard* was the right one. A reply to her telegram got back early the next morning:

> SENDING DOUGH NEED GIRL SWORD CABINET
> ACT COME HOME SWEETHEART
>
> ZEENA

CARD XV

Justice

holds in one hand a balance, in the other a sword.

LILITH opened the door; she said nothing until they were in the office and she had seated herself behind the desk, asking softly, "Did she?"

Stan had discarded clerical bib and collar. He was sweating, his mouth cottony. "She went all the way. Then she blew up. I—I knocked out the pair of them and left them there."

Lilith's eyes half closed. "Was that necessary?"

"Necessary? Wounds of God! Don't you think I tried to weasel out of it? The old bastard was like a stallion kicking down a stall to get into a mare. I dropped both of them and beat it."

Lilith was drawing on her gloves. She took a cigarette from her purse. "Stan, it may be some time before I can meet you." She swung open the panel and dialed the safe combination. "He may come to me—I'll try to persuade him not to hunt for you." She laid the convincer wad and the two brown envelopes on the desk. "I don't want to keep this any longer, Stan."

When he had stuffed the money into his pockets Lilith smiled. "Don't get panicky. He won't be able to start any action against you for several hours. How hard did you hit him?"

"I just pushed him. I don't think he was all the way out."

"How badly is the girl hurt?"

"For God's sake, she isn't *hurt*! I just dropped her; she'll come out of it quick. If she stays groggy it will give the chump something to worry about: what to do with her. If she gets clear she'll head straight back to the flat and wait for me. She'll have a good long wait. I've got the keyster parked uptown in a check room. The phoney credentials and everything. If Molly had any brains she could put the con on that mark for hush money: claim he attacked her in the dark séance room. Christ, why didn't I think of that angle sooner? But it's sour now. I'm on my way."

He lifted Lilith's face and kissed her, but the lips were cool and placid. Stan was staring down into her eyes. "It's going to be a long time, baby, before we get together."

She stood up and moved closer to him. "Don't write to me, Stan. And don't get drunk. Take sedative pills if you have to, but don't get drunk. Promise me."

"Sure. Where you going to write to me?"

"Charles Beveridge, General Delivery, Yonkers."

"Kiss me."

This time her mouth was warm.

At the door he slid his arm around her, cupping her breast with his hand, and kissed her again. Suddenly he drew up, his face sharp with alarm. "Wait a minute, baby. He's going to start thinking back on who tipped me to that abortion. And he's going to think straight to you! Come on, sweetheart, we've both got to scram."

Lilith laughed: two sharp notes like the bark of a fox. "He doesn't know that I know that. I worked it out from things he *wouldn't* say." Her eyes were still laughing. "Don't tell me how to look out for myself, lover. Tell me—" A black-gloved hand pressed his arm. "Tell me how you made that precision balance move!"

He grinned and said over his shoulder, "Yonkers," as he walked swiftly out of the door.

Mustn't use the car. Cab drivers remember people. Subway to Grand Central. Walk, do not run, to the nearest exit. One hundred and fifty grand. Christ, I could hire a flock of private cops myself.

In a dressing room under the station he opened the traveling bag and pulled out a shirt and a light suit. There was a fifth of Hennessy; he uncapped the bottle for a short one.

A hundred and fifty grand. Standing in his underwear he fastened on a money vest with twelve pockets. Then he took up the roll of currency—one handful—his profits from the church racket. Take a fifty and a few twenties and stash the rest away.

Snapping off the rubber band from the fat roll he peeled off the fifty. The next bill was a single. And the one after it. But he hadn't cluttered up the convincer boodle with singles! Had he added any money to the pile that night in Lilith's office? Singles!

He spread out the wad, passing the bills from one hand to the other. Then he turned so that the light above the wash bowl would fall on them and riffled through them again. Except for the outside fifty the whole works was nothing but ones!

Stan's eyebrows began to itch and he dug at them with his knuckles. His hands smelled of money and faint perfume from bills carried by women.

The Great Stanton took another pull of brandy and sat down carefully on the white dressing stool. What the hell had gone sour now? Counting over showed three hundred and eighty-three dollars in the boodle. There had been eleven thousand—and the "take"? Good Christ!

He let the dollars fall to the floor and snatched at one of the brown envelopes, cutting his thumb as he tore it open.

There was a shuffle of feet outside and the attendant's white duck trousers appeared beneath the door. "You all right in there, sir?"

"Yeah, yeah, sure."

This pile ought to be all five-century notes—

"You ain't feeling faint, is you, mister?"

Oh, good God, leave me alone. "No. I'm okay, I tell you."

"Well, that's fine, sir. I just thought I heard noise like some gentleman having a fit. Gentleman have a fit in here last week and I had to crawl under the door and hold him down. Had to get the porter, mop up all the blood where he cut his self."

"For God's sake, man, *let me get dressed!*" Stan grabbed a dollar from the scattered bills at his feet and held it under the door.

"Oh—oh! Thank *you*, sir. Thank *you*."

Stan tore off the brown paper. Singles!

The other envelope was tough; he ripped into it with his teeth. Again—the thick packet contained nothing but one-dollar bills!

The pastor of the Church of the Heavenly Message crushed a handful of them in his fist, his eyes traveling along the black lines between the tiles of the floor. He let out an explosive sound like a cough; lifting his fist he beat the crumpled paper against his forehead twice. Then he fired the money into a corner and turned on both faucets of the washbowl. In the roaring water he let himself go; he sank his face in the basin and screamed, the sound bubbling up past his ears through the rush of water. He screamed until his diaphragm was sore and he had to stop and sit down on the floor, stuffing a towel in his mouth and tearing it with his teeth.

At last he hoisted himself up and reached for the brandy, swallowing until he had to stop and gasp for breath. In the mirror's merciless light he saw himself: hair streaming, eyes bloodshot, mouth twisted. Bleeding wounds of Christ!

The gypsy switch.

He stood, swaying, his hair falling damply over his eyes.

Dr. Lilith Ritter said, "Sit down, Mr. Carlisle."

Her voice was cold, kind, and sad—and as professional as the click of a typewriter.

His head began to shake as if he were saying no to a long series of questions. It went on shaking.

"I've done everything I can," said the sad voice through cigarette smoke. "When you first came to me you were in bad shape. I had hoped that by getting at the roots of your anxiety I could avert a serious upset. Well—" The hand gestured briefly with its star sapphire. "I failed."

He began rubbing his fingers along the top of the desk,

listening to the small whimpering noise of sweat against mahogany.

"Listen to me, Mr. Carlisle." The doctor leaned forward
earnestly. "Try to understand that these delusions are part of
your condition. When you first came to me you were tortured
by guilt connected with your father—and your mother. All of
these things you think you have done—or that have been
done to you lately—are merely the guilt of your childhood
projected. Do I make myself clear?"

The room was rocking, the lamps were double rings of
light, sliding back and forth through each other while the
walls billowed. His head shook: no.

"The symbolism is quite obvious, Mr. Carlisle. You were
filled with the unconscious desire to kill your father. You
picked up somewhere—I don't know where—the name of
Grindle, an industrialist, a man of power, and identified him
with your father. You have a very peculiar reaction to older
men with a stubble of white beard. It makes you think of
fungus on the face of a corpse—the corpse you wanted your
father to be."

The doctor's voice was very soft now; soothing, kind, un-
answerable.

"When you were a child you saw your mother having
intercourse. Therefore tonight in hallucination you thought
you saw Grindle, the father-image, in intercourse with your
mistress—who has come to represent your mother. And that's
not all, Mr. Carlisle. Since I have been your counselor you
have made a transference to me—you see me also as your
mother. That explains your sexual delusions with regard to
me."

He slid his hands over his face, mashing the palms into his
eyes, gripping strands of hair between his fingers and wrench-
ing until pain freed his frozen lungs and let him draw a breath.
His thoughts ran over and over, playing the same words until
they became meaningless: grindle grindle grindle grindle
mother mother mother stop stop stop. The voice didn't stop.

"There is one thing more you must face, Mr. Carlisle: the
thing that is destroying you. Ask yourself why you wanted to
kill your father. Why was there so much guilt connected with
that wish? Why did you see me—me, the mother-image—in

hallucinations both as your mistress and as a thief who had cheated you?"

She was standing up now and leaning across the desk, her face quite near him. She spoke gently.

"You wanted intercourse with your mother, didn't you?"

His hand went up to cover his eyes again, his mouth opened to make a wordless noise that could have been anything, a yes, a no, or both. He said, "Uh—uh—uh—uh." Then it seemed that all the pain in him was concentrated in the back of his right hand in a sudden, furious stab like a snake bite. He dropped it and stared at the doctor, momentarily in focus again. She was smiling.

"One other thing, Mr. Carlisle." She blew cigarette smoke. "The man you claimed to have killed in Mississippi—I thought at first that was merely another delusion involving the father-image. On investigation, however, I discovered there really was such a death—Peter Krumbein, Burleigh, Mississippi. I know you'll be glad to know *that,* at least, really did happen. It was quite easy to trace. Not so many years ago, was it, Mr. Carlisle?"

She turned away suddenly and picked up the telephone, the smooth voice brisker now. "Mr. Carlisle, I've done all I can for you, but you *must* have hospital care. These hallucinations— We can't have you wandering about and getting into trouble. Just put yourself in my hands; you can trust me absolutely.

"Bellevue Hospital? Psychiatric Division, please."

The buzzer hummed; a latch clicked in the foyer. Then the door into the waiting room opened and closed. Someone coming.

He backed away, looking at her, his mouth hanging open, his eyes bulging. Door. Have to get out. People. Danger.

"Psychiatric Division? This is Dr. Lilith Ritter. Please send an ambulance . . ."

The door, rushing behind him, shut off her voice.

Get out. Street. Hide. He clung to the knob, holding the door shut so she couldn't follow him.

Dream. Nightmare. Delusion. Nothing . . . nothing real. Tongue . . . naked . . . talk . . . money . . . dream . . . nightmare.

Dimly, through wood, he heard the telephone click into its cradle. Snap of a latch . . . waiting room. Then her voice. "Will you come in, please?"

Silence.

He sucked without thinking at the back of his right hand, where there was a red, smarting mark like a cigarette burn.

Safe? People coming! Got to get—

Another voice beyond the panels, high-pitched. Man. "Doctor—a ghastly mess . . ."

"Lie straight on the couch, please. Let me take your glasses, Mr. Grindle."

The Devil

Beneath his bat-wings the lovers stand in chains.

THERE was a plate of glass shaped like a star in the floor where the dancers swayed and shuffled. When the band went into a sweet one the house lights dimmed out and the star glowed, shining up the girls' skirts, leaving their faces in darkness, but X-raying their clothes from the hips down. They screamed and giggled as their partners pushed them across the star and back into obscurity.

In one corner of the room the mentalist rose from his chair, steadying himself by a hand on its back. "Thank you, sir, and your charming girl friend, for your interest and for the drink. You understand, folks, I've got other people waiting . . ."

The drunk slid a silver dollar along the table and the mind reader took it in his finger tips. It vanished in a quick movement. He bowed and turned away.

The girl snickered, the noise bubbling in her glass as she drank. "Daddy, isn't he spooky?" She kept on chuckling. "Now, then, sweetheart, you heard what he said! He said, 'A man who has a good head for business will give you the thing nearest to your heart, something which once lived in a wire cage.' You heard him, daddy. What d'you s'pose he meant?''

The man said thickly, "Anything you say, kid, goes. You know that. Anything. Gee, honey, you got the prettiest lil pair of—" He remembered the slip of paper that the mind reader had told him to tuck under the strap of his wrist watch and he pulled it out, unfolding it and trying to focus on it. The girl struck a match.

In her affected scrawl, using small circles for dots, was written, "Will Daddy buy me that red-fox jacket?" He stared at the slip and then grinned. "Sure, kid. Anything for you, kid. You know that. Le's get outa here—go up t'your place. C'mon, honey, 'fore I'm too lit—too lit t'enjoy"—he broke wind but never noticed it—"anything."

At the bar Stan knocked off another quick one on the house. Even through the curtain of alky the maggot in his mind kept burrowing. How long will this joint last? They get crummier and crummier. That shiny-haired bastard—private. Private. Private information. Private investigations. Private reports, private shellackings. Private executions?

The thought turned and twisted in his mind, burning the alcohol out of it. Jesus, why did I ever have to tangle with that old crumb? How was I to know that Molly— Oh, God, here we go again.

A waiter stepped close and said, "Table eighteen, bud. The gal's named Ethel. Had three husbands and the clap. The guy with her is a drummer. Plumbers' supplies."

Stanton finished his drink and dropped a quarter in the waiter's vest pocket as he brushed past him.

On his way to the table Stan saw the boss, his navy-blue shirt sleeves rolled up and canary yellow tie pulled down, talking to two men in rumpled suits. They had not removed their hats. Both necks were thick.

A cold ripple slipped down his back. Wind seemed to whistle inside his undershirt. Cold. Oh, Jesus, here they come. Grindle. Grindle. Grindle. The old man's power covered the country like a pair of bat-wings, flapping cold and black.

Stan walked slowly to the back of the room, ducked behind a partition and squeezed his way through the kitchen and out into the alley at the rear of the Pelican Club, breaking into a run when he was clear of the building. He didn't dare go back for his hat. Christ, I ought to hang it on a nail right by the back door. But they'll block that the next time.

Always different faces, different guys. They must hire private dicks in every state, all of them different. Anderson sits inside that barbed-wire fort and spins it out like a spider, millions of bucks to smash one guy. Mexico. I've got to jump the border if I'm ever going to shake them. Three thousand miles of this damn country and no hole to duck into. How do those goons do it so quick? Mind readers—they must chase after every guy doing a mental act and take a sample of his hair, see if it's blond.

Across the dark rooftops a train whistled, long and mournfully. Stan ducked down another alley and leaned against the wall, listening to the roaring jolt of his own heart, fighting to get his breath. Lilith, Lilith. Across two thousand miles stretched the invisible golden wire still, and one end was buried in his brain.

Back in the Pelican Club the boss said, "Now you fellas run along. You tell McIntyre I'm not putting in no cig or novelty girls and I'm holding on to the hat check myself. It ain't for sale."

CARD XVII

The Hermit

An old man follows a star that burns in his lantern.

In the light of the fire the cards fell, forming the pattern of a cross. Stan dealt them slowly, watching them fall.

The gully was shielded from wind, the fire hidden from the tracks a quarter of a mile away across fields standing high with brittle weed-stalks. Weeds grew to the edge of the gully, the fire turning them yellow against the sky where stars hung, icy and remote.

The Empress. She smirked at him from beneath her crown of stars, holding a scepter with a golden ball on its end. The pomegranates embroidered on her robe looked like strawberries. Beyond her, trees stood stiffly—like the trees on a theater backdrop in a tank town. At her feet the ripening wheatheads. Smell of ripening wheat. Venus sign on the couch where she sat. Smell of ripening wheat.

What did they think, the wriggling bugs of the scum, jetting into the world to meet acids, whirling douches, rubber scum bags, upholstery of cars, silk drawers, clotted handkerchief . . . two hundred million at a shot . . .

758

Across the fire the fat man lifted a steaming can from the embers with a pair of pliers. "Got yourself a can, bud? Java's done."

Stan knocked tobacco crumbs from a tin and twisted a rag around it. "In there, pal."

The coffee set his stomach churning again. Christ, I need a drink. But how to snake out the bottle without that bastard cutting himself in?

He eased the bottle neck from his coat and pretended to be studying the cards while the white mule trickled into the steaming can.

The squat hobo raised his face. "My, *my!* What is this that gives off so heavenly an aroma?" His voice was like sandpaper. "Could it be *Odeur de Barleycorn?* Or is it a few drops—just the merest suggestion behind the ears—of that rare and subtle essence, 'Parfum Pourriture d'Intestin— You never know she wears it until it's . . . too late'? *Come on, blondy, gimme the bottle!*"

Through his smile Stan said, "Sure. Sure, pal. I was going to break it out later. I'm waiting for another pal of mine. He's out trying to get a lump."

The fat man took the bottle of rotgut, measured it by eye, and very accurately drank half of it, handing it back and returning to his coffee. "Thanks, bud. The only pal you got is right in there. You better soak it up before some other bo muscles in on us." He shifted his weight, crossed his legs, and took a long drink of coffee, which trickled down the shiny blue surface of his jowls. A two days' growth of beard made him look like a pirate.

He rested the can on his knee and wiped his chin, running his tongue around between his lips and gums. Then he said, "That's right, bud—kill the bottle. How would you like it if we had an unexpected guest?" His voice took on a reedy, mincing tone and he held his head coyly on one side, lifting bushy eyebrows. "He'd find us in a dither—it being the maid's day off. All we'd have to offer him would be a drink of that fine, mellow, wood-aged polecat piss." The jowls swayed as he shook his head in mock concern. Then the dark face brightened. "Or perhaps he would be that priceless gem—the guest-who-always-fits-in—ready at a moment's notice to don an apron (one of your frilly best, naturally, kept just for those special people) and join you in the kitchen, improvising a snack.''

Stan brought the bottle to his mouth again and tilted it; the raw whisky found holes in his teeth and punished him, but he finished it and heaved the bottle into the weeds.

The fat man threw another branch on the fire and squatted beside Stan. "What kind of cards are those, bud?"

The man's shirt was almost clean, pants cuffs scarcely frayed. Probably rode the plush a lot. In his lapel was a tiny steering-wheel emblem of a boat club.

Stan gazed up into his face. "My friend, you are a man who has seen life. I get the impression that somewhere in your life has been an office with a broad carpet. I see a window in an office building with something growing in it. Could it be little cedar trees—in a window box?"

The fat hobo stood up, swishing the coffee in his can. "Everybody had cedars. I had a better idea—an inspiration. Grass hummocks—just plain grass tufts. But this will show you the *genius.* What do you think I put in them? *Katydids!* I'd bring up a client late at night—town all dark there below us. Tell him to step back from the window and listen. You couldn't believe you were in the city." He looked down and his face tightened. "Wait a minute, bud. How'd you know about them grass tufts?"

The Great Stanton smiled thinly, pointing to the cards before him. "This is the Tarot of the Romany cartomancers. A set of symbols handed down from remote antiquity, preserving in their enigmatic form the ancient wisdom through the ages."

"What d'you do with 'em? Tell fortunes?" The gravel voice had lost its hostility.

"I receive impressions. You have two children. Is that correct?"

The fat man nodded. "Christ knows, I had once. If that bitch hasn't let 'em kill themselves while she was out whoring around."

"Your third wife?"

"Yeah, that's right. Wait a minute. How'd you know I was a three-time loser?"

"I drew the impressions from your mind, my friend, using the cards of the Tarot as a concentrative. Now, if you wish me to continue, I shall be glad to. The fee will be twenty-five cents, or its equivalent in merchandise."

The hobo scratched his scalp. "Okay, bud. Go ahead." He threw a quarter beside the cards and Stan picked it up. Five shots. Gathering the cards he shuffled them, having the fat man cut them with his left hand.

"You see, the first to appear is the *Hermit*. An old man, leaning on a staff, follows a star that burns in his lantern. That is your quest—your journey through life, always seeking something just out of your reach. Once it was wealth. It became the love of women. Next, you sought security—for yourself and others. But misfortune descended on you. Things inside you began to tear in opposite directions. And you would have five or six drinks before you took the train home at night. Isn't that right?"

The glowering, dark face nodded.

"The *Hermit* is the card of the Search. The Search for the Answer."

"Come again, bud." The fat man's tone was subdued and hopeless. "What brains I ever had was knocked loose by yard dicks years ago."

Stan closed his eyes. "Man comes into the world a blind, groping mite. He knows hunger and the fear of noise and of falling. His life is spent in flight—flight from hunger and from the thunderbolt of destiny. From his moment of birth he begins to fall through the whistling air of Time: down, down into a chasm of darkness . . ."

The hobo stood up cautiously and edged around the fire. He watched the cartomancer warily. Nuts can blow their tops easy—and this one still held a can of hot coffee.

The Great Stanton spoke aloud to himself. The jolt of whisky had loosened his stomach and drawn it out from his backbone. Now he rambled; with a foolish, drunken joy he let his tongue ride, saying whatever it wanted to say. He could sit back and rest and let his tongue do the work. Why beat my brains out reading for a bum that was probably too crooked and phoney even for the advertising racket? The tongue does the work. Good old tongue, man's best friend—and woman's second best. What the hell am I talking about?

". . . we come like a breath of wind over the fields of morning. We go like a lamp flame caught by a blast from a darkened window. In between we journey from table to table, from bottle to bottle, from bed to bed. We suck, we chew, we swallow, we lick, we try to mash life into us like an am-am-*amoeba* God damn it! Somebody lets us loose like a toad out of a matchbox and we jump and jump and jump and the guy always behind us, and when he gets tired he stomps us to death and our guts squirt out on each side of the boot of All Merciful Providence. The son-of-a-bitch!"

The world began to spin and he opened his eyes to keep his balance. The fat man wasn't listening. He was standing with his back to the fire, throwing pebbles at something beyond the circle of light.

When he turned around he said, "A goddamned, mangy, fleabitten abortion of a *dog* was trying to horn in on our fire. The stinking abomination. I hate 'em! They come up to you, smelling, groveling, please-kick-my-ass-mister. I *hate* 'em! They slaver all over you. You rub 'em behind the ears and they practically come in your face out of gratitude."

Stanton Carlisle said, "My friend, at some time a dog did you an injury. I think the dog was not yours but that it belonged to another—to a woman."

The bo, moving agilely with the grace of an athlete gone fat, was standing beside him now, fists working, the knuckles rippling as he spoke. "Sure it was a dog—a toadying, cringing, vomit-eating, goddamned abortion of a dog! Sure he belonged to a woman, you crazy bastard! And the dog was *me*!"

They held the pose like figures in a tableau. Only the firelight moved, jumping and flickering on the weeds and on the two faces, the pudgy one dark and tormented, the gaunt face of the blond hobo a blank.

There was a whining scuffle from the bank overhead and both men turned. An emaciated dog slid down and tremblingly approached the warmth, tail flattened between his haunches, eyes rolling.

Stan chirped between his teeth. "Come here, boy. Here. Over here by me."

The dog bounded toward him, yelping with delight at the sound of a friendly voice. He had almost reached Stan when the squat hobo drew back his foot. The kick lifted the animal, squirming and squealing, into the air; it fell, legs spraddled, in the middle of the fire, screamed, and shot away into the dark, trailing sparks from singed fur.

Stan swept the coffee in a curve; it glistened in the firelight, a muddy arc, and caught the fat man in the eyes. He stumbled back, wiping his sleeve across them. Then he lowered his head, resting his jowl on his left shoulder and stepping in with a rocking motion, left fist forward, right hand half open, ready to defend his face. In a soft, cultured voice he said, "Get your hands up, brother. You are in for a very unpleasant three minutes. I'll play with you that long and then send you off to dreamland."

The Rev. Carlisle had doubled in the middle, as if taken by a violent stomach cramp. He moaned, bending over, and the fat man dropped his guard an inch. It was low enough.

When Stan sprang he carried a thick faggot from the fire and with one lunge caught the hobo with its burning point just below the breast bone. The man went down limply and heavily, like a dummy stuffed with sand.

Stan watched him gape, fighting for breath. Then he smashed the torch into the open mouth, feeling the teeth crush under it.

The alcohol was draining out of his mind. He was alone and cold, under an immensity of sky—naked as a slug, as a tadpole. And the shadow of the crushing foot seemed to move closer. Stan began to run.

Far away, up on the drag, he heard the hoot of a whistle and he ran faster, staggering, a stitch in his side. Oh, Jesus— the Tarot. I left it by the fire. One more signpost pointing to the Rev. Carlisle.

A freight was slowing. He ran, his breath scorching, looking ahead, through the dark, for obstructions on the line. An iron step came whipping by him and he reached for it, but it tore from his fingers. The job was picking up speed.

A wide-open boxcar door slid up to him and he leaped.

Then, with the scalding panic rushing over him, he knew that he had missed and was swinging under.

A hand from the car gripped his shoulder and held him, half inside the car and half out, while under his feet the earth flew past.

The freight high-balled along.

Time

One foot on earth and one on water,
an angel pours eternity from cup to cup.

IN THE parking lot the Maryland sun beat down, flashing from rows of windshields, from chromium handles and the smooth curves of enameled mudguards.

Cincinnati Burns eased the battered convertible into line while Molly, standing out on the gravel, shouted, "Cut her left, honey. More left."

He drew out the ignition key and it was suddenly snatched from his hand and hurled out between the cars. Cincy said, "You little devil! You're mighty sassy. Ain't you? Ain't you?" He boosted the child high in the air while it screamed with joy.

Molly came running up. "Let me hold him, Cincy, while you get the key." He passed the baby to her and it grabbed a damp handkerchief from the gambler's coat pocket and waved it triumphantly.

"Come on, precious. Let's let Daddy get the key. Hey, quit kicking me in the tummy."

The big man set the boy on his shoulder, handing Molly his hat for safekeeping, and they headed for the grandstand. The gambler shifted the baby and looked at the stop watch on his wrist. "Plenty of time, kitten. The third race is our spot."

They stopped to buy paper cups of raspberry sherbet and Cincinnati whispered suddenly, "You hold the bambino, Molly. There's Dewey from St. Louis."

Treading softly, he approached from the rear and squatted down behind a glum, lantern-jawed man in a seersucker suit. Cincy took a pack of matches and holding his thick fingers, knuckles covered with red hair, as delicately as if he were threading a needle, he stuck a match between Dewey's shoe sole and the upper. Lighting the match, he sneaked back a few steps and then strolled over to where his wife and son were watching from behind the refreshment stand.

When the match burned down the long-faced horse player shot into the air as if hoisted by a rope and began smacking at his foot.

Molly, Cincy, and young Dennis, peeking around the corner of the stand, began to shout in unison. Molly dropped her cup of sherbet, and Dennis Burns, seeing it fall, threw his after it gleefully.

"Hey, what goes on?" Cincy rattled change in his pocket and said, "You go on. I'll catch up to ye's."

When he joined them he held four cups of sherbet. "Here, kids—one to suck on and one to drop. Dewey is sure a sucker for the hotfoot. This must be a thousand times somebody gives him the hotfoot. It's a dozen times, at least, that I give him the hotfoot myself. Let's get up in the stand, kitten. I'll get you organized and then I've got to get the roll down on that hay-burner in the third; he shouldn't drop dead, *kenna-hurra*. You wouldn't know that, that's Gaelic. If he breaks a leg we're going to have to talk fast back at that fleabag. What the hell, it's time we was pulling out of that trap anyhow. Every time I wake up in the morning and get a glim full of that wallpaper I feel like I ought to slip you five bucks."

The Wheel of Fortune

spins past Angel, Eagle, Lion, and Bull.

S TAN lay on the splintery boards, feeling the vibration against his elbows, smelling the acrid odor of machine oil rising from the planks. The freight thundered along, gaining speed.

The hands drew him further in and then slid under his armpits and helped him to sit up. "You all right, son? You sure come near swinging yourself into Kingdom Come." The voice was soft and friendly.

Now they were passing the outskirts of a town, lonely street lamps sending bars of light winking through the door. The man who had dragged him in was a Negro, dressed in denim overalls and a denim work coat. Above the bib of the overalls a white shirt was visible in the shadows. His smile was the only part of his face Stan could see.

Getting to his feet he braced himself against the sway of the car under him and worked his fingers and arms, easing the strain out of them. "Thanks, pal. It was too dark for me to put on any speed myself—couldn't see what was ahead of me on the drag."

"It's tough, dark night like this. You can't see the grab-irons. You can't hardly see *nothing*. How about a smoke?"

Stan felt a bag of tobacco pressed into his hand. He twisted himself a cigarette and they shared the match. The Negro was a young fellow, slim, with smooth, handsome features and close-cropped hair.

Stan drew in smoke and let it dribble from his nose. Then he began to shake, for the steady pound of the wheels under him brought back the stab of that hopeless, desperate fear, "This is it," and he trembled harder.

"You cold, mister? Or you got a fever?"

"Just shaken up. I thought I was going to hand in my checks."

Their cigarettes perfumed the darkness. Outside the rising moon rode with them, dipping beyond treetops.

"You a working stiff, mister, or just on the road?"

"On the road."

"Plenty fellows likes it that way. Seem like I'd rather work than knock myself out hustling."

"What kind of work do you do?"

"Any kind. Porter work, handyman. I run a freight elevator once. I can drive pretty good. Biggest old truck you can find, I'll drive her. I've shipped out: cook's helper and dishwasher. I can chop cotton. Reckon there ain't anything you can't do, you set your mind on it."

"Bound north?"

"New Jersey. Going to try and get me a job at Grindle's. What I hear, they taking on men. Taking on colored."

Stan braced his back against the closed door on the other side of the car and drew a final puff from the cigarette, sending the butt flipping through the open door, trailing sparks.

Grindle. Grindle. Grindle. To drown out the chatter of the wheels he said, "Why are they hiring guys all of a sudden? Business must be picking up."

The youth laughed a little. "Business staying right where she is. They hiring because they done a whole mess of firing a while back. They hiring all colored, this new bunch, what I hear."

"What's the idea of that?" Tame lawyers, tame psychologists, tame muscle-men. Bastards.

"What you s'pose? They get all the colored boys in there, and then they stir up the white boys, and pretty soon they all messing around with each other and forget all about long hours and short pay."

Stan was only half listening. He crawled into the corner next to the Negro and sat down, stretching his legs out in front of him. "Hey, bud, you wouldn't happen to have a drink in your pocket, would you?"

"Hell, no. All I got is four bits and this bag of makings. Traveling fast and light."

Four bits. Ten shots of nickel whisky.

The Great Stanton ran his hands over his hair.

"My friend, I owe you a great debt for saving my life."

"You don't owe me nothing, mister. What you expect me to do? Let you slide under and make hamburg steak out of yourself? You forget all about it."

Stan swallowed the cottony saliva in his mouth and tried again. "My friend, my ancestors were Scotch, and the Scotch are known to possess a strange faculty. It used to be called second sight. Out of gratitude, I want to tell you what I see in the future about your life. I may be able to save you many trials and misfortunes."

His companion chuckled. "You better save that second sight. Get it to tell you when you going to miss nailing a freight."

"Ah, but you see, my friend, it led me to the very car where I would find assistance. I *knew* you were in this car and would help me."

"Mister, you ought to play the races and get rich."

"Tell me this—I get a decided impression that you have a scar on one knee. Isn't that so?"

The boy laughed again. "Sure, I got scars on *both* my knees. I got scars on my ass, too. Anybody got scars all over him, he ever done any work. I been working since I could walk. I was pulling bugs off potato plants, time I quit messing my britches."

Stan took a deep breath. He couldn't let this wisenheimer townie crawl all over him.

"My dear friend, how often in your life, when things looked bad, have you thought of committing suicide?"

"Man, you sure got it bad. Everybody think they like to die sometime—only they always wants to be hanging around afterwards, watching all the moaning and grieving they folks going to do, seeing them laid out dead. They don't want to die. They just want folks to do a little crying and hollering over 'em. I was working on a road gang once and the captain like to knock me clean out of my skin. He keep busting me alongside the head whether I raise any hell or not—just for fun. But I didn't want to kill myself. I wanted to get loose. And I *got* loose, and here I am—sitting here. But that captain get his brains mashed out with a shovel a couple months later by a big crazy fellow, worked right next to me on the chain. Now that captain's dead and I ain't mourning."

A fear without a form or a name was squirming inside Stanton Carlisle. Death and stories of death or brutality burrowed under his skin like ticks and set up an infection that worked through him to his brain and festered in it.

He forced his mind back to the reading. "Let me tell you this, friend: I see your future unrolling like thread from a spool. The pattern of your days ahead. I see men—a crowd of men—threatening you, asking questions. But I see another man, older than yourself, who will do you a good turn."

The Negro stood up and then squatted on his haunches to absorb the vibration of the car. "Mister, you must of been a fortuneteller sometime. You talk just like 'em. Why don't you relax yourself? You last a lot longer, I'm telling you."

The white hobo jumped to his feet and lurched over to the open door, bracing his hand against the wall of the car and staring out across the countryside. They roared over a concrete bridge; a river flashed golden in the moonlight and was gone.

"You better stand back a little, son. You go grabbing scenery that way and somebody spot you if we pass a jerk stop. They phone on ahead, and when she slow down you got the bulls standing there with oak towels in their hands, all ready to rub you down."

Stan turned savagely. "Listen, kid, you got everything figured out so close. What sense does it all make? What sort of

God would put us here in this goddamned, stinking slaughterhouse of a world? Some guy that likes to tear the wings off flies? What use is there in living and starving and fighting the next guy for a full belly? It's a nut house. And the biggest loonies are at the top."

The Negro's voice was softer. "Now you talking, brother. You let all that crap alone and come over here and talk. We got a long run ahead of us and ain't no use trying to crap each other up."

Dully Stan left the doorway and crumpled into the corner. He wanted to shout out, to cry, to feel Lilith's mouth again, her breasts against him. Oh, Jesus, there I go. God damn her, the lying, double-crossing bitch. They're all alike. But Molly, the dumb little tomato. Quickly he wanted her. Then disgust mounted—she would leech on to him and drain the life out of him. Dull, oh, Christ, and stupid. Oh, Jesus . . . Mother. Mark Humphries, God damn his soul to hell, the thieving bastard. Mother . . . the picnic . . .

The Negro was speaking again and the words filtered through. ". . . take on like that. Why don't you tell me what you moaning about? You never going to see me again. Don't make no difference to me what you done. I mind my own business. But you'll feel better a hundred per cent, get it off your mind."

The prying bastard. Let me alone . . . He heard his own voice say, "Stars. Millions of them. Space, reaching out into nothing. No end to it. The rotten, senseless, useless life we get jerked into and jerked out of, and it's nothing but whoring and filth from start to finish."

"What's the matter with having a little poontang? Nothing dirty about that, 'cept in a crib you likely get crabs or a dose. Ain't anything dirty about it unless you feels dirty in your mind. Gal start whoring so as to get loose from cotton-chopping or standing on their feet ten, eleven hours. You can't blame no gal for laying it on the line for money. On her back she can rest."

Stan's torrent of despair had dried up. For a second he could draw breath—the weight seemed to have been lifted from his chest.

"But the purpose back of it all—why are we put here?"

"Way I look at it, we ain't put. We growed."

"But what started the whole stinking mess?"

"Didn't have to start. It's always been doing business. People ask me: how this world get made without God make it? I ask 'em right back: who make God? They say he don't need making; he always been there. I say: well then, why you got to go bringing him in at all? Old world's always been there, too. That's good enough for me. They ask me: how about sin? Who put all the sin and wickedness and cussedness in the world? I say: who put the boll weevil? He growed. Well, mean people grow where the growing's good for 'em—same as the boll weevil."

Stan was trying to listen. When he spoke his voice was thick and flat. "It's a hell of a world. A few at the top got all the dough. To get yours you got to pry 'em loose from some of it. And then they turn around and knock your teeth out for doing just what they did."

The Negro sighed and offered Stan the tobacco, then made himself another cigarette. "You said it, brother. You said it. Only they ain't going have it forever. Someday people going to get smart *and* mad, same time. You can't get nothing in this world by yourself."

Stan smoked, watching the gray thread sail toward the door and whip off into the night. "You sound like a labor agitator."

This time the Negro laughed aloud. "God's sake, man, labor don't need agitation. You can't agitate people when they's treated right. Labor don't need stirring up. It need squeezing together."

"You think they've got sense enough to do it?"

"They *got* to do it. I *know*."

"Oh. You *know*."

The lad in denims was silent for a moment, thinking. "Looky here—you plant four grains of corn to a hill. How you *know* one going to come up? Well, the working people, black *and* white—their brains growing just like corn in the hill."

The freight was slowing.

God, let me get out of here . . . this damn, slap-happy darkie, whistling in the lion's den. And Grindle . . . every second, moving closer to the fort . . .

"Hey, watch yourself, son. She's still traveling."

The train lost speed quickly. It was stopping. Stan jumped to the ground and the Negro followed, looking left and right. "This ain't good. Got no business stopping here. Oh—oh—it's a frisk."

At either end of the train, lights appeared, brakemen walking the tops carrying lanterns; flashlights of railroad bulls playing along the body rods and into open boxcars.

The young hobo said, "Something funny—this division ain't never been hostile before. And they frisking from both ends at once . . ."

On the other side of the freight a train whistled in, hissing, glowing, the red blaze of the engine shining under the boxcar and throwing the hoboes' shadows across the cinders ahead of them.

"Hey, son, let's try and jump that passenger job. You a fast rambler?"

The Rev. Carlisle shook his head. The furies were drawing close, Anderson's web was tangling him. This was the end of it. Dully he clambered back into the boxcar and sank down into a corner, burying his face in his bent elbow, while with hoarse voices and a stamp of feet the furies moved in . . .

"Hey, bo—" The whisper through the door barely penetrated. "Come on—let's nail that rattler. We make better time too."

Silence.

"So long, boy. Take it easy."

Doom had stepped onto the roof; then a light stabbed into the car, searching the corners. Oh, Jesus, this is it—this is it.

"Come on, you bastard, unload. And get your hands up."

He stood, blinking in the glare of the flashlight, and raised his arms.

"Come on, hit the grit!"

Stan stumbled to the door and sat down, sliding his feet into darkness. A big hand gripped his arm and jerked him out.

From the top of the car the head-end shack peered over, holding his brake club under one arm. "You got him?"

A voice behind the flashlight said, "I got one. But he ain't no coon. Way we got the tip, the guy was a coon."

The brakeman above them signaled with his lantern and

from the dark came the chug of a gasoline-driven handcar. It sped up and Stan could see that it was crowded with men—dark clothes—it was no track gang. When it stopped the men piled off and hurried across the rails.

"Where is he? On the freight? Who's shaking down the rattler?"

"We got boys frisking the rattler, don't worry."

"But we got it from Anderson . . ."

This is it. This is it. This is it.

". . . that the guy was colored." One of the newcomers came closer and brought out a flashlight of his own. "What's that in your pocket, bud?"

Stanton Carlisle tried to speak but his mouth was gritty.

"Keep your hands up. Wait a minute. This isn't a weapon. It's a Bible."

His lungs loosened; he could draw half a breath. "Brother, you hold in your hand the most powerful weapon in the world—"

"Drop it!" Big Hand shouted. "Maybe it's a pineapple made to look like a Bible."

The other voice was cool. "It's just a Bible." He turned to the white hobo. "We're looking for a colored lad. We know he boarded this train. If you can give us information which might lead to his arrest, you would be serving the forces of justice. And there might be something in it for you."

Justice. *Something in it* could mean folding money. Justice. A buck—ten cans of alky . . . justice. White-stubble justice . . . a buck—twenty shots . . . oh, frig them with their razorstrops, their *brake clubs* . . .

He opened his eyes wide, staring straight ahead in the light-beam. "Brother, I met a colored brother-in-God when I was waiting to nail this job. I tried to bring him to Jesus, but he wouldn't listen to the Word. I gave him my last tract—"

"Come on, parson, where did he go? Was he riding here in the car with you?"

"Brother, this colored brother-in-God nailed her somewhere up at the head-end. I was hoping we could ride together so I could tell him about our Lord and Savior Jesus Christ who died for our sins. I've rode from coast-to-coast a dozen times, bringing men to Christ. I've brought only a couple thousand so far . . ."

"Okay, parson, give Jesus a rest. We're looking for a goddamned nigger Red. You saw him grab her up front? Come on, guys, let's spread out. He's here someplace . . ."

The man with big hands stayed with Stanton while the others swarmed over the freight, swung between the cars and moved off into the darkness. The Rev. Carlisle had slipped into a low mutter which the yard dick made out to be a sermon, addressed either to an invisible congregation or to the air. The goddamned Holy Joe had thrown them off; now the coon had a chance of getting clear.

At last the freight whistled, couplings started and clanked, and it groaned off. Beyond it the passenger train, sleek and dark, waited while flashlights sprayed into the blinds, the side boxes of the diner, and along the tops.

Then it too began to move. As the club car slid past, Stan glimpsed through long windows a waiter in a white coat. He was uncapping a bottle while an arm in a tweed coat held a glass of ice.

A drink. Good Christ, a drink. Could I put the bite on this bull? Better not try it, no time to build it.

The railroad detective spat between his teeth. "Look here, parson, I'm going to give you a break. I ought to send you over. But you'd probably have the whole damn jail yelling hymns. Come on, crumb, take the breeze."

The big hands turned Stan around and pushed; he stumbled over tracks and up an embankment. In the distance the light of a farmhouse glowed. A drink. Oh, Jesus—

The passenger flyer picked up speed. In the club car a wrist shot from a tweed sleeve, revealing a wrist watch. Ten minutes' delay! Confound it, the only way to travel was by plane.

Under the club car, squeezed into a forest of steel springs, axles, brake rods and wheels, a man lay hidden. As the rattler gained speed, Frederick Douglass Scott, son of a Baptist minister, grandson of a slave, shifted his position to get a better purchase as he rolled on toward the North and the fort with its double fence of charged wire.

Shoulders braced against the truck frame, feet against the opposite side, he balanced his body on an inch-thick brake rod which bent under him. Inches below, the roadbed raced by, switches clawing up at him as the car pounded past them. The truck hammered and bucked. A stream of glowing coals, thrown down by the engine, blew over him and he fought them with his free hand, beating at the smoldering denim, while the train thundered on; north, north, north.

A specter was haunting Grindle. It was a specter in overalls.

CARD XX

Death

wears dark armor; beside his horse
kneel priests and children and kings.

THE PITCHMAN rounded a corner, looking both ways down the main street for the cop, and then slid into the darkened vestibule of the bank building. If the rain held off he might get a break at that. The movie theater was about to let out; fellows would be coming out with their girls.

As the first of the crowd drifted past him he drew a handful of gaudy envelopes from a large pocket inside his coat and fanned them in his left hand so that the brightly printed zodiac circle and the symbols stood out, a different color for each sign.

He ran his free hand once over his hair and took a breath. His voice was hoarse; he couldn't get it much above a whisper. "My friends if you'll just step this way for a single moment you may find that you have taken a step which will add to your health happiness and prosperity for the rest of your lives . . ."

One couple stopped and he spoke directly to them. "I

777

wonder if the young lady would mind telling me her birth date it costs you nothing folks because the first astrological chart this evening will be given away absolutely free of charge . . ."

The young fellow said, "Come on." They walked on past. The goddamned townies.

Need a drink. Jesus, I've got to pitch. I got to unload five of them.

"Here you are folks everybody wants to know what the future holds in store come in a little closer folks and I'll tell you what I'm going to do I'm going to give each and every one of you a personal reading get your astronomical forecast which shows your lucky numbers, days of the month and tells you how to determine the right person for you to marry whether you've got anybody in mind or not . . ."

They moved by him, some staring, some laughing, none stopping.

Hideous. Their faces suddenly became distorted, like caricatures of human faces. They seemed to be pushed out of shape. Some of them looked like animals, some like embryo chicks when you break an egg that is half incubated. Their heads bobbed on necks like stalks and he waited for their eyes to drop out and bounce on the sidewalk.

The pitchman started to laugh. It was a chuckle, bubbling up inside of him at first, and then it split open and he laughed, screaming and stamping his foot.

A crowd began to knot around him. He stopped laughing and forced out the words. "Here you are folks while they last." The laugh was fighting inside of him, tearing at his throat. "A complete astrological reading giving your birthstones, lucky numbers." The laugh was hammering to get out. It was like a dog tied to the leg of a workbench, fighting to get free of a rope. Here it came. "Whah, whah, whah, whah! Hooooooooooooooo!"

He beat the handful of horoscopes against his thigh, leaning his other hand against the stone lintel of the vestibule. The crowd was giggling at him or with him, some wondering when he was going to stop suddenly and try to sell them something.

One woman said, "Isn't it disgusting! And right in the doorway of the bank! It's indecent."

The pitchman heard her and this time he sat down limply on the marble steps, letting the horoscopes scatter around him, holding his belly as he laughed.

Something hit the crowd at its edge and mashed it forward and to each side. Then the blue legs moved in.

"I told you to beat it out of town."

The face of the cop seemed a mile above him, as if it were looking over the rim of a well.

Same cop. Two-dollar fine and get out of town.

"Wheeeeeeee! Ho—ho. Hah. Officer . . . officer . . . whah-hoooooooo!"

The hand that jerked him to his feet seemed to plunge out of the sky. "I told you to scram, bum. Now you going to walk down to the lockup or you going on a stretcher?"

A quick thrust and his hand was twisted halfway up his back; he was walking bent over to keep from getting his wrist broken. Through waves of laughter the world seeped in, coming in slices, as if the laughter split at the seams and showed a little raw and bloody reality before it closed up again.

"Where we going, officer? No, no, don't tell me. Let me guess. Down cellar?"

"Shut up, bum. Keep walking or you'll get your arm broke. I've got a good mind to work you over before we get down there."

"But, officer, they've seen me once down there. They'll get awfully tired of seeing me. They'll think it ridiculous, me showing up there so often. Won't they? Won't they? Won't they? You've got no rope around my neck. How can you be sure I won't run? Wait for the moon—it's coming out from under the rain pretty soon; any minute now. But you don't understand that. Officer, wait . . ."

They had left the crowd and cut down a side street. To the left was an alley, dark, but with a light at the other end of it. The cop shifted his grip on the prisoner's hand, letting go for a fraction of a second, and the pitchman spun free and began to run. He was sailing through air; he couldn't feel his feet touching the stones. And behind him the heavy splat of shoes on cobbles. He raced toward the light at the end of the alley, but there was nothing to be afraid of. He had always been here, running down the alley and it didn't matter; this was all there was any time, anywhere, just an alley and a light and the footsteps spanging on the cobbles but they never catch you, they never catch you, they never catch— A blow between his shoulders knocked him forward and he saw the stones, in the faint light ahead, coming up toward him, his own hands spread out, fingers bent a little on the left hand, thumbs at an eager angle, all spraddled out as if he were making shadows on a wall, of two roosters' heads, the thumbs forming the beaks and the spread fingers the notches of the combs.

The nightstick had struck him, whirling through the space between the two men. It bounded off, hitting a brick wall with a clear, wooden ping as the cobbles met his hands and the jar of the fall snapped his neck back. He was on his hands and knees when the foot caught him in the ribs and sent him sprawling on his side.

The great oval face ducked out of sight. The cop had bent to pick up the nightstick and the top of his cap cut off the sight of the face, above its V of shirt and black tie. That was all you could see.

He heard the shattering crack of the nightstick across his shoulders before the pain fought its way down the clogged nerves and went off, spraying around inside his brain like a hose jet of hot steel. He heard his own breath pop out between his teeth and he drew his feet under him. He was halfway erect when the stick knocked the rest of the breath out of him, smashing against his ribs.

It was somebody else's voice. "Officer . . . oh, Jesus . . . I ain't done nothing . . . gimme a break . . . oh, Jesus . . ."

"I'll give ye a break. I'll break every bone in your head, you stinking crumb. You as'd for it. Now you're gonna get it."

The stick landed again and the pain was white and incandescent this time as it slowly slid up his spine toward the brain on top.

The world came back and Stanton Carlisle, his mind sharpened to a point, saw where he was. He saw the lift of the cop's upper lip, revealing a gold crown. And in the faint light, behind him now, he noticed that the cop needed a shave. He was not over forty; but his hair and the beard beginning to sprout over the jowls were pearly. Like fungus on a corpse. At that instant pain from the blow across his buttocks reached his mind and a thousand tumblers fell into place; a door swung open.

Stan closed in, clamping one hand on the cop's lapel. His other hand crossed it, under the jowls, seizing the opposite lapel in its fist. Then, twisting sideways to protect his groin, Stanton began to squeeze. He heard the nightstick drop and felt the big hands tearing at his forearms, but the harder they pulled the tighter his fists dug into the throat. The day-old beard was like sandpaper on the backs of his hands.

Stan felt the wall of the alley jar against his shoulder, felt his feet leave the ground and the dark weight fall on him; but the only life in him now was pouring out through his hands and wrists.

The mountain on him wasn't moving. It was resting. Stan got one foot free and rolled both of them over so he was on top. The massive body was perfectly still. He tightened the choke still more, until his knuckles felt as if they would burst, and he began to tap the cop's head against the cobbles. Rap. Rap. Rap. He liked the sound. Faster.

Then his hands let go of themselves and he stood up, the hands falling to his sides. They wouldn't work any more, wouldn't obey him.

A bundle of astro-readings had fallen out and lay scattered on the stones, but he couldn't pick them up. He walked, very straight and precise, toward the light at the other end of the alley. Everything was sharp and clear now and he didn't even need a drink any more.

The freights would be risky. He might try the baggage rack of a long-haul bus, under the tarpaulin. He had traveled there once before.

Nothing more to bother about. For the cop was dead.

I can kill him again. I can kill him again. Any time he starts after me I can keep killing him. He's mine. My own personal corpse.

They'll bury him, just like you bury a stiff, clotted handkerchief.

I can kill him again.

But he won't come again. He's a dead pigeon.
I can kill him again.
But he's dead from a bum ticker.
I can kill him.

Strength

*A rose-crowned woman closes
a lion's jaws with her bare hands.*

IN THE EVENING light a tall figure, gaunt, with matted yellow hair, leaned over the top fence rail, watching a man and woman planting corn. The woman thrust a hoe handle into the earth and the man, who seemed to have no legs, hopped along on his hands, dropping grains of corn into the hills and smoothing the earth over them.

"Wait a minute, Joe. There's somebody wants us."

The big woman strode over plowed ground, pulling off her gloves. "I'm sorry, bud, but we ain't got nothing in the icebox to give you for a lump. And I ain't got time now to fix you a sit-down. You wait till I get my pocketbook from the house and I'll let you have four bits. There's a lunch wagon down the road." She stopped and caught her breath, then said hoarsely, "Glory be, it's Stan Carlisle!" Over her shoulder she called, "Joe! Joe! Come here this minute!"

The hobo was leaning on the fence, letting it carry his weight. "Hi, Zeena. Saw your ad—magazine."

The man drew near them, hopping along on his hands. His legs, twisted into a knot out of the way, were hidden by a burlap sack which he had drawn over them and tied around his waist. He swung up and sat looking at Stan silently, smiling as Lazarus must have smiled, newly risen. But his eyes were wary.

Zeena pushed back her straw hat and recovered her voice. "Stanton Carlisle, I swore if I ever set eyes on you again I'd sure give you a piece of my mind. Why, that child was pretty near out of her head, time she got to the carny. Everybody there thought she was touched, way she'd stumble around. I had her working the sword-box layout and she could just about step in and out of it, she was that bad. You sure done yourself proud by that girl, I must say. Oh, you was going to be mighty biggety—make a star out of her and everything. Well, you got there. But what good did it ever do her? Don't think I've ever forgot it." Her voice faltered and she sniffed, rubbing the back of a work-glove across her nose. "And what do you do but end up putting that kid, that sweet kid, on the turf—same as any two-bit pimp. It ain't any fault of yours that the kid pulled out of it so good. Oh, no. I hope she's forgot every idea she ever had about you. It ain't your fault she's married now to a grand guy and's got the cutest little kid of her own you ever laid eyes on. Oh, no, you done your best to land that girl in a crib house."

She stopped for breath, then went on in a different tone, "Oh, for God's sake, Stan, come in the house and let me fry you a slice of ham. You look like you ain't had a meal in a week."

The hobo wasn't listening. His knees had sagged; his chin scraped the fence rail and then he sank in a heap, like a scarecrow lifted from its pole.

Zeena dropped her gloves and began to climb the fence. "Joe, go down and hold the gate open. Stan's passed out. We got to get him in the house."

She lifted the emaciated body easily in her arms and carried it, legs dangling, toward the cottage.

Morning sun struck through the dotted curtains of the kitchen, falling on the golden hair of a man at the table, busy shoveling ham and eggs into his mouth. He stopped chewing and took a swallow of coffee.

". . . that skull buster was known all the way up and down the line. He beat two old stiffs to death in the basement of the jug last year. I knew when he got me up that alley that the curtain was going down."

Zeena turned from the stove with a skillet in one hand and a cake turner in the other. "Take it easy, Stan. Here's some more eggs. I reckon you got room for 'em." She filled his plate again.

Near the door Joe Plasky sat on a cushion, sorting mail into piles by states. It came in bundles; the mailman left it in a small barrel out on the road. On the barrel was painted: "ZEENA—PLASKY." They had outgrown an R.F.D. box long ago.

"He started working me over with the club." Stan paused with a forkful of egg in the air, looking at Joe. "So I let him have it. I clamped the *nami juji* on him and hung on. He went out for good."

Zeena stopped, holding the cake turner. She said, "Oh, my God." Then her eyes moved to Joe Plasky, who went on calmly sorting mail.

Joe said, "If it happened the way you tell it, kid, it was him or you. That Jap choke is a killer, all right. But you're a hot man, Stan. You've got to move quiet. And fast."

Zeena shook herself. "Well, he ain't moving till we get him fed up some. The boy was starved. Have some more coffee, Stan. But, Joe, what's he going to do? We can't—"

Joe smiled a little wider but his eyes were dark and turned inward, thinking. Finally he said, "They got your prints up there?"

Stan swallowed. "No. They don't print you on vag and peddling falls. Not in that town, anyway. But they know it was a blond pitchman working horoscopes."

Joe thought some more. "They didn't mug you?"

"No. Just a fine and a boot in the tail."

The half-man acrobat pushed aside the piles of letters and hopped over to the stairway, which led to the attic bedrooms. He swung up the stairs and out of sight; overhead they could hear a scrape as he crossed the floor.

Stan pushed back his plate and took a cigarette from the pack on the window sill. "Zeena, I've been living in a god-damned nightmare—a dream. I don't know what ever got into me. When vaudeville conked out we could have worked the night clubs. I don't know yet how I ever got tangled up with the spook racket."

The big woman was piling dishes in the sink. She was silent.

Stanton Carlisle's voice went on, getting back something of the old resonance. "I don't know what ever got into me. I don't expect Molly ever to forgive me. But I'm glad the kid got herself a good spot. I hope he's a swell guy. She deserves it. Don't tell her you ever saw me. I want her to forget me. I had my chance and I fluffed, when it came to Molly. I've fluffed everything."

Zeena turned back to him, her hands shining from the soapy water. "What you going to do, Stan, when you leave here?"

He was staring at the ember of his cigarette. "Search me, pal. Keep on bumming, I guess. The pitch is out. Everything's out. Good God, I don't know—"

On the stairs Joe Plasky made a scraping noise, coming down slowly. When he entered the kitchen he held a large roll of canvas under his arm. He spread it on the linoleum and unrolled it in two sections—gaudily painted banners showing enormous hands, the mounts and lines in different colors with the characteristics ascribed to each.

"Sophie Eidelson left these with us last season," he said. "Thought maybe you could use 'em. McGraw and Kauff-man's is playing a town down the line from here—be there all this week. There's worse places to hole up in than a carny."

Zeena dried her hands hastily and said, "Stan, give me a cigarette, quick. I've got it! Joe's got the answer. You could work it in a Hindu makeup. I've got an old blue silk kimono I can fix over for a robe. I reckon you know how to tie a turban."

The Great Stanton ran his hands over his hair. Then he knelt on the floor beside the half-man, pulling the palmistry banners further open and examining them. In his face Zeena could see the reflection of the brain working behind it. It seemed to have come alive out of a long sleep.

"Jesus God, this is manna from heaven, Joe. All I'll need is a bridge table and a canvas fly. I can hang the banners from the fly. They're looking for a pitchman, not a mitt reader. Oh, Jesus, here we go."

Joe Plasky moved away and picked up a burlap sack containing outgoing mail. He slung it over his shoulder and held the top of it in his teeth, setting off for the door on his hands. "Got to leave this for the pickup," he said, around the burlap. "You folks stay here—I've got it."

When he had gone Zeena poured herself a cup of coffee and offered one to Stan, who shook his head. He was still examining the banners.

"Stan—" She began to talk as if there was something which had to be said, something which was just for the two of them to hear. She spoke quickly, before Joe could return. "Stan, I want you to tell me something. It's about Pete. It don't hurt me to talk about him now. That was so long ago it seems like Pete never hit the skids at all. Seems like he died while we were still at the top of the heap. But I got to thinking—a kid will do an awful lot to lay some gal he's all steamed up about. And you were a kid, Stan, and hadn't ever had it before. I expect old Zeena looked pretty good to you in them days, too. Pete wouldn't ever have drank that bad alky. And you didn't know it was poison. Now come clean."

The Great Stanton stood up and thrust his hands into his pockets. He moved until the sun, shining through the window of the kitchen door, struck his hair. Soap and hot water had turned it from mud to gold again. His voice this time filled the kitchen; subtly, without increasing in power, it vibrated.

"Zeena, before you say another word, do me one favor. You remember Pete's last name?"

"Well— Well, he never used it. He wrote it on our marriage license. Only I ain't thought of it for years. Yes, I can remember it."

"And it's something I could never guess. Am I right? Will you concentrate on that name?"

"Stan— What—"

"Concentrate. Does it begin with *K*?"

She nodded, frowning, her lips parted.

"Concentrate. *K* . . . *R* . . . *U* . . . *M*—"

"Oh, my God!"

"The name was *Krumbein*!"

Joe Plasky pushed at the door and Stan moved aside. Zeena buried her mouth in the coffee cup and then set it down and hurried out of the room.

Joe raised his eyebrows.

"We were cutting up old times."

"Oh. Well, in that outfit I know McGraw a little—only you better not use my name, Stan. A guy as hot as you."

"What's calluses on the ends of the fingers, left hand?"

"Plays a stringed instrument."

"What's a callus here, on the right thumb?"

"A stonecutter."

"How about a callus in the bend of the first finger, right hand?"

"A barber—from stropping the razor."

"You're getting it, Stan. There's lots more that I forget— I ain't read mitts steady in many a year. If Sophie was here she could give you hundreds of things like that. She's got a whole notebook full of stuff. It locks with a key. But you'll make out all right. You always could read."

Zeena and Joe were sitting in the shade of the porch, opening letters and shaking out dimes. The woman said, "Hand me some more Scorpios, hon. I'm fresh out."

Joe ripped open a carton. The astrological booklets came in stamped-and-sealed envelopes. They addressed them quickly with fountain pens and threw them in a wire basket to be bundled up later for the postman.

Zeena said, "Beats all, Stan, how this mail-order business snowballs up. We put in one little ad and plowed back the dimes into the business. Now we got five chains of magazines covered and we can't hardly stop shaking out dimes to tend to the place here."

The Great Stanton reached into a saucepan by the side of the steamer chair where he lay in the sun. Taking a handful of dimes he counted out five batches of ten and rolled them into a red paper wrapper—five dollars' worth. The little red cylinders piled up in a china bowl on the other side of the chair, but he had carelessly allowed several to fall beside him. They were hidden between his thigh and the canvas chair-seat.

Joe hopped off the porch and over toward Stan, holding a basket of dimes in his teeth. He emptied them into the sauce-pan, smiling. "Little more and we're going to buy another place—farm next to this one. We've pretty near got this place mortgage-free. Long as people want horoscopes, I mean, astro-readings—you can't call 'em horoscopes through the mail unless they're drawn to the hour and minute of birth—long as they keep going like this we're set. And if they slack off, we've still got the farm."

Stan leaned back and let the sun strike through his eyelids. He was gaining. A week had filled him out. Almost back to his old weight. His eyes had cleared and his hands hardly shook at all. He hadn't had anything but beer in a week. A guy who's good at the cold reading will never starve. When Joe turned back to the porch Stanton slid the red cylinders from the chair to his pants pocket.

The truck bounced off the side road in a cloud of dust, white under the full moon, and turned into a state highway. Zeena drove carefully to spare the truck and Joe sat next to her, one arm on her shoulders to steady himself when they stopped suddenly or slowed down. Stan was next to the door of the cab, his palmistry banners in a roll between his knees.

Town lights glittered ahead as they topped a gradual rise. They coasted down it.

"Almost there, Stan."

"You'll make it, kid," Joe said. "McGraw's a hard cookie, but he ain't a nickel-nurser once you got him sold."

Stan was quiet, watching the bare streets they were rolling through. The bus station was a drugstore which kept open all night. Zeena stopped down the block and Stan opened the door and slid out, lifting out the banners.

"So long, Zeena—Joe. This—this was the first break I've had in a hell of a while. I don't know how—"

"Forget it, Stan. Joe and me was glad to do what we could. A carny's a carny and when one of us is jammed up we got to stick together."

"I'll try riding the baggage rack on this bus, I guess."

Zeena let out a snort. "I knew I'd forgot something. Here, Stan." From the pocket of her overalls she took a folded bill and, leaning over Joe, pressed it into the mentalist's hand. "You can send it back at the end of the season. No hurry."

"Thanks a million." The Great Stanton turned, with the rolled canvas under his arm, and walked away toward the drugstore. Halfway down the block he paused, straightened, threw back his shoulders and then went on, holding himself like an emperor.

Zeena started the truck and turned it around. They drove out of town in a different direction and then took a side road which cut into the highway further south, turning off it to mount a bluff overlooking the main drag. "Let's wait here, snooks, and try to get a peek into the bus when it goes by. I feel kind of funny, not being able to see him to the station and wait until it came along. Don't seem hospitable."

"Only smart thing to do, Zee. A fellow as hot as him."

She got out of the cab and her husband hopped after her; they crossed a field and sat on the bank. Above them the sky had clouded over, the moon was hidden by a thick ceiling.

"You reckon he'll make it, Joe?"

Plasky shifted his body on his hands and leaned forward. Far down the pale concrete strip the lights of a bus rose over the grade. It picked up speed, tires singing on the roadbed, as it bore down toward them. Through its windows they could make out the passengers—a boy and a girl, in a tight clinch on the back seat. One old man already asleep. It roared below the bank.

Stanton Carlisle was sharing a seat with a stout woman in a gay flowered-print dress and a white sailor straw hat. He was holding her right hand, palm up, and was pointing to the lines.

Joe Plasky sighed as the bus tore past them into darkness with a fading gleam of ruby taillights. "I don't know what'll happen to him," he said softly, "but that guy was never born to hang."

The Hanged Man

hangs head downward from the living wood.

IT WAS a cheap straw hat, but it added class. He was the type of guy who could wear a hat. The tie chain came from the five-and-ten, but with the suit and the white shirt it looked like the real thing. The amber mirror behind the bar always makes you look tanned and healthy. But he was tanned. The mustache was blackened to match the hair-dyeing job Zeena had done.

"Make mine a beer, pal."

He took it to a table, put his hat on an empty chair and unfolded a newspaper, pretending to read it. Forty-five minutes before the local bus left. They don't know who they're looking for up there—no prints, no photo. Stay out of that state and they'll look for you till Kingdom Come.

The beer was bitter and he began to feel a little edge from it. This was all right. Keep it at beer for a while. Get a stake, working the mitt camp. Get a good wad in the grouchbag and then try working Mexico. They say the language is a cinch to learn. And the damn country's wide open for ragheads.

They advertise in all the papers down there. Give that mess with the cop time to cool and I can come back in a few years and start working California. Take a Spanish name maybe. There's a million chances.

A guy who's good at the cold reading will never starve.

He opened the newspaper, scanning the pictures, thinking his way along through the days ahead. I'll have to hustle the readings and put my back into it. In a carny mitt camp you got to spot them quick, size 'em up and unload it in a hurry. Well, I can do it. I should have stayed right with the carny.

Two pages of the paper stuck and he went back and pried them apart, not caring what was on them, just so as not to skip any. In Mexico . . .

The picture was alone on the page, up near the top. He looked at it, concentrating on the woman's face, his glance merging the screen of black dots that composed it, filling in from memory its texture, contour, color. The scent of the sleek gold hair came back to him, the sly twist of her little tongue. The man looked twenty years older; he looked like a death's head—scrawny neck, flabby cheeks . . .

They were together. They were together. Read it. Read what they're doing.

PSYCHOLOGIST WEDS MAGNATE

In a simple ceremony. The bride wore a tailored . . . Best man was Melvin Anderson, long-time friend and advisor . . . Honeymoon cruise along the coast of Norway . . .

Somebody was shaking him, talking at him. Only it wasn't any grass tuft—it was a beer glass. "Jees, take it easy, bud. How'd ya bust it? Ya musta set it down too hard. We ain't responsible, you go slinging glasses around and get cut. Why don't ya go over to the drugstore. We ain't responsible . . ."

Darkness of street darkness with the night's eyes up above the roof cornices oh Jesus he was bleeding suitable for a full evening's performance gimme a rye and plain water, yeah, a rye make it a double.

It's nothing, I caught it on a nail, doc. No charge? Fine, doc. Gimme a rye—yeah, and plain water better make it a double rye and plain water seeping into the tire tracks where the grownups were everywhere.

I ain't pushing, bud, let's have no hard feelings, I'm your friend, my friend I get the impression that when you were a lad there was some line of work or profession you wanted to follow and furthermore you carry in your pocket a foreign coin or lucky piece you can see Sheriff that the young lady cannot wear ordinary clothes because thousands of volts of electricity cover her body like a sheath and the sequins rough against his fingers as he unhooked the smoothness of her breasts trembling pressing victory into we'll make a team right to the top and they give you a handout like a tramp at a back door but the doors have been closed, gentlemen, let them look for threads till Kingdom Come and the old idiot gaping there in the red light of the votive candle oh Jesus you frozen-faced bitch give me that dough yeah make it a rye, water on the side . . .

You could hardly see the platform for the smoke and the waiter wore a butcher's apron his sleeves were rolled up and his arms had muscles like Bruno's only they were covered with black hair you had to pay him every time and the drinks were small get out of this crummy joint and find another one but the dame was singing while the guy in a purple silk shirt rattled on the runt piano the old bag had on a black evening dress and a tiara of rhinestones

Put your arms around me, honey, hold me tight!

She drew the mike toward her and her tits bulged on each side of the rod Christ what an old bag . . .

Cuddle up and cuddle up with all your might!

She rubbed her belly against the microphone . . .

Oh! Oh! I never knew
any boy
like
you!

"Waiter—waiter, tell the singer to let me buy her a drink . . ."

When you look at me my heart . . . begins to float,
Then it starts a-rocking like a . . . a motor boat!
Oh! Oh! I never knew
Any boy . . . like . . . you!

"Whew, I'm all winded. Ya like that number? The old ones always the best, ain't they? Thanks, sport—same as ever for me, Mike. Ain't I seen you in here before, honey? Gee, you been missin' a good time . . ."

All hallways look alike and the lights burning black dressers and yellow bedspreads kiss me "Yeah, sure, honey, keep your pants on long enough for me to catch my breath. Them stairs—whew!"

Smell of face powder sweat perfume "Yeah, honey, I'll peel. Wait a minute, can't you? Never mind a chaser, just lean on the bottle, sport. Boy, this ain't bad. C'mon over and get friendly, honey, mamma's going to treat you right. Gee, ain't you the handsome one! Hey, honey, how about giving me my present now, huh? Where'd you get all them dimes? Holy gee, you musta stuck up a streetcar company. No more jumpsteady for me, honey, let's 'make a baby'—I got to get back."

Groping in the dark he found it, lying on its side there was still a drink in it oh Jesus I got to get out of here before they see this room . . .

The sun blinding him, feel in the lining, maybe some of them slipped down . . . one more roll of dimes . . . tie them in the tail of the undershirt this damn fleabag's a fleabag but the bottle don't need any corkscrew and to hell with water I fixed 'em all, the bastards, they'll never find me . . . covered my tracks too smart for 'em the bastards I bashed him right in the face and he fell back on the divan with his mouth hanging open the old bastard never knew what hit him but I'll slip them yet and work it in a Hindu outfit with dark makeup but there was one more drink the damn thieves somebody sneak in here and lap it up let me out of here got to get air oh Jesus the goddamned chairs are sliding back and forth back and forth and if I hold on tight to the carpet I won't slide and hit the wall with his fist beating away on the mantelpiece she sits straight up on the edge of the sofa looking at herself in the glass sign in front of the church when they boarded up the attic door and his hands bunching up the tablecloth as I rammed it into him, Gyp. That fat bastard I hope I blinded him following the star that burns in his lantern head down from the living wood.

In the office trailer McGraw was typing out a letter when he heard a tap on the screen door. He shaded his eyes against the desk lamp and said out of the side of his mouth, "Yeah, what?"

"Mis'er McGraw?"

"Yeah, yeah. What d'ya want? I'm busy."

"Wanna talk t'you, 'bout a 'traction. Added 'traction."

McGraw said, "Come on in. What you got to sell?"

The bum was hatless, shirt filthy. Under his arm he carried a roll of canvas. "Allow me t'introduce myself—Allah Rahged, top-money mitt reader. Got m'banners all ready t'go t'work. Best cold reader in the country. Lemme give you demonstration."

McGraw took the cigar out of his mouth. "Sorry, brother, I'm full up. And I'm busy. Why don't you rent a vacant store and work it solo?" He leaned forward, rolling up the paper in the typewriter. "I mean it, bud. We don't hire no boozers! Jesus! You smell like you pissed your pants. Go on, beat it!"

"Jus' give me chance make a demonstration. Real, old-time, A-number-one mitt reader. Take one look at the mark, read past, present—"

McGraw was letting his cold little eyes slide over the man whose head came within an inch of the trailer roof. The hair was dirty black, but at the temples and over the forehead was a thin line of yellow. Dyed. A lammister.

The carny boss suddenly smiled up at his visitor. "Take a seat, bud." From a cupboard behind him he lifted a bottle and two shot glasses. "Have a snort?"

"I thank you, sir. Very refreshing. I'll need only a fly and a bridge table—hang my banners on the edges of the fly."

McGraw shook his head. "I don't like a mitt camp. Too much trouble with the law."

The bum was eyeing the bottle, his red eyes fastened on it.

"Have another? No, I don't like mitt camps. Old stuff. Always got to have something new. Sensational."

The other nodded absently, watching the bottle. McGraw put it back in the cupboard and stood up. "Sorry, bud. Some other outfit, maybe. But not us. Good night."

The rum-dum pushed himself up, hands on the chair arms, and stood, swaying, blinking down at McGraw. Then he ran the back of his hand across his mouth and said, "Yeah. Sure." He stumbled, reached the screen door, and pulled it open, gripping it with his hand to keep his balance. He had forgotten the soiled canvas banners with their gaudily painted hands. "Well, so long, mister."

"Hey, wait a minute."

The lush was already back in the chair, leaning forward, his hands spread against his chest, elbows on the chair arms, head lolling. "Hey, mister, how 'bout 'nother li'l shot 'fore I go?"

"Yeah, sure. But I just happened to think of something. I got one job you might take a crack at. It ain't much, and I ain't begging you to take it; but it's a job. Keep you in coffee and cakes and a shot now and then. What do you say? Of course, it's only temporary—just until we get a real geek."

I MARRIED A DEAD MAN

by Cornell Woolrich

THE SUMMER NIGHTS are so pleasant in Caulfield. They smell of heliotrope and jasmine, honeysuckle and clover. The stars are warm and friendly here, not cold and distant, as where I came from; they seem to hang lower over us, be closer to us. The breeze that stirs the curtains at the open windows is soft and gentle as a baby's kiss. And on it, if you listen, you can hear the rustling sound of the leafy trees turning over and going back to sleep again. The lamplight from within the houses falls upon the lawns outside and copperplates them in long swaths. There's the hush, the stillness of perfect peace and security. Oh, yes, the summer nights are pleasant in Caulfield.

But not for us.

The winter nights are too. The nights of fall, the nights of spring. Not for us, not for us.

The house we live in is so pleasant in Caulfield. The blue-green tint of its lawn, that always seems so freshly watered no matter what the time of day. The sparkling, aerated pinwheels of the sprinklers always turning, steadily turning; if you look at them closely enough they form rainbows before your eyes. The clean, sharp curve of the driveway. The dazzling white-ness of the porch-supports in the sun. Indoors, the curving white symmetry of the bannister, as gracious as the dark and glossy stair it accompanies down from above. The satin finish of the rich old floors, bearing a telltale scent of wax and of lemon-oil if you stop to sniff. The lushness of pile carpeting. In almost every room, some favorite chair waiting to greet you like an old friend when you come back to spend a little time with it. People who come and see it say, "What more can there be? This is a home, as a home should be." Yes, the house we live in is so pleasant in Caulfield.

But not for us.

Our little boy, our Hugh, his and mine, it's such a joy to watch him growing up in Caulfield. In the house that will some day be his, in the town that will some day be his. To watch him take the first tottering steps that mean—now he

can walk. To catch and cherish each newly minted word that
fumblingly issues from his lips—that means, now he's added
another, now he can talk.

But even that is not for us, somehow. Even that seems
thefted, stolen, in some vague way I cannot say. Something
we're not entitled to, something that isn't rightfully ours.

I love him so. It's Bill I mean now, the man. And he loves
me. I know I do, I know he does, I cannot doubt it. And yet
I know just as surely that on some day to come, maybe this
year, maybe next, suddenly he'll pack his things and go away
and leave me. Though he won't want to. Though he'll love
me still, as much as he does on the day that I say this.

Or if he doesn't, it will be I who will. I'll take up my valise
and walk out through the door, never to come back. Though
I won't want to. Though I'll love him still, as much as I do
on the day that I say this. I'll leave my house behind. I'll leave
my baby behind, in the house that will some day be his, and
I'll leave my heart behind, with the man it belongs to (How
could I take it with me?), but I'll go and I'll never come back.

We've fought this thing. How bitterly we've fought it, in
every way that we know how. In every way there is. We've
driven it away, a thousand times we've driven it away, and it
comes back again in a look, a word, a thought. It's there.

No good for me to say to him, "You didn't do it. You've
told me so once. Once was enough. No need to repeat it now
again, this late. I *know* you didn't. Oh, my darling, my Bill,
you don't lie. You don't lie, in money, or in honor, or in
love—"

(But this isn't money, or honor, or love. This is a thing
apart. This is murder.)

No good, when I don't believe him. At the moment that
he speaks, I may. But a moment later, or an hour, or a day or
week, again I don't. No good, for we don't live just within a
single moment, we can't. The other moments come, the
hours, weeks, and, oh God, the years.

For each time, as he speaks, I know it wasn't I. That's all I
know. So well, too well, I know. And that leaves only—

And each time, as I speak, perhaps he knows that it wasn't
he (but I cannot know that, I cannot; there is no way for him

to reach me). So well he knows, so well. And that leaves only—

No good, no good at all.

One night six months ago I dropped upon my knees before him, with the boy there between us. Upon my bended knees. I put my hand on the little boy's head, and I swore it to him then and there. Speaking low, so the child wouldn't understand.

"By my child. Bill, I swear to you on the head of my child, that I didn't. Oh Bill, I didn't do it—"

He raised me up, and held me in his arms, and pressed me to him.

"I know you didn't. I know. What more can I say? In what other way can I tell you? Here, lie against my heart, Patrice. Perhaps that can tell you better than I— Listen to it, can't you tell that it believes you?"

And for a moment it does, that one moment of our love. But then the other moment comes, that one that always comes after. And he has already thought, "But I know it wasn't I. I know so well it wasn't I. And that leaves only—"

And even while his arms go tighter than ever about me, and his lips kiss the wetness from my eyes, he already doesn't again. He already doesn't.

There's no way out. We're caught, we're trapped. The circle viciously completes itself each time, and we're on the inside, can't break through. For if he's innocent, then it has to be me. And if I am, it has to be he. But I *know* I'm innocent. (Yet he may know he is too.) There's no way out.

Or, tired with trying to drive it away, we've rushed toward it with desperate abandon, tried to embrace it, to be done with it once and for all in that way.

One time, unable to endure its long-drawn, unseen, ghostly vigil over our shoulders any longer, he suddenly flung himself out of the chair he'd been in, though nothing had been said between us for an hour past. Flung the book he hadn't been reading, only pretending to, far from him like a brickbat. Flung himself up as wildly as though he were going to rush forward to grapple with something he saw there before him. And my heart flung itself wildly up with him.

He surged to the far end of the room and stopped there—
at bay. And made a fist, and raised his arm, and swung it with
a thundering crash against the door, so that only the panel's
thickness kept it from shattering. Then turned in his helpless
defiance and cried out:

"I don't care! It doesn't matter! Do you hear me? It doesn't
matter! People have done it before. Lots of times. And lived
out their happiness afterward. Why shouldn't we? He was no
good. It was what he deserved. He wasn't worth a second
thought. The whole world said so then, and they'd still say so
now. He isn't worth a single minute of this hell we've gone
through—"

And then he poured a drink for each of us, lavish, reckless,
and came back toward me with them. And I, understanding,
agreeing, one with him, rose and went to meet him halfway.

"Here, take this. Drink on it. Drown it. Drown it until it's
gone. One of us *did* do it. It doesn't matter. It's done with.
Now let's get on with living."

And striking himself on the chest, "All right, *I* did it. There.
I was the one. Now it's settled. Now it's over at last—"

And then suddenly our eyes looked deep into one another's, our glasses faltered in mid-air, went down, and it was
back again.

"But you don't believe that," I whispered, dismayed.

"And you do," he breathed, stricken.

Oh, it's everything, it's everywhere.

We've gone away, and it's where we go. It's in the blue
depths of Lake Louise, and high up in the fleecy cloud for-
mations above Biscayne Bay. It rolls restlessly in with the surf
at Santa Barbara, and lurks amid the coral rocks of Bermuda,
a darker flower than the rest.

We've come back, and it's where we've come back to.

It's between the printed lines on the pages of the books we
read. But it peers forth dark, and they fade off to illegibility.
"Is he thinking of it now, as I read? As I am? I will not look
up at him, I will keep my eyes to this, but—is he thinking of
it now?"

It's the hand that holds out its coffee-cup across the break-
fast-table in the mornings, to have the urn tipped over it.
Bloody-red for a moment in fancy, then back again to pale as

it should be. Or maybe, to the other, it's that other hand opposite one, that does the tipping of the urn; depending upon which side of the table the beholder is sitting.

I saw his eyes rest on my hand one day, and I knew what he was thinking at that instant. Because I had looked at his hand much the same way on a previous day, and I had been thinking then what he was thinking now.

I saw him close his eyes briefly, to efface the sickly illusion; and I closed mine to dispel the knowledge of it that his had conveyed to me. Then we both opened them, and smiled at one another, to tell one another nothing had happened just then.

It's in the pictures that we see on the theatre-screen. "Let's get out of here, I'm—tired of it, aren't you?" (Somebody is going to kill somebody, up there, soon, and he knows it's coming.) But even though we do get up and leave, it's already too late, because he knows why we're leaving, and I know too. And even if I didn't know until then, this—the very fact of our leaving—has told me. So the precaution is wasted after all. *It's* back in our minds again.

Still, it's wiser to go than to stay.

I remember one night it came too quickly, more suddenly than we could have foretold, there was less warning given. We were not able to get all the way out in time. We were still only making our way up the aisle, our backs to the screen, when suddenly a shot rang out, and then a voice groaned in accusation, "You've—you've killed me."

It seemed to me it was *his* voice, and that he was speaking to us, to one of us. It seemed to me, in that moment, that every head in the audience turned, to look our way, to stare at us, with that detached curiosity of a great crowd when someone has been pointed out to them.

My legs for a moment seemed to refuse to carry me any further. I floundered there for a minute as though I were going to fall down helpless upon the carpeted aisle. I turned to look at him and I saw, unmistakably, that his head had cringed for a moment, was down defensively between his shoulders. And he always carried it so straight and erect. A moment later it *was* straight again, but just for that instant it hadn't been, it had been hunched.

Then, as though sensing that I needed him just then, be- cause, perhaps, he needed me, he put his arm around my waist, and helped me the rest of the way up the aisle that way, steadying me, promising me support rather than actually giving it to me.

In the lobby, both our faces were like chalk. We didn't look at one another, it was the mirrors on the side told us that.

We never drink. We know enough not to. I think we sense that, rather than close the door on awareness, that would only open it all the wider and let full horror in. But that particular night, I remember, as we came out, he said, "Do you want something?"

He didn't say a drink; just "something." But I understood what that "something" meant. "Yes," I shuddered quietly.

We didn't even wait until we got home; it would have taken us too long. We went in to a place next door to the theatre, and stood up to the bar for a moment, the two of us alike, and gulped down something on the run. In three minutes we were out of there again. Then we got in the car and drove home. And we never said a word the whole way.

It's in the very kiss we give each other. Somehow we trap it right between our lips, each time. (Did I kiss him too strongly? Will he think by that I forgave him, again, just then? Did I kiss him too weakly? Will he think by that I was thinking of it, again, just then?)

It's everywhere, it's all the time, it's *us*.

I don't know what the game was. I only know its name; they call it life.

I'm not sure how it should be played. No one ever told me. No one ever tells anybody. I only know we must have played it wrong. We broke some rule or other along the way, and never knew it at the time.

I don't know what the stakes are. I only know we've for- feited them, they're not for us.

We've lost. That's all I know. We've lost, we've lost.

One

THE DOOR was closed. It had a look of pitiless finality about it, as though it would always be closed like this from now on. As though nothing in the world could ever make it open again. Doors can express things. This one did. It was inert, it was lifeless; it didn't lead anywhere. It was not the beginning of anything, as a door should be. It was the ending of something.

Above the push-button there was a small oblong rack, of metal, affixed to the woodwork, intended to frame a name-card. It was empty. The card was gone.

The girl was standing still in front of the door. Perfectly still. The way you stand when you've been standing for a long time; so long, you've forgotten about moving, have grown used to not moving. Her finger was to the push-button, but it wasn't pushing any more. No pressure was being exerted; no sound came from the battery behind the door-frame. It was as though she had been holding it that way so long, she had forgotten to take that, too, away.

She was about nineteen. A dreary, hopeless nineteen, not a bright, shiny one. Her features were small and well turned, but there was something too pinched about her face, too wan about her coloring, too thin about her cheeks. Beauty was there, implicit, ready to reclaim her face if it was given the chance, but something had beaten it back, was keeping it hovering at a distance, unable to alight in its intended realization.

Her hair was hazel-colored, and limp and listless, as though no great heed had been paid to it for some time past. The heels of her shoes were a little run-down. A puckered darn in the heel of her stocking peered just over the top of one. Her clothing was functional, as though it were worn for the sake of covering, and not for the sake of fashion, or even of appeal. She was a good height for a girl, about five-six or seven. But she was too thin, except in one place.

Her head was down a little, as though she were tired of carrying it up straight. Or as though invisible blows had lowered it, one by one.

She moved at last. At long last. Her hand dropped from the push-button, as if of its own weight. It fell to her side, hung there, forlorn. One foot turned, as if to go away. There was a wait. Then the other turned too. Her back was to the door now. The door that wouldn't open. The door that was an epitaph, the door that was finality.

She took a slow step away. Then another. Her head was down now more than ever. She moved slowly away from there, and left the door behind. Her shadow was the last part of her to go. It trailed slowly after her, upright against the wall. Its head was down a little, too; it too was too thin, it too was unwanted. It stayed on a moment, after she herself was already gone. Then it slipped off the wall after her, and *it* was gone too.

Nothing was left there but the door. That remained silent, obdurate, closed.

Two

IN the telephone-booth she was motionless again. As motionless as before. A telephone pay-station, the door left shunted back in order to obtain air enough to breathe. When you are in one for more than just a few moments, they become stifling. And she had been in this one for more than just a few moments.

She was like a doll propped upright in its gift-box, and with one side of the box left off, to allow the contents to be seen. A worn doll. A leftover, marked-down doll, with no bright ribbons or tissue wrappings. A doll with no donor and no recipient. A doll no one bothered to claim.

She was silent there, though this was meant to be a place for talking. She was waiting to hear something, something that never came. She was holding the receiver pointed toward her ear, and it must have started out by being close to it, at right angles to it, as receivers should be. But that was a long time before. With the passage of long, disappointing minutes it had drooped lower and lower, until now it was all the way down at her shoulder, clinging there wilted, defeated, like some sort of ugly, black, hard-rubber orchid worn for corsage.

The anonymous silence became a voice at last. But not the one she wanted, not the one she was waiting for.

"I am sorry, but I have already told you. There is no use waiting on the line. That number has been discontinued, and there is no further information I can give you."

Her hand dropped off her shoulder, carrying the receiver with it, and fell into her lap, dead. As if to match something else within her that was dead, by the final way it fell and stirred no more.

But life won't grant a decent dignity even to its epitaphs, sometimes.

"May I have my nickel back?" she whispered. "*Please.* I didn't get my party, and it's—it's the last one I've got."

Three

SHE climbed the rooming-house stairs like a puppet dangling from slack strings. A light bracketed against the wall, drooping upside-down like a withered tulip in its bell-shaped shade of scalloped glass, cast a smoky yellow glow. A carpet-strip ground to the semblance of decayed vegetable-matter, all pattern, all color, long erased, adhered to the middle of the stairs, like a form of pollen or fungus encrustation. The odor matched the visual imagery. She climbed three flights of them, and then turned off toward the back.

She stopped, at the last door there was, and took out a long-shanked iron key. Then she looked down at the bottom of the door. There was a triangle of white down by her foot, protruding from under the seam. It expanded into an envelope as the door swept back above it.

She reached into the darkness, and traced her hand along the wall beside the door, and a light went on. It had very little shine. It had very little to shine on.

She closed the door and then she picked up the envelope. It had been lying on its face. She turned it over. Her hand shook a little. Her heart did too.

It had on it, in hasty, heedless pencil, only this:

"Helen Georgesson."

No Miss, no Mrs., no other salutation whatever.

She seemed to come alive more fully. Some of the blank hopelessness left her eyes. Some of the pinched strain left her face. She grasped the envelope tight, until it pleated a little in her hold. She moved more briskly than she had until now. She took it over with her to the middle of the room, beside the bed, where the light shone more fully.

She stood still there and looked at it again, as though she were a little afraid of it. There was a sort of burning eagerness in her face; not joyous, but rather of desperate urgency.

She ripped hastily at the flap of it, with upward swoops of her hand, as though she were taking long stitches in it with invisible needle and thread.

Her hand plunged in, to pull out what it said, to read what it told her. For envelopes carry words that tell you things; that's what envelopes are for.

Her hand came out again empty, frustrated. She turned the envelope over and shook it out, to free what it must hold, what must have stubbornly resisted her fingers the first time.

No words came, no writing.

Two things fell out, onto the bed. Only two things.

One was a five-dollar bill. Just an impersonal, anonymous five-dollar bill, with Lincoln's picture on it. And over to the side of that, the neat little cachet they all bear, in small-size capitals: "This certificate is legal tender for all debts public and private." For all debts, public and *private*. How could the engraver guess that that might break somebody's heart, some day, somewhere?

And the second thing was a strip of railroad-tickets, running consecutively from starting-point to terminus, as railroad tickets do. Each coupon to be detached progressively en route. The first coupon was inscribed "New York"; here, where she was now. And the last was inscribed "San Francisco"; where she'd come from, a hundred years ago—last spring.

There was no return-ticket. It was for a one-way trip. There and—to stay.

So the envelope *had* spoken to her after all, though it had no words in it. Five dollars legal tender, for *all* debts, public and private. San Francisco—and no return.

The envelope plummeted to the floor.

She couldn't seem to understand for a long time. It was as though she'd never seen a five-dollar bill before. It was as though she'd never seen an accordion-pleated strip of rail-road-tickets like that before. She kept staring down at them.

Then she started to shake a little. At first without sound. Her face kept twitching intermittently, up alongside the eyes and down around the corners of the mouth, as if her expression were struggling to burst forth into some kind of fulminating emotion. For a moment or two it seemed that when it did, it would be weeping. But it wasn't.

It was laughter.

Her eyes wreathed into oblique slits, and her lips slashed back, and harsh broken sounds came through. Like rusty laughter. Like laughter left in the rain too long, that has got all mildewed and spoiled.

She was still laughing when she brought out the battered valise, and placed it atop the bed, and threw the lid back. She was still laughing when she'd filled it and closed it again.

She never seemed to get through laughing. Her laughter never stopped. As at some long-drawn joke, that goes on and on, and is never done with in its telling.

But laughter should be merry, vibrant and alive.

This wasn't.

Four

THE train had already ticked off fifteen minutes' solid, steady headway, and she hadn't yet found a seat. The seats were full with holiday crowds and the aisles were full and the very vestibules were full; she'd never seen a train like this before. She'd been too far behind at the dammed-up barrier, and too slow and awkward with her cumbersome valise, and too late getting on. Her ticket only allowed her to get aboard, it gave her no priority on any place to sit.

Flagging, wilting, exhausted, she struggled down car-aisle after car-aisle, walking backward against the train-pull, eddying, teetering from side to side, leaden valise pulling her down.

They were all packed with standees, and this was the last one now. No more cars after this. She'd been through them all. No one offered her a seat. This was a through train, no stops for whole States at a time, and an act of courtesy now would have come too high. This was no trolley or bus with a few moments' running time. Once you were gallant and stood, you stood for hundreds and hundreds of miles.

She stopped at last, and stayed where she'd stopped, for sheer inability to turn and go back again to where she'd come from. No use going any further. She could see to the end of the car, and there weren't any left.

She let her valise down parallel to the aisle, and tried to seat herself upon its upturned edge as she saw so many others doing. But she floundered badly for a moment, out of her own topheaviness, and almost tumbled in lowering herself. Then when she'd succeeded, she let her head settle back against the sideward edge of the seat she was adjacent to, and stayed that way. Too tired to know, too tired to care, too tired even to close her eyes.

What makes you stop, when you have stopped, just where you have stopped? What is it, what? Is it something, or is it nothing? Why not a yard short, why not a yard more? Why just there where you are, and nowhere else?

Some say: It's just blind chance, and if you hadn't stopped there, you would have stopped at the next place. Your story would have been different then. You weave your own story as you go along.

But others say: You could not have stopped any place else but this even if you had wanted to. It was decreed, it was ordered, you were meant to stop at this spot and no other. Your story is there waiting for you, it has been waiting for you there a hundred years, long before you were born, and you cannot change a comma of it. Everything you do, you have to do. You are the twig, and the water you float on swept you here. You are the leaf and the breeze you were borne on blew you here. This is your story, and you cannot escape it; you are only the player, not the stage manager. Or so some say.

On the floor before her downcast eyes, just over the rim of the seat-arm, she could see two pairs of shoes uptilted, side by side. On the inside, toward the window, a diminutive pair of pumps, pert, saucy, without backs, without sides, without toes, in fact with scarcely anything but dagger-like heels and a couple of straps. And on the outside, the nearer side to her, a pair of man's brogues, looking by comparison squat, bulky, and tremendously heavy. These hung one above the other, from legs coupled at the knee.

She did not see their faces and she did not want to. She did not want to see anyone's face. She did not want to see anything.

Nothing happened for a moment. Then one of the pumps edged slyly over toward one of the brogues, nudged gently into it, as if in a deft little effort to communicate something. The brogue remained oblivious; it didn't get the message. It got the feeling, but not the intent. A large hand came down, and scratched tentatively at the sock just above the brogue, then went up again.

The pump, as if impatient at such obtuseness, repeated the effort. Only this time it delivered a good sharp dig, with a bite to it, and on the unprotected ankle, above the armor-like brogue.

That got results. A newspaper rattled somewhere above, as if it had been lowered out of the way, to see what all this unpleasant nipping was about.

A whispered remark was voiced above, spoken too low to be distinguishable by any but the ear for which it was intended.

An interrogative grunt, in masculine timbre, answered it.

Both brogues came down even on the floor, as the legs above uncoupled. Then they swivelled slightly toward the aisle, as if their owner had turned his upper body to glance that way.

The girl on the valise closed her eyes wearily, to avoid the gaze that she knew must be on her.

When she opened them again, the brogues had come out through the seat-gap, and the wearer was standing full-height in the aisle, on the other side of her. A good height too, a six-foot height.

"Take my seat, miss," he invited. "Go ahead, take my place for awhile."

She tried to demur with a faint smile and a halfhearted shake of the head. But the velour back looked awfully good.

The girl who had remained in it added her insistence to his. "Go ahead, honey, take it," she urged. "He wants you to. We want you to. You can't stay out there like that, where you are."

The velour back looked awfully good. She couldn't take her eyes off it. But she was almost too tired to stand up and effect the change. He had to reach down and take her by the arm and help her rise from the valise and shift over.

Her eyes closed again for a moment, in ineffable bliss, as she sank back.

"There you are," he said heartily. "Isn't that better?"

And the girl beside her, her new seat-mate, said: "Why, you *are* tired. I never saw anyone so all-in."

She smiled her thanks, and still tried to protest a little, though the act had already been completed, but they both overrode her remonstrances.

She looked at the two of them. Now she at least wanted to see their two faces, if no others, though only a few moments ago she hadn't wanted to see any faces, anywhere, ever again. But kindness is a form of restorative.

They were both young. Well, she was too. But they were both happy, gay, basking in the world's blessings, that was the difference between them and her. It stood out all over them. There was some sort of gilded incandescence alight within both of them alike, something that was more than mere good spirits, more than mere good fortune, and for the first few moments she couldn't tell what it was. Then in no time at all, their eyes, and every turn of their heads, and every move they made, gave it away: they were supremely, brimmingly in love with one another. It glowed out all over them, almost like phosphorus.

Young love. New untarnished love. That first love that comes just once to everyone and never comes back again.

But, conversationally, it expressed itself inversely, at least on her part if not his; almost every remark she addressed to him was a friendly insult, a gentle slur, an amiable depreciation. Not so much as a word of tenderness, or even ordinary human consideration, did she seem to have for him. Though her eyes belied her. And he understood. He had that smile for all her outrageous insolences, that worshipped, that adored, that understood so well.

"Well, go on," she said with a peremptory flick of her hand. "Don't stand there like a dope, breathing down the backs of our necks. Go and find something to do."

"Oh, pardon me," he said, and pretended to turn the back of his collar up, as if frozen out. He looked vaguely up and down the aisle. "Guess I'll go out on the platform and smoke a cigarette."

"Smoke two," she said airily. "See if I care."

He turned and began to pick his way down the thronged aisle.

"That was nice of him," the newcomer said appreciatively, glancing after him.

"Oh, he's tolerable," her companion said. "He has his good points." She gave a shrug. But her eyes made a liar out of her.

She glanced around to make sure he'd gone out of earshot. Then she leaned slightly toward the other, dropped her voice confidentially. "I could tell right away," she said. "That's why I made him get up. About you, I mean."

The girl who'd been on the valise dropped her eyes for an instant, confused, deprecating. She didn't say anything.

"I am too. You're not the only one," her companion rushed on, with just a trace of vainglory, as if she couldn't wait to tell it quickly enough.

The girl said, "Oh." She didn't know what else to say. It sounded flat, superficial; the way you say "Is that so?" or "You don't say?" She tried to force a smile of sympathetic interest, but she wasn't very good at it. Out of practice at smiling, maybe.

"Seven months," the other added gratuitously.

The girl could feel her eyes on her, as though she expected some return in kind to be made, if only for the record.

"Eight," she said, half-audibly. She didn't want to, but she did.

"Wonderful," was her companion's praise for this arithmetical information. "Marvelous." As though there were some sort of a caste system involved in this, and she unexpectedly found herself speaking to one of the upper brackets of nobility: a duchess or a marquise, who outranked her by thirty days. And all around them, snobbishly ignored, the commonality of the female gender.

"Wonderful, marvelous," echoed the girl inwardly, and her heart gave a frightened, unheard sob.

"And your husband?" the other rushed on. "You going to meet him?"

"No," the girl said, looking steadily at the green velour of the seat-back in front of them. "No."

"Oh. D'dyou leave him back in New York?"

"No," the girl said. "No." She seemed to see it written on the seat-back in transitory lettering, that faded again as soon as it was once read. "I've lost him."

"Oh, I'm sor—" Her vivacious companion seemed to know grief for the first time, other than just grief over a broken doll or a school-girl crush betrayed. It was like a new experience passing over her radiant face. And it was, even now, bound to be someone else's grief, not her own; that was the impression you had. That she'd never had any grief of her own, had none now, and never would have. One of those star-blessed rarities, glittering its way through the world's dark vale.

She bit off the rest of the ejaculation of sympathy, gnawed at her upper lip; reached out impulsively and placed her hand upon her companion's for a moment, then withdrew it again.

Then, tactfully, they didn't speak any more about such things. Such basic things as birth and death, that can give such joy and can give such pain.

She had corn-gold hair, this sun-kissed being. She wore it in a hazy aureole that fluffed out all over her head. She had freckles that were like little flecks of gold paint, spattered from some careless painter's brush all over her apricot cheeks, with a saddle across the bridge of her tiny, pert nose. It was her mouth that was the beautiful part of her. And if the rest of her face was not quite up to its matchless beauty, that mouth alone was sufficient to make her lovely-looking, unaided, drawing all notice to itself as it did. Just as a single light is enough to make a plain room bright; you don't have to have a whole chandelier. When it smiled, everything else smiled with it. Her nose crinkled, and her eyebrows arched, and her eyes creased, and dimples showed up where there hadn't been any a minute before. She looked as though she smiled a lot. She looked as though she had a lot to smile about.

She continually toyed with a wedding-band on her third finger. Caressed it, so to speak, fondled it. She was probably unconscious of doing so by this time; it must have become a fixed habit by now. But originally, months ago, when it was first there, when it was new there, she must have taken such a fierce pride in it that she'd felt the need for continually displaying it to all the world—as if to say, "Look at *me*! Look what I've got!"—must have held such an affection for it that she couldn't keep her hands off it for very long. And now, though pride and affection were in nowise less, this had formed itself into a winning little habit that persisted. No matter what move her hands made, no matter what gesture they expressed, it always managed to come uppermost, to be foremost in the beholder's eye.

It had a row of diamonds, and then a sapphire at each end for a stop. She caught her new seat-mate's glance resting upon it, so then she turned it around her way a little more, so she could see it all the better, gave it a pert little brush-off with her fingers, as if to dispel the last, lingering, hypothetical grain of dust. A brush-off that pretended she didn't care any more about it just then. Just as her attitude toward him pretended she didn't care anything about him either. A brush-off that lied like the very devil.

They were both chatting away absorbedly, as new-found friends do, by the time he reappeared some ten minutes later. He came up to them acting secretive and mysterious in a rather conspicuous way. He looked cautiously left and right first, as if bearing tidings of highest secrecy. Then screened the side of his mouth with the edge of one hand. Then leaned down and whispered, "Pat, one of the porters just tipped me off. They're going to open up the dining-car in a couple of minutes. Special, inside, advance information. You know what that'll mean in this mob. I think we better start moving up that way if we want to get in under the rope on the first shift. There'll be a stampede under way as soon as word gets around."

She jumped to her feet with alacrity.

He immediately soft-pedalled her with the flats of both hands, in comic intensity. "Sh! Don't give it away! What are you trying to do? Act indifferent. Act as if you weren't going anywhere in particular, were just getting up to stretch your legs."

She smothered an impish chuckle. "When I'm going to the dining-car, I just *can't* act as if I weren't going anywhere in particular. It stands out all over me. You're lucky if you hold me down to a twenty-yard dash." But to oblige his ideas of Machiavellian duplicity, she exaggeratedly arched her feet and tiptoed out into the aisle, as though the amount of noise she made had any relation to what they were trying to do.

In passing, she pulled persuasively at the sleeve of the girl beside her. "Come on. You're coming with us, aren't you?" she whispered conspiratorially.

"What about the seats? We'll lose them, won't we?"

"Not if we put our baggage on them. Here, like this." She raised the other girl's valise, which had been standing there in the aisle until now, and between them they planked it lengthwise across the seat, effectively blocking it.

The girl was on her feet now, dislodged by the valise, but she still hung back, hesitant about going with them.

The young wife seemed to understand; she was quick that way. She sent him on ahead, out of earshot, to break trail for them. Then turned to her recent seat-mate in tactful reassurance. "Don't worry about—anything; *he'll* look after everything." And then, making confidantes of the two of them about this, to minimize the other's embarrassment, she promised her: "I'll see that he does. That's what they're for, anyway."

The girl tried to falter an insincere denial, that only proved the surmise had been right. "No, it isn't that—I don't like to—"

But her new friend had already taken her acceptance for an accomplished fact, had no more time to waste on it. "Hurry up, we'll lose him," she urged. "They're closing in again behind him."

She urged her forward ahead of herself, a friendly hand lightly placed just over her outside hip.

"You can't neglect yourself now, of all times," she cautioned her in an undertone. "I *know*. They told me that myself."

The pioneering husband, meanwhile, was cutting a wide swath for them down the center of the clogged aisle, causing people to lean acutely in over the seats to give clearance. And yet with never a resentful look. He seemed to have that way about him; genial but firm.

"It's useful to have a husband who used to be on the football team," his bride commented complacently. "He can run your interference for you. Just look at the width of that back, would you?"

When they had overtaken him, she complained petulantly, "Wait for me, can't you? I have two to feed."

"So have I," was the totally unchivalrous remark over his shoulder. "And they're both me."

They were, by dint of his foresight, the first ones in the dining-car, which was inundated within moments after the doors had been thrown open. They secured a choice table for three, diagonal to a window. The unlucky ones had to wait on line in the aisle outside, the door inhospitably closed in their faces.

"Just so we won't sit down to the table still not knowing each other's names," the young wife said, cheerfully unfolding her napkin, "he's Hazzard, Hugh, and I'm Hazzard, Patrice." Her dimples showed up in depreciation. "Funny name, isn't it?"

"Be more respectful," her young spouse growled, without lifting his forehead from the bill of fare. "I'm just trying you out for it. I haven't decided yet whether I'll let you keep it or not."

"It's mine now," was the feminine logic he got. "I haven't decided whether I'll let *you* keep it or not."

"What's your name?" she asked their guest.

"Georgesson," the girl said. "Helen Georgesson."

She smiled hesitantly at the two of them. Gave him the outside edge of her smile, gave her the center of it. It wasn't a very broad smile, but it had depth and gratitude, the little there was of it.

"You've both been awfully friendly to me," she said.

She looked down at the menu card she held spread between

her hands, so they wouldn't detect the flicker of emotion that made her lips tremble for a moment.

"It must be an awful lot of fun to be—you," she murmured wistfully.

Five

By the time the overhead lights in their car had been put out, around ten, so that those who wanted to sleep could do so, they were already old and fast friends. They were already "Patrice" and "Helen" to one another; this, as might have been surmised, at Patrice's instigation. Friendship blooms quickly in the hothouse atmosphere of travel; within the space of hours, sometimes, it's already full-blown. Then just as suddenly is snapped off short, by the inevitable separation of the travelers. It seldom if ever survives that separation for long. That is why, on ships and trains, people have fewer reticences with one another, they exchange confidences more quickly, tell all about themselves; they will never have to see these same people again, and worry about what opinion they may have formed, whether good or bad.

The small, shaded, individual sidelights provided for each seat, that could be turned on or off at will, were still on for the most part, but the car was restfully dimmer and quieter, some of its occupants already dozing. Patrice's husband was in an inert, hat-shrouded state on the valise that again stood alongside his original seat, his crossed legs precariously slung upward to the top of the seat ahead. However, he seemed comfortable enough, judging by the sonorous sounds that escaped from inside his hat now and then. He had dropped out of their conversation fully an hour before, and, an unkind commentary this on the importance of men to women's conversations, to all appearances hadn't even been missed.

Patrice was acting the part of a look-out, her eyes watchfully and jealously fastened on a certain door, far down the aisle behind them, in the dim distance. To do this, she was kneeling erect on the seat, in reverse, staring vigilantly over the back of it. This somewhat unconventional position, however, did nothing whatever to inhibit her conversational flow, which proceeded as freely and blithely as ever. Only, owing to her elevated stance, the next seat back now shared the benefit of most of it, along with her own. Fortunately, however, its occupants were disqualified from any great amount of interest in it by two facts; they were both men, and they were both asleep.

A ripple of reflected light suddenly ran down the sleek chromium of the door that had her attention.

"She just came out," she hissed with an explosive sibilance, and executed an agitated series of twists, turns, and drops on the seat, as though this were something vital that had to be acted upon immediately. "Hurry up! *Now!* Now's our chance. Get a move on. Before somebody else gets there ahead of us. There's a fat woman three seats down been taking her things out little by little. If she ever gets in first, we're sunk!" Carried away by her own excitement (and everything in life, to her, seemed to be deliciously, titillatingly exciting), she even went so far as to give her seat-mate a little push and urge her: "Run! Hold the door for us. Maybe if she sees you there already, she'll change her mind."

She prodded her relaxed spouse cruelly and heartlessly in a great many places at once, to bring him back to awareness.

"Quick! Hugh! The overnight-case! We'll lose our chance. Up there, stupid. Up there on the rack—"

"All right, take it easy," the somnolent Hugh grunted, eyes still completely buried under his obliterating hat-brim. "Talk, talk, talk, Yattatta, yattatta, yattatta. Woman is born to exercise her jaw."

"Man is born to get a poke on his, if he doesn't get a move on."

He finally pushed his hat back out of the way. "What do you want from me now? You got it down yourself."

"Well, get your big legs out of the way and let us by! You're blocking the way—"

He executed a sort of drawbridge maneuver, folding his legs back to himself, hugging them, then stretching them out again after the passage had been accomplished.

"Where y'going, in such a hurry?" he asked innocently.

"Now, isn't that stupid?" commented Patrice to her companion.

The two of them went almost running down the aisle, without bothering to enlighten him further.

"He takes a thirty-six sleeve, and it doesn't do me a bit of good in an emergency," she complained en route, swinging the kit.

He had turned his head to watch them curiously, and in perfectly sincere incomprehension. Then he went, "Oh." Understanding their destination now, if not the turmoil attendant on it. Then he pulled his hat down to his nose again, to resume his fractured slumbers where they had been broken off by this feminine logistical upheaval.

Patrice had closed the chromium door after the two of them, meanwhile, and given its inside lock-control a little twist of defiant exclusion. Then she let out a deep breath. "There. We're in. And possession is nine-tenths of the law. I'm going to take as long as I want," she announced determinedly, setting down the overnight-case and unlatching its lid. "If anybody else wants to get in, they'll just have to wait. There's only room enough for two anyway. And even so, they have to be awfully good friends."

"We're nearly the last ones still up, anyway," Helen said.

"Here, have some?" Patrice was bringing up a fleecy fistful of facial tissues from the case; she divided them with her friend.

"I missed these an awful lot on the Other Side. Couldn't get them for love nor money. I used to ask and ask, and they didn't know what I meant—"

She stopped and eyed her companion. "Oh, you have nothing to rub off, have you? Well, here, rub some of this on; then you'll have that to rub off."

Helen laughed. "You make me feel so giddy," she said with a wistful sort of admiration.

Patrice hunched her shoulders and grimaced impishly. "It's my last fling, sort of. From tomorrow night on I may have to be on my best behavior. Sober and sedate." She made a long face, and steepled her hands against her stomach, in mimicry of a bluenosed clergyman.

"Oh, on account of meeting your in-laws," Helen remembered.

"Hugh says they're not like that at all; I have absolutely nothing to worry about. But of course he just may be slightly prejudiced in their favor. I wouldn't think much of him if he wasn't."

She was scouring a mystic white circle on each cheek, and then spreading them around, mouth open the whole while, though it played no part in the rite itself.

"Go ahead, help yourself," she invited. "Stick your finger in and dig out a gob. I'm not sure what it does for you, but it smells nice, so there's nothing to lose."

"Is that really true, what you told me?" Helen said, following suit. "That they've never even seen you until now? I can't believe it."

"Cross my heart and hope to die, they've never laid eyes on me in their lives. I met Hugh on the Other Side, like I told you this afternoon, and we were married over there, and we went on living over there until just now. My folks were dead, and I was on a scholarship, studying music, and he had a job with one of these government agencies; you know, one of these initialed outfits. They don't even know what I *look* like!"

"Didn't you even send them a picture of yourself? Not even after you were married?"

"We never even had a wedding-picture taken; you know how us kids are nowadays. Biff, bing, bang! and we're married. I started to send them one of myself several times, but I was never quite satisfied with the ones I had. Self-conscious, you know; I wanted to make *such* a good first impression. One time Hugh even arranged a sitting for me at a photographer, and when I saw the proofs I said, 'Over my dead body you'll send these!' Those French photographers! I knew I was going to meet them eventually, and snapshots are so—so— Anyway the ones *I* take. So finally I said to him, 'I've waited this long, I'm not going to send any to them at all now. I'll save it up for a surprise, let them see me in the flesh instead, when they finally do. That way, they won't build up any false hopes and then be disappointed.' I used to censor all his letters too, wouldn't let him describe me. You can imagine how he would have done it. 'Mona Lisa,' Venus on the half-shell. I'd say, 'No you don't!' when I'd catch him at it, and scratch it out. We'd have more tussles that way, chase each other around the room, trying to get the letter back or trying to get it away from me.''

She became serious for a moment. Or at least, approached as closely to it as she seemed capable of.

"Y'know, now I wish I hadn't done that, sort of. Played hide and seek with them like this, I mean. Now I *have* got cold feet. Do you think they'll really like me? Suppose they don't? Suppose they have me built up in their expectations as someone entirely different, and—''

Like the little boy in the radio skit who prattles about a self-invented bugaboo until he ends up by frightening himself with it.

"How on earth do you make the water stay in this thing?'' she interrupted herself. She pounded lightly on the plunger set into the washbasin. "Every time I get it to fill, it runs right out again.''

"Twist it a little, and then push down on it, I think.''

Patrice stripped off her wedding-band before plunging her hands in. "Hold this for me, I want to wash my hands. I have a horror of losing it. It slipped down a drain on the Other Side, once, and they had to take out a whole section of pipe before they could get it out for me.''

"It's beautiful,'' Helen said wistfully.

"Isn't it, though?'' Patrice agreed. "See? It has our names, together, around it on the inside. Isn't that a cute idea? Keep it on your finger for me a minute, that's the safest.''

"Isn't it supposed to be bad luck to do that? I mean, for you to take it off, and for me to put it on?''

Patrice tossed her head vaingloriously. "I *couldn't* have bad luck,'' she proclaimed. It was almost a challenge.

"And I,'' thought Helen sombrely, "couldn't have good.''

She watched it curiously as it slowly descended the length of her finger, easily, without forcing. There was a curiously familiar feeling to it, as of something that should have been there long ago, that belonged there and had been strangely lacking until now.

"So this is what it feels like,'' she said to herself poignantly.

The train pounded on, its headlong roar deadened, in here where they were, to a muted jittering.

Patrice stepped back, her toilette at last completed. "Well, this is my last night," she sighed. "By this time tomorrow night we'll already be there, the worst'll be over." She clasped her own arms, in a sort of half-shiver of fright. "I hope they like what they're getting." She nervously stole a sidelong look at herself in the glass, primped at her hair.

"You'll be all right, Patrice," Helen reassured her quietly. "Nobody could help but like you."

Patrice crossed her fingers and held them up to show her. "Hugh says they're very well-off," she rambled on. "That makes it all the worse sometimes." She tittered in recollection. "I guess they must be. I know they even had to send us the money for the trip home. We were always on a shoestring, the whole time we were over there. We had an awful lot of fun, though. I think that's the only time you have fun, when you're on a shoestring, don't you?"

"Sometimes—you don't," remembered Helen, but she didn't answer.

"Anyway," her confidante babbled on, "as soon as they found out I was Expecting, that did it! They wouldn't hear of my having my baby over there. I didn't much want to myself, as a matter of fact, and Hugh didn't want me to either. They should be born in the good old U.S.A., don't you think so? That's the least you can do for them."

"Sometimes that's *all* you can do for them," Helen thought wryly. "That—and seventeen cents."

She had finished now in turn.

Patrice urged, "Let's stay in here long enough to have a puff, now that we're here. We don't seem to be keeping anybody else out. And if we try to talk out there, they might shush us down; they're all trying to sleep." The little lighter-flame winked in coppery reflection against the mirrors and glistening chrome on all sides of them. She gave a sigh of heartfelt satisfaction. "I love these before-retiring talks with another girl. It's been ages since I last had one. Back in school, I guess. Hugh says I'm a woman's woman at heart." She stopped short and thought about it with a quizzical quirk of her head. "Is that good or bad? I must ask him."

Helen couldn't repress a smile. "Good, I guess. I wouldn't want to be a man's woman."

"I wouldn't either!" Patrice hastily concurred. "It always makes me think of someone who uses foul language and spits out of the corner of her mouth."

They both chuckled for a moment in unison. But Patrice's butterfly-mind had already fluttered on to the next topic, as she dropped ash into the waste-receptacle. "Wonder if I'll be able to smoke openly, once I'm home?" She shrugged. "Oh well, there's always the back of the barn."

And then suddenly she had reverted to their mutual condition again.

"Are you frightened? About *it*, you know?"

Helen made the admission with her eyes.

"I am too." She took a reflective puff. "I think everyone is, a little, don't you? Men don't think we are. All I have to do is look at Hugh—" she deepened the dimple-pits humorously—"and I can see he's frightened enough for the two of us, so then I don't let on that I'm frightened too. And *I* reassure *him*."

Helen wondered what it was like to have someone to talk to about it.

"Are *they* pleased about it?"

"Oh sure. They're tickled silly. First grandchild, you know. They didn't even ask us if we *wanted* to come back. 'You're coming back,' and that was that."

She pointed the remnant of her cigarette down toward one of the taps, quenched it with a sharp little jet of water.

"Ready? Shall we go back to our seats now?"

They were both doing little things. All life is that, the continuous doing of little things, all life long. And then suddenly a big thing strikes into their midst—and where are the little things, what became of them, what were they?

Her hand was to the door, reversing the little hand-latch that Patrice had locked before, when they first came in. Patrice was somewhere behind her, replacing something in the uplidded dressing-kit, about to close it and bring it with her. She could see her vaguely in the chromium sheeting lining the wall before her. Little things. Little things that life is made up of. Little things that stop—

Her senses played a trick on her. There was no time for them to synchronize with the thing that happened. They played her false. She had a fleeting impression, at first, of having done something wrong to the door, dislodged it in its entirety. Simply by touching that little hand-latch. It was as though she were bringing the whole door-slab down inward on herself. As though it were falling bodily out of its frame, hinges and all. And yet it never did, it never detached itself, it never came apart from the entire wall-section it was imbedded in. So the second fleeting impression, equally false and equally a matter of seconds only, was that the entire wall of the compartment, door and all, was toppling, threatening to come down on her. And yet that never did either. Instead, the whole alcove seemed to upend, shift on a crazy axis, so that what had been the wall before her until now, had shifted to become the ceiling over her; so that what had been the floor she was standing on until now, had shifted to become the wall upright before her. The door was gone hopelessly out of reach; was a sealed trap overhead, impossible to attain.

The lights went. All light was gone, and yet so vividly explosive were the sensory images whirling through her mind that they glowed on of their own incandescence in the dark; it took her a comparatively long time to realize she was steeped in pitch-blackness, could no longer see physically. Only in afterglow of imaginative terror.

There was a nauseating sensation as if the tracks, instead of being rigid steel rods, had softened into rippling ribbons, with the train still trying to follow their buckling curvature. The car seemed to go up and down, like a scenic railway performing foreshortened dips and rises that followed one another quicker and quicker and quicker. There was a distant rending, grinding, coming nearer, swelling as it came. It reminded her of a coffee-mill they had had at home, when she was a little girl. But that one didn't draw you into its maw, crunching everything in sight, as this one was doing.

"Hugh!" the disembodied floor itself seemed to scream out behind her. Just once.

Then after that the floor fell silent.

There were minor impressions. Of seams opening, and of heavy metal partitions being bent together over her head, until the opening that held her was no longer foursquare, but tent-shaped. The darkness blanched momentarily in sudden ghostly pallor that was hot and puckery to breathe. Escaping steam. Then it thinned out again, and the darkness came back full-pitch. A little orange light flickered up somewhere, far off. Then that ebbed and dimmed again, and was gone, too.

There wasn't any sound now, there wasn't any motion. Everything was still, and dreamy, and forgotten. What was this? Sleep? Death? She didn't think so. But it wasn't life either. She remembered life; life had been only a few minutes ago. Life had had lots of light in it, and people, and motion, and sound.

This must be something else. Some transitional stage, some other condition she hadn't been told about until now. Neither life, nor death, but something in-between.

Whatever it was, it held pain in it; it was *all* pain, only pain. Pain that started small, and grew, and grew, and grew. She tried to move, and couldn't. A slim rounded thing, cold and sweating, down by her feet, was holding her down. It lay across her straight, like a water pipe sprung out of joint.

Pain that grew and grew. If she could have screamed, it might have eased it. But she couldn't seem to.

She put her hand to her mouth. On her third finger she encountered a little metal circlet, a ring that had been drawn over it. She bit on it. That helped, that eased it a little. The more the pain grew, the harder she bit.

She heard herself moan a little, and she shut her eyes. The pain went away. But it took everything else with it; thought, knowledge, awareness.

She opened her eyes again, reluctantly. Minutes? Hours? She didn't know. She only wanted to sleep, to sleep some more. Thought, knowledge, awareness, came back. But the pain didn't come back; that seemed to be gone for good. Instead there was just this lassitude. She heard herself whimpering softly, like a small kitten. Or was it she?

She only wanted to sleep, to sleep some more. And they were making so much noise they wouldn't let her. Clanging, and pounding on sheets of loose tin, and prying things away. She rolled her head aside a little, in protest.

An attenuated shaft of light peered through, from somewhere up over her head. It was like a long thin finger, a spoke, prodding for her, pointing at her, trying to find her in the dark.

It didn't actually hit her, but it kept probing for her in all the wrong places, all around her.

She only wanted to sleep. She mewed a little in protest—or was it she?—and there was a sudden frightened flurry of activity, the pounding became faster, the prying became more hectic.

Then all of it stopped at once, there was a complete cessation, and a man's voice sounded directly over her, strangely hollow and blurred as when you talk through a tube.

"Steady. We're coming to you. Just a minute longer, honey. Can you hold out? Are you hurt? Are you bad? Are you alone under there?"

"No," she said feebly. "I've—I've just had a baby down here."

Six

RECOVERY was like a progressive equalization of badly unbalanced solstices. At first time was all nights, unbroken polar nights, with tiny fractional days lasting a minute or two at a time. Nights were sleep and days were wakefulness. Then little by little the days expanded and the nights contracted. Presently, instead of many little days during the space of each twenty-four hours, there was just one long one in the middle of it each time, the way there should be. Soon this had even begun to overlap at one end, to continue beyond the setting of the sun and impinge into the first hour or two of evening. Now, instead of many little fragmentary days in the space of one night, there were many little fragmentary nights in the space of one day. Dozes or naps. The solstices had reversed themselves.

Recovery was on a second, concurrent plane as well. Dimension entered into it as well as duration. The physical size of her surroundings expanded along with the extension of her days. First there was just a small area around her that entered into awareness each time; the pillows behind her head, the upper third of the bed, a dim face just offside to her, bending down toward her, going away, coming back again. And over and above everything else, a small form allowed to nestle in her arms for a few moments at a time. Something that was alive and warm and hers. She came more alive then than at any other time. It was food and drink and sunlight; it was her lifeline back to life. The rest remained unfocussed, lost in misty gray distances stretching out and around her.

But this core of visibility, this too expanded. Presently it had reached the foot of the bed. Then it had jumped over that, to the wide moat of the room beyond, its bottom hidden from sight. Then it had reached the walls of the room, on all three sides, and could go no further for the present; they stopped it. But that wasn't a limitation of inadequate awareness any more, that was a limitation of physical equipment. Even well eyes were not made to go through walls.

It was a pleasant room. An infinitely pleasant room. This could not have been a haphazard effect achieved at random. It was too immediate, too all-pervading; every chord it struck was the right one: whether of color, proportion, acoustics, bodily tranquility and well-being, and above all, of personal security and sanctuary, of belonging somewhere at last, of having found a haven, a harbor, of being let be. The height of scientific skill and knowledge, therefore, must have entered into it, to achieve that cumulative effect that her mind could only label pleasant.

The over-all effect was a warm glowing ivory shade, not a chill, clinical white. There was a window over to her right, with a Venetian blind. And when this was furled, the sun came through in a solid slab-like shaft, like a chunk of copper-gold ore. And when it was unfurled, the dismembered beams blurred and formed a hazy mist flecked with copper-gold motes that clung to the whole window like a halo. And still at other times they brought the slats sharply together, and formed a cool blue dusk in the room, and even that was grateful, made you close your eyes without effort and take a nap.

There were always flowers standing there, too, over to her right near the head of the bed. Never the same color twice. They must have been changed each day. They repeated themselves, but never in immediate succession. Yellow, and then the next day pink, and then the next day violet and white, and then the next day back to yellow again. She got so she looked for them. It made her want to open her eyes and see what color they would be this time. Maybe that was why they were there. The Face would bring them over and hold them closer for her to see, and then put them back again.

The first words she spoke each day were: "Let me see my little boy." But the second, or not far behind, were always: "Let me see my flowers."

And after awhile there was fruit. Not right at first, but a little later on when she first began to enjoy appetite again. That was in a different place, not quite so close, over by the window. In a basket, with a big-eared satin bow standing up straight above its handle. Never the same fruit twice, that is to say, never the same arrangement or ratio of the various species, and never any slightest mark of spoilage, so she knew it must be new fruit each day. The satin bow was never the same twice, either, so presumably the basket was a different one too. A new basketful of fresh fruit each day.

And if it could never mean quite as much to her as the flowers that is because flowers are flowers and fruit is fruit. It was still good to look at in its way. Blue grapes and green, and purple ones, with the sunlight shining through them and giving them a cathedral-window lustre; bartlett pears, with a rosy flush that almost belonged to apples on their yellow cheeks; plushy yellow peaches; pert little tangerines; apples that were almost purple in their apoplectic full-bloodedness.

Every day, nestled in cool, crisp, dark-green tissue.

She hadn't known that hospitals were so attentive. She hadn't known they provided such things for their patients; even patients who only had seventeen cents in their purses— or would have, had they had purses—when they were admitted.

She thought about the past sometimes, remembered it, reviewed it, the little there was of it. But it brought shadows into the room, dimmed its bright corners, it thinned even the thick girder-like shafts of sunlight coming through the window, it made her want the covers closer up around her shoulders, so she learned to avoid thinking of it, summoning it up.

She thought:

I was on a train. I was closeted in the washroom with another girl. She could remember the metallic sheen of the fixtures and the mirrors. She could see the other girl's face; three dimples in triangular arrangement, one on each cheek, one at the chin. She could even feel the shaking and vibration, the slight unsteadiness of footing, again, if she tried hard enough. But it made her slightly nauseated to do so, because she knew what was coming next, in a very few seconds. She knew now, but she hadn't known then. She usually snapped off the sensory image, as if it were a light-switch, in a hurry at this point, to forestall what was surely coming next.

She remembered New York. She remembered the door that wouldn't open. She remembered the strip of one-way tickets falling out of an envelope. That was when the shadows really formed around, good and heavy. That was when the temperature of the room really went down. When she went back behind the train-trip, to remember New York, on the other side of it.

She quickly shut her eyes and turned her head aside on the pillow, and shut the past out.

The present was kinder by far. And you could have it so easy, any given moment of the day. You could have it without trying at all. Stay in the present, let the present do. The present was safe. Don't stray out of it—not in either direction, forward or backward. Because there was only darkness, way out there all around it, and you didn't know what you'd find. Sit tight; lie tight, right where you were.

She opened her eyes and warmed to it again. The sunlight coming in, thick and warm and strong enough to carry the weight of a toboggan from the window-sill to the floor. The technicolored burst of flowers, the beribboned basket of fruit. The soothing quiet all around. They'd bring the little form in pretty soon, and let it nestle against her, and she'd know that happiness that was something new, that made you want to circle your arms and never let go.

Let the present do. Let the present last. Don't ask, don't seek, don't question, don't quarrel with it. Hang onto it for all you were worth.

Seven

IT was really the flowers that were her undoing, that brought the present to an end.

She wanted one of them one day. Wanted to separate one from the rest, and hold it in her hand, and smell its sweetness directly under her nose; it wasn't enough any longer just to enjoy them visually, to look at them in the abstract, in group-formation.

They'd been moved nearer by this time. And she herself could move now more freely. She'd been lying quietly on her side admiring them for some time when the impulse formed.

There was a small one, dangling low, arching over in her direction, and she thought she'd get that. She turned more fully, so that she was completely sideward, and reached out toward it.

Her hand closed on its stalk, and it quivered delicately with the pressure. She knew she wouldn't have been able to break the stalk off short just with one hand alone, and she didn't want to do that anyway; didn't want to damage the flower, just borrow it for awhile. So she started to withdraw the stalk vertically from the receptacle, and as it paid off and seemed never to come to an end, this swept her hand high upward and at last back over her own head.

It struck the bed back, that part that was so close to her that she could never have seen it without making a complete head-turn, and something up there jiggled and quivered a little, as if threatening to detach itself and come down.

She made the complete head-turn, and even withdrew out from it a little, into a half-sitting position, something she had never attempted before, to bring it into focus.

It was a featherweight metal frame, a rectangle, clasped to the top bar of the bed, loose on its other three sides. Within was held a smooth mat of paper, with fine neat writing on it that blurred until it had stopped the slight swaying that her impact had set in motion.

It had been inches from her head, just over her head, all this time, but she'd never seen it until now.

Her chart.

She peered at it intently.

Suddenly the present and all its safety exploded into fragments, and the flower fell from her extended hand onto the floor.

There were three lines at the top, in neat symmetry. The first part of each was printed and left incomplete; the rest was finished out in typescript.

It said at the top: "Section—"

And then it said: "Maternity."

It said below that: "Room—"

And then it said: "25."

It said at the bottom: "Patient's Name—"

And then it said: "Hazzard, Patrice (Mrs.)."

Eight

THE nurse opened the door, and her face changed. The smile died off on it. You could detect the change in her face from all the way over there, even before she'd come any closer to the bed.

She came over and took her patient's temperature. Then she straightened the chart.

Neither of them said anything.

There was fear in the room. There was shadow in the room. The present was no longer in the room. The future had taken its place. Bringing fear, bringing shadow, bringing strangeness; worse than even the past could have brought.

The nurse held the thermometer toward the light and scanned it. Then her brows deepened. She put the thermometer down.

She asked the question carefully, as though she had gauged its tone and its tempo before allowing herself to ask it. She said, "What happened? Has something upset you? You're running a slight temperature."

The girl in the bed answered with a question of her own. Frightenedly, tautly. "What's that doing on my bed? Why is it there?"

"Everyone who's ill has to have one," the nurse answered soothingly. "It's nothing, just a—"

"But look—the name. It says—"

"Does the sight of your own name frighten you? You mustn't look at it. You're really not supposed to see it there. Sh, don't talk now any more."

"But there's something I— But you have to tell me, I don't understand—"

The nurse took her pulse.

And as she did so, the patient was suddenly looking at her own hand, in frozen, arrested horror. At the little circlet with diamonds, enfolding the third finger. At the wedding-band. As though she'd never seen it before, as though she wondered what it was doing there.

The nurse saw her trying to take it off, with flurried little tugs. It wouldn't move easily.

The nurse's face changed. "Just a moment, I'll be right back," she said uneasily.

She brought the doctor in with her. Her whispering stopped as they crossed the threshold.

He came over to the bed, put his hand to her forehead.

He nodded to the nurse and said, "Slight."

He said, "Drink this."

It tasted salty.

They put the hand under the covers, out of sight. The hand with the ring on it.

They took the glass from her lips. She didn't want to ask any questions, any more. She did, but some other time, not right now. There was something they had to be told. She'd had it a minute ago, but now it had escaped her again.

She sighed. Some other time, but not right now. She didn't want to do anything right now but sleep.

She turned her face toward the pillow and slept.

Nine

IT came right back again. The first thing. With the first glimpse of the flowers, the first glimpse of the fruit, right as her eyelids first went up and the room came into being. It came right back again.

Something said to her: Tread softly, speak slow. Take care, take care. She didn't know what or why, but she knew it must be heeded.

The nurse said to her, "Drink your orange juice."

The nurse said to her, "You can have a little coffee in your milk, starting from today on. Each day a little more. Won't that be a pleasant change?"

Tread softly, speak with care.

She said, "What happened to—?"

She took another sip of beige-colored milk. Tread warily, speak slow.

"To whom?" the nurse finally completed it for her.

Oh, careful now, careful. "There was another girl in the train washroom with me. Is she all right?" She took another sip of milk for punctuation. Hold the glass steady, now; that's right. Don't let it shake. Down to the tray again, even and slow; that's it.

The nurse shook her head reticently. She said, "No."

"She's dead?"

The nurse wouldn't answer. She too was treading softly. She too felt her way, she too wouldn't rush in. She said, "Did you know her very well?"

"No."

"You'd only met her on the train?"

"Only on the train."

The nurse had paved her own way now. It was safe to proceed. The nurse nodded. She was answering the question two sentences before, by delayed action. "She's gone," she said quietly.

The nurse watched her face expectantly. The pavement held; there was no cave-in.

The nurse ventured a step farther.

"Isn't there anyone else you want to ask about?"

"What happened to—?"

The nurse took the tray away, as if stripping the scene for a crisis.

"To *him*?"

Those were the words. She adopted them. "What happened to him?"

The nurse said, "Just a moment." She went to the door, opened it, and motioned to someone unseen.

The doctor came in, and a second nurse. They stood waiting, as if prepared to meet an emergency.

The first nurse said, "Temperature normal." She said, "Pulse normal."

The second nurse was mixing something in a glass.

The first nurse, her own, stood close to the bed. She took her by the hand and held it tightly. Just held it like that, tight and unyielding.

The doctor nodded.

The first nurse moistened her lips. She said, "Your husband wasn't saved either, Mrs. Hazzard."

She could feel her face pale with shock. The skin pulled as though it were a size too small.

She said, "No, there's something wrong— No, you're making a mistake—"

The doctor motioned unobtrusively. He and the second nurse closed in on her swiftly.

Somebody put a cool hand on her forehead, held her pressed downward, kindly but firmly; she couldn't tell whose it was.

She said, "No, please let me tell you!"

The second nurse was holding something to her lips. The first one was holding her hand, tight and warm, as if to say, "I am here. Don't be frightened, I am here." The hand on her forehead was cool but competent. It was heavy, but not too heavy; just persuasive enough to make her head lie still.

"Please—" she said listlessly.

She didn't say anything more after that. They didn't either.

Finally she overheard the doctor murmur, as if in punctuation: "She stood that very well."

Ten

IT came back again. How could it fail to now? You cannot sleep at all times, only at small times. And with it came: Tread softly, speak with care.

The nurse's name was Miss Allmeyer, the one she knew best.

"Miss Allmeyer, does the hospital give everyone those flowers every day?"

"We'd like to, but we couldn't afford it. Those flowers cost five dollars each time you see them. They're just for you."

"Is it the hospital that supplies that fruit every day?"

The nurse smiled gently. "We'd like to do that too. We only wish we could. That fruit cost ten dollars a basket each time you see it. It's a standing order, just for you."

"Well, who—?" Speak softly.

The nurse smiled winningly. "Can't you guess, honey? That shouldn't be very hard."

"There's something I want to tell you. Something you must let me tell you." She turned her head restlessly on the pillows, first to one side, then the other, then back to the first.

"Now, honey, are we going to have a bad day? I thought we were going to have such a good day."

"Could you find out something for me?"

"I'll try."

"The handbag; the handbag that was in the train-washroom with me. How much was in it?"

"*Your* handbag?"

"The handbag. The one that was there when I was in there."

The nurse came back later and said, "It's safe; it's being held for you. About fifty dollars or so."

That wasn't hers, that was the other one.

"There were two."

"There is another," the nurse admitted. "It doesn't belong to anyone now." She looked down commiseratingly. "There was just seventeen cents in it," she breathed almost inaudibly.

She didn't have to be told that. She knew by heart. She remembered from before boarding the train. She remembered from the train itself. Seventeen cents. Two pennies, a nickel, a dime.

"Could you bring the seventeen cents here? Could I have it just to look at it? Could I have it here next to the bed?"

The nurse said, "I'm not sure it's good for you, to brood like that. I'll see what they say."

She brought it, though, inside a small envelope.

She was alone with it. She dumped the four little coins from the envelope into the palm of her hand. She closed her hand upon them tightly, held them gripped like that, fiercely, in a knot of dilemma.

Fifty dollars, symbolically. Symbol of an untold amount more.

Seventeen cents, literally. Symbol of nothing, for there wasn't any more. Seventeen cents and nothing else.

The nurse came back again and smiled at her. "Now, what was it you said you wanted to tell me?"

She returned the smile, wanly. "It can keep for awhile longer. I'll tell you some other time. Tomorrow, maybe, or the next day. Not—not right today."

Eleven

THERE was a letter on the breakfast-tray.

The nurse said, "See? Now you're beginning to get mail, just like the well people do."

It was slanted toward her, leaning against the milk glass. On the envelope it said:

"Mrs. Patrice Hazzard"

She was frightened of it. She couldn't take her eyes off it. The glass of orange juice shook in her hand. The writing on it seemed to get bigger, and bigger, and bigger, as it stood there.

"MRS. PATRICE HAZZARD"

"Open it," the nurse encouraged her. "Don't just look at it like that. It won't bite you."

She tried to twice, and twice it fell. The third time she managed to rip one seam along its entire length.

"Patrice, dear:

"Though we've never seen you, you're our daughter now, dear. You're Hugh's legacy to us. You're all we have now, you and the little fellow. I can't come to you, where you are; doctor's orders. The shock was too much for me and he forbids my making the trip. You'll have to come to us, instead. Come soon, dear. Come home to us, in our loneliness and loss. It will make it that much easier to bear. It won't be long now, dear. We've been in constant touch with Dr. Brett, and he sends very encouraging reports of your progress—"

The rest didn't matter so much; she let it fade from her attention.

It was like train-wheels going through her head.

Though we've never seen you.

Though we've never seen you.

Though we've never seen you.

The nurse eased it from her forgetful fingers after awhile, and put it back in its envelope. She watched the nurse fearfully as she moved about the room.

"If I weren't Mrs. Hazzard, would I be allowed to stay in this room?"

The nurse laughed cheerfully. "We'd put you out, we'd throw you right outside into one of the wards," she said, bending close toward her in mock threat.

The nurse said, "Here, take your young son."

She held him tightly, in fierce, almost convulsive protectiveness.

Seventeen cents. Seventeen cents lasts such a short time, goes such a short way.

The nurse felt in good humor. She tried to prolong their little joke of a moment ago. "Why? Are you trying to tell me you're not Mrs. Hazzard?" she asked banteringly.

She held him fiercely, protectively close.

Seventeen cents, seventeen cents.

"No," she said in a smothered voice, burying her face against him, "I'm not trying to tell you that. I'm not trying."

Twelve

She was in a dressing-robe, sitting by the window in the sun. It was quilted blue silk. She wore it every day when she got up out of bed. On the breast-pocket it had a monogram embroidered in white silk; the letters "PH" intertwined. There were slippers to match.

She was reading a book. On the flyleaf, though she was long past it, it was inscribed "To Patrice, with love from Mother H." There was a row of other books on the stand beside the bed. Ten or twelve of them; books with vivacious jackets, turquoise, magenta, vermilion, cobalt, and with vivacious, lighthearted contents to match. Not a shadow between their covers.

There was a scattering of orange peel, and two or three seeds, in a dish on a low stand beside her easy chair. There was a cigarette burning in another, smaller dish beside that one. It was custom-made, it had a straw tip, and the initials "PH" on it had not yet been consumed.

The sunlight, falling from behind and over her, made her hair seem hazily translucent, made it almost seem like golden foam about her head. It skipped the front of her, from there on down, due to the turn of the chair-back, and struck again in a little golden pool across one outthrust bare instep, lying on it like a warm, luminous kiss.

There was a light tap at the door and the doctor came in.

He drew out a chair and sat down facing her, leaving its straight back in front of him as an added note of genial informality.

"I hear you're leaving us soon."

The book fell and he had to pick it up for her. He offered it back to her, but when she seemed incapable of taking it, he put it aside on the stand.

"Don't look so frightened. Everything's arranged—"

She had a little difficulty with her breathing. "Where—? Where to?"

"Why, home, of course."

She put her hand to her hair and flattened it a little, but then it sprang up again, gaseous as before, in the sun.

"Here are your tickets." He took an envelope out of his

pocket, tried to offer it to her. Her hands withdrew a little, each one around a side of the chair toward the back. He put the envelope between the pages of the discarded book finally, leaving it outthrust like a place-mark.

Her eyes were very large. Larger than they had seemed before he came into the room. "When?" she said with scarcely any breath at all.

"Wednesday, the early afternoon train."

Suddenly panic was licking all over her, like a shriveling, congealing, frigid flame.

"No, I can't! No! Doctor, you've got to listen—!" She tried to grab his hand with both of hers and hold onto it.

He spoke to her playfully, as if she were a child. "Now, now, here. What's all this? What *is* all this?"

"No, doctor, no—!" She shook her head insistently.

He sandwiched her hand between both of his, and held it that way, consolingly. "I understand," he said soothingly. "We're a little shaky yet, we've just finished getting used to things as they are— We're a little timid about giving up familiar surroundings for those that are strange to us. We all have it; it's a typical nervous reaction. Why, you'll be over it in no time."

"But I can't *do* it, doctor," she whispered passionately. "I can't *do* it."

He chucked her under the chin, to instill courage in her. "We'll put you on the train, and all you have to do is ride. Your family will be waiting to take you off at the other end."

"My family."

"Don't make such a face about it," he coaxed whimsically.

He glanced around at the crib.

"What about the young man here?"

He went over to it, and lifted the child out; brought him to her and put him in her arms.

"You want to take him home, don't you? You don't want him to grow up in a hospital?" He laughed at her teasingly. "You want him to *have* a home, don't you?"

She held him to her, lowered her head to him.

"Yes," she said at last, submissively. "Yes, I want him to have a home."

Thirteen

A TRAIN again. But how different it was now. No crowded aisles, no jostling figures, no flux of patient, swaying humanity. A compartment, a roomette all to herself. A little table on braces, that could go up, that could go down. A closet with a full-length mirrored door, just as in any ground-fast little dwelling. On the rack the neat luggage in recessive tiers, brand-new, in use now for the first time, glossy patent finish, hardware glistening, "PH" trimly stencilled in vermilion on the rounded corners. A little shaded lamp to read by when the countryside grew dark. Flowers in a holder, going-away flowers—no, coming-homeward flowers—presented by proxy at the point of departure; glazed fruit-candies in a box; a magazine or two.

And outside the two wide windows, that formed almost a single panel from wall to wall, trees sailing peacefully by, off a way in a single line, dappled with sunshine; dark green on one side, light apple-green on the other. Clouds sailing peacefully by, only a little more slowly than the trees, as if the two things worked on separate, yet almost-synchronized, belts of continuous motion. Meadows and fields, and the little ripples that hillocks made off in the distance every once in awhile. Going up a little, coming down again. The wavy line of the future.

And on the seat opposite her own, and more important by far than all this, snug in a little blue blanket, small face still, small eyes closed—something to cherish, something to love. All there was in the world to love. All there was to go on for, along that wavy line outside.

Yes, how different it was now. And—how infinitely preferable the first time had been to this one. Fear rode with her now.

There hadn't been fear then. There hadn't been a seat, there hadn't been a bite to eat, there had only been seventeen cents. And just ahead, unguessed, rushing ever nearer with the miles, there had been calamity, horror, the beating of the wings of death.

But there hadn't been fear. There hadn't been this gnawing

inside. There hadn't been this strain and counterstrain, this pulling one way and pulling the other. There had been the calm, the certainty, of going along the right way, the only way there was to go.

The wheels chattered, as they always chatter, on every train that has ever run. But saying now, to her ear alone:

> "You'd better go back, you'd better go back,
>   Clicketty-clack, clicketty-clack,
>   Stop while you can, you still can go back."

A very small part of her moved, the least part of her moved. Her thumb unbracketed, and her four fingers opened slowly, and the tight white knot they'd made for hours past dissolved. There in its center, exposed now—
An Indian-head penny.
A Lincoln-head penny.
A buffalo nickel.
A Liberty-head dime.
Seventeen cents. She even knew the dates on them by heart, by now.

> "Clicketty-clack,
>   Stop and go back,
>   You still have the time,
>   Turn and go back."

Slowly the fingers folded up and over again, the thumb crossed over and locked them in place.

Then she took the whole fist and struck it distractedly against her forehead and held it there for a moment where it had struck.

She stood up suddenly, and tugged at one of the pieces of luggage, and swivelled it around, so that its outermost corner was now inward. The "PH" disappeared. Then she did it to the piece below. The second "PH" disappeared.

The fear wouldn't disappear. It wasn't just stencilled on a corner of her, it was all over her.

There was a light knock outside the door, and she started as violently as though it had been a resounding crash.

"Who's there?" she gasped.

A porter's voice answered, "Five mo' minutes fo' Caulfield."

She reared from the seat, and ran to the door, flung it open. He was already going down the passage. "No, wait! It can't be—"

"It sho' enough is, though, ma'm."

"So quickly, though. I didn't think—"

He smiled back at her indulgently. "It always comes between Clarendon and Hastings. That's the right place fo' it. And we've had Clarendon already, and Hastings's comin' right after it. Ain't never change since I been on this railroad."

She closed the door, and swung around, and leaned her whole back against it, as if trying to keep out some catastrophic intrusion.

> "Too late to go back,
> Too late to go back—"

"I can still ride straight through, I can ride past without getting off," she thought. She ran to the windows and peered out ahead, at an acute angle, as if the oncoming sight of it in itself would resolve her difficulty in some way.

Nothing yet. It was coming on very gradually. A house, all by itself. Then another house, still all by itself. Then a third. They were beginning to come thicker now.

"Ride straight through, don't get off at all. They can't make you. Nobody can. Do this one last thing, that's all there's time for now."

She ran back to the door and hurriedly turned the little finger-latch under the knob, locking it on the inside.

The houses were coming in more profusion, but they were coming slower too. They didn't sail any more, they dawdled. A school-building drifted by; you could tell what it was even from afar. Spotless, modern, brand-new looking, its concrete functionalism gleaming spic-and-span in the sun; copiously glassed. She could even make out small swings in motion, in the playground beside it. She glanced aside at the small blanketed bundle on the seat. That would be the kind of school she'd want—

She didn't speak, but her own voice was loud in her ears. "Help me, somebody; I don't know what to do!"

The wheels were dying, as though they'd run out of lubrication. Or like a phonograph record that runs down.

"Cli-ck, cla-ck,
Cli-i-ck, cla-a-a-ck."

Each revolution seemed about to be the last.

Suddenly a long shed started up, just outside the windows, running along parallel to them, and then a white sign suspended from it started to go by, letter by letter in reverse.

"D-L-E-I-"

It got to the F and it stuck. It wouldn't budge. She all but screamed. The train had stopped.

A knock sounded right behind her back, the vibration of it seeming to go through her chest.

"Caulfield, ma'm."

Then someone tried the knob.

"Help you with yo' things?"

Her clenched fist tightened around the seventeen cents, until the knuckles showed white and livid with the pressure.

She ran to the seat and picked up the blue blanket and what it held.

There were people out there, just on the other side of the window. Their heads were low, but she could see them, and they could see her. There was a woman looking right at her.

Their eyes met; their eyes locked, held fast. She couldn't turn her head away, she couldn't withdraw deeper into the compartment. It was as though those eyes riveted her where she stood.

The woman pointed to her. She called out in jubilation, for the benefit of someone else, unseen. "There she is! I've found her! Here, this car up here!"

She raised her hand and she waved. She waved to the little somnolent, blinking head coifed in the blue blanket, looking solemnly out the window. Made her fingers flutter in that special wave you give to very small babies.

The look on her face couldn't have been described. It was as when life begins all over again, after an interruption, a hiatus. It was as when the sun peers through again at the end, at the end of a bleak wintry day.

The girl holding the baby put her head down close to his, almost as if averting it from the window. Or as if they were communing together, exchanging some confidence in secret, to the exclusion of everyone else.

She was.

"For you," she breathed. "For you. And God forgive me."

Then she carried him over to the door with her, and turned the latch to let the harassed porter in.

Fourteen

SOMETIMES there is a dividing-line running across life. Sharp, almost actual, like the black stroke of a paintbrush or the white gash of a chalk-mark. Sometimes, but not often.

For her there was. It lay somewhere along those few yards of car-passage, between the compartment-window and the car-steps, where for a moment or two she was out of sight of those standing waiting outside. One girl left the window. Another girl came down the steps. A world ended, and another world began.

She wasn't the girl who had been holding her baby by the compartment-window just now.

Patrice Hazzard came down those car-steps.

Frightened, tremulous, very white in the face, but Patrice Hazzard.

She was aware of things, but only indirectly; she only had eyes for those other eyes looking into hers from a distance of a few inches away. All else was background. Behind her back the train glided on. Bearing with it its hundreds of living passengers. And, all unknown, in an empty compartment, a ghost. Two ghosts, a large one and a very small one.

Forever homeless now, never to be retrieved.

The hazel eyes came in even closer to hers. They were kind; they smiled around the edges; they were gentle, tender. They hurt a little. *They were trustful.*

She was in her fifties, their owner. Her hair was softly graying, and only underneath had the process been delayed. She was as tall as Patrice, and as slim; and she shouldn't have been, for it wasn't the slimness of fashionable effort or artifice, and something about her clothes revealed it to be recent, only the past few months.

But even these details about her were background, and the man of her own age standing just past her shoulder was background too. It was only her face that was immediate, and the eyes in her face, so close now. Saying so much without a sound.

She placed her hands lightly upon Patrice's cheeks, one on each, framing her face between them in a sort of accolade, a sacramental benison.

Then she kissed her on the lips, in silence, and there was a lifetime in the kiss, the girl could sense it. The lifetime of a man. The many years it takes to raise a man, from childhood, through boyhood, into a grown son. There was bitter loss in the kiss, the loss of all that at a single blow. The end for a time of all hope, and weeks of cruel grief. But then too there was the reparation of loss, the finding of a daughter, the starting over with another, a smaller son. No, with the same son; the same blood, the same flesh. Only going back and starting again from the beginning, in sweeter sadder sponsorship this time, forewarned by loss. And there was the burgeoning of hope anew.

There were all those things in it. They were spoken in it, they were felt in it; and they were meant to be felt in it, they had been put into it for that purpose.

This was not a kiss under a railroad-station shed; it was a sacrament of adoption.

Then she kissed the child. And smiled as you do at your own. And a little crystal drop that hadn't been there before was resting on its small pink cheek.

The man came forward and kissed her on the forehead. "I'm Father, Patrice."

He stooped and straightened, and said, "I'll take your things over to the car." A little glad to escape from an emotional moment, as men are apt to be.

The woman hadn't said a word. In all the moments she'd been standing before her, not a word had passed her lips. She saw, perhaps, the pallor in her face; could read the shrinking, the uncertainty, in her eyes.

She put her arms about her and drew her to her now, in a warmer, more mundane, more everyday greeting than the one that had passed before. Drew the girl's head to rest upon her own shoulder for a moment. And as she did so, she spoke for the first time, low in her ear, to give her courage, to give her peace.

"You're home, Patrice. Welcome home, dear."

And in those few words, so simply said, so inalterably meant, Patrice Hazzard knew she had found at last all the goodness there is or ever can be in this world.

Fifteen

AND so this was what it was like to be home; to be in a home of your own, in a room of your own.

She had another dress on now, ready to go down to table. She sat there in a wing chair waiting, very straight, looking a little small against its outspread back. Her back was up against it very straight, her legs dropped down to the floor very straight and meticulously side by side. She had her hand out resting on the crib, the crib they'd bought for him and that she'd found already here waiting when she first entered the room. He was in it now. They'd even thought of that.

They'd left her alone; she would have had to be alone to savor it as fully as she was doing. Still drinking it in, hours after; basking in it, inhaling the essence of it; there was no word for what it did to her. Hours after; and her head every now and then would still give that slow, comprehensive, marvelling sweep around from side to side, taking in all four walls of it. And even up overhead, not forgetting the ceiling. A roof over your head. A roof to keep out rain and cold and loneliness— Not just the anonymous roof of a rented building, no; the roof of home. Guarding you, sheltering you, keeping you, watching over you.

And somewhere downstairs, dimly perceptible to her acutely attuned ears, the soothing bustle of an evening meal in preparation. Carried to her in faint snatches now and then at the opening of a door, stilled again at its closing. Footsteps busily crossing an uncarpeted strip of wooden floor, then coming back again. An occasional faint clash of crockery or china. Once even the voice of the colored housekeeper, for an instant of bugle-like clarity. "No, it ain't ready yet, Miz' Hazzard; need five mo' minutes."

And the laughingly protesting admonition that followed, miraculously audible as well: "Sh, Aunt Josie. We have a baby in the house now; he may be napping."

Someone was coming up the stairs now. They were coming up the stairs now to tell her. She shrank back a little in the chair. Now she was a little frightened, a little nervous again. Now there would be no quick escape from the moment's confrontation, as at the railroad station. Now came the real meeting, the real blending, the real taking into the fold. Now was the real test.

"Patrice dear, supper's ready whenever you are."

You take *supper* in the evening, when you're home, in your own home. When you go out in public or to someone else's home, you may take *dinner*. But in the evening, in your own home, it's *supper* you take, and never anything else. Her heart was as fiercely glad as though the trifling word were a talisman. She remembered when she was a little girl, those few brief years that had ended so quickly— The call to *supper*, only *supper*, never anything else.

She jumped from the chair and ran over and opened the door. "Shall I—shall I bring him down with me, or leave him up here in the crib till I come back?" she asked, half-eagerly, half-uncertainly. "I fed him already at five, you know."

Mother Hazzard slanted her head coaxingly. "Ah, why don't you bring him down with you just tonight, anyway? It's the first night. Don't hurry, dear, take your time."

When she came out of the room holding him in her arms moments later, she stopped a moment, fingered the edge of the door lingeringly. Not where the knob was, but up and down the unbroken surface where there was no knob.

Watch over my room for me, she breathed unheard. I'm coming right back. Take care of it. Don't let anyone— Will you?

She would come down these same stairs many hundreds of times to come, she knew, as she started down them now. She would come down them fast, she would come down them slowly. She would come down them blithely, in gayety. And perhaps she might come down them in fear, in trouble. But now, tonight, this was the very first time of all that she was coming down them.

She held him close to her and felt her way, for they were new to her, she hadn't got the measure of them, the feel of them, yet, and she didn't want to miss her step.

They were standing about in the dining-room waiting for her. Not rigidly, formally, like drill-sergeants, but in unself-conscious ease, as if unaware of the small tribute of consideration they were giving her. Mother Hazzard was leaning forward, giving a last-minute touch to the table, shifting something a little. Father Hazzard was looking up toward the lights through the spectacles with which he'd just been reading, and polishing them off before returning them to their case. And there was a third person in the room, somebody with his back half to her at the moment of entrance, surreptitiously pilfering a salted peanut from a dish on the buffet.

He turned forward again and threw it away when he heard her come in. He was young and tall and friendly-looking, and his hair was— A camera-shutter clicked in her mind and the film rolled on.

"There's the young man!" Mother Hazzard revelled. "There's the young man himself! Here, give him to me. You know who this is, of course." And then she added, as though it were wholly unnecessary even to qualify it by so much, "Bill."

But who—? she wondered. They hadn't said anything until now.

He came forward, and she didn't know what to do, he was so close to her own age. She half-offered her hand, hoping that if it was too formal the gesture would remain unnoticed.

He took it, but he didn't shake it. Instead he pressed it between both of his, held it warmly buried like that for a moment or two.

"Welcome home, Patrice," he said quietly. And there was something about the straight, unwavering look in his eyes as he said it that made her think she'd never heard anything said so sincerely, so simply, so loyally, before.

And that was all. Mother Hazzard said, "You sit here, from now on."

Father Hazzard said unassumingly, "We're very happy, Patrice," and sat down at the head of the table.

Whoever Bill was, he sat down opposite her.

The colored housekeeper peeked through the door for a minute and beamed. "Now this look right! This what that table been needing. This just finish off that empty si—"

Then she quickly checked herself, clapping a catastrophic hand to her mouth, and whisked from sight again.

Mother Hazzard glanced down at her plate for a second, then immediately looked up again smiling, and the hurt was gone, had not been allowed to linger.

They didn't say anything memorable. You don't say anything memorable across the tables of home. Your heart speaks, and not your brain, to the other hearts around you. She forgot after awhile to notice what she was saying, to weigh, to reckon it. That's what home is, what home should be. It flowed from her as easily as it did from them. She knew that was what they were trying to do for her. And they were succeeding. Strangeness was already gone with the soup, never to return. Nothing could ever bring it back again. Other things could come—she hoped they wouldn't. But never strangeness, the unease of unfamiliarity, again. They had succeeded.

"I hope you don't mind the white collar on that dress, Patrice. I purposely saw to it there was a touch of color on everything I picked out; I didn't want you to be too—"

"Oh, some of those things are so lovely. I really hadn't seen half of them myself until I unpacked just now."

"The only thing that I was afraid of was the sizes, but that nurse of yours sent me a complete—"

"She took a tapemeasure all over me one day, I remember that now, but she wouldn't tell me what it was for—"

"Which kind for you, Patrice? Light or dark?"

"It really doesn't—"

"No, tell him just this once, dear; then after that he won't have to ask you."

"Dark, then, I guess."

"You and me both."

He spoke a little less frequently than the remaining three

of them. Just a touch of shyness, she sensed. Not that he was strained or tonguetied or anything. Perhaps it was just his way; he had a quiet, unobtrusive way.

The thing was, who exactly was he? She couldn't ask outright now any longer. She'd omitted to at the first moment, and now it was twenty minutes too late for that. No last name had been given, so he must be—

I'll find out soon, she reassured herself. I'm bound to. She was no longer afraid.

Once she found he'd just been looking at her when her eyes went to him, and she wondered what he'd been thinking while doing so. And yet not to have admitted that she knew, that she could tell by the lingering traces of his expression, would have been to lie to herself. He'd been thinking that her face was pleasant, that he liked it.

And then after a little while he said, "Dad, pass the bread over this way, will you?"

And then she knew who he was.

Sixteen

EPISCOPAL CHURCH OF ST. BARTHOLOMEW, social kingpin among all the churches of Caulfield, on a golden April Sunday morning.

She stood there by the font, child in her arms, immediate family and their close friends gathered beside her.

They had insisted upon this. She hadn't wanted it. Twice she had postponed it, for two Sundays in succession now, after all the arrangements had been made. First, by pleading a cold that she did not really have. Secondly, by pleading a slight one that the child actually did have. Today she hadn't been able to postpone it any longer. They would have finally sensed the deliberation underlying her excuses.

She kept her head down, hearing the ceremony rather than seeing it. As though afraid to look on openly at it. As though afraid of being struck down momentarily at the feet of all of them for her blasphemy.

She had on a broad-brimmed hat of semi-transparent horsehair and that helped her, veiling her eyes and the upper part of her face when she cast it down like that.

Mournful memories, they probably thought. Grief-stricken.

Guilty, in reality. Scandalized. Not brazen enough to gaze at this mockery unabashed.

Arms reached out toward her, to take the child from her. The godmother's arms. She gave him over, trailing the long lace ceremonial gown that—she had almost said "his father"—that a stranger named Hugh Hazzard had worn before him, and that *his* father, Donald, had worn before *him*.

Her arms felt strangely empty after that. She wanted to cross them protectively over her breast, as though she were unclad. She forced herself not to with an effort. It was not her form that was unclad, it was her conscience. She dropped them quietly, clasped them before her, looked down.

"Hugh Donald Hazzard, I baptize thee—"

They had gone through the parody of consulting her preferences in this. To her it was a parody; not to them. She wanted him named after Hugh, of course? Yes, she had said demurely, after Hugh. Then how about the middle name? After her own father? Or perhaps two middle names, one for each grandfather? (She actually hadn't been able to recall her own father's name at the moment; it came back to her some time after, not without difficulty. Mike: a scarcely remembered figure of a looming longshoreman, killed in a drunken brawl on the Embarcadero when she was ten.)

One middle name would do. After Hugh's father, she had said demurely.

She could feel her face burning now, knew it must be flushed with shame. They mustn't see that. She kept it steadily down.

"—in the name of the Father, and of the Son, and of the Holy Ghost. Amen."

The minister sprinkled water on the child's head. She could see a stray drop or two fall upon the floor, darken into coin dots. A dime, a nickel, two pennies. Seventeen cents.

The infant began to wail in protest, as numberless infants before it since time immemorial. The infant from a New York furnished rooming house who had become heir to the first, the wealthiest family in Caulfield, in all the county, maybe even in all that State.

"You have nothing to cry about," she thought morosely.

Seventeen

THERE was a cake for him, on his first birthday, with a single candle standing defiantly in the middle of it, its flame like a yellow butterfly hovering atop a fluted white column. They made great to-do and ceremony about the little immemorial rites that went with it. The first grandson. The first milestone.

"But if he can't make the wish," she demanded animatedly, "is it all right if I make it for him? Or doesn't that count?"

Aunt Josie, the cake's creator, instinctively deferred to in all such matters of lore, nodded pontifically from the kitchen-doorway. "You make it for him, honey; he git it just the same," she promised.

Patrice dropped her eyes and her face sobered for a moment.

Peace, all your life, Safety, such as this. Your own around you always, such as now. And for myself—from you, someday—forgiveness.

"You got it? Now blow."

"Him or me?"

"It count just like for him."

She leaned down, pressed her cheek close to his, and blew softly. The yellow butterfly fluttered agitatedly, shrivelled into nothingness.

"Now cut," coached the self-imposed mistress of ceremonies.

She closed his chubby little hand around the knife-handle, enfolded it with her own, and tenderly guided it. The mystic incision made, she touched her finger to the sugary icing, scraped off a tiny crumb, and then placed it to his lips.

A great crowing and cooing went up, as though they had all just been witnesses to a prodigy of precocity.

A lot of people had come in, they hadn't had so many

people all in the house at one time since she'd first been there. And long after the small honor-guest had been withdrawn from the scene and taken upstairs to bed, the festivities continued under their own momentum, even accelerated somewhat. In that way grown-ups have of appropriating a child's party, given the slightest encouragement.

She came down again, afterward, to the lighted, bustling rooms, and moved about among them, chatting, smiling, happier tonight than she ever remembered being before. A cup of punch in one hand, in the other a sandwich with one bite gone, that she never seemed to get around to taking a second bite out of. Every time she raised it toward her mouth somebody said something to her, or she said something to somebody. It didn't matter, it was more fun that way.

Bill brushed by her once, grinning. "How does it feel to be an *old* mother?"

"How does it feel to be an *old* uncle?" she rejoined pertly over her shoulder.

A year ago seemed a long time away; just a year ago tonight, with its horror and its darkness and its fright. That hadn't happened to her; it *couldn't* have. That had happened to a girl named— No, she didn't want to remember that name, she didn't even want to summon it back for a fleeting instant. It had nothing to do with her.

"Aunt Josie's sitting up there with him. No, he'll be all right; he's a very *good* baby about going to sleep."

"Coming from a detached observer."

"Well, I *am* detached at this minute, so I'm entitled to say so. He's all the way upstairs and I'm down here."

She was in the brightly lighted living-room of her home, here, with her friends, her family's friends, all gathered about her, laughing and chatting. A year ago was more than a long time away. It had never happened. No, it had never happened. Not to her, anyway.

A great many of the introductions were blurred. There were so many firsts, on an occasion like this. She looked about, dutifully recapitulating the key-people, as befitted her role of assistant hostess. Edna Harding and Marilyn Bryant, they were those two girls sitting one on each side of Bill, and vying with one another for his attention. She suppressed a mischievous grin. Look at him, sober-faced as a totem pole. Why, it was enough to turn his head—if he hadn't happened to have a head that was unturnable by girls, as far as she'd been able to observe. Guy Ennis was that dark-haired young man over there getting someone a punch-cup; he was easy to memorize because he'd come in alone. Some old friend of Bill's, evidently. Funny that the honeybees didn't buzz around him more thickly, instead of unresponsive Bill. He looked far more the type.

Grace Henson, she was that stoutish, flaxen-haired girl over there, waiting for the punch-cup. Or was she? No, she was the less stout but still flaxen-haired one at the piano, softly playing for her own entertainment, no one near her. One wore glasses and one didn't. They must be sisters, there was too close a resemblance. It was the first time either one of them had been to the house.

She moved over to the piano and stood beside her. She might actually be enjoying doing that, for all Patrice knew, but she should at least have somebody taking an appreciative interest.

The girl at the keyboard smiled at her. "Now this." She was an accomplished player, keeping the music subdued, like an undertone to the conversations going on all over the room.

But suddenly all the near-by ones had stopped. The music went on alone for a note or two, sounding that much clearer than it had before.

The second flaxen-haired girl quitted her companion for a moment, stepped up behind the player's back, touched her just once on the shoulder, as if in some kind of esoteric remonstrance or reminder. That was all she did. Then she went right back to where she'd been sitting. The whole little pantomime had been so deft and quick it was hardly noticeable at all.

The player had broken off, uncertainly. She apparently had understood the message of the tap, but not its meaning. The slightly bewildered shrug she gave Patrice was evidence of that.

"Oh, finish it," Patrice protested unguardedly. "It was lovely. What's it called? I don't think I've ever heard it before."

"It's the Barcarolle, from *Tales of Hoffman*," the other girl answered unassumingly.

The answer itself was in anticlimax. Standing there beside the player, she became conscious of the congealing silence immediately about her, and knew it wasn't due to that, but to something that must have been said just before. It had already ended as she detected it, but awareness of it lingered on—in her. Something had happened just then.

I've said something wrong. I said something that was wrong just now. But I don't know what it was, and I don't know what to do about it.

She touched her punch-cup to her lips, there was nothing else to do at the moment.

They only heard it near me. The music left my voice stranded, and that only made it all the more conspicuous. But who else in the room heard? Who else noticed? Maybe their faces will tell—

She turned slowly and glanced at them one by one, as if at random. Mother Hazzard was deep in conversation at the far end of the room, looking up over her chair at someone. She hadn't heard. The flaxen-haired girl who had delivered the cautioning tap had her back to her; she might have heard and she might not. But if she had, it had made no impression; she was not aware of her. Guy Ennis was holding a lighter to a cigarette. He had to click it twice to make it spark, and it had all his attention. He didn't look up at her when her glance strayed lightly past his face. The two girls with Bill, they hadn't heard, it was easy to see that. They were oblivious of everything else but the bone of contention between them.

No one was looking at her. No one's eyes met hers.

Only Bill. His head was slightly down, and his forehead was querulously ridged, and he was gazing up from under his brows at her with a strange sort of inscrutability. Everything they were saying to him seemed to be going over his head. She couldn't tell if his thoughts were on her, or a thousand miles away. But his eyes, at least, were.

She dropped her own.

And even after she did, she knew that his were still on her none the less.

Eighteen

As they climbed the stairs together, after, when everyone had gone, Mother Hazzard suddenly tightened an arm about her waist, protectively.

"You were so brave about it," she said. "You did just the right thing; to pretend not to know what it was she was playing. Oh, but my dear, my heart went out to you, for a moment, when I saw you standing there. That look on your face. I wanted to run to you and put my arms around you. But I took my cue from you, I pretended not to notice anything either. She didn't mean anything by it, she's just a thoughtless little fool."

Patrice moved slowly up the stairs at her side, didn't answer.

"But at the sound of the very first notes," Mother Hazzard went on ruefully, "he seemed to be right back there in the room with all of us again. So *present*, you could almost see him in front of your eyes. The Barcarolle. His favorite song. He never sat down to a piano but what he played it. Whenever and wherever you heard that being played, you knew Hugh was about someplace."

"The Barcarolle," Patrice murmured almost inaudibly, as if speaking to herself. "His favorite song."

Nineteen

"—DIFFERENT now," Mother Hazzard was musing comfortably. "I was there once, as a girl, you know. Oh, many years ago. Tell me, has it changed much since those days?"

Suddenly she was looking directly at Patrice, in innocent exclusive inquiry.

"How can she answer that, Mother?" Father Hazzard cut in drily. "She wasn't there when you were, so how would she know what it was like then?"

"Oh, you know what I mean," Mother Hazzard retorted indulgently. "Don't be so hanged precise."

"I suppose it has," Patrice answered feebly, turning the

handle of her cup a little further toward her, as if about to lift it, and then not lifting it after all.

"You and Hugh were married there, weren't you, dear?" was the next desultory remark.

Again Father Hazzard interrupted before she could answer, this time with catastrophic rebuttal. "They were married in London, I thought. Don't you remember that letter he sent us at the time? I can still recall it: 'married here yesterday.' London letterhead."

"Paris," said Mother Hazzard firmly. "Wasn't it, dear? I still have it upstairs, I can get it and show you. It has a Paris postmark." Then she tossed her head at him arbitrarily. "Anyway, this is one question Patrice *can* answer for herself."

There was suddenly a sickening chasm yawning at her feet, where a moment before all had been security of footing, and she couldn't turn back, yet she didn't know how to get across.

She could feel their three pairs of eyes on her, Bill's were raised now too, waiting in trustful expectancy that in a moment, with the wrong answer, would change to something else.

"London," she said softly, touching the handle of her cup as if deriving some sort of mystic clairvoyance from it. "But then we left immediately for Paris, on our honeymoon. I think what happened was, he began the letter in London, didn't have time to finish it, and then posted it from Paris."

"You see," said Mother Hazzard pertly, "I was partly right, anyhow."

"Now isn't that just like a woman," Father Hazzard marvelled to his son.

Bill's eyes had remained on Patrice. There was something almost akin to grudging admiration in them; or did she imagine that?

"Excuse me," she said stifledly, thrusting her chair back. "I think I hear the baby crying."

Twenty

AND then, a few weeks later, another pitfall. Or rather the same one, ever-present, ever lurking treacherously underfoot as she walked this path of her own choosing.

It had been raining, and it grew heavily misted out. A rare occurrence for Caulfield. They were all there in the room with her and she stopped by the window a moment in passing to glance out.

"Heavens," she exclaimed incautiously, "I haven't seen everything look so blurry since I was a child in San Fran. We used to get those fogs th—"

In the reflection on the lighted pane she saw Mother Hazzard's head go up, and knew before she had even turned back to face them she had said the wrong thing. Trodden incautiously again, where there was no support.

"In San Francisco, dear?" Mother Hazzard's voice was guilelessly puzzled. "But I thought you were raised in— Hugh wrote us you were originally from—" And then she didn't finish it, withholding the clue; no helpful second choice was forthcoming this time. Instead a flat question followed. "Is that where you were born, dear?"

"No," Patrice said distinctly, and knew what the next question was sure to be. A question she could not have answered at the moment.

Bill raised his head suddenly, turned it inquiringly toward the stairs. "I think I hear the youngster crying, Patrice."

"I'll go up and take a look," she said gratefully, and left the room.

He was in a soundless sleep when she got to him. He wasn't making a whimper that anyone could possibly have heard. She stood there by him with a look of thoughtful scrutiny on her face.

Had he really thought he heard the baby crying?

Twenty-One

THEN there was the day she was slowly sauntering along Congress Avenue, window-shopping. Congress Avenue was the main retail thoroughfare. Looking at this window-display, looking at that, not intending to buy anything, not needing to. But enjoying herself all the more in this untrammelled state. Enjoying the crowd of well-dressed shoppers thronging the sunlit sidewalk all about her, the great majority of them women at that forenoon hour of the day. Enjoying the bustle, the spruce activity, they conveyed. Enjoying this carefree moment, this brief respite (an errand for Mother Hazzard, a promise to pick something up for her, was what had brought her downtown), all the more for knowing that it was a legitimate absence, not a dereliction, and that the baby was safe, well taken care of while she was gone. And that she'd enjoy returning to it all the more, after this short diversion.

It was simply a matter of taking the bus at the next stop ahead, instead of at the nearer one behind her, and strolling the difference between the two.

And then from somewhere behind her she heard her name called. She recognized the voice at the first syllable. Cheerful, sunny. Bill. She had her smile of greeting ready before she had even turned her head.

Two of his long, energetic strides and he was beside her.

"Hello there. I thought I recognized you."

They stopped for a minute, face to face.

"What are you doing out of the office?"

"I was on my way back just now. Had to go over and see a man. And you?"

"I came down to get Mother some imported English yarn she had waiting for her at Bloom's. Before they send it out, I can be there and back with it."

"I'll walk with you," he offered. "Good excuse to loaf. As far as the next corner anyhow."

"That's where I'm taking my bus anyway," she told him.

They turned and resumed their course, but at the snail's pace she had been maintaining by herself before now.

He crinkled his nose and squinted upward appreciatively. "It does a fellow good to get out in the sun once in awhile."

"Poor abused man. I'd like to have a penny for every time you're out of that office during hours."

He chuckled unabashedly. "Can I help it if Dad sends me?

Of course, I always happen to get right in front of him when he's looking around for someone to do the leg-work."

They stopped.

"Those're nice," she said appraisingly.

"Yes," he agreed. "But what are they?"

"You know darned well they're hats. Don't try to be so superior."

They went on, stopped again.

"Is this what they call window-shopping?"

"This is what they call window-shopping. As if you didn't know."

"It's fun. You don't get anywhere. But you see a lot."

"You may like it now, because it's a novelty. Wait'll you're married and get a lot of it. You won't like it then."

The next window-display was an offering of fountain pens, a narrow little show-case not more than two or three yards in width.

She didn't offer to stop there. It was now he who did, halting her with him as a result.

"Wait a minute. That reminds me. I need a new pen. Will you come in with me a minute and help me pick one out?"

"I ought to be getting back," she said halfheartedly.

"It'll only take a minute. I'm a quick buyer."

"I don't know anything about pens," she demurred.

"I don't myself. That's just it. Two heads are better than one." He'd taken her lightly by the arm by now, to try to induce her. "Ah, come on. I'm the sort they sell anything to when I'm alone."

"I don't believe a word of it. You just want company," she laughed, but she went inside with him nevertheless.

He offered her a chair facing the counter. A case of pens was brought out and opened. They were discussed between him and the salesman, she taking no active part. Several were uncapped, filled at a waiting bottle of ink at hand on the counter, and tried out on a pad of scratch-paper, also at hand for that purpose.

She looked on, trying to show an interest she did not really feel.

Suddenly he said to her, "How do you like the way this

writes?" and thrust one of them between her fingers and the block of paper under her hand, before she quite knew what had happened.

Incautiously, her mind on the proportions and weight of the barrel in her grasp, her attention fixed on what sort of a track the nib would leave, whether a broad bold one or a thin wiry one, she put it to the pad. Suddenly "Helen" stood there on the topmost leaf, almost as if produced by automatic writing. Or rather, in the fullest sense of the word, it was just that. She checked herself just in time to prevent the second name from flowing out of the pen. It was already on the preliminary upward stroke of a capital G, when she jerked it clear.

"Here, let me try it a minute myself." Without warning he'd taken both pen and pad back again, before she could do anything to obliterate or alter what was on it.

Whether he saw it or not she couldn't tell. He gave no indication. Yet it was right there under his eyes, he must have, how could he have failed to?

He drew a cursory line or two, desisted.

"No," he said to the salesman. "Let me see that one."

While he was reaching into the case, she managed to deftly peel off the topmost leaf with that damaging "Helen" on it. Crumpled it surreptitiously in her hand, dropped it to the floor.

And then, belatedly, realized that perhaps this was even worse than had she left it on there where it was. For surely he'd seen it anyway, and now she'd only pointed up the fact that she did not want him to. In other words, she'd doubly damned herself; first by the error, then by taking such pains to try to efface it.

Meanwhile, his interest in the matter of pens had all at once flagged. He looked at the clerk, about to speak, and she could have almost predicted what he was about to say—had he said it—his expression conveyed it so well. "Never mind. I'll stop in again some other time." But then instead he gave her a look, and as though recalled to the necessity for maintaining some sort of plausibility, said hurriedly, almost indifferently, "All right, here, make it this one. Send it over to my office later on."

He scarcely looked at it. It didn't seem to matter to him which one he took.

And, she reminded herself, after making such to-do about her coming in with him to help him select one.

"Shall we go?" he said, a trifle reticently.

Their parting was strained. She didn't know whether it was due to him or due to herself. Or just due to her own imagining. But it seemed to her to lack the jaunty spontaneity of their meeting just a few minutes ago.

He didn't thank her for helping him select a pen, and she was grateful for that at least. But his eyes were suddenly remote, abstracted, where until now they had been wholly on her at every turn of speech. They seemed to be looking up this way toward the top of a building, looking down that way toward the far end of the street, looking everywhere but at her any more, even while he was saying "Here's your bus," and arming her into it, and reaching in from where he stood to pay the driver her fare. "Goodbye. Get home all right. See you tonight." And tipped his hat, and seemed to have already forgotten her even before he had completed the act of turning away and going about his business. And yet somehow she knew that just the reverse was true. That he was more conscious of her than ever, now that he seemed least so. Distance had intervened between them, that was all.

She looked down at her lap, while the bus swept her along past the crowded sidewalks. Funny how quickly a scene could change, the same scene; the sunlit pavements and the bustling shoppers weren't fun any more to watch.

If it had been a premeditated test, a trap— But no, it couldn't have been that. That much at least she was sure of, though it was no satisfaction. He *couldn't* have known that he was going to run into her just where he had, that they were going to walk along just as they had, toward that pen emporium. At the time he'd left the house this morning, she hadn't even known herself that she was coming downtown like this; that had come up later. So he couldn't have lain in wait for her there, to accost her. That much at least had been spontaneous, purely accidental.

But maybe as they were strolling along, and he first looked

up and saw the store sign, that was when it had occurred to him, and he'd improvised it, on the spur of the moment. What was commonly said must have occurred to him then, as it only occurred to her now. That when people try out a new pen, they invariably write their real names. It's almost compulsory.

And yet, even for such an undeliberated, on-the-spot test as that, there must have been some formless suspicion of her already latent in his mind, in one way or another, or it wouldn't have suggested itself to him.

Little fool, she said to herself bitterly as she tugged at the overhead cord and prepared to alight, why didn't you think of that before you went in there with him? What good was hindsight now?

A night or two later his discarded coat was slung over a chair and he wasn't in the room with it at the moment. She needed a pencil for something for a moment anyhow, that was her excuse for it. She sought the pocket and took out the fountain pen she found clasped to it. It was gold and had his initials engraved on it; some valued, long-used birthday or Christmas present from one of his parents probably. Moreover, it was in perfect writing order, couldn't have been improved on, left a clear, deep, rich trace. And he wasn't the sort of man who went around displaying two fountain pens at a time.

It had been a test, all right. And she had given a positive reaction, as positive as he could have hoped for.

Twenty-Two

SHE'D heard the doorbell ring some time before, and dim sounds of conglomerate greeting follow it in the hall below, and knew by that some visitor must have arrived, and must still be down there. She didn't think any more about it. She'd had Hughie in his little portable tub at the moment, and that, while it was going on, was a full-time job for anyone's attention. By the time she'd finished drying and talcuming and dressing him, putting him to bed for the night, and then lingering treacherously by him awhile longer, to watch her opportunity and worm the last celluloid bath-duck out of his tightly closed little fist, the better part of an hour had gone by. She felt sure the caller, whoever he was, must already be long gone by that time. That it had been a masculine visitor was something she could take for granted; anyone feminine from six to sixty would automatically have been ushered up-stairs by the idolatrous Mother Hazzard to look in on the festive rite of her grandson's bath. In fact it was the first time she herself had missed attending one in weeks, if only to hold the towel, prattle in an unintelligible gibberish with the small person in the tub, and generally get in the uncomplaining mother's way. Only something of importance could have kept her away.

She thought they were being unusually quiet below, when she finally came out of her room and started down the stairs. There was a single, droning, low-pitched voice going on, as if somebody were reading aloud, and no one else was audible.

They were all in the library, she discovered a moment later; a room that was never used much in the evenings. And when it was, never by all of them together, at one time. She could see them in there twice over, the first time from the stairs themselves, as she came down them, and then in an after-glimpse, through the open doorway at nearer range, as she doubled back around the foot of the stairs and passed by in the hall just outside.

The three of them were in there, and there was a man with them whom she didn't know, although she realized she must have seen him at least one or more times before, as she had everyone who came to this house. He was at the table, the reading-lamp lit, droning aloud in a monotonous, singsong voice. It wasn't a book; it seemed more like a typed report. Every few moments a brittly crackling sheet would sweep back in reverse and go under the others.

No one else was saying a word. They were sitting at varying distances and at varying degrees of attention. Father Hazzard was drawn up to the table with the monologist, following every word closely, and nodding in benign accord from time to time. Mother Hazzard was in an easy chair, a basket on her lap, darning something and only occasionally looking up in sketchy aural participation. And Bill, strangely present, was off on the very outskirts of the conclave, a leg dangling over the arm of his chair, head tilted all the way back with a protruding pipe thrust ceilingward, and giving very little indication of listening at all. His eyes had a look of vacancy, as though his mind were elsewhere while his body was dutifully and filially in the room with them.

She tried to get by without being seen, but Mother Hazzard looked up at just the wrong time and caught the flicker of her figure past the door-gap. "There she is now," she said. A moment later her retarding call had overtaken and halted her. "Patrice, come in here a moment, dear. We want you."

She turned and went back, with a sudden constriction in her throat.

The droning voice had interrupted itself to wait. A private investigator? No, no, he couldn't be. She'd met him here in the house on a friendly basis, she was sure of it. But those voluminous briefs littered in front of him—

"Patrice, you know Ty Winthrop."

"Yes, I know we've met before." She went over and shook hands with him. She kept her eyes carefully off the table. And it wasn't easy.

"Ty is Father's lawyer," Mother Hazzard said indulgently. As though that were really no way to describe an old friend, but it was the shortest one for present purposes.

"And golf rival," supplied the man at the table.

"Rival?" Father Hazzard snorted disgustedly. "I don't call that rivalry, what you put up. A rival has to come up somewhere near you. Charity-tournament is more what I'd call it."

Bill's head and pipe had come down to the horizontal again. "Lick him with one hand tied behind your back, eh Dad?" he egged him on.

"Yeah, *my* hand," snapped the lawyer, with a private wink for the son. "Especially last Sunday."

"Now, you three," reproved Mother Hazzard beamingly. "I have things to do. And so has Patrice. I can't sit in here all night."

They became serious again. Bill had risen and drawn up a chair beside the table for her. "Sit down, Patrice, and join the party," he invited.

"Yes, we want you to hear this, Patrice," Father Hazzard urged, as she hesitated. "It concerns you."

Her hand tried to stray betrayingly toward her throat. She kept it down by sheer will-power. She seated herself, a little uneasily.

The lawyer cleared his throat. "Well, I think that about takes care of it, Donald. The rest of it remains as it was before."

Father Hazzard hitched his chair nearer. "All right. Ready for me to sign now?"

Mother Hazzard bit off a thread with her teeth, having come to the end of something or other. She began to put things away in her basket, preparatory to departure. "You'd better tell Patrice what it is first, dear. Don't you want her to know?"

"I'll tell her for you," Winthrop offered. "I can put it in fewer words than you." He turned toward her and gazed friendlily over the tops of his reading-glasses. "Donald's changing the provisions of his will, by adding a codicil. You see, in the original, after Grace here was provided for, there was an equal division of the residue made between Bill and Hugh. Well now we're altering that to make it one-quarter of the residue to Bill and the remainder to you."

She could feel her face beginning to flame, as though a burning crimson light were focussed on it, and it alone, that they could all see. An agonizing sensation of wanting to push away from the table and make her escape, and of being held trapped there in her chair, came over her.

She tried to speak quietly, quelling her voice by moistening her lips twice over. "I don't want you to do that. I don't want to be included."

"Don't look that way about it," Bill said with a genial laugh. "You're not doing anybody out of anything. I have Dad's business—"

"It was Bill's own suggestion," Mother Hazzard let her know.

"I gave both the boys a lump sum in cash, to start them off, on the day they each reached their twenty-first—"

She was on her feet now, facing all of them in turn, almost

panic-stricken. "No, please! Don't put my name down on it at all! I don't want my name to go down on it!" She all but wrung her clasped hands toward Father Hazzard. "Dad! Won't you listen to me?"

"It's on account of Hugh, dear," Mother Hazzard let him know in a tactful aside. "Can't you understand?"

"Well, I know; we all feel bad about Hugh. But she has to go on living just the same. She has a child to think of. And these things shouldn't be postponed on account of sentiment; they have to be taken care of at the right time."

She turned and fled from the room. They made no attempt to follow her.

She closed the door after her. She stormed back and forth, two, three times, holding her head locked in her upended arms. "Swindler!" burst from her muffledly. "Thief! It's just like someone climbing in through a window and—"

There was a low knock at the door about half an hour later. She went over and opened it, and Bill was standing there.

"Hello," he said diffidently.

"Hello," she said with equal diffidence.

It was as though they hadn't seen one another for two or three days past, instead of just half an hour before.

"He signed it," he said. "After you went up. Winthrop took it back with him. Witnessed and all. It's done now, whether you wanted it or not."

She didn't answer. The battle had been lost, downstairs, before, and this was just the final communiqué.

He was looking at her in a way she couldn't identify. It seemed to have equal parts of shrewd appraisal and blank incomprehension in it, and there was just a dash of admiration added.

"You know," he said, "I don't know why you acted like that about it. And I don't agree with you, I think you were wrong in acting like that about it." He lowered his voice a little in confidence. "But somehow or other I'm glad you acted like that about it. I like you better for acting like that about it." He shoved his hand out to her suddenly. "Want to shake goodnight?"

Twenty-Three

SHE was alone in the house. That is, alone just with Hughie, in his crib upstairs, and Aunt Josie, in her room all the way at the back. They'd gone out to visit the Michaelsons, old friends.

It was nice to be alone in the house once in awhile. Not too often, not all the time, that would have run over into loneliness. And she'd known what that was once, only too well, and didn't want to ever again.

But it was nice to be alone like this, alone *without* loneliness, just for an hour or two, just from nine until eleven, with the sure knowledge that they were coming back soon. With the whole house her own to roam about in; upstairs, down, into this room, into that. Not that she couldn't at other times—but this had a special feeling to it, doing it when no one else was about. It did something to her. It nourished her feeling of *belonging*, replenished it.

They'd asked her if she didn't want to come with them, but she'd begged off. Perhaps because she knew that if she stayed home alone she'd get this very feeling from it.

They didn't importune her. They never importuned, never repeated any invitation to the point of weariness. They respected you as an individual, she reflected, that was one of the nice things about them. Only one of the nice, there were so many others.

"Then next time, maybe," Mother had smiled in parting, from the door.

"Next time without fail," she promised. "They're very nice people."

She roamed about for awhile first, getting her "feel" of the place, saturating herself in that blessed sensation of "belonging." Touching a chair-back here, fingering the texture of a window-drape there.

Mine. My house. My parents' house and mine. Mine. Mine. My *home*. My chair. My window-drape. No, hang back like that, that's the way I want you to.

Silly? Childish? Fanciful? No doubt. But who is without childishness, fancies? What is life without them? Or, *is* there life without them?

She went into Aunt Josie's pantry, took the lid off the cookie-jar, took one out, took a big bite out of it.

She wasn't hungry. They'd all finished a big dinner only a couple of hours ago. But—

My house. I can do this. I'm entitled to them. They're waiting there for me, to help myself whenever I feel like it.

She put the lid on the jar, started to put the light out.

She changed her mind suddenly, went back, took out a second one.

My house. I can even take two if I want to. Well, I *will* take two.

And one in each hand, each with a big defiant bite taken out of it, she came out of there. They weren't food for the mouth, actually, they were food for the soul.

The last crumbs brushed off her fingers, she decided to read a book finally. Utter repose had come to her now, a sense of peace and well-being that was almost therapeutic in its depth. It was a sensation of *healing*; of becoming one, becoming whole again. As though the last vestiges of an old ache, from an old split in her personality (as indeed there was one in the fullest sense), had been effaced. A psychiatrist could have written a learned paper on this; that just roaming about a house, in utter security, in utter relaxation, for half an hour or so, could achieve such a result for her, beyond all capacity of cold-blooded science, in the clinic, to have done likewise. But, human beings are human beings, and science isn't what they need; it's a home, a house of their own, that no one can take away from them.

It was the right time, almost the only time, for reading a book. You could give it your full attention, you could lose yourself in it. You became one with it for awhile, selfless.

In the library, it took her some time to make a definitive selection. She did a considerable amount of leaf-fluttering along the shelves, made two false starts back to the chair for an opening paragraph or two, before she'd finally settled on something that gave an indication of suiting her.

Marie Antoinette, by Katharine Anthony.

She'd never cared much for fiction, somehow. Something about it made her slightly uncomfortable, perhaps a reminder of the drama in her own life. She liked things (her mind expressed it) *that had really happened*. Really happened, but long ago and far away, to someone entirely else, someone that never could be confused with herself. In the case of a fictional character, you soon, involuntarily, began identifying yourself with him or her. In the case of a character who had once been an actual living personage, you did not. You sympathized objectively, but it ended there. It was always, from first to last, someone else. Because it had once, in reality, *been* someone else. (Escape, they would have called this, though in her case it was the reverse of what it was for others. They escaped from humdrum reality into fictional drama. She escaped from too much personal drama into a reality of the past.)

For an hour, maybe more, she was one with a woman dead a hundred and fifty years; she lost track of time.

Dimly, with only a marginal part of her faculties, she heard brakes go on somewhere outside in the quiet night.

". . . Axel Fersen drove swiftly through the dark streets." (They're back. I'll finish this chapter first.) "An hour and a half later, the coach passed through the gate of Saint-Martin. . . ."

A key turned in the front door. It opened, then it closed. But no murmur of homecoming voices eddied in. Vocal silence, if not the total kind. Firm, energetic footsteps, a single pair, struck across the preliminary gap of bare flooring adjacent to the door, then blurred off along the hall carpeting.

". . . A little way beyond, they saw a large travelling-carriage drawn up at the side of the road." (No, that's Bill, not they. He's the one just came in. I forgot, they didn't take the car with them, the Michaelsons live just around the corner) "a large travelling-carriage drawn up at the side of the road. . . ."

The tread went to the back. Aunt Josie's pantry-light flashed on again. She couldn't have seen it from where she was, but she knew it by the click of its switch. She knew all the lights by the clicks of their switches. The direction from which the click came, and its sharpness or faintness of tone. You can learn those things about a house.

She heard water surge from a tap, and then an emptied glass go down. Then the lid of the cookie-jar went down, with its heavy, hollowed, ringing, porcelain thud. It stayed down for some time, too, was in no hurry to go back on again.

". . . drawn up at the side of the road." (Aunt Josie'll have a fit. She always scolds him. She never scolds me, for doing the very same thing. I guess she used to when he was a boy, and can't get over the habit) "The pseudo Madame Korff and her party entered the carriage. . . ."

The lid went back on again at long last. The footsteps started forward again, emerged into the back of the hall. They stopped short, backed up a step, the floor creaked slightly with doubled weight in one place.

". . ." (He dropped a chunk on the floor, stopped to pick it up. Doesn't want her to see it lying there in the morning, and know what he's been up to. I bet he's still afraid of Aunt Josie in his heart, in a little-boy way.) ". . ."

But her thoughts were not consciously of him or on him. They were on her book. It was the perimeter of her mind, the unused residue, that kept up a running commentary to itself, and which the center of her attention paid no heed to.

He subsided for awhile, was lost to awareness. Must have been slumped somewhere, finishing his cookies. Probably with a leg thrown over a chair-arm, if he was in a chair at all.

He had known they were going over to the Michaelsons, and must have thought she had gone with them, that he was alone in the house. The library was to the right of the stairs, and he had taken the left channel, to the pantry and returned, hadn't come near here as yet, so he couldn't have known that she was in here. The shaded lamp she was beside had a limited radius of reflection that did not reach past the room-doorway.

Suddenly his lithe footfalls were underway again, had re-commenced, the nibbling interlude at an end. They struck out into the hall again, clarifying as they emerged from wherever it was he had been, rounded the bottom of the stairs, and turned in on this side. They were coming straight toward here, toward this room she was unsuspectedly in.

She went ahead steadily reading, trapped by the mounting interest of the passage she had just entered upon, held fast. Didn't even raise her eyes.

His tread reached the threshold. Then it stopped short there, almost with a recoil.

For perhaps a moment he stood stock-still, looking at her.

Then, abruptly, he took an awkward step in retreat, a full step to the rear, turned, went away again.

It was almost subconsciously that she knew all this; not in full consciousness, at least not as yet. It was there, clinging to her awareness, but it hadn't penetrated it as yet.

". . ." (Why did he turn and go away like that, when he saw me in here alone?) ". . . and disposed themselves upon the comfortable cushions. . . ." (He intended coming in here. He did come as far as the door. Then when he saw that I was in here, and didn't seem to have seen him yet, he backed away. Why? Why was that?) "Axel Fersen took the reins. . . ."

Slowly the spell of the book unravelled, disintegrated. Her eyes left its pages for the first time. She raised her head questioningly, still holding the book open before her.

Why? Why did he do that?

It isn't that he was afraid of disturbing me. We're all one family, we don't stand on ceremony like that with one another. We all go from room to room as we like without a by-your-leave, except in the upstairs-rooms, and this isn't upstairs, this is down here. He didn't even say hello. When he saw that I didn't see him, he wanted it left that way, did his best to keep it that way, tried not to attract my attention. Withdrew *backward* the first step, and only then turned around.

The front door had reopened, but without closing behind him. He'd gone out front for a moment, to put the car away. She heard the thump of its door as he shut it on himself, heard its gears mesh into motion.

Doesn't he like me? Is that why he doesn't want to find himself alone in a room with me, when no one else is here? Is he holding something against me? I thought—it seemed—as if his full confidence had been given to me long ago, but—To balk like that, curb himself, almost swerve away, at the very threshold.

And then suddenly, quite simply, almost matter-of-factly, she knew. It came to her. Some indefinable something had told her. Something that no word could explain. Something too tenuous to bear the weight of *any* words.

No, it's not because he doesn't like me. It's because he does like me, *does* like me, that he backed away like that, doesn't want to be in the room alone with me if he can avoid it. Likes me too well. Is already beginning to fall in love with me. And—and thinks he shouldn't. Is fighting it. That hopeless, last-ditch fight that's never won.

Determinedly, but quite unhurriedly, she closed her book, carried it over to the gap from which she'd extracted it, pushed it in. She left the lamp on for him (since he had seemed to want to come in here), but quitted the room herself, left it to him, went out into the hall, went up the stairs and into her own room, closed the door of that for the night.

She undid her hair, brushed it for retiring.

She heard the rumble of the garage-doors, heard the padlock strike against them as he let it fall back to rest, heard him come into the house again. He went straight back toward the library, and went in, this time unhesitatingly (to accost her now, to face it, to bring it out, his decision taken during those few minutes' breathing spell?)—to find it empty. The lamp on, the reader gone.

Seconds later she remembered that she'd left her cigarette burning there, on the table, under the lamp, beside where she'd been sitting. Had forgotten to pick it up when she came out. It must be burning still, she'd only just lit it before she'd first heard the car drive up outside.

It wasn't that she was alarmed about possible damage. He'd see it at a glance, and put it out for her.

But it would tell him. For, just as he had intended coming in when he hadn't, it would reveal to him that she *hadn't* intended getting up and leaving when she had.

She not only knew, now, that he was beginning to love her, but, by token of that telltale cigarette, he knew that she knew.

Twenty-Four

IN the light of the full-bodied moon the flower-garden at the back of the house was as bright as noon when she stepped out into it. The sanded paths that ran around it foursquare, and through it like an X, gleamed like snow, and her shadow glided along them azure against their whiteness. The little rock-pool in the center was polka-dotted with silver disks, and the wafers coalesced and separated again as if in motion, though they weren't, as her point of perspective continually shifted with her rotary stroll.

The perfume of the rose-bushes was heavy on the June night, and sleepy little insects made a somnolent humming noise, as though they were talking in their sleep.

She hadn't wanted to sleep yet, and she hadn't wanted to read, it was too close in the library with the lamp on. She hadn't wanted to sit alone on the front porch any longer, once Mother and Father Hazzard had left her and gone up to their room. She'd gone up a moment and looked in at Hughie, to see if he was all right, and then she'd come out here. To the flower-garden in the back, safely secluded behind its tall surrounding hedge.

Eleven struck melodiously from the little Reformed church over on Beechwood Drive, and the echoes lingered in the still air, filling her with a sense of peace and well-being.

A quiet voice, seeming to come from just over her shoulder, said: "Hello; I thought that was you down there, Patrice."

She turned, startled, and couldn't locate him for a minute. He was above her, perched edgewise on the sill of his open window.

"Mind if I come down and join you for a cigarette?"

"I'm going in now," she said hastily, but he'd already disappeared.

He stepped down from the back porch and the moonlight sifted over his head and shoulders like talcum as he came toward her. She turned in company with him, and they walked slowly on together side by side. Once all around the outside path, and then once through a bisecting middle one.

She reached out and touched a flower once in passing; bent it a little toward her, then let it sway back again undamaged.

A full-blown white rose; the perfume was almost like a bomb-shell in their faces for a moment.

He didn't even do that much; didn't do anything. Didn't say anything. Just walked beside her. One hand slung in his pocket. Looking steadily down, as though the sight of the path fascinated him.

"I hate to tear myself away, it's so lovely down here," she said at last.

"I don't give a hang about gardens," he answered almost gruffly. "Nor walking in them. Nor the flowers in them. You know why I came down here. Do I have to tell you?"

He flung his cigarette down violently, backhand, with the same gesture as if something had angered him.

Suddenly she was acutely frightened. She'd stopped short. "No, wait, Bill. Bill, wait— Don't—"

"Don't what? I haven't said anything yet. But you know already, don't you? I'm sorry, Patrice, I've got to tell you. You've got to listen. It's got to come out."

She was holding out her hand protestingly toward him, as if trying to ward off something. She took a backward step away, broke their proximity.

"*I* don't like it," he said rebelliously. "It does things to me that are new. I was never bothered before. I never even had the sweetheart-crushes that they all do. I guess that was my way to be. But this is it, Patrice. This is it now, all right."

"No, wait— Not now. Not yet. This isn't the time—"

"This is the time, and this is the night, and this is the place. There'll never be another night like this, not if we both live to be a hundred. Patrice, I love you, and I want you to ma—"

"Bill!" she pleaded, terrified.

"Now you've heard it, and now you're running away. Patrice," he asked forlornly, "what's so terrible about it?"

She'd gained the lower-porch step, was poised on it for a moment in arrested flight. He came after her slowly, in a sort of acquiescent frustration, rather than in importunate haste.

"I'm no lover," he said. "I can't say it right—"

"Bill," she said again, almost grief-strickenly.

"Patrice, I see you every day and—" He flung his arms

apart helplessly. "What am I to do? I didn't ask for it. I think it's something good. I think it's something that should be."

She leaned her head for a moment against the porch-post, as if in distress. "Why did you have to say it yet? Why couldn't you have— Give me more time. Please, give me more time. Just a few months—"

"Do you want me to take it back, Patrice?" he asked ruefully. "How can I now? How could I, even if I hadn't spoken? Patrice, it's so long since, now. Is it Hugh, is it still Hugh?"

"I've never been in love bef—" she started to say, penitently. She stopped suddenly.

He looked at her strangely.

I've said too much, flashed through her mind. Too much, or not enough. And then in sorrowful confirmation: Not enough by far.

"I'm going in now." The shadow of the porch dropped between them like an indigo curtain.

He didn't try to follow. He stood there where she'd left him.

"You're afraid I'll kiss you."

"No, that isn't what I'm afraid of," she murmured almost inaudibly. "I'm afraid I'll want you to."

The door closed after her.

He stood out there in the full bleach of the moonlight, motionless, looking sadly downward.

Twenty-Five

IN the morning the world was sweet just to look at from her window. The sense of peace, of safety, of belonging, was being woven about her stronger all the time. Soon nothing could tear its fabric apart again. To wake up in your own room, in your own home, your own roof over your head. To find your little son awake before you and peering expectantly out through his crib, and giving you that crowing smile of delight that was already something special he gave to no one but you. To lift him up and hold him to you, and have to curb yourself, you wanted to squeeze so tightly. Then to carry him over to the window with you, and hold the curtain back, and look out at the world. Show him the world you'd found for him, the world you'd made for him.

The early sunlight like goldenrod pollen lightly dusting the sidewalks and the roadway out front. The azure shadows under the trees and at the lee sides of all the houses. A man sprinkling a lawn a few doors down, the water fraying from the nozzle of his hose twinkling like diamonds. He looked up and saw you, and he gave you a neighborly wave of the hand, though you didn't know him very well. And you took Hughie's little hand at the wrist, and waved it back to him in answering greeting.

Yes, in the mornings the world was sweet all right.

Then to dress, to dress for two, and to go downstairs to the pleasant room waiting for you below; to Mother Hazzard, and her fresh-picked flowers, and her affectionate, sunny greeting, and the mirror-like reflection of the coffee-percolator (that always delighted him so) showing squat, pudgy images seated around it on its various facets: an elderly lady, and a much younger lady, and a very young young-man, the center of attraction in his high chair.

To be safe, to be at home, to be among your own.

Even mail for you, a letter of your own, waiting for you at your place. She felt a pleased little sense of completion at sight of it. There was no greater token of permanency, of belonging, than that. Mail of your own, sent to your home.

"Mrs. Patrice Hazzard," and the address. Once that name had frightened her. It didn't now. In a little while she would no longer even remember that there had been another name, once, before it. A lonely, frightened name, drifting ownerless, unclaimed, about the world now—

"Now Hughie, not so fast, finish what you've got first."

She opened it, and there was nothing in it. Or rather, nothing written on it. For a moment she thought there must have been a mistake. Just blank paper. No, wait, the other way around—

Three small words, almost buried in the seam that folded

the sheet in two, almost overlooked in the snowy expanse that surrounded them.

"Who are you?"

Twenty-Six

IN the mornings the world was bitter-sweet to look at from her window. To wake up in a room that wasn't rightfully yours. That you knew—and you knew somebody else knew— you had no right to be in. The early sunlight was pale and bleak upon the ground, and under all the trees and on the lee side of all the houses, tatters of night lingered, diluted to blue but still gloomy and forbidding. A man sprinkling the lawn a few doors down was a stranger; a stranger you knew by sight. He looked up, and you hurriedly shrank back from the window, child and all, lest he see you. Then a moment later, you already wished you hadn't done that, but it was too late, it was done.

Was he the one? Was he?

It isn't as much fun any more to dress for two. And when you start down the stairs with Hughie, those stairs you've come down so many hundreds of times, now at last you've learned what it's like to come down them heavyhearted and troubled, as you said you might some day have to, that very first night of all. For that's how you're coming down them now.

Mother Hazzard at the table, beaming; and the flowers; and the gargoyle-like reflections on the percolator-panels. But you only have eyes for one thing, furtive, straining eyes, from as far back as the threshold of the doorway. From farther back than that, even; from the first moment the table has come into sight. Is there any white on it, over on your side of it? Is there any rectangular white patch showing there, by or near your place? It's easy to tell, for the cloth has a printed pattern, with dabs of red and green.

"Patrice, didn't you sleep well, dear?" Mother Hazzard asked solicitously. "You look a little peaked."

She hadn't looked peaked out on the stairs a moment ago. She'd only been heavyhearted and troubled then.

She settled Hughie in his chair, and took a little longer than was necessary. Keep your eyes away from it. Don't look at it. Don't think about it. Don't try to find out what's in it, you don't want to know what's in it; let it stay there until after the meal, then tear it up un—

"Patrice, you're spilling it on his chin. Here, let me."

She had nothing to do with her own hands, from that point on. And she felt as though she had so many of them; four or five at least. She reached for the coffee-pot, and a corner of it was in the way. She reached for the sugar-bowl, and another corner of it was in the way. She drew her napkin toward her, and it sidled two or three inches nearer her, riding on that. It was all about her, it was everywhere at once!

She wanted to scream, and she clenched her hand tightly, down beside her chair. I mustn't do that, I mustn't. Hughie's right here next to me, and Mother's just across the table—

Open it, open it fast. Quick, while you still have the courage.

The paper made a shredding sound, her finger was so thick and maladroit.

One word more this time.

"Where are you from?"

She clenched her hand again, down low beside her chair. White dissolved into it, disappearing through the finger-crevices.

Twenty-Seven

IN the mornings the world was bitter to look at from the window. To wake up in a strange room, in a strange house. To pick up your baby—that was the only thing that was right-fully yours—and edge toward the window with him, creeping up slantwise and peering from the far side of it, barely lifting the curtain; not stepping forward to the middle of it and throwing the curtain widely back. That was for people in their own homes, not for you. And out there, nothing. Nothing that belonged to you or was for you. The hostile houses of a hostile town. An icy wash of sun upon a stony ground. Dark shadows like frowns under each tree and leeward of each house. The man watering the lawn didn't turn around to greet you today. He was more than a stranger now, he was a potential enemy.

She carried her boy with her downstairs, and every step was like a knell. She was holding her eyes closed when she first went into the dining-room. She couldn't help it; she couldn't bring herself to open them for a moment.

"Patrice, you don't look right to me at all. You ought to see your color against that child's."

She opened her eyes.

Nothing there.

But it would come. It would come again. It had come once, twice; it would come again. Tomorrow maybe. The day after. Or the day after that. It would surely come again. There was nothing to do but wait. To sit there, stricken, helpless, waiting. It was like holding your head bowed under a leaky faucet, waiting for the next icy drop to detach itself and fall.

In the mornings the world was bitter, and in the evenings it was full of shadows creeping formlessly about her, threatening from one moment to the next to close in and engulf her.

Twenty-Eight

SHE hadn't slept well. That was the first thing she was conscious of on awakening. The cause, the reason for it, that came right with it. That was what really mattered; not the fact that she hadn't slept well, but knowing the cause, the reason for it. Only too well.

It wasn't new. It was occurring all the time lately, this not sleeping well. It was the rule rather than the exception.

The strain was beginning to tell on her. Her resistance was wearing away. Her nerves were slowly being drawn taut, a little more so each day. She was nearing a danger-point, she knew. She couldn't stand very much more of it. It wasn't when they came; it was in-between, waiting for the next one to come. The longer it took to come, the greater her tension, instead of the less. It was like that well-known simile of the second dropped shoe, prolonged ad infinitum.

She couldn't stand much more of it. "If there's another one," she told herself, "something will snap. Don't let there be another one. Don't."

She looked at herself in the glass. Not through vanity, conceit, to see whether damage had been done her looks. To confirm, objectively, the toll that was being taken. Her face was pale and worn. It was growing thinner again, losing its roundness, growing back toward that gauntness of cheek it had had in New York. Her eyes were a little too shadowed underneath, and just a little too bright. She looked tired and frightened. Not acutely so, but chronically. And that was what was being done to her by this.

She dressed herself, and then Hughie, and carried him down with her. It was so pleasant in the dining-room, in the early morning like this. The new-minted sun pouring in, the color of champagne; the crisp chintz curtains; the cheery colored ware on the table; the fragrant aroma of the coffee-pot; the savory odor of fresh-made toast seeping through the napkin thrown over it to keep it warm. Mother Hazzard's flowers in the center of the table, always less than an hour old, picked from her garden at the back. Mother Hazzard herself, spruce and gay in her printed morning-dress, beaming at her. Home. Peace.

"Leave me in peace," she pleaded inwardly. "Let me be. Let me have all this. Let me enjoy it, as it's meant to be enjoyed, as it's waiting around to be enjoyed. Don't take it from me, let me keep it."

She went around the table to her and kissed her, and held Hughie out to her to be kissed. Then she settled him in his highchair, between the two of them, and sat down herself.

Then she saw them, waiting for her.

The one on top was a department-store sales brochure, sealed in an envelope. She could identify it by the letterhead in the upper corner. But there was something under it, another one. Its corners stuck out a little past the top one.

She was afraid to bring it into fuller view, she postponed it.

She spooned Hughie's cereal to his mouth, took alternating sips of her own fruit juice. It was poisoning the meal, it was tightening up her nerves.

It mightn't be one of those, it might be something else. Her hand moved with a jerk, and the department-store folder was out of the way.

"Mrs. Patrice Hazzard."

It was addressed in pen and ink, a personal letter. She never got letters like that from anyone; who wrote to her, whom did she know? It must be, it was, one of those again. She felt a sick, cold feeling in her stomach. She took in everything about it, with a sort of hypnotic fascination. The three-cent purple stamp, with wavy cancellation-lines running through it. Then the circular postmark itself, off to the side. It had been posted late, after twelve last night. Where? She wondered. By whom? She could see in her mind's eye an indistinct, furtive figure slinking up to a street mail-box in the dark, a hand hastily thrusting something into the chute, the clang as the slot fell closed again.

She wanted to get it out of here, take it upstairs with her, close the door. But if she carried it away with her unopened, wouldn't that look secretive, wouldn't that call undue attention to it? It was safe enough to open it here in the very room; they never pried in this house, they never asked questions. She knew she could even have left it lying around open after having read it herself, and it would have been safe, nobody would have put a hand to it.

She ran her knife through the flap, slit it.

Mother Hazzard had taken over Hughie's feeding, she had eyes for no one but him. Every mouthful brought forth a paean of praise.

She'd opened the once-folded inner sheet now. The flowers were in the way, they screened the shaking of her hand. So blank it was, so much waste space, so little writing. Just a line across the middle of the paper, where the crease ran.

"What are you doing there?"

She could feel her chest constricting. She tried to quell the sudden inordinate quickness of her breathing, lest it betray itself.

Mother Hazzard was showing Hughie his plate. "All gone. Hughie ate it all up! Where *is* it?"

She'd lowered it into her lap now. She managed to get it back into its envelope, and fold that over, singly and then doubly, until it fitted into the span of her hand.

"One more and something will snap." And here it was, the one more.

She could feel her self-control ebbing away, and didn't know what catastrophic form its loss might take. "I've got to get out of this room," she warned herself. "I've got to get away from this table—now—quickly!"

She stood up suddenly, stumbling a little over her chair. She turned and left the table without a word.

"Patrice, aren't you going to have your coffee?"

"I'll be right down," she said smotheredly, from the other side of the doorway. "I forgot something."

She got up there, into her room, and got the door closed.

It was like the bursting of a dam. She hadn't known what form it would take. Tears, she'd thought, or high-pitched hysterical laughter. It was neither. It was anger, a paroxysm of rage, blinded and baffled and helpless.

She went over to the wall and flailed with upraised fists against it, held high over her head. And then around to the next wall and the next and the next, like somebody seeking an outlet, crying out distractedly: "Who are you yourself? Where are you sending them from? Why don't you come out? Why don't you come out in the open? Why don't you come out where I can see you? Why don't you come out and give me a chance to fight back?"

Until at last she'd stopped, wilted and breathing fast with spent emotion. In its wake came sudden determination. There was only one way to fight back, only one way she had to rob the attacks of their power to harm—

She flung the door open. She started down the stairs again. Still as tearless as she'd gone up. She was going fast, she was rippling down them in a quick-step. She was still holding it in her hand. She opened it up, back to its full size, and started smoothing it out as she went.

She came back into the dining-room still at the same gait she'd used on the stairs.

"—drank all his milk like a good boy," Mother Hazzard was crooning.

Patrice moved swiftly around the table toward her, stopped short beside her.

"I want to show you something," she said tersely. "I want you to see this."

She put it down on the table squarely in front of her and stood there waiting.

"Just a moment, dear; let me find my glasses," Mother Hazzard purred acquiescently. She probed here and there among the breakfast things. "I know I had them with me when Father was here at the table; we were both reading the paper." She looked over toward the buffet on the other side of her.

Patrice stood there waiting. She looked over at Hughie. He was still holding his spoon, entire fist folded possessively around it. He flapped it at her joyously. Home. Peace.

Suddenly she'd reached over to her own place at the table, picked up the department-store circular still lying there, replaced the first letter with that.

"Here they are, under my napkin. Right in front of me the whole time." Mother Hazzard adjusted them, turned back to her. "Now what was it, dear?" She opened the folder and looked at it.

Patrice pointed. "This pattern, right here. The first one. Isn't it—attractive?"

Behind her back, held in one hand, the abducted missive slowly crumpled, deflated, was sucked between her fingers into compressed invisibility.

Twenty-Nine

QUIETLY and deftly she moved about the dimly lighted room, passing back and forth, and forth and back, with armfuls of belongings from the drawers. Hughie lay sleeping in his crib, and the clock said almost one.

The valise stood open on a chair. Even that wasn't hers. It was the one she'd first used on the train-ride here, new-looking as ever, the one with "PH" on its rounded corner. She'd have to borrow it. Just as she was borrowing the articles she picked at random, to throw into it. Just as she was borrowing the very clothes she stood in. There were only two things in this whole room with her now that were rightfully hers. That little bundle sleeping quietly there in the crib. And that seventeen cents lying spread out on a scrap of paper on the dresser-top.

She took things for him, mostly. Things he needed, things to keep him warm. They wouldn't mind, they wouldn't begrudge that; they loved him almost as much as she did, she reasoned ruefully. She quickened her movements, as if the danger of faltering in purpose lay somewhere along this train of thought if she lingered on it too long.

For herself she took very little, only what was of absolute necessity. Underthings, an extra pair or two of stockings—

Things, things. What did things matter, when your whole world was breaking up and crumbling about you? *Your* world? It wasn't *your* world, it was a world you had no right to be in.

She dropped the lid of the valise, latched it impatiently on what it held, indifferent to whether it held enough, or too much, or too little. A little tongue of white stuff was trapped, left protruding through the seam, and she let it be.

She put on the hat and coat she'd left in readiness across the foot of the bed. The hat without consulting a mirror, though there was one right at her shoulder. She picked up her handbag, and probed into it with questing hand. She brought out a key, the key to this house, and put it down on the dresser. Then she brought out a small change-purse and shook it out. A cabbagy cluster of interfolded currency fell out soundlessly, and a sprinkling of coins, these last with a tinkling sound and some rolling about. She swept them all closer together, and then left them there on top of the dresser. Then she picked up the seventeen cents and dropped that into the change-purse instead, and replaced it in the handbag, and thrust that under her arm.

She went over beside the crib, then, and lowered its side. She crouched down on a level with the small sleeping face.

She kissed it lightly on each eyelid. "I'll be back for you in a minute," she whispered. "I have to take the bag down first and stand it at the door. I can't manage you both on those stairs, I'm afraid." She straightened up, lingered a moment, looking down at him. "We're going for a ride, you and I; we don't know where, and we don't care. Straight out, along the way the trains go. We'll find someone along the road who'll let us in next to him—"

The clock said a little after one now.

She went over to the door, softly opened it, and carried the valise outside with her. She eased it closed behind her, and then she started down the stairs valise in hand, with infinite slowness, as though it weighed a lot. Yet it couldn't have been the valise alone that seemed to pull her arm down so, it must have been the leadenness of her heart.

Suddenly she'd stopped, and allowed the valise to come to rest on the step beside her. They were standing there without a sound, down below her by the front door, the two of them. Father Hazzard and Doctor Parker. She hadn't heard them until now, for they hadn't been saying anything. They must have been standing there in a sort of momentary mournful silence, just preceding leavetaking.

They broke it now, as she stood there unseen, above the bend of the stairs.

"Well, goodnight, Donald," the doctor said at last, and she saw him put his hand to Father Hazzard's shoulder in an attempt at consolation, then let it trail heavily off again. "Get some sleep. She'll be all right." He opened the door, then he added: "But no excitement, no stress of any kind from now on, you understand that, Donald? That'll be your job, to keep all that away from her. Can I count on you?"

"You can count on me," Father Hazzard said forlornly.

The door closed, and he turned away and started up the stairs, to where she stood riveted. She moved down a step or two around the turn to meet him, leaving the valise behind her, doffed hat and coat flung atop it now.

He looked up and he saw her, without much surprise, without much of anything except a sort of stony sadness.

"Oh, it's you, Patrice," he said dully. "Did you hear him? Did you hear what he just said?"

"Who is it—Mother?"

"She had another of those spells soon after we retired. He's been in there with her for over an hour and a half. It was touch and go, for a few minutes, at first—"

"But Father! Why didn't you—?"

He sat down heavily on the stair-step. She sat down beside him, slung one arm about his shoulders.

"Why should I bother you, dear? There wouldn't have been anything you could have— You have the baby on your hands all day long, you need your rest. Besides, this isn't anything new. Her heart's always been weak. Way back before the boys were born—"

"I never knew. You never told me— But is it getting worse?"

"Things like that don't improve as you get on in years," he said gently.

She let her head slant to rest against his shoulder, in compunction.

He patted her hand consolingly. "She'll be all right. We'll see that she is, you and I, between us, won't we?"

She shivered a little, involuntarily, at that.

"It's just that we've got to cushion her against all shocks and upsets," he said. "You and the young fellow, you're about the best medicine for her there is. Just having you around—"

And if in the morning she had asked for Patrice, asked for her grandchild, and he'd had to tell her— She fell strangely silent, looking down at the steps under their feet, but no longer seeing them. And if she'd come out of her room five minutes later, just missing the doctor as he left, she might have brought death into this house, in repayment for all the love that had been lavished on her. Killed the only mother she'd ever known.

He misunderstood her abstraction, pressed her chin with the cleft of his hand. "Now don't take it like that; she wouldn't want you to, you know. And Pat, don't let her know you've found out about it. Let her keep on thinking it's her secret and mine. I know she'll be happier that way."

She sighed deeply. It was a sigh of decision, of capitulation to the inevitable. She turned and kissed him briefly on the side of the head and stroked his hair a couple of times. Then she stood up.

"I'm going up," she said quietly. "Go down and put out the hall-light after us, a minute."

He retraced his steps momentarily. She picked up the valise, the coat, the hat, and quietly reopened the door of her own room.

"Goodnight, Patrice."

"Goodnight, Father; I'll see you in the morning."

She carried them in with her, and closed the door, and in the darkness on the other side she stood still a minute. A silent, choking prayer welled up in her.

"Give me strength, for there's no running away, I see that now. The battle must be fought out here where I stand, and I dare not even cry out."

Thirty

THEN they stopped suddenly. There were no more. No more came. The days became a week, the week became a month. The month lengthened toward two. And no more came.

It was as though the battle had been won without striking a blow. No, she knew that wasn't so; it was as though the battle had been broken off, held in abeyance, at the whim of the crafty, shadowy adversary.

She clutched at straws—straws of attempted comprehension—and they all failed her.

Mother Hazzard said: "Edna Harding got back today; she's been visiting their folks in Philadelphia the past several weeks."

But no more came.

Bill remarked: "I ran into Tom Bryant today; he tells me his older sister Marilyn's been laid up with pleurisy; she only got out of bed for the first time today."

"I *thought* I hadn't seen her."

But no more came.

Caulfield: Population 203,000, she thought. That was what the atlas in the library said. And a pair of hands to each living soul of them. One to hold down the flap of a letter-box, on some secret shadowy corner; the other to quickly, furtively slip an envelope through the slot.

No more came. Yet the enigma remained. What was it? Who was it? Or rather, what had it been? Who had it been?

Yet deep in her innermost heart she knew somehow the present tense still fitted it, none other would do. Things like that didn't just happen and then stop. They either never began at all, or else they ran on to their shattering, destructive conclusion.

But in spite of that, security crept back a little; frightened off once and not so bold now as before, but crept tentatively back toward her a little.

In the mornings the world was bitter-sweet to look at, seeming to hold its breath, waiting to see—

Thirty-One

MOTHER HAZZARD knocked on her door just as she'd finished tucking Hughie in. There wasn't anything exceptional about this, it was a nightly event, the filching of a last grandmotherly kiss just before the light went out. Tonight, however, she seemed to want to talk to Patrice herself. And not to know how to go about it.

She lingered on after she'd kissed him, and the side of the crib had been lifted into place. She stood there somewhat uncertainly, her continued presence preventing Patrice from switching out the light.

There was a moment's awkwardness.

"Patrice."

"Yes, Mother?"

Suddenly she'd blurted it out. "Bill wants to take you to the Country Club dance with him tonight. He's waiting down there now."

Patrice was so completely taken back she didn't answer for a moment, just stood there looking at her.

"He told me to come up and ask you if you'd go with him." Then she rushed on, as if trying to talk her into it by sheer profusion of wordage, "They have one about once each month, you know, and he's going himself, he usually does, and—why don't you get dressed and go with him?" she ended up on a coaxing note.

"But I—I—" Patrice stammered.

"Patrice, you've got to begin sooner or later. It isn't good for you not to. You haven't been looking as well as you might lately. We're a little worried about you. If there's something troubling you— You do what Mother says, dear."

It was apparently an order. Or as close to an order as Mother Hazzard could ever have brought herself to come. She had opened Patrice's closet-door, meanwhile, and was peering helpfully inside. "How about this?" She took something down, held it up against herself to show her.

"I haven't very much—"

"It'll do nicely." It landed on the bed. "They're not very formal there. I'll have Bill buy you an orchid or gardenia on the way, that'll dress it up enough. You just go and get the *feel* of it tonight. It'll begin coming back to you little by little." She smiled reassuringly at her. "You'll be in good hands." She patted her on the shoulder as she turned to go outside. "Now that's a good girl. I'll tell Bill you're getting ready."

Patrice overheard her call down to him from above-stairs, a moment later, without any attempt at modulating her voice: "The answer is yes. I talked her into it. And you be very nice to her, young man, or you'll hear from me."

He was standing waiting for her just inside the door when she came downstairs.

"Am I all right?" she asked uncertainly.

He was suddenly overcome with some sort of awkwardness. "Gee, I—I didn't know how you could look in the evening," he said haltingly.

For the first few moments of the drive, there was a sort of shyness between them, almost as though they'd only just met tonight for the first time. It was very impalpable, but it rode with them. He turned on the radio in the car. Dance music rippled back into their faces. "To get you into the mood," he said.

He stopped, and got out, and came back with an orchid.

"The biggest one north of Venezuela," he said. "Or wherever they come from."

"Here, pin it on for me." She selected a place. "Right about here."

Abruptly, he balked at that, for some strange reason. All but shied away bodily. "Oh no, that you do yourself," he said, more forcefully than she could see any reason for.

"I might stick myself," he added lamely as an afterthought. A little too long after.

"Why, you great big coward."

The hand that would have held the pin was a trifle unsteady, she noticed, when he first put it back to the wheel. Then it quieted.

They drove the rest of the way. The rest of the way lay mostly through open country. There were stars overhead.

"I've never *seen* so many!" she marvelled.

"Maybe you haven't been looking up enough," he said gently.

Toward the end, just before they got there, a peculiar sort of tenderness seemed to overcome him for a minute. He even slowed the car a little, as he turned to her.

"I want you to be happy tonight, Patrice," he said earnestly. "I want you to be *very* happy."

There was a moment's silence between them, then they picked up speed again.

Thirty-Two

And for the next one, right after that, the tune they played was "Three Little Words." She remembered that afterward. That least of all things about it, the tune they had been playing at the time. She was dancing it with Bill. For that matter she'd been dancing them all with him, steadily, ever since they'd arrived. She wasn't watching, she wasn't looking around her, she wasn't thinking of anything but the two of them.

Smiling dreamily, she danced. Her thoughts were like a little brook running swiftly but smoothly over harmless pebbles, keeping time with the tinkling music.

I like dancing with him. He dances well, you don't have to keep thinking about your feet. He's turned his face toward me and is looking down at me; I can feel it. Well, I'll look up at him, and then he'll smile at me; but I won't smile back at him. Watch. There, I knew that was coming. I will *not* smile back. Oh, well, what if I did? It slipped out before I could stop it. Why shouldn't I smile at him, anyway? That's the way I feel about him; smilingly fond.

A hand touched Bill's shoulder from behind. She could see the fingers slanted downward for a second, on her side of it, without seeing the hand or arm or person it belonged to.

A voice said: "May I cut in on this one?"

And suddenly they'd stopped. Bill had stopped, so she had to, too.

His arms left her. A shuffling motion took place, Bill stepped aside, and there was someone else there in his place. It was like a double exposure, where one person dissolves into another.

Their eyes met, hers and the new pair. His had been waiting for hers, and hers had foolishly run into his. They couldn't move again.

The rest was horror, sheer and unadulterated. Horror such as she'd never known she could experience. Horror under the electric lights. Death on the dance floor. Her body stayed upright, but otherwise she had every feeling of death coursing through it.

"Georgesson's the name," he murmured unobtrusively to Bill. His lips hardly seemed to stir at all. His eyes didn't leave hers.

Bill completed the ghastly parody of an introduction. "Mrs. Hazzard, Mr. Georgesson."

"How do you do?" he said to her.

Somehow there was even worse horror in the trite phrase than there had been in the original confrontation. She was screaming in silent inward panic, her lips locked tight, unable even to speak Bill's name and prevent the transfer.

"May I?" Georgesson said, and Bill nodded, and the transfer had been completed; it was too late.

Then for a moment, blessed reprieve. She felt his arms close about her, and her face sank into the sheltering shadow of his shoulder, and she was dancing again. She no longer had to stand upright, unsupported. There, that was better. A minute to think in. A minute to get your breath in.

The music went on, their dancing went on. Bill's face faded away in the background.

"We've met before, haven't we?"

Keep me from fainting, she prayed, keep me from falling.

He was waiting for his answer.

Don't speak; don't answer him.

"*Who'd* he say you were?"

Her feet faltered, missed.

"Don't make me keep on doing this, I can't. Help me—outside someplace—or I'm—"

"Too warm for you?" he said politely.

She didn't answer. The music was dying. She was dying.

He said, "You went out of step, just then. My fault, I'm afraid."

"Don't—" she whimpered. "Don't—"

The music stopped. They stopped.

His arm left her back, but his hand stayed tight about her wrist, holding her there beside him for a moment.

He said, "There's a veranda outside. Over there, out that way. I'll go out there and wait for you, and we can—go ahead talking."

She hardly knew what she was saying. "I can't— You don't understand—" Her neck wouldn't hold firm; her head kept trying to lob over limply.

"I think I do. I think I understand perfectly. I understand you, and you understand me." Then he added with a grisly sort of emphasis that froze her to the marrow: "I bet we two understand one another better than any other two people in this whole ballroom at the moment."

Bill was coming back toward them from the sidelines.

"I'll be out there where I said. Don't keep me waiting too long, or—I'll simply have to come in and look you up again." His face didn't change. His voice didn't change. "Thanks for the dance," he said, as Bill arrived.

He didn't let go her wrist; he transferred it to Bill's keeping, as though she were something inanimate, a doll, and bowed, and turned, and left them.

"Seen him around a few times. Came here stag, I guess."
Bill shrugged in dismissal. "Come on."

"Not this one. The one after."

"Are you all right? You look pale."

"It's the lights. I'm going in and powder. You go and dance
with someone else."

He grinned at her. "I don't want to dance with someone
else."

"Then you go and—and come back for me. The one after."

"The one after."

She watched him from just outside the doorway. He went
out front toward the bar. She watched him go in there. She
watched him sit down on one of the tall stools. Then she
turned and went the other way.

She walked slowly over to the doors leading outside onto
the veranda, and stood in one of them, looking out into the
fountain-pen-ink blueness of the night. There were wicker
chairs, in groups of twos and threes, spaced every few yards,
encircling small tables.

The red sequin of a cigarette-coal had risen perpendicularly
above one, all the way down at the end, imperiously summoning her. Then it shot over the balustrade laterally, cast
away in impatient expectancy.

She walked slowly down that way, with the strange feeling
of making a journey from which there was to be no return,
ever. Her feet seemed to want to take root, hold her back of
their own volition.

She came to a halt before him. He slung his hip onto the
balustrade, and sat there askew, in insolent informality. He
repeated what he'd said inside. "*Who*'d he say you were?"

The stars were moving. They were making peculiar eddying
swirls like blurred pinwheels all over the sky.

"You abandoned me," she said with leashed fury. "You
abandoned me, with five dollars. Now what do you want?"

"Oh, then we have met before. I *thought* we had. Glad you
agree with me."

"Stop it. What do you want?"

"What do I want? I don't want anything. I'm a little confused, that's all. I'd like to be straightened out. The man introduced you under a mistaken name in there."

"What do you want? What are you doing down here?"

"Well, for that matter," he said with insolent urbanity, "what are you doing yourself down here?"

She repeated it a third time. "What do you want?"

"Can't a man show interest in his ex-protégée and child? There's no way of making children ex, you know."

"You're either insane or—"

"You know that isn't so. You wish it were," he said brutally.

She turned on her heel. His hand found her wrist again, flicked around it like a whip. Cutting just as deeply.

"Don't go inside yet. We haven't finished."

She stopped, her back to him now. "I think we have."

"The decision is mine."

He let go of her, but she stayed there where she was. She heard him light another cigarette, saw the momentary reflection from behind her own shoulder.

He spoke at last, voice thick with expelled smoke. "You still haven't cleared things up," he purred. "I'm as mixed-up as ever. This Hugh Hazzard married—er—let's say you, his wife, in Paris, a year ago last June fifteenth. I went to considerable expense and trouble to have the exact date on the records there verified. But a year ago last June fifteenth you and I were living in our little furnished room in New York. I have the receipted rent-bills to show for this. How could you have been in two such far-apart places at once?" He sighed philosophically. "Somebody's got their dates mixed. Either he had. Or I have." And then very slowly, "Or *you* have."

She winced unavoidably at that. Slowly her head came around, her body still remaining turned from him. Like one who listens hypnotized, against her will.

"It was you who's been sending those—?"

He nodded with mock affability, as if on being complimented on something praiseworthy. "I thought it would be kinder to break it to you gently."

She drew in her breath with an icy shudder of repugnance.

"I first happened on your name among the train-casualties, when I was up in New York," he said. He paused. "I went down there and 'identified' you, you know," he went on matter-of-factly. "You have that much to thank me for, at any rate."

He puffed thoughtfully on his cigarette.

"Then I heard one thing and another, and put two and two together. I went back for awhile first—got the rent-receipts together and one thing and another—and then finally I came on the rest of the way down here, out of curiosity. I became quite confused," he said ironically, "when I learned the rest of the story."

He waited. She didn't say anything. He seemed to take pity on her finally. "I know," he said indulgently, "this isn't the time nor place to—talk over old times. This is a party, and you're anxious to get back and enjoy yourself."

She shivered.

"Is there anywhere I can reach you?"

He took out a notebook, clicked a lighter. She mistakenly thought he was waiting to write at her dictate. Her lips remained frozen.

"Seneca 382," he read from the notebook. He put it away again. His hand made a lazy curve between them. In the stricken silence that followed he suggested after awhile, casually: "Lean up against that chair so you don't fall; you don't seem very steady on your feet, and I don't want to have to carry you bodily inside in front of all those people."

She put her hands to the top of the chair-back and stood quiet, head inclined.

The rose-amber haze in the open doorway down at the center of the terrace blotted out for a moment, and Bill was standing there looking for her.

"Patrice, this is our dance."

Georgesson rose for a second from the balustrade in sketchy etiquette, immediately sank back against it.

She made her way toward him, the blue pall of the terrace covering her uncertainty of step, and went inside with him. His arms took charge of her from that point on, so that she no longer had to be on her own.

"You were both standing there like statues," he said. "He can't be very good company."

She lurched against him in the tendril-like twists of the rumba, her head dropped to rest on his shoulder.

"He isn't very good company," she agreed sickly.

Thirty-Three

THE phone-call came at a fiendishly unpropitious moment.

He'd timed it well. He couldn't have timed it better if he'd been able to look through the walls of the house and watch their movements on the inside. The two men in the family were out. She'd just finished putting Hughie to sleep. She and Mother Hazzard were both up on the second floor, separately. Which meant that she was the only one fully eligible to answer.

She knew at the first instant of hearing it who it was, what it was. She knew too, that she'd been expecting it all day, that she'd known it was coming, it was surely coming.

She stood there rooted, unable to move. Maybe it would stop if she didn't go near it, maybe he would tire. But then it would ring again some other time.

Mother Hazzard opened the door of her room and looked out.

Patrice had swiftly opened her own door, was at the head of the stairs, before she'd fully emerged.

"I'll get it on this phone, dear, if you're busy."

"No, never mind, Mother, I was just going downstairs, anyway, so I'll answer it there."

She knew his voice right away. She hadn't heard it for over two years, until just last night, and yet it was again as familiar to her as if she'd been hearing it steadily for months past. Fear quickens the memory.

He was as pleasantly aloof at first as any casual caller on the telephone. "Is this the younger Mrs. Hazzard? Is this Patrice Hazzard?"

"This is she."

"I suppose you know, this is Georgesson."

She did know, but she didn't answer that.

"Are you—where you can be heard?"

"I'm not in the habit of answering questions like that. I'll hang up the receiver."

Nothing could seem to make him lose his equanimity. "Don't do that, Patrice," he said urbanely. "I'll ring back again. That'll make it worse. They'll begin wondering who it is keeps on calling so repeatedly. Or, eventually, someone else

will answer—you can't stay there by the phone all evening—
and I'll give my name if I have to and ask for you." He waited
a minute for this to sink in. "Don't you see, it's better for
you this way."

She sighed a little, in suppressed fury.

"We can't talk very much over the phone. I think it's better
not to, anyway. I'm talking from McClellan's Drugstore, a few
blocks from you. My car's just around the corner from there,
where it can't be seen. On the left side of Pomeroy Street,
just down from the crossing. Can you walk down that far for
five or ten minutes? I won't keep you long."

She tried to match the brittle formality of his voice with
her own. "I most certainly can not."

"Of course you can. You need cod-liver-oil capsules for
your baby, from McClellan's. Or you feel like a soda, for yourself. I've seen you stop in there more than once, in the evening."

He waited.

"Shall I call back? Would you rather think it over awhile?"

He waited again.

"Don't do that," she said reluctantly, at last.

She could tell he understood: her meaning had been a positive and not a negative one.

She hung up.

She went upstairs again.

Mother Hazzard didn't ask her. They weren't inquisitive
that way, in this house. But the door of her room was open.
Patrice couldn't bring herself to reenter her own without at
least a passing reference. Guilty conscience, this soon? she
wondered bitingly.

"That was a Steve Georgesson, Mother," she called in. "Bill
and I ran into him there last night. He wanted to know how
we'd enjoyed ourselves."

"Well, that was real thoughtful of him, wasn't it?" Then
she added, "He must be a decent sort, to do that."

Decent, Patrice thought dismally, easing the door closed
after her.

She came out of her room again in about ten minutes' time.
Mother Hazzard's door was closed now. She could have gone
on down the stairs unquestioned. Again she couldn't do it.

She went over and knocked lightly, to attract attention.

"Mother, I'm going to take a walk down to the drugstore and back. Hughie's out of his talc. And I'd like a breath of air. I'll be back in five minutes."

"Go ahead, dear. I'll say goodnight to you now, in case I'm asleep by the time you're in again."

She rested her outstretched hand helplessly against the door for a minute. She felt like saying, Mother, don't let me go. Forbid me. Keep me here.

She turned away and went down the stairs. It was her own battle, and no proxies were allowed.

She stopped beside the car, on darkened Pomeroy Street.

"Sit in here, Patrice," he said amiably. He unlatched the door for her, from where he sat, and even palmed the leather cushion patronizingly.

She settled herself on the far side of the seat. Her eyes snapped refusal of the cigarette he was trying to offer her.

"We can be seen."

"Turn this way, toward me. No one'll notice you. Keep your back to the street."

"This can't go on. Now once and for all, for the first time and the last, what is it you want of me, what is this about?"

"Look, Patrice, there doesn't have to be anything unpleasant about this. You seem to be building it up to yourself that way, in your own mind. I have no such— It's all in the way you look at it. I don't see that there has to be any change in the way things were going along—before last night. You were the only one knew before. Now you and I are the only ones know. It ends there. That is, if you want it to."

"You didn't bring me out here to tell me that."

He went off at a tangent. Or what seemed to be a tangent. "I've never amounted to—as much as I'd hoped, I suppose. I mean, I've never gotten as far as I should. As I once expected to. There are lots of us like that. Every once in awhile I find myself in difficulties, every now and then I get into a tight squeeze. Little card-games with the boys. This and that. You know how it is." He laughed deprecatingly. "It's been going on for years. It's nothing new. But I was wondering if you'd care to do me a favor—this time."

"You're asking me for money."

She almost felt nauseated. She turned her face away.

"I didn't think there were people like you outside of—outside of penitentiaries."

He laughed in good-natured tolerance. "You're in unusual circumstances. That attracts 'people like me.' If you weren't, you *still* wouldn't think there were any, you wouldn't know any different."

"Suppose I go to them now and tell them of this conversation we've just been having, of my own accord. My brother-in-law would go looking for you and beat you within an inch of your life."

"We'll let the relationship stand unchallenged. I wonder why women put such undue faith in a beating-up? Maybe because they're not used to violence themselves. A beating doesn't mean much to a man. Half an hour after it's over, he's as good as he was before."

"You should know," she murmured.

He tapped a finger to the points of three others. "There are three alternatives. You go to them and tell them. Or I go to them and tell them. Or we remain in status quo. By which I mean, you do me a favor, and then we drop the whole thing, nothing further is said. But there isn't any fourth alternative."

He shook his head slightly, in patient disapproval. "You overdramatize everything so, Patrice. That's the unfailing hallmark of cheapness. You're a cheap girl. That's the basic difference between us. I may be, according to your lights, a rotter, but I have a certain tone. As you visualize it, I'd stride in there, throw my arms out wide in declamation, and blare, 'This girl is not your daughter-in-law!' Not at all. That wouldn't work with people like that. It would overreach itself. All I'd have to do would be to let you accuse yourself out of your own mouth. In their presence. You couldn't refuse the house to me. 'When you were in Paris with Hugh, Patrice, which bank did you live on, Left or Right?' 'What was the name of the boat you made the trip back on, again?' 'Well, when I ran into you over there that day with him—oh, you forgot to mention that we'd already met before, Pat?—why is it you looked so different from what you do today? You don't look like the same girl at all.' Until you crumpled and caved in."

He was capable of it. He was too cold about the whole thing, that was the dangerous feature. No heat, no impulse, no emotion to cloud the issue. Everything planned, plotted, graphed, ahead of time. Drafted. Charted. Every step. Even the notes. She knew their purpose now. Not poison-pen letters at all. They had been important to the long-term scheme of the thing. Psychological warfare, nerve warfare, breaking her down ahead of time, toppling her resistance before the main attack had even been made. The research-trip to New York in-between, to make sure of his own ground, to make sure there was no flaw, to leave her no loophole.

He skipped the edge of his hand off the wheel-rim, as if brushing off a particle of dust. "There's no villain in this. Let's get rid of the Victorian trappings. It's just a business trans-action. It's no different from taking out insurance, really." He turned to her with an assumption of candor that was almost charming for a moment. "Don't you want to be practical about it?"

"I suppose so. I suppose I should meet you on your own ground." She didn't try to project her contempt; it would have failed to reach him, she knew.

"If you get rid of these stuffy fetishes of virtue and villainy, of black and white, the whole thing becomes so simple it's not even worth the quarter of an hour we're giving it here in the car."

"I have no money of my own, Georgesson." Capitulation. Submission.

"They're one of the wealthiest families in town, that's com-mon knowledge. Why be technical about it? Get them to open an account for you. You're not a child."

"I couldn't *ask* them outright to do such a—"

"You don't *ask*. There are ways. You're a woman, aren't you? It's easy enough; a woman knows how to go about those things—"

"I'd like to go now," she said, reaching blindly for the door-handle.

"Do we understand one another?" He opened it for her. "I'll give you another ring after awhile."

He paused a moment. The threat was so impalpable there was not even a change of inflection in the lazy drawl.

"Don't neglect it, Patrice."

She got out. The crack of the door was the unfelt slap-in-the-face of loathing she gave him.

"Goodnight, Patrice," he drawled after her amiably.

Thirty-Four

"—PERFECTLY plain," she was saying animatedly. "It had a belt of the same material, and then a row of buttons down to about here."

She was purposely addressing herself to Mother Hazzard, to the exclusion of the two men members of the family. Well, the topic in itself was excuse enough for that.

"Heaven sakes, why didn't you take it?" Mother Hazzard wanted to know.

"I couldn't do that," she said reluctantly. She stopped a moment, then she added: "Not right—then and there." And played a lot with her fork. And felt low.

They must have thought the expression on her face was wistful disappointment. It wasn't. It was self-disgust.

You don't have to ask openly. There are ways; it's easy enough. A woman knows how to go about those things.

This was one of them now.

How defenseless those who love you are against you, she thought bitterly. How vicious and how criminal it is to trade on that self-imposed defenselessness. As I am doing now. Tricks and traps and wiles, those are for strangers. Those should be used against such only. Not against those who love you; with their guard down, with their eyes trustfully closed. It made her skin crawl in revulsion. She felt indecent, unclean, obscene.

Father Hazzard cut into the conversation. "Why didn't you just charge it up and have it sent? You could have used Mother's account. She deals there a lot."

She let her eyes drop. "I wouldn't have wanted to do that," she said reticently.

"Nonsense—" He stopped suddenly. Almost as though someone had trodden briefly on his foot under the table.

She caught Bill glancing at her. He seemed to be holding

the glance a moment longer than was necessary. But before she could verify this, it had stopped, and he resumed bringing the suspended forkful of pie-fill up to his mouth.

"I think I hear Hughie crying," she said, and flung her napkin down and ran out to the stairs to listen.

But in the act of listening upward, she couldn't avoid over-hearing Mother Hazzard's guarded voice in the dining-room behind her, spacing each word with strictural severity.

"Donald Hazzard, you ought to be ashamed of yourself. Do you men-folk have to be told *every*thing? Haven't you got a grain of tact in your heads?"

Thirty-Five

IN the morning Father Hazzard had lingered on at the table, she noticed when she came down, instead of leaving early with Bill. He sat quietly reading his newspaper while she finished her coffee. And there was just a touch of secretive self-satis-faction in his attitude, she thought.

He rose in company with her when she got up. "Get your hat and coat, Pat, I want you to come with me in the car. This young lady and I have business downtown," he an-nounced to Mother Hazzard. The latter tried, not altogether successfully, to look blankly bewildered.

"But what about Hughie's feeding?"

"I'll give him his feeding," Mother Hazzard said serenely. "You'll be back in time for that. I'm just borrowing you."

She got in next to him a moment later and they started off.

"Did poor Bill have to walk to the office this morning?" she asked.

"Poor Bill indeed!" he scoffed. "Do him good, the big lug. If I had those long legs of his, I'd walk it myself, every morning."

"Where are you taking me?"

"Now just never you mind. No questions. Just wait'll we get there, and you'll see."

They stopped in front of the bank. He motioned her out and led her inside with him. He said something to one of the guards in an aside, and he and she sat down to wait for a moment on a bench.

For the briefest moment only. Then the guard had come back with a noticeable deference. He led them toward a door marked "Manager, Private." Before they could reach it it had already opened and a pleasant-faced, slightly stout man wearing horn-rimmed spectacles was waiting to greet them.

"Come in and meet my old friend Harve Wheelock," Father Hazzard said to her.

They seated themselves in comfortable leather chairs in the private office, and the two men shared cigars.

"Harve, I've got a new customer for you. This is my boy Hugh's wife. Not that I think your mangy old bank is any good, but—well, you know how it is. Just habit, I reckon."

The manager shook appreciatively all over, as if this were some joke between them that had been going on for years. He winked for Patrice's benefit. "I agree with you there. Sell it to you real cheap."

"How cheap?"

"Quarter of a million." Meanwhile he was penning required entries on a filing-form, as though he had all the information called for at his fingers' tips, didn't need to ask anything about it.

Father Hazzard shook his head. "Too cheap. Can't be any good." He offhandedly palmed an oblong of light blue paper onto the desk, left it there face down.

"You think it over and let me know," the manager said drily. And to her, reversing his pen, "Sign here, honey."

Forger, she thought scathingly. She handed it back, her eyes downcast. The strip of light blue was clipped to it and it was sent out. A midget black book came back in its stead.

"Here you are, honey." The manager tendered it to her across his desk.

She opened it and looked at it, unnoticed, while the two resumed their friendly bickering hammer and tongs. It was so spotless, so unused yet. At the top it said "Mrs. Hugh Hazzard." And there was just one entry, under today's date. A deposit.

"5000.00"

Thirty-Six

SHE stood there holding the small round canister, staring frozenly at it as though she couldn't make out what was in it. She'd been holding it like that for long moments, without actually seeing it. She tilted it at last and dumped its contents into the washbowl. It had been better than half-full.

She went out, and closed the door, and went across the hall and knocked softly.

"I'm stepping out for just a moment, Mother. Hughie upset his whole can of talc in the bath just now, and I want to get another before I forget."

"All right, dear. The walk'll do you good. Oh—bring me back a bottle of that shampoo while you're in there, dear. I'm on the last of it now."

She got that slightly sickened feeling she was beginning to know so well. It was so easy to fool those who loved you. But who were you really fooling—them or yourself?

His arm was draped negligently atop the car-door, elbow out. The door fell open. He made way for her by shifting leisurely over on the seat, without offering to rise. His indolent taking of her for granted was more scathingly insulting than any overt rudeness would have been.

"I'm sorry I had to call. I thought you'd forgotten about our talk. It's been more than a week now."

"Forgotten?" she said drily. "I wish it were that easy."

"I see you've become a depositor of the Standard Trust since our last meeting."

She shot him an involuntary look of shock, without answering.

"Five thousand dollars."

She drew a quick breath.

"Tellers will chat for a quarter cigar." He smiled. "Well?"

"I haven't any money with me. I haven't used the account yet. I'll have to cash a check in the morning and—"

"They give a checkbook with each account, don't they? And you have that with you, most likely—"

She gave him a look of unfeigned surprise.

"I have a fountain pen right here in my pocket. I'll turn on the dashboard-lights a minute. Let's get it over and done with; the quickest way's the best. Now; I'll tell you what to write. To Stephen Georgesson. Not to Cash or Bearer. Five hundred."

"Five hundred?"

"That's academic."

She didn't understand what he meant, and was incautious enough to let him go on past that point without stopping him.

"That's all. And then your signature. The date, if you want."

She stopped short. "I can't do this."

"I'm sorry, you'll have to. I don't want it any other way. I won't accept cash."

"But this passes through the bank with both our names on it, mine as payer, yours as payee."

"There's such a flood of checks passing through the bank every month, it's not even likely to be noticed. It could be a debt of Hugh's, you know, that you're settling up for him."

"Why are you so anxious to have a check?" she asked irresolutely.

A crooked smile looped one corner of his mouth. "Why should you object, if I don't? It's to your advantage, isn't it? I'm playing right into your hands. It comes back into your possession after it clears the bank. After that you're holding tangible evidence of this—of blackmail—against me if you should ever care to prosecute. Which is something you haven't got so far. Remember, up to this point, it's just your word against mine, I can deny this whole thing happened. Once this check goes through, you've got living proof."

He said, a little more tartly than he'd yet spoken to her, "Shall we get through? You're anxious to get back. And I'm anxious to pull out of here."

She handed him the completed check and pen.

He was smiling again now. He waited until she'd stepped out and he'd turned on the ignition. He said above the low throb of the motor, "Your thinking isn't very clear, nor very quick, is it? This check is evidence against *me*, that *you*'re holding, if it clears the bank and returns to you. But if it doesn't— if it's kept out, and never comes up for payment at all—then it's evidence against *you*, that *I'm* holding."

The car glided off and left her standing behind looking after it in her shattered consternation.

Thirty-Seven

SHE all but ran toward the car along the night-shaded street, as if fearful it might suddenly glide into motion and escape her, instead of directing her steps toward it grudgingly as she had the two previous times. She clung to the top of the door with both hands when she'd reached it, as if in quest of support.

"I can't stand this! What are you trying to do to me?"

He was smugly facetious. His brows went up. "Do? I haven't done anything to you. I haven't been near you. I haven't seen you in the last three weeks."

"The check wasn't debited."

"Oh, you've had your bank statement. That's right, yesterday was the first of the month. I imagine you've had a bad twenty-four hours. I must have overlooked it—"

"No," she said with fierce rancor, "you're not the kind would overlook anything like that, you vicious leech! Haven't you done enough to me? What are you trying to do, drive me completely out of my mind—"

His manner changed abruptly, tightened. "Get in," he said crisply. "I want to talk to you. I'll drive you around for a quarter of an hour or so."

"I can't *ride* with you. How can you ask me to do that?"

"We can't just stand still in this one place, talking it over. That's far worse. We've done that twice already. We can circle the lake drive once or twice; there's no one on it at this hour and no stops. Turn your collar up across your mouth."

"Why are you holding the check? What are you meaning to do?"

"Wait until we get there," he said. Then when they had, he answered her, coldly, dispassionately, as though there had been no interruption.

"I'm not interested in five hundred dollars."

She was beginning to lose her head. Her inability to fathom

his motives was kindling her to panic. "Give it back to me, then, and I'll give you more. I'll give you a thousand. Only, give it back to me."

"I don't want to be *given* more. I don't want to be *given* any amount. Don't you understand? I want the money to belong to *me*, in my own right."

Her face was suddenly stricken white. "I don't understand. What are you trying to say to me?"

"I think you're beginning to, by the look on your face." He fumbled in his pocket, took something out. An envelope, already sealed and stamped for mailing. "You asked me where the check was. It's in here. Here, read what it says on it. No, don't take it out of my hand. Just read it from where you are."

"Mr. Donald Hazzard
Hazzard and Loring
Empire Building
Caulfield."

"No—" She couldn't articulate, could only shake her head convulsively.

"I'm mailing it to him at his office, where you can't intercept it." He returned it to his pocket. "The last mail-collection, here in Caulfield, is at nine each night. You may not know that, but I've been making a study of those things recently. There's a mail-box on Pomeroy Street, just a few feet from where I've been parking the last few times I've met you. It's dark and inconspicuous around there, and I'll use that one. It takes the carrier until nine-fifteen to reach it, however; I've timed him several nights in a row and taken the average."

He silenced her with his hand, went on: "Now, if you reach there before the carrier does, this envelope stays out of the chute. If you're not there yet when he arrives, I drop it in. You have a day's grace, until nine-fifteen tomorrow night."

"But what do you want me to be there for—? You said you didn't want more—"

"We're going to take a ride out to Hastings, that's the next town over. I'm taking you to a justice of the peace there, and he's going to make us man and wife."

He slowed the car as her head lurched soddenly back over the top of the seat for a moment.

"I didn't think they swooned any more—" he began. Then as he saw her straighten again with an effort and pass the back of her hand blurredly before her eyes, he added: "Oh, I see they don't; they just get a little dizzy, is that it?"

"Why are you doing this to me?" she said smotheredly.

"There are several good reasons I can think of. It's a good deal safer, from my point of view, than the basis we've been going on so far. There's no chance of anything backfiring. A wife, the law-books say, cannot testify against her husband. That means that any lawyer worth his fee can whisk you off the stand before you can so much as open your mouth. And then there are more practical considerations. The old couple aren't going to be around forever, you know. The old lady's life is hanging by a thread. And the old man won't last any time without her. Old Faithful, I know the type. When they go, you and Bill share unequally between you— Don't look so horrified; that lawyer of theirs hasn't exactly talked, but this is a small town, those things sort of seep around without even benefit of word-of-mouth. I can wait that year, or even two or three if I have to. The law gives a husband one-third of his wife's property. Three-quarters of—I may be underestimating, but ʳᵒᵘghly I'd say four hundred thousand, that's three hundred thousand. And then a third of that again— Don't cover your ears like that, Patrice; you look like someone out of a Marie Corelli novel."

He braked. "You can get out here, Patrice. This is close enough." And then he chuckled a little, watching her flounder to the pavement. "Are you sure you're able to walk steady? I wouldn't want to have them think I'd plied you with—"

The last thing he said was, "Make sure your clock isn't slow, Patrice. Because the United States Mail is always on time."

Thirty-Eight

THE headlight-beams of his car kept slashing up the road ahead of them like ploughshares, seeming to cast aside its topsoil of darkness, reveal its borax-like white fill, and spill that out all over the roadway. Then behind them the livid furrows would heal again into immediate darkness.

It seemed hours they'd been driving like this, in silence yet acutely aware of one another. Trees went by, dimly lit up from below, along their trunks, by the passing reflection of their headlight-wash, into a sort of ghostly incandescence. Then at times there weren't any trees, they fell back, and a plushy black evenness took their place—fields or meadows, she supposed—that smelled sweeter. Clover. It was beautiful country around here; too beautiful for anyone to be in such a hell of suffering in the midst of it.

Roads branched off at times, too, but they never took them. They kept to this wide, straight one they were on.

They passed an indirectly lighted white sign, placed at right angles to the road so that it could be read as you came up to it. It said "Welcome to Hastings," and then underneath, "Population—" and some figures too small to catch before they had already gone by.

She glanced briefly after it, in a sort of fascinated horror.

He'd apparently seen her do it, without looking directly at her. "That's across the State line," he remarked drily. "Travel broadens one, they say." It was nine forty-five now according to her wristwatch. It had taken them only half an hour's drive to get here.

They passed through the town's nuclear main square. A drugstore was still open, two of the old-fashioned jars of colored water that all drugstore-windows featured once upon a time flashing emerald and mauve at them as they went by. A motion-picture theatre was still alive inside, but dying fast externally, its marquee already dark, its lobby dim.

He turned up one of the side streets, a tunnel under leafy shade trees, its houses all set back a lawn-spaced distance so that they were almost invisible in the night-shade from the roadway. A dim light peering through from under the recesses of an ivy-covered porch seemed to attract him. He shunted over to the walk suddenly, and back a little, and stopped opposite it.

They sat for awhile.

Then he got out on his side, came around to hers, and opened the door beside her.

"Come in," he said briefly.

She didn't move, she didn't answer.

"Come on in with me. They're waiting."

She didn't answer, didn't move.

"Don't just sit there like that. We had this all out before, back at Caulfield. Move. Say something, will you?"

"What do you want me to say?"

He gave the door an impatient slap-to again, as if in momentary reprieve. "Get yourself together. I'll go over and let them know we got here."

She watched him go, in a sort of stupor, as though this were happening to someone else; heard his tread go up the wooden plank-walk that led up to the house. She could even hear the ring of the bell, from within the house, all the way out here where she was. It was no wonder, it was so quiet. Just little winged things buzzing and humming in a tree overhead.

She wondered: How does he know I won't suddenly start the car and drive off? She answered that herself: He knows I won't. He knows it's too late for that. As I know it. The time for stopping, for drawing back, for dashing off, that was long ago. So long ago. Long before tonight. That was in the compartment on the train coming here, when the wheels tried to warn me. That was when the first note came. That was when the first phone-call came, the first walk down to the drugstore. I am as safely held fast here as though I were manacled to him.

She could hear their voices now. A woman saying, "No, not at all; you made very good time. Come right in."

The doorway remained open, lighted. Whoever had been standing in it had withdrawn into the house. He was coming back toward her now. The sound of his tread along the wooden walk. She gripped the edge of the car-seat with her hands, dug them in under the leather cushions.

He was up to her now, standing there.

"Come on, Patrice," he said casually.

That was the full horror of it, his casualness, his matter-of-factness. He wasn't acting the part.

She spoke quietly too, as quietly as he, but her voice was as thin and blurred as a thrumming wire.

"I can't do it. Georgesson, don't ask me to do this."

"Patrice, we've been all over this. I told you the other night, and it was all settled then."

She covered her face with cupped hands, quickly uncovered it again. She kept using the same four words; they were the only ones she could think of. "But I can't do it. Don't you understand? I can't *do* it."

"There's no impediment. You're not married to anyone. Even in your assumed character, you're not married to anyone, much less as yourself. I investigated all that in New York."

"Steve. Listen, I'm calling you Steve."

"That doesn't melt me," he assured her jocosely. "That's my name, I'm supposed to be called that." He lidded his eyes at her. "It's my *given* name, not one that I took for myself—*Patrice.*"

"Steve, I've never pleaded with you before. In all these months, I've taken it like a woman. Steve, if there's anything human in you at all I can appeal to—"

"I'm only too human. That's why I like money as much as I do. But your wires are crossed. It's my very humanness, for that reason, that makes your appeal useless. Come on, Patrice. You're wasting time."

She cowered away edgewise along the seat. He drummed his fingers on the top of the door and laughed a little.

"Why this horror of marriage? Let me get to the bottom of your aversion. Maybe I can reassure you. There is no personal appeal involved; you haven't any for me. I've got only contempt for you, for being the cheap, tricky little fool you are. I'm leaving you on the doorstep of your ever-loving family again, just as soon as we get back to Caulfield. This is going to be a paper marriage, in every sense of the word. But it's going to stick, it's going to stick to the bitter end. Now does that take care of your mid-Victorian qualms?"

She cast the back of her hand across her eyes as though a blow had just blinded her.

He wrenched the door open.

"They're waiting for us in there. Come on, you're only making it worse."

He was beginning to harden against her. Her opposition was commencing to inflame him against her. It showed inversely, in a sort of lethal coldness.

"Look, my friend, I'm not going to drag you in there by the hair. The thing isn't worth it. I'm going inside a minute and call the Hazzard house from here, and tell them the whole story right now. Then I'll drive you back where I got you from. They can have you—if they want you any more." He leaned toward her slightly across the door. "Take a good look at me. Do I look like I was kidding?"

He meant it. It wasn't an empty bluff, with nothing behind it. It might be a threat that he would prefer not to have to carry out, but it wasn't an idle threat. She could see that in his eyes, in the cold sullenness in them, the dislike of herself she read in them.

He turned and left the car-side and went up the plank-walk again, more forcefully, more swiftly, than he'd trod it before.

"Excuse me, could I trouble you for a minute—" she heard him start to say as he entered the open doorway, then the rest was blurred as he went deeper within.

She struggled out, clinging to the flexing door like somebody walking in his sleep. Then she wavered up the plank-walk and onto the porch, and the ivy rustled for a minute as she teetered soddenly against it. Then she went on toward the oblong of light projected by the open doorway, and inside. It was like struggling through knee-deep water.

A middle-aged woman met her in the hallway.

"Good evening. Are you Mrs. Hazzard? He's in here."

She took her to a room on the left, parted an old-fashioned pair of sliding doors. He was standing in there, with his back to them, beside an old-fashioned telephone-box bracketed to the wall.

"Here's the young lady. You can both come into the study when you're ready."

Patrice drew the doors together behind her again. "Steve," she said.

He turned around and looked at her, then turned back again.

"Don't—you'll kill her," she pleaded.

"The old all die sooner or later."

"Has it gone through yet?"

"They're ringing Caulfield for me now."

It wasn't any sleight-of-hand trick. His finger wasn't anywhere near the receiver-hook, holding it shut down. He was in the act of carrying it out.

A choking sound broke in her throat.

He looked around again, less fully than before. "Have you decided once and for all?"

She didn't nod, she simply let her eyelids drop closed for a minute.

"Operator," he said, "cancel that call. It was a mistake." He replaced the receiver.

She felt a little sick and dizzy, as when you've just looked down from some great height and then drawn back again.

He went over to the sliding-doors and swung them vigorously back.

"We're ready," he called into the study across the hall.

He crooked his arm toward her, backhand, contemptuously tilting up his elbow for her to take, without even looking around at her as he did so.

She came forward and they went toward the study together, her arm linked in his. Into where the man was waiting to marry them.

Thirty-Nine

IT was on the way back that she knew she was going to kill him. Knew she must, knew it was the only thing left to be done now. She should have done it sooner, she told herself. Long before this; that first night as she sat with him in his car. It would have been that much better. Then this, tonight's ultimate horror and degradation, would at least have been avoided. She hadn't thought of it then; that was the one thing that had never occurred to her. It had always been flight, escape from him in some other way; never safety in this way— his removal.

But she knew she was going to do it, now. Tonight.

Not a word had passed between them, all this way, ever since leaving the justice's house. Why should one? What was there to say? What was there to do, now—except this one final thing, that came to her opposite a white-stockinged telegraph-pole, about four miles out of Hastings. Just like that it came: click, snap, and it was there. As though she had passed through some electric-eye beam stretched across the road, there from that particular telegraph-pole. On the one side of it, still, just passive despair, fatalism. On the other, full-grown decision, remorseless, irrevocable: I'm going to kill him. To-night. Before this night ends, before the light comes again.

Neither of them said anything. He didn't, because he was content. He'd done what he'd set out to do. He did whistle lightly, once, for a short while, but then he stopped that again. She didn't say anything, because she was undone. Destroyed, in the fullest sense of the word. She'd never felt like this before. She didn't even feel pain of mind any more. Struggle was ended. She was numb now. She'd even had more feeling left in her after the train-crash than now.

She rode all the way with her eyes held shut. Like a woman returning from a funeral, at which everything worth keeping has been interred, and to whom nothing left above ground is worth looking at any longer.

She heard him speak at last. "There, was that so bad?" he said.

She answered him mechanically, without opening her eyes. "Where are you—? What do you want me to do now?"

"Exactly nothing. You go on just as you were before. This is something between the two of us. And I want it to stay that way, understand? Not a word to the Family. Not until I'm ready. It'll be Our Little Secret, yours and mine."

He was afraid if he took her with him openly, they'd change the will, she supposed. And afraid if he left her with them, and they learned of it, they'd have it annulled for her.

How did you kill a man? There was nothing here, no way. The country was flat, the road level, straight. If she snatched at the wheel, tried to throw the car out of control, nothing much would happen. You needed steep places, hairbreadth turns. And the car was only trundling along, not going fast.

It would only roll off into the dirt maybe, strike a telegraph-pole, shake them up a little.

Besides, even if that had been the feasible way, she didn't want to die with him. She only wanted him to die. She had a child she was devoted to, a man she loved. She wanted to live. She'd always had an unquenchable will to live, all her life; she still had it now. Numbed as she was, it was still flickering stubbornly inside her. Nothing could put it out, or—she would already have contemplated another alternative, probably, before now.

Oh God, she cried out in her mind, if I only had a—

And in that instant, she knew how to do it. Knew how she was going to do it. For the next word-symbol flashing before her senses was "gun," and as it appeared it brought its own answer to the plea.

In the library, at home. There was one in there, somewhere.

A brief scene came back to mind, from many months ago. Buried until now, to suddenly reappear, as clear as if it had just taken place a moment ago. The reading-lamp, comfortably lit and casting its cheerful glow. Father Hazzard, sitting there by it, lingering late over a book. The others gone to bed, all but herself. She the last one to leave him. A brief kiss on his forehead.

"Shall I lock up for you?"

"No, you run along. I will, in a moment."

"You won't forget, though?"

"No, I won't forget." And then he'd chuckled, in that dry way of his: "Don't be nervous, I'm well-protected down here. There's a revolver in one of the drawers right by me here. We keep it specially for burglars. That was Mother's idea, once, years ago—and there hasn't been hide nor hair of one in all the time since."

She'd laughed at this melodramatic drollery, and told him quite truthfully: "It wasn't prowlers I was thinking of, but a sudden rainstorm in the middle of the night and Mother's best drapes."

She'd laughed. But now she didn't.

Now she knew where there was a gun.

You crooked your finger through. You pulled. And you had peace, you had safety.

They stopped, and she heard the car-door beside her clack open. She raised her eyes. They were in a leafy tunnel of the street trees. She recognized the symmetrical formation of the trees, the lawn-slopes on either side of them, the dim contours of the private homes in the background. They were on her own street, but further over, about a block away from the house. He was being tactful, letting her out at a great enough distance from her own door to be inconspicuous.

He was sitting there, waiting for her to take the hint and get out. She looked at her watch, mechanically. Not even eleven yet. It must have been around ten when it happened. It had taken them forty minutes coming back; they'd driven slower than going out.

He'd seen her do it. He smiled satirically. "Doesn't take long to marry, does it?"

It doesn't take long to die, either, she thought smoulderingly.

"Don't you—don't you want me to come with you?" she whispered.

"What for?" he said insolently. "I don't want you. I just want what eventually—comes with you. You go upstairs to your unsullied little bed. (I trust it is, anyway. With this Bill in the house.)"

She could feel heat in her face. But nothing much mattered, nothing counted. Except that the gun was a block away, and he was here. And the two of them had to meet.

"Just stay put," he advised her. "No unexpected little trips out of town, now, Patrice. Unless you want me to suddenly step forward and claim paternity of the child. I have the law on my side, now, you know. I'll go straight to the police."

"Well—will you wait here a minute? I'll—I'll be right out. I'll get you some money. You'll need some—until—until we get together again."

"Your dowry?" he said ironically. "So soon? Well, as a matter of fact, I don't. Some of the men in this town play very poor cards. Anyway, why give me what's already mine? Piecemeal. I can wait. Don't do me any favors."

She stepped down, reluctantly.

"Where can I reach you, in case I have to?"

"I'll be around. You'll hear from me, every now and then. Don't be afraid of losing me."

No, it had to be tonight, tonight, she kept telling herself grimly. Before the darkness ended and the daybreak came. If she waited, she'd lose her courage. This surgery had to be performed at once, this cancer on her future removed.

No matter where he goes in this city tonight, she vowed, I'll track him down, I'll find him, and I'll put an end to him. Even if I have to destroy my own self doing it. Even if I have to do it in sight of a hundred people.

The car-door swung closed. He tipped his hat satirically.

"Good night, Mrs. Georgesson. Pleasant dreams to you. Try sleeping on a piece of wedding-cake. If you haven't wedding-cake, try a hunk of stale bread. You'll be just as crummy either way."

The car sidled past her. Her eyes fastened on the rear license-plate, clove to it, memorized it, even as it went skimming past. It dwindled. The red tail-light coursed around the next corner and disappeared. But it seemed to hang there before her eyes, like a ghost-plaque, suspended against the night, for long minutes after.

NY09231

Then that, too, dimmed and went out.

Somebody was walking along the quiet night sidewalk, very close by. She could hear the chip-chipping of the high heels. That was she. The trees were moving by her, slowly rearward. Somebody was climbing terraced flagstone steps. She could hear the gritty sound of the ascending tread. That was she. Somebody was standing before the door of the house now. She could see the darkling reflection in the glass opposite her. It moved as she moved. That was she.

She opened her handbag and felt inside it for her doorkey. Hers, was good. The key they'd given her. It was still there. For some reason this surprised her. Funny to come home like this, just as though nothing had happened to you, and feel for your key, and put it into the door, and—and go into the house. To *still* come home like this, and *still* go into the house.

I have to go in here, she defended herself. My baby's asleep in this house. He's asleep upstairs in it, right now. This is where I have to go; there isn't any other place for me to go.

She remembered how she'd had to lie, earlier tonight, asking Mother Hazzard to mind Hughie for her while she visited a new friend. Father had been at a business meeting and Bill had been out.

She put on the lights in the lower hall. She closed the door. Then she stood there a minute, her breath rising and falling, her back supine against the door. It was so quiet, so quiet in this house. People sleeping, people who trusted you. People who didn't expect you to bring home scandal and murder to them, in return for all their goodness to you.

She stood there immobile. So quiet, so still, there was no guessing what she had come back here for, what she had come back here to do.

Nothing left. Nothing. No home, no love, even no child any more. She'd even forfeited that prospective love, tarnished it for a later day. She'd lose him too, he'd turn against her, when he was old enough to know this about her.

He'd done all this to her, one man. It wasn't enough that he'd done it once, he'd done it twice now. He'd wrecked two lives for her. He'd smashed up the poor inoffensive seventeen-year-old simpleton from San Francisco who had had the bad luck to stray his way. Smashed her up, and wiped his feet all over her five-and-ten-cent-store dreams, and spit on them. And now he'd smashed up the cardboard lady they called Patrice.

He wouldn't smash up anybody more!

A tortured grimace disfigured her face for a moment. The back of her wrist went to her forehead, clung there. An inhalation of terrible softness, yet terrible resolve, shook her entire frame. Then she tottered on the bias toward the library entrance, like a comic drunk lacking in sufficient coordination to face squarely in the direction in which he is hastening.

She put on the big reading-lamp in there, center-table.

She went deliberately to the cellarette, and opened that, and poured some brandy and downed it. It seemed to blast its way down into her, but she quelled it with a resolute effort.

Ah, yes, you needed that when you were going to kill a man.

She went looking for the gun. She tried the table-drawers first, and it was not in there. Only papers and things, in the way. But he'd said there was one in here, that night, and there must be, somewhere in this room. They never told you anything that was untrue, even lightly; he, nor Mother, nor—nor Bill either for that matter. That was the big difference between them and her. That was why they had peace—and she had none.

She tried Father Hazzard's desk next. The number of drawers and cubicles was greater, but she sought them all out one by one. Something glinted, as she moved a heavy business-ledger aside, in the bottommost under-drawer, and there it lay, thrust in at the back.

She took it out. Its inoffensive look, at first, was almost a disappointment. So small, to do so great a thing. To take away a life. Burnished nickel, and bone. And that fluted bulge in the middle, she supposed, was where its hidden powers of death lay. In her unfamiliarity, she pounded at its back with the heel of her hand, and strained at it, trying to get it open, risking a premature discharge, hoping only that if she kept fingers clear of the trigger she would avert one. Suddenly, with astonishing ease at the accidental right touch, it had broken downward, it slanted open. Round black chambers, empty.

She rummaged in the drawer some more. She found the same small cardboard box, half-noted in her previous search, that she had hastily cast aside. Inside, cotton-wool, as if to hold some very perishable medicinal capsule. But instead, steel-jacketed, snub-nosed, the cartridges. Only five of them.

She pressed them home, one by one, into the pits they were meant for. One chamber remained empty.

She closed the gun.

She wondered if it would fit into her handbag. She tried it spadewise, the flat side up, and it went in.

She closed the handbag, and took it with her, and went out of the room, went out to the back of the hall.

She took out the classified directory, looked under "Garages."

He might leave it out in the streets overnight. But she didn't think he would. He was the kind who prized his cars and his hats and his watches. He was the kind of man prized everything but his women.

The garages were alphabetized, and she began calling them alphabetically.

"Have you a New York car there for the night, license 09231?"

At the third place the night attendant came back and said: "Yes, we have. It was just brought in a few minutes ago."

"Mr. Georgesson?"

"Yeah, that's right. What about it, lady? Whaddya want from us?"

"I—I was out in it just now. The young man just brought me home in it. And I find I left something with him. I have to get hold of him. Please, it's important. Will you tell me where I can reach him?"

"We ain't supposed to do that, lady."

"But I can't get in. He has my doorkey, don't you understand?"

"Whyn'tcha ring your doorbell?" the gruff voice answered.

"You fool!" she exploded, her fury lending her plausible eloquence. "I wasn't supposed to be out with him in the first place! I don't want to attract any attention. I *can't* ring the doorbell!"

"I getcha, lady," the voice jeered, with that particular degree of greasiness she'd known it would have, "I getcha." And a double tongue-click was given for punctuation. "Wait'll I check up."

He left. He got on again, said: "He's been keeping his car with us for some time now. The address on our records is 110 Decatur Road. I don't know if that's still—"

But she'd hung up.

Forty

She used her own key to unlock the garage-door. The little roadster that Bill habitually used was out, but the big car, the sedan, was in there. She backed it out. Then she got out a moment, went back to refasten the garage-door.

There was the same feeling of unreality about this as before; a sort of dream-fantasy, a state of somnambulism, yet with over-all awareness. The chip-chip of footsteps along the cement garage-driveway that were someone else's, yet were her own—sounding from under her. It was as though she had experienced a violent personality split, and one of her selves, aghast and helpless, watched a phantom murderess issue from the cleavage and start out upon her deadly quest. She could only pace this dark thing, this other self, could not recapture nor reabsorb it, once loosed. Hence (perhaps) the detached objectivity of the footsteps, the mirror-like reproduction of her own movements.

Reentering the car, she backed it into the street, reversed it, and let it flow forward. Not violently, but with the suave pick-up of a perfectly possessed driver. Some other hand, not hers—so firm, so steady, so pure—remembered to reach for the door-latch and draw the door securely closed with a smart little clout.

Outside, the street-lights went spinning by like glowing bowls coming toward her down a bowling-alley. But each shot was a miss, they went alternately too far out to this side, too far out to that. With herself and the car, the kingpin in the middle that they never knocked down.

She thought: That must be Fate, bowling against me. But I don't care, let them come.

Then the car had stopped again. So easy it was to go forth to kill a man.

She didn't study it closely, to see what it was like. It didn't matter what it was like; she was going in there, it was going to happen there.

She pedalled the accelerator again, went on past the door and around the corner. There she made a turn, for the right-of-way was against her, pointed the car forward to the way from which she had just come, brought it over against the sidewalk, stopped it there, just out of sight.

She took up her bag from beside her on the seat, as a woman does who is about to leave a car, secured it under her arm.

She shut off the ignition and got out. She walked back around the corner, to where she'd just come from, with the quick, preoccupied gait of a woman returning home late at night, who hastens to get off the street. One has seen them that way many times; minding their own business with an added intentness, for they know they run a greater risk of being accosted then than during the daylight hours.

She found herself alone on a gloomy nocturnal strip of sidewalk in front of a long rambling two-story structure, hybrid, half commercial and half living quarters. The ground floor was a succession of unlighted store-fronts, the upper a long row of windows. The white shape of a milk bottle stood on the sill of one of these. One was lighted, but with the shade drawn. Not the one with the milk bottle.

Between two of the store-fronts, recessed, almost secretive in its inconspicuousness, there was a single-panel door, with a waffle-pattern of multiple small panes set into it. They could be detected because there was a dim hall-light somewhere beyond them, doing its best to overcome the darkness.

She went over to it and tried it, and it swung out without any demur, it had no lock, was simply a closure for appearances' sake. Inside there was a rusted radiator, and a cement stair going up, and at the side of this, just as it began, a row of letter boxes and push-buttons. His name was on the third she scanned, but not in its own right, superimposed on the card of the previous tenant, left behind. He had pencil-scratched the name off, and then put in his own underneath. "S. Georgesson." He didn't print very well.

He didn't do anything very well, except smash up people's lives. He did that very well, he was an expert.

She went on up the stairs and followed the hall. It was a jerry-built, makeshift sort of a place. During the war shortage they must have taken the attic or storage-space part of the stores below and rigged it up into these flats.

What a place to live, she thought dimly.

What a place to die, she thought remorselessly.

She could see the thin line the light made under his door. She knocked, and then she knocked again, softly like the first time. He had his radio on in there. She could hear that quite distinctly through the door.

She raised her hand and smoothed back her hair, while waiting. You smoothed your hair—if it needed it—just before you were going to see anyone, or anyone was going to see you. That was why she did it now.

They said you were frightened at a time like this. They said you were keyed-up to an ungovernable pitch. They said you were blinded by fuming emotion.

They said. What did they know? She felt nothing. Neither fear nor excitement nor blind anger. Only a dull, aching determination all over.

He didn't hear, or he wasn't coming to open. She tried the knob, and this door too, like the one below, was unlocked, it gave inward. Why shouldn't it be, she reasoned, what did he have to fear from others? They didn't take from him, he took from them.

She closed it behind her, to keep this just between the two of them.

He didn't meet her eyes. The room was reeking with his presence, but it was a double arrangement, bed- and living-quarters, and he must be in the one just beyond, must have just stepped in as she arrived outside. She could see offside light coming through the opening.

The coat and hat he'd worn in the car with her tonight were slung over a chair, the coat broadside across its seat, the hat atop that. A cigarette that he'd incompletely extinguished a few short moments ago was in a glass tray, stubbornly smouldering away. The drink that he'd started, then left, and was coming back to finish any second now—the drink with which he was celebrating tonight's successful enterprise—stood there on the edge of the table. The white block of its still-unmelted ice cube peered through the side of the glass, through the straw-colored whiskey it floated in.

The sight of it brought back a furnished room in New York. He took his drinks weak; he liked them strong, but he took them weak when it was his own whiskey he was using. "There's always another one coming up," he used to say to her.

There wasn't now. This was his last drink. (You should have made it stronger, she thought to herself wryly.)

Some sort of gritty noise was bothering her. A pulsation, a discord of some sort. It was meant for music, but no music could have reached her as music, as she was now. The hyper-tension of her senses filtered it into a sound somewhat like a scrubbing-brush being passed over a sheet of ribbed tin. Or maybe, it occurred to her, it was on the inside of her, and not outside anywhere.

No, there it was. He had a small battery-portable standing against the side wall. She went over to it.

"*Che gelida mannina*—" some far-off voice was singing; she didn't know what that meant. She only knew that this was no love-scene, this was a death-scene.

Her hand gave a brutal little wrench, like wringing the neck of a chicken, and there was a stupor of silence in his two shoddy rooms. This one out here, and that one in there.

Now he'd step out to see who had done that.

She turned to face the opening. She raised her handbag frontally to her chest. She undid it, and took out the gun, and fitted her hand around it, the way her hand was supposed to go. Without flurry, without a tremor, every move in perfect coordination.

She sighted the gun toward the opening.

"Steve," she said to him, at no more than room-to-room conversational pitch in the utter stillness. "Come out here a second. I want to see you."

No fear, no love, no hate, no anything at all.

He didn't come. Had he seen her in a mirror? Had he guessed? Was he that much of a coward, cringing away even from a woman?

The fractured cigarette continued to unravel into smoke-skeins. The ice cube continued to peer through the highball glass, foursquare and uneroded.

She went toward the opening.

"Steve," she rasped. "Your wife is here. Here to see you."

He didn't stir, he didn't answer.

She made the turn of the doorway, gun wheeling before her like some sort of foreshortened steering-gear. The second room was not parallel to the first, it was over at a right angle to it. It was very small, just an alcove for sleeping in. It had a bulb up above, as though a luminous blister had formed on the calcimined surface of the ceiling. There was also a lamp beside the iron cot, and that was lit as well, but it was upside-down. It was standing on its head on the floor, its extension-wire grotesquely looped in air.

She'd caught him in the act of getting ready for bed. His shirt was lying over the foot of the cot. That was all he'd taken off. And now he was trying to hide from her, down on the floor somewhere, below cot-level, on the far side of it. His hand peered over it—he'd forgotten that it showed—clutching at the bedding, pulling it into long, puckered lines. And the top of his head showed, burrowed against the cot—just a glimpse of it—bowed in attempt at concealment, but not inclined deeply enough. And then, just on the other side of that, though his second hand *didn't* show, more of those puckered wrinkles ran over the edge of the bedding at one place, as though it were down below there somewhere out of sight, but hanging on for dear life.

And when she looked at the floor, out beyond the far side of the cot, she could glimpse the lower part of one leg, extended out behind him in a long, lazy sprawl. The other one didn't show, must have been drawn up closer under his body.

"Get up," she sneered. "At least I thought I hated a man. Now I don't know what you are." She passed around the foot of the cot, and his back came into view. He didn't move, but every line of his body expressed the arrested impulse to get away.

Her handbag sprang open and she pulled something out, pitched it at him. "Here's the five dollars you gave me. Remember?" It fell between his shoulderblades, and lay there lengthwise across his spine, caught in the sharp up-curve his back made, oddly like a label or tag loosely pasted across him.

"You love money so," she said scathingly. "Now here's the interest. Turn around and get it."

She'd fired before she'd known she was going to. As though there were some cue in the words for the gun to take of its own accord, without waiting for her. The crash surprised her, she could feel it go up her whole arm, as though someone had stingingly slapped her wristbone, and the fiery spittle that gleamed for a moment at the muzzle made her blink her eyes and swerve her head aside involuntarily.

He didn't move. Even the five-dollar bill didn't flutter off him. There was a curious low moaning sound from the tubular rod forming the head of the cot, as when a vibration is slowly dimming, and there was a black pockmark in the plaster of the wall, sharply off to one side of it, that seemed to leap up into being for the first time only as her eyes discovered it.

Her hand was at his shoulder now, while her mind was trying to say "I didn't—I didn't—" He turned over lazily, and ebbed down to the floor, in a way that was almost playful, as if she had been threatening to tickle him and he was trying to avoid it.

Indolent dalliance, his attitude seemed to express. There was even a sort of gashed grin across his mouth.

His eyes seemed to be fixed on her, watching her, with that same detached mockery they'd always shown toward her. As if to say, "What are you going to do now?"

You could hardly tell anything was the matter. There was only a little dark streak by the outside corner of one eye, like a patch of patent leather used instead of court plaster; as though he'd hurt himself there and then covered it over. And where that side of his head had come to rest against the lateral thickness of the bedding, there was a peculiar sworled stain, its outer layers of a lighter discoloration than its core.

Somebody screamed in the confined little room. Not shrilly, but with a guttural wrench, almost like the bark of a terrified dog. It must have been she, for there was no one in there to scream but her. Her vocal chords hurt, as though they had been strained asunder.

"Oh, God!" she sobbed in an undertone. "I didn't need to come—"

She cowered away from him, step by faltering step. It wasn't that little glistening streak, that daub of tar, nor yet the way he lay there, relaxed and languid, as if they had had such fun he was exhausted, and it was too much trouble to get up off his back and see her out. It was his eyes that knifed her with fear, over and over, until panic had welled up in her, as though gushing through a sieve. The way they seemed fixed on her, the way they seemed to follow her backward, step by step. She went over a little to one side, and that didn't get her away from them. She went over a little to the other, and that didn't get her away from them either. Contemptuous, patronizing, mocking, to the end; with no real tenderness in them for her, ever. He looked on her in death as he'd looked on her in life.

She could almost hear the drawled words that went with that look. "Where d'you think you're going now? What's your hurry? Come back here, you!"

Her mind screamed back: "Away from here—! Out of here—! Before somebody comes—! Before anybody sees me!"

She turned and fled through the opening, and beat her way through the outside room, flailing with her arms, as though it were an endless treadmill going the other way, trying to carry her back in to him, instead of a space of a brief few yards.

She got to the door and collided against it. But then, after the first impact, after her body was stopped against it, instead of stilling, it kept on thumping, and kept on thumping, as though there were dozens of her hurling themselves against it in an endless succession.

Wood shouldn't knock so, wood shouldn't bang so— Her hands flew up to her ears and clutched them. She was going mad.

The blows didn't space themselves and wait between. They were aggressive, demanding, continuous. They were already angered, and they were feeding on their own anger with every second's added delay. They drowned out, in her own ears, her second, smothered scream of anguish. A scream that held more real fear in it than even the first one had, in the other room just now. Fear, not of the supernatural now, but of the personal; a fear more immediate, a fear more strong. Agonizing fear, trapped fear such as she'd never known existed before. *The fear of losing the thing you love.* The greatest fear there is.

For the voice that riddled the door, that welled through, bated but flinty with stern impatience, was Bill's.

Her heart knew it before the sound came, and then her ears knew it right as it came, and then its words told her after they had come.

"Patrice! Open. Open this door. Patrice! Do you hear me? I knew I'd find you here. Open this door and let me in, or I'll break it down!"

A moment too late she thought of the lock, and just a moment in time he thought of it too. That it had been unlocked the whole while, just as she had found it to be earlier. She crushed herself flat against it, with a whimper of despair, just too late, just as the knob gave its turn and the door-seam started to widen.

"No!" she ordered breathlessly. "No!" She tried to hold it closed with the full weight of her whole palpitating body.

She could almost feel the currents of his straining breath beating into her face. "Patrice, you've—got—to—let—me—in—there!"

And between each word she lost ground, her heels scraped futilely backward over the surface of the floor.

He could see her now, and she could see him, through the fluctuating gap their opposing pressures made, widening a little, then narrowing again, then widening more than ever. His eyes, so close to her own, were a terrible accusation, far worse than that dead man's had been inside. Don't look at me, don't look at me! she implored them despairingly in her mind. Oh, turn away from me, for I can't bear you!

Back she went, steadily and irresistibly, and still she tried to bar him, to the last, after his arm was in and his shoulder, straining her whole body insensately against him, flattening her hands till they showed bloodless against the door.

Then he gave one final heave to end the unequal contest, and she was swept back along the whole curved arc of the door's path, like a leaf or a piece of limp rag that got caught in the way. And he was in, and he was standing there next to her, his chest rising and falling a little with quickened breath.

"No, Bill, no!" she kept pleading mechanically, even after the cause of her plea was lost. "Don't come in. Not if you love me. Stay out."

"What're you doing here?" he said tersely. "What brought you?"

"I want you to love me," was all she could whimper, like a distracted child. "Don't come in. I want you to love me."

He took her suddenly, and shook her fiercely by the shoulder for a moment. "I saw you. What did you come here to do? What did you come here for, at this hour?" He released her again. "What's this?" He picked up the gun, which she had completely lost track of until now in her turmoil. It must have fallen, or she must have flung it to the floor, in her flight from the inner room.

"Did you bring it with you?" He came back toward her again. "Patrice, *answer* me!" he said with a flinty ferocity she hadn't known he possessed. "What did you come here for?"

Her voice kept backing and filling in her throat, as if unable to rise to the top. At last it overflowed. "To—to—to kill him." She toppled suddenly against him, and his arm had to go around her, tight and firm, to keep her up.

Her hands tried to crawl up his lapels, up his shirt-front, toward his face, like wriggling white beggars pleading for alms.

A swipe of his hand and they were down again.

"And did you?"

"Somebody—did. Somebody—has already. In there. He's dead." She shuddered and hid her face against him. There is a point beyond which you can't be alone any more. You have to have someone to cling to. You have to have someone to hold you, even if he is to reject you again in a moment or two and you know it.

Suddenly his arm dropped and he'd left her. It was terrible to be alone, even just for that minute. She wondered how she'd stood it all these months, all these years.

Life was such a crazy thing, life was such a freak. A man was dead. A love was blasted into nothingness. But a cigarette still sent up smoke in a dish. And an ice cube still hovered unmelted in a highball glass. The things you wanted to last, they didn't; the things it didn't matter about, they hung on forever.

Then he reappeared from the other room, stood in the opening looking at her again. Looking at her in such a funny way. A little too long, a little too silent—she couldn't quite make out what it was she didn't like about it, but she didn't like him to look at her that way. Others, it didn't matter. But not him.

Then he raised the gun, which he was still holding, and put it near his nose.

She saw his head give a grim nod.

"No. No. I didn't. Oh, please believe me—"

"It's just been fired," he said quietly.

There was something rueful about the expression of his eyes now, as if they were trying to say to her: Why don't you want to tell me? Why don't you get it out of the way by telling me, and then I'll understand. He didn't say that, but his eyes seemed to.

"No, I didn't. I fired it at him, but I didn't hit him."

"All right," he said quietly, with just that trace of weariness you show when you don't believe a thing, but try to gloss it over to spare someone.

Suddenly he'd thrust it into the side-pocket of his coat, as though it were no longer important, as though it were a past detail, as though there were things of far greater moment to be attended to now. He buttoned his coat determinedly, strode back to her; his movements had a sort of lithe intensity to them now that they'd lacked before.

An impetus, a drive.

He swept a sheltering arm around her again. (That sanctuary that she'd been trying to find all her life long. And only had now, too late.) But this time in hurried propulsion toward the door, and not just in support. "Get out of here, quick," he ordered grimly. "Get down to the street again fast as you can."

He was pulling her along, hurrying her with him, within the curve of his protective arm. "Come on. You can't be found here. You must have been out of your mind to come here like this!"

"I was," she sobbed. "I am."

She was struggling against him a little now, trying to keep herself from the door. She pried herself away from him suddenly, and stood back, facing him. Her hands kept rebuffing his arms each time they tried to reclaim her.

"No, wait. There's something you've got to hear first. Something you've got to know. I tried to keep you out, but now you're in here with me. I've come this far; I won't go any further." And then she added, "The way I was."

He reached out and shook her violently, in his exasperation. As if to get some sense into her. "Not now! Can't you understand? There's a man dead in the next room. Don't you know what it means if you're found here? Any minute somebody's apt to stick his head into this place—"

"Oh, you fool," she cried out to him piteously. "You're the one who doesn't understand. The damage has been done already. Can't *you* see that? I *have* been found here!" And she murmured half-audibly, "By the only one who matters to me. What's there to run away and hide from now?" She brushed the back of her hand wearily across her eyes. "Let them come. Bring them on now."

"If you won't think of yourself," he urged her savagely, "think of Mother. I thought you loved her, I thought she meant something to you. Don't you know what a thing like this will do to her? What are you trying to do, kill her?"

"Somebody used that argument before," she told him vaguely. "I can't remember who it was, or where it was."

He'd opened the door cautiously and looked out. Narrowed it again, came back to her. "No sign of anyone. I can't understand how that shot wasn't heard. I don't think these adjoining rooms are occupied."

She wouldn't budge. "No, this is the time, and this is the place. I've waited too long to tell you. I won't go a step further, I won't cross that door-sill—"

He clenched his jaw. "I'll pick you up and carry you out of here bodily, if I have to! Are you going to listen to me? Are you going to come to your senses?"

"Bill, I'm not entitled to your protection. I'm not—"

His hand suddenly clamped itself to her mouth, sealing it. He heaved her clear of the floor, held her cradled in his arms. Her eyes strained upward at him in muted helplessness, above his restraining hand.

Then they dropped closed. She didn't struggle against him.

He carried her that way out the door, and along the hall, and down those stairs she'd climbed so differently a little while ago. Just within the street-entrance he set her down upon her feet again.

"Stand here a minute, while I look out." He could tell by her passiveness now that her recalcitrance had ended.

He withdrew his head. "No one out there. You left the car around the corner, didn't you?" She didn't have time to wonder how he knew that. "Walk along close to me, I'm going to take you back to it."

She took his arm within a doublecoil of her own two, and clinging to him like that, they came out unobtrusively and hurried along together close in beside the building-front, where the shadow was deepest.

It seemed a long distance. No one saw them; better still, no one was there to see them. Once a cat scurried out of a basement-vent up ahead of them. She crushed herself tighter against him for a moment, but no sound escaped her. They went on, after the brief recoil.

They rounded the corner, and the car was there, only its own length back away from the corner.

They crossed on a swift diagonal to it, and he unlatched the door for her and armed her in. Then suddenly the door was closed again, between them, and he'd stayed on the outside.

"Here are the keys. Now take it home and—"

"No," she whispered fiercely. "No! Not without you! Where are you going? What are you going to do?"

"Don't you understand? I'm trying to keep you out of it. I'm going back up there again. I have to. To make sure there's nothing there linking you. You've got to help me. Patrice, what was he doing to you? I don't want to know why, there isn't time for that now, I only want to know *what*."

"Money," she said laconically.

She saw his clenched hand tighten on the rim of the door, until it seemed to be trying to cave it in. "How'd you give it to him, cash or check?"

"A check," she said fearfully. "Only once, about a month ago."

He was speaking more tautly now. "You destroyed it when it came back, of c—?"

"I never got it back. He purposely kept it out. He must still have it someplace."

She could tell by the way he stiffened and slowly breathed in, he was more frightened by that than he had been by anything else she had told him so far. "My God," he said batedly. "I've got to get that back, if it takes all night." He lowered his head again, leaned it in toward her. "What else? Any letters?"

"None. I never wrote him a line in my life. There's a five-dollar bill lying in there, by him, but I don't want it."

"I'd better pick it up anyway. Nothing else? You're sure? Now, think, Patrice. Think hard."

"Wait; that night at the dance—he seemed to have my telephone number. Ours. Jotted down in a little black notebook he carries around with him." She hesitated. "And one other thing."

"What? Don't be afraid; tell me. What?"

"Bill—he made me marry him tonight. Out at Hastings."

This time he brought his hand up, let it pound back on the door-rim like a mallet. "I'm glad he's—" he said balefully. He didn't finish it. "Did you sign your own name?"

"The family's. I had to. That was the whole purpose of it. The justice is mailing the certificate in to him, here at this address, in a day or two."

"There's still time enough to take care of that, then. I can drive out tomorrow and scotch it out there, at that end. Money works wonders."

Suddenly he seemed to have made up his mind what he intended doing. "Go home, Patrice," he ordered. "Go back to the house, Patrice."

She clung fearfully to his arm. "No— What are you going to do?"

"I'm going back up there. I have to."

She tried to hold him back. "No! Bill, no! Someone may come along. They'll find *you* there. Bill," she pleaded, "for *me*—don't go back up there again."

"Don't you understand, Patrice? Your name has to stay out of it. There's a man lying dead upstairs in that room. They mustn't find anything linking you to him. You never knew him, you never saw him. I have to get hold of those things— that check, that notebook. I have to get rid of them. Better still, if I could only move him out of there, leave him somewhere else, at a distance from here, he mightn't be identified so readily. He might never be identified at all. He's not from town here, there isn't anybody likely to inquire in case of his sudden disappearance. He came and he went again; bird of passage. If he's found in the room there, it'll be at once established who he is, and then that'll bring out of lot of other things."

She saw him glance speculatively along the length of the car, as if measuring its possibilities as a casket.

"I'll help you, Bill," she said with sudden decision. "I'll help you—do whatever you want to do." And then, as he looked at her dubiously, "Let me, Bill. Let me. It's a small way of—making amends for being the cause of the whole problem."

"All right," he said. "I can't do it without the car, anyway. I need that." He crowded in beside her. "Give me the wheel a minute. I'll show you what I want you to do."

He drove the car only a yard or two forward, stopped it again. It now stood so that only the hood projected beyond the corner building-line, the rest of it still remained sheltered behind that. The driver's seat was exactly aligned with the row of store-fronts around the turn.

"Look down that way, from where you sit," he instructed her. "Can you see that particular doorway from here?"

"No. I can see about where it is, though."

"That's what I mean. I'll stand in it, light up a cigarette. When you see that, bring the car on around in front of it. Until then, stay back here where you are. If you see anything else, if you see something go wrong, don't stay here. Drive straight out and away, without making the turn. Drive for home."

"No," she thought stubbornly, "no, I won't. I won't run off and leave you here." But she didn't tell him so.

He'd gotten out again, was standing there facing her, looking cautiously around on all sides of them, without turning his head too much, just holding his body still, glancing over his shoulders, first on this side, then on that.

"All right," he said finally. "It's all right now. I guess I can go now."

He touched the back of her hand consolingly for a minute.

"Don't be frightened, Patrice. Maybe we'll be lucky, at that. We're such novices at anything like this."

"Maybe we'll be lucky," she echoed, abysmally frightened.

She watched him turn and walk away from the car.

He walked as he always walked, that was one nice thing about him. He didn't slink or cringe. She wondered why that should have mattered to her, at such a time as this. But it made what he, what they, were about to attempt to do a little less horrible, somehow.

He'd turned and he'd gone inside the building where the man was lying dead.

Forty-One

IT seemed like an eternity that he'd been up there. She'd never known time could be so long.

That cat came back again, the one that had frightened her before, and she watched its slow, cautious circuitous return to the place from which they had routed it. She could see it while it was still out in the roadway, but then as it closed in toward the building-line, the deeper shading swallowed it.

You can kill a rat, she found herself addressing it enviously in her mind, and they praise you for it. And your kind of rat only bites, they don't suck blood.

Something glinted there, then was gone again.

It was surprising how clearly she could see the match-flame. She hadn't expected to be able to. It was small, but extremely vivid for a moment. Like a luminous yellow butterfly held pinned for a second at full wing-spread against a black velvet backdrop, then allowed to escape again.

She promptly bore down on the starter, trundled around the corner, and brought the car down to him with facile stealth. No more than a soft whirr and sibilance of its tires.

He'd turned and gone in again before she'd reached him. The cigarette that he'd used to attract her lay there already cast down.

She didn't know where he wanted to—wanted to put what he was bringing out. Front or back. She reached out and opened the rear door on his side, left it that way, ready and waiting for him.

Then she stared straight ahead through the windshield, with

a curious sort of rigidity, as though she were unable to move her neck.

She heard the building-door open, and still couldn't turn her neck. She strained, tugged at it, but it was locked in some sort of rigor of mortal terror, wouldn't carry her head around that way.

She heard a slow, weighted tread on the gritty sidewalk—his—and accompanying it a softer sound, a sort of scrape, as when two shoes are turned over on their softer topsides, or simply on their sides, and trail along that way, without full weight to press them down.

Suddenly his voice breathed urgently (almost in her ear, it seemed), "The front door. The front."

She couldn't turn her head. But she could move her arms at least. She extended them without looking, broke the latch open for him. She could hear her own breath singing in her throat, like the sound a teakettle-spout makes when it is simmering toward a catastrophic overflow.

Someone settled on the seat beside her. Just the way anyone does, with the same crunchy strain on the leather. He touched her side, he nudged her here and there.

The muscular block shattered, and her head swung around.

She was looking into his face. Not Bill's, not Bill's. The mocking eyes wide open in the dark. *His* head had had to swing toward her, just as hers had toward him—it couldn't have remained inert!—to make the grisly face-to-face confrontation complete. Even in death he wouldn't let her alone.

A strangled scream wrenched at her windpipe.

"Now, none of that," the voice of Bill said, from just on the other side of him. "Get in back. I want the wheel. I want him next to me."

The sound of his voice had a steadying effect on her. "I didn't mean it," she murmured blurredly. She got out, got in again, holding onto the car for support in the brief transit between the two places. She didn't know how she did it, but she did.

He must have known what she was going through, though he didn't look at her.

"I told you to go home," he reminded her quietly.

"I'm all right," she said. "I'm all right. Go ahead." It came out tinny, like something on a worn-out disk played by a feathered needle.

The door cracked shut, and they were in motion.

Bill kept the car down to a laggard crawl the first few moments, using only one hand to the wheel. She saw him reach over with the other and tilt down the hat-brim low over the face beside him.

He found time for a word of encouragement to her, conscious of her there behind him, though still he didn't turn to glance at her.

"Can you hear me?"

"Yes."

"Try not to be frightened. Try not to think of it. We've been lucky so far. The check and the notebook were on him. Either we make it or we don't. Look at it that way. It's the only way. You're helping me, too, that way. See, if you're too tense, then I'm too tense too. You react on me."

"I'm all right," she said with that same mechanical bleat as before. "I'll be quiet. I'll be controlled. Go ahead."

After that, they didn't talk. How could you, on such a ride?

She kept her eyes away. She'd look out the side as long as she could; then when that became a strain, she'd look up at the car ceiling for a moment to rest. Or down at the floor directly before her. Anywhere but straight ahead, to where those two heads (she knew) must be lightly quivering in synchronization to the same vibration.

She tried to do what he'd told her. She tried not to think of it. "We're coming home from a dance," she said to herself. "He's bringing me home from the Country Club, that's all. I'm wearing that black net with the gold disks. Look, see? I'm wearing that black dress with the gold disks. We had words, so I'm—I'm sitting in the back, and he's sitting alone up front."

Her forehead was a little cold and damp. She wiped it off.

"He's bringing me home from the movies," she said to herself. "We saw—we saw—we saw—" Another of those blocks, this time of the imagination, occurred; it wouldn't come. "We saw—we saw—we saw—"

Suddenly she'd said to him, aloud, "What was the name of that picture we just now came away from?"

"Good," he answered instantly. "That's it. That's a good idea. I'll give you one. Keep going over it." It took him a moment to get one himself. "Mark Stevens in *I Wonder Who's Kissing Her Now*," he said suddenly. They'd seen that together back in the sunlight, a thousand years ago (last Thursday). "Start in at the beginning, and run through it. If you get stuck, I'll help you out."

She was breathing laboredly, and her forehead kept getting damp again all the time. "He wrote songs," she said to herself, "and he took his foster-sister to a—to a variety-show, and he heard one of them sung from the stage—"

The car made a turn, and the two heads up front swung together, one almost landed on the other's shoulder. Somebody pried them apart.

She hurriedly squeezed her eyes shut. "When—when did the title-song come into it?" she faltered. "Was that the opening number, they heard from the gallery?"

He'd halted for a light, and a taxicab had halted beside him, wheel-cap to wheel-cap. "No, that was—" He looked at the taxicab. "That was—" He looked at the taxicab again, the way you look vaguely at some external object when you're trying to remember something that has nothing to do with it. "That was 'Hello, Ma Baby.' Cakewalk number, don't you remember? The title-song didn't come until the end. He couldn't get words for it, don't you remember?"

The light had changed. The taxicab had slipped on ahead, quicker to resume motion. She crushed the back of her hand against her mouth, sank her teeth into it. "I can't," she sighed to herself. "I can't." She wanted to scream to him, "Oh, open the door! Let me out! I'm not brave! I thought I could, but I can't— I don't care, only let me get out of here, now, right where we are!"

Panic, they called this panic.

She bit deeper into her own skin, and the hot frenzied gush subsided.

He was going a little faster now. But not too fast, not fast enough to attract suspicion or catch any roving eye. They were in the outskirts now, running along the turnpike that breasted the sunken railroad right-of-way. You were supposed to go a little faster along there.

It took her several moments to realize that the chief hazard was over. That they were already out of Caulfield, clear of it; or at least clear of its built-up heart. Nothing had happened. No untoward event. They hadn't grazed any other car. No policeman had come near them, to question them over some infraction, to look into the car. All those things that she had dreaded so, had failed to materialize. It had been a ride completely without incident. The two of them might have been alone in the car, for all the risk they'd run—outwardly. But inwardly—

She felt all shrivelled-up inside, and old; as though there were permanent wrinkles on her heart.

"He wasn't the only one that died tonight," she thought. "I died too, somewhere along the way, in this car. So it didn't work, it was all for nothing. Better to have stayed back there, still alive, and taken the blame and the punishment."

They were out in open country now. The last cardboard-box factory, kept at a civic-minded distance away from the city limits, the last disused-brewery stack, even those had long slipped by. The embankment that carried the turnpike had started a very gradual rise, the broad swath of railroad-tracks, by illusory contrast, seemed to depress still further. The neat, clean-cut concrete-facing that had been given the embankment further in toward town didn't extend this far out; here there was just a natural slope, extremely steep, but with weeds and bushes clinging to it.

He'd stopped all of a sudden, for no apparent reason. Run the two outside wheels off the road on the railroad's side, and stopped there. That was all the space that was allowed, just two wheels of the car; even that was an extremely precarious position to take. The downslope began almost outside the car door.

"Why here?" she whispered.

He pointed. "Listen. Hear it?" It was a sound like the cracking of nuts. Like a vast layer of nuts, all rolling around and being cracked and shelled.

"I'd like to get him out of town," he said. He got out, and scrambled down the slope a way, until she could only see him from the waist up, and stood looking down. Then he picked up something—a stone, maybe, or something—and she saw him throw. Then he turned his head a little, and seemed to be listening.

Finally he fought his way back up to her again, digging his feet in sideways to gain leverage.

"It's a slow freight," he said. "Outbound. It's on the inside track, I mean the one right under us here. I could see a lantern go by on the roof of one of the cars. It's unearthly long—I think they're empties—and it's going very slow, almost at a crawl. I threw a stone, and I heard it hit one of the roofs."

She had already guessed, and could feel her skin crawling.

He was bending over the form on the front seat, going through its pockets. He ripped something out of the inside coat-pocket. A label or something.

"They don't always get right of way like the fast passengers do. It may have to stop for that big turnpike crossing not far up, you know the one I mean. The locomotive must be just about reaching it by now—"

She'd fought down her repulsion; she'd made up her mind once more, though this was going to be even worse than back there at the doorway. "Shall I— Do you want me to—?" And she got ready to get out with him.

"No," he said, "no. Just stay in it and watch the road. The slope is so steep, that when you get down below a certain point with—anything—it will plunge down the rest of the way by itself. It's been sheared off at the bottom, it's a sheer drop."

He'd swung the front door out as far as it would go, now.

"How's the road?" he asked.

She looked back first, all along it. Then forward. The way it rose ahead made it even easier to sight along.

"Empty," she said. "There's not a moving light on it anywhere."

He dipped down, did something with his arm, and then the two heads and the two pairs of shoulders rose together. A minute later the front seat was empty.

She turned away and looked at the road, looked at the road for all she was worth.

"I'll never be able to sit on the front seat of this car again," it occurred to her. "They'll wonder why, but I'll always balk, I'll always think of what was there tonight."

He had a hard time getting him down the slope, he had to be a brake on the two of them at once, and the weight was double. Once the two of them went down momentarily, in a stumble, and her heart shot up into her throat, as though there were a pulley, a counterweight, working between them and it.

Then he regained his balance again.

Then when she could only see him from the waist up, he bent over, as if laying something down before him, and when he'd straightened up again, he was alone, she could only see him by himself.

Then he just stood there waiting.

It was a gamble, a wild guess. A last car, a caboose, could have suddenly come along, and—no more train to carry their freight away. Just trackbed left below, to reveal what lay on it as soon as it got light.

But he'd guessed right. The sound of cracking nuts thinned, began to die out. A sort of rippling wooden shudder, starting way up ahead, ran past them and to the rear. Then a second one. Then silence.

He dipped again.

Her hands flew up to her ears, but she was too late. The sound beat her to it.

It was a sick, hollow thud. Like when a heavy sack is dropped. Only, a sack bursts from such a drop. This didn't.

She put her head down low over her lap, and held her hands pressed to her eyes.

When she looked up again, he was standing there beside her. He looked like a man who has himself in hand, but isn't sure that he isn't going to be sick before long.

"Stayed on," he said. "Caught on that catwalk, or whatever it is, that runs down the middle of each roof. I could see him even in the dark. But his hat didn't. That came off and went over."

She wanted to scream: "Don't! Don't *tell* me! Let me not know! I know too much already!" But she didn't. And by that time it was over with, anyway.

He got in again and took the wheel, without waiting for the train to recommence its run.

"It'll go on again," he said. "It has to. It was already

on its way once. It won't just stand there the rest of the night."

He ran the car back onto the rim of the road again, and then he brought it around in a U-turn, facing back to Caulfield. And still nothing came along, nothing passed them. On no other night could this road have been so empty.

He let their headlight beams shoot out ahead of them now.

"Do you want to come up here and sit with me?" he asked her quietly.

"No!" she said in a choked voice. "I couldn't! Not on *that* seat."

He seemed to understand. "I just didn't want you to be all alone," he said compassionately.

"I'll be all alone from now on, anyway, no matter where I sit," she murmured. "And so will you. We'll both be all alone, even together."

Forty-Two

SHE heard the brakes go on, and felt the motion of the car stop. He got out and got into the back next to her. They stayed just the way they were for several long moments. She with her face pressed against the bosom of his shirt, buried against him as if trying to hide it from the night and all that had happened in the night. He with one hand to the back of her head, holding it there, supporting it.

They didn't move nor speak at first.

Now I have to tell him, she kept thinking with dread. Now the time is here. And how shall I be able to?

She raised her head at last, and opened her eyes. He'd stopped around the corner from their own house. (*His* own. How could it ever be hers again? How could she ever go in there, after what had happened tonight?) He'd stopped around the corner, out of sight of it, and not right at the door. He was giving her the chance to tell him; that must be why he had done it.

He took out a cigarette, and lit it for her in his mouth, and offered it to her inquiringly. She shook her head. So then he threw it out the side of the car.

His mouth was so close to hers, she could smell the aroma of the tobacco freshly on his breath. It'll never be this close again, she thought, never; not after I'm done with what I have to tell him now.

"Bill," she whispered.

It was too weak, too pleading. That feeble a voice would never carry her through. And it had such rocky words ahead of it.

"Yes, Patrice?" he answered quietly.

"Don't call me that." She turned toward him with desperate urgency, forcing her voice to be steady. "Bill there's something you've got to know. I don't know where to begin it, I don't know how— But, oh, you've got to listen, if you've never listened to me before!"

"Sh, Patrice," he said soothingly. "Sh, Patrice." As though she were a fretful child. And his hand gently stroked her hair; downward, and then downward again, and still downward.

She moaned, almost as though she were in pain. "No— don't—don't—don't."

"I know," he said almost absently. "I know what you're trying so hard, so brokenheartedly, to tell me. That you're not Patrice. That you're not Hugh's wife. Isn't that it?"

She sought his eyes, and he was gazing into the distance, through the windshield and out ahead of the car. There was something almost abstract about his look.

"I know that already. I've always known it. I think I've known it ever since the first few weeks you got here."

The side of his face came gently to rest against her head, and stayed there, in a sort of implicit caress.

"So you don't have to try so hard, Patrice. Don't break your heart over it. There isn't anything to tell."

She gave an exhausted sob. Shuddered a little with her own frustration. "Even the one last chance to redeem myself, you've taken away from me," she murmured hopelessly. "Even that little."

"You don't have to redeem yourself, Patrice."

"Every time you call me that, it's a lie. I can't go back to that house with you. I can't go in there ever again. It's too late now—two years too late, two years—but at least let me tell it to you. Oh God, let me get it out! Patrice Hazzard was

killed on the train, right along with your brother. I was deserted by a man named—"

Again he placed his hand over her mouth, as he had at
Georgesson's place. But more gently than he had then.

"I don't want to know," he told her. "I don't want to hear.
Can't you understand, Patrice?" Then took his hand away, but
now she was silent, for that was the way he wanted her to be.
And that was the easier way to be. "*Won't* you understand
how I feel?" He glanced about for an instant, this way and
that, as if helplessly in search of some means of convincing
her. Some means that wasn't there at hand. Then back to her
again, to try once more; speaking low and from the heart.

"What difference does it make if there once was another
Patrice, another Patrice than you, a girl I never knew, some
other place and some other time? Suppose there *were* two?
There are a thousand Marys, a thousand Janes; but each man
that loves Mary, he loves only his Mary, and for him there are
no others in the whole wide world. And that's with me too.
A girl named Patrice came into my life one day. And that's
the only Patrice there is for me in the world. I don't love the
name, I love the girl. What kind of love do you think I have,
anyway? That if she got the name from a clergyman, it's on;
but if she helped herself to it, it's off?"

"But she *stole* the name, took it away from the dead. And
she lay in someone else's arms first, and then came into your
house with her child—"

"No, she didn't; no," he contradicted her with tender stub-
bornness. "You still don't see, you still won't see; because
you're not the man who loves you. She couldn't have; because
she *wasn't*, until I met her. She only began then, she only
starts from then. She only came into existence, as my eyes first
took her in, as my love first started in to start. Before then
there wasn't any she. My love began her, and when my love
ends, she ends with it. She has to, because she *is* my love.
Before then, there was a blank. A vacant space. That's the way
with any love. It can't go back before itself.

"And it's you I love. The you I made for myself. The you
I hold in my arms right now in this car. The you I kiss like
this, right now . . . right now . . . and now.

"Not a name on a birth-certificate. Not a name on a Paris

wedding-license. Not a bunch of dead bones taken out of a railroad-car and buried somewhere by the tracks.

"The name of my love is Patrice to me. My love doesn't know any other name, my love doesn't want any."

He swept her close to him, this time with such quivering violence that she was almost stunned. And as his lips found hers, between each pledge he told her:

"You are Patrice. You'll always be Patrice. You'll *only* be Patrice. I give you that name. Keep it for me, forever."

They lay that way for a long while; one now, wholly one. Made one by love; made one by blood and violence.

Presently she murmured, "And you knew, and you never—?"

"Not right away, not all in a flash. Life never goes that way. It was a slow thing, gradual. I think I first suspected inside of a week or two after you got here. I don't know when I was first sure. I think that day I bought the fountain pen."

"You must have hated me that day."

"I didn't hate you that day. I hated myself, for stooping to such a trick. (And yet I couldn't have kept from doing it, I couldn't have, no matter how I tried!) And do you know what I got from it? Only fear. Instead of *you* being the frightened one, I was. I was afraid that you'd take fright from it, and that I'd lose you. I knew *I'd* never be the one to expose you; I was too afraid I'd lose you that way. A thousand times I wanted to tell you, 'I know; I know all about it,' and I was afraid you'd take flight and I'd lose you. The secret wasn't heavy on you; it was me it weighted down."

"But in the beginning. How is it you didn't say anything in the very beginning? Surely you didn't condone it from the very start?"

"No; no, I didn't. My first reaction was resentment, enmity; about what you'd expect. But for one thing, I wasn't sure enough. And the lives of too many others were involved. Mainly there was Mother. I couldn't risk doing that to her. Right after she'd lost Hugh. For all I knew it might have killed her. And even just to implant seeds of suspicion, that would have been just as bad, that would have wrecked her happiness. Then too, I wanted to see what the object was, the game. I thought if I gave you enough rope— Well, I gave you rope and rope, and there was no game. You were just you. Every day it became a little harder to be on guard against you. Every day it became a little easier to look at you, and think of you, and like you. Then that night of the will—"

"You knew what you did, and yet you let them go ahead and—"

"There was no real danger. Patrice Hazzard was the name they put down in black and white. If it became necessary, it would have been easy enough to break it; or rather restrict it to its literal application, I should say. Prove that you and Patrice Hazzard were not identically one and the same and, therefore, that you were not the one intended. The law isn't like a man in love; the law values names. I pumped our lawyer a little on the q.t., without of course letting on what I had on my mind, and what he told me reassured me. But what that incident did for me once and for all, was to show me there was no game, no ulterior motive. I mean, that it wasn't the money that was at the bottom of it. Patrice, the fright and honest aversion I read on your face that night, when I came to your door to tell you about it, couldn't have been faked by the most expert actress in creation. Your face got as white as a sheet, your eyes darted around as though you wanted to run out of the house for dear life then and there; I touched your hand, and it was icy-cold. There is a point at which acting stops, and the heart begins.

"And that gave me the answer. I knew from that night on what it was you really wanted, what it was that had made you do it: safety, security. It was on your face a hundred times a day, once I had the clue. I've seen it over and over. Every time you looked at your baby. Every time you said, 'I'm going up to my room.' The way you said '*my* room.' I've seen it in your eyes even when you were only looking at a pair of curtains on the window, straightening them out, caressing them. I could almost hear you say, 'They're mine, I belong here.' And every time I saw it, it did something to me. I loved you a little more than I had the time before. And I wanted you to have all that rightfully, permanently, beyond the power of anyone or anything to ever take it away from you again—"

He lowered his voice still further, till she could barely hear the message it breathed.

"At my side. As my wife. And I still do. Tonight more than ever, a hundred times more than before. Will you answer me now? Will you tell me if you'll let me?"

His face swam fluidly before her upturned eyes.

"Take me home, Bill," she said brokenly, happily. "Take Patrice home to your house with you, Bill."

Forty-Three

FOR a moment, as he braked and as she turned her face toward it, her overtired senses received a terrifying impression that it was on fire, that the whole interior was going up in flame. And then as she recoiled against him, she saw that bright as the light coming from it was, brazier-bright against the early-morning pall, it was a steady brightness, it did not quiver. It poured from every window, above and below, and spilled in gradations of intensity across the lawn, and even as far as the frontal walk and the roadway beyond, but it was the static brightness of lighted-up rooms. Rooms lighted up in emergency.

He nudged and pointed wordlessly, and on the rear plate of the car already there, that they had just drawn up behind, stood out the ominous "MD." Spotlighted, menacing, beetling, within the circular focus of their own headlights. Prominent as the skull and crossbones on a bottle label. And just as fear-inspiring.

"Doctor Parker," flashed through her mind.

He flung open the door and jumped down, and she was right behind him.

"And we sat talking back there all this time," she heard him exclaim.

They chased up the flagstone walk, she at his heels, outdistanced by his longer legs. He didn't have time to use his key. By the time he'd got it out and put it to where the keyhole had last been, the keyhole was already back out of reach and Aunt Josie was there instead, frightened in an old flowered bathrobe, face as gray as her hair.

They didn't ask her who it was; there was no need to.

"Ever since happass eleven," she said elliptically. "*He's* been with her from midnight straight on through."

She closed the door after them.

"If you'd only phoned up," she said accusingly. "If you'd only leff word where I could reach you." And then she added, but more to him than to Patrice, "Daybreak. I hope the party was wuth it. It sure must have been a good one. I know one thing, it sure coss more than any party you ever went to in your life. Or ever likely to go to."

Patrice screamed out within herself, wincing: How right you are! It wasn't good, no, it wasn't—but oh, how costly!

Dr. Parker accosted them in the upper hall. There was a nurse there with him. They had thought he'd be in with her.

"Is she asleep?" Patrice breathed, more frightened than re-assured at this.

"Ty Winthrop's been in there alone with her for the past half-hour. She insisted. And when people are quite ill, you overrule them; but when they're even more ill than that, you don't. I've been checking her pulse and respiration at ten-minute intervals."

"That bad?" she whispered in dismay. She caught the stricken look on Bill's face, and found time to feel parenthet-ically sorry for him even while she asked it.

"There's no immediate danger," Parker answered. "But I can't make you any promises beyond the next hour or two." And then he looked the two of them square in the eyes and said, "It's a bad one this time. It's the daddy of them all."

It's the last one, Patrice knew then with certainty.

She crumpled for a moment, and a scattered sob or two escaped from her, while he and Bill led her over to a hall-chair, there beside the sickroom-door, and sat her down.

"Don't do that," the doctor admonished her, with just a trace of detachment—perhaps professional, perhaps per-sonal— "There's no call for it at this stage."

"It's just that I'm so worn-out," she explained blurredly.

She could almost read his answering thought. Then you should have come home a little earlier.

The nurse traced a whiff of ammonia past her nose, eased her hat from her head, smoothed her hair soothingly.

"Is my baby all right?" she asked in a moment, calmer.

It was Aunt Josie who answered that. "I know how to look after him," she said a trifle shortly. Patrice was out of favor right then.

The door opened and Ty Winthrop came out. He was putting away his glasses.

"They back yet—?" he started to say. Then he saw them. "She wants to see you."

They both started up at once.

"Not you," he said to Bill, warding him off. "Just Patrice. She wants to see her alone, without anyone else in the room. She repeated that several times."

Parker motioned her to wait. "Let me check her pulse first."

She looked over at Bill while they were standing there waiting, to see how he was taking it. He smiled untroubledly. "I understand," he murmured. "That's her way of seeing *me*. And a good way it is, too. Just about the best."

Parker had come out again.

"Not more than a minute or two," he said disapprovingly, with a side look at Winthrop. "And then maybe we'll all get together to see that she gets a little rest."

She went in there. Somebody closed the door after her.

"Patrice, dear," a quiet voice said.

She went over to the bed.

The face was still in shadow, because of the way they'd left the lamp.

"You can raise that a little, dear. I'm not in my coffin yet."

Her eyes looked up at Patrice in the same way they had that first day at the railroad station. They were kind. They smiled around the edges. They hurt a little, they were so *trustful*.

"I didn't dream—" she heard herself saying. "We drove out further than we'd intended to— It was such a beautiful night—"

Two hands were feebly extended for her to clasp.

She dropped suddenly to her knees and smothered them with kisses.

"I love you," she pleaded. "That much is true; oh, that much is true! If I could only make you believe it. My mother. You're my mother."

"You don't have to, dear. I know it already. I love you too, and my love has always known that you do. That's why you're my little girl. Remember that I told you this: *you're my little girl*."

And then she said, very softly, "I forgive you, dear. I forgive my little girl."

She stroked Patrice's hand consolingly.

"Marry Bill. I give you both my blessing. Here—" She gestured feebly in the direction of her own shoulder. "Under my pillow. I had Ty put something there for you."

Patrice reached under, drew out a long envelope, sealed, unaddressed.

"Keep this," Mother Hazzard said, touching the edge for a moment. "Don't show it to anyone. It's just for you. Do not open until—after I'm not here. It's in case you need it. When you're in greatest need, remember I gave it to you— open it then."

She sighed deeply, as though the effort had tired her unendurably.

"Kiss me. It's late. So very late. I can feel it in every inch of my poor old body. *You* can't feel how late it is, Patrice, but *I* can."

Patrice bent low above her, touched her own lips to hers.

"Goodbye, my daughter," she whispered.

"Goodnight," Patrice amended.

"Goodbye," she insisted gently. There was a faint, prideful smile on her face, a smile of superior knowledge, as of one who knows herself to be the better informed of the two.

Forty-Four

LONELY vigil by the window, until long after it had grown light. Sitting there, staring, waiting, hoping, despairing, dying a little. Seeing the stars go out, and the dawn creep slowly toward her from the east, like an ugly gray pallor. She'd never wanted to see daybreak less, for at least the dark had covered her sorrows like a cloak but every moment of increasing light diluted it, until it had reached the vanishing-point, it was gone, there wasn't any more left.

Motionless as a statue in the blue-tinged window, forehead pressed forward against the glass, making a little white ripple of adhesion across it where it touched. Eyes staring at nothing, for nothing was all there was out there to see.

I've found my love at last, only to lose him; only to throw him away. Why did I find out tonight I loved him, why did I have to know? Couldn't I have been spared that at least?

The day wasn't just bitter now. The day was ashes, lying all around her, cold and crumbled and consumed. No use for pinks and blues and yellows to try to tint it, like watercolors lightly applied from some celestial palette; no use. It was dead. And she was sitting there beside its bier.

And if there was such a thing as penance, absolution, for mistakes that, once made, can never be wholly undone again, can only be regretted, she should have earned it on that long vigil. But maybe there is none.

Her chances were dead and her hopes were dead, and she couldn't atone any further.

She turned and slowly looked behind her. Her baby was awake, and smiling at her, and for once she had no answering smile ready to give him. She couldn't smile, it would have been too strange a thing to fit upon her mouth.

She turned her face away again, so that she wouldn't have to look at him too long. Because, what good did crying do? Crying to a little baby. Babies cried to their mothers, but mothers shouldn't cry to their babies.

Outside, the man came out on that lawn down there, pulling his garden-hose after him. Then when he had it all stretched out, he let it lie, and went back to the other end of it, and turned the spigot. The grass began to sparkle, up where the nozzle lay inert, even before he could return to it and take it up. You couldn't see the water actually coming out, because the nozzle was down too flat against the ground, but you could see a sort of iridescent rippling of the grass right there, that told there was something in motion under it.

Then he saw her at her window, and he raised his arm and waved to her, the way he had in the beginning, that first day. Not because she was she, but because his own world was all in order, and it was a beautiful morning, and he wanted to wave to someone to show them how he felt.

She turned her head away. Not to avoid his friendly little salutation, but because there was a knocking at her door. Someone was knocking at her door.

She got up stiffly and walked over toward it, and opened it.

A lonely, lost old man was standing out there, quietly, unassumingly. Bill's father was standing out there, very wilted, very spent. A stranger, mistaking her for a daughter.

"She just died," he whispered helplessly. "Your mother just died, dear. I didn't know whom to go to, to tell about it—so I came to your door." He seemed unable to do anything but just stand there, limp, baffled.

She stood there without moving either. That was all she was able to do too. That was all the help she could give him.

Forty-Five

THE leaves were dying, as she had died. The season was dying. The old life was dying, was dead. They had buried it back there just now.

"How strange," Patrice thought. "To go on, before one can go on to something new, there has to be death first. Always, there has to be a kind of death, of one sort or another, first. Just as there has been with me."

The leaves were brightly dying. The misty black of her veil dimmed their apoplectic spasms of scarlet and orange and ochre, tempered them to a more bearable hue in the fiery sunset, as the funeral limousine coursed at stately speed homeward through the countryside.

She sat between Bill and his father.

"I am the Woman of the Family now," she thought. "The only woman of their house and in their house. That is why I sit between them like this, in place of prominence, and not to the outside."

And though she would not have known how to phrase it, even to herself, her own instincts told her that the country and the society she was a part of were basically matriarchal, that it was the woman who was essentially the focus of each home, the head of each little individual family-group. Not brazenly, aggressively so, not on the outside; but within the walls, where the home really was. She had succeeded to this primacy now. The gangling adolescent who had once stood outside a door that wouldn't open.

One she would marry and be his wife. One she would look after in filial devotion, and ease his loneliness and cushion his decline as best she could. There was no treachery, no deceit, in her plans; all that was over with and past.

She held Father Hazzard's hand gently clasped in her own, on the one side. And on the other, her hand curved gracefully up and around the turn of Bill's stalwart arm. To indicate: You are mine. And I am yours.

The limousine had halted. Bill got out and armed her down. Then they both helped his father and, one on each side of him, walked slowly with him up the familiar terraced flagstones to the familiar door.

Bill sounded the knocker, and Aunt Josie's deputy opened the door for them with all the alacrity of the novice. Aunt Josie herself, of course, a titular member of the family, had attended the services with them, was on her way back now in the lesser of the two limousines.

She closed the door in respectful silence, and they were home.

It was she who first saw them, Patrice. They were in the library.

Bill and his father, going on ahead, supporting arm about waist, had passed the open doorway obliviously. She had lingered behind for a moment, to give some muted necessary orders.

"Yes, Mrs. Hazzard," Aunt Josie's deputy said docilely.

Yes, Mrs. Hazzard. That was the first time she had heard it (Aunt Josie always called her "Miss Pat"), but she would have that now all her life, as her due. Her mind rolled it around on its tongue, savoring it. Yes, Mrs. Hazzard. Position. Security. Impregnability. The end of a journey.

Then she moved forward and, passing the doorway, saw them.

They were sitting in there, both facing it. Two men. The very way they held their heads—they were not apologetic, they were not disclaiming enough, for such a time and such a place and such a visit. Their faces, as she met them, did not say: "Whenever you are ready." Their faces said: "*We* are ready for you now. Come in to us."

Fear put out a long finger and touched her heart. She had stopped.

"Who are those two men?" she breathed to the girl who had let her in. "What are they doing in there?"

"Oh, I forgot. They came here about twenty minutes ago, asking to see Mr. Hazzard. I explained about the funeral, and suggested maybe they'd better come back later. But they said no, they said they'd wait. I couldn't do anything with them. So I just let them be."

She went on past the opening. "He's in no condition to speak to anyone now. You'll have to go in there and—"

"Oh, not old Mr. Hazzard. It's Mr. Hazzard his son they want."

She knew then. Their faces had already told her, the grim way they had both sized her up that fleeting second or two she had stood in the doorway. People didn't stare at you like that, just ordinary people. Punitive agents did. Those empowered by law to seek out, and identify, and question.

The finger had become a whole icy hand now, twisting and crushing her heart in its grip.

Detectives. Already. So soon, so relentlessly, so fatally soon. And today of all days, on this very day.

The copybooks were right, the texts that said the police were infallible.

She turned and hurried up the stairs, to overtake Bill and his father, nearing the top now, still linked in considerate, toiling ascent.

Bill turned his head inquiringly at sound of her hasty step behind them. Father Hazzard didn't. What was any step to him any more? The only one he wanted to hear would never sound again.

She made a little sign to Bill behind his father's back. A quick little quirk of the finger to show that this was something to be kept between the two of them alone. Then said, trying to keep her voice casual, "Bill, as soon as you take Father to his room, I want to see you for a minute. Will you come out?"

He came upon her in her own room, in the act of lowering an emptied brandy-jigger from her lips. He looked at her curiously.

"What'd you do, get a chill out there?"

"I did," she said. "But not out there. Here. Just now."

"You seem to be shaking."

"I am. Close the door." And when he had, "Is he sleeping?"

"He will be in another minute or two. Aunt Josie's giving him a little more of that sedative the doctor left."

She kneaded her hands together, as though she were trying to break each bone separately. "They're here, Bill. About the other night. They're here already."

He didn't have to ask, he knew what she meant by "the other night." There was only one other night for them, there would always be only one, from now on. As the nights multiplied, it would become "that night," perhaps; that was the only alteration.

"How do you know? Did they tell you?"

"They don't have to. I know." She snatched at his coat-lapels, as though she were trying to rip them off him. "What are we going to do?"

"*We* are not going to do anything," he said with meaning. "*I'll* do whatever is to be done about it."

"Who's that?" she shuddered, and crushed herself close to him. Her teeth were almost chattering with nervous tension.

"Who is it?" he asked at full voice.

"Aunt Josie," came through the door.

"Let go of me," he cautioned in an undertone. "All right, Aunt Josie."

She put her head in and said, "Those two men that're down there, they said they can't wait for Mr. Hazzard any more."

For a moment a little hope wormed its way through her stricken heart.

"They said if he don't come down, they'll have to come up here."

"What do they want? Did they tell you?" he said to Aunt Josie.

"I asked 'em twice, and each time they said the same thing.

'Mr. Hazzard.' What kind of an answer is that? They're bold ones."

"All right," he said curtly. "You've told us."

She closed the door again.

He stood for awhile irresolute, his hand curled around the back of his neck. Then straightened with reluctant decision, squared off his shoulders, hitched down his cuffs, and turned to face the door. "Well," he said, "let's get it over with."

She ran to join him. "I'll go with you."

"You won't!" He took her hand and put it off his arm, in rough rejection. "Let's get that straight right now. You're staying up here, and you're staying out of it. Do you hear me? No matter what happens, you're staying out of it."

He'd never spoken to her like that before.

"Are you taking me to be your husband?" he demanded.

"Yes," she murmured. "I've already told you that."

"Then that's an order. The first and the last, I hope, that I'll ever have to give you. Now look, we can't tell two stories about this. We're only telling one: mine. And it's one that you're not supposed to know anything about. So you can't help me, you can only harm me."

She seized his hand and put her lips to it, as a sort of godspeed.

"What are you going to tell them?"

"The truth." The look he gave her was a little odd. "What did you expect me to tell them? *I* have nothing to lie about, as far as it involves me alone."

He closed the door and he went out.

Forty-Six

As she found her hands leading the way down for her, one over the other, along the bannister-rail, while her feet followed them more slowly, a step behind all the way, she realized how impossible it would have been to follow his injunction, remain immured up there, without knowing, without listening; how futile of him to expect it of her. She couldn't have been involved as she was, she couldn't have been a woman at all, and obeyed him. This wasn't prying; you didn't pry into something that concerned you as closely as this did her. It was your right to know.

Hand over hand down the bannister, the rest of her creeping after, body held at a broken crouch. Like a cripple struggling down a staircase.

A quarter of the way down, the murmur became separate voices. Halfway down, the voices became words. She didn't go beyond there.

Their voices weren't raised. There was no blustering or angry contradiction. They were just men talking quietly, politely together. Somehow, it struck more fear into her that way.

They were repeating after him something he must have just now said.

"Then you do know someone named Harry Carter, Mr. Hazzard."

She didn't hear him say anything. As though he considered one affirmation on that point enough.

"Would you care to tell us what relationship—what connection—there is between you and this man Carter?"

He sounded slightly ironical, when he answered that. She had never heard him that way toward herself, but she caught a new inflection to his voice, and recognized it for irony. "Look, gentlemen, you already know. You must, or why would you be here? You want me to repeat it for you, is that it?"

"What we want is to hear it from you yourself, Mr. Hazzard."

"Very well, then. He is a private detective. As you already know. I selected and hired him. As you already know. And he was being paid a fee, he was being retained, to watch, to keep his eye on, this man Georgesson whom you're concerned with. As you already know."

"Very well, we do already know, Mr. Hazzard. But what we don't already know, what he couldn't tell us, because he didn't know himself, was what was the nature of your interest in Georgesson, why you were having him watched."

And the other one took up where the first had left off: "Would *you* care to tell us that, Mr. Hazzard? Why were you having him watched? What was your reason for doing that?"

Out on the stairs, her heart seemed to turn over and lie down flat on its face. "My God," went echoing sickly through her mind. "Now I come into it!"

"That's an extremely private matter," he said sturdily.

"I see; you don't care to tell us."

"I didn't say that."

"But still, you'd rather not tell us."

"You're putting words into my mouth."

"Because you don't seem to supply us with any of your own."

"It's essential for you to know this?"

"We wouldn't be here if it weren't, I can assure you. This man of yours, Carter, was the one who reported Georgesson's death to us."

"I see." She heard him take a deep breath. And she took one with him. Two breaths, one and the same fear.

"Georgesson was a gambler," he said.

"We know that."

"A crook, a confidence man, an all-around shady operator."

"We know that."

"Then here's the part you don't. Back about—it must be four years ago—three, anyway—my older brother Hugh was a senior at Dartmouth College. He started down here to spend the Christmas holidays at home, with us. He got as far as New York, and then he never got any further. He never showed up. He wasn't on the train that was to have brought him in the next day. We got a long-distance phone-call from him, and he was in trouble. He was practically being held there against his will. He'd gotten into a card-game, it seems, the night before with this Georgesson and a few of his friends—set-up, of course—and they'd taken him for I don't know how many thousands, which he didn't have, and they wanted a settlement before they'd let him go. They had him good, it had the makings of a first-class mess in it. Hugh was just a high-spirited kid, used to associating with decent people, gentlemen, not that kind of vermin, and he hadn't known how to handle himself. They'd built him up for it all evening long, liquored him up, thrown a couple of mangy chorus-girls at him in the various spots they'd dragged him around to first—well, anyway, because of my mother's health and the family's good name, there could be no question of calling the police into it, it would have been altogether too smelly. So my father went up there in person—I went along with him, incidentally—and squared the thing off for him. At about fifty cents to the dollar, or something like that. Got back the I.O.U.'s they'd extorted from the kid. And brought him home with us.

"That's about all there was to it. Not a very new story, it's happened over and over. But naturally, I wasn't likely to forget this Georgesson in a hurry. Well, when I learned he was down here in Caulfield a few weeks ago, showing his face around, I didn't know if it was a coincidence or not, but I wasn't taking any chances. I got in touch with a detective agency in New York and had them send Carter down here, just to try to find out what he was up to.

"And there you have it. Now does that answer your question? Is that satisfactory?"

They didn't say it was, she noticed. She waited, but she didn't hear them say it was.

"He didn't approach you or your family in any way? He didn't molest you?"

"He didn't come near us."

(Which was technically correct, she agreed wryly; she'd had to go to him each time.)

"You would have heard about it before now, if he had," he assured them. "I wouldn't have waited for you to look me up, I would have looked you up."

With catastrophic casualness a non-sequitur followed. She suddenly heard one of them ask him, "Do you want to bring along a hat, Mr. Hazzard?"

"It's right outside in the hall," he answered drily. "I'll pick it up as we go by."

They were coming out of the room. With an infantile whimper, that was almost like that of a little girl running away from goblins in the dark, she turned and fled up the stairs again, back to her room.

"No—! No—! No—!" she kept moaning with feverish reiteration.

They were arresting him, they were accusing him, they were taking him with them.

Forty-Seven

DISTRACTED, she flung herself down on the bench before her
dressing-table. Her head rolled soddenly about on her shoulders, as though she were drunk. Her hair was displaced, burying one eye.

"No—! No—!" she kept insisting. "They can't— It isn't
fair—"

They wouldn't let him go— They'd never let him go
again— He wouldn't come back— He'd never come back to
her—

"Oh, for the love of God, help me! I can't take any more
of this!"

And then, as in the fairy tales, as in the story-books of old,
where everything always comes out all right, where good is
good and bad is bad, and the magic spell is always broken just
in time for the happy ending, there it was—right under her
eyes—

Lying there, waiting. Only asking to be picked up. A white
oblong, a sealed envelope. A letter from the dead.

A voice trapped in it seemed to whisper through the seams
to her, faint, far away: "When you're in the most need, and
I'm not here, open this. When your need is the greatest, and
you're all alone. Goodbye, my daughter; my daughter, good-
bye . . ."

"I, Grace Parmentier Hazzard, wife of Donald Sedgwick
Hazzard, being on my death-bed, and in the presence
of my attorney and lifelong counsellor Tyrus Winthrop,
who will duly notarize my signature to this and bear
witness to it if called upon to do so by the legally constituted authorities, hereby make the following statement, of my own free will and volition, and declare it
to be the truth:

"That at approximately 10.30 P.M. on the evening of
24th September, being alone in the house with just my
devoted friend and housekeeper, Josephine Walker, and
my grandchild, I received a long-distance telephone-call
from Hastings, in the neighboring State. That the caller

was a certain Harry Carter, known to me as a private investigator and employed by my family and myself as such. That he informed me that just a few moments earlier my beloved daughter-in-law, Patrice, the widow of my late son, Hugh, had been driven against her will to Hastings by a man using the name of Stephen Georgesson, and had there been compelled to enter into a marriage-ceremony with him under duress. And that at that time, while he spoke to me, they were on their way back here, to this city, together.

"Upon receipt of this information, and having obtained from this Mr. Carter the address of the aforementioned Stephen Georgesson, I dressed myself, called Josephine Walker to me, and told her I was going out, and would be away for only a short time. She tried to dissuade me, and to prevail upon me to reveal my purpose and where I was going, but I would not. I instructed her to wait for me close beside the front door, in order to admit me at once upon my return, and under no circumstances, then or at any later time, to reveal to anyone that I had left the house at that time or under those circumstances. I caused her to take an oath upon the Bible, and knowing the nature of her religious beliefs and early upbringing knew she would not break it afterward no matter what befell.

"I removed and carried with me a gun which habitually was kept in a desk in the library of my home, having first inserted into it the cartridges. In order to lessen recognition as much as possible, I put on the heavy veil of mourning which I had worn at the time of the death of my elder son.

"I walked a short distance from my own door, entirely alone and unaccompanied, and at the first opportunity engaged a public taxicab. In it I went to the quarters of Stephen Georgesson, to seek him out. I found he had not yet returned when I first arrived, and I therefore waited, sitting in the taxi a short distance from his door, until I saw him return and enter. As soon as he had, I immediately entered in turn, right after him, and was admitted by him. I raised my veil in order to let him see my face, and I could see that he guessed who I was, although he'd never seen me before.

"I asked him if it was true that he had just now forced my dead son's wife to enter a marriage-pact with him, as had been reported to me.

"He readily admitted it, naming the place and time.

"Those were the only words that passed between us. Nothing further was said. Nothing further needed to be.

"I immediately took out the gun, held it close toward him, and fired it at him as he stood there before me.

"I fired it only once. I would have fired it more than once, if necessary, in order to kill him; it was my full intention to kill him. But having waited to see if he would move again, and seeing that he did not, but lay as he had fallen, then and only then I refrained from firing it any more and left the place.

"I had myself returned to my own home in the same taxi that had brought me. Within a short time after, I became extremely ill from the excitement and strain I had undergone. And now, knowing that I am dying, and being in full possession of my faculties and with full re-alization of what I am doing, I wish to make this state-ment before I pass away and have it, in the case of wrongful accusation of others, should that occur, brought to the attention of those duly constituted to deal with the matter. But only in such case, not other-wise.

(*Signed*) Grace Parmentier Hazzard.
(*Witnessed and attested*)
Tyrus Winthrop, Att'y at Law."

She reached the downstairs doorway with it too late. The doorway was empty by the time she swayed that far, and clung there, all dazed and disheveled. They'd gone, and he'd gone with them.

She just stood there in the doorway. Empty in an empty doorway.

Forty-Eight

AND then, there he was at last.

He was so very real, so photographically real down there, that paradoxically, she couldn't quite believe she was seeing him. The very herringbone weave of his coat stood out, as if a magnifying glass were being held to the pattern, for her special inspection. The haggardness of his face, the faint trace of shadow where he needed a shave, she could see everything about him so clearly, as if he were much nearer than he was. Fatigue, maybe, did that, by some reverse process of concentration. Or eyes dilated from long straining to see him, so that now they saw him with abnormal clarity.

Anyway, there he was.

He turned, and came in toward the house. And just before he took the final step that would have carried him too far in under her to be in sight any more, his eyes went up to the window and he saw her.

"Bill," she said silently through the glass, and her two hands flattened to the pane, as if framing the unheard word into a benediction.

"Patrice," he said silently, from down below; and though she didn't hear him, didn't even see his lips move, she knew that was what he said. Just her name. So little, so much.

Suddenly she'd fled from the room as madly as though she'd just been scalded. The upflung curtain settled down again to true, and the backflung door ricocheted back again toward closure, and she was already gone. The baby's wondering head turned after her far too slowly to catch her in her flight.

Then she stopped short again, below the turn of the stairs, and waited for him there, unable to move any further. Stood waiting for him to come to her.

He left his hat, just as though this were any other time he was returning home, and came on up to where she was standing. And somehow her head, as if it were tired of being all alone, went down upon his shoulder and stayed there against his own.

They didn't speak at first. Just stood there pressed together, heads close. There was no message; there was only—being together.

"I'm back, Patrice," was all he said at last.

She shuddered a little and nestled closer. "Bill, now what will they—?"

"Nothing. It's over. It's already through. At least, as far as I'm concerned. That was just for purposes of identification. I had to go with them and look at him, that was all."

"Bill, I opened this. She says—"

She gave it to him. He read it.

"Did you show it to anyone else?"

"No."

"Don't." He tore it once across, and stuffed the remnants into his pocket.

"But suppose—?"

"It's not needed. His gambler-friends are already down on the books for it, by this time. They told me they found evidence to indicate that a big card-game had taken place up there earlier that night."

"I didn't see any."

He gave her an eloquent look. "They did. By the time they got there."

She widened her eyes a little at him.

"They're willing to let it go at that. So let us let it go at that too, Patrice." He sighed heavily. "I'm all-in. Feel like I've been on my feet for a week straight. I'd like to sleep forever."

"Not forever, Bill, not forever. Because I'll be waiting around, and that would be so long—"

His lips sought the side of her face, and he kissed her with a sort of blind stupefaction.

"Walk me up as far as the door of my room, Patrice. Like to take a look at the youngster, before I turn in."

His arm slipped wearily around her waist.

"*Our* youngster from now on," he added softly.

Forty-Nine

"MR. WILLIAM HAZZARD was married yesterday to Mrs. Patrice Hazzard, widow of the late Hugh Hazzard, at a quiet ceremony at St. Bartholomew's Episcopal Church, in this city, performed by the Reverend Francis Allgood. There were no attendants. Following their marriage Mr. and Mrs. Hazzard left immediately for a honeymoon trip through the Canadian Rockies."—*All Caulfield morning and evening newspapers.*

Fifty

WHEN the reading of the will had been concluded—that was on a Monday following their return, about a month later—Winthrop asked the two of them to remain behind a moment after the room had been cleared. He went over and closed the door after the others present had left. Then he went to the wall, opened a built-in safe, and took out an envelope. He sat down at his desk.

"Bill and Patrice," he said, "this is meant for you alone."

They exchanged a look.

"It is not part of the estate, so it concerns no one else but the two of you.

"It is from her, of course. It was transcribed on her death-bed, less than an hour before she died."

"But we already—" Bill tried to say.

Winthrop silenced him with upturned hand. "There were two of them. This is the second. Both dictated to me during the hours of that same night, or I should say, early morning. This follows the other. The first she gave you herself that same night, as you know. The other she turned over to me. I was to hold it until today, as I have done. Her instructions to me were: It is for the two of you alike. It is not to be delivered to the one without the other. When delivered, it is not to be opened by the one without the other. And finally, it is only to be delivered in the case of your marriage. If you were not married at this time, as she wanted you to be—and you know she did, very much—then it was to be destroyed by me, un-opened. Singly, it is not for either one of you. United in mar-riage, it is a last gift to the two of you, from her.

"However. You need not read it if you do not want to. You can destroy it unopened. I am under pledge not to reveal what is in it, even though I naturally know, for I took her words down at the bedside, and witnessed and notarized her signature in my capacity as her attorney. You must, therefore, either read it or not read it for yourselves. And if you do read it, then when you have read it, you are to destroy it just the same."

He waited a moment.

"Now, do you want me to deliver it to you, or do you prefer that I destroy it?"

"We want it, of course," Patrice whispered.

"We want it," Bill echoed.

He extended it to them lengthwise. "You kindly place your fingers on this corner. You on this." He withdrew his own fingers, and they were left holding it.

"I hope it brings you the extra added happiness she wanted you both to have. I know that that is why she did it. She asked me to bless you both, for her, as I gave it to you. Which I do now. That concludes my stewardship in the matter."

They waited several hours, until they were alone together in their room that night. Then when he'd finished putting on his robe, and saw that she had donned a silken bridal something over her nightdress, he took it out of his coat-pocket and said:

"Now. Shall we? You do want to, don't you?"

"Of course. It's from her. We want to read it. I've been counting the minutes all evening long."

"I knew you'd want to. Come on over here. We'll read it together."

He sat down in an easy chair, adjusted the hood of the lamp over one shoulder. She perched beside him on the arm of the chair, slipped an arm about his shoulders.

The sealing-wax wafers crumbled and the flap shot upright, under his fingers.

In silent intensity, heads close together, they read:

"My beloved children:

"You are married by now, by the time this reaches you. (For if you are not, it will not reach you; Mr. Winthrop will tell you all about that.) You are happy. I hope I have given you that happiness. I want to give you even a little more. And trust and pray that out of your plenty, you will spare a little of it for me, even though I am gone and no longer there with you. I do not want a shadow to cross your minds every time you recall me. I cannot bear to have you think ill of me.

"I did not do that thing, of course. I did not take that young man's life. Perhaps you have already guessed it. Perhaps you both know me well enough to know I could not have done such a thing.

"I knew that he was doing something to threaten Patrice's happiness, that was all. That was why we were having Mr. Carter investigate him. But I never actually set eyes on him, I never saw him.

"I was alone in the house last night (for as Mr. Winthrop writes this for me, it is still last night, though you will not read it for a long time to come). Even Father, who never goes out without me, had to attend an important emergency meeting at the plant. It meant settling the strike that much sooner, and I pleaded with him to go, though he did not want to. I was alone, just Aunt Josie and the child and I.

"Mr. Carter phoned around ten-thirty o'clock and told me he had bad news; that a marriage-service had just been performed joining the two of them at Hastings. I had taken the call on the downstairs phone. The shock brought on an attack. Not wishing to alarm Aunt Josie, I tried to get up the stairs to my room unaided. By the time I had reached the top, I became exhausted and could only lie there, unable to move any further or to call out.

"While I was lying there helpless like that, I heard the outside door open and recognized Bill's step below. I tried to attract his attention, but my voice was too weak, I couldn't reach him with it. I heard him go into the library, stay there several moments, then come out again. Afterward I remembered hearing something click between his hands right then, as he stood there by the door. And I knew he never uses a cigarette-lighter. Then he left the house.

"When Aunt Josie had come out some time later,

found me there, and carried me to my bed, and while we were waiting for the doctor, I sent her to the library to see if that gun that belonged there was still there. She did not understand why I wanted her to do this, and I did not tell her. But when she came back and told me that the gun was missing, I was afraid what that might mean.

"I knew by then that I was dying. One does. I had time to think, lying there during those next long hours. I could think so clearly. I knew that there was a way in which either my Bill or my Patrice might need my protection, once I was no longer there to give it. I knew I had to give it none the less, as best I could. I wanted them to have their happiness. I wanted above all my little grandchild to have his security, his start in life without anything to mar it. I knew what the way was in which I could give this to them.

"So as soon as Dr. Parker would allow it, I had Ty Winthrop called to my bedside. To him, in privacy, I dictated the sworn statement which you have had by now.

"I hope, my dear ones, you have not had to use it. I pray you have not, and never will have to.

"But this is its retraction. This is the truth, just meant for you two alone. One tells the truth to one's loved ones, one does not have to swear to and notarize it. There is no guilt upon me. This is my wedding gift to you. To make your happiness even more complete than it is already.

"Burn it after you have read it. This is a dying woman's last wish. Bless you both.

Your devoted Mother."

The match made a tiny snap. Stripes of black crept up the paper, then ran together, before any flame could be seen. Then there was a little soundless puff, and suddenly yellow light glowed all around it.

And as it burned, over this yellow light, they turned their heads and looked at one another. With a strange, new sort of fright they'd never felt before. As when the world drops away, and there is nothing left underfoot to stand on.

"*She* didn't do it," he whispered, stricken.

"*She* didn't," she breathed, appalled.

"Then—?"

"Then—?"

And each pair of eyes answered, "You."

THE SUMMER NIGHTS are so pleasant in Caulfield. They smell of heliotrope, of jasmine, and of clover. The stars are warm and close above us. The breeze is gentle as a baby's kiss. The soothing whisper of the leafy trees, the lamplight falling on the lawns, the hush of perfect peace and security.

But not for us.

The house we live in is so pleasant here in Caulfield. Its blue-green lawn, always freshly watered; the dazzling whiteness of the porch-supports in the sun; the gracious symmetry of the bannister that curves down from above; the gloss of rich old floors; the lushness of pile carpeting; in every room some favorite chair that's an old friend. People come and say, "What more can there be? This is a home."

But not for us.

I love him so. More than ever before, not less. So bitterly I love him. And he loves me. And yet I know that on some day to come, maybe this year, maybe next, but surely to come, suddenly he'll pack and go away and leave me. Though he'll love me still, and never stop even after he's gone.

Or if he doesn't, I will. I'll take up my valise, and walk out through the door, and never return. I'll leave my heart behind, and leave my child behind, and leave my life behind, but I'll never come back.

It's certain, it's assured. The only uncertainty is: which one of us will be the first to break.

We've fought this thing. In every way we know, in every way there is. No good, no good at all. There's no way out. We're caught, we're trapped. For if he's innocent, then it has to be me. And if I am, it has to be he. But I *know* I'm innocent. (Yet he may know he is too.) We can't break through, there's no way out.

It's in the very kiss we give each other. Somehow we trap it right between our lips, each time. It's everywhere, it's all the time, it's *us*.

I don't know what the game was. I'm not sure how it should be played. No one ever tells you. I only know we must have played it wrong, somewhere along the way. I don't even know what the stakes are. I only know they're not for us.

We've lost. That's all I know. We've lost. And now the game is through.

The End.

BIOGRAPHICAL NOTES

NOTE ON THE TEXTS

NOTES

Biographical Notes

JAMES M. CAIN Born July 1, 1892, in Annapolis, Maryland. Moved with family in 1903 to Chestertown, Maryland, where father served as president of Washington College. Graduated from Washington College 1910. Studied singing, but eventually abandoned musical career. Taught English and mathematics at Washington College, 1914–17. Worked as reporter for Baltimore *American* and then Baltimore *Sun* before enlisting in army; served in France with headquarters of 79th Division and edited the weekly divisional newspaper, *The Lorraine Cross*. Resumed work with Baltimore *Sun* after the war. Married Mary Rebekah Clough in 1920. Published articles in *Atlantic Monthly* and *Nation*; worked briefly as coal miner in 1922. Marriage ended in divorce in 1923. Taught journalism at St. John's College, Annapolis, 1923–24. Moved to New York in 1924 and wrote for New York *World* and other publications. Married Elina Sjosted Tyszecka in 1927. Published fiction and articles in *The American Mercury*, including satirical political dialogues collected in 1930 as *Our Government*. Worked for ten months in 1931 as managing editor of *The New Yorker*. Moved to Hollywood, where he worked for 17 years as screenwriter for most of the major studios (credits include *Hot Saturday*, 1932; *Dr. Socrates*, 1935; *Algiers*, 1938; *Stand Up and Fight*, 1939; *Money and the Woman*, 1940; *The Bridge of San Luis Rey*, 1943; *The Great Gatsby*, 1945; *The Glass Heart*, 1946). First novel, *The Postman Always Rings Twice*, published 1934 (a stage version written by Cain ran on Broadway in 1936). *Double Indemnity* serialized in *Liberty* magazine in 1938. Published novels *Serenade* (1937), *Mildred Pierce* (1941), *Love's Lovely Counterfeit* (1942). Second marriage ended in divorce in 1942. *Double Indemnity* successfully filmed in 1943, directed by Billy Wilder and starring Barbara Stanwyck and Fred MacMurray; magazine serials *Double Indemnity*, *Career in C Major* (1938), and *The Embezzler* (1940) collected in *Three of a Kind* (1943). Married movie actress Aileen Pringle in 1944; divorced the following year. Movie versions of *Mildred Pierce*, directed by Michael Curtiz and starring Joan Crawford, and *The Postman Always Rings Twice*, directed by Tay Garnett and starring Lana Turner and John Garfield, appeared, 1945–46. Civil War novel *Past All Dishonor* published 1946. Campaign organized by Cain in 1946 to establish American Authors Authority, organization intended to protect and administer authors' copyrights, met with intense opposition from studios, publishers, and other writers, some of whom accused Cain of being a pawn of Communists;

he abandoned plan the following year. Married opera singer Florence MacBeth in 1947 and moved with her to Hyattsville, Maryland. Published novels *Sinful Woman* (1947), *The Moth* (1948), *Jealous Woman* (1950), *The Root of His Evil* (1951, revision of 1938 magazine serial), *Galatea* (1953), *Mignon* (1963), *The Magician's Wife* (1965). Wife died in 1966. Reputation revived by publication of *Cain × 3* (1969), omnibus of early novels with introduction by Tom Wolfe. Published novels *Rainbow's End* (1975) and *The Institute* (1976); other late novels rejected for publication, *Cloud Nine* and *The Enchanted Isle*, were published posthumously (1984–85). Died October 27, 1977.

HORACE MCCOY   Born April 14, 1897, in Pegram, Tennessee. Moved with family to Nashville at age two. Worked as auto mechanic and traveling salesman after dropping out of high school. Moved with family to Dallas in 1915. Enlisted in Texas National Guard in 1917; received training as aerial observer, and served in France in 1918 as bombardier and aerial photographer. Returned to Dallas, worked as reporter for *Dallas Dispatch*, and then joined *Dallas Journal* as sports editor. Married Loline Scherer in 1921; son Stanley born 1924. Active as actor in acclaimed Dallas Little Theatre, 1925–31. Began contributing stories to *Black Mask* in 1927; published 16 stories, 1927–34, most concerning the adventures of Texas Ranger Jerry Frost and his Air Border Patrol; also published in other pulps including *Battle Aces*, *Action Stories*, *Western Trails*, and *Man Stories*. Marriage broke up; lost newspaper job in 1929. Became editor in 1930 of recently launched magazine *The Dallasite*, which soon failed. Eloped with a Dallas socialite, but marriage was quickly annulled. Went to Hollywood in 1931 to pursue an acting career; was cast only in a few minor roles. Became contract screenwriter with RKO in 1932. Married Helen Vinmont, daughter of wealthy oilman, in 1933 (they had a daughter, Amanda, born 1940, and a son, Peter, born 1945). First novel, *They Shoot Horses, Don't They?*, published 1935. Second novel, *No Pockets in a Shroud*, based on Dallas experiences as actor and reporter, was rejected by American publishers but appeared in England in 1937 with substantial changes demanded by English publisher; third novel, *I Should Have Stayed Home*, published 1938. Worked steadily as screenwriter for RKO, Paramount, and Warner Brothers for the next two decades; credits include *Postal Inspector*, 1936; *The Trail of the Lonesome Pine*, 1936; *The Texans*, 1938; *Gentleman Jim*, 1942; *Appointment in Berlin*, 1943; *Montana Belle*, 1952; *The Turning Point*, 1952 (his screen treatment was posthumously published in 1956 as novel *Corruption City*); *The Lusty Men*, 1952; *The World in His Arms*, 1952; *Rage at Dawn*, 1955. Became aware in the late 1940s that his work was highly appreciated in Europe, particularly France. Published novel *Kiss Tomorrow Good-bye* in 1948; it received weak reviews but sold well (film version, starring James Cagney, released 1950); issued in paperback by New American Library along with three earlier novels (most in abridged versions). Visited France in 1951. Final novel *Scalpel* (1952), based on screen treatment about a doctor's career, became bestseller. Worked on novel *The Hard-Rock Man*, never completed. Died of a heart attack on December 15, 1955.

EDWARD ANDERSON Born June 19, 1905, in Weatherford, Texas. Moved with family through many small towns in Texas and Oklahoma before his father, an itinerant printer, settled in Ardmore, Oklahoma. Worked as freelance newspaperman during 1920s. Traveled to Europe in 1930, working on freighter; visited Belgium, France, and Germany. On return to U.S. settled in Abilene, Texas, where his family was living. Formed close friendship with writer John Knox, who introduced him to writings of Knut Hamsun, Maxim Gorky, Karl Marx, and others. Left Abilene to live hobo life, traveling around U.S. and spending time in San Francisco, Boston, and New York; returned to Abilene in late 1933. Sold short stories based on hobo experiences to *Story*. Married Polly Anne Bates in 1934 and moved to New Orleans; wrote articles for *True Detective* and other magazines, and subsequently took newspaper job at the *New Orleans States*. Novel *Hungry Men* won *Story* prize for best first novel and was published by Doubleday in 1935. Daughter Helen Ann born 1935; son Dick Edward born 1936. Returned to Texas and wrote second novel, *Thieves Like Us*, based partly on interviews with cousin Roy Johnson, who was serving life sentence for armed robbery. Went to Denver to work for *Rocky Mountain News*; also wrote for local radio shows. *Thieves Like Us* published by Frederick A. Stokes in 1937. At suggestion of agent Adeline Schulberg, went to Los Angeles to write for movies; worked briefly at Paramount and Warner Brothers before joining staff of *Los Angeles Examiner*. Sold movie rights to *Thieves Like Us* for $500. Subsequent fiction remained unpublished. Son Ross born 1941. Marriage broke up in 1946. After losing job with *Examiner* worked successively for *Sacramento Bee* and *Fort Worth Star-Telegram*. Remarried Polly Anne in 1949. Film version of *Thieves Like Us*, titled *They Live By Night* (directed by Nicholas Ray), opened in 1950 after two-year delay; the novel was reissued in paperback. Marriage broke up again in 1950 as a result of Anderson's heavy drinking; he resumed a drifting life, working sporadically at newspapers in different parts of the U.S., marrying twice more. With third wife, Lupe, settled again in Texas; daughter Sarita born 1956. Espoused extreme right-wing political views along with religious beliefs based on Swedenborgianism. Died from heart attack September 5, 1969.

KENNETH FEARING   Born July 28, 1902, in Oak Park, Illinois; father, Harry Fearing was successful Chicago attorney; mother, Oliver Flexner, a newspaper reporter, was member of Jewish family originally from Bohemia. Parents' marriage broke up a year after Fearing's birth and he was raised mostly by father's sister. Attended University of Illinois for two years, then transferred to University of Wisconsin, where he met writers Carl Rakosi and Margery Latimer, and was editor of the college literary magazine; graduated in 1924. Settled in New York City; maintained close relationship with Latimer until 1928. Worked sporadically at odd jobs but mostly devoted himself to writing; wrote prolifically for pulp magazines under pseudonyms; contributed poetry and reviews to periodicals including *New Masses*, *Poetry*, and *The New Yorker*. First book of poems, *Angel Arms*, published 1929. Married medical social worker Rachel Meltzer in 1933; son Bruce born 1935. Published *Poems* (1935) and *Dead Reckoning* (1938); wrote a number of unpublished novels before *The Hospital* appeared in 1939. Awarded Guggenheim fellowship (1937–38) and prize from American Academy of Arts and Letters (1944); stayed in Europe (mostly in London) with Rachel for nine months, 1936–37. In addition to other volumes of poetry—*Collected Poems of Kenneth Fearing* (1940), *Afternoon of a Pawnbroker* (1943), *Stranger at Coney Island* (1948)—published novels *Dagger of the Mind* (1941), *Clark Gifford's Body* (1942), *The Big Clock* (1946). Marriage broke up in 1942; married artist Nan Lurie in 1945. Film version of *The Big Clock*, directed by John Farrow and starring Ray Milland and Charles Laughton, released 1948 (Fearing had negotiated disadvantageous contract signing away future rights). Interviewed by FBI on his political associations in 1950, said he was "not yet" a member of the Communist Party. Second marriage broke up in 1952; in later years suffered from effects of poverty and long-term heavy drinking. Later novels were *Loneliest Girl in the World* (1951), *The Generous Heart* (1954), and *The Crozart Story* (1960); final poetry collection, *New and Selected Poems*, appeared in 1956. Worked on staff of *Newsweek*, 1952–54, and as publicist for Muscular Dystrophy Association of America, 1955–58. Died of cancer on June 26, 1961.

WILLIAM LINDSAY GRESHAM   Born August 20, 1909, in Baltimore, Maryland. Moved with family to Fall River, Massachusetts, and then to New York City in 1917; graduated Erasmus Hall High School in Brooklyn, 1926. Worked at odd jobs and as folk singer in Greenwich Village cafés; joined Civilian Conservation Corps in 1933. Married after leaving the CCC. After brief stint as reviewer for New York *Evening Post*, worked as advertising copy writer; contributed stories to pulp magazines. Joined Communist Party in 1936; went to Spain the following year and served for 15 months as medic with the Abraham Lincoln Brigade. Returning to U.S. in January 1939, spent time in tuberculosis ward, attempted suicide, underwent lengthy psychoanalysis, and worked as editor for true crime magazine. After divorcing first wife, married poet Joy Davidman in 1942; they had two sons, David and Douglas, born in 1944 and 1945, and lived successively in Ossining and Staatsburg, New York. Gresham's first novel, *Nightmare Alley*, published in 1946; it was a bestseller and was filmed the following year, directed by Edmund Goulding and starring Tyrone Power. His second novel, *Limbo Tower*, appeared in 1949. Gresham and his wife were deeply influenced by ideas of C. S. Lewis, and announced their joint conversion in articles published in 1951 anthology *These Found the Way: Thirteen Converts to Protestant Christianity*. Struggled with alcoholism, was occasionally violent, and engaged frequently in extramarital affairs; stopped attending Presbyterian church and pursued interests in Zen Buddhism, occult traditions, and L. Ron Hubbard's Dianetics. Divorced Joy Davidman in 1954 and married her cousin Renee Pierce (Davidman resettled with children in England, married C. S. Lewis in 1956, and died in 1960). Gresham's later books included *Monster Midway: An Uninhibited Look at the Glittering World of the Carny* (1953), *Houdini: The Man Who Walked Through Walls* (1959), and *The Book of Strength*. Lived in New Rochelle; became partially blind and was diagnosed with cancer in 1962. Committed suicide with overdose of sleeping pills in Dixie Hotel in New York City, where he had registered under a false name, on September 14, 1962.

CORNELL WOOLRICH Born Cornell George Hopley-Woolrich on December 4, 1903, in New York City. Moved with parents to Mexico in 1907, where father worked as engineer; marriage soon broke up, and Woolrich remained with father while mother returned to New York. After several years rejoined mother, living with her and her family in luxurious house on Manhattan's Upper West Side. First novel, *Cover Charge*, written while an undergraduate at Columbia and published 1926, followed by *Children of the Ritz* (1927), *Times Square* (1929), *A Young Man's Heart* (1930), *The Time of Her Life* (1931), and *Manhattan Love Song* (1932). Went to Hollywood in 1928 to work on movie version of *Children of the Ritz*. Married Gloria Blackton, daughter of pioneering filmmaker J. Stuart Blackton, in December 1930; marriage ended three months later (break-up may have been precipitated by wife's discovery of Woolrich's homosexual activities). Woolrich returned to New York to rejoin his mother; traveled with her to Europe in April 1931, staying mostly in France, and returned to U.S. in 1933. Moved with mother into apartment in Hotel Marseilles in New York City, where they lived for the next 25 years. Began to write crime stories for pulp magazines, contributing prolifically to *Detective Fiction Weekly, Dime Detective, Argosy, Black Mask*, and others. First crime novel, *The Bride Wore Black*, published 1940. Published series of crime novels, sometimes under names William Irish and George Hopley: *The Black Curtain* (1941), *Black Alibi* (1942), *Phantom Lady* (1942, as William Irish), *The Black Angel* (1943), *Deadline at Dawn* (1944, as William Irish), *The Black Path of Fear* (1944), *Night Has a Thousand Eyes* (1945, as George Hopley), *Waltz into Darkness* (1947, as William Irish), *Rendezvous in Black* (1948), *I Married a Dead Man* (1948, as William Irish), *Fright* (1950, as George Hopley), *Savage Bride* (1951), *Strangler's Serenade* (1951, as William Irish). Many of his novels and stories were adapted into movies, including *The Leopard Man, Phantom Lady, Deadline at Dawn, Black Angel, The Chase, Fear in the Night, Night Has a Thousand Eyes, The Window, No Man of Her Own* (based on *I Married a Dead Man*), and *Rear Window*, and for radio and television. Productivity diminished drastically in final two decades of life; suffered from alcoholism and became even more reclusive. Mother died in October 1957. *Hotel Room*, collection of stories without a crime theme, published 1958. Final completed novel, *Death Is My Dancing Partner*, published 1959; *The Doom Stone* (1960), reprint of a 1939 pulp novella, was last book to appear in his lifetime. (An unfinished novel, *Into the Night*, was completed by Lawrence Block and published in 1987.) Changed name legally to William Irish in 1961. Untreated infection became gangrenous, necessitating amputation of right leg in January 1968. Died September 25, 1968, six days after suffering a stroke.

Note on the Texts

This volume collects six American novels of the 1930s and 1940s that have come to be identified with the "noir" genre of crime fiction: *The Postman Always Rings Twice* by James M. Cain (1934); *They Shoot Horses, Don't They?* by Horace McCoy (1935); *Thieves Like Us* by Edward Anderson (1937); *The Big Clock* by Kenneth Fearing (1946); *Nightmare Alley* by William Lindsay Gresham (1946); and *I Married a Dead Man* by Cornell Woolrich (1948).

James M. Cain began work on his first novel in the late autumn of 1932, writing the narrative in the third person until early in 1933, when he decided to use a first-person narration. Cain showed an early version of the novel to screenwriter Vincent Lawrence, who persuaded him to rewrite and shorten the section of the book dealing with the court proceedings against Cora. In the summer of 1933 Cain submitted a 159-page typescript to Alfred A. Knopf under the title *Bar-B-Q*. Knopf asked for significant revisions, which Cain refused to make; after H. L. Mencken and Blanche Knopf recommended publication of the novel, Knopf reversed himself and accepted the version Cain had submitted. Cain did agree to change the title and chose *The Postman Always Rings Twice* after considering *Black Puma* and *The Devil's Checkbook*. *The Postman Always Rings Twice* was published by Alfred A. Knopf on February 19, 1934. Cain did not revise the novel after its initial publication. The text printed here is that of the first edition.

Horace McCoy began writing a short story titled "Marathon Dance" sometime after he moved to southern California in early 1931. He later retitled the story "They Shoot Horses, Don't They?" and wrote at least three different manuscript versions that varied in length from 3,500 to 6,000 words. In 1932 and 1933 McCoy submitted the story to magazines, but it was rejected for reasons of length and profanity. (He also submitted a proposal for a film titled "Marathon Dancers" to Universal in the summer of 1932; the relationship between the film proposal and "They Shoot Horses, Don't They?" is not known.) McCoy then expanded the story into a novel and apparently completed an initial draft by November 1933. He continued to work on the novel until early in 1935, when he sent the manuscript to Harold Matson, his New York literary agent. Simon and Schuster accepted the novel for publication, and McCoy corresponded with the book's designer, Philip Van Doren Stern, about the typographical presentation of the judge's sentencing speech. *They Shoot Horses,*

Don't They?, Horace McCoy's first novel, was published by Simon and Schuster on July 25, 1935. McCoy did not make any revisions in the novel after its publication. This volume prints the text of the first edition and follows its typographical presentation of the courtroom scenes.

Edward Anderson began writing *Thieves Like Us*, his second novel, in 1935. After interviewing a cousin who was imprisoned for armed robbery in the Texas state penitentiary in Huntsville, Anderson worked on the book, then titled *They're Thieves Like Us*, in a rented cabin near Kerrville, Texas. In 1936 he sent a manuscript to Bernice Baumgarten, his New York literary agent, who suggested that the book be submitted to *True Detective* magazine for serialization. Anderson rejected this suggestion and, after revising the manuscript, had Baumgarten submit the novel to hardcover book publishers. *Thieves Like Us* was published by Frederick A. Stokes Company in 1937. Anderson made no changes in the novel after its publication. This volume prints the text of the first edition.

Kenneth Fearing wrote *The Big Clock*, his fourth published novel, between August 1944 and October 1945. A condensed version of the book appeared in *The American Magazine* in October 1946 under the title "The Judas Picture." *The Big Clock* was published by Harcourt, Brace, and Company in the fall of 1946. Fearing did not make changes in the novel after its publication. This volume prints the text of the first edition.

William Lindsay Gresham attributed the origin of *Nightmare Alley* to conversations he had with a former carnival worker while they were both serving as volunteers with the Loyalist forces in the Spanish Civil War. Gresham wrote the novel, his first, while working as an editor for a "true crime" pulp magazine in New York City during the 1940s. He outlined the plot and wrote the first six chapters over a period of two years, then finished the book in four months. *Nightmare Alley* was published by Rinehart and Company, Inc., in 1946. Gresham did not revise the novel after its initial publication. This volume prints the text of the first edition.

Cornell Woolrich began publishing crime stories in pulp magazines in 1934 and became a prolific writer of suspense novels during the 1940s. Between 1940 and 1948 Woolrich published six novels under his own name, four novels under the name William Irish, and one novel as George Hopley, while continuing to write short stories for magazines. *I Married a Dead Man* is an expanded and rewritten version of "They Call Me Patrice," a novella that appeared in *Today's Woman* in April 1946. Woolrich used the characters and basic plot of the novella but made significant revisions, including adding passages of first-person narration and writing a new ending (in the novella a character introduced at the end of the story confesses to the murder). *I Married a Dead Man* was published as a Story Press Book by J. B. Lippincott Company in July 1948; it appeared, as had all three of the Woolrich novels previously published by Lippincott, under the name William Irish. Woolrich made no changes in the novel after its publication. The text presented in this volume is that of the first edition.

This volume presents the texts of the original printings chosen for inclusion here, but it does not attempt to reproduce features of their typographic design, such as display capitalization of chapter openings. The texts are printed without change, except for the correction of typographical errors. Spelling, punctuation, and capitalization are often expressive features, and they are not altered, even when inconsistent or irregular. The following is a list of typographical errors corrected, cited by page and line number: 6.32, potatoes.; 46.3, around?; 53.24, Sackett.; 75.30, that?; 87.6, dowstairs; 185.9, Mother's; 233.35, .12-gauge; 245.36, a two; 248.22, .12-gauge; 248.28, .12-gauge; 259.35, twelve; 267.28, boy; 275.21, Stoctor; 304.5, sung; 304.30, Bowie.; 309.31, said,; 313.27, a such; 318.40, his coat; 320.4, Chickamaw; 349.33, curb."; 354.31, everyday; 356.15, gone done; 356.23, of; 494.24, it's; 495.20, breath; 718.11, very; 743.26, heards; 762.26, agily; 803.3, it; 803.36, unmisakably; 838.26, last; 845.28, passengers,; 859.17, guilessly; 872.26, return; 877.1, helplessly,; 878.36, in it,; 881.16, had came; 891.5, I"; 892.1, where-/ever; 902.37, if; 931.20, of two; 943.13, carboose; 951.31, saying,; 953.34, irridescent; 968.21, doned; 968.36, You.

Notes

In the notes below, the reference numbers denote page and line of this volume (the line count includes headings). No note is made for material included in standard desk-reference books such as Webster's *Collegiate*, *Biographical*, and *Geographical* dictionaries. For references to other studies and further biographical background than is contained in the Biographical Notes, see Roy Hoopes, *Cain* (New York: Holt, Rinehart and Winston, 1982); John Thomas Sturak, "The Life and Writings of Horace McCoy, 1897–1955" (unpublished dissertation, The University of California Los Angeles, 1966); Mark Roydan Winchell, *Horace McCoy* (Boise: Boise State University, 1982); Patrick Bennett, *Rough and Rowdy Ways: The Life and Hard Times of Edward Anderson* (College Station: Texas A&M University Press, 1988); Kenneth Fearing, *Complete Poems* (Orono, Maine: The National Poetry Foundation, 1994), edited by Robert M. Ryley; Patricia B. Santora, "The Life of Kenneth Flexner Fearing (1902–1961)," *CLA Journal 32* (1989); William Lindsay Gresham, "From Communist to Christian," *Presbyterian Life*, February 18, 1950; Francis M. Nevins, Jr., *Cornell Woolrich: First You Dream, Then You Die* (New York, London, Tokyo: The Mysterious Press, 1988); *Blues of a Lifetime: The Autobiography of Cornell Woolrich* (Bowling Green: Bowling Green State University Press, 1991), edited by Mark T. Bassett; *Tough Guy Writers of the Thirties* (Carbondale and Edwardsville: Southern Illinois University Press, 1968), edited by David Madden; and Geoffrey O'Brien, *Hardboiled America: Lurid Paperbacks and the Masters of Noir* (revised edition, New York: Da Capo Press, 1997).

THE POSTMAN ALWAYS RINGS TWICE

2.2   *Vincent Lawrence*]   Playwright and screenwriter (1890–1946) known in Hollywood for his mastery of plot construction; he was a close friend of Cain and advised him during the writing of *The Postman Always Rings Twice*.

4.34   wind wing]   A small panel in a car window that can be adjusted for ventilation.

11.14   the Chief]   The Super Chief, a luxury train running between Los Angeles and Chicago.

14.36   Mother Machree]   Song (1910) by Rida Johnson Young, Ernest R. Ball, and Chauncey Olcott; it was the theme song of the popular Irish tenor John McCormack.

25.33   Hoppe] William F. Hoppe (1887–1959), American billiards champion.

25.36–37   Blind Tom the Sightless Piano Player] Thomas Greene Bethune (1849–1908), pianist and composer born in slavery in Columbus, Georgia. He was a child prodigy and amazed audiences with his total musical and verbal recall and his ability to mimic natural and instrumental sounds; he could perform more than 700 pieces from memory.

31.12–19   "There's a long . . . long trail with you."] Song (1913) by Stoddard King and Zo Elliott, popular with troops in World War I.

54.5   Cadona] Mexican trapeze artist Alfredo Codona (1893–1937) became famous for doing the triple aerial somersault.

61.28–29   Dempsey-Firpo fight] Heavyweight boxing champion Jack Dempsey defeated challenger Luis Angel Firpo ("The Wild Bull of the Pampas") at the Polo Grounds in New York City on September 14, 1923. The fight ended in the second round after three minutes and 57 seconds of fighting time.

THEY SHOOT HORSES, DON'T THEY?

98.2–4   *Michael Fessier . . . Harry Clay Wither*] Michael Fessier (1907–88), novelist (*Fully Clothed and in His Right Mind*, 1935) and Hollywood screenwriter whose credits included *Women Are Trouble*, *Song of the City*, and *Wings of the Navy*; Harry Clay Wither, managing editor of the *Dallas Journal*, was a close friend and mentor of McCoy.

109.28   von Sternberg . . . a Russian picture] Josef von Sternberg's *The Scarlet Empress*, starring Marlene Dietrich as Catherine the Great, was released in 1934.

109.30–31   Mamoulian . . . Boleslawsky] Rouben Mamoulian (1898–1987) and Richard Boleslawsky (1889–1937) were prestigious Hollywood directors of the early sound period.

112.40–113.1   Margaret Sullavan . . . Josephine Hutchinson] Margaret Sullavan (1911–60), movie actress whose films included *Only Yesterday* (1933) and *Little Man, What Now?* (1934); Josephine Hutchinson (b. 1904), movie actress whose films included *Happiness Ahead* (1934) and *Oil for the Lamps of China* (1935).

128.8   Alice Faye] Movie star (b. 1912) who appeared in a long series of musicals beginning with *George White's Scandals* (1934).

THIEVES LIKE US

216.4–5   ROY . . . ANNE] Anderson's cousin, Roy Johnson, was serving a life sentence for armed robbery when Anderson interviewed him as background for *Thieves Like Us*; Polly Anne Bates was Anderson's first wife.

217.1–3   "Men do not . . . of his house."]   Proverbs 6:30–31.

249.14   pratt]   Buttocks.

276.1   *La Golondrina*]   Mexican song written in 1883 by Narciso Serradell.

304.34–35   that woman up in Canada]   Elzire Dionne, mother of quin-tuplets, born in Ontario in 1934, who became the object of intense public interest.

326.8   *El Rancho Grande*]   Song (1934) by Silvano Ramos.

355.23   *La Paloma*]   Traditional Mexican song.

356.11   *La Cucaracha*]   Traditional Mexican song which became a popular hit in 1934.

THE BIG CLOCK

380.1   *Nan*]   Fearing's second wife, Nan Lurie.

418.11   WPA   stuff]   Art   commissioned   by   the   Works   Projects Administration.

442.2   M.E.]   Managing Editor.

463.16   *mot de passe*]   French: password.

NIGHTMARE ALLEY

518.2   *Joy Davidman*]   Gresham's second wife (1915–60), a poet who won the Yale Series of Younger Poets award in 1938 for *Letter to a Comrade*.

521.1–13   Madame Sosostris . . . death by water]   T. S. Eliot, *The Waste Land*, lines 43–55.

521.15–17   For at Cumae . . . "I want to die."]   The anecdote is re-counted, in Petronius' novel, by the wealthy freedman Trimalchio during his banquet.

548.33   soup and fish]   Tuxedo.

606.15   *Prosit, Liebchen*]   German: Cheers, darling.

639.4–7   *Shall we gather . . . throne of God.*]   Cf. Robert Lowry, "Beau-tiful River."

653.21–34   "Hark, hark the lark . . . at those springs . . ."]   Shakespeare, *Cymbeline*, Act II, scene iii, lines 20–22.

657.27–28   Sir Oliver Lodge, Sir Arthur Conan Doyle, Camille Flam-marion, Sir William Crookes]   Sir Oliver Lodge (1851–1940), English physi-cist; Sir Arthur Conan Doyle (1859–1930), English novelist; Camille Flammarion (1842–1925), French astronomer; Sir William Crookes (1832–1919), English physicist and chemist.

716.15   Daniel Douglas Home]   Daniel Dunglas Home (1833–86), Scottish spiritualist medium.

793.24–32   *"Put your arms around me . . . you!"*]   *Put Your Arms Around Me Honey*, 1910 song by Junie McCree and Albert Von Tilzer.

I MARRIED A DEAD MAN

856.1   *Tales of Hoffman*]   *Les Contes d'Hoffmann*, opera by Jacques Offenbach (1819–80); never completed by the composer, it had its first performance in Paris in 1881.

870.37   *Marie Antoinette* by Katharine Anthony]   Anthony (1877–1965) published her biography in 1932; she also wrote biographies of Margaret Fuller, Catherine the Great, and Louisa May Alcott.

871.17   Axel Fersen]   Count Hans Axel von Fersen (1755–1810), Swedish officer resident at Versailles who aided the royal family in their unsuccessful attempt to flee France in 1791.

872.6   Madame Korff]   Name assumed by Mme. de Tourzel, the governess of the French royal family, during their attempted flight.

892.28   "Three Little Words."]   Song (1930) by Harry Ruby and Bert Kalmar.

926.8   "*Che gelida mannina—*"]   Aria sung by Rodolfo to Mimi in Puccini's *La Boheme* (Italian: "What a frozen little hand").

940.3–4   Mark Stevens in *I Wonder Who's Kissing Her Now*]   Stevens played the songwriter Joseph E. Howard in the 1947 Warner Brothers musical directed by Lloyd Bacon.

Library of Congress Cataloging-in-Publication Data

Crime novels : American noir of the thirties and forties.
     p. cm. — (The Library of America ; 94)
     Contents: The postman always rings twice / James M.
Cain — They shoot horses, don't they / Horace McCoy —
Thieves like us / Edward Anderson — The big clock /
Kenneth Fearing — Nightmare alley / William Lindsay
Gresham — I married a dead man / Cornell Woolrich.
     ISBN 1–883011–46–9
     1. Detective and mystery stories, American. 2. American
fiction—20th century. 3. Crime—Fiction. I. Cain,
James M. (James Mallahan), 1892–1977. Postman always
rings twice. II. McCoy, Horace, 1897–1955. They shoot
horses, don't they? III. Anderson, Edward, 1905–1969.
Thieves like us. IV. Fearing, Kenneth, 1902–1961.
Big clock. V. Gresham, William Lindsay, 1909–1962.
Nightmare alley. VI. Woolrich, Cornell, 1903–1968. I
married a dead man. VII. Series.
PS648.D4C695 1997
813′.087208052—dc21   97–2485
                                          CIP

THE LIBRARY OF AMERICA SERIES

1. Herman Melville, *Typee, Omoo, Mardi* (1982)
2. Nathaniel Hawthorne, *Tales and Sketches* (1982)
3. Walt Whitman, *Poetry and Prose* (1982)
4. Harriet Beecher Stowe, *Three Novels* (1982)
5. Mark Twain, *Mississippi Writings* (1982)
6. Jack London, *Novels and Stories* (1982)
7. Jack London, *Novels and Social Writings* (1982)
8. William Dean Howells, *Novels 1875–1886* (1982)
9. Herman Melville, *Redburn, White-Jacket, Moby-Dick* (1983)
10. Nathaniel Hawthorne, *Collected Novels* (1983)
11. Francis Parkman, *France and England in North America* vol. I, (1983)
12. Francis Parkman, *France and England in North America* vol. II, (1983)
13. Henry James, *Novels 1871–1880* (1983)
14. Henry Adams, *Novels, Mont Saint Michel, The Education* (1983)
15. Ralph Waldo Emerson, *Essays and Lectures* (1983)
16. Washington Irving, *History, Tales and Sketches* (1983)
17. Thomas Jefferson, *Writings* (1984)
18. Stephen Crane, *Prose and Poetry* (1984)
19. Edgar Allan Poe, *Poetry and Tales* (1984)
20. Edgar Allan Poe, *Essays and Reviews* (1984)
21. Mark Twain, *The Innocents Abroad, Roughing It* (1984)
22. Henry James, *Essays, American & English Writers* (1984)
23. Henry James, *European Writers & The Prefaces* (1984)
24. Herman Melville, *Pierre, Israel Potter, The Confidence-Man, Tales & Billy Budd* (1985)
25. William Faulkner, *Novels 1930–1935* (1985)
26. James Fenimore Cooper, *The Leatherstocking Tales* vol. I, (1985)
27. James Fenimore Cooper, *The Leatherstocking Tales* vol. II, (1985)
28. Henry David Thoreau, *A Week, Walden, The Maine Woods, Cape Cod* (1985)
29. Henry James, *Novels 1881–1886* (1985)
30. Edith Wharton, *Novels* (1986)
31. Henry Adams, *History of the United States during the Administrations of Jefferson* (1986)
32. Henry Adams, *History of the United States during the Administrations of Madison* (1986)
33. Frank Norris, *Novels and Essays* (1986)
34. W. E. B. Du Bois, *Writings* (1986)
35. Willa Cather, *Early Novels and Stories* (1987)
36. Theodore Dreiser, *Sister Carrie, Jennie Gerhardt, Twelve Men* (1987)
37. Benjamin Franklin, *Writings* (1987)
38. William James, *Writings 1902–1910* (1987)
39. Flannery O'Connor, *Collected Works* (1988)
40. Eugene O'Neill, *Complete Plays 1913–1920* (1988)
41. Eugene O'Neill, *Complete Plays 1920–1931* (1988)
42. Eugene O'Neill, *Complete Plays 1932–1943* (1988)
43. Henry James, *Novels 1886–1890* (1989)
44. William Dean Howells, *Novels 1886–1888* (1989)
45. Abraham Lincoln, *Speeches and Writings 1832–1858* (1989)
46. Abraham Lincoln, *Speeches and Writings 1859–1865* (1989)
47. Edith Wharton, *Novellas and Other Writings* (1990)
48. William Faulkner, *Novels 1936–1940* (1990)
49. Willa Cather, *Later Novels* (1990)
50. Ulysses S. Grant, *Personal Memoirs and Selected Letters* (1990)
51. William Tecumseh Sherman, *Memoirs* (1990)
52. Washington Irving, *Bracebridge Hall, Tales of a Traveller, The Alhambra* (1991)
53. Francis Parkman, *The Oregon Trail, The Conspiracy of Pontiac* (1991)
54. James Fenimore Cooper, *Sea Tales: The Pilot, The Red Rover* (1991)

55. Richard Wright, *Early Works* (1991)
56. Richard Wright, *Later Works* (1991)
57. Willa Cather, *Stories, Poems, and Other Writings* (1992)
58. William James, *Writings 1878–1899* (1992)
59. Sinclair Lewis, *Main Street & Babbitt* (1992)
60. Mark Twain, *Collected Tales, Sketches, Speeches, & Essays 1852–1890* (1992)
61. Mark Twain, *Collected Tales, Sketches, Speeches, & Essays 1891–1910* (1992)
62. *The Debate on the Constitution: Part One* (1993)
63. *The Debate on the Constitution: Part Two* (1993)
64. Henry James, *Collected Travel Writings: Great Britain & America* (1993)
65. Henry James, *Collected Travel Writings: The Continent* (1993)
66. *American Poetry: The Nineteenth Century,* Vol. 1 (1993)
67. *American Poetry: The Nineteenth Century,* Vol. 2 (1993)
68. Frederick Douglass, *Autobiographies,* (1994)
69. Sarah Orne Jewett, *Novels and Stories* (1994)
70. Ralph Waldo Emerson, *Collected Poems and Translations* (1994)
71. Mark Twain, *Historical Romances* (1994)
72. John Steinbeck, *Novels and Stories 1932–1937* (1994)
73. William Faulkner, *Novels 1942–1954* (1994)
74. Zora Neale Hurston, *Novels and Stories* (1995)
75. Zora Neale Hurston, *Folklore, Memoirs, and Other Writings* (1995)
76. Thomas Paine, *Collected Writings* (1995)
77. *Reporting World War II: American Journalism 1938–1944* (1995)
78. *Reporting World War II: American Journalism 1944–1946* (1995)
79. Raymond Chandler, *Stories and Early Novels* (1995)
80. Raymond Chandler, *Later Novels and Other Writings* (1995)
81. Robert Frost, *Collected Poems, Prose, & Plays* (1995)
82. Henry James, *Complete Stories 1892–1898* (1996)
83. Henry James, *Complete Stories 1898–1910* (1996)
84. William Bartram, *Travels and Other Writings* (1996)
85. John Dos Passos, *U.S.A.* (1996)
86. John Steinbeck, *The Grapes of Wrath and Other Writings 1936–1941* (1996)
87. Vladimir Nabokov, *Novels and Memoirs 1941–1951* (1996)
88. Vladimir Nabokov, *Novels 1955–1962* (1996)
89. Vladimir Nabokov, *Novels 1969–1974* (1996)
90. James Thurber, *Writings and Drawings* (1996)
91. George Washington, *Writings* (1997)
92. John Muir, *Nature Writings* (1997)
93. Nathanael West, *Novels and Other Writings* (1997)
94. *Crime Novels: America Noir of the 1930s and 40s* (1997)
95. *Crime Novels: America Noir of the 1950s* (1997)
96. Wallace Stevens, *Collected Poetry and Prose* (1997)

This book is set in 10 point Linotron Galliard,
a face designed for photocomposition by Matthew Carter
and based on the sixteenth-century face Granjon. The paper is
acid-free Ecusta Nyalite and meets the requirements for permanence
of the American National Standards Institute. The binding
material is Brillianta, a woven rayon cloth made by
Van Heek-Scholco Textielfabrieken, Holland.
The composition is by The Clarinda
Company. Printing and binding by
R.R.Donnelley & Sons Company.
Designed by Bruce Campbell.